CONTRARIAN

TOR BOOKS BY L. E. MODESITT, JR.

THE GRAND ILLUSION

Isolate
Councilor
Contrarian

THE SAGA OF RECLUCE

The Magic of Recluce
The Towers of the Sunset
The Magic Engineer
The Order War
The Death of Chaos
Fall of Angels
The Chaos Balance
The White Order
Colors of Chaos
Magi'i of Cyador
Scion of Cyador
Wellspring of Chaos
Ordermaster
Natural Ordermage
Mage-Guard of Hamor
Arms-Commander
Cyador's Heirs
Heritage of Cyador
Recluce Tales
The Mongrel Mage
Outcasts of Order
The Mage-Fire War
Fairhaven Rising
From the Forest

THE COREAN CHRONICLES

Legacies
Darknesses
Scepters
Alector's Choice
Cadmian's Choice
Soarer's Choice
The Lord-Protector's Daughter
Lady-Protector

THE IMAGER PORTFOLIO

Imager
Imager's Challenge
Imager's Intrigue
Scholar
Princeps
Imager's Battalion
Antiagon Fire
Rex Regis
Madness in Solidar
Treachery's Tools
Assassin's Price
Endgames

L.E. MODESITT JR.

CONTRARIAN

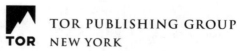

TOR PUBLISHING GROUP
NEW YORK

CONTRARIAN

Copyright © 2023 by Modesitt Family Revocable Living Trust

A Tor Book
Published by Tom Doherty Associates / Tor Publishing Group
120 Broadway
New York, NY 10271

www.tor-forge.com

Tor® is a registered trademark of Macmillan Publishing Group, LLC.

The Library of Congress Cataloging-in-Publication Data is available upon request.

ISBN 978-1-250-84701-0 (hardcover)
ISBN 978-1-250-84702-7 (ebook)

Our books may be purchased in bulk for promotional, educational, or business use. Please contact your local bookseller or the Macmillan Corporate and Premium Sales Department at 1-800-221-7945, extension 5442, or by email at MacmillanSpecialMarkets@macmillan.com.

First Edition: 2023

Printed in the United States of America

0 9 8 7 6 5 4 3 2 1

FOR ALL THOSE *whose advice and support
helped me survive the Washington years,
particularly Bill Armstrong, Bob Lee,
Ken Kramer, and Jim Tozzi.*

MAJOR CHARACTERS

Steffan Delos Dekkard Isolate and Councilor, Former Security Aide for Premier Obreduur

Avraal Ysella-Dekkard Empath, Former Security Aide for Premier Obreduur, wife of Dekkard

Emrelda Ysella-Roemnal District Patroller, sister of Avraal

Nincya Gaaroll Pattern-sensor, empath-in-training for Dekkard

Svard Roostof Senior Legalist

Luara Colsbaan Junior Legalist

Shuryn Teitryn Engineering Aide

Margrit Pettit Personal Secretary

Axel Obreduur Former Premier (assassinated)

Ingrella Obreduur Councilor from Oersynt (Craft), widow of Axel Obreduur

Fredrich Hasheem Premier, Councilor from Port Reale (Craft)

Guilhohn Haarsfel Councilor from Kathaar, Craft Party Floor Leader

Hansaal Volkaar Councilor from Uldwyrk, Commerce Party Floor Leader

Saandaar Vonauer Councilor from Plaatz, Landor Party Floor Leader

Laureous XXIV Imperador of Guldor

Kaliara Bassaana Councilor from Caylaan (Commerce)

Villem Baar Councilor from Suvion (Commerce)

Breffyn Haastar Councilor from Brekaan (Landor)

Eyril Konnigsburg Councilor from Veerlyn (Commerce), former admiral

Erskine Mardosh Military Affairs Committee Chair, Councilor from Siincleer (Craft)

Kharl Navione Councilor from Seibryg (Landor)

Pohl Palafaux Councilor from Point Larmat (Commerce)

Gerhard Safaell   Waterways Committee Chair, Councilor from Enke (Craft)
Harleona Zerlyon   Justiciary Committee Chair, Councilor from Ondeliew (Craft)

Oskaar Ulrich   Former Premier (Commerce), Vice-Presidente, Suvion Industries
Jaime Minz   Isolate, Former Security Aide for Ulrich, Assistant Security Director for Northwest Industrial Chemical (deceased)
Izaak Trujillo   Guard Captain, Council Guards

CONTRARIAN

PROLOGUE

THE QUESTIONABLE COUNCILOR DEKKARD

Exactly who is Councilor Steffan Delos Dekkard? Some facts we know. He is a graduate of the Military Institute. He is also an isolate and the former security aide to the late Premier Axel Obreduur, but only for the last two years, a position that allowed him to fulfill his naval service obligation without ever going to sea. Once appointed as councilor, he immediately masterminded the passage of the Security and Public Safety Reorganization Act that effectively destroyed the Security Ministry and disarmed Special Agents, thus removing their ability to deal with threats to public safety, such as the so-called New Meritorists.

What is not so widely known is that Councilor Dekkard was selected as a councilor from Gaarlak after the first candidate for councilor died in a suspicious fire and then after the man elected to replace him died of a heart attack that some claim was foul play. What is also not widely known is that, although Councilor Dekkard's office was one of those targeted and destroyed by the New Meritorists, the councilor and his entire staff escaped untouched, while the councilors and staff in the other four offices targeted were killed, including the Premier, an amazing feat under the circumstances. Councilor Dekkard, it is said, was the one who suggested that new premier select Premier Obreduur's widow fill her husband's seat, apparently overriding suggestions from the Craft Party of Oersynt.

Before last summer, no one in Gaarlak had even heard of Steffan Dekkard, not until he gave a brief talk at a Craft Party gathering, accompanying then Councilor Obreduur on a tour of Gaarlak, perhaps to pave the way for Dekkard to become a councilor? In addition to these circumstances, Dekkard owns neither property nor a home in Gaarlak or the surrounding area, and his parents are Argenti immigrants who live in Oersynt.

That's the brief and amazing story of Steffan Dekkard, at least to date.

The Machtarn Tribune
30 Winterfirst 1267

Duadi
32 Winterfirst 1267

DEKKARD glanced out the carriage window at the ironway station platform, the predawn darkness only dimly lit by the tall gas lamps, then back toward the slender but trimly muscular black-haired woman sitting beside him on the dark blue velvet seat. "Well, Ritten Ysella-Dekkard, how does it feel to embark on the next major event of our life?"

"We've had enough major events already, dear," she replied in the slightly sweet tone that suggested he was edging toward a spoutstorm.

"Buying a house together in Gaarlak will be a major *domestic* event," he replied in a tone he hoped was conciliatory, "not a catastrophic one like the shelling of the Council Office Building." *And the assassination of the Premier.* The man who had given him the chance to become a councilor— and to meet Avraal. *If only . . . but who could have foreseen the method of the Meritorist attack?*

Avraal shook her head. "I'd never thought we'd end up where we are."

"I certainly never expected to be a councilor, or to be married to an empath who's descended from ancient royalty," Dekkard replied wryly.

"Everyone's forgotten about the kings of Aloor . . . except my father and brother."

The first-class steward, wearing a deep blue uniform trimmed with silver piping, strode down the center corridor, saying, "The express will be leaving immediately."

Less than a minute later, a steam whistle sounded, and with a slight jolt, the carriage began to move.

Since there was little to see through the wide window, at least not clearly, Dekkard studied, as best he could in the dim light, the wooden paneling, a dark stained cherry, rather than the yellow cedar, or even the older black walnut. "I think the paneling in this carriage is the new cherry, most likely from dowry lands Jareem Saarh sold to Guldoran Ironway."

"He'll end up losing everything in the long run, and I wouldn't care in the slightest, except that it wouldn't be fair to Maelle."

"At the Yearend Ball, he did say that she was likely running the lands better than he could."

"He believed it. I could sense that," replied Avraal. "For her sake, I hope he was right . . . but he's been wrong about more than a few things, like getting together with Palafaux and Schmidtz."

"Exactly, and I have the feeling that that trio has something else planned."

"No doubt connected to Ulrich and Siincleer Shipbuilding. Speaking of those two . . . do you think Ulrich might have been the one behind that story in the *Tribune*?"

"Our most honorable former premier, who likely ordered the assassination of his devoted former aide to keep anyone from tying corporacion aid to the New Meritorists? How could you possibly believe that?" Dekkard's voice dripped with sardonicism.

"I don't feel that sorry for Jaime Minz, not after the times he tried to get others to kill you, and his funneling explosives to the New Meritorists. But still . . . he did all of Ulrich's dirty work, and Ulrich or one of his cronies just disposed of him like that, and no one's even looking at Ulrich."

"Guard Captain Trujillo is, but there's no hard evidence," Dekkard pointed out. "Just like with Lamarr's and Decaro's deaths. I still wonder about how much Jens Seigryn was involved with Decaro's death." Thinking of the Craft Party political coordinator for the Gaarlak district, Dekkard couldn't help but shake his head. "I wasn't the one who schemed to make me councilor instead of him. That was Gretna Haarl, and I didn't even know about it. Jens had to know that."

"I'm not sure that will make him any happier. I don't like it that you had to use him to organize tomorrow's breakfast meeting with all the guildmeisters."

"What else could we do? We don't have much choice, not with so little time, especially since he's the Advisory Committee's representative in Gaarlak, in addition to being the Craft Party coordinator."

"I still wish there had been another way, without involving him." Avraal frowned. "I'll be carrying my knives, and so will you."

"All the time now. I did bring my personal truncheon, in case it appears necessary." He smiled wryly. "It may be that the safest place I'll be is at Plainfields on Findi afternoon."

"It was kind of Emilio and Patriana to invite us for an early dinner."

"I suspect he wants to hear about the Landor councilors we both know. Patriana may not miss his being a councilor, but I suspect he does at times."

After a short silence, Avraal said, "How do you think Nincya and Emrelda will get along?"

"Without us there, you mean? They'll do fine. Nincya respects your sister, and she's enough of an empath that she can sense if something's troubling Emrelda, and Emrelda's direct without being overbearing. If you want to worry about something, worry about whether we can find a decent house in the right place." Dekkard shook his head. "I just hope that the property legalist that Namoor Desharra recommended understands our particular situation."

"Our limitations, you mean?"

"I know your parents gave you that personal bond, but . . ." *I don't want you using it all, even if we do have to buy something in Gaarlak because I'm a councilor.*

"Stop feeling guilty. Part of the reason they sent it was because I married a man whom they could brag about, rather than avoid talking about."

"As in," Dekkard continued in an archly haughty tone, imitating an arrogant Landor, "'Avraal did marry a councilor of the Sixty-Six, not *quite* the same as a Landor heir, but given that she's an *empath*, she did quite well'?"

Avraal tried . . . and failed . . . to hide a sardonically amused smile. "You did that rather well . . . almost like Cliven."

Dekkard winced.

Avraal laughed, then leaned over and kissed his cheek.

2

JUST before the first morning bell, Dekkard and Avraal left their second-floor room at the Ritter's Inn and started down the wide staircase, the heavy maroon carpeting on the steps muffling the sound of their boots.

Dekkard hadn't slept well after waking up in the middle of the night from another nightmare about the shelling of the Council Office Building. *At least the nightmares are getting less frequent.* With that thought, he looked out over the lobby, but didn't yet see Jens Seigryn.

For the coming breakfast meeting, Dekkard wore one of his gray winter suits with the red cravat unofficially suggesting a councilor, while Avraal wore a conservative dark blue suit with trousers and a light blue head-scarf, draped over her shoulders. She also wore a golden lapel pin with a small red stone in the center, a quiet but necessary statement that she was a certified security empath.

Dekkard couldn't help noticing that the brass lighting fixtures on the wall didn't seem quite as well-polished as when they had stayed at the inn the previous summer. He also hoped he could put the names he'd studied to the faces of the guildmeisters he and Avraal would shortly encounter, since they'd only met several briefly.

From the staircase, the two walked across the smooth dark gray slate floor, past the small restaurant, already more than half full, toward the private dining room.

Jens Seigryn—short and wiry, with thinning brown hair and a high forehead—waited beside the open door. As he caught sight of the couple, he smiled broadly.

"Steffan, Avraal . . . or should I say Councilor and Ritten?"

"Steffan and Avraal is fine, Jens," said Dekkard cheerfully. "I appreciate your arranging the breakfast for us, especially on such short notice."

"That's what political coordinators do. Everyone wanted to come, and that's unusual." Seigryn paused. "Gretna Haarl . . . insisted . . ."

"That she wanted to be seated next to me . . . or Avraal?"

Seigryn looked surprised at Dekkard's last words. "Avraal . . . you really thought she might want to be next to Avraal?"

"It was a definite possibility. When she wrote to congratulate me, she only had two questions. When was I coming to Gaarlak and was I smart enough to listen to Avraal." That wasn't how Haarl had written it, but it was definitely what she'd meant. Then Dekkard looked directly at Seigryn. "I trust you know that I had no idea what Gretna had in mind."

Seigryn smiled ruefully. "I knew that from the moment she became guildmeister she wouldn't support anyone either Axel or I proposed. You were the only one of those she proposed that anyone else would accept." After a moment, he went on, his voice both subdued and slightly cautious. "Later, when you have a moment, could we talk . . . about Axel?"

"We'd be more than happy to. He always spoke well of you."

"Thank you." After a momentary hesitation, Seigryn said, "We'd better go in . . . several of the guildmeisters are already here."

"Including Gretna?" asked Avraal.

"She was the first."

Seigryn led the way into the private dining room, just an oblong chamber some eight yards long and six wide. Dark oak paneled the walls below the chair rail, with cream plaster walls above the rail. The maroon carpeting was the same as that on the main stairs, and the crown molding matched the carpet.

Three people stood beside the large round table, set with silver cutlery and a plain white linen cloth. Dekkard immediately picked out the thin, almost frail figure of Gretna Haarl, and the stocky Yorik Haansel of the Stonemasons, but had to mentally struggle a moment to place the other woman before finally coming up with the name of Arleena Desenns, the head of the Weavers Guild.

"Councilor and Ritten Dekkard were a bit early," announced Seigryn. "We'll wait a few more minutes before we sit down, but I thought you'd all like a few words."

Dekkard immediately went to Gretna Haarl, smiled, and said, "I got here at the first opportunity, and, as I wrote you, I'd already taken your counsel in not letting go of Avraal."

"You've been a most pleasant surprise as a councilor, Steffan," replied Haarl. "You pushed through Security reforms. Myram Plassar tells me you're pushing reforms for working women."

"We're also working on broader pay reform legislation. That might take longer." Dekkard regretted that Plassar couldn't have been at the breakfast, but since she was only a regional steward and not a guildmeister, her inclusion would have raised the hackles of the other regional stewards, and including everyone would have made the breakfast too large . . . and too costly for his expense account.

"That's good to hear." Haarl looked to Avraal. "How much of that was your idea?"

Avraal smiled. "Steffan came up with it all."

"Not that she hasn't been encouraging . . . and kept me from making certain mistakes," added Dekkard.

"Amazing . . . a man with initiative who also listens."

"It happens occasionally." Dekkard gave a slight chuckle, then sobered. "Premier Obreduur did both."

"Look where it got him," interjected Yorik Haansel, who then smiled at Dekkard and added, "It's good to see you here, Councilor."

"As I said, I came as soon as it was possible."

"The newssheets said that the Meritorists destroyed your office. How did you escape and Premier Obreduur didn't?" asked Haansel. "There was some question . . ."

Dekkard managed to maintain a pleasant expression, despite his dismay at the possibility that the *Tribune* story had reached Gaarlak. "They fired at his office first and at mine last. When I heard and saw the first explosion I got my staff out of the office and into the stone-walled stairwell. The attack didn't last more than ten minutes."

"Why did they stop that soon?" asked Haarl.

"Either their makeshift steam cannon or one of their handmade shells exploded as they fired, and that destroyed the cannon, any remaining explosives, and them. Otherwise, it could have been much, much worse." Dekkard saw two more guildmeisters arrive—Alastan Cleese, of the Farmworkers, and Charlana Boetcher, who had replaced Johan Lamarr as guildmeister of the Crafters.

Jens Seigryn closed the door to the private dining room and walked toward the table. Then he stopped and said, "If you'd find your seats . . . we'll have the blessing." Seigryn nodded to Dekkard. "Councilor . . ."

From his time visiting and campaigning with Obreduur, Dekkard knew that the Trinitarian faith was stronger in smaller cities, and that a blessing before a meal was expected. He found the card bearing his name and stood behind the chair while the others sorted themselves out. He did notice that Avraal was across the table from him flanked by Gretna Haarl and Arleena Desenns, while Charlana Boetcher stood on his right and Alastan Cleese on his left.

Dekkard bowed his head slightly, then began. "Almighty and Trinity of Love, Power, and Mercy, in this time of trial and upheaval, we thank you for the solidity you bring to this world. We humbly ask that you grant us the wisdom to see illusions for what they are and to understand that all material goods are fleeting vanities, and that the greatest vanity of all is to seek and hoard power, rather than to share it in doing good. We humbly ask you to bless this gathering and the food we will partake, in the name of the Three in One."

"The Three in One," murmured those around the table.

"Good short blessing," declared Yorik Haansel to no one in particular, as he sat down between Boetcher and Desenns.

Immediately, servers appeared and poured café for everyone, then provided two platters of croissants, and one with ham strips.

"Councilor," began Cleese, as soon as everyone had served themselves, his tone of voice almost apologetic, "I'm sure you've followed the weather . . ."

"It's been terrible all across Guldor. I've been worried about the impact on farmworkers and what will happen to food prices."

"You say that so easily . . ."

"I'm not casual about it. There have been at least four large disturbances in Machtarn in recent weeks over food prices. One ended in such violence that an entire block burned to the ground, and a score of people died. Girls are selling themselves on the streets in poor neighborhoods to earn marks for food. That doesn't count events in other cities across Guldor. I imagine similar problems have happened in Gaarlak. That's one reason we're here. I need to know what I don't see and the newssheets don't cover."

"You were elected two months ago."

"Alastan," said Desenns, "stop being a complete idiot. The councilor is new. Despite that, he did manage to pass reforms to get rid of the Security Ministry. Last year you were complaining about that. Don't you read the newssheets? He's been the target of the New Meritorists and the Commercers. His office was destroyed. The Council has been in session the whole time since he was elected. What exactly do you expect?"

"We've still got problems here, Arleena. Close to a quarter of my farmworkers don't have enough marks to feed their families right now."

"That's the sort of thing I need to know," Dekkard said quietly. "I personally read every single letter and petition, but no one has yet written me and told me what you just said. I want to find someone I can put on my staff here in Gaarlak, someone that you can talk to so that I'll learn about issues sooner."

"If you do that," said Desenns, "it'll be the first time in my life."

"Sounds like a good idea," boomed out Haansel. "Why didn't Raathan do that?"

"I don't know," replied Dekkard. "Perhaps he relied on his family."

"Exactly," declared Cleese. "All he heard about was Landor problems. Nothing about farmworkers, crafters, millworkers . . . the ones who need to be heard."

"Don't forget about the artisans," said Charlana Boetcher, her voice almost acid.

"You artisans have it easy. You're not out in the weather all the time."

"Do we have it easy, Councilor?" asked Boetcher sweetly.

Dekkard was beginning to wish that Jon Eliver, the Farmworkers assistant guildmeister, whom he'd met during his previous visit, had come in place of Cleese, but he replied pleasantly, "The five years I spent as a plasterer's apprentice were the hardest of my life. Artisans don't have it easy, but most people who work with their hands and bodies don't. I've never forgotten that."

"You did that? Nobody told me," declared Cleese defensively.

Boetcher sighed loudly. "I was there when Jon Eliver told you that. So was Gretna Haarl. That's why we all wanted Steffan as councilor."

"I heard it, too," declared Gretna Haarl loudly.

Cleese looked as if he might dispute it, when Yorik Haansel grinned and said, "Give it up, Alastan. My ears are bad, and I heard it."

Cleese closed his mouth and shook his head.

For a moment, there was silence, and Dekkard let it draw out for a moment, then said, quietly but firmly, "Both Avraal and I do understand. She understands, partly because she's an empath and partly because she worked her way up, starting in the prisons as a parole screener." He paused to let that sink in. "We don't know all that you and the hardworking people you represent have gone through, and the Council has to do better. I'll do the best I can. For too long the Council has listened only to corporacion and Landor needs and problems, but the current Council has already made a good start in changing that. To keep that momentum, we need to know specific problems and needs that the Council can address. The Council can't change the weather, but we can look into and seek change in work practices or freight rates . . . or in safety rules. You know where your problems are. So let me know. But remember, we can't fix everything at once, just like you can't craft a desk overnight, or get in a harvest in a few bells."

"If there even is a harvest," replied Cleese. "More failed this year than in past years."

For a moment, Dekkard didn't know what to say that wouldn't sound flippant or uncaring, but he finally managed to say, "It's been a hard year everywhere for growers."

"The Commercers don't make it easier," said Haarl. "Premier Obreduur's wife won a legal action against Gaarlak Mills. They have to pay women as much as the men for the same jobs, but Lakaan Mills still won't do it. Their legalists file motion after motion, and each motion costs the guild hundreds of marks."

Dekkard nodded, then said, "Ritten Obreduur told me that mill owners and others would force legal action for every mill corporacion until and unless the Council made the law specifically adhere to the ruling of the High Justiciary. I'm already working on legislation that will do that, but it's likely to take a while to get such a law through the Council."

"There are real problems in the Lakaan Brickworks. Others, too, I'd wager," declared Haansel. "They've got new steam driers, and it's giving the setters consumption . . . leastwise they call it consumption . . ."

After that, it seemed to Dekkard that every guildmeister had a problem or two, sometimes three, but he listened carefully, then responded, ending with a polite request that they send him a letter with as many details as they could.

By the time Dekkard had heard them all out, it was close to third bell, and he was just grateful that there weren't any frowns or scowls . . . at least, not that he had seen. He just hoped that Avraal had sensed anyone unhappy so that he could follow up with them, although he also hoped that wouldn't be necessary.

Dekkard then immediately turned to Alastan Cleese. "I'm sorry. I didn't realize just how bad . . ."

Cleese shook his head. "Not your fault. You're a fair-minded young fellow trying to do your best . . . unlike some."

"I am concerned about farmworkers and those who work with their hands. The rest of the winter is going to be hard. I'll do what I can to improve working conditions, but, as I said earlier, if you have any other specific ideas about what would help, especially on a permanent basis, I'd like to hear from you."

"Let me think about it. You'll hear when I have." Cleese stood.

So did Dekkard, as he said, "Thank you." Then he turned to Charlana Boetcher as soon as Cleese moved away.

She rose from the table.

Dekkard inclined his head and said, "I trust you won't mind if I visit some of the crafters' shops and businesses over the next week."

"I'd hoped you would." She smiled and handed him a card. "Come by if you have any questions."

"Thank you." Before slipping the card into his suit pocket, Dekkard took a quick look at the name on the card—Boetcher Silver. "Is there any place or area you'd recommend where I might start . . . in addition to yours, of course?"

"It doesn't really matter where you start, just so long as it's not with us and that you visit several areas so that people won't get the impression that you just made a few token appearances."

"What you're suggesting, I think," Dekkard replied wryly, "is that token appearances might be worse than no appearances."

"I didn't say that," Boetcher replied with an amused smile, "but I didn't have to."

After Boetcher stepped away, Gretna Haarl appeared. "I had a very good talk with Avraal. Keep listening to her."

"I've never stopped listening to her, and I don't intend to now." *Especially now.*

"Excellent. I look forward to seeing you on Furdi."

"Avraal has the details?"

"She does." Haarl smiled. "You do well in difficult situations. Until Furdi."

Dekkard thought she seemed satisfied as she left, although he wondered just what Avraal had committed them to.

Yorik Haansel was the last to come up to Dekkard. "Glad to see you talked to Alastan before he left. I'll talk to him, too. He's a good man. He just doesn't like to admit that his ears aren't what they used to be." He paused, then said, "Guldor lost a great man when those idiots killed Axel."

Dekkard lowered his voice and said, "They weren't idiots; they were corporacion tools out to weaken the Council. Part of that was already proved, but there isn't evidence to go further."

Haansel nodded slowly. "Doesn't surprise me. Seemed unlikely that Meritorists would do that by themselves. You just be careful." He smiled. "It was a good breakfast." Then he turned and headed for the door.

In moments, Dekkard and Avraal were alone in the room with Jens Seigryn.

"You sounded like Obreduur . . . a younger Obreduur," said Seigryn.

"Who do you think I learned it from?" Dekkard paused. "They certainly had a lot of pointed questions."

"This is the first time in more than a century that guildmeisters here in Gaarlak have a chance to question their own councilor in person. The Landor councilors avoided meeting with them like this."

"Jens," said Dekkard, "you wanted to talk about Axel . . ."

For just an instant, Seigryn looked surprised, as if he hadn't expected

Dekkard to bring up Obreduur. "How did it really happen? He was always so careful."

"The New Meritorists had help building a steam cannon and make-shift shells. Then they hid it inside a canvas-topped stake lorry, drove it down the service road behind the Council Office Building, stopped, and targeted his office from about fifty yards. In less than a sixth they took out five offices. The Justiciary Ministry and the head of the Council Guards suspect the help and expertise came from corporacions, but there was no hard evidence. They captured one low-level corporate officer, and he was immediately assassinated. Officially, it was all his doing."

"The bastards . . . Axel was the best chance they had of a better life."

"The Meritorist leaders are fanatics, and the corporate types are very good at manipulation," replied Dekkard. "You've seen more than a little of that."

"Landors . . . Commercers . . . they'll never change."

Dekkard smiled. "Then . . . I guess it's up to us Crafters." He paused, then said, "Thank you for arranging the breakfast. We appreciate it."

"You're welcome. You paid for it," said Seigryn with a touch of humor. "Now . . . if you need anything else . . ."

"We'll let you know. This is just a low-key visit. We need to get more familiar with Gaarlak and look into the possibilities of fashioning a 'permanent tie to the district' . . . as the Great Charter phrases it." Dekkard inclined his head. "Thank you, again. We'll walk out with you." He gestured toward the door.

"What are your plans?" asked Seigryn as he walked beside Dekkard.

"First, to sign for a steamer, and then we'll see. We have some exploring to do." Dekkard turned and looked to Avraal. "Shall we go?"

Once they saw Seigryn off at the inn's lobby doors, Dekkard looked to Avraal. "How bad was the damage?"

"From what I sensed, you contained it all."

"With your help."

"Jens definitely tried to set you up," said Avraal quietly. "He must have suggested that they all bring their problems . . . saying something like now that they had a Crafter councilor they should let you know what really needed to be done. Gretna also didn't request to be seated by me."

"You sorted that out, I take it."

Avraal smiled. "We sorted it out. She seemed irritated. So I just asked her if she had any questions for me because Jens had indicated that she wanted to be seated near me. She managed not to explode. After a long moment, she asked if he'd really said that. I told her exactly what you said and Jens's reply."

"And?"

"She asked that neither of us do anything unless we heard from her. Right now, it's probably better that she handles it."

"I don't think this is going to turn out well for Jens," said Dekkard.

"He's having trouble realizing that Guldor's changing. That's another reason why he shouldn't have been councilor. I promised that you'd show up at Gaarlak Mills, outside the larger building, at fourth bell on Furdi, to meet any millworkers who wanted to see you. After that, Arleena Desenns, Gretna, and I decided that you should do the same thing on Unadi afternoon outside the buildings at Lakaan Mills. Arleena said she'd come up with a banner and have it at Gaarlak Mills tomorrow afternoon."

"That was kind and helpful of her."

"She knows that you're the only kind of Crafter who can hold the Gaarlak district, and that otherwise it would go to the Commercers."

"I can see that. In the last election, the Commercer candidate, Wheiter, had twice the votes of the Landor candidate, and was less than two thousand votes behind Decaro." Dekkard paused, then said, "I committed to Charlana that we'd visit craft establishments all around the city while we're here."

"Good."

"How was Alastan Cleese feeling when he left? I tried to smooth that over, and Yorik Haansel said he'd talk to Cleese."

"He was mainly feeling a little embarrassed when he left."

"We should find him and drop by in a day or so, or maybe on Findi."

"Findi," said Avraal. "I already got his home address from Arleena."

"Thank you. It's going to take both of us to do my job . . . but then, you already knew that."

"I did." She smiled warmly. "But it's nice to hear you say it."

"I'll finish the paperwork for the steamer, and we need to go see Namoor."

"I'll get our overcoats from the room while you're doing that." She paused. "Do you have your cards with you, or do I need to get them?"

"I remembered them, but thank you."

As Avraal headed for the staircase, Dekkard went to the lobby desk, where he signed for the small Gresynt steamer that he had arranged for, knowing that he and Avraal needed to become more familiar with the city, and they couldn't do that by being driven around. Having a steamer would allow for much more flexibility, given all that they needed to do in the limited time they had.

"The steamer's out front, sir," said the concierge as he handed over the keys. "It's the dark blue one."

"Thank you." Then Dekkard turned to join Avraal near the foot of the staircase, where he donned his overcoat and Avraal eased the headscarf over her hair, before the two walked out to the Gresynt. It was much like Emrelda's model, but the dark blue paint was more subdued than Emrelda's brilliant teal.

In minutes, Dekkard headed east just past the center square, and its imposing marble statue of Laureous the Great, before turning north through the few blocks containing banques and office buildings. Most of the façades of the three- and four-story buildings looked tired, worn, and grimy. Shortly, he turned left, driving through the North Quarter's grand houses, some of which had definitely seen better days. He tried to remember the route to the more modest dwelling that had been converted to hold the legal offices of Namoor Desharra. Three turns later—one of them wrong, necessitating the other two—Dekkard brought the Gresynt to a stop in front of the three-story, brownish brick dwelling on West Oak Street with the small sign in front reading DESHARRA & ASSOCIATES.

"That wasn't too bad from memory." Dekkard grinned ruefully, then got out, closed his door, and walked around to open the steamer door on Avraal's side.

They walked up three steps and then another five yards to the door. Dekkard was about to try the bellpull when Avraal pointed to a small sign.

IF THE DOOR IS UNLOCKED, PLEASE ENTER.

Dekkard tried the door. It was unlocked. He opened it and motioned for Avraal to precede him.

Before either of them had taken three steps into the foyer, which had a closed door on the right and one on the left that stood open to an empty sitting room, the gray-haired Namoor Desharra appeared and walked through the sitting room toward them.

"Councilor and Ritten Dekkard, you're a bit earlier than I expected. Jens said it might be after fourth bell."

Her words reminded Dekkard that part of Desharra's legal practice was as the legalist for the Craft Party of Gaarlak. He smiled. "Lately, Jens has been a bit confused, at least where we've been concerned. I wouldn't be surprised if that continued."

"You did know that he wanted to be councilor?"

"Not until after I'd been sworn in. I could tell that Axel was stunned that I'd been recommended by the Gaarlak Craft Party."

"I understand that acrimonious would not have been an inappropriate description for the selection meeting, although that might even have understated feelings." Desharra smiled warmly. "It's good that you're here." She motioned to the sitting room. "We have some time before Kelliera Heimdell will be here."

"She's the legalist property agent?" asked Dekkard.

"She's very good . . . and trustworthy." Desharra settled into the armchair facing the dark blue couch.

Dekkard and Avraal took the couch, and Avraal eased the scarf off her hair.

"Before we get to that," Dekkard began, "Gretna Haarl mentioned the legal difficulty with getting Lakaan Mills to comply with the terms the High Justiciary imposed on Gaarlak Mills. Ingrella had mentioned that legal action against each mill corporacion might be necessary . . . unless the Council acted to legislate that change."

"They'll try to litigate that as well." Desharra smiled sardonically.

"Sometime during this session of the Council, I'd thought I'd try to introduce legislation to cut any stalling short. Do you have any suggestions that would reduce the scope of litigation?"

"I like the way you said that, Councilor."

"Steffan . . . please."

"I could send you the language of our brief and the language of the High Justiciary affirming the lower justiciary ruling."

"My legalists would find that incredibly useful, especially since much of their earlier work went up in smoke . . . literally."

"Ingrella wrote me that your office was one of those destroyed. She thinks highly of you, by the way."

"I think incredibly highly of her."

"I'm glad you do. You should."

"I know I've imposed on you, but I'd like your thoughts on another matter." Dekkard leaned forward. "I really need someone here in Gaarlak whom people can contact and who can relay information and concerns to me. Previous councilors relied on family, I suspect."

"If they even bothered." Desharra's lips curled in contempt.

"I don't have inherited wealth, and neither does Avraal. That means any pay for an assistant, an office, and any expenses have to come out of my office account, and it's not exactly capacious."

Desharra frowned for a moment. "We might be able to help. You could sublet from us. There's a tiny room on the other side of the foyer. We've used it as a storage area, but anyone coming would have direct access."

"So they wouldn't be going through your space."

"Exactly. Let me talk to the others, and we'll see what would cover the expense. Much as I'd like to, under the law we can't donate it, even for the official business of a councilor."

"I can see that . . . and if you know of any young legalists who might like a low-paying position . . ."

Desharra laughed. "That will be the least of your problems. Entry-level legalist or legal clerk positions are hard to come by. Some, if it were legal, would pay you."

"I need someone honest enough to tell me what is actually happening, whether they think I want to hear it or not."

"I can think of several possibilities, and you can talk to them later this week."

"Both of us will talk to them," said Dekkard.

"I thought as much," replied the legalist.

"Do you have an address where I could reach Myram Plassar? Her contact information vanished in the attack on the office."

"She mentioned you were looking into expanding the rights to a legalist for working women who weren't eligible to join the guild. She has a small office west of the central square, on Goldenwood Avenue, as I recall. I'll get the exact address while you talk to Kelliera."

The three discussed setting up the office for another third, when a red-haired woman in a gray overcoat walked through the front door, wearing a matching gray headscarf.

"Kelliera . . . come meet the Councilor and Ritten Ysella-Dekkard."

Dekkard immediately stood as the property legalist entered the sitting room, realizing as he did that Kelliera Heimdell was even shorter than Avraal.

At that point Avraal and Desharra stood as well, and the legalist said, "I'll leave you in Kelli's very capable hands. I'll have the documents ready for your office by tomorrow afternoon, and I'm here most of the time if you need anything else."

Heimdell smiled pleasantly. "I understand you're looking for a house. What are your requirements and expectations?"

"It's not so much expectations as limitations." Dekkard gestured to the armchair. "We might as well sit down." Once all three were seated, he went on. "We're not endowed with inherited wealth. So we're looking for something modest in a decent neighborhood, preferably with three bedrooms, a sitting room, a dining room, a study, and two bathrooms . . . and a garage. What would something like that in good repair run . . . or is there anything?"

"Houses here are cheaper than in Machtarn. I'd say, based on what I've reviewed, you could get all of that in a nice neighborhood for around four thousand marks. Five thousand bordering the North Quarter."

Dekkard looked to Avraal.

"What would another thousand marks possibly gain us?" asked Avraal. "And what would be the additional fees and taxes?"

"You'd have to make a deposit to cover half the house taxes for the year, and the property legalist fees are included in the house price. Usually the additional costs are less than five percent. Another thousand marks would give you more space or more rooms . . . or a slightly better location. It just depends on the property." Heimdell shrugged and paused. "It might be better if we took a drive, and I show you houses that are possibilities. If any interest you, I can arrange for you to see them."

Avraal nodded.

"With one condition," added Dekkard. "One of us drives. We also need to learn to get around Gaarlak."

Kelliera Heimdell offered an amused smile. "Of course. Now?"

"Now," said Avraal firmly, rising to her feet.

Before the three left the office Dekkard turned to accept a card from Namoor Desharra, with the address of Myram Plassar, then hurried to catch up to Avraal.

3

O VER the next two bells, Dekkard drove through what seemed to be every street on the north side of Gaarlak. After the last house that Kelliera Heimdell showed them, a squarish boxlike structure with white paint peeling off the brown brick, Dekkard eased the Gresynt to the curb and looked at Avraal. "What do you think?"

"The second house might be worth a second look. That was the one with the double garage and the covered veranda. And the one before this one."

"Those are the two largest of those you looked at," said the property legalist evenly from where she sat in the rear seat of the leased Gresynt.

"It wasn't the size," said Avraal, "but the feel."

"All of the ones you've seen you could move into immediately. Would you be interested in a house that needs some work . . . but could be quite something?"

"It won't hurt to look," said Dekkard.

"It's in the North Quarter, on a quiet street, with quite a few advantages, but . . . you'll see."

As Dekkard followed Heimdell's guidance, he saw that they were headed back toward the part of the North Quarter which contained the more imposing dwellings. *Is this house a converted carriage house or the like?* Not that he had any problem with that. It just had to be something Avraal liked.

"Turn right on the next street, Sunrise Lane."

As Dekkard turned, he realized that the lane was well-named because it was only a block long. Facing each other at both ends of the lane were mansions that dwarfed anything around the Obreduurs' house in Machtarn, and the Obreduurs' house wasn't small. "This is close to our price range?"

"The houses here are spacious, but not enormous," replied Heimdell. "Just look."

Dekkard slowed the steamer and looked. The "lane" was wider than most of the streets in the North Quarter, and the sidewalks were set flush with the curbstones, while the area between the sidewalks and the dwellings was only about six or seven yards. The dwellings were all two-storied, with slate roofs, and looked to be roughly the same size, perhaps a fifth larger than Emrelda's house, but each was distinctively different from its neighbor.

"The next house on the right, the gray stone one. You can just stop in front and see what you think."

Dekkard's first impression was that the house didn't belong, even though it was neither larger nor smaller than the other houses on Sunrise Lane. The obvious difference was that it was built of cut gray stone, rare in Gaarlak, from what he'd seen previously, while the other houses were of brick. The wooden trim was painted a forest green, and the front door looked to be solid oak. Behind the closed shutters, the windows appeared generous in size.

"It looks lovely," said Avraal. "Why is it even available?"

"There was a kitchen fire."

"So everything inside smells like smoke?" asked Dekkard.

"Why don't I just show you? After you've seen it, I'll answer any questions that I can, and then you can make up your own minds."

"Now?" asked Dekkard.

"It's empty. I picked up a key, just in case you were interested. I have the keys for the other two currently vacant houses you saw. Since you didn't appear interested in either, I didn't mention that I had keys."

Dekkard shut down the steamer. "We're here. We might as well look." He got out of the Gresynt and stretched, which felt good after all the driving, chilly as the air was.

As he and Avraal followed Heimdell up the stone walk, small flakes of snow drifted down from the greenish-gray clouds, a reminder that Gaarlak was definitely colder than Machtarn. The brass numbers on the stone wall beside the door indicated that the house was 19 Sunrise Lane, which was definitely odd, given that the numbers on the other nearby north-south streets were in the low two thousands.

"The gas and water have been turned off. It's unfurnished," said Heimdell as she unlocked the solid-oak door and opened it, gesturing for them to step inside.

Dekkard was surprised to discover that the entry foyer was octagonal, and floored with gray and black stone tiles, the black providing a border and marking where the entry ended and the center hall began. The doorway on the left opened into a study, but Dekkard didn't see a door, which struck him as peculiar, until he realized that pocket doors were contained within the archway.

"The original builder was fond of pocket doors," said Heimdell. "They all appear to be in working order."

Dekkard surveyed the study in the dim light that seeped through the closed shutters, taking in the cabinetry on the wall opposite the front window, with the empty bookshelves above it. Then he turned to the other door, where Avraal studied the spacious front parlor.

From there, they moved to the center hall with the staircase to the second floor, and the door to the small powder room on the left, beyond which was a sitting or music room, and then the dining room. Past the parlor, a narrow hallway led to the door to the covered portico and drive. Beyond the side hallway was the breakfast room. As they neared the kitchen, Dekkard tried to see if he could discern any trace of smoke. He could not. When they stepped into the space that should have been the kitchen . . . there was nothing except the wall timbers. Even the plaster and lath had been stripped away on the two exterior walls.

"What happened?" asked Dekkard.

"An older couple bought the house. Rather than just repairing the fire damage, they decided that the entire kitchen needed to be redone. They got this far . . . and they both caught simmeral fever and died. They were from Enke. Their only child, a daughter, wanted nothing to do with it. An . . . investor bought it, and he went bankrupt, and the Lakaan Valley Banque was left with it. They've had it for sale for over a year."

"What are they asking?" Dekkard was mostly curious.

"I can't say. They're open to offers. It would likely cost fifteen hundred to two thousand marks to put a good kitchen in. The previous owners replaced the furnace and the water boilers."

"What do houses on the lane run . . . or would they likely run?" asked Avraal.

"Eight to twelve thousand marks, from past sales. As you saw, they're all about the same size. Do you want to see the upstairs?"

"We've come this far . . ." said Dekkard with a smile, gesturing back in the direction of the hall staircase.

The upper level held a spacious master bedroom with two closets and an en suite bathroom with a separate tub and shower, and a sitting room that could be accessed from the master bedroom or the hall, with another bathroom and three modest bedrooms. From there they went to the basement, which held the laundry tubs, and a separate water boiler, various storerooms, and a wine cellar. Their last stop was the double garage with a small attached workroom.

When they returned to the Gresynt, Heimdell asked, "What do you think?"

Dekkard said nothing, just looked to Avraal.

"It has possibilities, but we need to think it over."

Heimdell handed over a card, to Avraal. "Just let me know if you want to look at those other two houses or what you think about this one, or if you want to look at something entirely different."

"We will," said Avraal.

Beyond pleasantries, Dekkard said very little until after they returned the property legalist to her steamer. Once they were alone in the leased steamer, he asked, "What do you think?"

"I like it. She's right. It could really be something, but we need to know more. The area looks prosperous enough . . . but is it? And what would it really cost to rebuild that kitchen?"

Dekkard grinned. "Why don't we combine finding out with a visit I need to make."

Avraal frowned, then smiled. "Hrald Iglis! That makes sense."

"It does. We know he's good, and he's honest. He won't be cheap, though."

"If we decide to buy that house, the last thing we need is cheap. Do you remember how to get there?"

"His shop is on River Avenue, roughly a mille northeast of the Gaarlak Mills. So all I have to do is head back east until I run into the river."

Getting through the North Quarter to River Avenue was more involved than Dekkard had thought, simply because many through streets *weren't*, and because of North Park, a tree-lined expanse five blocks square whose existence had been unknown to Dekkard—until he encountered it.

"It does look like a pleasant park," said Avraal, "except in winter."

"At least the snow's only coming down in flurries." *So far.* Dekkard had known that they'd likely encounter snow in Gaarlak, but he and Avraal hadn't much choice about when they'd been able to come.

Finally, he turned the steamer north on River Avenue, noting that he was well north of the Gaarlak Mills. Less than a third of a mille later he turned off into the brick-paved parking area in front of the red brick building that held Gaarlak Cabinetry. He parked the steamer beside the door, and they both entered the small front room with its black walnut counter, and the same chair rail, created in the style that was Iglis's less ornate version of old Imperial, that topped black walnut wainscoting.

"There's only one person in back," said Avraal.

Before Dekkard could call out, the stocky but somehow angular Iglis stepped into the front room, absently brushing back his thinning gray hair. His eyes widened as he took in the two.

"You said to stop by when we came to Gaarlak. We got here late yesterday, and I had meetings earlier today."

Iglis shook his head. "Almighty take me. Like I wrote you, never thought I'd see an artisan councilor here in Gaarlak."

"I wouldn't be if Axel hadn't brought me here last summer . . . but I never thought . . ."

"Why did it have to be him? He was working toward some of what those Meritorists wanted."

"It wasn't really the Meritorists . . ." Dekkard went on to give a brief explanation of what had happened and what had been hidden by the sniper's killing of Jaime Minz.

Iglis nodded slowly, then said, "That makes frigging brutal sense. Newssheets said you were targeted, but escaped. Made it sound almost like you were involved."

"That's because the Commercers tried and failed to kill Steffan at least four times," snapped Avraal. "Then they planted that story."

"Sounds about right," said Iglis sardonically.

"You asked how it really happened," said Dekkard. "They aimed for his office first. I saw, then heard the impact, yelled loudly, and got everyone out of the office and into the stairwell—it's solid stone—before they targeted my office."

"You going to carry on what he started?" Iglis's tone of voice held a hint of challenge as he looked directly at Dekkard.

"As best I can . . . along with Ingrella. Together . . . well . . . we'll do everything we can."

"Kind of you to stop by . . ."

"Like someone else, I make every effort to keep my promises . . . and besides, you say what you mean." Dekkard smiled.

Iglis looked surprised.

"You know," Dekkard went on, "Axel never did get to have any of your cabinets."

"That's so. Talked about it . . . more than once."

"We're looking at a house. There's this little provision in the Great Charter that stipulates something about a councilor having a place in his district."

"Think I heard something about that." Iglis's voice was deadpan.

Dekkard caught the glint in his eye and said, "The thing is . . . it needs an entire kitchen. I thought maybe you could give us some advice."

"You talking about the old Tadwyrth place on Sunrise Lane?"

Dekkard laughed softly. "It figures you'd know."

"I turned it down when that pair of fancy-dancers from Enke asked me to do it."

"They didn't want to pay for your work?"

"Not that. They wanted to look over my shoulder every frigging day. Don't work that way."

"If we decided to buy the house and you agreed to do it, I can guarantee you wouldn't have us looking over your shoulder. The Council would be guaranteeing we wouldn't be there."

Iglis looked to Avraal.

"He's already been the target of assassins at least four times. I'm not about to be anywhere except where he is."

This time Iglis laughed. "Axel picked the right man."

"You know the kitchen," said Avraal. "How much would it cost to do it right?"

"I bid eighteen hundred. Should be able to do it for less. Staark cleaned out all the damaged plaster and lath and dumped the old sinks and stuff. The stove was what caused the fire, and it's gone. Bid would include the necessary plaster and lath, sinks, and hookups for stove and anything else."

"Second question . . . or questions," asked Dekkard. "What do you think of the house?"

"If you can buy it at your price, do it. Younger folks with marks are moving back there. The only reason the Tadwyrth place hasn't sold is no one sees beyond the emptiness of the kitchen."

"Thank you. If we decide to buy it—"

Iglis laughed loudly and looked at Avraal. "I think someone else already made that decision."

Dekkard shook his head. "Then . . . if we can persuade them to sell it at a price we can afford . . . meaning that we have enough marks left to fix it, we'll look forward to you giving us a kitchen." He paused. "You wouldn't mind arranging for the stove and a gas cooler."

"Be better that way. Cabinets'll fit cleaner."

"One way or another, we'll let you know."

"From what I've seen of you two, you'll be having a fine house in Gaarlak."

"We'll have to see." Dekkard grinned.

"Go make it work out. You need a house, and I could use the work."

"We'll talk to you when we know," said Avraal.

"Until later," added Dekkard, turning toward the door.

Once they were outside in the intermittent snow, Avraal said quietly, "You made his day, maybe his month."

"His work is outstanding, and he's honest. Shall we head back to find Kelliera?" Dekkard opened the steamer door for her.

"I thought you'd never ask." Avraal slipped into the front passenger seat of the Gresynt.

Dekkard smiled.

Before he started the steamer, he checked the address on Kelliera Heimdell's card—890 West Beech Street.

Once they were headed back to the northwest side of Gaarlak, Dekkard said, "How much should we offer?"

"As little as we have to. The Lakaan Valley Banque won't meet personally with us. Kelliera will present our offer, and they'll accept, reject, or counter."

Although Dekkard had never bought a house before, he'd assumed the negotiations would be at arm's length, particularly since Avraal was an empath. "Five thousand marks?"

She frowned. "Six, I think. They won't take less. They might not take that. It will cost us at least three thousand to make it livable, and that still would put the total worth at nine thousand. Then we'll have to think about furniture."

"Of which we have none," said Dekkard dryly. "Unless you have a stash of that somewhere."

"Alas, my dear," replied Avraal, clutching her headscarf pseudo-dramatically, "I am but a disinherited Landor maid, with no property to my name."

"Outside of a bond that will provide almost all of the marks going toward a house," Dekkard replied in an ironically amused tone.

"I wouldn't have those if you weren't a councilor," said Avraal, her tone firm.

"And if other Landor councilors hadn't written your parents."

"For a moment I was tempted to send it back."

"I wondered about that," admitted Dekkard.

"You didn't say anything."

"If I said anything until you did, anything I said would have sounded self-serving. I think you deserve more than you got, but if I said so . . ." He shook his head. "And if I told you to send it back, then it would make matters even worse with your parents and you'd have nothing but more unhappiness."

After several moments, Avraal nodded, then said, "It also would have made matters worse for Emrelda."

"I could have said that any comment would be self-serving . . . but that would have been almost as bad, because without you saying anything . . ."

She leaned over and kissed his cheek. "So we might as well spend some of it."

"Some of it should go in an account in your name, at the Lakaan Valley Banque . . . if they sell us the house. I'll also open an account there. It will make transferring funds easier."

"What happens if . . ."

"If there's an election and I lose? If Hrald is right, we shouldn't lose money on the house . . . and that's if we don't want to move here permanently."

"Do you think we would? Honestly?" Avraal sounded slightly appalled.

"Did you ever think you'd be a premier's security aide who married a failed artisan who was a security aide? Did I ever think I'd be a councilor?"

She smiled wryly. "You have a point. It would be good to have somewhere to go just in case . . . even though what we'd do here is problematical."

"Then . . . why . . ." *do you want to buy this house?*

"Because buying a tiny place indicates we're doing it because we must. Because, in Gaarlak, we'll definitely lose marks if we buy small and cheap. Because buying this house will show your immediate commitment to Gaarlak." She paused. "And because it feels right in a way I can't explain." She paused. "And when we have it the way we want it, I can have a photograph taken or an etching made and send it to my parents as a thank-you." She grinned.

"That's if the banque accepts our offer." *Your offer, really.*

"They will. Kelliera as much as said they wanted to get it off their books, but they have to be able to justify it as being close to market value, less repairs."

Since Avraal was usually right in what she felt, Dekkard just nodded.

A sixth or so later, Dekkard brought the Gresynt to a halt in front of another imposing dwelling that had been converted into offices. When they walked up to the double doors and then into the small foyer, Dekkard checked the building directory. Heimdell & Bader was on the first floor. By the time Dekkard had consulted the directory, Avraal had found and opened the office door. Dekkard had to hurry to catch her.

The secretary/receptionist looked up at the couple, then smiled. "Might you be Councilor and Ritten Dekkard?"

"We are," said Dekkard.

"Legalist Heimdell said you might come by. If you'd come with me . . ."

In moments, the two were seated in a small office with two narrow windows that only offered a view of the portico of the adjoining dwelling.

Behind a desk with several neatly stacked folders sat Kelliera Heimdell. "You've made a decision, I take it."

"We'll make an offer on Nineteen Sunrise Lane."

Heimdell nodded. "What sort of offer?"

"Six thousand marks, drawn on a personal bond from the Banque of Sudaen," said Avraal. "We did some research, and replacing the kitchen will likely cost two thousand marks, plus the cost of a stove and a cooler. There are likely other repairs necessary as well."

"That may be slightly less than the banque hopes for."

"They'll obviously be getting new account holders as well," replied Avraal evenly.

"Then I'll have the papers prepared."

"When will they be ready?" asked Dekkard.

"Around third bell. If you come back then and sign the offer sheet, I can get them to the banque today. I need a few details from you two, beginning with your full names and occupations." Heimdell smiled as she looked at Dekkard. "Your occupation is obvious."

"Steffan Delos Dekkard."

Then Heimdell turned to Avraal.

"Avraal Mikaila Ysella-Dekkard. I'm a certified consulting empath for Baartol Associates in Machtarn."

"Ysella . . . that's an old name . . . ?"

"Yes," replied Avraal. "My father is the Ritter Mikail Ysella."

"Will the title be joint?"

"Yes," said Avraal.

"If I might see the bond . . ."

Avraal handed it over.

Heimdell's eyes widened slightly, but she returned it and asked, "How do you plan to have the balance handled?"

"Three thousand marks in an interest-bearing account in my name at the Lakaan Valley Banque, and the balance, after legal expenses and fees, in a bond back to me."

"Just your name for the account?"

"Just her name," said Dekkard. "I'll be opening an account in my name."

In less than another sixth, Avraal and Dekkard left the office of the property legalist.

"We have several bells," said Avraal. "Do you have something in mind?"

"I do. I'd like to stop by Julian Baurett's house."

"The stipended patroller?"

"He'd know as well as anyone how the Security reforms worked out here, and I'd like his views before I encounter anyone in Public Safety in Gaarlak."

Once again it took Dekkard longer than he anticipated to locate Baurett's older red brick house, located several blocks west and almost a score south of Heimdell's office. As Dekkard and Avraal got out of the leased steamer, he noticed that the snow flurries had stopped and that the greenish-gray clouds were lighter in color and higher, suggesting that there wouldn't be a heavy snow. *At least not for a while.*

He knocked on the door. There was no reply. After a moment, he knocked harder.

A gruff voice called out from inside, "Who is it?"

Dekkard decided to handle Baurett the way Obreduur had. "The pretty boy who became councilor."

"Let yourself in. Need to see if your head's swelled."

Dekkard opened the door, followed Avraal in, then closed the door behind himself.

Baurett was sitting in the same armchair as the last time Dekkard and Avraal had seen him, except there was a fire in the hearth. He did not stand as he looked from Avraal to Dekkard. "Pretty boy or not, you were smart to marry her. Why are you two bothering with an old has-been?" He leaned forward slightly and seemed to wince, but gestured to the armchair and the worn cream and maroon settee.

Dekkard and Avraal took the settee, and Dekkard replied, "Because you're not a has-been and you know a lot. Besides, who else would tell me where I've screwed up?"

Baurett laughed. "Sounds like something Axel would have said."

"We both learned a lot from him."

"You know you weren't his choice?"

"I knew, and I told him I knew, and he admitted it."

"Is Jens outside?"

"No."

"Good thing. Frigging good thing."

"We did have to use him to set up the guild breakfast this morning. There wasn't another way because I couldn't get things together soon enough." *And couldn't figure out any way to go around Jens that wouldn't have made matters worse.*

"What do you want to know . . . or was that just lager froth?"

"What should I know about Jens that I don't?"

"Couldn't prove it, but he had to be the one behind Decaro's death . . ."

Not the cobbler? Or did Jens blackmail her?

". . . pretty sure he was the one who set up Marjoy. Only met her once, when Lewes came through. Mean woman, but she didn't know the butt of a pistol from the barrel. No way she could have shot Lewes, then herself."

For a long moment, Dekkard managed not to swallow. "He did that to get Obreduur's position as regional coordinator?"

"No other way he was going to get it, not so long as Axel was there. Axel suspected, I think, but there wasn't any proof. With Jens, there never is."

Dekkard could see that, and there had been more than enough hints that there was a darker side to Jens Seigryn. "I suspected there was more to Jens, but not as much as you're indicating."

"Most folks think the way you did. Not much more to say about that. What else do you want to know?"

Dekkard had to think, trying to get his thoughts back in order. "What did your boys in the Benevolent Society think of the Security reforms?"

"Most of 'em wondered why someone hadn't done it sooner. You really the one who put that together?"

"For better or worse. The ideas were mine. My legalists made sure the language was correct."

Baurett looked to Avraal. "That right?"

"It is. Axel never saw what Steffan had drafted until it came up for a vote. They never talked about it, either."

The former patroller looked back to Dekkard. "You could have done a lot worse. Axel didn't listen to you on some things, did he?"

"Not on everything. Some things we couldn't get the votes for. How did it work out here?"

Baurett offered an amused smile. "We never had any STFs. Only a squad of SAs. Half of 'em quit. The others went to work for the regional Justiciary office as investigators. It'll be like that except in the bigger cities. Biggest impact had to be in Machtarn." He looked once more to Avraal. "How many attempts on your pretty boy? Besides the shelling?"

"Too many."

Baurett turned back to Dekkard. "You figure it's over?"

Dekkard smiled sardonically. "Hardly. The only question is when the Commercers and corporacions climb back out of their holes."

"Another month. Sometime in spring. How good is the latest Councilor Obreduur?"

"Very good, but in a quieter way."

Baurett nodded approvingly, then asked, "You two house-hunting?"

"Yes."

"Stay in the city."

"We're looking at a place not far from here."

"Make it modestly impressive, if you can. Too big, and they'll think you're a Commercer posing as a Crafter. Too small, and you don't really care about Gaarlak."

"We figured that."

"I can't say that surprises me. What are your plans while you're here?"

Over the next third of a bell, Dekkard and Avraal told him, as well as asked questions and for suggestions.

Finally, Baurett smiled, almost tiredly, and said, "I can't tell you how much I appreciated the visit. Almost makes me feel useful again." He held up a hand. "No protests. You could have asked a lot of others."

"But they wouldn't have been as direct," replied Dekkard. "We need that . . . and we appreciate it."

"Sometime . . . not necessarily now—I know you've got a lot to do— stop in and talk with Josiah Arkham. He's a lieutenant at the main patroller station in Gaarlak. Joe's good people. Tell him that his worst critic sent you."

"We'll do that." Dekkard smiled as he stood. "Thank you again."

Baurett looked to Avraal. "You're his security, right."

"He also has an emotional-pattern sensor in Machtarn."

"Smart. Now . . . get on your way. I've taken enough of your time."

"We won't argue . . . this time," said Dekkard as he moved to the door, waiting for Avraal as Baurett murmured something to her that Dekkard couldn't make out.

Once they were in the steamer heading back to Heimdell's office, he asked, "What did he say to you?"

"That I was to keep you safe, that there weren't enough like you."

"There aren't enough like you."

"I'll accept that," she replied with a hint of a smile, "but I'm not the target you are, and Julian knows it." She paused, then added, "He doesn't want to show it, but he's not well."

"He's a lot weaker than when we saw him last summer." Dekkard paused, then said, "That bit about Jens . . . I don't doubt Julian, but still it's hard to believe that Axel didn't say more . . . or do something . . . except . . . without proof . . ."

"And if he did," Avraal pointed out, "he'd be thought of as an accessory."

Dekkard could see that, but it still bothered him.

He stopped the Gresynt outside Heimdell's office at a half before third bell. "We might as well go in. They might even have the papers ready."

Avraal adjusted the headscarf before getting out of the Gresynt, and the two walked to the converted small mansion.

When they entered the office, the receptionist stood. "I'll take you back. She thought you might be early."

Kelliera Heimdell stood by her desk as Avraal and Dekkard arrived. "We just finished a few minutes ago." She picked up the two-page document and handed it to Avraal, then gestured to the chairs. "Please read it carefully."

Avraal sat down and began to read. Dekkard seated himself in the other chair in front of the desk. When she finished, she handed the two sheets to Dekkard.

He read the document twice, but couldn't find anything wrong with it. He looked to Heimdell. "Avraal can give you the bond, but it's drawn on the Banque of Sudaen."

"That's not a problem. Avraal will sign over the bond to the banque, and receive a certificate of deposit for it. The banque will hold the property in escrow until the funds clear. From Sudaen, that's likely to take from two to four days. At that point, the deed will be executed, and she will receive the balance of funds in whatever form she specifies, which could be in mark notes, a personal bond, an account in the banque, or some combination, less the legal and registration fees, which will be approximately a hundred marks."

Dekkard looked to Avraal, who nodded, then said, "We'll sign."

After both signed the offer, Heimdell said, "I might have an answer this afternoon, but it's more likely that it won't be until midday tomorrow. Where are you staying?"

"At the Ritter's Inn."

Heimdell nodded. "I'll send a message there if I get an answer this afternoon. What about tomorrow?"

"We'll be making the rounds most of the day," said Dekkard. "If we don't hear before we set out on our day's schedule tomorrow morning, we'll stop by here when we can." He inclined his head. "Thank you."

"Thank you, Ritten Ysella-Dekkard, Councilor."

Neither Dekkard nor Avraal spoke until they reached the steamer, when Dekkard looked to Avraal. "What do you think?"

She smiled wryly. "We either made a great decision or a terrible mistake."

"Only if the banque accepts the offer."

"They'll accept it." She paused. "We have some time before dinner."

"I did promise Charlana Boetcher I'd visit shops. We could go back to the inn, park the Gresynt, and see what shops are around."

"Why don't we drive around the blocks near the inn first and see what's there?"

Dekkard laughed. "That's more practical, especially in this weather."

4

A SIXTH past fourth bell found Dekkard and Avraal, having left the Gresynt in the hotel parking area, walking west toward Alycia's, which had appeared to be a shop catering to women a little less than a block away.

"Somehow, it feels different doing this for myself," said Dekkard.

"You met people without Obreduur present."

"But he could always save the situation if I mishandled it. Now . . ." Dekkard shrugged.

"You never did," said Avraal, "but I understand."

The store window featured modest suits, one in bright blue and the other in a deep rose, on two female mannequins, with a display of handbags in between.

"There's only one person inside," said Avraal.

Dekkard opened the glass-fronted door, then followed Avraal. The shop was a good ten yards wide and semi-divided into front and rear sections, with what appeared to Dekkard to be blouses and casual wear in the front, with more formal wear toward the rear. Two short angled display cases were set in the middle to form a V with a small bronze mechanical cash register resting on the short case that joined them.

The blond woman in a tasteful security-blue suit and a white blouse, who had been replacing a jacket on a rack, immediately turned and said to Avraal, "Good afternoon. I love your coat. Might I ask where you got it?"

Dekkard took in her face, judging that she was roughly fifteen years older than he was, or perhaps a little less.

"Julieta, in Machtarn," replied Avraal.

"I've heard that it's very stylish. Were you visiting Machtarn?"

Avraal smiled and turned to Dekkard. "If you would explain, dear?"

"I'm Steffan Dekkard, the councilor recently appointed to represent Gaarlak. We're here hunting for an appropriate house, since it was suggested that the city was most appropriate for a Craft councilor."

For just an instant, there was a hint of surprise on the woman's face. "And you're here?"

"I'm here to find out about where to shop," said Avraal.

"And I'm here to introduce myself . . . and to find out what you need from a councilor."

"You're really a councilor? Really?"

"For better or worse." He handed her one of his engraved cards, which bore his Council Office Building address.

"I'm pleased to meet you."

"Are you Alycia? Or was the name chosen for effect?" Dekkard smiled. "Or perhaps both?"

"My mother thought it was an effective and beautiful name. I'll settle for effective. The full name is Alycia Elisabet Kerguellen. Are you honestly house-hunting?"

"We've put in an offer," replied Dekkard. "How long have you had this shop?"

"Eight years in Springfirst. I love clothes, and there wasn't a shop like this in Gaarlak. I thought I'd give it a try. The first years were . . . uneasy, but now it's working well. I even have some regular customers who come from Enke." Kerguellen paused. "Wasn't there a story about your wedding . . . and that you two were . . . was it security . . . for the Premier, the one who the radicals killed, I mean."

"Yes, there was a story," replied Dekkard. "And we were security for Premier Obreduur, until I became a councilor. But since I'm here as a councilor, I'd like to know your thoughts about matters involving the Council."

"I don't know that the Council has much to do with shops like mine."

"Not directly, but how we regulate the ironways or the waterways affects how much goods cost you. And if something does come up, feel free to write me. In a few weeks, I'll have a small office here in Gaarlak where you can tell someone if you don't feel like writing."

Kerguellen nodded, thoughtfully.

"I won't take any more of your time, Alycia, and I wish you the best with your shop."

"It was good to see a councilor in person. I never have. Good fortune with your house offer."

"Thank you," said Avraal warmly, before she eased Dekkard away from the display case and out of the shop.

The next stop had a name painted across the glass—THE FURNITURE EMPORIUM—and from the table and chairs in the display window looked to carry modest wooden furniture of the sort manufactured in quantity either in Eshbruk or Nolaan, or perhaps Aaken.

Dekkard took a slow deep breath, then stepped inside.

A heavyset, blond young man strode up to him, wearing a less-than-expensive brown woolen suit. "Welcome to the Furniture Emporium. If you need it, we have it . . . or we can get it."

"That's good to know," said Dekkard pleasantly. "We're not buying at present, but we might in the future."

"Can I show you what we have? That way, you'll know when you come back."

"We're here for a different reason." Dekkard handed the young man a card. "I'm the new councilor for Gaarlak. I stopped in to let you know that. The card has my office address in Machtarn, and that's where you can contact me."

"You're the councilor?"

"I am, and this is my wife. You are . . . ?"

"Haarys Duuvrey, sir. I wish my uncle were here. It's his store. He went out on a delivery. You're really the councilor?"

"That's right. The former councilor was Emilio Raathan. I'm the new one."

"I'll tell him you were here."

"Thank you, Haarys."

After they left the store, Dekkard asked, "What did you think of the furniture?"

"Some of it would be appropriate for the breakfast room. Other than that, I didn't see anything that demanded to be bought. Did you?"

Dekkard shook his head.

The next shop, adjacent to an alley, was small, no more than four yards wide, and belonged to a cobbler, thankfully not Myshella Degriff, who just might have been Jens Seigryn's agent in setting up the "heart attack" that killed Haasan Decaro.

When Avraal and Dekkard entered, he could see that the cobbler, who didn't look to be that much older than Dekkard, was working with a pedal treadle sewing machine. He called out, "I'll be with you in a minute."

"Finish what you're doing," Dekkard called back, as he looked around the front room with barely enough space for three people to stand in front of the oil-finished wooden counter.

Several minutes passed before the cobbler left the sewing machine and walked to the counter. "You don't have any shoes with you, and I'm not buying anything."

Dekkard smiled pleasantly. "I'm not selling anything. I'm Steffan Dekkard, the new councilor for Gaarlak. Now that the Council's in recess, I'm here to meet people."

"I only vote Craft."

"I am a Crafter. I started out as a decorative plasterer. After military training, I worked as a security aid for former Premier Obreduur—the one who was assassinated last month."

"I heard his name. What do you want?"

"Nothing . . . just to introduce myself . . . and to give you someone to complain to when you don't like what the Council's doing." Dekkard handed him a card.

The cobbler glanced at it, then dropped it into a small drawer behind the counter. "Anything else?"

"Not until I need my boots resoled."

"I'll see you then, Councilor."

Dekkard nodded. "Thank you for your time."

When they were back on the sidewalk and past the alley, Dekkard asked, "Was he angry inside or just rude?"

"I couldn't tell, but trying to shift his mood would have made him suspicious . . . or even more suspicious."

Dekkard could see that. "Are all cobblers angry . . . or just the ones I've met?"

"I've met one or two who were quite nice."

Dekkard shook his head.

The next stop was at a shop with a modest sign reading SILVER & GOLD, which was clearly a pawnshop, with various items in old but clean glass cases or hung on the wall.

"You two are right stylish. Looking for old jewelry, perhaps?" asked a white-haired man, attired in pressed gray trousers, a white shirt, and a security-blue sweater over the shirt.

"No. I'm here to make your acquaintance, and I'm not selling anything." Dekkard handed him a card. "I'm the new councilor for Gaarlak."

"Alphons Giiltjens, owner and proprietor." He grinned. "And you are selling something. Yourself."

Dekkard grinned back. "Absolutely. Except that I'm also giving you someone to write and complain to if you have problems the Council might be able to fix."

"You're a brave man," replied Giiltjens. "Most folks either want to complain or to be left alone. You two were in the newssheets last summer, weren't you?"

"We were."

"How'd you get to be councilor?"

"Most of the guilds chose me. I still don't know precisely why."

"Because Haasan Decaro was a swindling scoundrel and Jens Seigryn was worse. Just had nicer manners. I'm guessing folks figured no one bothered to get to you. That right?"

"Some of them tried very hard after he became councilor," said Avraal. "They didn't much like his Security reforms."

Giiltjens glanced toward the golden pin in her lapel, barely visible because of her overcoat. "That's why you're with him now?"

Avraal smiled. "Partly . . . but also because we got married."

"Still a team, then." The pawnshop proprietor grinned. "You sure you wouldn't like to look at jewelry?"

Avraal smiled back warmly. "Not right now, but I might the next time."

"I'll take that as a maybe . . . and I'll keep the card, just in case."

When they left the pawnshop. Dekkard looked to Avraal.

"He was what he seemed. He doesn't like Jens very much."

Over the next bell, Dekkard and Avraal visited another six establishments, including a menswear shop, a watchmaker, a butcher shop, a dry goods store, and a tiny shop that only sold women's headscarves. Then they started back toward the inn, walking into a chill wind.

"I'm getting the feeling that for these people," said Dekkard, "Emilio Raathan was almost invisible."

"That's not surprising. He's a Landor," replied Avraal dryly.

Dekkard laughed, if softly. "We need to go have some dinner . . . someplace warm."

"And get something to drink."

Dekkard just nodded. After less than two bells of meeting people, he was ready for a break.

When they stepped into the Ritter's Inn, Dekkard was grateful, not so much for the warmth of the lobby as for the lack of wind. "Do you want to go up to the room before we eat?"

"I do. Why don't you check the desk first, just in case there's a message? I'll wait by the staircase."

Dekkard walked over to the desk.

"Yes, Councilor?" asked the clerk.

"Do we have any messages?"

"I believe there's one. Let me check."

In a moment, he returned with a single large messenger-service envelope, which he handed to Dekkard. "That's all, sir."

"Thank you." Dekkard walked back to where Avraal waited at the foot of the staircase, then said, "There's one message. I can't tell from the envelope."

"Let's walk up to the room. I'm getting warm in this coat."

Less than a sixth later, the two stood in their room, coats off and hung up.

Dekkard extracted one of his throwing knives from its waist sheath and used the sharpened tip to open the messenger-service envelope. Inside was a business-sized envelope bearing the engraved return address of Heimdell & Bader. "You should open it. You're going to be paying for it." He extended the knife to her and watched as she carefully slit open the inner envelope, then returned his knife before taking out the single sheet.

Then she smiled. "The banque accepted our offer without any changes. The documents will be ready by fourth bell tomorrow morning. We're to go to her office first."

"Congratulations. Now . . . shall we go have something to eat?"

"We should." She smiled ruefully and added, "Either to celebrate good fortune or to console ourselves for tying ourselves to Gaarlak at a very uncertain time."

"Both," replied Dekkard, his smile as rueful as hers.

5

J UST before fourth bell, Dekkard brought the Gresynt to a halt outside the offices of Heimdell & Bader, somewhat later than intended because of the delay in warming up the steamer. As the two walked toward the converted dwelling, Dekkard could see the steam of his own breath in the cold clear air. He was glad he'd thought to bring gloves.

"At least we won't have any illusions about winter in Gaarlak," said Dekkard as he opened the building door. "We're fortunate it hasn't snowed more than it did."

"It still could. We're going to be here for another week."

Kelliera Heimdell met them in the foyer, pulling on her leather gloves as she said, "It might be best if we each took our own steamers. I have some other matters later, and I'm sure you have a crowded schedule."

"We'll follow you," said Dekkard. "Is there anything we should know?"

"It's fairly standard. I know you understand this, but it's my obligation as a property legalist to point out that you can't take possession or make any physical changes to the house until the funds clear, because you won't technically be the owners until then."

Dekkard glanced to Avraal.

"Since we have no furniture and need to work out restoring the kitchen, that's not a problem."

The two left the foyer behind Heimdell, got in the Gresynt, and followed the legalist back into the southwest end of the banking section of central Gaarlak past the imposing red brick structure of the Banque of Gaarlak, with its gray stone quoins, to a much smaller brown brick building farther to the southwest, where they parked in the small lot beside the banque. The brick walls weren't grimy, but they looked worn, although the bronze doors were polished.

Heimdell led them through the front entrance into a foyer. On the left side were the teller cages, on the right a door that the property legalist held open, then closed after Avraal and Dekkard entered. Avraal let her headscarf slip off her hair, as did Heimdell.

The secretary at the desk adjacent to the door looked to the legalist.

"Ritten Ysella-Dekkard and Councilor Dekkard."

"The small conference room, Legalist Heimdell. I'll let Director Raensyn know you're here."

In moments, the three were in a small, oak-paneled room, with dark green drapes flanking the single frosted glass window. The circular table and the chairs were also oak. The only other furniture was a long and narrow side table set against the left wall.

Dekkard wondered whether they should stand or sit, but didn't have to choose because an older white-haired man and a somewhat younger woman entered the chamber.

Heimdell immediately spoke, "Ritten, Councilor, I'd like to introduce Pietr Raensyn, director of real estate for the banque, and Patrice Ellisyn. She's the legalist who handles mortgages and property transfers. Pietr, Patrice, Ritten Avraal Ysella-Dekkard and Councilor Steffan Delos Dekkard."

"I'm pleased to meet you both," declared Raensyn. "I don't believe Gaarlak has had a Craft councilor in a long time, not in my lifetime, anyway. Certainly not a couple as distinguished as you both are." He smiled briefly. "Given that this is essentially a marks-only transaction, there's far less paperwork involved. Patrice will go over that with you, and then I'll make sure that the financial aspects are correct . . ."

In less than a third, Dekkard and Avraal were walking out of the banque.

"The house is yours once the funds clear," said Heimdell. "It might be as soon as late on Quindi, but will more likely be sometime on Unadi. Conceivably, it might take a day or two longer, depending on the Banque of Sudaen. I'll send a message to the Ritter's Inn as soon as I know, but feel free to check with me anytime."

"How did it end up in the Lakaan Valley Banque, instead of the Banque of Gaarlak?" asked Dekkard.

"The man who bought the property had a large line of credit with the banque for his engineering business. He had severe difficulties in meeting deadlines. That put him in default and led to bankruptcy. He took his life. The banque was awarded the property as partial compensation. What was left of his business was turned over to his other creditor."

"I'm surprised that he didn't go to the Banque of Gaarlak for a business line of credit," said Dekkard.

"The Banque of Gaarlak seldom lends to those without considerable assets, preferably liquid assets, or impressive non-liquid assets . . . or, occasionally, to offspring of those with such assets. The Lakaan Valley Banque charges higher rates for such loans, which usually offset the higher risks. It's quite solid, and most crafters and smaller businesses bank with it."

"Thank you for helping us with the house," said Dekkard, "and explaining about the banques."

"It was definitely my pleasure. I think you'll be much happier there than anyplace else I could have shown you. From what I've read in the newssheets, you might even be happier in your house here than in Machtarn."

"That's a possibility, at least at times," agreed Dekkard.

"We'll be in touch," said Avraal warmly.

When Dekkard and Avraal were alone in the Gresynt, he asked, "What did you sense in the banque?"

"Mild interest, and a certain wonderment on the part of the banque legalist that she was even there. Sr. Raensyn was pleased that it all went well, but not the kind of pleased where he just wanted it out of his hands."

"Even after buying the house and restoring the kitchen," said Dekkard, "you'll still have close to half—"

"Forty percent, more likely, after unanticipated expenses, and that doesn't include furniture."

"Right now, I have over three thousand marks—"

"Just save it for now," said Avraal. "We'll worry about furniture later."

"You need to save what's left of the bond. We can buy furniture bit by bit . . . or save the marks to buy it, bit by bit."

"That's what I meant, dear." She paused. "Now . . . what are we going to do until fourth bell . . . as if I don't know?"

"Visiting more small shops, of course. I'd thought we ought to do an area on the southeast side closer to the river, then take a break for café and a little something to eat before we go to the mills."

"It's a good thought. People need to see their councilor, and you need to be able to mention that at lunch tomorrow with Martenya Oguire. It can't hurt to have her mention it somewhere."

"I'd still like to know how she found out so quickly when we were coming. She sent that heliogram even before we finished making arrangements, not that I hadn't planned to see her."

Avraal laughed. "She's the owner and publisher of the *Gaarlak Times*, and you have to ask? After all the people you contacted?"

Dekkard offered a sheepish smile as he started the Gresynt. "There is that." After several minutes, he eased the steamer out of the parking area and headed east.

They'd only traveled a few blocks when Avraal asked, "Why did you ask about the banques?"

"I was curious. I was very glad the Banque of Gaarlak didn't have the property. That would have cost us a fair bit more."

"Why do you think that?"

"Because the Commercer candidate in the last election lost to Decaro by less than two thousand votes, and he was the son of the presidente of the Banque of Gaarlak."

Avraal just shook her head.

The first stop was Gaarlak Cabinetry. When they walked in, Iglis was behind the counter.

"Yes or no?" he asked.

"They took our offer," said Dekkard. "We don't get possession until the funds clear."

"Raensyn won't stall on that. They're not making marks on a property they couldn't move, and they're partial to Crafters anyway."

"What sort of wood would you suggest for the kitchen?" asked Avraal.

"Depends on how light or dark you want the room. Light . . . and I'd go with maple or golden oak. Goldenwood's a shade lighter, but maple and oak are tougher, and in a kitchen you need that. Oak has a more obvious grain. That's a personal choice . . ."

"I'm inclined to go with a lighter wood . . ." began Avraal.

Dekkard just listened as Avraal and Iglis talked about wood, while his thoughts went to Jens Seigryn. He still wondered whether Seigryn would try something more direct than the setup at the breakfast with the guildmeisters.

"Steffan . . . don't you think it would be best if Hrald brought wood samples to the house?"

"We're fairly flexible on Duadi, and funds should clear by then." Dekkard turned to Iglis. "What if we came by in the afternoon?"

"I can do that. I could also do Unadi if you get possession earlier."

"Then we'll see you whenever we take possession," said Avraal warmly.

"I'll not be going anywhere."

Once they left Iglis and were in the Gresynt headed south, Avraal asked, "You weren't all there when I was talking to Hrald."

"I'm sorry. I was thinking about Jens Seigryn and what he might be up to."

"No good, but all we can do is keep our eyes open."

Dekkard hoped that would be enough.

For the next two bells, the two walked through the shops that lay well east of the center square—and the imposing marble statue of Laureous the Great—then stopped at a small bistro for café and chorzipan. By that time, even with his gloves, Dekkard's hands felt cold.

After that, Dekkard drove north to another shop area, this one midway between the eastern edge of the North Quarter and the Lakaan River. After walking and talking to shop owners and clerks and others for well over a bell, they returned to the Gresynt and drove east to the river and the largest building of the Gaarlak Mills complex.

Dekkard had barely parked on River Avenue when a much older Ferrum pulled up behind the Gresynt. Gretna Haarl and another woman, whom Dekkard didn't recall meeting, got out of the older steamer.

"Councilor—" began Haarl.

"Steffan, Gretna," said Dekkard cheerfully. "I can't spend however long I'm councilor having you address me that way. Especially since you're a guildmeister. At the infrequent formal events, as necessary, but on River Avenue in the middle of winter?"

Dekkard was both surprised and pleased that Haarl laughed.

Then she said, "Steffan, this is Ladora Ingelstaat. She's one of the assistant guildmeisters."

Dekkard inclined his head slightly. "I'm pleased to meet you, Ladora. I appreciate your coming out in this weather."

"Thank you." Ingelstaat grinned. "For winter, this is warm."

"Steffan," added Haarl, "we have the banner that Arleena had made. I thought we'd go to the omnibus shelter and prop it up where workers will see it as they leave the mill."

"That makes sense to me."

Immediately, Ingelstaat removed a bundle from the rear seat of the Ferrum, and all four crossed River Avenue. When they reached the omnibus shelter, Haarl and Ingelstaat immediately set up the banner, each end fastened to a two-part pole a little more than two yards long. Dekkard studied the banner. All it said was COUNCILOR STEFFAN DEKKARD. That was all it had to say.

A few minutes passed, and an omnibus pulled up beside the shelter. Then the mill whistle blew, signifying the shift change, and before long, workers began to leave the mill building. A few headed toward the parking area that held a score of older steamers, but most walked toward the waiting omnibus. The first few workers looked at the banner curiously.

Dekkard stepped forward slightly and declared heartily, "It's not a joke or an illusion. I'm the new councilor for Gaarlak. I'm here to meet you and, if you want, to answer any questions you have."

"Are you really a councilor? You look young for that," said a woman with a weathered face.

"I am one of the younger councilors, but, yes, I'm really a councilor."

". . . thought so," murmured the younger woman beside her.

"Why are you here?"

"I'm the first Craft councilor from Gaarlak in a long time." *Like never.* "I may look a bit dressy, but I started out as a decorative plasterer. I'm here because I wanted you to see and meet someone representing you who knows what hard physical work is."

"You really start as plasterer?"

"I did. Then I got military training and went into security. I became a security aide for Councilor Obreduur from Oersynt. When he became premier, I became the councilor for Gaarlak."

"What's the minister who's in charge of waterways going to do to stop all the flooding?"

"I don't know what the ministry plans. I do know that they're concerned, and I'll make a point of looking into it when I get back to Machtarn."

"Just looking into it won't help."

"No, it won't, but I have to find out what they plan before I can do anything."

After that the questions came faster, some angry, some curious.

"Folks are hungry. What are you going to do about it?"

"Why haven't you fixed the levees to stop the flooding?"

"Never saw no councilors before. What do you really want?"

"Not enough food, but the Council keeps the Landors in style. Why don't you do something?"

"What happened to the old councilor?"

For not quite two-thirds of a bell Dekkard talked to whoever stopped, possibly as many as forty millworkers, and that didn't count those who asked no questions, but who just listened, mostly to pass the time waiting for the next omnibus. Then, the sidewalk and shelter were empty.

Dekkard coughed and cleared his throat, feeling a little hoarse.

"That went better than I thought it might," said Haarl.

"You don't sound like a new councilor," said Ingelstaat.

"Is that good or bad?" asked Dekkard humorously.

"Good," said Haarl.

The two women lowered the banner, took the poles apart, and in minutes wrapped it all into a compact bundle.

"Unadi at Lakaan Mills?" Haarl's words were more statement than question.

"Unadi at fourth bell," confirmed Dekkard as the four waited for a steam lorry to pass before crossing River Avenue.

After they saw the two guild officials off, Dekkard and Avraal got into the Gresynt and headed back to Namoor Desharra's office to pick up the documents she had promised. While the legalist wasn't there, the documents were.

Dekkard asked for a note card and wrote a grateful appreciation to the legalist for the materials, then carried the documents out to the Gresynt.

"I'm more than ready to get back to the inn . . . and a hot meal, with a lager . . . possibly two."

"Just one . . . and we can read another section in *The City of Truth*."

"You brought it with us?"

"Of course. I thought we'd have time to read."

Dekkard liked the way she smiled after she spoke, which suggested other possibilities as well.

6

On a clear winter dawn, the sun's first light infuses the icicles hanging from the eaves outside the kitchen window with a red-gold glow that changes into sparkling white as the sun rises. By midday those icicles become nearly colorless, only to find themselves tinted rosy gold at sunset, finally darkening as they partake of the violet-black of evening. While the icicles may grow or shrink with the warmth or cold of the day, the ice itself changes little, yet the pattern of colors varies with the light of the sun.

So, too, is it with the sculptures comprising the Fountain of the Seasons, whose waters spring from the centers of white marble flowers and urns, the color our eyes perceive depending on the effects of sun and weather. Yet the marble itself does not change.

The crimson tunic of an Alooran hussar, so bright in full sunlight, turns subdued in the candlelight of a palace ball, while the harsh angles of the Hall of Commerce in Teknar are softened by the autumn fog.

The young man beholds a woman, fair of face and figure, perceiving her as vital and filled with grace, while his grandsire sees her eyes as calculating and her hands as grasping.

For all that, none of these are changed, although how we perceive them is altered by the time and circumstances under which we behold them.

One man reads a scroll of verse. He finds the thoughts expressed therein move heart and mind, and commends it to his friend, who, declaring the words abstruse and overly complex, dismisses it as pedagogic illogic. The words have not changed from the time the first read the scroll until the second did. They remain the same. The first man claims the scroll proclaims wisdom, and the second sees the words as meaningless jargon, or even nonsense.

What is . . . is. The illusion is in our minds.

AVERRA
The City of Truth
Johan Eschbach
377 TE

7

O N Quindi morning, after two bells of walking through another craft
area and talking to proprietors and workers at various machine
shops, a plumbing supply house, a tinsmith's shop, a hardware store, an
older mechanic working at a repair facility for agricultural steam engines
and pumps, and other craft businesses, Dekkard and Avraal got back in
the Gresynt and headed for Myram Plassar's office on Goldenwood Avenue. That area turned out to be a somewhat less prosperous section of
the central business district, but not that far from several smaller hotels,
barely larger than rooming houses.

But then, she is the regional steward for the Working Women Guild,
reflected Dekkard.

The office itself was squeezed in between a small pawnshop with barred
windows and a small restaurant that had no name Dekkard could discern
and scarcely looked able to accommodate a score of patrons elbow-to-
elbow, even with a counter and five tiny tables.

The sign beside the door to Plassar's office read: WW GUILD OFFICE.

Dekkard opened the door, gestured for Avraal to enter, then followed.

A dark-haired woman wearing a maroon jacket and matching trousers
turned from the wooden filing cabinet and smiled. "Councilor . . ."

"Steffan, Myram, except on stuffy formal occasions."

"I'm glad to see you both. Namoor told me that you might be stopping
by. Is there something specific I could help you with . . . or is this social?"

"A little of both," replied Dekkard. "You were very kind to provide
information to Luara Colsbaan. Unfortunately, it was destroyed—"

"Was your office that badly damaged that even records didn't survive?"

"Between the explosion and the water damage . . . not much was readable. We'd sent copies of the draft legislation to another committee, and
some of the summarized background survived, but everything you sent,
as well as most of Luara's other research, didn't survive. I don't want to
impose . . ."

Plassar offered a sardonically amused laugh. "You've barely escaped
being blown up and you're apologizing. I can certainly have my clerk
type up another copy. She's not exactly overworked at the moment." She
paused. "Do you think what you have in mind has a chance?"

"The three Craft councilors on the Justiciary Committee will back the idea, and Ingrella Obreduur is also ex officio to the committee. It certainly has a chance. It's too early to say beyond that."

Plassar looked to Avraal quizzically.

Avraal shook her head. "It was Steffan's idea from the beginning, after meeting you and the guild legalist in Oersynt."

"Tarisha Vereen, I take it? She wrote me that Legalist Colsbaan had written her."

"It was Tarisha," Dekkard affirmed. "How are working women doing here in Gaarlak right now?"

"It's better than last winter. The weather's not quite as cold, but the big difference is that the women aren't getting hassled by the Special Agents." She smiled and added, "That's because they've all been removed from anything to do with patrols. The regular patrollers usually aren't a problem. The SAs could be nasty . . ."

After about another third of pleasant but professional conversation, Dekkard and Avraal took their leave.

By then, he was more than ready for a break and something to eat. The lunch with Martenya Oguire might not be that much of a break, but since he and Avraal were meeting Oguire at the Seasprite, he could hope that the food would be good, and that the questions from the owner and publisher of the *Gaarlak Times* wouldn't be too pointed.

They reached the foyer of the restaurant just a few minutes before the first bell of afternoon. Dekkard took in the thin malachite wall panels edged with polished brass trim that gave the foyer and the dining room a sense of light.

"Councilor and Ritten Dekkard . . ." offered the maître d'hôtel, "if you'd come with me."

Perhaps because Dekkard was still thinking about Jens Seigryn, as well as wondering when the next corporacion attack might surface—and in what form—he was especially alert as they were escorted to a small private dining room, albeit one with two long and narrow windows that left the room every bit as light as the main dining room. Martenya Oguire rose from a circular table set for three. "I'm so glad to see you both. I have to admit I was stunned when you were selected as councilor, and pleasantly surprised to hear that you two had married."

"You ran a very complimentary story," replied Dekkard as the three seated themselves.

"Everyone loves to read about unexpected marriages, particularly when it involves a descendant of royalty and someone who's gained power apparently through struggle and ability." Oguire offered an amused smile, then gestured to the server standing by the door. "What would you like to drink?"

"Just café," said Avraal.

"The same," added Dekkard.

"The usual," said Oguire. When the server departed, she said to Dekkard, "Not that you don't have great ability, and you doubtless struggled for the well-earned honors at the Military Institute, as well as putting yourself in harm's way to protect others . . . but really, should that have led to being selected councilor?"

"I was more surprised than anyone," replied Dekkard. "Even more than Premier Obreduur, and he was stunned."

"Everyone agrees on those two points," said Oguire amiably. "After that . . . there's much less agreement. Why do you think you were selected?"

"I don't know. I could guess. I won't because I simply don't know." He offered an amused smile. "Guessing when you don't know all the facts can be very dangerous."

"Do you think you're more qualified than others who might have been considered?"

"Again, I have no idea, because I never knew who else was under consideration. I did meet the two original candidates. Sr. Decaro and I exchanged less than a score of words. I certainly felt that Johan Lamarr was qualified."

"Did you know that Jens Seigryn was one of those under consideration?"

"I was never told that," *which is perfectly true,* "but if that's the case, I'm not surprised."

"Would you admit that Sr. Seigryn is more qualified than you?"

"I'd say we both have qualifications, but they're different. I strongly doubt that he could have gotten the Security reform legislation through the Council, but there are doubtless areas where he has great experience. Since we've never talked at length, I have no idea what his strengths or weaknesses might be."

"What are your weaknesses?"

"We all have strengths and weaknesses, but I'd rather let others make those judgments based on my actions."

At that moment, the server returned with their beverages and a menu for each of them.

Dekkard took a sip of the café, then glanced at the menu.

"What have you two been doing with your time?" asked Oguire, looking at Avraal.

"Mostly, we've been meeting people, hearing their questions and concerns."

"You don't have a house here, I understand."

"We do now," Avraal replied. "We just closed on a house on Sunrise Lane."

"That area is coming back, but it's not inexpensive."

"The house we bought needs some work," said Avraal. "That made it possible for us."

"I can see where that might help," replied Oguire in a reserved tone. "I suppose we should order. The braised chicken is quite good, and so is the hearty vegetable soup."

Dekkard decided to try the chicken, while both women ordered the soup.

Once the server left, Oguire turned back to Dekkard. "You mentioned your part in getting the Security reforms passed in the Council. Could you go into that a little more?"

"Because of my experience in security, the chairman asked the committee members to offer suggestions. I made my suggestions as draft legislation. Since no other committee member did, my proposal was the one that the committee worked from . . ." Dekkard was very careful in describing the process and in answering Oguire's follow-up questions, which took until their meal arrived. Then, in between mouthfuls of chicken and golden rice—Dekkard ignored the spiced carrots—he answered pointed questions about the New Meritorists and the shelling of the Council Office Building. He and Avraal passed on dessert, although the apple tart looked inviting, largely because dessert would likely subject him to more questions.

As the three rose to leave, Oguire smiled and said, "Thank you for indulging my curiosity. You both speak well, and, despite my initial doubts, and your skillful reticence, I have a feeling that you two will be much better for Gaarlak than any of the possible alternatives." The smile remained as she added, "That doesn't mean I won't take you to task if I think it necessary."

Dekkard smiled in return. "I appreciate your listening, and I'm well aware that you won't hesitate to speak out. I'd only ask that, if you think it necessary, your tasking be based on verified facts and not on rumor accepted unthinkingly as fact."

"That's a fair request."

Dekkard noted that she didn't agree to abide by the request, but saw no point in pressing the issue. He also realized he had no recollection of how the braised chicken had tasted.

When they were back in the Gresynt, Dekkard glanced at Avraal for an instant, then said, "That wasn't a lunch. It was an interrogation."

"What else did you expect?" asked Avraal in an amused tone.

"A bit more civility and a little less of an attack."

"She wasn't angry," replied Avraal, "but by the end, she was feeling a little frustrated. I tried to blunt that by giving her the sense that we were doing the best we could. Did you notice that she never took notes?"

"She didn't when she interviewed us before, either, and she got all the details right. That kind of memory gives her a definite advantage."

8

O N the way to breakfast on Findi, wearing a jacket and various shades of gray that qualified as "winter casual," Dekkard stopped by the lobby desk to pick up the morning edition of the *Gaarlak Times,* which he tucked under his arm as they walked into the small restaurant. He wasn't about to look to see if there was a story until he was sitting down, and he certainly wasn't about to let Avraal read it until she'd had at least one mug of café.

He'd barely seated himself before she said, "Well . . . are you going to read it?"

"After I've had my café. I need some fortification."

"You? The one who reads *Gestirn* before even *pouring* café?"

"Most of those stories are about other people. After yesterday's luncheon and interrogation, this might be different."

Avraal offered an amused smile, but waited until they'd been served café and Dekkard had taken several sips before she asked, "Now? Or do you want me to read it first?"

Dekkard set down his mug and picked up the newssheet. While the story wasn't the lead, it was on page one, and the headline was simple:

NEW COUNCILOR, NEW STYLE

Almost as soon as the Council of Sixty-Six declared its Midwinter Recess, our new councilor, Steffan Dekkard, and his bride, Avraal, were on the express to Gaarlak. His purpose? To talk to and meet as many people as possible . . . and to find a house here.

Ritter Dekkard was the surprise choice of the Gaarlak Craft Party to replace Councilor-elect Haasan Decaro, who died of a heart attack before he could be sworn in. Unlike many new councilors, Ritter Dekkard actually has experience with the Council, both as a security aide and economic specialist for the late Premier Obreduur . . .

Dekkard couldn't help frowning. Despite all of Oguire's pointed questions, the entire story was positive, even about the shelling of the Council Office Building. He handed the newssheet to Avraal. "It's not what I expected."

After Avraal read it, she said, "It's positive because of how you handled the questions."

"The way *we* handled the questions, I think." He paused. "Given the story, the interview was a warning of sorts."

"I can see that. Don't lie or mislead her or even the Almighty won't be able to save you."

Dekkard smiled faintly. "At least my croissants and ham won't give me indigestion now."

"They wouldn't have anyway," Avraal pointed out. "You can eat anything."

"Mostly," he said amiably. He frowned and picked up the newssheet again.

"What is it?"

"I thought I saw something . . . yes . . . Here it is." He read the short article.

> . . . after two days, Machtarn patrollers, with the help of two companies from the Imperial Army, finally quelled the rioting in the Southtown and Rivertown areas of Machtarn. More than fifty rioters were killed and eleven patrollers were injured . . .

When he finished, he handed it to Avraal, knowing she'd immediately be worried, given that Emrelda was assigned to one of the patrol stations responsible for patrolling Southtown.

Dekkard could see Avraal frown as she began to read, and he said, "No patrollers were killed, and she's not used for riot duty."

"Do you think that would stop her if she thought she was needed?" Avraal did not quite snap her words.

"No . . . but I did tell Gaaroll to send a heliogram if anything happened. We haven't gotten one, and they finished putting down the riots yesterday."

"I still worry."

"I know." Dekkard waited until she set down the newssheet and had several more sips of café before he asked, "Do you think we should visit Alastan Cleese this morning?"

"It can't hurt to try."

"And visit some nice shops after that, since we don't need to get bedraggled before going to Plainfields?"

"If we have time," agreed Avraal.

The two didn't hurry over their breakfast, but neither did they dawdle, and it was still before third bell when they finished. Before leaving the inn, while Avraal went up to the room to get their overcoats, Dekkard stopped by the concierge's desk and asked for directions to the address for Alastan Cleese that Avraal had obtained from Arleena Desenns.

The clerk frowned for just an instant. "You'll have to take the southeast bridge. This is an Eastown address."

"Will that be a problem?"

"No, sir. I wouldn't go much farther than that, not at night."

"We're going this morning."

"Then it should be fine, sir."

"Thank you." Dekkard walked back to the wide staircase and glanced to the left side at the top, thinking about the assassin who had attempted to shoot Obreduur the previous summer. It could have turned out very differently without Avraal's warning. *But then, so much could have turned out differently without her . . . and not for the better.*

He smiled as she appeared at the top of the staircase.

Within minutes, he had his coat and gloves on and they were walking out to the Gresynt. "Apparently, Cleese doesn't live in the most prosperous section of Gaarlak. It's on the southeast side of the river, but the neighborhood is called Eastown."

"It's good we're going now. We'll have plenty of time to get back."

There was still frost in the shade, and it took longer than usual to get the pressure up in the steamer, but it was just after third bell when Dekkard reached the southeast bridge, a narrow stone structure barely wide enough for two lorries side by side, with uneven bitumen paving.

The far smaller dwellings on the southeast side of the river sat closer together than any Dekkard had seen elsewhere in Gaarlak, but most were of the same brown brick. Little more than a third later, Dekkard pulled up in front of a dwelling slightly larger than most he had passed, but all were set back from the street only about five yards.

Because the street was so narrow, Dekkard took the liberty of parking in the drive, behind a well-kept but definitely not new Ferrum. The two had not even reached the front door when it opened, and the gray-haired Alastan Cleese stood there.

"Never thought I'd see a Craft councilor walking up to my door," declared Cleese. "Not one here in Gaarlak." He smiled at Avraal, adding, "Especially one with a wife as lovely as you."

"We really didn't have time to talk as much as we should have on Tridi," said Dekkard.

"Being as this is endday . . . we're not set up . . ."

"You're talking to two people who, until a little more than two months ago, were security aides who were lucky to have a room to themselves," said Dekkard.

"It's a bit cold here," added Avraal, "and I'm from Sudaen, where it never even frosts."

"Alastan," said a voice from within the house, "invite them in. They're here to see you."

Cleese offered a slightly embarrassed smile. "I'm not minding my manners, according to Emmelyn. Do come in." He stepped back and held the door open, then ushered them in to the small front parlor. "Have a seat."

Dekkard and Avraal took the straight-backed wooden armchairs, leaving the upholstered armchairs for their hosts.

Avraal smiled at Emmelyn, who stood in the narrow archway. "You should join us."

"Might as well, Em," said Cleese. "Otherwise, you'll have me repeating it all after they go, and you'll fuss at me because I missed something."

Once both Cleeses were seated, Dekkard said, "We really didn't have a chance for you to go over the specific problems your guild members are having. You said that a quarter of your farmworkers don't have enough marks to feed their families. Is this because *all* growers are laying off a quarter of their workers, or are, say, potato farmers not laying off that many, but wheat-corn growers have cut their workers by half. I'm over-simplifying, but . . ."

"That's a good point, Councilor . . ."

"Steffan, please. Save the titles for public functions."

Cleese chuckled. "Old Councilor Raathan'd never say that, not that we ever saw him. Well . . . you got the point. Past year the maize and wheat-corn growers got rain at the wrong times and no rain when they needed it. Yields were about half of normal, except for the Landors who've got steam-powered pumps and sprinkler systems, and more water rights than they know what to do with. Only a few of the spud crops matured and got harvested before the heavy fall rains, and the water rot . . ."

For nearly a bell, Dekkard just let Cleese talk, prompting him with an occasional question. Once or twice Emmelyn corrected her husband.

Finally, Cleese looked at Dekkard, grinned, and said, "I've talked a lot. But you asked."

"I did. You gave me a much better idea of the problems. Finding ways to help isn't going to be easy. I do have a question for you that might seem strange since no one grows rice around here. Landors are very much opposed to lowering the tariffs on swampgrass rice, but Sargassan swampgrass rice is a lot cheaper than rice grown in places like Encora and Khasaar. What do you think about it?"

Cleese laughed. "Get rid of the tariff, for all we care. There're maybe two or three districts in all Guldor that grow rice. It's one of the worst jobs a farmworker could have. Labor's hard in anything, but they flood the fields once the plants mature, and that draws the bloodflies . . . you get infected, you won't live to forty. Most of the workers are beetles, you know, ones who escape from Atacama, but I wouldn't wish bloodflies on my worst enemy."

"Do you know what districts those might be?"

"Khasaar, Khuld, and Daal." Cleese paused. "Why'd you ask?"

"People are going hungry. Swampgrass rice would be cheap without the tariff. Seems to me that a few Landors are getting rich, while their workers suffer. Poorer Guldorans pay more for food or go hungry, and if the tariff isn't helping anyone but a few Landors . . ."

"I like the way you think, Steffan."

Cleese and Dekkard talked for another third before Dekkard stood and said, "I'd like to stay, but we have more visits to make."

"You know where to find me." Cleese looked to Avraal. "You didn't say much, Ritten."

"I don't learn when I'm talking," replied Avraal with a smile.

"Smart lady," said Cleese.

"Very smart." Dekkard paused, then said, "And please let me know if something important comes up."

"I'll make sure he does," said Emmelyn.

Dekkard didn't doubt that for a moment, but he just said, "Thank you very much for filling us in." Then he looked back to Emmelyn and added, "It was a pleasure meeting you."

After leaving the small house, Dekkard was very careful backing the leased steamer out of the narrow drive and heading back across the southeast bridge into central Gaarlak.

"Those three rice-growing districts . . . they're well south on the Khulor River," said Dekkard. "Khuld . . . that's Saarh's district."

"He must be on higher ground, because I don't think he grows rice."

"At the moment, I don't recall the councilor from Daal, but he has to be a Landor. Olaaf Sturmsyn is from Khasaar, and he's definitely a Landor."

They then spent the next two bells visiting shops near Namoor Desharra's office, after which they drove to another area father north and east and did the same. Slightly after third bell, Dekkard headed west looking for Northwest Boulevard, which he found, after one wrong turn and a correction by Avraal, and turned onto it, heading out of the city.

Dekkard kept looking for the two red brick posts that marked the entry to Plainfields, but Avraal was the one who called out, "There they are, just past those trees."

With an amused smile Dekkard turned and drove past the posts onto a bitumened lane, flanked by a chest-high and well-trimmed boxwood hedge, the leaves of which had turned the yellow-green of winter. After about a half mille, the lane rose through the stubbled fields to a low ridge that held the long two-story mansion. Traces of snow lingered in shady places untouched by the weak winter sun. Dekkard drove under the covered portico at the south end of the dwelling and brought the Gresynt to a stop.

As before, the one who greeted them was Emilio Raathan's son, Georg, wearing security-blue trousers and a dark maroon jacket over a rich cream shirt. "Welcome back!"

"We're glad to be here," replied Dekkard. "I never thought I'd be coming back as a councilor."

"Or married?"

"We were beginning to get serious when we were here last," said Dekkard.

"*You* were beginning," added Avraal with a mischievous smile.

"Well . . . let's get you inside," declared Georg, who opened the heavy golden oak door, then closed it while they were taking off their overcoats. "Just hang them on the wall pegs—we're very practical."

From there, they walked down the beige-tiled hallway, past the receiving parlor and all the way to the salon, where Emilio Raathan stood as the three entered. Patriana and Georg's wife, Katryna, remained seated.

"After what I've read about what you've been through, Steffan," said Emilio Raathan, "you look to be in fine shape."

Dekkard waited for everyone to be seated before he replied. "I've been in Gaarlak for four days, and no one's tried to kill me. People have been friendly. It makes a difference."

"The *Times* story this morning said you found a house," said Patriana.

"It's in the North Quarter—a nice place, but no mansion."

"That was once *the* place to live in town," said Katryna. "I understand it's coming back."

"So we heard," said Avraal cheerfully. "It needs some work, but that will be finished while we're in Machtarn. We hope to have it livable by the next time we're here."

"We invited you for a pleasant dinner," said Raathan, "but I do have one question. Why would the New Meritorists assassinate Axel and try to kill you? The Craft Party is far more likely to address at least some of their concerns."

"Did you read about Jaime Minz, the former aide to Premier Ulrich?"

"I thought he was an influencer for Northwest Industrial Chemical," said Georg.

"He was a longtime aide to Ulrich . . ." Dekkard gave a summary of Minz's involvement with Capitol Services and the ties to the New Meritorists, then said, "To me, that indicates that Ulrich and others used the New Meritorists to remove the Premier."

"Why did they go after you?" asked Katryna, her tone curious.

"Katryna," said Emilio Raathan, drawing out her name, "exactly who was the councilor who effectively removed the Security Ministry as a tool for corporacion interests."

Katryna stiffened, then said, "I hadn't thought of it that way."

"I'm quite sure certain corporacion types knew who that councilor was," said Patriana.

That had always been Dekkard's belief, but it surprised him to hear Emilio Raathan say it. From his one earlier meal at Plainfields, he wasn't that surprised at Patriana's comment. *But then the Landors weren't any happier with the growth of Commercer and corporacion power than the Crafters were.*

"Thank you, Steffan," said Emilio Raathan. "From what Breffyn Haastar has written and from what has been in the newssheets, I suspected something along those lines." He paused. "I do believe that's enough of politics for the evening."

Dekkard was more than certain it would be, and that anything but politics could and would be discussed.

9

IT was barely light on Unadi morning when Dekkard woke. He glanced over at Avraal to see if she happened to be awake, only to find her looking at him.

"You almost never wake before me," he said quietly. "Is something the matter?"

"Are we doing the right thing?"

"You mean . . . are you doing the right thing in spending the only inheritance you're likely to get to support your husband's career?"

"Dear . . . I wouldn't have even that if it weren't for you. No . . . it's the house."

"You think we shouldn't have bought it? Or we should have bought something smaller?"

"It's not that . . ."

Dekkard waited.

"It's already a lovely place. It's a shame that we'll spend so little time here. It's . . ." She shook her head.

"Almost a luxury?"

She nodded. "I feel guilty. I marry you, and because all their Landor friends approve, I get an inheritance of sorts . . . and so does Emrelda . . . and she's been through so much more. It doesn't make any sense . . . not really."

"The letter said that they had come to realize how much you had accomplished," Dekkard pointed out.

"It also said how much more we had accomplished together."

"That's true, but condescending. While I wouldn't be a councilor without you and all you taught me, there's still the implication that you got that wedding present because of who you married, and Emrelda got it because they felt sorry for her. They're almost saying that not only did she marry just an engineer, but he's vanished and likely dead." He paused. "Your parents live in a different world. You told me that. At least they made an effort."

"I suppose I should look at it that way."

"But it's hard after all these years?"

Avraal nodded.

"And I feel guilty because you're spending most of your inheritance on a house that I need to remain a councilor."

"I like the house, and we're both better off now."

"I know . . . but it still has to be annoying."

"I'm glad you understand." She paused. "I'm actually hungry."

"You *have* been awake a long time, worrying. You take the first shower."

Two-thirds of a bell later, they were seated at a table at the inn's restaurant, drinking café.

"What are we doing today?" asked Avraal.

"Besides meeting workers at Lakaan Mills this afternoon, nothing's exactly set . . . unless your funds have cleared. That should happen today, but we'll have to see." Dekkard picked up a croissant, which held apricot preserves, as opposed to quince paste, and took a bite. "Not too bad."

"Much better than your usual," teased Avraal.

"How would you know?" Dekkard grinned. "You never tried one with quince paste."

"I didn't have to."

When they finished breakfast, the two left the restaurant and walked to the lobby desk.

"Are there any messages for either of us?" asked Dekkard.

"Just one, Councilor. Just a moment." The desk clerk returned almost immediately and handed Dekkard a messenger-service envelope.

"Thank you." Dekkard immediately turned and handed the envelope to Avraal.

She opened it and withdrew a smaller envelope bearing the return address of Heimdell & Bader, which she opened in turn, extracting and reading the single sheet. "Everything's cleared."

"Then we know what we're doing next. Shall we get our coats and finish assuring a continued commitment to Gaarlak?"

Between getting ready, driving to meet Kelliera Heimdell, and then driving to the Lakaan Valley Banque, it was third past fourth bell when Avraal, Dekkard, and Heimdell walked into the same small conference room where they'd signed the last paperwork.

Pietr Raensyn appeared almost instantly, smiling. "It's much simpler this time. A copy of the deed has been recorded with the regional Justiciary office. Here's the original deed, and all the keys to the house. This is your receipt for half a year's house taxes in advance—one hundred seventy-four marks. You'll only owe for three months, next Yearend, since the banque had to pay for the first month of the year. The various fees are itemized here, for another two hundred ninety marks. The banque owes you eight thousand five hundred thirty-six marks." Raensyn paused. "You had mentioned opening an account here?"

"You offer an interest-bearing account?" asked Avraal.

"We do. There are certain limitations. The account must be maintained over a thousand marks to draw interest and the minimum initial deposit is fifteen hundred. The account allows five withdrawals a month without a fee. Each withdrawal after that costs three marks. Interest is paid at the end of each season, based on the average balance for the season. The current rate is three point two-five percent."

"Then I'd like three thousand marks to go into such an account."

"In her name," said Dekkard firmly.

"Four thousand marks in a personal bond to me, and the balance in mark notes."

"Very good, Ritten," replied Raensyn.

"Could I open a smaller account, say starting with five hundred marks?" asked Dekkard.

"Absolutely," said Raensyn. "If you choose to add to it, once the balance exceeds one thousand marks, we will pay interest at the rate of two percent, three point two-five percent if it exceeds fifteen hundred marks."

"Can I make banque-to-banque fund transfers from the Council Banque?"

Raensyn smiled. "Any banque will accept those."

Little more than two-thirds of a bell later, Dekkard and Avraal were back in the steamer, and Dekkard's wallet was considerably thinner, unlike Avraal's.

"Hrald Iglis?" asked Dekkard.

"Where else?" replied Avraal with a smile.

"After Hrald, I'd like to stop by Namoor Desharra's office to see if she's had any responses about possible staff . . . and see what we can do about furniture and supplies."

In the end, nothing went as swiftly as at the Lakaan Valley Banque.

It took nearly three bells to take Iglis to the house on Sunrise Lane, have him measure and take notes, then return and go over his original plans, make the general changes that Avraal wanted . . . as well as leave a deposit. Avraal also got the cabinetmaker to agree to accept any furniture deliveries to the house.

Then, at the meeting with Namoor Desharra, the legalist had a list of fifteen people interested in working for Dekkard. While she quickly went over the names before recommending three that he should talk to, that took time, as did arranging and setting up payment details for the small room and its associated logistics, including a small outside sign identifying the GAARLAK OFFICE OF COUNCILOR DEKKARD.

By then Dekkard and Avraal had to hurry to get to Lakaan Mills. They arrived at less than a sixth before fourth bell.

Both Arleena Desenns and Gretna Haarl were standing next to the banner, once more propped up against the side of an omnibus stop. Dekkard could see the relief on Desenns's face as he and Avraal walked swiftly across River Avenue, reaching the other side as an omnibus approached the stop for the mills.

"I'm sorry," said Dekkard. "We were arranging for a small office here in Gaarlak, and the details took a little longer than we'd planned."

The two exchanged glances.

"You're going to have an office here, with someone in it?"

"That's the general idea. That way, if you have a problem, or there's something you think I should know, you can go there, and they'll send word to me. Also, that person will be sending me regular reports on important events that happen in Gaarlak."

"I thought that was part of Jens's job," said Desenns.

"I've never heard a word from him."

"Jens has never felt he had to report to anyone," said Haarl evenly.

"He never had a Craft councilor here," said Desenns, then asking after a hesitation, "How do you know that whoever takes the job will do it well?"

"I'm hoping that the fact that the office is across the entry from Legalist Namoor Desharra's office, and that she went over the list of applicants with me, will prove helpful. I'll be interviewing the top three tomorrow."

Both guildmeisters smiled.

Then Arleena said, "How did you manage that?"

"I just told her that I needed a small office and one reliable person."

Haarl shook her head in an amused fashion.

At that moment, the mill's steam whistle blew, and workers poured out of the mill. Dekkard moved closer to the banner, but not directly in front of it because he didn't want to block the workers' view.

As had been the case at Gaarlak Mills, a few millworkers headed for steamers, with most heading for the omnibus, but a few stopped to talk to Dekkard. Once the first omnibus departed, a few more joined the small group around Dekkard, Avraal, and the two guildmeisters.

Many of the questions were like those he'd answered before. Some were not, but the general feel was much the same—some anger, some frustration, and, occasionally, just curiosity.

"Why do women supervisors and line leaders get paid less than the men here? It's not that way at Gaarlak Mills."

"Because there's no law to require it . . ." Dekkard explained that briefly.

"What does the Imperador think about that?" returned the woman almost belligerently.

"I don't know. I've never met with the Imperador. To my knowledge he's never said anything about it one way or another."

"Hummphhh." The woman just shook her head, then stepped away.

After that the questions came faster.

"There's no election. Why are you here?"

"How did a young man like you get to be a councilor?"

"What happened to the old councilor?"

"Can't you do something about the mill dust?"

"The price of flour is too high. What do you intend to do about it?"

After more than a third, the area around the omnibus station was deserted except for the four. As the two guildmeisters took down the banner and packed it up, Dekkard looked to Desenns. "What do you think?"

"You do this every time you're here, and after a few years, they might be voting for you and not the party."

"We'll see if we can manage it a little sooner," Dekkard replied wryly. Then he smiled. "Thank you both for setting these up. I hope I'll be able to give a little more notice next time."

"You two are leaving on Quindi?" asked Desenns.

"Unfortunately," replied Dekkard.

"The Midwinter Recess lasts until the end of next week," said Haarl.

"That's true," replied Dekkard, "but my expense account doesn't stretch that far. That won't be as much of a problem the next time because the house will be ready, and we won't be paying for lodging."

"You bought a house?" asked Desenns.

"I did. A certain guildmeister suggested that it was a good idea."

Haarl tried to look innocent.

Desenns turned to Haarl. "You told him that?"

"She wrote me, and she was very polite. She was right."

"You have two houses?" asked Desenns.

"No, we don't," said Avraal. "One is all we can afford. We live with my sister in Machtarn."

"Remember," said Dekkard, with what he hoped was humorous sardonicism, "we're working Crafters, not wealthy Landors or Commercers."

"So your only house is here?"

"That's right."

"It might not take a few years," said Desenns, "especially once that gets around."

Dekkard hoped not, and he also had the feeling Desenns just might help spread the word.

"It's looking like snow," said Haarl. "We better let you go."

"Until later," replied Dekkard before he and Avraal turned and headed for the Gresynt. The clouds to the northeast did indeed look dark green and threatening.

10

WHEN Dekkard woke on Duadi morning and looked out the window of their room, everything was white with snow, although it had stopped falling, and the accumulation seemed only a few digits deep.

"You're definitely going to need that overcoat."

"It snowed, didn't it?"

"Some."

"Do I have to get up?" asked Avraal in a mournful tone of voice.

"Not if you don't want café . . . or if you'd prefer to skip my interviews with the young people looking to be a staff assistant."

"Young people?" said Avraal as she sat up in the wide bed. "The ones you and Namoor chose to interview were all women."

"You agreed with every choice."

"Might I have the first shower?" she asked sweetly.

"Of course."

After Avraal took her shower, Dekkard shaved, showered, and dressed in his heavier gray suit, and then they went downstairs for a moderately quick breakfast. Dekkard did scan the *Gaarlak Times,* but there was nothing about riots or unrest in Machtarn—and a brief mention of a demonstration in Uldwyrk.

After breakfast, they donned overcoats and ventured out into the snow, which, as Dekkard suspected, turned out to be ankle-deep, but the air was cold enough that the snow was crunchy, rather than slushy. He lit off the Gresynt, then began to brush the snow off the steamer. By the time he finished, the steamer was ready to go.

Dekkard took his time in driving to Desharra's office. He saw only one steamer—an older Ferrum—that had slid off the street and ended up wedged against the curb, but traffic was light, partly because many older steamers lacked heat and the ability to defrost the windscreen.

He parked the Gresynt carefully. Then he and Avraal got out and took the cleared sidewalk to the legalist's office. One of the secretaries appeared immediately. "Councilor, Ritten, Legalist Desharra will join you in the conference room shortly. If I could take your coats?"

"Thank you."

Once the woman returned, Dekkard and Avraal followed her to the conference room, which held a circular table with four chairs placed around it, three on one side and one on the other side opposite the middle chair of three.

"You sit in the middle," said Avraal. "You are the councilor."

Dekkard didn't argue.

Less than a sixth passed before Namoor Desharra entered the room. After handing six sheets of paper each to Avraal and then to Dekkard, she said, "Those provide the background information on the three, and a typed report each did this morning here in the office. As we discussed the other day, I asked each to type up what they thought was the most important legal or political event that had happened here in Gaarlak in the last year."

"I think I'll wait to read the reports until after the interviews," said Dekkard.

Desharra nodded. "Arvylla Dejaenes is the first applicant. I told Maranda to escort her here in a few minutes."

Dekkard looked over the background sheet on Dejaenes, who had graduated from the Gaarlak Women's Seminary in 1265 and who worked as a shop clerk in a dry goods store. According to what Desharra had said on Unadi, the seminary was almost as good as Imperial University. As was the case with all three being interviewed, she had adequate typing skills.

"If it's amenable to you both," added Desharra, "I thought it would be easier if I introduced you and asked each of them why they applied for the position and what skills they would bring to it. After that, the questions would be yours."

Dekkard smiled. "That sounds fine, but, if you think we've missed something or that something important needs to be brought up, I'd like you to do so. You have far more experience in interviewing than we do."

"I agree with Steffan," added Avraal immediately.

"I appreciate your kindness."

Dekkard laughed. "It's not kindness, Namoor. It's self-interest and self-preservation. I should have said immediately how much we appreciate your kindness and thoughtfulness."

The legalist offered a warm but amused smile. "Then we should begin."

Within a minute or so, the conference room door opened, and a young woman dressed in a long blue skirt, a cream blouse, and a brown jacket entered the conference room.

"Please take the seat, Arvylla. I'm Legalist Namoor Desharra. Steffan Dekkard is the councilor for Gaarlak, and his wife, Ritten Avraal Ysella-Dekkard, is a certified empath."

Arvylla inclined her head politely and seated herself.

"Why did you apply to be the local clerk for Councilor Dekkard, and what skills do you have that would serve well in such a position?" Desharra's voice was firm, but pleasant.

The young woman swallowed, then said, "I applied because I'd like my education to count for more than being a shop clerk. I studied government at the seminary, but there aren't many government positions in Gaarlak, especially for women, unless you can study law. I like meeting people. I feel like I'm good at helping them. Maybe I'm guessing, but it seems like that's what I'd be doing for you, Councilor."

"Sometimes," answered Dekkard. "And sometimes people just want to complain, and your job will require you to be friendly and polite without promising more than that you'll let me know. Then you'll have to write me with their address and their complaint or problem." He paused, then asked, "Why do you feel you're good at helping people?"

"In the store, I always ask what they need . . . and I listen."

"How well do you know Gaarlak and the surrounding area?" asked Dekkard.

"I know the city as well as most, sir. I've learned more since I've been at the store. Sr. Pena sometimes has me use the little store lorry to deliver purchases all over the city, and, when Nardall isn't available, I'll pick up shipments from the freight depot at the ironway station . . ."

Dekkard, Avraal, and Desharra asked questions and listened for perhaps a sixth, when Dekkard said, "Thank you very much, Arvylla. If you'd wait out front. After we finish talking with all three of you, we'll let you know."

The second applicant was Zenya Onswyrth. She wore dark maroon trousers, a white blouse, and a maroon jacket in a shade just a trace lighter than her trousers. Dekkard saw that her boots were polished, but far from new.

In response to Desharra's opening question, she replied, "I applied for the position because I've been a legal clerk for the last two years. I don't see that I'll ever be more than that if I stay in Gaarlak. All my family is here, and I don't want to leave, but I'd like to be in a position where I could help people personally. I'd also like to spend more time with people."

"You do understand what the pay is?" asked Dekkard. "If you do the job right, it's likely to be more demanding in some ways than being a legal clerk."

"Yes, sir. It's less than I'm making now."

Dekkard wasn't quite sure what to ask, but Desharra spoke. "What is it that doesn't satisfy you in your present position?"

"I don't have any complaints. Everyone is pleasant, and the pay is good. The legalists are considerate, and I've learned a lot."

"But somehow . . . it's unsatisfying?" asked Dekkard.

"I feel like something's missing, sir."

Avraal asked, "Why do you think that working for the councilor will fill that lack?"

"I don't know for certain. There hasn't been a district clerk for a councilor ever, so far as I could discover, but if people come to you for help, they would have to have different problems, wouldn't they?"

"The problems are different," replied Dekkard, "but the techniques for dealing with them are limited and similar, somewhat like the law, I'd imagine. You'll be required to write a weekly report of important events and problems here and to send newssheet clippings which report on such events, and all stories reporting on what the Council or the Imperador have done."

Zenya looked puzzled for a moment.

"What the *Gaarlak Times* reports may not include the entire story or may include the reaction of people in Gaarlak to an event in Machtarn. I'll need to know that." Dekkard smiled, then asked, "What do you know about the political parties in Gaarlak?"

"We have a Landor Party, a Commercer Party, and a Craft Party, just like everywhere."

"Do you know who ran for councilor from each party?"

Zenya paused, then said, "Haasan Decaro was the one who ran for the Craft Party, and Elvann Wheiter for the Commercer Party."

"Do you recall the Landor candidate?"

"No, sir."

After another sixth of questions and replies, Dekkard glanced at Desharra, who gave the smallest of headshakes, and then to Avraal, who shook her head.

"Thank you, Zenya. If you'd wait in the front sitting room."

"Thank you, sir, for giving me the chance to talk to you about the position."

The third applicant was Printempa Desoordha, neatly attired in a bluish-gray jacket over black trousers. Her pale blue blouse set off her red hair. Even before Namoor Desharra could speak, Printempa said, "Thank you so much for this opportunity."

Desharra merely said, "You're welcome. If you'd take the seat at the table." Then she asked the same two questions that she'd posed to the earlier applicants.

"Working for Councilor Dekkard would allow me to use my skills and education to help people in a way that's seldom possible except in Machtarn itself." Printempa smiled warmly. "As for skills, I'm a good typist, and I can write quickly and correctly. I try to listen intently, and I enjoy helping people. I admit I don't have any work experience to speak of because I just finished classes at the seminary."

"This isn't a high-paying position," Dekkard said mildly.

"I'm just starting out, and I don't expect more than what was listed. I know I have a lot to learn, but I'm a quick study, and I know how to work hard."

"What's your greatest strength?" asked Avraal.

"I like to learn, and I've usually been able to integrate what I've learned to broaden my abilities."

"There will be a great deal of routine requirements in this position," Dekkard pointed out, "such as weekly reports and newssheet clippings being sent to me. You'll have to summarize people's problems and refer them to me in Machtarn, and you will only be able to promise people that we'll do our best."

"I thought that might be so, sir. In time, I'd hope to learn enough to reduce the effort of your office in Machtarn."

"Where do you see working for the councilor taking you?" asked Desharra.

"I hadn't thought much about that, Legalist Desharra. I have a great deal to learn before even thinking that far in the future."

The three asked questions and listened to Printempa's replies for not quite a third longer before Dekkard, after looking to Avraal and Desharra, said, "Thank you very much. If you'd wait in the sitting room while we talk matters over, we'll let you know what we decide."

Printempa rose gracefully and inclined her head. "Thank you again for giving me a chance at this opportunity."

After she left and the conference room door was firmly closed, Dekkard said, "I'd like a few minutes to read what each wrote."

"So would I," added Avraal.

"I've read them, because I had one of my typists make letter-for-letter copies, mistakes and all, not that any of them made many. But it will be interesting to reread them after hearing them reply to questions."

Dekkard read each report carefully, then set them side by side on the table, and again compared them. Finally, he looked to Desharra, then Avraal. "Thoughts? Observations? Things I might have missed while asking questions?"

Namoor Desharra said quietly, "What do you feel, Steffan?"

"I'm inclined toward the second young woman. I don't know that she's perfect, but . . . the first, I think, would be overwhelmed, and she struggles with the writing. And the last one . . . there's something a little . . . off . . . there. She's too bright . . . too talented."

"Why do you think that?" asked Desharra.

"I read what she wrote. It's too good, as if it were prepared for an exam."

Desharra nodded. "I suspect she wants the experience until next year's legalist training program begins. That's just a guess, of course."

"What do you two think? Am I missing something?"

"For someone who's not an empath," said Avraal, "you read people well. Printempa . . . she was emotionally walling off a lot."

"You've had a great deal of experience with legal clerks, Namoor. What do you think of Zenya Onswyrth?"

"You could do much, much worse. From her writing and typing, she's likely a good clerk, but she won't last if she stays a clerk."

"She needs more personal contact in her work," said Avraal. "And she'll get it, if not always favorably."

"Then we'll bring her back here." Dekkard paused. "I think I'd better be the one doing that."

Neither woman objected.

Dekkard left the conference room and walked to the front sitting room. All three women looked at him. "Arvylla, Printempa, thank you for your time and effort, I do appreciate it, but I've made a different decision." Then he looked at Zenya Onswyrth. "If you'd come with me."

Zenya looked totally stunned. "Me, sir?"

"You," replied Dekkard with a smile. He gestured toward the conference room.

After spending another two bells with Zenya Onswyrth, and ascertaining that she could begin work full-time on Unadi the thirteenth of Winterend, Dekkard and Avraal spent the rest of the morning with Namoor Desharra working out the last details of setting up his Gaarlak office, and arranging for Desharra to send an invoice to his Machtarn office for services, equipment, and supplies provided, as well as a small amount for petty cash for Zenya.

When they left the legalist's office, Avraal looked to Dekkard and said, "There's something else we need to do."

"There are likely quite a few other matters we need to address. Which one do we need to address first?"

"Bedroom furniture. You've said that we could save marks by staying in the house the next time we come, but we need something to sleep on."

"I thought we were going to get—"

"Dear . . . the house has four bedrooms. We get an adequate bedroom suite immediately. When we can afford something special, most likely from Hrald, the adequate set goes into one of the other bedrooms."

"That makes sense, but I've never known you not to. You had that in mind when you asked Hrald about dealing with furniture deliveries, didn't you?"

"I wasn't exactly hiding it from you." Avraal smiled.

"No . . . but I was thinking that such a purchase might be somewhat further into the future." *When I'd saved up a few more marks.*

"Dear . . . once we get back to Machtarn, how are we going to be able to shop in Gaarlak? Besides . . . the quiet that followed Minz's shooting isn't likely to last much longer."

Dekkard couldn't dispute her words or logic. "Where are we going, then?"

"Gaarlak Fine Furniture. That's the store Hrald recommended. It's in a shop area we haven't visited."

Dekkard smiled wryly. He'd definitely need to visit as many shops as possible . . . after buying whatever bedroom suite Avraal chose . . . and after that . . . doubtless at least some linens.

11

O N Tridi, Dekkard and Avraal trudged through more shops and craft businesses, along with a stop at the main Gaarlak patrol station to see Josiah Arkham, only to discover that he was on leave until the following Unadi. So Dekkard left a brief note.

That evening Avraal wrote a letter to her parents, thanking them for their wedding gift and telling them about the house—why it was necessary and that it likely would appreciate in value.

Except for the letters, Furdi was much the same, although the two took a break on Furdi afternoon to meet the two deliverymen from Gaarlak Fine Furniture, who unloaded and set up a "modest" bedroom suite that included a bedstead, two night tables, one dressing table with a mirror, and two matching chests of drawers, as well as a mattress and box springs.

Modest as the furniture was considered, it was certainly better than anything Dekkard had ever used before, and he almost felt guilty—and somewhat of a spendthrift, since it wouldn't even be utilized for at least a month and a half, if not longer. The linens remained wrapped in the smaller bedroom closet, the one Dekkard knew without asking was his, and the mattress remained covered in brown paper.

Once everything was set up and in place, Avraal and Dekkard locked the house and went back to making the rounds of shops and small businesses until well after fifth bell that evening when they returned to the Ritter's Inn.

Just before first bell on Quindi morning, after rising early, eating quickly, and taking a steamhack to the ironway station, having turned in the leased Gresynt the night before, Dekkard and Avraal entered their first-class compartment on Guldoran Ironway's Machtarn Day Express.

After the porter stowed their luggage and the two were alone in the compartment, Dekkard looked to Avraal. "How are you feeling?"

"A little tired." Avraal tried—and failed—to stifle a yawn. "What about you?"

"A little tired as well . . . and I can't help wondering what's happened in Machtarn that didn't show up in the *Gaarlak Times*."

"Most likely, not much . . . or did you mean whatever Ulrich and Juan del Larrano might be doing that the newssheets won't discover?"

"I meant the first, but I ought to be more worried about the second. Del Larrano's public statement after the killing of Pietro Venburg was a not-so-veiled warning that the Siincleer corporacions don't intend to change their practices. We'll have to find a way to get the Council to require some changes, and we'll still have to deal with Ulrich and the New Meritorists." Dekkard stopped as the carriage offered a slight jolt, then began to move, and he turned his eyes out the window as the express accelerated out of the ironway station and within minutes crossed the ironway bridge across the Lakaan River.

"How do you plan to deal with Ulrich?" asked Avraal. "Premier Hasheem isn't keen on allowing an investigation and hearings."

"That was before the New Meritorists shelled the Council Office Building. I made a point of not pressing him before the Midwinter Recess. I can't afford not to press him once the Council's back in session." Dekkard yawned.

"You need to take a nap."

"So do you."

"That's why I suggested you take one."

Dekkard offered an amused smile and closed his eyes.

He wasn't exactly surprised to find three bells had passed when he woke from the nap, nor was he surprised that Avraal was still asleep.

While practically every minute of their time in Gaarlak had been filled, largely out of the necessity for Dekkard to establish a legal and physical presence in the district, there hadn't been any significant problems, but what Julian Baurett revealed had certainly given Dekkard pause. Although Seigryn had never said a word, it was clear that Seigryn felt he should have been the one selected as councilor after Decaro's "heart attack." *But you'll likely never know the details of what actually happened with Decaro, and certainly not anytime soon.*

A little before fifth bell in the afternoon, the express began to slow, and to the west Dekkard could catch glimpses of the Rio Azulete, which meant they would arrive in Machtarn in less than a sixth. "We'll be just about on time. At least Emrelda and Gaaroll won't have had to wait in the cold long."

"I just hope Emrelda wasn't hurt in the Southtown riots."

"Gaaroll would have messaged us," said Dekkard.

"With the snow, any heliograph messages could have been delayed."

"There's no point in worrying. We'll find out when we get off the express."

Dekkard could tell that Avraal was even more concerned than she was saying, because she had her overcoat and gloves on even before the carriage came to a halt in the Machtarn station.

Since the express wasn't full—few people came to the capital before an endday in winter—Dekkard had no trouble quickly obtaining a porter, and in minutes they were walking away from the ironway carriage.

Just beyond the gate at the end of the platform stood a woman in the security-blue winter jacket and uniform of an Imperial patroller. Emrelda's worried expression turned to a broad smile as Avraal and Dekkard walked toward her, followed by the porter pushing the luggage dolly that held their suitcases. Not for the first time, the similarity of the two sisters, almost identical, struck Dekkard, Emrelda's light brown hair and height being the only difference. Although Emrelda was five years older, no one could have told it by looking at them together.

"I'm so glad to see you!" exclaimed Avraal. "We read about the riots in Southtown, and I worried . . ."

"It turned out all right for me," said Emrelda, "but Georg got his arm broken. Thank the Almighty it wasn't a compound fracture. Sammel made sure that it didn't go any further."

For a moment, Dekkard was lost, but then recalled the pair of patrollers he'd met in Elfredo's taverna.

"You were there?" asked Avraal.

"Pretty much all of us were. I was there to deal with the women and children forced out by the fires . . . but I can tell you everything once we get home." Emrelda turned and started to walk toward the exit.

Avraal shot a glance at Dekkard, one that he had no trouble interpreting. *Don't tell me I didn't have reason to worry.* The two were close enough that, at times, they seemed to know when something wasn't right with the other—even when they were milles apart. *Or in this case, hundreds of milles apart.*

Dekkard leaned forward and murmured, "You were right to worry, but I was right in that she wasn't injured."

"She could have been," hissed Avraal.

Dekkard wasn't about to argue. "You're right. She could have been, but let's just be glad she wasn't." Dekkard knew that Emrelda was as stubborn as Avraal, and that most likely, Emrelda had insisted on being involved in order to help the women and children. He also felt momentarily surprised by a damp chill that felt colder than the snow and frost of Gaarlak.

When Avraal, Dekkard, and Emrelda reached the large gray Gresynt that Avraal had bought from her sister, the short and muscular Gaaroll, who was waiting, insisted on taking the luggage from the porter and stowing it in the third row of seats, while Dekkard paid the porter.

Then he turned to Emrelda, noting the dark circles under her eyes, and said, "You had a long week. I'll drive back to the house. We got naps on the express. We're just happy to see you, and we're glad you're safe." He added in a lower voice, "You can tell how worried Avraal's been."

"A little worry's good for her," replied Emrelda dryly. "You've both been in more danger than I have." She handed the Gresynt's keys to Dekkard. "But I would appreciate your driving."

"Is there any place to avoid?"

"No. Not tonight."

Emrelda took the seat immediately behind Dekkard, while Avraal took the front passenger seat, and Gaaroll the one behind her. Dekkard turned east on Council Avenue until he reached Imperial Boulevard, where he turned south. Traffic was comparatively light, and in a third of a bell he turned off Florinda into the drive of Emrelda's house. A trail of smoke came from the house to the east, the dwelling of the temperamental Sr. Waaldwud and his family.

"Just drive to the garage," murmured Avraal. "I'll get the garage door."

Dekkard followed directions, driving under and through the covered portico on the east side of the house. Before long he and Gaaroll collected the suitcases, and Avraal closed the garage door.

"There's a hearty soup on the stove that will only take a few minutes to warm up," declared Emrelda.

"You didn't have to—" began Avraal.

"I didn't," replied Emrelda. "Gaaroll did."

"Mostly," added Gaaroll. "I just followed her directions, and then she seasoned and improved it when she got back from duty."

"Take your cases upstairs and wash up," said Emrelda, "and we'll have everything ready in a few minutes. Over dinner we can catch up on what you two did in Gaarlak, and what's happened here."

"Are you sure?" asked Avraal, her tone worried.

"I'm sure," replied Emrelda. "There's almost nothing to do."

Dekkard had his doubts, but he carried the suitcases up to their bedroom, setting them down before shedding his overcoat and gloves. By the time that he and Avraal washed up and made their way back to the breakfast room, where they ate most meals, Dekkard could definitely smell the aroma of the soup.

"All of you sit down," said Gaaroll. "You're tired, and I'll serve." She grinned. "I haven't been working that hard while you two were gone."

In few minutes, everyone had a bowl of soup, and a basket of warm bread sat in the middle of the table. Emrelda and Avraal had Silverhills white wine, and Dekkard and Gaaroll had Kuhrs lager. No one spoke much for a time.

Then Avraal said, "However you two managed it, this is excellent."

"Very, very good," added Dekkard, taking another piece of bread.

A bit later, Emrelda set down her spoon and said, "You two go first. What happened in Gaarlak?"

Dekkard nodded to Avraal. "You have the most important news."

"We bought a house."

"What's it like . . . and what's the neighborhood like?" asked Emrelda.

"It's two full stories, gray stone . . ." Avraal went on to describe 19 Sunrise Lane, beginning with the nonexistent kitchen—and what it would be like once Hrald Iglis finished it.

"That sounds like a swell's mansion," said Gaaroll.

Avraal shook her head. "It's a little bit bigger than here, but prices are so much lower."

"How do you feel about the house?" Emrelda asked Dekkard.

"He feels guilty," Avraal answered before Dekkard could, but she followed her words with an amused smile.

"You shouldn't," said Emrelda. "Neither of us would have anything from them, if you two hadn't married."

"That's partly why I feel that way," replied Dekkard. "Who Avraal marries shouldn't affect how your parents feel about either of you and your accomplishments."

"We won't change them, and, unfortunately, neither will you." Her voice lightened as she asked, "What else happened in Gaarlak?"

Avraal looked to Dekkard and said, "Your turn."

Dekkard summarized the breakfast and the rest of their time in Gaarlak.

"You make it sound so uneventful," said Emrelda, "even the house."

"It was," replied Dekkard. "We just met as many people as we could and let them know who I am and that I'll listen."

"It was hard work in its way," said Avraal. "I wouldn't be surprised if he talked to more than five hundred people, even a thousand, and he arranged for, set up, and staffed an office there."

"I can see why you both took a nap on the express back," said Emrelda.

"Now, it's your turn," said Dekkard, "and we need to know the details."

"It all started the day after you left, late on that Tridi. Two patrollers— Allayn and Lowes—caught two men breaking into a small grocery shop in Southtown. Early on Furdi morning, more than twenty men broke into the same store and began to loot it. Captain Narryt brought two squads. The looters attacked with knives and hammers. One thing led to another and before it was all over, fires and looting broke out everywhere. The captain asked the Army for help, and it took three companies two more days to restore order. Four whole blocks burned. I'd guess that close to five hundred people lost their homes."

"How did Georg get hurt?" asked Avraal.

"Someone threw a chunk of stone from a rooftop. Sammel shot the thrower." Emrelda's voice was matter-of-fact.

"What was behind it all?" Dekkard suspected he already knew.

"The same as before. Too many people don't have work or marks. Every week food prices are a little higher. Some of the junior patrollers complain that it's harder to make ends meet. Georg and his wife have his sister living in their cellar. A good third of the patrollers assigned to the Erslaan station spend two-thirds of a bell each way on the omnibus from where they can afford to live."

"Has there been more trouble in Rivertown?" asked Dekkard.

"Not as bad as what happened in Southtown, but it could *get* that bad, according to the captain." Emrelda took a healthy swallow of her wine and turned to her sister. "Tell me more about the house."

Dekkard kept his smile to himself, but he was happy to listen to the sisters talk about the Gaarlak house.

12

WHEN Dekkard finally woke on Findi morning, he could tell that he'd slept late, both from the fact that the bedroom was light and that Avraal was awake . . . and smiling.

"I didn't realize I was that tired," he said.

"Everything you did in Gaarlak took more than you realized . . . or than you wanted to admit."

"I'm still not used to talking to that many people, bell after bell."

"You do it well, though."

"I still have a lot to learn. And I owe Obreduur. Without having accompanied him last summer, and without his forcing me to write out what I needed to say, I definitely would have been fumbling this past week."

"You didn't fumble. A few times you could have done better, but you were always personable without being false or condescending. I liked it that you weren't afraid to say you didn't know, but that you'd look into it."

"I hate saying that," Dekkard admitted.

"You're still a new councilor, and people shouldn't expect you to know everything."

"But many of them do. It's as if they're thinking, 'This is a government problem, and you made the laws. So why don't you know about it?'" Dekkard grinned. "But that's why I'm getting paid a lot more, isn't it?"

"Not really," replied Avraal sardonically. "You're getting paid that much because it's the lowest amount that Landors or Commercers would accept. Councilors really should be paid more. The Obreduurs couldn't have lived where they do on a councilor's pay. That's why most of the Craft councilors are much older, and either former guild officials or legalists."

"We're only making it because both of us work and your sister supplies our lodging here." He cleared his throat, then asked, "Are you ready to have breakfast?"

"I am hungry."

"Then we should eat." But when Dekkard got out of bed, he realized that it was colder in the bedroom than he'd thought . . . and that the faint patter against the window wasn't wind, rain, or leaves. "It's sleeting."

"I know." Avraal smiled sweetly. "Would you mind getting my robe?"

Dekkard retrieved her heavy robe from the closet, then pulled on an old set of security grays and an even older set of boots. He'd never even had a robe until Emrelda had given him one after he and Avraal were married, which he only used on his way to and from the bathroom.

In a few minutes, they were both headed downstairs.

Both Gaaroll and Emrelda were at the breakfast room table, although, like Avraal, Emrelda was wearing a robe, rather than endday clothes or her uniform.

Avraal looked to her sister. "You don't have a shift later today, I hope?"

Emrelda shook her head. "I traded shifts with Georg. With his broken arm, he's helping with dispatch now. He had some things he needed to take care of on Tridi night."

"You did two shifts on Tridi?" asked Avraal.

"Why not? That way, I could sleep late this morning and spend some time with you two."

Dekkard couldn't resist looking toward the morning edition of *Gestirn* on the side table.

Emrelda caught his glance and said, "There's nothing in there about the Council or wayward councilors . . . or corporacion misfeasance. There is an article about another riot, this time at Woodlake."

"Where they broke into a brewery last month, wasn't it, and set a fire that spread to several blocks of cold-water row houses?"

Emrelda nodded, then added, "Woodlake's not quite as bad as South-town or Rivertown, but they burned another couple of blocks."

Dekkard shook his head. "Any stories in the newssheets about food prices?"

"The usual crap," said Gaaroll, "about bad weather and poor crops. Never mention the frigging tariffs on Sargassan swampgrass rice or emmer wheat-corn."

Emrelda smiled. "You've been listening to Steffan."

"He makes sense. Some councilors don't."

Emrelda turned to Avraal. "The food and wine critic has a nice article about Don Miguel's, calls it an undiscovered, if expensive, gem."

"Aren't gems usually expensive?" asked Dekkard sardonically.

"Just because you don't read the section about food and wine," said Avraal, "you don't have to disparage their comments."

Dekkard snorted. "I didn't. I merely commented on the redundancy."

Emrelda and Avraal exchanged glances.

Dekkard ignored their looks and poured two mugs of café, then set one in front of Avraal and one at his place, before heading for the cooler in the pantry.

"There's quince paste in there," called Emrelda.

"Thank you," replied Dekkard, with a smile as he imagined Avraal's expression in response to her sister's words.

Given the weather, he had the feeling that the day would be quiet . . . and slow, and that was definitely fine with him.

13

O N Unadi morning, at slightly before the third morning bell, Dek-kard drove the gray Gresynt to the Council Office Building, where he pulled up in front of the west doors and turned to Avraal. "Lunch at noon?"

"Unless I send a message by fifth bell."

Dekkard then opened the driver's door and stepped out, wearing his overcoat over his gray suit. He carried his gray leather folder with him, checking once more to make sure that he was wearing the gold councilor's pin, while Avraal slid behind the wheel.

Gaaroll stepped out of the steamer's middle door, wearing the heavy security-blue winter jacket she'd received from Emrelda, and said, "No strong feelings anywhere near, sir."

"Good." Not that Dekkard had expected any, since the Council wouldn't even be in session until Unadi of the next week. He watched the Gresynt for a moment as Avraal turned back onto Council Avenue heading east. Then he and Gaaroll walked toward the bronze doors of the building. He glanced up, noticing what looked to be small stone towers atop the two corners of the building he could see.

Permanent watchtowers, no doubt added by Guard Captain Trujillo. Dekkard glanced toward the covered parking and was surprised to see that a heavy iron fence had been added on top of the low walls, with iron gates at all the openings in the low walls, although the gates were pres-ently all open. As he walked toward the building, he shifted his eyes to the pair of Council Guards in their heavy green-and-black winter uniforms.

Once inside, Dekkard noticed that the main first-floor corridor leading to the wide central staircase to the second level was almost empty, unsur-prisingly, since not many councilors were likely to be around and the few staffers who hadn't been given time off during the Midwinter Recess were already at work. The walk to Dekkard's office couldn't have been any longer, since his office, as that of the most junior councilor after the last election, was on the far east end of the second level.

As Dekkard reached the top of the staircase, his eyes went to his left, toward the office where he'd spent more than two years, Obreduur's office, the one that the Premier's wife now occupied. *He's gone . . . and you can't do anything to bring him back.* He forced his thoughts back to the day ahead and kept moving toward his own office.

The moment he and Gaaroll walked in, Margrit immediately said, "Welcome back, Councilor. You, too, Nincya, even if you weren't as far away."

"Thank you," replied Dekkard. "It's good to see you. I hope you got some rest."

"I took off last week and slept late every morning."

Svard Roostof appeared from the staff office. "How does it look, sir? We finally got all the replacement desks and typewriters."

"Much better than what we had before . . . but I'd rather have the old furniture and all those we lost."

"We all would, sir."

"Who's off this week?"

"Luara's off, and so is Illana. Shuryn will be back on Tridi."

Dekkard nodded then gestured toward his office. "We need to talk."

Once inside the modest office, Dekkard took off his overcoat and hung it on one of the hooks in the alcove that led to the small washroom and toilet, then walked to the window and glanced out. He immediately saw that an iron gate had been erected to close off the service road behind the building and a new guard post stood beside the gate.

More precautions. He nodded, then turned, seated himself behind the desk, and asked Roostof, "What else should I know that likely didn't get to Gaarlak or into the pages of *Gestirn*?"

"You heard about the fires and disturbances in Southtown, Rivertown, and Woodlake, didn't you?"

"I read about them."

"It's been quiet except there. No broadsheets or demonstrations from the New Meritorists. No explosions or deaths."

"Have there been any other disruptions in other cities that you know of?"

"The stevedores refused to work all last week in Neewyrk. They said the ice rain made loading and unloading too dangerous. I wouldn't be surprised if there were problems in other places with all the bad weather and poor harvests, but they haven't been in the newssheets."

"Speaking of poor harvests . . . I have another project for you. I've done a little research on rice, and I've been told that the tariffs on Sargassan swampgrass rice really only benefit Landors in about three Council districts in the southwest. I need to find out how accurate those figures are. It might be a good task for Shuryn, but I'll leave that up to your discretion. If they turn out to be largely correct, you'll be drafting a legislative proposal to repeal the tariffs."

"The Landors won't like that."

"I'm aware of that, but the Commercers will, and according to the Farmworkers guildmeister, working the rice fields is about the worst task possible. More important, it will bring food prices down, and that could reduce the unrest we're seeing." Dekkard paused. "And could you or Shuryn look into the impact of the emmer wheat-corn tariff as well?"

"We can do that."

"I'm going to add to your workload in another way. We now have a very small office in Gaarlak staffed by one former legal clerk. Her name is Zenya Onswyrth. I told her to show up on Unadi the thirteenth. Her salary is thirty marks a month. I have the post and street address and the forms filled out for her to go on the payroll. You said that the Council Banque will pay district employees by fund transfers to accounts in other chartered banques. I have that information for you, as well as the name of the landlord for the office . . ." As Dekkard continued to talk he extracted the forms containing the necessary information and laid them on the desk.

"You didn't offer her very much . . ."

"You told me we couldn't afford more than forty-five. Salaries in Gaarlak are low. This way, if we're pleased with her after a month or two we can increase her pay to thirty-five marks. One other thing. Since Luara isn't here, you're to watch for information about working women coming from Myram Plassar and some background legal information on the Gaarlak Mills litigation that required equal pay for women doing the same job as men. It's from Namoor Desharra, who was the legalist Ingrella Obreduur worked with on that case."

"Luara will be very pleased to get that. While you were gone, Bretta typed up more copies of the background-information material on the extension of guild legalist representation to . . . unassociated . . . working women."

Dekkard was just glad he'd had that material in his folder, because it would have been a chore for Colsbaan to re-create from scratch, given what had been lost in the damage to the office from the shelling. "At the breakfast meeting with the guildmeisters . . ." He went on to fill Roostof in on all the functionaries and individuals with whom he and Avraal had met during the time in Gaarlak so that the names would be at least passingly familiar.

When Dekkard finished, Roostof nodded, then said, "You and Ritten Dekkard must have spent the entire time working."

"Mostly. Councilor Raathan and his wife did have us to dinner. Outside of that . . ."

Roostof asked, almost apologetically, "Did you have any success in establishing . . . ah . . . a permanent connection—"

"We did buy a house. In Gaarlak proper in a good neighborhood, something neither too small nor extravagant, not that we could afford extravagant. It will be ready by the next recess."

Roostof offered a quizzical look.

"It needed significant repairs and rebuilding of the kitchen. That was one reason we could afford it." Dekkard then grinned and asked, "It's strictly personal, and you don't have to answer, but have you seen any more of the charming Bettina Safaell?"

Roostof smiled in return. "You set it up so that she'd meet me, didn't you?"

"She sounded like someone you'd like, and from what her father said, you seemed to fit what she might like. I thought it couldn't hurt to offer her the possibility to meet you. She did want to know about what other councilors' legalists do."

"I do appreciate that thoughtfulness. I'm being very cautious . . . and so is she, but . . . whatever happens, just being with her has been wonderful so far."

"I'd hoped you'd both at least appreciate each other." Dekkard took a deep breath. "I should get started on reading through all those replies you, Luara, and Shuryn drafted for me."

"We do have a stack of letters and replies for you." Roostof grinned. "Margrit's been waiting to see your face when she delivers them." He stood. "I'll let her bring them in."

In less than a minute after Roostof departed, Margrit appeared with a modest stack of replies, each reply on top of the original letter or petition. Dekkard glanced at the stack of perhaps fifteen to twenty letters and replies. "That's not too bad."

"No, sir, but there are nine more stacks."

"*Nine* more?"

"Yes, sir. People have started to realize that you actually answer, and say something when you do."

"The reward for diligence. I'll take them a stack at a time."

"Just let me know when you're ready for more, sir."

"I will." Once Margrit left his office, Dekkard lifted the first reply and the attached letter off the stack, and began to read. After the first polite lines, he reached the key section.

. . . *understand the need to repair the damage to the Council Office Building quickly. Why can't the Council apply the same speed to repairing the failing levees on the Lakaan River? We've been flooded and lost crops to high water for three out of the last four years . . .*

If true, that was a good question, and he turned to the reply Roostof had crafted for him to sign or modify.

> *. . . in the latest appropriations legislation, the Council added significant additional funding for levee repairs. I have written the Minister of Waterways to suggest strongly that those on the Lakaan River be given a high priority . . .*

Dekkard frowned, knowing that existing legislation prioritized funding repairs on previous damage, then smiled as he saw the attached letter to the Transportation Ministry, and read the critical wording.

> *. . . while funds for levee repair are prioritized under law according to past damage, I'm requesting that this year's extensive damage be included in the forthcoming repair schedule . . .*

After reading that, he signed both and picked up the next letter and response. By the time Avraal arrived at a sixth before noon, Dekkard had made his way through three stacks and was working on the fourth. He'd only had to make changes to a handful, although he had penned notes at the bottom of several others.

"How are you coming?" she asked, eyeing the stack of letters on one side of the desk and those he'd dealt with on the other.

"A little more than a third through the letters and petitions. What about you?"

"I'm hungry. We can talk about it at lunch."

Dekkard didn't bother with his overcoat, but Avraal wore hers as the two left his office, took the main staircase, and then crossed the open courtyard between the Council Office Building and the Council Hall. A chill wind had come up since morning, and Dekkard was close to shivering when he and Avraal stepped out of the courtyard and into the Council Hall and began to walk toward the councilors' dining room.

The dining room held only a handful of councilors. At one table were Elyncya Duforgue and Harleona Zerlyon, two of the four female Craft Party councilors, and at another was Villem Baar with a striking blond woman, who had to be his wife.

Baar immediately said something to his wife, then stood and gestured.

As Dekkard and Avraal reached the table, Baar said, "Would you join us? We just got here and haven't even ordered."

"We'd love to," declared Avraal.

"Oh, this is Gretina," said Baar as Avraal and Dekkard seated themselves at the circular table. "Dear, might I introduce Steffan Dekkard and Avraal Ysella-Dekkard?"

"I'm so happy to meet you both," declared Gretina, in a voice that sounded like she meant it. "Villem's talked a great deal about both of you."

"He's mentioned you to us," replied Dekkard, "and how he was looking forward to your arrival."

"The children and I are very glad to be here, and it's nice to have a little more space, even if we are leasing. I understand that you two live in the Hillside area." Gretina looked to Avraal.

"We do. We're living with my older sister on Florinda Way."

"That's only a few blocks from our house. We're on Astragalis Way, on the west side of Jacquez. Once we get a bit more settled, you *must* come over for dinner . . . with your sister."

"We'd like that very much," replied Avraal.

When the server appeared, the conversation paused, if only long enough for the four to order.

Then Villem said, "I haven't seen you since the recess began. In fact, I haven't seen many other councilors, but then, most have gone back to their districts. It didn't make much sense for me to do that." He smiled wryly.

Dekkard could see that, given that Baar had been a practicing legalist in Suvion and had been selected as a replacement councilor only two months earlier. "We went to Gaarlak." He looked to Avraal, who just nodded. "We bought a house there, since . . . there is this requirement for a property tie to the district."

"Will you rent it when you're not there?" asked Baar.

"Not at present," said Dekkard. "It needed some repairs. It was being updated, and the owners died in the middle of the project, and their family wanted nothing to do with the house."

"That's good." Gretina nodded.

"How old are your children?" asked Avraal.

"They're fourteen and eleven."

"Boy and girl?" asked Dekkard.

"Girl and boy," replied the other councilor. "Karlotta is fourteen going on twenty-four, and Matteus is eleven going on twelve."

"He's likely to be the happier for it," replied Dekkard, "although she may not think so."

Avraal just shook her head.

"I see a little disagreement there," said Gretina in an amused tone.

"That's because we both have sisters, each about five years older," replied Dekkard. "Our experiences were a bit different."

"But, from what Villem has told me, you're both incredibly accomplished."

Dekkard just looked at Avraal.

She looked back at him. "You said it. You explain it." Her tone was light, but not malicious, as if she enjoyed telling him to explain.

"I was granted a largely worry-free childhood. Avraal wasn't. I happen to believe that children who are mature beyond their years often worry excessively. Since I wasn't mature beyond my years"—*and still am not*—"I wasn't burdened with excessive worries." He looked to Avraal again and smiled.

She laughed softly. "I'll concede on that point."

"That's an interesting observation," said Gretina, glancing at her husband.

Villem Baar offered a rueful smile. "It's also one similar to what Gretina has suggested more than once." He nodded to Dekkard. "I do, however, have some doubts about your not being mature beyond your years as a youth."

"I'll grant you half of that," admitted Dekkard. "My reasoning was somewhat beyond my years; my emotions were definitely not."

Gretina began to laugh, shaking her head as she did. Then, so did Avraal.

When the two women stopped laughing, Dekkard looked to Villem and said, "I think I'll stop while I'm still behind."

Avraal blotted the tears from her eyes with a handkerchief that she'd materialized from somewhere.

Gretina looked to Avraal and simply said, "Dinner at our house this coming Findi, with your sister? Fourth bell."

"We'll be there," replied Avraal.

"If I might be practical," said Dekkard, "the house number would be useful."

"Third house west from Jacquez on the north side, number thirty-one-thirty-one," declared Villem.

Dekkard smiled faintly, amused that the house number was the same as that of Emrelda's house, but that made sense, he supposed, since both were third from the corner and on the north side of the street.

"What can you tell us about Gaarlak and your new house?" asked Gretina.

"You tell them about Gaarlak, and I'll tell them about the house," Avraal suggested to Dekkard.

From that point on, after they were served, the conversation centered on Gaarlak and the house.

After Dekkard and Avraal finished lunch and took their leave of the Baars, once they were outside walking back across the courtyard toward the Council Office Building, Avraal said, "I really like her. She's warm and honest all the way through."

"She might be why I've come to respect him," said Dekkard.

Avraal nodded. "I can see that. They're also about the closest in age to us of all the other councilors."

"Ellus Fader might be close."

"I don't recall that name."

"He's Quentin Fader's younger brother, and the Landors named him to succeed his brother. They're from Silverhills. Now . . . you never said what happened at your work today."

"One of Carlos's trackers—he has several—was killed last Quindi night. He was beaten outside his house. Two other trackers, working for other businesses or legalists here in Machtarn, have been killed over the past month. The only thing they have in common is that all of the businesses for whom they worked primarily serve guilds or smaller businesses."

"It could be either Ulrich or del Larrano . . . or someone else who's opposed to the Council looking into Commercer abuses. Del Larrano did offer that veiled warning, and Ulrich had to be behind Minz's death. Should I bring this up with Hasheem?"

"Carlos wants you to think about it and see if you hear anything once the Council reconvenes. He also wants me to ask Emrelda if there have been any other deaths where the victim has been brutally beaten."

"I did say that it's been quiet for too long, but that's the sort of thing where I'd rather not be proven right." After a moment, Dekkard asked, "Is Carlos looking for another empath?"

"He was even before the shelling, but really good empaths aren't easy to find, even with what he can pay."

"There might be a couple of councilors' empaths who'd be interested."

"Are you thinking about Alympiana Nhord?" asked Avraal as they entered the Council Office Building.

"I was." Dekkard knew Nhord had been in the main corridor outside Councilor Waarfel's office when the New Meritorists had shelled that office. She'd been thrown into something and broken an arm, but she'd been Waarfel's only surviving staffer and had decided to take time off after that. She hadn't been that happy working for Waarfel, but never said why.

"She might be a possibility. I'll let Carlos know."

"Is there anything else?"

"Not so far." Avraal stopped at the base of the center staircase. "I don't see any point in my going up to your office—"

"Actually, I thought we might stop by Ingrella's office. It's easier to drop in here than to drive to her house."

"We also won't be tempted to stay as long," said Avraal.

After the two climbed the center staircase and stepped inside the refurbished office, the middle-aged woman sitting at the personal secretary's desk looked up, took in Dekkard's pin, then Avraal's, and asked politely, "How can I help you, Councilor . . . Ritten?"

Dekkard paused, then said, "I'm Steffan Dekkard, and this is my wife Avraal. Ingrella suggested that we drop by once we got back from Gaarlak."

The woman smiled pleasantly. "I believe she's free. Let me tell her you're both here."

In moments, Ingrella appeared. "Avraal, Steffan . . . I was hoping you'd come by."

"We got back on Quindi," said Dekkard, "but getting reorganized and, frankly, getting some sleep, took up most of yesterday."

"I've been rather busy myself. Let me introduce you to everyone. Leyala, here, was kind enough to come from the firm to keep me organized and on schedule."

"It's an incredibly difficult task, requiring almost no effort," replied the woman standing beside her desk with a broad smile.

"Right now, in addition to Leyala, I have one legalist and two typists. Carlos is helping me look for security aides, and I'm still looking for an economic aide."

After giving Dekkard and Avraal a brief introduction to the three women in the staff office, Ingrella escorted them back into her office, motioning for Dekkard to close the door, which he did before sitting in the chair next to Avraal and across the desk from Ingrella.

"Was your house-hunting successful?"

Dekkard smiled and nodded to Avraal.

"We bought a house in the northwest section of Gaarlak . . ." Avraal gave a brief description of the house, as well as the fact that Hrald Iglis was redoing the cabinets.

"That sounds as though you did well," replied Ingrella. "Did you see Emilio and Patriana Raathan? They sent a lovely letter."

About Axel's death, no doubt. "We did," replied Dekkard. "We had dinner with them a week ago last Findi."

"And Jens Seigryn?"

"He arranged a breakfast for the morning after we arrived." Dekkard hesitated, then added, "We had to clear up a few misunderstandings at the breakfast and afterward."

"If he stays as the district coordinator for the Craft Party, there might be more of those," said Ingrella evenly.

"We got that feeling," said Avraal before Dekkard could speak. "Several of the guildmeisters remarked on it as well. Julian Baurett was more . . . forthcoming."

"What do you think of Jens?" asked Dekkard quietly.

"He's always wanted to be a councilor, at almost any cost. I'd rather not say more."

"Of course." Dekkard understood . . . or thought he did. *Axel Obreduur felt he had to support Seigryn if his name came up, but not to the extent of overriding the district Craft Party . . . and Ingrella wants the reason not to come up . . . ever.*

"How else did your visit go?"

Over the next sixth Avraal and Dekkard summarized what happened.

After that, he said, "We don't want to take any more of your time, but we thought this might be the best time to see you."

Ingrella smiled warmly. "I'm so glad that you did. In another week or so, perhaps we could get together."

"This time at our expense," suggested Avraal. "You've hosted us too many times without us returning the favor."

"I'd like that very much."

Dekkard glanced at Avraal, and they both stood.

"We'll be in touch," said Avraal as she and Dekkard left the inner office.

Once outside the office, Dekkard walked with Avraal to the top of the central staircase.

There she stopped and said, "I'll see you after fourth bell."

"You don't have to hurry. I have a lot of responses to go through." He leaned forward and kissed her cheek, then watched for several moments as she walked down the green marble steps, then turned toward the west doors.

Less than a sixth later, Dekkard was back at his desk going through the seemingly endless responses.

14

D UADI, Tridi, and Furdi were all very similar to Unadi as far as Dekkard and Avraal were concerned. Svard did confirm that swampgrass rice growing appeared to be confined primarily to the three districts Alastan Cleese had mentioned but cautioned Dekkard that very small amounts might be grown elsewhere in Guldor.

When Dekkard woke on Quindi morning, he had the definite feeling that the quiet couldn't continue, and that had nothing to do with the scattered sleet pelting the bedroom window.

He sat up and turned to Avraal. "It's sleeting."

"I can hear it."

"If we were still in Gaarlak, it would be snow."

"Don't remind me. Go take your shower and leave some warm water."

Dekkard smiled. "I always do."

She smiled in return. "I know."

Although the house was chilly, Dekkard did feel some heat wafting up the stairs, most likely from the kitchen. Once he was shaved, showered, and dressed, he hurried down to the breakfast room.

Emrelda, fully uniformed and about ready to leave, gestured to the newssheet. "You shouldn't have said anything about it being quiet. We should go to services tonight."

"I'll tell Avraal."

Emrelda nodded and headed for the side hall and her winter patrol jacket.

Gaaroll watched as Dekkard picked up the morning edition of *Gestirn* and began to read.

FORMER PREMIER KILLED IN FIRE

Former Premier Johan Grieg and his wife Maryanna are believed to have died in a raging blaze at their house in East Quarter on Furdi evening. The flames were so intense that the firefighters could not enter the dwelling . . .

Ritter Grieg was dismissed by the Imperador in the wake of the Kraffeist Affair, when it was revealed that Jhared Kraffeist, as Minister of Public Resources, had illegally leased sections of the Eshbruk Naval Coal

Reserve to Eastern Ironway . . . Kraffeist died from a fall in his home last Summerend . . .

The cause of the blaze has not been identified . . . Machtarn fire officials plan a thorough investigation . . .

Dekkard read the article a second time, then laid the newssheet beside Avraal's place at the table and went to pour their cafés, after which he got the croissants and quince paste. He was about to sit down when Avraal hurried into the breakfast room.

"It's even chilly down here."

Dekkard pointed to the newssheet.

"You have that look on your face," said Avraal. "What happened?"

"Just read it," replied Dekkard evenly. "After a few sips of café, of course."

"Then it's serious." Avraal seated herself, ignored Dekkard's advice, as they both knew she would, and picked up the newssheet.

Dekkard sat down, took a swallow of café, then split his croissants, and applied the requisite amount of quince paste. He waited for Avraal's reaction.

After a minute or so, she set the newssheet aside. "Ulrich, I'd say. Indirectly, of course. Very indirectly."

"Maybe not so indirectly. I'd wager that it was handled by former Special Agents, from the fifty that never reported for duty at the Justiciary or Treasury Ministry."

"How do you propose to find which agents are the guilty ones?" asked Avraal dryly.

"The guilty part is easy. They're all guilty of dereliction of duty. Finding the ones involved in Ulrich's schemes will be harder, but the first step is to follow the marks. Your boss found the banque account for Capitol Services." Dekkard paused. "Do you think that might be why someone killed experienced trackers before Grieg and his wife were killed?"

"What else?" snorted Gaaroll.

"I agree with Nincya," said Avraal.

Dekkard nodded, then realized something else. The story never mentioned the councilor who had replaced Grieg after the elections—Aestyn Zeigland. In fact, no one ever mentioned Zeigland. Dekkard doubted he could even recognize the man at a distance. Yet he represented Neewyrk, and Neewyrk was where Eastern Ironway had its headquarters. Had Eastern pressed for a low-profile candidate after the Kraffeist Affair? Or had that been Ulrich's doing?

You'll likely never know.

After a moment, he picked up one of the croissants.

Once they finished eating, Dekkard, Avraal, and Gaaroll quickly washed their dishes and cleaned up the breakfast room. Then Dekkard and Avraal hurried upstairs to finish dressing—in Dekkard's case, to strap his throwing knives in place and put on his winter suit coat.

As he watched Avraal finish dressing, he said, "I've been thinking. Without hard proof, we can't get at the financial records of Northwest Industrial Chemical or Suvion Industries, but, there is one set of financial records we might be able to access . . . or the Security Committee or Guard Captain Trujillo can."

"The Griegs'?"

Dekkard shook his head. "Jaime Minz's . . . and Capitol Services'."

"Trujillo and the Justiciary Ministry have already looked at them."

"From what Trujillo told me, they didn't compare the two in any detail. They looked at totals. By comparing them, we just might find out something." *If you can persuade them to share the records . . . or do a certain kind of analysis.*

"But Guard Captain Trujillo said all the large transactions were made in marks or with banque cheques made out to Capitol Services."

"I still think the flow of funds—and the dates—could indicate something. It's likely to be easier at the moment than pushing for hearings about dunnite and military contracting. Anyway, I'm going to talk to Trujillo."

"What will you tell Hasheem?"

"I promised to inform him of any new evidence about dunnite. Assuming that I can even get access to Minz's financial records, I strongly doubt that they'll show direct evidence of involvement with dunnite. Besides, he has his hands full."

"That's an indirect way of saying you won't need to tell him anything. Is he being too cautious?"

"I don't know," admitted Dekkard. "It could be that, if I hadn't pushed the Security reforms and if Obreduur hadn't prosecuted the former Security minister and the others, the Commercer plants in the New Meritorist movement wouldn't have attacked so soon. Or, maybe, if we'd stopped and looked more into the lorry—"

"Even if we'd stopped and investigated," replied Avraal firmly, "we would have found nothing, and, at most, the attack would have been delayed perhaps a third of a bell."

And, Obreduur, three other councilors, and their staffs would still be dead.

Avraal slipped into her gray jacket and said, "We need to go."

Dekkard opened the bedroom door for her, then closed it behind himself and followed her down the stairs.

In minutes, the three were in the gray Gresynt, headed west on Florinda Way. Dekkard turned north at the corner, then, after three blocks, east on Astragalis Way.

"You want to see where the Baars live, I take it?" asked Avraal.

"It's only a little out of the way, but I'll cross Jacquez and head north on Vergaellen," explained Dekkard, because he was wary of taking Jacquez, given the two assassination attempts on him there. When he drove past the Baars' leased residence, Dekkard took a quick glance. It looked to be a mirror version of Emrelda's house, with the portico on the west side, rather than the east.

He had to wait a bit before he could cross Jacquez, but even with the delay and the detour, less than a third of a bell had passed when he brought the Gresynt to a stop outside the west doors of the Council Office Building.

"I'll see you sometime around noon?"

"I'll make it as close to then as I can."

Dekkard and Gaaroll got out of the steamer. He watched for several moments as Avraal headed west on Council Avenue toward Imperial Boulevard, then turned. In minutes, he and Gaaroll entered his office.

He stopped at the doorway to the staff office and said, "Svard, when you have a moment."

"Yes, sir.

Once the two were in Dekkard's private office with the door closed, Dekkard seated behind the desk and Roostof in the middle chair, Dekkard asked evenly, "You saw the story about former Premier Grieg this morning? What are your thoughts?"

"I doubt it was an accident," replied Roostof, his voice slightly cynical.

"And?"

"He knew something someone didn't want to come out."

"Some of it already came out. That was how Obreduur and Justiciary Minister Kuta were able to charge Minz with conspiracy, in addition to manslaughter."

"What about the murder charge?"

"Grieg didn't know anything about Venburg's murder. He did know about Capitol Services, and Minz's role in funneling resources to the New Meritorists. He told Obreduur." Dekkard wasn't about to mention his own role in getting Grieg's admission. "Now, both Obreduur and Grieg are dead."

Roostof just looked at Dekkard attentively.

"Minz is a deceased individual charged with serious offenses. Under the law, can't the Council or the Guard captain obtain his banque records? Both from the Council Banque and from the Imperial Banque of Machtarn?"

"I believe so, if the Council has a legitimate reason," said Roostof. "I'd have to check the specifics."

"I'd appreciate your doing that, preferably without talking to anyone. Those records might provide a clue as to how Minz funneled all that dunnite to the New Meritorists."

"Do you intend to bring it up before the Security Committee, sir?"

"It's been suggested that I not even try without a great deal more hard evidence."

Roostof frowned.

"Svard . . . we can't track who ordered whom to do what, but I'm hoping that who paid whom for what might give us a place to begin. We know marks went to Minz through Capitol Services, but, from what I've learned, those appear to be pass-throughs. I'm hoping to find a pattern in the dates *if* I can get access to those records." Dekkard stood.

So did Roostof. "I'll check the Council regulations and the criminal disclosure provisions and get back to you, sir."

"Thank you." Dekkard looked at the two stacks on his desk—one of replies he needed to read and sign, or revise, and one of incoming unread letters and petitions. "You know what I'll be doing."

Going through both stacks took close to three bells. After handing the signed replies to Margrit for posting and the revised replies and the incoming letters to Roostof, he returned to his personal office. He walked to the window nearest his desk, taking in the recently replaced windows and stonework, then looked out to the north, taking in what he could see of the Imperador's Palace before his eyes dropped to the now-gated service roadway less than thirty yards from the building.

He could almost see the scarred and scratched lorry that had stopped and, in moments, started to fire shells into the building. *What else could you have done besides get everyone out of the office?*

He shook his head and walked back to his desk.

Less than a third later, Roostof knocked and opened the door slightly. "Do you have a moment, sir?"

"Come on in, Svard."

The senior legalist entered, closed the door, and took the middle chair. "What did you find out?"

"There's nothing that applies directly to the Minz situation. Both the Justiciary Ministry and the Security Ministry can obtain access to financial records to determine financial crimes or to ascertain whether funds were employed in an illegal fashion or in support of criminal activity. The financial records of a deceased person are available to the executor or the administrator of the deceased person's estate. But there's nothing in legislated law about obtaining records for possible past criminality, and the law is unclear about the Council obtaining such records without a committee order. I'm sure there are case law precedents, but since that was never my specialty, I don't know them. I hope you don't mind, but I asked Luara if she knew. The only case she could recall was when her firm obtained access to financial records of a widow to determine that the estate executor had been embezzling funds."

Dekkard nodded slowly, then said, "I'm glad you asked her. Thank you. I'll need to think about this."

Several minutes after Roostof left, Dekkard wrote out a short note, which he placed in an envelope that he slipped into his jacket pocket. Then he stood and walked to the window, looking out through the winter coal haze toward the Palace, before making his way out into the anteroom. "Margrit, I'm going over to the Council Hall. I don't know how long I'll be gone, but I doubt it will be longer than two bells. In any event, I'll be back by noon." Then he looked to Gaaroll, who was already donning her security-blue winter jacket. "Ready, Nincya?"

"Yes, sir."

From the office, Dekkard and Gaaroll walked to the central staircase, down to the main level, and then to the doors to the courtyard and covered portico running between the Council Office Building and the Council Hall. While he saw several staffers, he didn't encounter any councilors.

Whether Guard Captain Trujillo would be in his small office Dekkard had no idea, but he could always slip the note under the door if Trujillo was elsewhere.

Fortunately, Trujillo was in his office, and Dekkard turned to Gaaroll. "Wait somewhere near and practice your sensing." Then Dekkard stepped into the office and closed the door.

"What can I do for you, Councilor?" The Guard captain stood and gestured to the single chair across from his narrow desk.

Dekkard seated himself, as did Trujillo, then said, "There were more than a few unresolved issues connected with the shelling of the Council Office Building. The Security Committee, or at least this member, is still worried that there may be more dunnite in the hands of the New Meritorists. Since the late Sr. Minz seemed to be involved, I've been thinking about how we could look into the matter . . . quietly."

"What exactly did you have in mind?" Trujillo's voice was even, reserved, but not wary.

"There are two things. I had Minz followed after he began work as an influencer. He didn't require an escort when visiting councilors' offices. So who put him on the access list?"

"I thought you might ask that," replied Trujillo.

Meaning that you should have brought it up earlier.

"Two councilors gave him access. Councilor Kuuresoh and Councilor Schmidtz. What was the other matter?"

"I was wondering if you'd analyzed the pattern of financial transactions in Sr. Minz's personal accounts and the accounts of Capitol Services, comparing them to see if there might be a pattern corresponding to New Meritorist activities, or those of the renegade Special Agents."

Trujillo's smile contained a hint of amusement. "Exactly what would you hope to discover?"

"I can't think of any other way to gain even a hint of those behind Sr. Minz and those involved in the attack. Minz certainly had to obtain the funds from elsewhere. Even if some transactions or transfers of funds were in the form of banque cheques or drafts, finding out who purchased the cheques might offer a general idea. Or have you already attempted that?"

"We've thought about it, but . . . right now, the Council Guard has a few other priorities, Councilor."

"Pardon me, if I'm treading where I shouldn't, but that suggests that anyone who can be trusted with that information doesn't have the time to spend, and those who do have the time . . ." Dekkard left the sentence unfinished.

"Premier Hasheem is most concerned that the Council Guard concentrate its planning and resources on protecting the Council against possible further attacks."

"I can see that you've already taken a number of steps." Dekkard paused. "What if a junior councilor on the Security Committee looked over such records, one with a background in security, of course, and attempted such an analysis for the Guard?"

"So long as the analysis remained in the hands of the Council Guard, I don't believe that would contravene any existing orders or procedures. The material being analyzed would necessarily also have to remain within the physical purview of the Guard. No findings can be released without the permission of the Guard and the Premier."

"I can't see how it could be otherwise," agreed Dekkard.

Trujillo laughed softly. "When do you want to start?"

"When would be convenient?"

"The sooner the better." The Guard captain's smile vanished.

"You think there will be more trouble soon?"

"Why else are you here?" returned Trujillo. "I will require one assurance from you, Councilor."

"And that is?"

"You let me know immediately of *any* insights or suspicions you have about danger bearing on the Council or councilors." Trujillo looked squarely at Dekkard. "Without your warning about the lorry, I wouldn't have alerted the guards and the roof sentries, and matters could have been much, much worse."

"Did the Guards' efforts result in the explosion that destroyed the steam cannon?"

"We're fairly sure of that . . ."

It would have been good to know that earlier. But then, Dekkard knew Trujillo tended not to reveal anything he didn't have to, unless it was in the Council's interest or he was pressed.

"We're also taking other steps to further secure all Council buildings." Trujillo stood. "Let me take you down to the records room. Any notes you take will have to remain with the records until you finish and the Premier and I both agree as to what leaves the chamber. Also, your security aide will have to wait outside the door."

Dekkard stood and followed the Guard captain from the office out to the main corridor. Gaaroll joined Dekkard, and they followed Trujillo to a nondescript door some fifteen yards away, opening into a narrow stairway leading to the lower level, with a central corridor under the main-level corridor. The entrance to the records room seemed to be under the entrance to the Premier's floor office. Behind the door was a small space with an equally small desk manned by a clerk and an armed guard beside a locked iron door.

Trujillo looked to Gaaroll. "You can wait here." Then he turned to the clerk. "Councilor Dekkard is to have access to a particular set of records, and only those. His access is unlimited, but he needs to sign in every time he comes, and his notes are to remain with the files."

"Yes, sir." The clerk stood and walked to the door, which he unlocked, then led the way into the chamber beyond, stopping immediately to light the bronze lamp on the wall above a bare table desk. "There are pens and paper in the desk drawer."

Trujillo turned toward the three rows of black-painted steel filing cabinets and made his way to the row on the far right, where he opened a drawer and extracted four large folders, which he brought to the table and laid out side by side on the dark oak surface. "There are four sets of financial records—the accounts for the Machtarn office of Northwest Industrial Chemical, the records for Capitol Services, and Sr. Minz's personal accounts, one here at the Council Banque, which he closed the week after the last election, and one at the Imperial Banque of Machtarn. Leave whatever notes you make beside the files, and Courben here will put them in a separate file. They'll be kept with these four until you're finished."

Nearly two bells later, after the duty guard returned the records to the vault and Dekkard left the records room, he definitely understood Trujillo's smile. He also knew that, before returning to study the records, he needed to create a detailed timeline of various events.

As he and Gaaroll walked up the narrow staircase to the main level, Dekkard said, "I'm sorry. I didn't realize it would take that long."

"Real secret, sir?"

"Very secret."

Avraal was waiting when Dekkard walked into his office. She offered an amused smile. "The one time I'm early, you're not here, and even Margrit doesn't know where you went."

"I'll tell you all about it at lunch. It took much longer than I realized."

"What did?"

"What I'm going to tell you at lunch. Shall we go?"

Once the two of them were out in the main corridor, Avraal said quietly, "I think you should have Gaaroll accompany you, even when I'm here, once the Council is back in session. She can sense farther than I can, and she's getting better."

"You're right."

"Did your little excursion have something to do with what you mentioned this morning?"

"It did. I met with Trujillo. I found out that Minz was granted access by both Kuuresoh and Schmidtz, and that the Guard captain has those records." Dekkard quickly explained the records and the conditions under which he could examine them.

"Did you discover anything?"

"I have to do more work on my own, and I'll need your help. I'll need to re-create an accurate timeline of what happened so that I can see if any of the transactions correlate with various events."

"How long do you think it will be before you can tell anything?"

"At least a few days, possibly longer. I got the feeling Trujillo would like to do it, but can't afford the time."

"Hasheem's looking to be far too cautious," replied Avraal.

"Mardosh might also be pressing for caution. I can see Siincleer Shipping exerting pressure." Dekkard frowned. "There was one thing Trujillo said that he hadn't before—that his guards were responsible for exploding the lorry, and that it would have been much worse without my warning him."

"Good of him to tell you now." There was a hint of acid in Avraal's voice.

"He's been told not to pursue the matter, and he's worried. I don't think he'd have said that or allowed me access otherwise. He's also tightening up security."

"Besides the roof towers, the guards are checking the delivery lorries, I noticed."

When they crossed the garden courtyard to the Council Hall, it was empty, except for the Council Guards posted outside the doors. By Unadi, Dekkard knew, that would change. The wind had picked up, and by the time they entered the Council Hall he was close to shivering. Avraal had kept her overcoat, but he'd left his in the office.

Once they were seated in the councilors' dining room and had ordered, Dekkard asked, "How was your morning?"

"Alympiana Nhord came in to see Carlos. Her arm is still in a cast. She doesn't want to work for a councilor, or even for the Council."

"That's understandable. I don't see her as working for Carlos, though."

"He doesn't either, but he has a client for whom she'd be a good fit."

"Low-level high-volume security screening?"

"Small building-loan banque, part administration and part screening. She was very interested."

"Good. Has he found anyone for Ingrella yet?"

"Not so far." Avraal paused as the server delivered their cafés and entrées, the white bean soup for Dekkard and onion soup for her. After the server left, she added, "For the first time ever, empaths and isolates aren't all that enthusiastic about working for councilors."

"Because six were killed in the shelling . . . and a few others vanished or quit?" asked Dekkard sardonically.

"I imagine that had something to do with it," replied Avraal in the overly sweet tone that made Dekkard want to wince.

"What is Carlos telling them?"

"He's politely saying that the higher-paying or higher-status positions come with more risk. Alympiana will likely take the lower-paying and lower-risk position." Avraal ate several spoonfuls of soup before continuing. "That means that the replacement councilors may have trouble obtaining security aides."

"And that could make them more cautious as well, which will play into Ulrich's hands and embolden the New Meritorists." Dekkard smiled wryly. "Do you have any cheerful news?"

"It's Quindi, and Presider Buusen's homilies aren't that long, and we are having dinner with the Baars tomorrow."

Dekkard decided to concentrate on those aspects, rather than on Unadi and the resumption of Council sessions.

15

DEKKARD spent most of the remainder of Quindi afternoon in his office, less than a bell of which was devoted to correspondence. The majority was spent working on a detailed timeline of events over the past year, particularly New Meritorist and student demonstrations. He ended up asking Shuryn Teitryn, his engineering aide, to research the exact dates for a list of events.

He, Avraal, Emrelda, and Gaaroll attended services at the Hillside Trinitarian Chapel, then had a quiet dinner at home.

On Findi morning, Dekkard woke to the sound of sleet pattering against the window, but by the time he and Avraal went downstairs for breakfast, the sleet had been replaced by wet heavy snowflakes. In turn, less than a bell later the snowflakes stopped, and by noon the sun was out, if without much warmth.

Before that long, or so it seemed to Dekkard, it was time to get ready for dinner with the Baars. Since Avraal deemed the dress for dinner as winter casual, Dekkard donned various shades of gray. Avraal wore her calf-length not-quite-formfitting dark green dress with a light gray jacket, and dark gray boots, with, of course, her small gold lapel pin with the crimson starburst. Emrelda opted for a regal blue dress and a pale green jacket.

When the three got into the Gresynt for the short drive, just before fourth bell, all traces of the snow and sleet had melted, except in the shaded spots around the house. Despite the sunlight, the brisk northwest wind confirmed that it was definitely winter.

Since the space under the portico of the Baars' house was empty, Dekkard took the drive and parked there.

Villem greeted them at the side door, escorted them in, and took their overcoats.

"No one could doubt that you two are sisters," said Gretina warmly as she led them into the front parlor.

Dekkard immediately noticed the furniture, with carving and lines that proclaimed that it was late Imperial. "Is the furniture from family?"

Gretina smiled. "How did you know?"

"It's late Imperial, and well-kept, but the upholstery is newer than the wood. The carving is too good to be replica, and it's all perfectly matched."

"It came from my grandparents," said Gretina. "Everyone else said it was old-fashioned. We had it reupholstered after we got it. I've always loved it."

Villem shook his head. "You continue to surprise me, Steffan." He gestured to the chairs and the settee.

"Almost everyone has surprises, if you look deeply enough."

"Hardly," said Avraal. "For some people, the surprise is that they have no depth."

"Or it's measured in mere digits," added Emrelda.

"If that," finished Gretina.

Villem looked to Dekkard and asked, genially, "How does it feel to be outnumbered?"

"I had an older sister," replied Dekkard. "I was always outnumbered." He grinned. "The good thing is that it's much harder to make a stupid mistake . . . especially a second time."

All three women laughed.

Dekkard sat beside Avraal on the settee.

Villem offered an amused smile. "Drinks? We have wine and lager."

"White wine," said Avraal.

"White, also," said Emrelda.

"Lager," added Dekkard.

"I'll be back in a moment," said Villem.

Gretina looked to Emrelda. "I understand you're a patroller. How did both of you end up in security fields?"

"By accident on my part," replied Emrelda. "When Avraal was a parole screener in Siincleer, we got to talking when she visited for Yearend, and she mentioned that the patrollers were always looking for women to be patrollers. So I looked into it. I had to take a yearlong program at Imperial University, and then six months at the Patroller Academy, but I found that I liked it. I ended up as a junior dispatcher, but I'm also a backup street patroller."

Emrelda had just finished explaining when Villem returned, carrying a tray of beverages. He offered a glass of white wine to Avraal, another to Emrelda, a beaker of lager to Gretina, a second beaker to Dekkard, and, after setting the tray on a side table, took the remaining glass, red wine, for himself.

"How did you two meet?" Dekkard asked Gretina.

"The meeting was easy," Gretina replied. "We met in university— Imperial University, of course. We were both studying law, but Villem never noticed me."

"Until she graduated third in the class," added Villem dryly. "I was fifth."

"You're a legalist, too, then?" Emrelda asked Gretina.

"Only part-time. I'd thought there might be more opportunities here in Machtarn, but we're still getting settled."

"Do you have a particular area of expertise?" asked Dekkard.

"I've mostly handled estate and property law—not property law as in selling or buying, but wills, probate, legatees, or commercial property complications and permitting."

To Dekkard, that made sense, since most of those didn't require immediate action by a legalist. *But you're presuming that's because she's the one doing all the child care.* "There's nothing political in any of that, I take it?"

Gretina offered an amused smile. "Not so far."

"Are you thinking what I am?" asked Avraal.

"I think so."

Villem showed a puzzled frown.

"Would you mind if we mentioned your name to a few people?" asked Dekkard. "It might not come to anything, but, at the least, they could offer other suggestions."

"I'd appreciate that very much."

"They aren't likely to be as numerous as the contacts your uncle might have," Dekkard added, "given that he's the presidente of the largest banque in Guldor."

After the slightest pause, Gretina replied, "Uncle Haarden is rather traditional, and I'd rather not impose on him."

"Nicely put," said Dekkard dryly. "I don't wish to assume, but does that mean that the most honorable Haarden Hallaam is not terribly enthused about women legalists or that he will reluctantly accept a niece who only works part-time?"

Villem barely managed not to choke on a sip of his red wine.

Gretina grinned, then said to Villem, "It's quite all right, dear. I'm already enjoying the evening."

Villem shook his head. "I didn't expect that, Steffan. You delivered that so perfectly."

"Uncle Haarden doesn't hire women legalists, part-time or otherwise," said Gretina. "Even if it weren't against banque rules to hire relatives, I wouldn't ever want to work for him." She hesitated. "I never did thank you for the way in which you introduced him to Premier Obreduur." After another pause, she added, "I know you two were close to the Premier, and it must have been a terrible loss."

"There's still an emptiness," replied Dekkard. "I saw it happen, yet even now it seems as much like a nightmare as real." He wasn't about to mention the nightmares that still plagued him.

"Better you than me," said Villem. "You knew what to do. I probably would have been still gawking at the attackers when the shells hit."

"I doubt that," replied Dekkard. "At that point, the only thing you can do is get out and get your staff out. I just did what was obvious. I'm sure you would have, too."

"Now that you've covered the obvious reaction to the horrible," said Avraal, "could we talk about something more cheerful?"

Knowing that Avraal's question was more like a command, Dekkard smiled and asked, "How are the children finding Machtarn?"

"As you might think," replied Gretina. "One day Karlotta is complaining about leaving all her friends behind, and a week later, there are two others in the sitting room, and they're acting like old friends. By then, Matteus had commandeered the study to play crowns with a schoolmate."

"They must be gregarious," observed Avraal.

"They take after Gretina, thank the Almighty," said Villem. "At his age, I would have been playing Impatience with myself in a corner. I'm not a great lover of crowns."

"You and Steffan are alike in that," said Avraal. "He refuses to play crowns."

"Why, if I might ask?" Gretina's words were warm and held honest curiosity.

"Neither personal combat nor warfare are neat, and crowns creates the illusions that strategy can overcome reality and that neither are ever bloody and messy, which they so often are. There are enough illusions in life without adding to them in the name of play or entertainment." Dekkard offered an embarrassed laugh. "The way I said that makes me sound like a withered, curmudgeonly pedant, I suppose."

"More like a cynical realist, I'd say," replied Villem.

"That's because you agree with him," said Gretina cheerfully. "I find some illusions are comforting. I know not all people are good, but I like to believe that most people are at heart."

"How about councilors?" asked Dekkard.

"There are likely a few who aren't that good, but I think most will do the right thing. Villem says I'm being overly generous. What do you think?"

Not about to comment on Villem's judgment, Dekkard said, "Some of those who might not be considered particularly good are no longer councilors. I have hopes for their replacements."

"Spoken like a true politician," declared Villem, with an amused smile.

"I'll endeavor to dispel that impression," replied Dekkard. "Eyril Konnigsburg is far superior to Oskaar Ulrich. You're an incredible improvement over Erik Marrak. Even Yordan Farris, who doesn't impress me, is far more honest than Kurtweil Aashtaan. Tomas Pajiin is so much better than Demarais Haaltf that Commercers voted for him. Those are the ones I know about so far. I also think some of the new Craft councilors are likely better than their predecessors, but I haven't seen enough to tell." Dekkard looked to Villem and smiled. "Is that less like a true politician, as you put it?"

Villem just shook his head, ruefully.

Gretina and Avraal exchanged glances, and Dekkard got the definite impression that both were amused, if not totally favorably.

He took a swallow of his untouched lager, then another, before he recognized the taste. "Where did you get Riverfall? It is Riverfall, isn't it? I didn't know it was available anywhere in Machtarn."

Villem nodded to Gretina. "She found it. I'm not much of a lager drinker."

"There's this specialty wine and spirits shop on Justiciary Avenue, buried between all those legalist offices," explained Gretina. "I'd read about it in the food and wine section of *Gestirn*. Since I was close, I stopped there just to see what they had."

"*Gestirn* has a good columnist for that," said Emrelda. "Especially about wines and where they come from."

Gretina's comment about where she'd been suggested to Dekkard that she'd been talking to a few legalist firms, but he merely asked, "Do you recall the name of the shop?"

"High Spirits, as I recall."

"I can see where Steffan might be shopping next," said Avraal.

"Possibly, if they haven't priced it exorbitantly."

Avraal smiled, and Dekkard knew she was recalling their first-month anniversary dinner at Estado Don Miguel, where he'd ordered a rather expensive beaker of Karonin.

After perhaps another third of light conversation, Gretina excused herself, returning in a few minutes to say, "Dinner is ready." Then she led the way to the dining room.

Dekkard couldn't help noting that the table, chairs, sideboard, and china cabinet were of the same late Imperial style as the furnishings in the parlor. *Someone in her family definitely had taste and marks.*

"You're having lamb Suvion," announced Gretina. "That's the elaborate title for lamb medallions in a mint cream sauce, with rice and carrots. The rolls are courtesy of Karlotta, as will be dessert, and she's serving."

Avraal, Dekkard, and Emrelda sat on one side of the table with Villem and Gretina on the other side. Villem seated himself last after refilling the wineglasses and beakers.

Immediately Karlotta appeared, blond, like both her parents, but with the piercing green eyes of her mother. She wore dark green trousers and a matching long-sleeved blouse and carried two plates, which she served to Emrelda and Avraal. The next two went to her mother and Dekkard, and the last to her father, accompanied by a basket of rolls, which she set on the table.

"Thank you, dear," said Gretina quietly.

Karlotta smiled, then left the dining room.

"She presents herself well," observed Emrelda.

"Always, at least in public," replied Villem.

Emrelda and Avraal exchanged amused glances, but neither spoke.

"I saw that look," declared Gretina. "You're right. Around the house without company is a bit different."

Dekkard also suspected that, often, Karlotta needed reminders about her room, but since that was merely a guess, based on how his own sister had acted, he refrained from commenting, instead waiting for Gretina to lift her fork so that he could sample the lamb.

After she did, and Dekkard had taken several bites, he said, "This is excellent. I've never had anything like it before."

"Thank you," replied Gretina. "I have to admit that I stole the recipe from Villem's mother."

"It didn't take much stealing," replied Villem. "She didn't have any daughters to pass it on to."

"But that wasn't why I copied it from her recipe book, then asked," said Gretina. "It was because I liked it, and so do you. Besides, I've fixed it for her, and she liked the way I did." She looked to Avraal. "Are there any family recipes that are your favorite?"

"Most likely the molasses nut pie," said Avraal, "but the past few months are the first time in years I've had a chance to cook, and neither of us has much time for anything elaborate except on Findis . . ."

For the remainder of the dinner, which included pear tarts for dessert, the conversation remained light and well removed from politics.

Almost two bells passed before Avraal, Emrelda, and Dekkard got back into the gray Gresynt to head back home.

"Villem and Gretina aren't at all what I expected," said Emrelda. "Even after what you told me."

"They're more like a younger version of the Obreduurs than like other Commercers I've met," said Avraal.

"I like them both," added Dekkard. "It'll be interesting to see how he reacts to what happens next in the Council."

"Such as?" asked Emrelda.

"When Ulrich does something nasty or when the New Meritorists' public demonstrations turn into attacks or riots. That could happen when the disturbances over food prices get worse."

"The one two weeks ago was bad enough," said Emrelda. "I wouldn't want to see anything worse."

"Enough," said Avraal. "We had a very good evening. All that can wait until tomorrow."

Dekkard agreed with that, but, as he turned the Gresynt onto Jacquez heading south, he realized that while the talk about politics had been brief, more time had been spent on Emrelda's being a patroller. *Most likely to avoid possible controversies in politics.*

16

UNADI morning was cold and windy, but that didn't stop Avraal, Dekkard, and Gaaroll from leaving the house on time, and Dekkard turning the Gresynt over to Avraal outside the west doors of the Council Office Building just before second bell.

"Sometime after fourth bell?" he asked as he got out of the steamer, checking his personal truncheon and picking up his leather folder.

"If I'll be terribly late, I'll send a message."

Dekkard smiled, closed the steamer door, and watched for a minute or so as Avraal drove off. Then he and Gaaroll turned and headed into the building, where there were definitely more staffers in the main hall than during the previous week.

Dekkard decided to stop by Ingrella Obreduur's office.

"Good morning, Councilor," said Leyala the moment Dekkard appeared.

"I just wanted to ask her a quick question, if she's here and free."

"She has a meeting in a third or so, but she might have a few minutes. Let me see."

In moments, Dekkard was in her office. He didn't bother to close the door. "I just stopped by to see if you were free for lunch."

"How about tomorrow, Steffan?" Ingrella replied warmly. "I'm meeting with Harleona over lunch today."

"That would be fine. Noon? Would you like me to meet you here? We could walk over together."

"I'd appreciate that, since I don't have security aides yet."

"Well . . . you'd likely be limited to me and Nincya."

"That should be more than sufficient. I see you're carrying a truncheon."

"And knives. Avraal insisted."

"She's right."

"I actually have one more question."

Ingrella offered an amused smile.

"I'm sure you've seen Villem Baar?"

"The councilor from Suvion? Yes. What about him?"

"It's not about him. It's about his wife. She's a legalist." Dekkard gave a quick explanation of Gretina Baar's situation, and his and Avraal's feelings about her, ending with, "I just thought you might have some thoughts."

"Let me think about that. We can talk about it at lunch tomorrow."

"That's all I ask. Until tomorrow."

Ingrella nodded, and Dekkard departed.

Minutes later, Dekkard and Gaaroll entered his office.

"Good morning, sir," offered Margrit. "You have just one message." She handed him the envelope.

"Thank you." Dekkard then walked into the staff office and to Shuryn Teitryn's desk.

"Yes, sir?"

"When you have a moment, give me the information you have so far on the events and their dates. I can add the rest as you get it."

"It's a bit piecemeal, sir. I can have something typed up in a bell."

"That would be fine."

When Dekkard entered his personal office, he shed his overcoat and hung it up, then opened the message. It was a form message from Hasheem, informing Security Committee members that the committee would meet at fourth bell on Duadi morning. Interestingly, there was no subject listed for the meeting.

What does Fredrich have in mind? Just to discuss possible hearings for the months ahead? Or has something come up?

Since Dekkard had no idea which might be the case, he turned his attention to the incoming letters and petitions neatly stacked in his inboxes. A little over a bell later, he was close to reading the last of the letters when Teitryn knocked on his door.

"Sir? I have what you asked for."

"Come on in and show me."

The engineering aide walked to the desk and handed Dekkard a short stack of papers.

Dekkard frowned.

"There are a lot of blank spaces there, sir. I put in each day with a space, even if there was no entry, and I had Britta type up two copies. That way either of us can add entries. Oh . . . the prices you asked for are on the last sheet."

Teitryn's approach made sense to Dekkard, although he suspected there would be more than a few days with no entries by the time he finished. *And you can't tell which ones they'll be right now.* For that matter, Dekkard knew that there was a strong possibility that a comparative analysis of Minz's financial records might only suggest other leads . . . or prove nothing at all. *But what else can you do?*

"Thank you. I appreciate it."

Once Teitryn left, Dekkard finished the incoming mail, then quickly went through the timeline before slipping the papers into his leather folder. He stood and left his office.

"Margrit, I'm going over to the Council Hall. I'll be on the lower level in the Council Guard's records room doing some research. You can tell anyone who asks I'm in the Council Hall, and you don't know when I'll be back, but it won't be until after the short Council session at the earliest. Don't tell anyone but Svard exactly where I am unless it's urgent."

"Yes, sir."

Dekkard looked to Gaaroll. "Let's go."

As he and Gaaroll walked from the office toward the central staircase, Dekkard said, "Once I'm in the records room, you can go back to the office. Come back right before noon."

He could see another councilor—Chiram Ghohal—walking toward the staircase from the west end of the building. "What do you sense about him?"

"He's not feeling strong about anything."

Ghohal walked past the west side of the staircase and continued eastward, reaching the top of the east side just about the same time Dekkard did. "How was the recess for you, Steffan?"

"Quietly eventful. We went to the district and also set up a small office there. What about you?"

"Pretty much the same. Where are you headed?" Ghohal's voice was even, and far from effusive.

"Over to the Council Hall."

"Committee meeting?"

"No. Just some errands . . . before the session and everything gets busy again," said Dekkard as they headed down the green marble steps.

"Doesn't seem like we'll be that busy."

"Not for a little while. We'll have to see."

"You don't sound convinced. What aren't you saying?"

"You remember Jaime Minz?"

Ghohal frowned for a moment. "Oh . . . the influencer who murdered the head legalist at Siincleer Shipbuilding and got shot? Why would that make the Council a busier place?"

"Because he was also behind the shelling of the Council, and neither the Council Guard, the Justiciary Ministry, nor the Ministry of Public Safety could ever find out from where he got all the marks or the dunnite for the shells. So far, no one's found whoever's leading the New Meritorists. I don't think they're going away. Do you?"

Ghohal shook his head. "Why am I always unsettled after talking to you?"

"Because you ask good questions that don't have settling answers," replied Dekkard with a smile, as he stepped away from the staircase. "I'll see you later."

Once Dekkard and Gaaroll were in the courtyard and walking under the covered portico toward the Council Hall, Dekkard asked, "Was Councilor Ghohal upset at all?"

"Some. A little, but not a whole lot. Seemed cool and distant."

Not surprising. He wasn't that happy about your pressing him to vote for Hasheem.

When they reached the records room, there was a Council Guard on duty that Dekkard didn't recognize, but the duty clerk was the same one who had signed him in previously.

"Thank you, Courben."

"You're welcome, sir . . . That folder . . . it will have to stay here."

Dekkard wasn't surprised, not after what Trujillo had said earlier. He opened the folder and extracted the sheets Teitryn had prepared. "I'll need these. They're a calendar of events, and I'll leave them with the files."

"So long as they stay with the files, sir."

"They will." Dekkard turned to Gaaroll. "A sixth before noon."

After Gaaroll left, Courben went to the door to the inner chamber, which he unlocked and opened, then retrieved the same four files that Dekkard had read through on Quindi, as well as a fifth folder containing Dekkard's notes.

The first thing Dekkard did was to go through the records of Minz's personal account at the Council Banque, which Minz had closed once he was no longer on the Council payroll. As Dekkard had surmised from his study on Quindi, the only cheques Minz had written from his personal account before the election on the twelfth of Fallfirst were to himself for marks. The only deposits were his salary. The same turned out to be true for Minz's personal account at the Imperial Banque of Machtarn, which Minz had opened back at the beginning of 1264—except, there were more deposits and withdrawals. The balance was continually almost twice that in his Council Banque account. *So he was double-dipping for years.*

The Capitol Services account was more interesting. That account had been established in 1264 almost at the same time as Minz's personal account, and the volume of transactions was far greater. Minz had written cheques for other than marks, although a significant number of cheques were still made out to Minz. These were likely cashed to obtain marks for services or equipment Minz hadn't wanted to appear in the banque records.

Dekkard wrote down the cheques made out to specific individuals and businesses, as well as the date they had been written. Then he began on a similar list for the large cheques made out to Capitol Services, but he'd barely started when he realized that it was almost noon.

He rapped on the door, and Courben appeared almost immediately.

"I replaced the materials in each file and left my notes in the other file."

"I appreciate that, sir."

"I might be back later today, but I can't say for sure."

"We're not going anywhere, sir. Neither are the files."

When Dekkard left the inner chamber, he found Gaaroll waiting. Once they were out of the outer chamber and headed up the narrow staircase to the main level, he said, "We're going to the councilors' dining room. You can get something to eat. Be outside the councilors' lobby at half after first bell. Did anything interesting happen while I was buried in the records room?"

"Not that I know of. No really strong feelings anywhere."

"Keep practicing on trying to sense more. I'm afraid we'll both need everything you can discern before that long."

"Something I should know, sir?"

"Just a feeling."

After Gaaroll escorted him to the councilors' dining room, Dekkard was about to ask for a table when Eyril Konnigsburg, who was seated with Kaliara Bassaana, beckoned to him. He was happy to walk toward them. On the way, he saw Ingrella Obreduur and Harleona Zerlyon together at a table, talking comfortably, or so it seemed.

After Dekkard seated himself, a server arrived and immediately took his order, then returned with three cafés.

"I take it that your wife is at work?" said Konnigsburg.

"She is."

"She must have a great deal of flexibility," said Bassaana.

"She does," replied Dekkard. "That was one reason she took the position she did. It's worked out moderately well."

"I've noticed another aide with you."

"She's an empath-in-training. She has great promise."

"That makes sense," said Bassaana evenly. "Good empaths who want to work for the Council are rare these days."

"So I've heard," replied Dekkard cheerfully.

"Do you have any idea what Fredrich will say this afternoon?" asked Bassaana.

"None whatsoever. I haven't even seen him since well before the Midwinter Recess."

"You didn't stay here, did you?" asked Bassaana in a casual tone.

"No. Like most councilors I went to my district, where it snowed several times, but it didn't stick."

"You're the fortunate one," she replied. "By the time I left Caylaan, the snow was over a yard deep. It'll keep piling up for another few weeks, and when it finally starts to warm up, it won't finish melting until the end of Springfirst."

"Did you go back to Veerlyn?" Dekkard asked Konnigsburg.

"Just for a week. That way I could check on the house as well."

"I don't imagine there were any disturbances there, the way there have been in other cities, were there?" asked Dekkard.

"There never are, not with the naval facilities there."

At that moment, the server arrived with their meals, and the conversation for the rest of the meal remained pleasant and about the weather and other innocuous subjects, largely because Dekkard was present. He suspected that Konnigsburg had invited him to the table for just that reason, and he wondered what Bassaana might want specifically from the former admiral.

The three left the dining room at a sixth before the first afternoon bell, and Dekkard was soon at his floor desk, beside that of Ingrella Obreduur.

"Was your luncheon productive?" Dekkard asked her pleasantly.

"Very much so. What about yours?"

"It was pleasant."

Ingrella offered an amused smile.

Both turned as Hasheem appeared on the dais, although the Premier did not walk forward to the lectern, clearly waiting.

Once the bell struck and the lieutenant-at-arms thumped his staff, Hasheem walked to the lectern. "The Council of Sixty-Six is now in session at a time when individual councilors are at greater risk than at any time in recent years. I want to assure you that the Justiciary Ministry, the Ministry of Public Safety, and the Council Guard are continuing their investigation of the New Meritorists. As some of you may have noticed, the Council Guard instituted a number of new measures designed to prevent a recurrence of last month's attack on the Council Office Building. There will be other changes over the coming weeks. In the meantime, the Council has much to do, not only in matters of security but also in addressing other issues of import, although we will need to be thorough and patient.

"For those of you who have not read about it, former Premier Johan Grieg and his wife died in a fire in their house last Furdi evening. His family has requested that there be no Council memorial service, and we will honor that request.

"I would also remind the Council that, in the event of a winter storm with snowfall greater than ten digits, all Council sessions and committee meetings will be put off until the main thoroughfares are cleared. This is likely an unnecessary reminder, since we seldom have heavy snow here, but with all the heavier snowfall to the north this winter, it remains a possibility."

After a series of procedural notices, Hasheem concluded, "There being no further business, the Council is recessed until Furdi at first afternoon bell."

Dekkard had barely stood when Tomas Pajiin turned and asked, "Do you know what Hasheem has in mind for the Security Committee meeting tomorrow?"

"If you know anything, it's more than I do," returned Dekkard with a cheerfully ironic tone. "I assume he'll tell us about upcoming hearings. Beyond that?" He shrugged. "The first months of the new year are usually slower, but with the New Meritorists, that could change, although they've been quiet so far."

"You think they might stay quiet until spring?"

"It's possible."

"You don't sound convinced, Steffan."

"I'm not, but it's just a feeling." *Partly based on the fact that there have been far too many disturbances in the poorer parts of Machtarn and other cities.*

Dekkard and Pajiin left the Council chamber together.

Gaaroll stood waiting outside the councilors' lobby. "Back to the office, sir?"

Dekkard momentarily debated going down to the records room, but decided against it. He wasn't getting anywhere quickly with the financial files, and he needed to rethink how to analyze them. He also didn't want to get behind on correspondence, and he needed to talk to Colsbaan about the working women's legislative proposals. "Yes, back to the office."

Because of the increasing wind, Dekkard walked swiftly through the courtyard, moving fast enough that the shorter-legged Gaaroll half walked, half jogged to keep up. He did slow down once they were inside the Council Office Building.

As soon as he reached his office, he asked Luara Colsbaan to join him. After she seated herself across the desk from him, he asked, "Where are you with the legal representation for working women who don't belong to the guild?"

"I've gotten all the backup material from Namoor Desharra and Myram Plassar, and I've finished reconstructing all the supporting documentation."

"Good. I'll need to talk to Chairman Haarsfel about it, and some of the other members on the Workplace Administration Committee. Then I'll know how to address the next steps. How are you coming on the equal pay and equivalent jobs proposal?"

"I'm still researching the existing statutory law."

Dekkard frowned. "Can't you draft something that says, 'notwithstanding any other provision in law'?"

"Without supporting annotations, such laws haven't had that good a record when they've been appealed to the High Justiciary." She added dryly, "The High Justiciary can be rather finicky about precedent and legislation that doesn't at least acknowledge that precedent."

"You mean we'll have to change every law that might enable pay discrimination? No wonder the Council gets so little done." Dekkard didn't conceal his consternation.

Colsbaan shook her head. "Not every law, but we'll have to address those bearing directly on matters of pay and other compensation, either by noting that existing statutory law does not enable discrimination or by changing any language that could conceivably permit it. Fortunately, the Great Charter doesn't address the matter."

Dekkard understood that. Amending the Great Charter took an overwhelming vote of two successively elected Councils—something that the New Meritorists seemed totally unaware of with their demands of immediately changing the Council's voting procedures, procedures set forth in the Charter.

"So it's going to take a while," he finally said.

"I'm getting there, sir, but I can't say yet how long it will take. Several weeks . . . possibly longer."

"Do what you can," he said with a wry smile, as he stood.

Once Colsbaan left, Dekkard turned his attention to the stack of correspondence replies.

He finished dealing with those slightly before fourth bell. Then he turned his attention to considering what other leads he might ferret out of Minz's financial records. He was still thinking over possibilities when Avraal arrived, almost two thirds past fourth bell.

"I'm sorry to be a bit late," she said. "Carlos had a late interview with another empath."

"Was she any good?" asked Dekkard as he stood.

"*He* was adequate, but not much more. Certainly not good enough for a Council security aide, although *he* thought he was."

"Are you ready to head home?"

"If you are."

"I'm more than ready."

In moments, Dekkard had his overcoat on and his gray leather folder in hand. Almost as quickly, Roostof and Margrit had closed up the office, and Dekkard, Avraal, and Gaaroll walked toward the central staircase.

"Did anything interesting happen in Council?" asked Avraal.

"Not much. Hasheem announced that there would be more improvements to Council security and that the Grieg family had requested that there not be a Council memorial. I studied the Minz records some more, but I'm not getting anywhere fast." *Or anywhere at all so far.*

"Button up your overcoat," suggested Avraal as the three neared the west doors. "It's cold out there."

"How cold?"

"Colder than any winter day I've felt in Machtarn. There are scattered ice crystals falling out of the sky."

"There aren't any clouds," said Dekkard. "Not anywhere to the north."

"Tell that to the crystals. It's a good thing that we didn't have rain. It'd be ice by now."

Dekkard winced as he stepped through the bronze doors and out into the wind. Once the three were in the steamer, while he waited for the flash boiler to heat up, he looked to Avraal and said, "I hope Emrelda didn't have to work late. Otherwise, you'll be buried in that coat for a bell . . . or huddled in front of the sitting room gas grate."

"After dinner, I may be anyway. It's a good night for sitting there and reading. We haven't done that in a while."

"We can do that," agreed Dekkard with a smile. Then he eased the Gresynt out of its space and toward the guarded gate of the covered parking.

Over the years, so much has been written about truth, word after word spilling across the pages, written in every language extant in the world, as well as in a few tongues no longer spoken or written. Each sage, each poet or playwright, even writers of fictional entertainment—all of them have declaimed upon truth, expanding upon it or trying to squeeze it into terse trimeter, explaining or refusing to explain how they saw what they defined as truth. Artists and sculptors often speak of embodying truth in their work, rather than letting the work present itself.

Words can but offer an incomplete description of even the most common objects. Take a nail, a common nail. Even if two wordsmiths agreed on a written description of the same nail, do they see exactly the same nail? We know some men see better than others. Some women see a greater range of colors than do men. A nail is among the simplest of objects, yet it is more than it seems, for it is forged through craft and can be employed in holding together a myriad of larger objects. Some wretches have used nails not for building, but for torture and torment. What then is the truth of a nail? Does its "truth" lie in its use? Or does the only "truth" of a nail lie in its existence as an object?

What then of truths proclaimed for the non-material?

Those purveyors of faith, seemingly without exception, each proclaim that their faith is the one true faith, not that anyone would expect them to admit their faith is false or even spurious. So many claim truth in faith, yet seldom have I ever seen or heard an explanation of what constitutes truth in faith, only that each believes in his faith as true.

The nail exists. It can be felt and observed, used or not. Faith itself cannot be observed; only believers of that faith can be observed. Does not that suggest that a nail holds more truth than a faith? Or that the nail is real and that faith is an illusion necessary to its believers?

AVERRA
The City of Truth
Johan Eschbach
377 TE

WHEN Dekkard woke on Duadi and sat up on the edge of the bed, he could see the steam of his breath. He immediately hurried to the bathroom, where a quick but warm shower helped.

Avraal was in the shower almost as soon as he left it.

He dressed quickly and made his way down to the breakfast room, where Emrelda was finishing her café, fully dressed, including her uniform jacket. Gaaroll wore her winter jacket, although the breakfast room didn't seem that cold to Dekkard, unlike the upstairs.

"Newssheet says it's going to get colder," grumbled Gaaroll.

"After last night, that figures," said Emrelda. "I need to get in early."

"You didn't say much, just that some of your patrollers were called out because of a disturbance near the ironway station. Your station is all the way across the city from there. Is there anything in *Gestirn* about that?"

"Not much. Just that there was an organized looting or theft from the terminal market next to the station." Emrelda shook her head. "It could be a long cold day."

"Because of the looting or because some patrollers can't make it in?" asked Dekkard.

Emrelda shook her head. "More likely because of fires. When it gets really cold, there are more fires. People get cold, and they get careless. You'd think they'd learn, but they don't. Fires mean more people on the streets, and people trying to get into warmer places where they're not wanted. That leads to trouble."

Dekkard nodded. It made sense, but he hadn't thought of it that way.

Emrelda took a last swallow of café and stood. "I'll see you sometime this afternoon or evening."

"Just be as careful as you can."

"Or as circumstances let us."

After Emrelda left, Dekkard picked up *Gestirn* and began to read the small lead story.

> Duadi and the next few days will be the coldest Machtarn has endured in years . . . heliograph service from Veerlyn north and east shut down yesterday afternoon because of heavy snow and high winds. Service may not

be resumed for several days . . . The number of ironway locals has been reduced throughout the north of Guldor to accommodate snow-removal locomotives . . .

Then he searched for the story on looting, but there wasn't much more than what Emrelda had said the night before. *But looting a terminal market of groceries and produce?*

Dekkard set the newssheet down and went to fix café for Avraal and himself. By the time he had both ready and on the breakfast table, he could hear her footsteps on the stairs. As she entered the breakfast room, her eyes went to the newssheet on the side table.

"Nothing of great interest," said Dekkard, "except that the next few days are likely to be the coldest in years. There wasn't much more about the disturbance Emrelda mentioned last night, other than someone looted the terminal market near the ironway station."

Avraal immediately seated herself and cradled the café mug in her hands before taking a small sip, then actually taking a bite of the croissant Dekkard had set before her. "I suppose I'll need this."

"I expect so."

After several minutes, Avraal asked, "Do you think Hasheem has a surprise for the Security Committee?"

"I doubt it. You know Hasheem doesn't like surprises."

"Then he's in for a long and disturbing year," Avraal replied.

Gaaroll laughed softly.

As soon as the three finished breakfast and cleaned up, Dekkard donned his overcoat and gloves, then picked up his leather folder. "I'm going out to warm up the Gresynt. Just wait inside until I pull up to the portico."

"I appreciate that," said Avraal.

"Me too, sir," added Gaaroll.

Dekkard was definitely glad for the overcoat and gloves as he walked through the chilling wind to the garage. As he expected, it took several minutes before the steamer was ready to go, and a few minutes after that before he pulled up to the portico. Both Avraal and Gaaroll hurried out of the house and into the Gresynt, closing the doors quickly.

Dekkard drove carefully, although the lack of recent rain or snow made it unlikely that the streets would be icy. When he reached the Council Office Building, he brought the steamer to a stop in front of the west doors. "After fourth bell?"

Avraal nodded.

In minutes, she was on her way, and Dekkard and Gaaroll were inside the building and headed to his office. Once there, with no messages awaiting him, Dekkard immediately started reading the incoming letters and infrequent petitions. In less than a bell, he had read it all and turned it over to Roostof for the staff to draft responses.

At a third before fourth bell, Dekkard and Gaaroll left the office for the Security Committee meeting. Dekkard did wear his overcoat and gloves.

As he neared the staircase, another councilor, dark-haired, balding, and wiry, approached, clearly intent on saying something. As the other neared, Dekkard finally realized that the man had to be Kastyn Heimrich, the replacement for Tedor Waarfel, one of the councilors killed in the New Meritorist shelling of the Council Office Building.

"Steffan, in case you don't recall, I'm Kastyn Heimrich. We haven't met formally, and I wanted to rectify that."

"There's no need to rectify anything, and I appreciate your making the effort. How are you finding the Council so far?"

"The procedures aren't that unfamiliar, since I was a district councilor for Aloor, but getting to know the committee structures and my way around, as well as having to re-create an office from nothing, have proved . . . daunting."

"I can understand that, and sympathize. I don't know if anyone told you, but any Craft councilors elected to replace Commercers or most Landors in the last election faced the same problem, since the premier before Premier Obreduur ordered all office records to be destroyed."

Heimrich's mouth opened momentarily. "Why . . . why would anyone do that?"

"Former Premier Ulrich did not deign to explain himself on that matter. Some committee records were also destroyed or removed." Dekkard paused, then added, "Those are the sort of details that briefings often don't cover."

Heimrich offered a wry smile in response, then said, "Councilor Nortak suggested I introduce myself. I can see why."

"That was kind of him, but Tomas Pajiin could also have told you, or Premier Hasheem, since they're both on the Security Committee."

"Nonetheless . . . I'm glad to meet you, and I appreciate the information."

"I hope we can get together later, perhaps for lunch," said Dekkard apologetically, "but I do need to be leaving now because I was on my way to a Security Committee meeting."

"Oh, I won't keep you."

"I've enjoyed meeting you, and I'll be in touch." After a parting smile, Dekkard turned and headed down the staircase. Once they were well away from Heimrich, he quietly asked Gaaroll, "What did you sense?"

"He had some feelings. Not strong. Some worry, I think."

When he and Gaaroll reached the committee room, Dekkard said, "Just wait here. I don't think the meeting will be that long. I hope not, anyway." Then he hurried inside, shedding his overcoat and hanging it on one of the wall pegs.

Haastar and Navione stood to one side of the long, curved desk on the dais, talking, while Baar nodded. Dekkard had barely taken his seat when Pajiin hurried in and took his seat to Dekkard's left. Then came Hasheem, followed quickly by Rikkard, who, as always, avoided even looking in Dekkard's vicinity.

Even before the last reverberations of the fourth bell sounded, Hasheem gaveled the committee to order. Then he surveyed the councilors, one at a time, beginning with Baar on his far left and continuing until his eyes left Dekkard. "What I'm about to say should not be discussed with anyone not present."

At that moment, Dekkard realized that there were no clerks in the chamber.

"In the last few days, at least two events have occurred that merit concern. First, the I.S. *Khuld,* a light cruiser, is missing. It had just arrived in Port Reale prior to entering dry dock for an update to its signaling heliographs and gunnery. Half the crew had been granted leave. A significant portion of those remaining aboard seized the ship and killed most of the officers aboard at the time. Crew members who would not join them were thrown overboard. The mutineers steamed off and commandeered coal from the civilian coaling station at Zeiryn. The whereabouts of the *Khuld* are currently unknown, but the mutineers are believed to be New Meritorists or sympathizers. For that reason, the dreadnought *Resolute* and several other warships will be patrolling the offshore approaches to Machtarn." Hasheem paused, then continued. "When I sent the notice for the hearing yesterday morning, the only matter to be discussed was the missing cruiser. Last night, however, unknown individuals, presumably New Meritorists, attacked and looted the Guldoran Ironway terminal market here in Machtarn. They did the same at terminal markets in Port Reale, Uldwyrk, Enke, Ondeliew, and possibly others. Here in Machtarn, they first stole an undetermined number of steam lorries, looted the terminal market, and then drove the lorries into less savory neighborhoods where they abandoned them with signs proclaiming 'Free Food.' The looters were armed and shot any duty security guards who resisted. None of them have been apprehended so far." Hasheem cleared his throat. "At the moment, that's all I have."

Dekkard glanced around, but no one spoke immediately. So he did. "Sir, can we assume that councilors on the Military Affairs Committee have also been briefed?"

"You can. They were briefed on the *Khuld* late yesterday. Chairman Mardosh is briefing them on the terminal markets now."

"Is there evidence that the New Meritorists conducted the lootings?" asked Villem Baar.

"No. That is a supposition based on the fact that four attacks occurred close to simultaneously."

"How much was taken?" asked Breffyn Haastar.

"The looters arrived with four lorries right after the market closed. They knew what they wanted, and filled the lorries quickly."

"Where did they abandon the lorries?" asked Dekkard.

"I don't recall the exact street locations, only that they were in River-town, Southtown, Woodlake, and Easthill."

After several other questions, which were essentially variations on those already asked, Hasheem said, "Once we have more information, the committee will meet to discuss the security implications." He rapped the gavel once.

Pajiin turned to Dekkard. "You think it was the Meritorists?"

"If it wasn't, we're facing an even bigger problem, plus the complications of Commercers hostile to a Craft government," Dekkard pointed out.

Pajiin nodded slowly.

Then the two stood. After getting their coats, they left the committee room, the last to depart. Dekkard was certain Hasheem had hurried back to his floor office. He did see Haastar and Navione walking in the direction of the councilors' lobby, but didn't see Baar or Rikkard.

Once clear of the doorway, Dekkard nodded to Pajiin, then stopped and turned to Gaaroll. "We'll go down to the records room. I can only stay there about a bell before I have to head back. We're escorting Ingrella Obreduur to lunch."

"Doesn't she have any security aides yet?"

"They seem to be hard to come by now that some have been killed, especially since the deaths included Commercers and Landors." Dekkard headed toward the doorway to the narrow staircase down to the lower level.

"That kind doesn't make good security types."

"What kind would that be?" asked Dekkard, wanting to know what Gaaroll's definition might be.

"The kind that want marks without work or danger."

"I don't think that kind work out well in anything," replied Dekkard as he opened the door to the stairwell.

Once in the records room, he spent most of a bell trying to find mark transactions in Minz's personal account that might indicate withdrawals for ironway fare, or other specific items, but had absolutely no success, deciding that was a dead end. In his personal accounts Minz had always withdrawn or deposited even hundreds of marks.

At a third before noon, he and Gaaroll left the records room and walked back to Ingrella's office in the Council Office Building.

Ingrella stood just outside her inner office, in her overcoat and talking to Leyala, when Dekkard entered the outer office. "You're always punctual, Steffan."

"I try, Ingrella."

The older woman just smiled, then said, "Shall we go?"

As they headed out of the office and toward the main staircase, Dekkard asked, "How are you coming with staff?"

"I have good legalists, an excellent personal secretary, and solid typists. Economic aides who understand Craft issues are rare. That was one reason why Axel pushed you in that direction. And, suddenly," her tone turned ironic, "good security aides are scarce."

"Nincya and I spoke about that earlier."

"You were wise to take her and train her," said Ingrella quietly.

"No. I was wise to listen to Avraal about it," replied Dekkard dryly. "Also wise enough not to ignore any recommendations she made."

"You're like Axel in that, except I think you learned younger than he did."

"That's only because I met Avraal when I was younger than Axel was when he met you." Dekkard beckoned for her to lead the way down the staircase, then followed her.

When they stepped out into the courtyard, Dekkard was definitely glad that he'd worn his overcoat, given the wind and the fact that it felt even colder outside than it had in the morning. He glanced toward the north. A greenish-black wall of clouds was definitely moving in.

"Fellow headed toward us," said Gaaroll quietly. "Strong red feelings. Real strong."

Dekkard shifted his eyes toward the figure striding quickly toward them, loosening his coat and putting one hand on his personal truncheon, even before he recognized the councilor—Gerard Schmidtz, the senior Commercer on the Military Affairs Committee, on which Ingrella also was a member.

Well before Schmidtz was that close, he moved to the north edge of the covered walkway without so much as glancing in Dekkard's or Ingrella's direction as he hurried past them.

"That was the walk of a very angry man," said Ingrella several moments later.

"I have to wonder just why he was that angry," said Dekkard. "I've never seen him like that. He's always seemingly pleasant, even when he's not feeling that way at all." *Which suggests that he was furious.* Dekkard couldn't help wondering who and/or what had upset Schmidtz.

"Most likely something Hasheem or Mardosh did or said," replied Ingrella. "They're the only ones with enough power to thwart him."

"He doesn't seem the type who'd like being thwarted."

"Really?" asked Ingrella, her tone amused.

"That was my impression, but I've only talked with him once, very briefly. How is he on the committee?"

"We've only had the one meeting since I became a councilor. He said very little."

Once they reached the entrance to the councilors' dining room, Dekkard said to Gaaroll, "Meet us here a sixth after first bell."

"Yes, sir."

Dekkard didn't say much until after they were seated and had ordered, when he asked, "Have you thought much about Gretina Baar?"

"I have some people looking into her. If they come to the same conclusions you and Avraal did, there are several firms that might be interested. There aren't that many women legalists who deal in the high-end technical aspects of property law and who are good. The good female legalists usually chose other fields."

"Thank you. I won't say anything except that I've passed on her name."

"I appreciate that, Steffan."

"You were at the Military Affairs Committee meeting this morning, I take it?"

"I was."

"What are your thoughts about the *Khuld* incident?"

"I doubt it was a mutiny," replied Ingrella evenly. "More like a planned takeover. Isn't that what you think?"

"It is. I also suspect that the *Khuld* is steaming toward Machtarn. From outside the harbor, they could shell the Council Hall. The Imperial Palace would be at the edge of its range."

"Have you mentioned that to anyone else?" asked Ingrella.

"Not so far. Fredrich mentioned that the *Resolute* and several other warships would be patrolling the sea approaches to Machtarn. It will take the *Khuld* two weeks to reach Machtarn at cruising speed. Longer, if the weather is bad. It's almost four thousand milles."

"Why do you think they didn't try to take over a warship at a nearer port?"

"The *Khuld* was about to undergo maintenance. At least half the crew was on leave. Maintenance on cruisers and corvettes is done at Port Reale. Siincleer is the only other port that does extensive maintenance, but it handles heavy cruisers and dreadnoughts. They have much larger crews, and it would have required a much greater force to capture even a heavy cruiser. Also, the *Khuld* is an older light cruiser, perhaps one with, shall I say, a less effective commander. Maintenance schedules are planned years out."

"You're saying this was planned well in advance."

"That's the only way it could have been accomplished. Just like the destruction of sixteen Security buildings."

"What else do you think they've planned?"

"I have no idea. As I told Axel, it will likely be something that makes perfect sense in hindsight, but something that's either so improbable or so obvious that we don't foresee it." Dekkard paused as the server appeared with their orders, white bean soup for him, onion soup for her, and cafés for both.

They both sampled their respective soups before Ingrella spoke.

"The way it appears, the Commercers have used the New Meritorists, but making even limited common cause with revolutionaries whose goals you despise seems foolhardy to me."

"They're worried, if not desperate," replied Dekkard. "They've held power for decades, but, despite all their recent efforts, the Craft Party keeps gaining seats."

Ingrella shook her head. "The New Meritorists are anything but stupid. They'll take anything they can get without any compunction and then destroy those who helped them."

"That's clear now," agreed Dekkard, "but the Commercers tend to equate marks with intelligence. On the other hand, I suspect revolutionaries equate marks with lack of perception. The fact that they're both wrong will make matters worse." He paused. "The New Meritorists are turning out to be much more dangerous than anyone thought." *Including me.* "They also have a much broader base of support than was apparent."

"I still find it unconscionable that Lukkyn Wyath never investigated them," said Ingrella.

"We don't know that," Dekkard pointed out. "We only know that there aren't any *records* of such an investigation. Wyath's dead; the director in charge of the Special Agents fled Guldor; and some fifty agents have vanished."

"Fredrich hasn't selected a Minister of Public Safety yet, either." Ingrella looked meaningfully at Dekkard.

Dekkard ignored the look, knowing he didn't have the knowledge or the inclination for such a post. "Someone like Captain Narryt—he's Emrelda's station captain—would be a good choice. He's knowledgeable, and he's survived under Wyath without losing his integrity."

"You might mention that to Fredrich."

"I will if the opportunity arises."

Ingrella merely nodded.

"Your colleague Namoor Desharra has been most helpful in providing material to my legalists," Dekkard offered. "We're working on a legislative proposal dealing with the rights of women in the workplace."

"Harleona Zerlyon mentioned that."

For the remainder of lunch, the two spoke of legal issues.

After escorting Ingrella back to her office, Dekkard returned to the records room, where he spent another two bells. He did discover, as Trujillo had told him earlier, that Minz had deposited a banque draft for fifteen thousand marks in the Capitol Services account two weeks before he withdrew ten thousand marks in notes, presumably the ten thousand that had gone to Sohl Hurrek, the clerk who had tried to kill Dekkard with Atacaman pepper dust. Interestingly enough, the banque draft had been drawn on the Banque of Siincleer. Again, a transaction suggesting that it came from Siincleer Shipbuilding through the late Pietro Venburg, but not exactly proof. There were also a number of banque drafts of two thousand five hundred marks from the Suvion Commerce Banque and the Banque of Siincleer, and after Fallfirst, the Northwest Banque of Chuive, as well as two from the Banque of Uldwyrk and several drawn on the Neewyrk Imperial Banque.

Incredibly suggestive of regular payments by corporacions in those cities, but not proof.

By a little after third bell he returned to his office, where he immediately began signing or revising replies to letters, occasionally looking out the window to the north where the looming greenish-black clouds continued to advance on Machtarn. He could also hear the wind outside. He finished dealing with the correspondence slightly before fourth bell, after which he pondered what other links might exist between the New Meritorists and Ulrich.

When he noticed snowflakes beginning to fall past the window, he walked out into the staff office and to Roostof's desk. "Svard, let everyone go right now. That snow is going to get heavy before long."

"I'd thought about it."

"Next time, interrupt me," replied Dekkard with a wry smile. "I was caught up in something."

In minutes, only Roostof, Gaaroll, and Dekkard remained.

Then Avraal arrived, bundled in her black overcoat with a black scarf. Before she could say anything, Dekkard spoke. "I know. We need to be going." He turned to Roostof. "You, too, Svard. Remember, if the snow's deeper than ten digits, the Council's closed until the main streets are clear." Then he walked back into his personal office, donned his overcoat and gloves, and picked up his gray leather folder. Abruptly, he stopped and shut off the gas lamp before joining Avraal in the outer office.

"The snow is already sticking to the side streets," Avraal said after the four left the office. "There aren't that many steamers on the roads. I think most people left work early."

"Good."

When they reached the west doors, Dekkard said, "Be careful on the drive home, Svard."

"You, too, sir."

Because Avraal had driven the Gresynt, it took no time at all for the steamer to pressure up, for which Dekkard was grateful, especially since the snow was beginning to come down more heavily. Thankfully, both Council Avenue and Jacquez were largely still clear because of the traffic, but Florinda already held more than a digit of snow when Dekkard turned onto it and, less than a hundred yards later, headed up the drive to the garage, where he stopped short of the door, got out and opened it, and then eased the Gresynt inside.

"Emrelda's not home," said Avraal. "She's not scheduled to work late. That means something went wrong."

"She might be late because the snow delayed her relief. We can't do anything here in the garage," Dekkard pointed out as he opened the steamer door. "I'll keep sweeping the drive every so often so the snow doesn't build up. She shouldn't be that long."

When everyone was inside, with the kitchen stove and sitting room gas grate turned on, Dekkard went back out into the snow and swept the drive, all the way from the garage doors to the street, while Avraal and Gaaroll worked on getting dinner. Almost a bell later, and after several more drive sweepings by Dekkard, with the snow close to four digits deep where Dekkard hadn't swept, Emrelda drove up the drive, and Dekkard hurried out and opened the garage door.

Once she was out of the steamer and the garage, he brushed off the snow still remaining on her teal Gresynt, then closed the door, and walked to the portico door with Emrelda.

"Thank you for clearing the way," she said. "All of the side streets are getting icy, and I was a little worried about Florinda and getting up the drive."

"I thought that might be the case." Dekkard opened the portico door, then followed Emrelda inside, closing the door firmly against the wind from the northeast.

Avraal hurried out of the kitchen and into the main hall where Emrelda was hanging up her patroller's winter jacket. "We've been worried about you."

"I'm fine. Tomorrow and Furdi will be the days to worry about, particularly if the snow keeps falling and it stays this cold." Emrelda smiled. "Whatever you're cooking smells good."

"It's a mash-up of sorts, with the leftover lamb, some boiled potatoes, and even a few turnips that Steffan won't eat but won't say anything about." Avraal smiled sweetly at her husband.

Dekkard smiled back. "I've never complained." *Especially since it wouldn't do any good.*

"How were your days?" asked Emrelda.

"We'll tell you at dinner. It's almost ready," said Avraal.

That was fine with Dekkard, although some of his day would be shared later, and only with Avraal.

EVEN before Dekkard was fully awake on Tridi morning, he could feel the chill in the bedroom and had the feeling that it was still snowing. One glance out the window told him that neither of them was likely to be going anywhere. Even so, he shaved and took a quick shower, but donned an old set of winter security grays before heading downstairs.

"I take it there's no *Gestirn* this morning?" he asked as he entered the breakfast room.

Gaaroll snorted. "Snow's more than knee-deep. Still coming down."

Dekkard looked to Emrelda, in full uniform. "You're going to work?"

"I said today and tomorrow would be hard."

"I can clear the drive."

"There's no hurry. I'll be walking today. The way the snow's coming down, it's safer to walk. It won't take that much longer, and the steamer would be buried by the time my shift is over. I was just getting ready to go." Emrelda smiled sardonically. "There is a snow shovel in the garage. Markell inherited it. We never used it. Have fun."

"It'll likely be easier than what you're doing." Dekkard walked with Emrelda into the hallway, where she donned her winter patrol jacket, gloves, and visor cap. He accompanied her to the portico door, which he opened for her. "Until this afternoon."

"It might be later."

Dekkard watched as she walked down the snow-covered drive. The snow looked deeper than even knee-high, and, if anything, was coming down more rapidly than the night before. He quickly shut the door and made his way back to the kitchen, where he made two cafés, then retrieved the croissants from the cooler and brought them and the cafés to the breakfast room.

"Where's Emrelda?" asked Avraal as she appeared.

"On her way to work." As Dekkard spoke, he noted that Avraal was also wearing winter security grays, as well as a gray pullover sweater.

"She's driving in this?"

"She's walking. She said it would be a long day."

"Are you going to work?" asked Avraal.

"The snow is well over ten digits deep already. That's when the Council is closed. Besides, nothing important is scheduled. No sessions and no hearings, not for any of my committees. What about you?"

"I'm not about to drive in this much snow. Not when it's coming down as hard as it is."

"Good idea," said Gaaroll.

Avraal seated herself and cradled the café mug in her hands. "How long will this last?"

"I'd wager it won't end soon. The heliographs were shut down early yesterday across most of the north." Dekkard settled across from her and smiled wryly. "Emrelda told me where the snow shovel is."

"That should keep you busy," replied Avraal.

"Some of the time. What will you do?"

"Read, and I'll write another letter to Mother. I can post it after the snow clears. Maybe she'll even reply."

Dekkard knew that Avraal's mother hadn't replied to the letter about the house in Gaarlak and thanking her parents for the gift that had made it possible, but he only said, "You're being the well-mannered daughter."

"At least you didn't say dutiful. I've never fulfilled their definition of that."

"How could you say that?" teased Dekkard. "You've married a Ritter, and all their friends approve."

Avraal said sweetly, "How would you like hot café in the face?"

Dekkard decided against saying, *You don't want their friends to approve?* Instead, he said, "I'd appreciate not having burns on my face."

"You were going to say something else, weren't you?"

"I thought better of it."

"Excellent idea."

Gaaroll failed to hide a grin.

"I thought so," replied Dekkard cheerfully.

After breakfast, he donned his old winter security jacket and gloves, then trudged through the snow on the upper drive to the garage, where he retrieved the shovel. Shoveling the drive down to the street took a good bell.

He wasn't the only one shoveling. Next door, to the east, while someone had shoveled the drive earlier, Sr. Waaldwud had obviously left earlier, because his wife and the young empath nanny took turns re-shoveling the drive. Young Tomas played in the snow while the nanny shoveled.

By the time Dekkard finished, another digit of the white stuff coated the area between the house and the garage. Dekkard shook his head and went inside to warm up, especially his hands. *At least the next time there won't be as much to shovel.*

Over the course of the morning and afternoon, he shoveled the drive twice more. In between he wrote out various possibilities for New Meritorist actions, forcing himself not to tear up those he decided were too far-fetched, even one where the revolutionaries managed to kill the Imperador. While Dekkard knew such an assassination was certainly possible, particularly if the Meritorists didn't mind the costs or repercussions, he couldn't see the point of such an assassination since the real power in Guldor lay in the Council and the provisions of the Great Charter. *And the Commercer-dominated corporacions.*

While Dekkard struggled with analyzing the Meritorist possibilities and battling the snow, Gaaroll spent the day helping Avraal in the kitchen.

At about a third before sixth bell, Dekkard went out again to shovel the drive. He'd almost reached the bottom when Emrelda trudged toward him. By then, the snow in front of the house was almost waist-deep—and still falling. "Are you all right?" he asked as he walked down to meet her.

"Jacquez is mostly cleared. That part wasn't hard." She offered a crooked smile. "I see that the sidewalk and drive at the Waaldwuds' are shoveled."

"Not by me. The poor nanny did most of it, but Tomas had a good time." Dekkard paused. "Do you know what Waaldwud does? He was gone long before you left this morning."

"I have no idea. He's always kept to himself, and after that business with his first nanny, I have no desire to know." Emrelda grinned and asked, "You didn't offer to help the nanny? You certainly noticed when she first arrived."

Dekkard grinned back. "I'm not feeling that generous. Keeping ahead of—or not too far behind—the snow on the drive and our sidewalk has been enough exercise."

"You mean Avraal didn't help?"

As the two walked up the drive, Dekkard could hear the amusement in her voice. "She's cooking. Gaaroll's helping. Avraal said you'd need a good hot meal."

"I need more than that, but a hot meal will be a good start."

"Lager, wine, or something like hot mulled wine?"

"Don't go to the trouble of hot mulled wine. A warm house and lager will be fine." Emrelda paused outside the portico door, where she brushed off most of the snow that had accumulated on her jacket and cap before opening the door and stepping inside.

Dekkard left the shovel outside beside the portico door and followed Emrelda.

Avraal immediately hurried from the kitchen. "I'm glad to see you weren't that late."

Emrelda eased off her jacket and cap. "I'll tell you all about it over dinner."

"It's ready," said Avraal. "We were waiting for you. Dinner is simple enough, just a stew. Dessert was what took the time."

"Desserts," corrected Gaaroll. "A four-level pudding cake and cinnamon apple tarts *and* some sweet rolls for breakfast tomorrow."

Emrelda smiled at her sister. "You couldn't just take it easy, could you?"

"From our background?" Avraal motioned and led the way to the breakfast room.

Dekkard followed the three women, then went to the pantry to get lager for everyone.

After he returned and was handing out the lagers, Avraal served the stew and brought out a loaf of warm bread.

"Fresh-baked bread yet," said Emrelda. "With all this, I almost hope it will keep snowing."

"Let's not think of that," replied Avraal. "Try the stew."

Although Dekkard had tasted the stew earlier and had found it better than just good, he knew that Avraal worried about whether her sister would like it.

"This is excellent, and the bread is perfect. Thank you. I can't tell you how much I appreciate this, especially after today."

"Was it as bad as you thought it might be?" asked Dekkard.

"It could have been worse," said Emrelda after taking another spoonful of stew and a small swallow of Kuhrs.

Dekkard waited for her to explain.

"A water main broke at the edge of Southtown sometime around midmorning. By the time the crews got that main shut off, parts of south Vergaellen were turning to ice, and by midafternoon all of it was frozen—"

"Didn't any of it drain off in the storm sewers?" asked Dekkard.

"They were already frozen with all the crap that people throw in them. It's Southtown, remember?"

Dekkard winced. "Then what?"

"A bunch of the locals used the diversion to break into shops. With the snow and ice, it took time to get more patrollers there. Another group attacked the first, and five people got killed. Likely more, but that's what I saw. There was a fight at Waalyn's that turned into a brawl, and there was a fire near the water-main break, and a whole line of row houses burned down."

"No water for fire lorries?" asked Gaaroll.

Emrelda shook her head. "Not just that. Water pressure's low in South-town anyway. So they couldn't hook fire hoses from the nearest hydrant that had water."

Dekkard looked to Emrelda. "You think tomorrow will be worse?"

"It could be. Especially if it gets really cold after the snow stops."

"Be bodies in the alleys," said Gaaroll. "There are even when it's not this cold. That's around the harbor. Be worse in Southtown or Rivertown."

Emrelda just nodded.

20

BY Furdi morning the snow wasn't falling as heavily, but the wind picked up and created chest-high snowdrifts in places. Emrelda left the house early—walking—and Dekkard gave up shoveling when it became clear that the wind blew even more snow into any place he cleared. The snow finally died away by the first afternoon bell, and the wind dropped to a light, but freezing, breeze.

By midafternoon, Dekkard finally had the drive and walks cleared, and immediately after that a lorry with a plow turned off Jacquez and cleared the north side of Florinda, turning at the end of the block and clearing the south side. In the process, the plow also dumped more snow on the end of the drive.

Dekkard put his overcoat back on and wrapped a heavy scarf around his neck and ears and prepared to head back out when Avraal came out of the kitchen.

"I thought you just cleared the drive."

"I did." Dekkard went on to explain, adding, "But the plow driver was clearing Jacquez, and he turned off and just cleared our block."

"That might just be because you live here," replied Avraal. "Council administration has all the councilors' addresses, and there are only sixty-six of you in the city."

"That definitely means we're headed back to work tomorrow," said Dekkard.

"It also means that Emrelda can drive to work."

"We'll have to preheat the steamers."

"That's better than walking."

Dekkard pulled on his gloves and headed back outside.

Because the plow compacted the snow it had pushed toward the curb, Dekkard had to labor to cut through the heavier and icier mass and carry it to one side of the drive or the other, a shovelful at a time. By the time he finished, the piled snow bordering the street end of the drive was more than chest-high, and he was sweating profusely, despite the chill and the wind.

He left the shovel beside the portico door and brushed the snow off his trousers and coat before he stepped into the house.

More than two bells passed before Emrelda finally arrived home.

"The snow's so deep I had to walk in the street," she said as she unwound her scarf and took off her winter uniform jacket. "Only Camelia Avenue and Jacquez are plowed. Did you know not another side street off Jacquez is plowed? And they only plowed one block. How did you manage that?" She smiled wryly at Dekkard.

"I imagine one block of Astragalis is also plowed," replied Dekkard. "Premier Hasheem might have something in mind for the Council. Or he wants to make sure that the Council can act in case emergency legislation is necessary." *Which it may well be after this much snow.*

"Or it just might be the standard snow-removal plan for Machtarn," suggested Avraal.

"That's even more likely," admitted Dekkard, who then turned to Emrelda. "Was your day as bad as yesterday?"

"Not quite. There weren't any more water-main breaks, and only one small fire in an abandoned house where squatters tried to use the fireplace. Jacquez was the only street in Southtown that got plowed, and the deep snow kept most people from going out. There weren't any brawls, but three men froze to death in the alley behind Waalyn's."

"Likely because they drank too much and passed out when the cold hit 'em," offered Gaaroll, as she joined the others.

"That's certainly the way the deaths will be recorded," said Emrelda evenly.

Dekkard didn't reply, except mentally. *Meaning that they were likely ejected for being rowdy or just hanging around and then passed out.*

"What do I smell?" asked Emrelda.

"Cinnamon-spiced hot wine," said Avraal. "It's even colder today than it was yesterday. I thought you might like it, especially since we're having the last of the stew for dinner."

Emrelda nodded thoughtfully. "I'll take you up on the hot cinnamon wine." Then she smiled. "And on the stew."

21

ON Quindi morning, everyone left the house early, not knowing how the streets would be, or what had happened anywhere, since there had been no delivery of *Gestirn* for the past three days.

Getting up the hill on Jacquez was tricky, but Dekkard managed it, although it had been years since he'd driven in snow, but Avraal never had, not surprisingly, since it had never snowed in Sudaen, or at least not in her lifetime. Council Avenue had been cleared down to bare bitumen, and Dekkard would have wagered the same of Imperial Boulevard.

Still, when he pulled up outside the west doors of the Council Office Building, he turned to Avraal. "If the Avenue of the Guilds hasn't been cleared—"

"I'll come back here for the day," Avraal interjected before Dekkard could finish, then added, "But I'd wager that it's been cleared."

Given that the teamsters driving the plows were guild members, Dekkard knew she was right, but he had one other concern. "If you are working with Carlos all day, I'd prefer that you aren't too late coming here."

"I'll be careful."

That wasn't quite what Dekkard had in mind, but he just replied, "Please do." Then he opened the door and got out of the Gresynt, retrieving his leather folder as he did.

As Avraal drove off, Dekkard smiled, noticing she wasn't speeding off nearly as fast as usual. On the way to the office, he and Gaaroll stopped by the post station, where Dekkard dispatched Avraal's letter to her mother. Then the two made their way up to the office.

Roostof was there, as were Margrit and Bretta.

"We're likely to be short of staff today," said Roostof. "The east side of the city got more snow and only certain omnibus routes are running today. It's a good thing that it's Quindi." He grinned at Gaaroll. "You can get in some practice typing and help Bretta with the filing."

"Better than sitting around."

"You have one message," said Margrit.

"From Premier Hasheem, I'm sure," replied Dekkard.

"I believe it is, sir." Margrit tried to hide a smile as she handed him the envelope.

Dekkard opened it and read the message. "Security Committee meeting at fourth bell this morning." Noting that, once again, Hasheem had not indicated a subject, Dekkard looked back to Roostof. "Has anything important happened beside the snow? We didn't get any newssheets."

"I don't think anyone did," replied Roostof. "I certainly didn't."

"Neither did I," said Margrit. "There's no mail, either. Not yet, anyway. This was the worst storm I've seen here in Machtarn."

"Something might have happened in Rivertown yesterday," added Roostof. "I heard steam whistles, the kind they use on patroller vans, headed that way, and there was a lot of smoke in the late afternoon."

"Another fire—or worse." Dekkard then related what he'd heard from Emrelda, before adding, "With this storm, the cold, less and more costly food, things are only going to get worse, and that's even if the New Meritorists don't do anything." *Which they will, sooner or later, especially with a light cruiser likely headed toward Machtarn.* He paused, then asked, "Is there anything I need to address immediately?"

"Nothing out of the ordinary."

"Let's hope it stays that way." Dekkard headed into his personal office, where he hung up his overcoat. On his desk was a small stack of replies to be signed, those to which he had made corrections on Duadi. He finished reading and signing them in little more than a third of a bell.

After giving the signed replies to Margrit, he spent the next bell on various matters, including thinking about what the New Meritorists might do, reviewing the background material on the legislative proposals Luara was developing, and trying to figure out what Ulrich and his shadowy cohort might next attempt.

At a third before fourth bell, Dekkard pulled on his overcoat, left his office, and beckoned to Gaaroll. The two walked through nearly deserted corridors, along the cleanly shoveled and swept walkway to the Council Hall, and then through the almost vacant main corridor to the Security Committee chamber.

"Just wait outside," Dekkard told Gaaroll. "I doubt that this meeting will be that long."

"Yes, sir. Will we be going to the records room next?"

"That might depend on what happens in the committee meeting."

When Dekkard stepped into the committee chamber, he wasn't exactly surprised that Tomas Pajiin was the only councilor there, not when the storm that had paralyzed Machtarn for two days would have been considered a matter of course in Pajiin's Eshbruk district.

"Good morning, Steffan," offered Pajiin cheerfully. "I thought you'd be one of the first to show up."

"I thought the same of you, possibly Jaradd Rikkard, since he's from Endor."

"Rikkard wouldn't arrive early. Not his way. That storm dropped real snow. Surprised me."

"I was about to say that you won't see another like it here any time soon, but it's gotten even colder, and there's been a lot of snow in the north."

"If it follows the patterns we get in Eshbruk, we'll get another on Duadi or early Tridi."

Dekkard was about to reply when Breffyn Haastar and Kharl Navione entered the chamber, followed shortly by Villem Baar and Rikkard. Then Hasheem appeared in the doorway from the adjoining staff room and immediately took his seat.

"I'm glad to see that you all weathered the storm," said Hasheem pleasantly. "The committee will come to order." He rapped the gavel once, then cleared his throat. "This storm arrived at a most inconvenient time. While the skies are clear to the north at present, the only heliographs operating north of Oersynt are those along major ironway routes, since the snow is too deep for operators to get to some of the connecting stations. Because of the heavy snowfall on the eastern side of the Silver Hills, we also do not have heliograph service to Port Reale. The latest information from the Navy had to come by ironway, and the Gilt Ridge pass was not reopened until late yesterday. As of Tridi, there had been no sightings of the light cruiser *Khuld*.

"First Marshal Bernotte has conveyed to me that the *Resolute* and the warships accompanying it are more than sufficient to intercept and destroy the *Khuld*, should the mutineers be foolish enough to approach Machtarn. The Justiciary Ministry and the Ministry of Public Safety have uncovered very little new information about the New Meritorists or the leadership of the group. The names so far discovered no longer are at the addresses they previously inhabited . . . Nor has the sole remaining witness in the Minz case been located."

Despite what First Marshal Bernotte had conveyed to Hasheem, Dekkard was far from convinced that the *Resolute* and its escorts would be able to find, let alone sink, the *Khuld*. Any mutineers skillful enough to engineer a successful mutiny and re-coaling needed to be taken far more seriously than suggested by the marshal's words, but bringing the matter up in committee would only anger Hasheem. There was also the possibility that the mutineers had very different plans. *After all, there's nothing really of military value here in Machtarn.* But then, no matter how well-crewed the light cruiser might be and how intelligent the head of the mutineers might be, a single warship could only accomplish so much against the fleets of Guldor. *Except any damage would reflect badly on the Council.*

"Sr. Chairman," asked Dekkard, "at what point do you plan to make the information about the I.S. *Khuld* public?"

"When the First Marshal and the Premier determine that such information is in the public interest, Councilor." Almost without stopping, Hasheem went on. "Next Tridi, the committee will hold a hearing dealing with the increasing number of individuals fleeing Atacama and crossing the Rio Doro. The witness at the hearing on Tridi will be River Commander Escobaar. He will address the specific problems facing the River Patrol."

Dekkard could understand Hasheem's interest, since the crossings had been occurring in his district, and Hasheem was likely facing local pressure to do something about it.

Hasheem stopped and cleared his throat once more before continuing. "Do any of you wish to suggest security interests into which the committee should inquire?" He turned to his left. "Councilor Navione?"

"Not at this time."

"Councilor Haastar?"

"At the appropriate time, perhaps the committee could hold hearings on the impact of tariffs on smuggling. High tariffs entice smugglers, particularly along the far southwest coast in the shallows where the Navy cannot patrol. In the past, the Navy has avoided even looking into the matter. This makes the coastal waters there less secure, and the Council gains no revenue from goods smuggled ashore. So far, the Military Affairs Committee has failed to address the matter. Since there is also a security implication . . . ?"

"You raise an interesting point. I'd prefer to discuss the matter with Chairman Mardosh before bringing the matter before this committee." Hasheem turned to Rikkard. "Councilor?"

"Let's bring back the Security agents. We'll need them before long."

"Councilor, the Council has already acted on that matter." Almost without pausing Hasheem turned and said, "Councilor Pajiin?"

"I'd like the committee to pass something forbidding the use of government forces or facilities against guilds over unsafe workplace practices."

"That would seem to be more suited to the Workplace Administration Committee, Councilor," replied Hasheem politely.

"The Workplace Administration Committee doesn't have jurisdiction over Justiciary agents or patrollers. In the past, it didn't have jurisdiction over Security agents, either. For years, every time guilds tried to stop work over unsafe practices, the corporacions claimed they were disturbing the peace or some such, and Security agents used firearms against men who just wanted the safety rules followed. We couldn't even get a hearing before the district justicer."

Dekkard thought he saw a flicker of either consternation or irritation cross Hasheem's face, if only for an instant.

"If you feel that strongly, Councilor, then you should draft legislation for the committee to consider. Once you present such a draft, the committee will indeed consider it and hold any necessary hearings."

"Thank you, Sr. Chairman."

"Councilor Dekkard?"

"At the appropriate time, should the New Meritorists create further damage with dunnite, it may be necessary to investigate how such dunnite came into their hands." Dekkard wasn't about to mention his other concern, not with anyone else present.

"If such occurs, the committee will indeed need to look into the matter. Councilor Baar?"

"I have no suggestions at present, but I would reserve the right to bring up matters of interest when appropriate."

"You always have that right, Councilor."

"Thank you, Sr. Chairman."

"If no councilor has further comments?" Hasheem looked at each man, then rapped the gavel. "The committee is dismissed until the next meeting."

As the other councilors began to leave the chamber, Pajiin turned to Dekkard. "Would you mind looking over what I come up with?"

"I'm sure you have good legalists, Tomas."

"They're good, but you look at things differently. Rikkard and maybe Baar will try to punch holes in it. I've seen you work. You anticipated everything they tried."

"That wasn't just me. If you want me to look something over, I'd also like to have my senior legalist look at it. He's one of the best."

"How'd you find him?"

"He'd been Premier Obreduur's junior legalist for years. He stayed with Obreduur out of loyalty, but Obreduur couldn't pay him more and recommended he come to work for me."

"He was fortunate, more ways than one. He can certainly look at it. I'll need all the help I can get. Thank you."

"We need to help each other, especially now." Dekkard knew the thought was trite, but also true.

When Dekkard donned his overcoat and left the committee room, he found Breffyn Haastar waiting outside in the corridor.

"Would you like to meet for lunch at a third past noon?" asked the Landor councilor.

"Absolutely," replied Dekkard.

Haastar smiled. "I'll see you then."

As the older councilor walked away, Dekkard turned to Gaaroll. "That means we're headed down to the records room." *Since there's no sense in walking back to the office, spending little more than a bell there, and walking back.*

"Won't get as cold that way."

"True." Dekkard glanced at the door to the Premier's floor office, and at the Council Guard posted there, then decided against stopping. *For now.* He had a little time to think over how to present his concerns about the *Khuld.* He continued toward the door and the stairwell to the lower level.

Once he signed in and began to consider the files before him on the table, Dekkard knew he'd been missing something. So he decided to write down the date and amount of every instance when Minz had withdrawn or written cheques to himself. Then he looked over the withdrawals and deposits of similar amounts and compared the dates. Several patterns were obvious. One he'd noted earlier—Minz had invariably deposited a cheque for two hundred fifty marks from Northwest Industrial Chemical on the third of each month, beginning in Fallend, presumably his monthly salary as an influencer. What was more interesting was that, beginning in Springfirst of 1265, on the last Quindi of every month, Minz had withdrawn five hundred marks from the Capitol Services account.

That had to be what he was paying himself. Dekkard shook his head. If his suspicion was correct, between Northwest Industrial Chemical and Capitol Services, Minz had been making more marks than a councilor, even when he'd been just a Security Committee aide, between his Council position and what he'd apparently withdrawn from the Capitol Services account.

The other pattern was that on the sixth Tridi of every month, fifty marks were withdrawn in notes. *So who is he paying that to?*

There was only one large transaction in Minz's personal account at the Imperial Banque of Machtarn, and that was on the thirtieth of Fallfirst, when he had withdrawn four thousand marks in a banque draft payable to the Landbanque of Machtarn.

That had to be when he bought the flat in Westpark!

By that time, it was already just past noon, and Dekkard needed to put his notes away and go meet Breffyn Haastar.

Once he and Gaaroll left the records room and were climbing the narrow staircase to the main level, Dekkard said, "After we get to the dining room, you get something to eat and meet me back at the dining room at a third past first bell. We'll be going back down to the records room for about a bell before heading to the office."

"You finding something, sir?"

"I'm finding, but what it all means I haven't quite figured out."

"You will. You always do," replied Gaaroll.

Except sometimes it's much later than I should have. Dekkard followed Gaaroll out of the upper door and into the main corridor. They continued until they reached the entrance to the councilors' dining room.

"A third after first bell?" Gaaroll asked.

"That's right." Dekkard walked through the open door, noticing that Gaaroll did not turn until she was sure he was inside.

He barely handed his overcoat over to one of the attendants when Haastar appeared and did the same.

"It's still cold out there," said Haastar as the two followed the maître d'hôtel to a table for two. "I'm glad Tatyanna was able to leave before the storm."

"I take it she's also from the southwest?"

"Her family's originally from Khasaar. Her grandfather—he was Kamreyn Klein—bought extensive holdings near Brekaan when he was a young man."

Dekkard just nodded, since about the only thing he knew about Khasaar was that it held the headquarters of Southwestern Ironway, and he'd never heard of Kamreyn Klein, but the way Haastar had mentioned the name, he decided he should find out. After they seated themselves, he asked, "How did you meet?"

"The way most Landor couples meet," said Haastar with an amused expression, "by arrangement. Unlike many, we actually liked each other from the first. I was very fortunate."

"It sounds like you both were."

Haastar shook his head. "Tatyanna is the one who runs the lands, and that's how it should be. The lands are hers. She was overseeing them from the time she was fifteen. My father inherited a holding barely sufficient for one son. Baaltar has added some lands through skillful management, but . . ."

"Is that why you worked to become a councilor?"

"What else would be better for a Landor trained as a legalist?"

"Were you already a legalist when you met Tatyanna?"

"Barely, but she liked the fact that I'd studied property and water law. It's been useful at times."

"I never would have guessed that," Dekkard admitted. He didn't say anything more because their server arrived.

Haastar ordered the duck cassoulet, while Dekkard chose the three-cheese chicken.

After the server departed, Haastar asked quietly, "What do you think the New Meritorists will do next?"

"Another attack on the Council, in some fashion. The seizure of a light cruiser is suggestive, even if First Marshal Bernotte has deployed a small flotilla."

"You sound doubtful."

"'Cynical' might be a better term. So far nothing has worked out as planned. Why should Bernotte's strategy?"

"Do you have a better one?"

"Hardly," replied Dekkard sardonically. "That's one reason why I'm not saying much in committee or to Premier Hasheem." After a slight hesitation, he asked, "What do you think?"

"I don't know what to think. I see that people are angry. Too many people who are hungry don't have jobs, but Tatyanna can't afford to hire more workers, especially now, with the new steam machinery getting so expensive. I overheard Gerard Schmidtz complaining that older manufactories can't buy new equipment unless they lay off workers. They have to buy new equipment because smaller manufactories are."

For a moment, Haastar's words didn't make sense, but then Dekkard understood, although he wondered if Schmidtz might have been exaggerating. Still . . . new equipment cost less to operate and took fewer workers. "That also might be why larger corporacions are trying to squeeze out smaller competitors."

"Is that really happening? I've heard some talk."

"It's occurring," confirmed Dekkard. "Quietly, but steadily. Sometimes, quietly brutal."

Haastar frowned. "Do you think that had anything to do with the killing of that Siincleer Shipbuilding legalist at the Yearend Ball?"

"The stories in *Gestirn* strongly suggested that. The Siincleer corporacions are known for those tactics. No proof has ever shown up, but I'd wager that Siincleer's squashing of smaller competitors had a lot to do with it." Dekkard paused, remembering something that Obreduur had mentioned after Markell had vanished. "Not only that, but Siincleer Engineering is undertaking building projects in Noldar. I wouldn't be surprised if some were for Guldoran corporacions wanting to use cheaper labor."

"So we're facing unhappy and unemployed workers and unhappy large and small corporacions, and the revolutionist New Meritorists. Is that how you see it?" asked Haastar.

"Is there any other way to look at it?" returned Dekkard quietly. "Guldor is changing in ways that no one foresaw. No one planned for it, either."

"You did, in a way. With the Public Safety reforms. What else do you have in mind?" Haastar smiled warmly. "Don't tell me you don't. You're not a one-shot pistol, Steffan."

"I do have a few proposals in the works, but they're likely not the ones we need now. Or the *only* ones we need now," Dekkard added after a moment.

"What do you think we need? Not what the New Meritorists are proposing, I hope?"

"Almighty, no. Their approach would be a disaster." Dekkard fingered his chin. "We need better worker safety and protection laws, not so much the standards, but the means to enforce them. We also need to find some way to stop . . ." He shook his head. "Not stop . . . exactly, but the larger corporacions are using marks and illegal subterfuges in all sorts of ways that aren't good. Workers know that, and they feel that those with marks get away with almost anything. That sets a bad example and gives support to the New Meritorists. We need to find a way to make corporacion presidentes and senior officers personally responsible and able to be prosecuted under criminal law for such illegal acts." He smiled sardonically. "I could go on and on, but that's more than enough. Why are you so interested in what I think?"

"I've always been interested, but . . ." Haastar offered a slightly embarrassed smile. "Tatyanna suggested I could do worse than listening to you."

"She esteems me too highly."

Haastar laughed softly. "Tatyanna is good-hearted, but she's an excellent judge of character and ability. That's why the holding is one of the most profitable in the southwest."

At that moment, the server reappeared with their orders and café for each.

Once the server left, Dekkard took a bite of his three-cheese chicken, then another, realizing that he was hungrier than he'd realized. Both men ate silently for several minutes.

Then Dekkard asked, "Did Tatyanna say anything else?"

"She didn't have to." Haastar paused. "How soon before matters will get worse?"

"I don't know . . . but I have the feeling it won't be long." *Possibly as soon as when the streets are clear.* Dekkard wasn't sure where that thought had come from, and he wasn't about to voice it.

"Did you have that feeling about the shelling of the Council Office Building?"

"I told Obreduur that the New Meritorists would attack it, not the Council Hall, but I had no idea the attack would be a shelling. I certainly didn't think it would happen as soon as it did."

"That's more than anyone else foresaw," Haastar pointed out.

"It wasn't enough, unfortunately. What do you think would be the worst thing the New Meritorists could do?"

"What about destroying the Palace and killing the Imperador?"

Dekkard almost nodded. If Haastar had come up with that . . . "So far, the New Meritorists have been targeting the Council, but that's not to say that they couldn't target the Imperador. Do you think that's a possibility?" Dekkard paused. "I'm asking honestly. I really don't have a good feel for that."

"I don't know, either, Steffan. Tatyanna has heard through some of the long-timers at the holding that some of the younger men who got laid off are angry not only at her, and other Landors, but at both the Council and the Imperador."

"If that's any indication, they just might target the Imperador. Still, it would be harder. The Council is on a main avenue. The Palace is a good third of a mille from the gates."

"You sound like you know your way. Have you actually been there?" asked Haastar.

"Twice. Only briefly when Avraal and I were Obreduur's security aides. We accompanied him to both confirmations."

"You continue to amaze me, Steffan."

"Breffyn, I know things you don't. You know things I don't. That's because we come from different backgrounds. It's also a good reason for sharing thoughts and information."

Haastar smiled cheerfully. "Why do you think I asked you to lunch?"

"What else do you have in mind?"

"Nothing, right now. Except that I worry Fredrich doesn't see how bad things could get."

"I have some concerns about that as well, especially when he as much as said he wasn't going to make information public on the *Khuld*— essentially until he had to. If he holds off too long, that will turn councilors and others against him."

"I imagine he knows that."

Dekkard wasn't that sure that Hasheem did.

"Do you still feel that there's a problem with some Commercers? I got that feeling when you mentioned the dunnite in committee."

"I do know that there were others behind Minz."

"The one who was arrested for the killing of the Siincleer legalist? Who got shot before he could be tried?"

"Besides being one of those behind the Council shelling, he used to work for Premier Ulrich, both as a Council aide, and, illegally, I believe, running a service business called Capitol Services on the side . . ." Dekkard went on to explain very briefly.

"That doesn't sound good," replied Haastar. "I can't say I'm surprised Ulrich likely turned on him. Ulrich often didn't keep promises to Saandaar."

Dekkard nodded. That Ulrich hadn't kept promises to the Landor floor leader was hardly unexpected.

"Axel was much better. We'll have to see about Fredrich," added Haastar.

The remainder of lunch was far more casual.

After leaving the dining room with Gaaroll, Dekkard immediately made his way to the Premier's floor office.

The guard looked at Dekkard, then Gaaroll. "Councilor Dekkard, the Premier's not seeing anyone."

"Please tell his secretary I'd like about one minute with him. Let her decide."

The guard frowned, then stepped inside, returning almost immediately. "You can go in, sir."

"Thank you." Dekkard turned to Gaaroll. "Just wait here." Then he stepped through the half-open door and looked to the woman behind the small desk.

"You said one minute, Councilor."

"What I have will take that. If he asks questions, it might take a bit longer."

"Go on in."

Dekkard walked into the inner office and closed the door.

Hasheem looked up from behind the desk. "Yes, Steffan?"

"You likely have thought of this, but in case you haven't, the *Khuld*'s eight-digit guns can reach the Council buildings—and the Palace—from just outside the Machtarn harbor entrance. The New Meritorists have already accomplished one shelling. I know the *Khuld* can't physically reach Machtarn for almost two weeks if not longer, but I thought I should bring the matter to your attention . . . just in case."

"First Marshal Bernotte has the matter well in hand, Steffan."

Dekkard held in a sigh. "We also thought we had the Council Office Building well-protected. We did, but not against attackers willing to die, if necessary. The same thing could happen with the *Khuld*. I hope not, but I thought it my duty to bring the matter to your attention, Fredrich. Early enough that some contingency plans could be worked out."

Hasheem offered a sour smile in return. "Axel told me that discounting what you said was dangerous. While I think it unlikely, you do make a good point about fanatics willing to die for an objective. I will convey your thoughts to the First Marshal, to Guard Captain Trujillo, and to the Palace Guard commander."

Dekkard inclined his head slightly. "That's all I had. I hope you have a good endday."

"The same to you, Steffan."

Dekkard turned and left, opening the door and then closing it behind himself. He turned to the secretary and smiled. "Thank you very much."

"I'll always convey your requests, Councilor." Her words were pleasant, neither cool nor warm.

Once Dekkard was out in the main corridor, he said, "Did you actually get anything to eat, Nincya?"

"I did. I even sat with some other security aides. They asked me to join them."

"Do I know them?"

Gaaroll smiled. "They know you, sir. Laurenz Korriah and Shaundara Keppel."

"They're good people. Did you learn anything from them?"

"They're worried about the New Meritorists. They wanted to know how it was working for you. She was glad you married the Ritten."

"So am I," replied Dekkard. "Did they say anything I should know?"

"Nothing that you haven't said, sir."

"I suppose that's good." Dekkard opened the door to the staircase and motioned for her to lead the way to the lower level.

Once Dekkard signed into the records room, he went to work, making a list of all the banque drafts of two thousand five hundred marks deposited to the Capitol Services account over the past two years. There were forty-three, totaling over a hundred thousand marks. Even if Minz had indeed paid himself five hundred marks a month, and the other regular cash payment had gone to someone else, Minz had spent ninety thousand marks in some other fashion or another, most likely at Ulrich's direction. A goodly amount had gone to the New Meritorists as well as the men who had built the steam cannon and fabricated the shells, and the purchase of one lorry, possibly another, given that the one that had held protest signs had been markedly different from the stake lorry. But even with the purchase of two lorries and the payment of ten thousand marks to Sohl Hurrek, and several thousand to other assassins, there had to be additional expenditures, and that worried Dekkard more than a little.

Could Minz just have stashed the notes somewhere, and his secretary made off with them?

That was certainly possible, but from what Dekkard had seen of Minz it seemed unlikely. While he knew he needed to get back to his office, he spent a few more minutes writing a list, matching the banque drafts and the banque on which they were drawn with the most likely corporacion to have made such payments.

Banque of Siincleer
    17 drafts   Siincleer Shipbuilding/Siincleer Engineering
Suvion Commerce Banque
    16 drafts   Suvion Industries
Neewyrk Imperial Banque
    6 drafts   Eastern Ironway
Banque of Uldwyrk
    2 drafts   Uldwyrk Systems
Northwest Banque of Chuive
    2 drafts   Northwest Industrial Chemical

Then he added his list to the notes in his note file, after which he replaced the other material he'd taken out in its appropriate file. He left the files on the table, stood, and stretched, before leaving the records room.

On the walk back through the Council Hall and the Council Office Building, the only other councilor he saw, and that was across the hallway, was Eduardo Nortak, who didn't even look in Dekkard's direction.

As Dekkard entered the office, he saw Roostof talking to Margrit. Both immediately looked up.

"We did get some letters," said Margrit. "They're on your desk."

"Other than that," added Roostof, "nothing of interest has happened."

"I suspect that's good," replied Dekkard. "Svard, does the name Kamreyn Klein mean anything to you?"

"You mean the founder of Southwestern Ironway?"

Dekkard smiled wryly. *At least you didn't ask Haastar.* "That's the one. Do you know why his family became Landors, rather than Commercers?"

"I have no idea, sir. Do you want me to look into it?"

Dekkard shook his head. "That doesn't matter. I was just curious."

In less than a bell, Dekkard read through the letters and turned them over to Svard, and Margrit handed him a message from Hasheem. After opening it, he said to her, "There's a Security Committee meeting at fourth bell on Unadi morning." He did not mention that the subject was an intelligence update.

Once back in his private office, he thought over his conversation with Breffyn Haastar, and what legislative changes would help defuse the anger of displaced workers so that they didn't blindly follow the New Meritorists. He couldn't help wondering how much worse the situation might be than what he'd thought.

He'd made a few notes when Avraal showed up just after third bell.

"How was your day?" he asked.

"I'll tell you later."

"That good?" He raised his eyebrows.

"What about your day?"

"Quietly disturbing, between the Security Committee meeting and a few other revelations."

"It's cold and icy outside. Is there any reason—"

"Why we can't leave now? Not at all."

In less than a sixth, after Roostof had closed down the office and sent everyone home, Dekkard and Avraal walked toward the central staircase. In another sixth, Dekkard pulled out of the covered parking and headed east on Council Avenue. He was especially careful on the drive home. Along the way he noticed that many of the larger side streets had been cleared.

Once they were home, Avraal raided the cooler, and she and Gaaroll made empanadas. In the process, Dekkard merely chopped or diced whatever was placed in front of him. They did wait for Emrelda to arrive before the empanadas went into the oven.

Still, it wasn't that long before everyone was seated around the breakfast table.

"The crust could be lighter," said Avraal, a hint of disappointment in her voice.

"They're hot, and they're good," declared Emrelda. "I could get used to your cooking very easily, especially on days like these."

"You've already had about everything I know how to cook," replied Avraal.

"Another difficult day?" Dekkard looked to Emrelda because he definitely wanted to steer the conversation away from who was cooking what and how well.

"Not as bad as it could have been. Not as bad as tomorrow might be."

"You have duty tomorrow?" asked Avraal.

"Day shift," confirmed Emrelda.

"What happened today?" pressed Dekkard.

"Not that much. Two butcher shops and a grocer were closed, likely because it's been hard for lorries to get around. A small mob tried to break into the smaller butcher's place. They scattered when a patrol squad arrived. Several men were cut up. The squad found a body in the alley. Dead long before the mob. The water main still hasn't been repaired. One small house caught fire and burned to ashes."

"That's not much?" asked Dekkard.

Emrelda shook her head. "Captain says that Southtown's too quiet, ready to go up in flames or explode like a powder keg."

"Soon?" asked Gaaroll.

"Could be a week, maybe two . . . or tomorrow. It's probably the same in Rivertown, Woodlake, and Easthill. People are hungrier, angrier, and it's colder."

"And more of them don't have jobs?" asked Dekkard.

"That, too," agreed Emrelda, after a healthy swallow of Kuhrs. "The captain says applications for the Patroller Academy have been way up this past year."

For a moment, Dekkard wondered what that had to do with anything. "Do they always go up in bad times?" *Because there are fewer alternatives with decent and steady pay?*

"Usually."

"Applications for Council security aides are down," said Dekkard.

"That's because private security positions are still open," replied Avraal, "and private security aides aren't getting killed."

"More that the deaths of the private aides aren't in the newssheets," added Dekkard sardonically.

"Softies," muttered Gaaroll.

Emrelda and Avraal both smiled.

Much later, after Dekkard and Avraal had retired to their definitely chill bedroom, he asked, "So what happened in your day?"

"Another investigator is missing. This time it was someone working for the Guilds' Advisory Committee. The committee has been investigating reports of worker deaths at Suvion Industries and Northwest Industrial Chemical. The local Chemical Workers Guilds claim that workers are being fired for failure to show up for work, but that they can't work because they're being slowly poisoned."

"It is that hard to examine the workers?"

"The company physicians claim that there's nothing wrong with the workers but laziness, or that they got some flux or another . . . or consumption. Other doctors say that they're ill or disabled from chemical exposure. Neither side believes the other, but safety inspectors are blocked by the Admiralty from examining parts of the works where munitions are compounded on grounds that would reveal military secrets. The former workers who died received death payments and free cremation."

"That reduces the evidence," suggested Dekkard.

"My thought as well."

"I also wonder if Ulrich is behind the missing investigators. Carlos should at least keep Ulrich in mind."

"I already told him that. What about your day?"

Dekkard recounted what had happened, including the Security Committee meeting, what Haastar had said at lunch, and the results of his list-making.

"Do you really think the mutineers will shell the Council or the Palace? Can they even get close enough?"

"After what's already happened, I don't think the possibility can be discounted. With the weather the way it is, there's always the chance of fog. That will make it harder for the *Resolute* to find the *Khuld*."

"The mutineers got rid of all the officers."

"Senior petty officers know more than junior officers, and sometimes more than some senior officers."

"You are cynical tonight," she said gently.

"Not about you," he replied with a warm smile.

22

Findi dawned cold and cloudless, if with a high haze that reduced the warmth of the white sun. With the direct light of sunrise, Dekkard woke out of an uneasy slumber, although he could not recall the source of that unease. Deciding to let Avraal sleep, he pulled on old clothes and headed downstairs.

Emrelda sat alone in the breakfast room, which, although still cold, was far warmer than the bedroom Dekkard had just left.

"I hope today is better than yesterday, or at least not as bad as you fear."

"So do I," she replied.

"We'll do some shopping. Is there anything you'd like or that we need?"

"I left a suggested list on the counter. Add anything you two think we need." Emrelda paused, then said, "Make sure you're carrying your truncheon where you can reach it quickly, and keep one hand free, even if it means Avraal's carrying more than you—unless you prefer to have her carry a truncheon."

Dekkard just nodded. Avraal could use a truncheon, and she did have one, but she'd seldom employed one in the last several years. "Lots of smash-and-grab right now?"

"It's been especially bad this winter." Emrelda took a last swallow of café and stood. "By the way, we finally got the morning newssheet." She gestured to the side table.

Once Emrelda left, Dekkard got the croissants, then picked up the morning edition of *Gestirn*. The front-page stories were all related to the snow. As he quickly read through the rest of the newssheet he also noticed that there was no mention of the *Khuld*, which meant that either the Admiralty had kept the matter from the newsies or that they'd leaned heavily on them. Dekkard would have wagered on the former. Once news got out, it always ended up in the newssheets, not always immediately. There also weren't any stories about the unrest in areas like Rivertown, Easthill, or Southtown.

He waited until he heard Avraal's steps on the stairs before he readied their cafés. Since Gaaroll stepped into the breakfast room before Avraal arrived, Dekkard ended up fixing three cafés.

Avraal arrived, wearing a robe, then immediately sat down and cradled the warm mug in her hands. Gaaroll followed Avraal's example.

Dekkard sat down across from his wife and sampled his café.

After several sips, Avraal looked at Dekkard. "How was Emrelda this morning?"

"Resigned and a bit apprehensive. She left a shopping list and told me to keep my truncheon handy and a hand free."

"Triple true," agreed Gaaroll.

"You can come, too," said Dekkard cheerfully. "If there's danger, it'd be good to know from a greater distance."

"Shouldn'ta said anything," muttered Gaaroll.

"I would have insisted," said Avraal. "It's getting so that nowhere in Machtarn is totally safe." Her eyes went to the side table and the morning newssheet.

"It's mostly about the storm."

"No surprise there." Avraal returned to sipping her café.

After breakfast, Dekkard showered and dressed in winter security grays and his old winter gray security jacket, as did Avraal. By fourth bell the three were in the Gresynt heading down Jacquez to the various shops in the Erslaan area. When Dekkard eased the Gresynt to a stop outside the butcher shop a block north and east of the omnibus stop on Camelia Avenue, the screeching of the high-pitched steam whistles used by patrollers penetrated the steamer, coming from the southeast, almost certainly from Southtown. Dekkard couldn't help but glance at Avraal.

"I just hope she's still at the station." Avraal's tone suggested doubts about that.

If women and children are involved, she'll be out there helping. That was a thought Dekkard knew he didn't need to voice.

As he got out of the steamer, thinking about what Emrelda had said, his hand went to his truncheon. *It can't hurt to be ready.*

"Strong feelings inside! Headed this way!" Gaaroll called out.

"Thieves! Stop!"

Almost instantly, Dekkard had his truncheon in hand, moving toward the entrance to the shop, where two men burst out, neither fully aware of Dekkard moving in from the side.

Dekkard tripped the first, jabbed the second in the celiac plexus with a force that went through the man's thin jacket, then kept the first down with a side kick to the knee before he could get back on his feet. A knife skittered away from the second man. "Move and you're dead!" he snapped.

Avraal had a knife out and ready.

The second man lay twitching on the brick walk in front of the shop, the short-bladed knife lying just beyond his hand, while the first lay crumpled on his side, looking up at Dekkard. Dekkard kicked the knife farther away.

A man appeared in the shop doorway, his mouth open as he saw a man and a woman in security grays watching the two fallen thieves.

Without taking his eyes off the two thieves, Dekkard said, "Send someone for the patrollers."

"One of 'em slashed up the boss."

"Take care of him, and send someone for patrollers. Now! The station's not that far away."

"Yes, sir."

In moments, a boy ran from the shop westward toward the patrol station, but it was close to a third of a bell later before a patrol steamer arrived, and two patrollers got out.

Dekkard recognized the older patroller, but couldn't recall the man's name. The second patroller looked barely old enough to be a recruit.

The older patroller looked at Avraal, then Dekkard, and smiled.

"When the boy said a man and a woman in grays had taken down two thieves, I had a feeling it might be you."

"We did what we could, Sammel," said Avraal. "How's Georg?"

"Still doing records at the station."

Sammel looked at the pair of thieves.

The man that Dekkard had tripped was lying on his side. "Bastard in gray broke my knee."

"Isn't that too bad," declared Sammel. "He's a councilor, you know. Assaulting a councilor can be a sentence to the work camps."

The other man had finally begun to move and struggled to sit up. His face was drawn and pale. He looked at Dekkard and then at Sammel.

"The knife over there was his," said Dekkard. "He used it on the shop owner, according to the clerk."

"Not only theft, but assault on a shopkeeper and a councilor." Sammel looked more intently at the man with the injured knee. "This time you won't get off so easy."

In minutes, the two patrollers had the pair in iron cuffs, after which they removed the marks taken from the shop, and then locked the two in the rear of the steamer, where the younger patroller remained watching them.

Dekkard, Avraal, and Gaaroll followed Sammel into the shop and stood to the side as the patroller talked to the shop owner.

Somewhat more than a third of a bell later, Dekkard and Avraal finished their shopping, turning down the shop owner's offer to give them what they had bought.

"Sr. Padilla," Dekkard said, since he'd heard the man's name when Sammel had questioned him, "you've been through enough today. You don't need to lose money on us as well. You were kind enough to show us some choice cuts, and we appreciate that."

Avraal smiled warmly and added, "We will take advantage of your knowledge in the future."

"That you will always have, Ritten." Padilla offered a small but amused smile, and added, "And I will be able to tell my children and their children how a Ritter and Ritten stopped thieves in my store. Their children will think I tell tall tales. I cannot thank you enough."

"We're just glad we could help," said Dekkard.

After loading the various meats into the Gresynt, Dekkard eased behind the wheel and took a deep breath. "Emrelda warned me, but I really didn't think anything would happen to us."

He shook his head. "I was too hard on them, but I was just reacting. I could have killed the second one."

"You didn't," Avraal pointed out. "He had a knife, and he'd already used it. Besides, they were already troublemakers. Sammel recognized one of them. And they will get fed in the work camp."

Dekkard couldn't help wondering how well they'd be fed. *But they chose to rob a butcher, for marks, not for food.*

"We still need to finish our errands," Avraal pointed out.

"We do," agreed Dekkard as he eased the Gresynt away from the butcher shop.

The remainder of their shopping—including the grocer's and the spirits shop—was uneventful, and the three returned to the house at a third past second afternoon bell. After a quick bite to eat, Avraal returned to the kitchen, and Dekkard went out to the garage to check over the Gresynt.

Emrelda actually stepped into the house at a third past fourth bell, certainly earlier than Dekkard had expected.

"I heard from Sammel that you two just couldn't stay out of trouble," said Emrelda as she took off her winter jacket.

"You told me to keep my truncheon handy," replied Dekkard. "They caught me by surprise. I might have been a little hard on them."

"Those two would have gotten caught sooner or later," said Emrelda. "They could have gotten shot and killed if a patroller had been there. Not that they'll thank you." She turned to Gaaroll. "You saw them in action. I never have. What did you think?"

"I never saw anyone move that quick. Those grabbers never saw it coming."

"That's because you haven't seen a trained security aide in action before," said Dekkard.

Avraal raised her eyebrows, but didn't say anything.

She didn't have to. Dekkard knew exactly what she was thinking. So he said to Emrelda, "What about your day?"

"Less eventful than yours. I spent it in the station with Georg. We got caught up on some of the reports. Southtown was mostly quiet. It won't be tomorrow, most likely."

"It won't be that long before dinner's almost ready," Avraal said. "We're having matambre with potatoes and leeks. And there's also some hot spiced cinnamon wine. I've even had some." She looked to Dekkard.

"I'll get you some. I turned on the grate in the front parlor. I'll bring it to you there."

Dekkard headed for the kitchen. He was definitely glad that there hadn't been any more unrest in Southtown, but, like Emrelda, he had to wonder how long the quiet would last.

23

W HEN Dekkard, Avraal, and Gaaroll left the house on Unadi, a light but bitterly cold wind blew out of the north under a high gray haze, and the air held the acrid odor of burning coal.

As he eased the Gresynt down the drive between the heaped snow on each side, Dekkard couldn't help but wonder how long it would be before the mutiny and seizure of the I.S. *Khuld* appeared in either *Gestirn* or *The Machtarn Tribune*.

"Really strong feelings to the north on Jacquez," Gaaroll said. "Two sets."

"Might be an accident, but we'll take Camelia this morning. Just make sure you concentrate on the university bell tower." Dekkard doubted that there would be another possible assassin posted there, especially after Minz's death, but there was no sense in not reminding Gaaroll to check.

"Yes, sir."

When Dekkard neared the university, he saw students trudging along the snow-lined sidewalks or over snow-packed tracks, but neither Avraal nor Gaaroll sensed any imminent danger there or on the remainder of the drive to the Council Office Building. As usual, Dekkard turned the Gresynt over to Avraal, and then he and Gaaroll made their way to the office.

His first words to Margrit were, "Good morning," followed by, "Did everyone make it in safely today?"

"Yes, sir, although I understand the omnibuses on the east side were packed and not terribly warm. The morning mail hasn't arrived yet, either."

"Just bring it in when it does."

Dekkard's office was chilly, but while he shed his overcoat, he was definitely glad for his gray winter suit coat as he began to go over the small stack of typed replies awaiting him. He finished those well before he again donned his overcoat for the walk to the Council Hall and the Security Committee meeting at fourth bell. The main corridors of the Council Office Building held a few more staffers than usual, some of whom just seemed to be talking to others. Then he realized why—the interior main corridor was much warmer than most councilors' offices, simply because the corridors had no outside windows and the gas lamps added a touch of heat.

As he and Gaaroll neared the Security Committee chamber, Dekkard caught sight of Rikkard and Baar standing outside the chamber, and he realized that he hadn't seen any security aides accompanying Baar, in the last week or so. *Did he decide to do without them, or is there some other reason?*

He might have asked Baar, but both Baar and Rikkard entered the committee chamber before Dekkard reached the door.

"Just wait here," he said to Gaaroll. "This meeting shouldn't be long. Then we'll go down to the records room."

When Dekkard entered, the only councilors in the chamber were Baar, Rikkard, and Kharl Navione. Given that Navione was already seated and writing something and that it was still a sixth before the committee was to convene, Dekkard approached the two Commercer councilors. "Good morning, Jaradd, Villem."

"Good morning, Steffan," replied Baar pleasantly.

Rikkard just nodded.

Dekkard smiled and asked Rikkard, "How does this snow compare to what you get in Endor?"

Rikkard looked momentarily surprised, as if he hadn't expected Dekkard to speak to him, then said, "This would be a big storm there as well. By now, Endor's probably had a half score smaller storms. The snow doesn't melt. Not until late spring."

"So it just keeps piling up all winter?"

"Mostly. What about Gaarlak—or do you know?"

Dekkard ignored the pleasantly voiced, but snide, comment and replied, "It's about the same as Oersynt. They get more snow than Machtarn, but it gets warm enough for some of it to melt. We were in Gaarlak for Midwinter Recess, and it snowed twice. Half of it was gone before we left."

"That's more like Jeeroh," said Baar, adding after a moment, "Here comes the chairman."

Rikkard immediately moved toward his seat behind the long, curved desk.

"Until later," Dekkard said to Baar, smiling as he finished, and turned back toward his own seat.

In less than a minute, all the councilors were seated, since Pajiin and Haastar had come in while Dekkard had been talking to the two Commercers.

Hasheem gaveled the committee to order and immediately said, "This meeting will be brief. There has only been one sighting of the *Khuld*. Early yesterday morning, she was spotted southeast of Surpunta, just offshore, steaming eastward toward Devult. Even at flank speed, she could not reach Point Larmat until a week from now. First Marshal Bernotte has again assured me that the *Resolute*'s flotilla is positioned to intercept and destroy the *Khuld*.

"On a less promising note, there have been three attacks on coaling towers belonging to Guldoran Ironway. No sizable amount of coal was removed. The drastic rise in coal prices last month may have prompted the attacks. Still, such attacks are worrisome.

"The Public Safety Ministry discovered what appears to have been an armory used by the New Meritorists near Rivertown. Most of the weapons had been removed, but patrollers caught two men loading the last of the firearms, and the patrollers have a number of leads."

The fact that the New Meritorists had almost managed to move weapons without getting caught bothered Dekkard. *On the other hand, the patrollers did move fast enough to catch someone, which they've never managed before.*

"Do any of you have questions or comments?" asked Hasheem, almost diffidently.

"Why did it take them so long?" demanded Rikkard.

Hasheem looked guilelessly at Dekkard. "Perhaps you could explain that more effectively, Councilor Dekkard."

Dekkard bit back what he wanted to say to Rikkard, pausing a moment before speaking. "It's very simple. The previous Security minister avoided investigating the New Meritorists and failed to keep any records about them . . ." From there, Dekkard went on to describe the publicly available information about Jaime Minz and his ties to the New Meritorists and to Northwest Industrial Chemical.

"Some of that information never came before this committee." Rikkard looked directly at Hasheem.

"That is because it was a criminal investigation by the Justiciary Ministry," replied Hasheem. "With the murder of Sr. Minz and the disappearance of his associates, further investigation has been rather hampered. Does that address your inquiry, Councilor?"

"It does not, Sr. Chairman, but it appears that, at present, the information that would address my inquiry is not available." Rikkard's words were clipped, but deliberate.

"Are there other questions?" asked Hasheem.

"Yes, Sr. Chairman," replied Baar. "Has there been any investigation of the sources of those funds that were directed to the New Meritorists?"

"That investigation is proceeding," replied Hasheem. "It will be time-consuming because the funds were transferred either in mark notes or by banque drafts that did not reveal the origin of the funds. The only names appearing in any financial records thus far discovered are those of the late Sr. Minz and his secretary, who is among the missing."

"Thank you, Sr. Chairman."

"Are there any other Imperial warships that might be compromised?" asked Navione.

"The Admiralty hasn't reported any others," replied Hasheem.

As soon as Hasheem gaveled the end of the committee meeting, Rikkard was on his feet and out of the chamber.

Pajiin leaned toward Dekkard. "Seems like the good Councilor Rikkard didn't like what you said. How did you know that much about Minz?"

"I knew him in passing when we were both security aides. When I became a councilor, I discovered that Ulrich had him remove a lot of the Security Committee records before Obreduur became premier. That made me suspicious. So I wasn't surprised when *Gestirn* reported he'd been charged with several crimes, one of which was setting up the Atacaman red pepper dust attack on me."

"You mentioned that before. Did you suspect him before it came out in the newssheets?"

"I thought it was possible, but there was no proof."

"Commercers are good at covering their tracks. Always have been," said Pajiin in a low but sardonic tone of voice.

"I imagine you've seen more than enough of that."

"Thought it was bad back in Eshbruk, but it's worse here." Pajiin stood. "I'll see you later."

Dekkard stood as well, picked up his gray leather folder, and followed Pajiin out of the committee chamber, where he found Villem Baar waiting for him, unaccompanied.

"Do you have a moment, Steffan?"

"As long as you need."

"You know more about former Premier Ulrich than you said today, don't you?"

"I know some more," replied Dekkard cautiously. "Why do you ask?"

"Because Jaradd didn't question you. He thought he was asking a question the chairman wouldn't really answer. When you answered, Jaradd didn't want you to say any more."

"Do you think that was why he left?"

"That would be my guess," replied Baar.

"Is he close to former Premier Ulrich?"

"I have no idea. He's never mentioned him."

Dekkard didn't see much point in pursuing that inquiry, but he did have one other question. "I noticed you don't seem to have any security aides, or am I missing something?"

"They were just temporary. They were on loan from the firm I was with until things settled down."

"Barthow, Juarez and . . ." Dekkard stopped because he couldn't remember the last name of the legalist firm, even though he recalled that the firm had represented Lukkyn Wyath, the former Security minister executed for treason, among other offenses.

"Whittsyn," supplied Baar. "I'm surprised that you remembered the firm's name. It's not exactly prominent in Machtarn."

"Except the firm represented Minister Wyath."

Baar winced slightly. "It wasn't quite like that. Paarsens and Alvara handle most of the actual work. They specialize in cases before the High Justiciary. Even so, it was regrettable."

"Let me guess," said Dekkard, with a wry smile. "The firm's largest client is Suvion Industries, and someone there asked."

"The first part is unarguable. Since I've had no contact with the firm since before I was sworn in, I don't know anything about how the firm came to represent Sr. Wyath, but I imagine something along the lines of your surmise occurred. Suvion Industries wasn't part of my practice, and I had no idea that Wyath had been director of security there until it came out in the newssheet articles about his trial."

"How did you feel about it?"

"I can see why the firm felt it had no choice, but it bothered me. It still does." Baar offered a rueful smile. "When I told Gretina about the firm representing Sr. Wyath, she said my becoming councilor could be for the best. That remains to be seen, but she might be right."

"I understand that," replied Dekkard.

For a moment, Baar looked puzzled.

"If I hadn't been selected, Avraal and I would still have been Obreduur's security aides . . . or one of us would have been."

"Oh."

"Exactly. And on a more cheerful note," added Dekkard, "I did pass on Gretina's name to a few people. If I hear anything, I'll let you know. But then, if anyone's interested, she might hear before I do."

"Gretina will appreciate that. I certainly do."

"Now . . . if you'll excuse me, I need to get to an appointment." That was a bit of a stretch, but he did need to see what else he might be able to puzzle out from the financial documents in the records room.

"Until later, then," said Baar before turning and heading in the direction of the courtyard and the Council Office Building.

Once he and Gaaroll were well away from Baar, Dekkard asked, "Could you tell if Councilor Baar was lying when we were talking?"

"He didn't feel that way, sir."

"Good." Dekkard began to walk in the same direction as Baar had gone, but only until he reached the stairwell to the lower level.

Once they were in the outer area of the records room, Dekkard said, "You'll have to wait. I don't know how long this will take."

"I'll be here, sir."

Dekkard left his leather folder with Gaaroll before the clerk unlocked the door to the records section.

He spent about two-thirds of a bell searching for other possible correlations between mark transactions and possible services, without a great deal of success, when the door opened and Guard Captain Trujillo appeared.

"How is your analysis coming, Councilor?"

"I've discovered a number of matters which are likely." Dekkard went on to detail his suppositions about pay and about the possible corporacions from which the banque drafts might have come—and the possible total amount of marks distributed by Minz. "Unfortunately, while I believe all those suppositions to be fact, unless supporting evidence can be found, they remain suppositions."

"You may have actual proof of one criminal activity," Trujillo pointed out.

"I do?"

"Criminal conspiracy. We know that Capitol Services was implicated in the shelling of the Council Office Building. That's definitely a capital criminal offense. The pattern of banque drafts suggests ongoing financial support of Capitol Services by five parties. You've provided some possible leads." He smiled politely, then asked, "Do you believe that you can learn any more from studying this information?"

"At the moment, probably not, but I'd like to be able to look at the files if something else occurs to me."

"You're welcome any time, sir. We might use your findings, but, if we do, your actual notes will remain here. I trust you'll find that satisfactory." The Guard captain's words were not a question.

"Of course. You can certainly use my notes. I would prefer that my name not be used."

"That shouldn't be a problem."

Trujillo waited until Dekkard replaced the materials in the appropriate files, then accompanied him from the records room.

Dekkard debated stopping at the dining room, but decided that he really wasn't hungry, and that nothing on the menu appealed to him.

When he reached his office, Margrit immediately said, "Sir, along with the regular mail, there was a large packet from Zenya Onswyrth in the Gaarlak office. It's on your desk. I didn't open it."

"You can in the future," said Dekkard. "She's forwarding letters and sending a weekly report. Just handle the letters the way you always do and put the report and anything else on top."

After Dekkard entered his personal office, he hung up his overcoat, then settled behind the desk. The packet contained nine letters and a precisely typed report, with a section for each day. Dekkard read through them carefully. Most of the entries were about the handful of people who stopped by, often just to express their surprise at the existence of the office, but several made comments about food prices, and two conveyed concerns about the New Meritorists. The most interesting, and disturbing, report was that some individuals had damaged the coaling tower serving the Guldoran Ironway station in Gaarlak, but that little, if any, coal had been removed.

New Meritorists? But why would they damage a coaling tower and not take much coal?

Dekkard had the feeling that, again, it would be obvious when he found out the reason for the damage.

Tridi, 15 Winterend, contained one politically interesting entry.

> . . . Sr. Jens Seigryn came to the office and visited. He asked how I got my job. I told him. Legalist Desharra saw him and talked to him. Afterward, she explained his roles as Advisory Committee liaison to the district Craft Party . . .

The entry for Furdi, 16 Winterend, simply stated that the office was closed because the snow was chest-high in places, but the only note about the snow in the entry for Quindi was that the office opened one bell late.

So far so good for Zenya. Dekkard nodded and turned his attention to the handful or so of unopened letters Zenya had forwarded, using one of his throwing knives to open them. After going through those and the letters Margrit had already slit, he carried the stack out to the staff office and deposited them in Roostof's inbox, then said, "Svard . . . Shuryn . . . I need to talk to both of you about a new project."

The two followed him back into his office, Shuryn coming last and closing the door.

Once they were all seated, Dekkard began, "I've been thinking, after a talk with another councilor, about the problems facing workers, especially those in large manufactories. Before the Midwinter Recess, Chairman Haarsfel held a number of hearings in the Workplace Administration Committee about dangerous conditions in various different industries. Seldom were those conditions because of deficiencies in existing law. More often they were the result of the laws not being enforced. In some cases, it appeared that the corporacions knew when inspectors were coming and they cleaned up the workplace for the inspections. Sometimes, there were no inspections, and sometimes the inspectors failed to report deficiencies. I'm thinking of legislating a Workplace Safety Enforcement Commission or Office with the power to require ongoing compliance with the laws and large and escalating fines for noncompliance as well as a prohibition on government contracts by corporacions who have more than one major violation in a running five-year period." Dekkard looked to Roostof.

"That's rather ambitious, sir. Do you think the Premier or Chairman Haarsfel would support it?"

"Not right now," admitted Dekkard, "but I have the feeling that there will be a time when they will." *Likely closer than anyone thinks.* "I'd like to have something ready before then."

"Like the Security reform bill?" replied Roostof.

"The need for Security reform was obvious for a long time. It was just that no one else wanted to touch it. With worker safety reforms, it's not as obvious."

"With Chairman Haarsfel holding hearings, wouldn't developing such a proposal be seen as presumptuous?"

"If that proposal is seen, it might, but Haarsfel hasn't mentioned anything about legislative changes. We need to have something ready in the next few weeks. If necessary, we can turn the draft over to him." *But from what I've seen, he'd rather have someone else introduce it.*

Roostof nodded slowly, then said, "You want us to start immediately, I take it?"

"That's right." Dekkard looked to Teitryn. "Shuryn, keep working on the corporacion project, as you can, but this takes priority." After a hesitation, he added, "You can go now. I have some other matters to talk over with Svard."

"Yes, sir."

Once Teitryn had left and closed the door, Dekkard said, "I have the feeling that there are more unhappy workers out there than most councilors suspect."

"Even the Craft councilors, sir?"

"Even most of them. The few that see the unhappiness, from what I can tell, are a few of the junior ones, like Pajiin, and the women. Premier Hasheem comes originally from the Fieldworkers Guild in Port Reale, but he tends to be cautious. I'm going by feelings, and I could be wrong. That's why you need to keep this quiet."

"Like the Security reforms?"

"Just like the Security reforms." Dekkard coughed, cleared his throat, then asked pleasantly, "What are you seeing on the streets in your part of Machtarn?"

"Right now, snow. But you mean more about people, especially people who aren't doing that well. There are more men in worn jackets and gloves wrapped in rags, usually in groups of two or three. All ages." Roostof paused, wetted his lips, then offered a smile that was almost embarrassed. "Just before the storm, there was a woman . . . really little more than a girl . . . almost pretty . . . she offered in a way . . . you know what I mean." He shook his head. "I'm not that type. She almost begged. I gave her two marks and told her to get something to eat. She probably didn't."

"I can see that. You're well-dressed, and you have a kind face."

"Bettina said something like that."

"I'm glad you two are getting along. Have you spoken with her father?"

"Only in passing. He seems to like me, but I can tell he's very protective of her."

"Right now, I get the impression she's about all he cares about besides being a councilor. Do you two talk about anything besides legalisms and law?"

"She talks about everything. She knows so much. She'll be a better legalist . . . I mean, a better pure legalist, than I am. I just . . . worry. A lot of the old-type legalists don't look favorably on really bright women legalists."

That comment reminded Dekkard of Gretina Baar. He just hoped that Ingrella's contacts would prove useful. "There are more women legalists in top positions now. Just look at Ingrella Obreduur and the new Justiciary minister."

"That's true, but it hasn't been easy for any of them."

"Svard, Bettina is intelligent, and she has contacts, including you. Take it one step at a time." Dekkard stood. "I won't keep you from organizing Shuryn on the new effort."

As soon as Roostof left, Margrit brought in a small stack of responses.

After signing a few, Dekkard stood and walked to the window, looking down through the glass at the stone outer lower sill, its clean and unmarked surface denying the reality of the carnage that had occurred little more than a month before. Then his eyes lifted to the north and the Palace of the Imperador.

Several minutes passed before he took a deep breath and returned to his desk and the necessary routine of signing letters, letters that could be rendered meaningless in an instant . . . yet the failure to take care of such mundane necessities, over time, would assure that he would be a one-term councilor.

And would that be so bad?

24

DESPITE Emrelda's concerns and Dekkard's fears, Duadi, Tridi, and Furdi were much like Unadi: cold, with a gloomy haze and the acrid odor of burned coal hanging everywhere and getting stronger day by day. There were two short pro forma sessions of the Council, necessary on weeks where the Council had no official business but was not in a declared recess. The only Security Committee meeting was on Tridi, when River Commander Escobaar testified about the problems facing the River Patrol in dealing with Atacaman refugees. As Dekkard anticipated, the commander wanted more funding and more men. Hasheem made no commitment except that the committee would review the matters. Other than that, there was nothing new to report on security matters, while Haarsfel couldn't summon more worker witnesses to Machtarn for Workplace Administration Committee hearings until ironway service was fully restored.

Avraal and Carlos Baartol and his remaining staff had not made any progress in finding any evidence concerning who was behind the disappearance and likely death of the missing investigators.

By Quindi morning, Dekkard definitely felt unsettled, not because something had occurred, but because it was too quiet. The only situation that had changed was the small story in *Gestirn* stating that the Admiralty had not replied to an inquiry about a light cruiser that appeared to have been delayed in reporting for a scheduled refit in Port Reale, but the story did not mention the name of the ship.

While Dekkard wondered when the rest of that story would appear, the drive to the Council Office Building was uneventful, as was Avraal's departure in the Gresynt.

Only a single message awaited him in his office, and it was from Eyril Konnigsburg, suggesting that the two of them have lunch at noon, if Dekkard happened to be free. Dekkard immediately wrote a note agreeing and dispatched Gaaroll with that reply.

Then he dealt with the incoming letters, after which he turned his attention to writing down thoughts on possible provisions for the worker safety enforcement proposal.

At a third before noon, he donned his overcoat and gloves, and he and Gaaroll headed out to walk to the Council Hall. Dekkard had only taken

a handful of steps into the courtyard when, along with the omnipresent odor of burning coal, he smelled something else burning. He glanced
around but didn't see any obvious smoke, possibly because of the heavy
green-tinged gray haze, but the haze looked darker to the east. Finally, he
asked Gaaroll, "Do you smell something else burning, besides coal?"

"Yes, sir. Couldn't tell you what, though."

Dekkard just hoped that what was burning was small and would be
quickly extinguished, but he had the feeling that wasn't going to be the
case. He also knew there wasn't anything he could do about it, and he
liked that even less.

Konnigsburg was waiting for him just inside the entrance to the councilors' dining room.

"You can tell you're an Institute graduate, Steffan. Always well-presented
and punctual."

"The same goes for you." Dekkard felt uncomfortable in addressing
Konnigsburg by his first name, given he was a retired admiral, but didn't
want to subordinate himself by using titles.

Konnigsburg gestured to the maître d'hôtel, who led them to one of the
tables for two.

Once they were seated, Konnigsburg said, "I've always wondered why
so few Institute graduates end up as councilors."

"Most, I suspect, can do much better in other fields, and those who
have been as successful as you likely don't want to deal with political intrigue, which is often petty."

The older councilor laughed softly. "You expressed that rather carefully."

"I've learned that everything said might appear in print. Unfortunately,
I've failed upon occasion to heed my own observation."

"Not often, from what I've heard and observed."

"Then I've been fortunate."

Konnigsburg looked up as their server reached the table, then said,
"Café and the white bean soup."

"I'll have the same," added Dekkard.

Once the server left, Konnigsburg said, "Your so-called fortune is
partly because there's a perception that it's unwise, and even unnecessary,
to make an enemy of you." He held up a hand. "I know. There are a few
senior Commercers who don't hold that view, but even they're wary of
you. That wasn't why I suggested we meet. You're on the Security Committee, Steffan. I understand you've been briefed on an 'occurrence' at
Port Reale?"

"The mutiny or takeover of the *Khuld,* you mean?"

"What are your thoughts about it?"

"I'd be interested in knowing how they managed it before I say much else."

Konnigsburg's smile conveyed wry amusement. "Tell me your assumptions, and I'll correct or add to them, as I can."

"I'm only guessing, but the *Khuld* is one of the older light cruisers. The ship's captain was likely a senior commander with an acceptable but not outstanding record. I suspect he was the type who obsessed over minor details personally, rather than letting department heads or senior petty officers deal with them—"

"That's accurate enough," interrupted the older councilor. "Within days, he was quietly relieved of command and immediately retired."

"Because a disciplinary hearing or court-martial would have suggested the mutineers had some basis for their action."

"I thought you'd understand. So what do you think the mutineers will do?"

"The *Khuld* is on its way to Machtarn," said Dekkard. "Those in command are likely New Meritorists trying to avoid the *Resolute* and those in its battle group. They'll attempt to use the eight-digit guns to shell either the Council or the Palace, if not both."

"What about the *Resolute*'s battle group?"

"I'd be willing to bet that the mutineers have detailed charts of the coast around Machtarn. They'll take advantage of favorable conditions— fog or sea mists—and approach under circumstances that the commander of the battle group believes aren't possible. They'll also have very experienced gunners."

Konnigsburg offered a wintry smile. "That's quite similar to what I wrote the First Marshal. I haven't heard back, and I doubt I will. I've heard, indirectly, of course, that they believe the mutineers will head for Noldar."

"Why there?" asked Dekkard.

"Because the Oligarch has become less and less . . . amenable . . . to requests from Guldor, and there are certain . . . commercial complications."

"You mean, all the manufactories Guldoran corporacions are building there?"

"Exactly."

"You and the First Marshal are only cordial?"

"You put it so politely, Steffan. Bernotte is politically adept in the military way. He was also a very effective battle group commander—some fifteen years ago, before the latest generation of ships and turbines."

"And he doubts that any mere seamen and petty officers can match the tactical and maneuvering abilities of the officers of the Imperial Navy of Guldor?"

"You *are* good," said Konnigsburg. "I heard him say something like that about the capabilities of the Polidoran Comity's navy, before several of their corvettes destroyed an entire Noldaran flotilla. Of course, that was before the Oligarch began to modernize his fleet." After a slight hesitation, Konnigsburg added, "The Imperador is quite fond of the First Marshal."

"You discovered that as the chief of Naval Intelligence?"

"I don't believe I ever said anything about that."

"You're an admiral. You were posted to Veerlyn. You heard that comment, *and* you doubtless warned Admiral Bernotte that the Polidoran Navy was better than its reputation. Although the name of the admiral in that position is never made public, it makes sense that you held the position." Dekkard decided to press a little harder, if politely. "Were you under consideration to be Bernotte's successor?"

Dekkard had always been curious about just where Konnigsburg had stood in the Admiralty, since the First Marshal was chosen by the Imperador and not by the Premier, the First Marshal being the only ministerial appointment granted to the Imperador by the Great Charter. The Imperador also chose the Fleet Marshal, the second-in-command of all Guldoran military forces. The only limitation was that any officer picked for either post could not serve for more than a total of nine years, the usual pattern being three years as Fleet Marshal before possibly being selected for six as First Marshal, although the Imperador or the Council could remove either at their pleasure, just not both in the same two-month period.

Dekkard paused as the server arrived with their meals. He had several mouthfuls of the soup while he waited for Konnigsburg to speak.

"As I've mentioned before, you would have done well in Naval Intelligence, Steffan," Konnigsburg said cheerfully, before taking a sip of his café.

"And you have a way of revealing matters without overtly doing so and while being able to deny doing so."

"One does learn a few things after thirty years in the Navy."

"I could check past records, but how much longer can the First Marshal theoretically remain in his present position?"

"A little more than two years, as I recall."

"What is your opinion of the Fleet Marshal?"

"From what I've seen, he will be appointed to succeed the First Marshal, and he will diligently continue policies similar to those of his predecessor."

"Unless something goes wrong or there's an inappropriate reaction to a situation?"

"That's a fair assumption, but the inappropriateness would have to be quite obvious."

The question that immediately came to Dekkard's mind was whether Konnigsburg had chosen to retire before he could be tied to a forthcoming inappropriate reaction or whether his retirement had been engineered or requested by the First Marshal or the Fleet Marshal.

Konnigsburg took several more spoonfuls of soup before he spoke. "You didn't ask what you were thinking."

"Because there was no appropriate way to ask it," replied Dekkard.

"You're also adept at asking questions without asking them."

"Only at times," replied Dekkard.

"I thought that resigning and hopefully becoming a councilor and possibly serving on the Military Affairs Committee would prove to be the best professional reaction to whatever disaster might be forthcoming. I did not foresee the New Meritorists, I must admit."

"I didn't, either," replied Dekkard, "but once I was tasked with looking into the Meritorists, I saw that the signs were all there. The previous Council shouldn't have been so surprised."

Konnigsburg raised his eyebrows. "What do you think were those signs?"

"Fieldworkers displaced by steam machinery, skilled crafters being replaced by cheaper manufacturing methods, the Council's growing disregard for worker safety, the destruction of small businesses by larger corporacions using unethical and often illegal means, the abuses of the Security Ministry's Special Agents, not to mention scandals like the Kraffeist Affair. There are others, but those are the ones that immediately come to mind."

Konnigsburg's soft laugh was ironic. "Those aren't signs that would come to the immediate attention of many councilors, especially Commercers and Landors. And none of them would seem that disturbing by itself, but together, especially with someone providing dunnite and expertise?" Konnigsburg shook his head.

"There was already a fair amount of expertise among the New Meritorists," Dekkard pointed out, "and more than a little anger about how little the Council seemed to care about the impact of its actions on those less fortunate."

"Such as?"

"The high tariffs on Sargassan swampgrass rice. Only two or three districts in all of Guldor raise rice, but that tariff increases food prices for everyone." Dekkard could also have mentioned military contracting, but after Mardosh's reaction, he decided not to.

"You don't ever bring up anything you haven't thought through, do you?" asked Konnigsburg.

"I often do, especially if I'm looking for information. No one knows everything. What about you?"

"A naval career leads one to focus on the relevant information, but too often apparent relevancy excludes pertinent information."

"I don't think that tendency is exclusive to the Navy," said Dekkard dryly.

"Unfortunately, neither do I," replied Konnigsburg, "nor to those overseeing the Navy."

Rather a backhanded way of suggesting it's a problem in the Military Affairs Committee. "Or to those involved with security," added Dekkard.

"You seemed to handle that well with the Security reforms."

"There were enough indisputable facts that connected the seemingly irrelevant to the perceived reality. In other areas, it's been harder, as I'm certain must be the case in naval and other military matters. Avraal has pointed out, more than once, that some people only see what they wish to see." *And not just family.*

"Emilya has offered similar counsel from the time I was a junior officer. There were definitely times when I should have listened more carefully."

"It was probably a good thing that we were a security team before we married. She was senior, and I had to listen. Eventually, I realized that was definitely a good thing."

From there the conversation was about wives and people, but Dekkard was left with the feeling that Konnigsburg hadn't grasped how big the "little" indications might turn out to be.

When Dekkard returned to the office, accompanied by Gaaroll, a stack of replies for him to sign or revise awaited him.

Avraal arrived in his personal office at a third past fourth bell.

Dekkard immediately stood, walked around the desk, and hugged her. "Is something wrong?"

"Not at all, but sometimes, I don't always show you how I look forward to seeing you . . . just seeing you."

"I'm glad." She held him to her for a long moment before stepping back, then watched as he went to retrieve his overcoat and gloves.

"How was your day?" he asked as he donned the overcoat.

"Nothing much new, except the air's gotten really bad. We haven't found any leads on the missing investigators, and the Advisory Committee told Carlos that they'll have to reduce his retainer beginning next month because guild dues payments are declining."

"That means more guilders are out of work, but that usually happens in the winter."

"Not this many, Carlos said."

"I take it that your pay will be reduced."

"I had to insist, but it wouldn't be fair otherwise."

"How much?"

"Fifteen percent for all the professionals. Five percent for the others. Carlos isn't saying, but I suspect he won't pay himself at all."

Dekkard turned off the wall sconce and motioned to the door, following Avraal out.

"Svard! Margrit, time to close up."

Dekkard did not move from where he stood beside Margrit's desk until only Svard and Gaaroll remained. "We'll wait out in the corridor for you, Svard."

The senior legalist grinned. "You aren't giving me any choice."

"I want you to have a bit of life besides here," replied Dekkard. "Not that I suspect you need much encouragement at present."

"It's good advice," added Avraal, "even if he doesn't always take it."

Dekkard heard a snicker from Gaaroll.

In minutes, the four were walking down the center staircase and toward the west doors.

Once Dekkard stepped out of the Council Office Building, he almost choked, so strong was the smoke and the acridity of the cold air. "You were right. Whatever's burning is more than coal from furnaces and boilers."

"More like a whole block," said Gaaroll.

"The wind's from the northeast," said Dekkard. "It could be from Woodlake or Easthill."

"You're assuming a poorer district is burning," said Avraal.

"That's a good assumption right now," Dekkard replied. "If things don't get better, it might not be." He turned to Roostof. "Be careful on the drive home. You're not that far from Rivertown."

"I'll be careful," replied Roostof, "but that goes for you as well."

The drive back to the house was without event, but when Dekkard eased the Gresynt into the drive, the garage doors were closed.

"Emrelda's working late," said Avraal.

"She still could be at the station because they sent patrollers to help other stations," Dekkard pointed out. "She's more valuable as a dispatcher when they're shorthanded."

"Let's hope you're right. The least we can do is fix dinner, even if it's leftovers."

"Your leftovers are better than most people's original dinners."

Avraal just shook her head as Dekkard stopped the Gresynt short of the garage, then got out and opened both doors. While the smoke and acridity that he smelled weren't as strong as they had been at the Council buildings, they were still much stronger than on previous days.

Avraal and Gaaroll walked back to the portico and let themselves into the house while Dekkard garaged the Gresynt. Then he closed the one garage door, leaving the other open for Emrelda, and made his way to the house, where he took off his overcoat and gloves, as well as his suit coat, before going to the kitchen to help Avraal fix dinner.

More than a bell passed before Dekkard heard the portico door open and then shut, followed by the words, "I'm home. Sorry I'm so late."

Dekkard let out a slow sigh of relief and followed Avraal out into the hall.

Emrelda looked at the three faces beholding her and said, "There's nothing to worry about here—or in Southtown. We had to send a squad to Woodlake to help with the riots, fires, and looting there. Captain Narryt said that the acting Minister of Public Safety requested two companies of army troopers."

"Not former STF, I hope," said Dekkard.

"I asked the same thing," replied Emrelda. "He said they were regular army because the STF troopers haven't finished retraining. They had to recruit more STF troopers because so many resigned."

That didn't exactly astound Dekkard. "So you ran the station while it was going on?"

"Pretty much. Administratively, that is. What's for dinner? It smells good."

"Assorted warmed-up leftovers," replied Avraal.

"It sounds wonderful. I'm starving."

"So are we all," replied Avraal, leading the way to the breakfast room.

25

DEKKARD woke at his normal time on Findi, knowing that Emrelda had duty as the head dispatcher, despite working the previous endday, because of the changes in shifts resulting from the riots in Woodlake, a fact she hadn't mentioned until after dinner the night before.

He was about to tiptoe to the shower when Avraal said, "Don't take all the warm water. I'll be up in a few minutes."

"I won't."

While Dekkard had doubts about Avraal getting up quickly, she was in the shower immediately after he left it. He did entertain certain thoughts, but she said, "Not now. It's too cold."

So Dekkard grinned sheepishly, finished getting dressed, then headed downstairs.

Emrelda sat at the breakfast table, in full uniform, except for her uniform jacket, sipping her café. She looked up and pointed to the morning *Gestirn*. "The captain didn't mention that there was more crap going on in Rivertown, not just in Woodlake."

"He might not have known."

"More like he was told not to say more than he had to. That doesn't happen as much now. Not after your reforms."

"Likely he couldn't avoid saying where your patrollers were sent, but not where those from other stations were headed. Someone above him is more than a little worried."

"They should be."

"How does the captain feel about it all?"

"He's gotten quiet. He's really worried. Who wouldn't be? We've barely been able to keep things under control in Southtown."

"Is there anything the Council can do?"

Emrelda shook her head. "More food and marks for the poorest would help some, but that's something the Council's never done. Another snowstorm might keep the violence down, but that will cause more deaths from the cold. Machtarn's not prepared for prolonged snow and cold. This is the longest freezing spell I can recall."

Dekkard had to agree, but he'd only been in Machtarn a little less than three years, unlike Emrelda's ten years. He also doubted that there was much more food to be had soon. Prolonged food shortages had never been a problem in recent years, not given how fertile much of Guldor was. So food wasn't really stockpiled to any degree, but the weather of the past year had been unusual, with frosts in the late spring, drought and then excessive rainfall, and early snows everywhere except in the far southwest. *So many talked about poor harvests, but you didn't realize just how bad they were.*

Emrelda stood and donned her uniform jacket. "Don't worry about dinner for me."

"Of course we will," interjected Avraal from the breakfast room door. "I'll do a hearty soup. That way it won't matter when you get home."

"So long as it's not leeks and beets," replied Emrelda with a smile.

Avraal walked to the portico door with her sister, and Dekkard began to fix cafés. After setting them on the table, while Avraal seated herself and began to sip from her mug, Dekkard picked up the morning edition of *Gestirn* and began to read about the riots, looting, and burning in Rivertown and Woodlake. From what he read, no one had determined a precise cause for either set of disturbances. *Suggesting that there's a great amount of unfocused anger.*

Dekkard wondered just how much of that was totally unrecognized by most councilors. *Most of it, in all probability.* Then he shook his head.

"What was that headshake all about?" asked Avraal.

"The Council. As I told you last night, Eyril Konnigsburg understands the danger the mutineers pose, but not the danger of hungry, angry, or desperate people."

"Do we, really?"

"I don't know what it's like to be in that position. I do realize that hundreds of thousands of people in that situation are a threat to the Council and to keeping order without having to use excessive force. I'm not sure that many councilors see it that way."

"Even after the shelling?"

"Too many think a few disgruntled revolutionaries got blown up in a badly organized plot to destroy the Council. They seem to have forgotten that the New Meritorists managed to destroy or damage sixteen Security buildings without anyone getting caught and have printed thousands and thousands of posters and broadsheets without being discovered."

"You've suggested that the New Meritorists used Ulrich and Minz, and I'd agree. Are they still using Ulrich?" There was a trace of skepticism behind Avraal's words.

"I doubt it. Shelling the Council had to go beyond what Ulrich had in mind, and Minz let his personal anger get in the way. If I had to wager,

Ulrich has destroyed every bit of evidence that he can get his hands on. The problem is that what Minz did revealed some real Council vulnerabilities. Hasheem and Trujillo are dealing with the physical vulnerabilities, but no one's dealing with the others."

"You did with the Security reforms, and you're working on others."

"I worry that I can't get them through the Council and that, even if I can, they'll be too little and too late."

"You're only one councilor—"

"You've made that point before. And you're right. But it still bothers me."

"It can bother you," replied Avraal firmly, "just so long as you don't take on the responsibility and weight of the whole Council. Especially when you've done your best to let others know. You just may have to avoid the damage and let the others see for themselves. In the meantime, we can do things together today." Her last words were resolutely cheerful.

"Like make a hearty soup?"

She smiled. "Along with a few other . . . diversions."

Dekkard couldn't help smiling in return.

26

WHEN Dekkard opened his eyes in the dim gloom on Unadi morning, he could immediately smell that, despite the closed and curtained windows, the odor of burning substances in addition to coal had not only continued, but increased. That wasn't unexpected, not after Emrelda's report the night before that disturbances had been reported in not only Rivertown and Woodlake, but in Easthill, and that matters weren't that much better in Southtown.

Yet when Dekkard reached the breakfast room, the morning edition of *Gestirn* only had a short article, which he reread after getting Avraal's café for her—just to make sure he'd read it correctly the first time, but the significant information was contained in one paragraph.

> . . . continuing and unexpected cold weather has resulted in a number of dwelling fires all across Machtarn, but primarily in the more densely populated areas, where firefighters and civic patrollers have been hampered by crowds of displaced persons and by a lack of water pressure caused by frozen pipes and leakages . . . According to city records this is the longest period of cold weather in Machtarn in over a century . . .

Without a word, Dekkard just handed the newssheet to Avraal to see what she had to say.

After a minute or so she handed it back. "That's about what Emrelda said. Unless it warms up, the problems with fires and crowds are going to get worse."

"It's colder out," said Gaaroll. "Leastwise, it felt that way when Emrelda left."

"We'll have to see what the day brings." *And if Hasheem has any plans for dealing with it all.*

He quickly went through the rest of the newssheet and discovered a story about the *Khuld,* the key section of which read:

> The Admiralty has so far refused to comment on the possibility that the light cruiser I.S. *Khuld,* which was scheduled for a refit at Port Reale, may indeed have been lost at sea. Other sources indicate that some of

the crewmen have been returned to Port Reale after being rescued. The Admiralty has refused comment . . .

Dekkard doubted that the mutiny would remain undisclosed much longer.

When he went out to light off the Gresynt, he paused outside the portico door and looked south, toward the ocean. Besides the haze and smoke, definitely stronger and more acrid than they had been on Findi night, he thought there were either low-lying clouds or banks of fog and sea mist over the water, but with the hampered visibility that was as much guess as calculation.

But the Khuld *should be close to Point Larmat by now, unless the* Resolute *and her battle group have been successful.*

Then he heard a screeching, possibly of brakes, and then more crunching sounds. Suspecting that he knew the cause, he still walked partway down the drive, far enough to ascertain that at least three steamers were smashed together in the middle of the intersection between Jacquez and Florinda.

Gaaroll immediately appeared. "What happened?"

"An accident on Jacquez. The steamers are jammed together, but not totally wrecked. What do you sense?"

"Doesn't feel like anyone's seriously hurt. Two people—men, I'd guess—are pretty angry, though."

Dekkard studied the accident, but it appeared that, despite all the arguing, no one seemed to be injured—and no one was even looking in his direction. Still . . . "Nincya, is anyone headed this way that we can't see?"

"No, sir. Not so far."

"Keep sensing while I get the Gresynt ready."

As he walked up the drive to the garage, Dekkard wondered if he might be overcautious. *But after all that's happened . . .*

Although neither Avraal nor Gaaroll sensed anything presaging danger, Dekkard wasn't about to tempt fate. So, after he drove down the drive, he turned west on Florinda and wound his way to Imperial Boulevard along the back streets on the north side of Imperial University.

He'd only been driving north on the boulevard for three blocks when Gaaroll said, "Lots of really, really strong emotions up ahead, especially to the left."

"How far away? Can you tell?"

"Hard to tell, sir. Might be half a mille, or if it's really strong, a mille."

Dekkard glanced to the northwest, but the combination of smoke and haze, and possibly even fog, made it impossible for him to tell if there was some sort of conflagration in the direction of Rivertown. "Just let me know."

While the traffic wasn't that heavy, Dekkard eased into the right lane, so that he could turn off Imperial to the east if the boulevard turned out to be blocked farther north, although the steamers and lorries ahead of him were moving at close to normal speed. He'd driven about another half mille when the steamers in front of him began to slow.

"Strong feelings moving east. Not quite straight ahead," said Gaaroll. "Might be on the west side of the boulevard."

Even before Gaaroll finished speaking, Dekkard turned, barely squeezing the Gresynt between the steamer coming to a stop in front of him and a delivery lorry, then going halfway onto the sidewalk for a good ten yards before turning onto a side way, one he hoped wasn't a dead end, at least not until he could reach a cross street.

"I can even sense those feelings," declared Avraal, "and they have to be more than a fifth of a mille away."

"People are getting hurt," said Gaaroll. "Maybe shot."

Dekkard kept the Gresynt moving eastward along the narrow street. "Are we gaining on those strong feelings?"

"So far," said Gaaroll.

The next cross street looked to be wider, and Dekkard turned north again, paralleling Imperial Boulevard. There was some traffic, but not a great deal, and Dekkard understood why when it ended at Justiciary Avenue. He glanced to his left, where he saw a line of patroller lorries blocking the avenue.

"The feelings are building up on the other side of the lorries," declared Gaaroll. "So many, has to be a mob."

"We'll see how it looks on Council Avenue," said Dekkard, turning east on Justiciary and accelerating to the next cross street, which he took to Council Avenue. Again, he looked west, where he saw another line of vehicles, but they looked to be Army lorries. He turned east on Council Avenue, but then had to slow as he neared the Council buildings because the new iron gates across the avenue were closed except in one place.

"I don't think you're going to work today," Dekkard said wryly as he brought the steamer to a halt before the gates.

"I hadn't noticed," Avraal replied sardonically.

The Council Guards checked the bumper emblem, looked at Dekkard, and then motioned him through. Only the main entrance to the covered parking was open, and there were three guards there, one of whom motioned for him to lower the window. Dekkard did.

"Councilor?"

Dekkard turned so that the guard could see his pin.

"Thank you, sir."

After Dekkard eased the Gresynt to a stop in his parking place, he raised the window, and looked to his left. The pedestrian gate was still open, if with two guards flanking it. He couldn't help wondering how many councilors and staffers wouldn't make it to work. *More likely staffers won't be here because most councilors live to the south and east.* But then Ingrella might have been caught in the traffic, unless she'd left even earlier.

"What's your feeling about being here or heading back home?" Dekkard asked.

"What's yours?" Avraal countered.

"We're safer from mobs here than at home, and we won't have patrollers and troopers protecting us at home."

"You're being logical, rather than feeling," replied Avraal, "but your logic and my feelings agree."

Dekkard made sure to lock the steamer, although he thought that the Army and the iron gates and fencing around the Council buildings would pose enough of a barrier that it was unlikely that the mob would get any farther. But, given the strength of the feelings that Avraal and Gaaroll had sensed, he had a sick feeling that the only question would be not whether there were casualties, but how many.

As the three walked through the pedestrian gate and across the drive to the Council Office Building, Dekkard said, "Does either of you sense how many demonstrators there are?"

"It's more than I've sensed in previous demonstrations, but how many exactly I couldn't tell," replied Avraal.

"Thousands, anyway," added Gaaroll.

Dekkard glanced toward the iron gates across the avenue, but he didn't hear or see any sign of demonstrators. He glanced up to the roof of the Council Office Building. There were definitely more guards there, in and around the new sentry boxes, and they carried rifles.

Once they were inside the building, Dekkard saw that there were fewer staffers in the main corridor, but not that many fewer.

"How are people feeling?" he asked Avraal quietly when they neared the central staircase.

"Some are nervous, as you'd expect. Some are undisturbed, but they may not know yet."

Dekkard could believe that, given that he hadn't been able to see or hear anything, and he'd known about the demonstrators, or what Gaaroll suggested was a massive mob.

Because Dekkard knew that Roostof, Margrit, and Bretta all lived to the west of Imperial Boulevard, when he entered the office he was relieved to see both Roostof and Margrit standing by the door to his personal office. "I'm glad you two are here. Did either of you have any trouble?"

"We didn't, but Bretta said she caught the last omnibus," replied Roostof. "She thought it was the last, anyway, because she could see the mob coming a block or so away."

"The Premier sent a notice warning about possible demonstrators," added Margrit. "It suggested that staff remain inside until the situation is resolved."

"What do you know, sir?" asked Roostof.

"The patrollers and Army units have blocked Justiciary and Council Avenues, and the Council Guard has closed the new gates across Council Avenue and has guards with rifles posted on the roof." After a moment, Dekkard asked, "Is there anything else new here besides the warning and the messages?"

"You do have a lot of mail," said Margrit. "That includes some letters delayed by last week's storm, by their postmarks, and there is a packet and report from Zenya Onswyrth."

"Let's see what the messages have to say." Dekkard opened the first. "There's an emergency meeting of the Council at fourth bell. So, the other must be a notice of a Security Committee meeting." He opened the second. "It's at third bell." That was just two-thirds of a bell away.

Dekkard had no doubt that the mob would be dispersed. The cost was another question, but unfettered populism, whether by mob rule, or even by direct representation and personal accountability, was no way to govern an empire or country. *Even if the anger represented by mobs is understandable and partially justified.*

"What do you think will happen, sir?" asked Margrit.

"If the crowds don't settle down and disperse, people will be shot. How many depends on whether they listen to the patrollers and Army and how violent the crowds are."

Dekkard motioned for Avraal to accompany him into his personal office. She closed the door, and he took off his overcoat and hung it up, then asked, "What do you think?"

"They shouldn't be shot."

"I don't think the patrollers or the Army want to do that. That's why they have lorries blocking the avenue, but we also can't let them rampage and destroy everything that's in their way. Who knows how many shops have already been looted? Once it gets to that point, how else can you stop them? The shop owners aren't to blame for their problems. Neither is the present Council. But they're hungry. They don't see things getting better soon, and they're angry. The Commercers created this mess, and the blame will end up on us."

"Hasn't Hasheem been able to find out anyone in the New Meritorists he—or you—could talk to?"

"Not that I'm aware of. Carlos would be more likely to discover someone like that, or maybe even Guard Captain Trujillo, but I don't see that talking is going to help so long as they want to dismantle the structure of government. There has to be another force for reason out there, and I don't see it."

"Why don't we create it?" asked Avraal quietly. "You speak well, and I can help convince people. Gaaroll can watch out for danger. Emrelda might be able to point to the less dangerous venues."

"What? Put on a false beard and old grays and preach in the less frequented squares?"

"A well-trimmed and stylish beard, not gray. Maybe auburn, and you'd need a matching wig. I do like the idea of plain grays."

"Even the four of us can't create a movement all that quickly."

"You don't have to. Just the illusion of something bigger. That might get the attention of the New Meritorists—*and* they might just want to talk, to join forces."

"More likely they'll want to eliminate me as quickly as possible."

"You don't stay in one place very long. Keep moving and persuading people."

"That could be dangerous."

"More dangerous than allowing the New Meritorists to grow into an even stronger revolutionary movement?"

"As always, you have a point." He paused. "We need to think about just how to do this, and we'll need catchy phrases and slogans and a name."

"You're very good with those, dear. Think about it. *Now* I'm going to wander around the building for a few minutes. I'll be back in time to accompany you to the committee meeting."

Dekkard sat down behind his desk. *Do you really want to foment another aspect of revolution, even if it's an illusion? Even for a good cause? Don't the New Meritorists think their cause is good?*

After a time, he took a deep breath and looked at the letters neatly stacked and waiting. He decided to begin with Zenya Onswyrth's report, which listed the concerns of the eight people who'd stopped by the office. Five of them wanted to know what Dekkard was doing about food shortages and higher prices. In addition to that, three of the five thought that postal charges were too high, which was why they were complaining in person.

Two others wanted the Council to use more force and put down the New Meritorists for good. One wanted the Council to look into the "exorbitant" freight charges of Guldoran Ironway.

Hrald Iglis had stopped by to leave a message that the kitchen work was coming, but slower than planned because of the snow. The last note was that Jens Seigryn had apparently vanished, sometime during the big storm, according to Namoor Desharra.

Vanished? Dekkard couldn't help but think about what Gretna Haarl had said, that Dekkard wasn't to do anything with regard to Jens unless she contacted him.

He shook his head, wondering if Jens had really disappeared, but he had the feeling that the disappearance was likely to be permanent, especially after what Julian Baurett had revealed. *But with what the* Tribune *has been publishing, they could make some nasty insinuations, especially if Jens shows up dead.*

But Dekkard couldn't do anything about Jens. *Except worry.*

So, after finishing Zenya Onswyrth's report, Dekkard started reading the letters. Most contained subjects with which he was becoming all too familiar: high food prices, more than shortages, which wasn't unexpected because those who wrote could afford pens, paper, and postage; prices of coal and kerosene; the New Meritorists, and particularly why the Council didn't just get rid of them all; the unfair pricing of produce rates by the ironways; and the failure of the Council to build more river levees. A few letters asked why the Council didn't just make councilors' votes public, since it shouldn't be that big a problem.

When Dekkard carried the letters out to Roostof, he saw Avraal and Gaaroll quietly talking, but he didn't ask until he came back into the front area. "Something I should know?"

"We'll tell you on the walk to the Security Committee meeting."

"Let me get my overcoat."

Once the three were walking toward the center staircase, Avraal said, "Nincya's fairly certain that quite a few protestors were shot. She sensed the feelings and deaths."

"Scores? Or hundreds?"

"Felt like hundreds, sir. Couldn't tell how many wounded or died."

"Is it still going on?"

"Not now. Stopped about a third ago."

"Are there any other strong feelings near? I mean scores, not a few."

"No, sir."

"That means that either the protestors tried to attack the patrollers and Army, and they shot the attackers, or the protestors wouldn't disperse and the Army shot them to disperse the crowd." Neither possibility was good, but from what he'd observed over the past months, Dekkard didn't think the patrollers would open fire unless attacked. "I'll hear what the Premier has to say, either in the committee meeting or in the Council meeting."

When the three stepped out into the courtyard, Dekkard saw several other councilors ahead of him—Breffyn Haastar and Kharl Navione, Tomas Pajiin with someone Dekkard didn't recognize from behind, and Villem Baar. None of them looked back as they walked swiftly through the bitter winter wind.

Villem Baar, however, stood outside the committee room, clearly waiting for Dekkard, who stepped away from Avraal and Gaaroll to talk with him.

"Both your personal and professional security aides, I see," said Baar quietly.

"They insisted, after the mass of protestors headed toward the Council."

"I got here before they closed off the avenues." Baar paused, then added, "I saw Eyril Konnigsburg this morning. He was rather . . . preoccupied."

"Did he say why?" asked Dekkard, even though he suspected he knew the reason.

"Not really. He said something about Chairman Mardosh not understanding, but that he couldn't go into it."

"Like the Security Committee, some matters have to stay within each committee."

"What do you think about Mardosh?"

"Having Siincleer Shipbuilding in his district presents a problem for him and the Military Affairs Committee."

"It's probably better that I'm not on that committee."

"You have fewer conflicts that way." *Considering that Suvion Industries is likely the largest corporacion in your district.* "We probably ought to go in now. The chairman won't be in the greatest of moods."

Dekkard and Baar had just seated themselves when Rikkard hurried into the chamber.

Hasheem immediately gaveled the committee to order, then said, "Most of you doubtless noticed the gates and guards this morning. For those of you who are not aware, a large, unruly, and sometimes violent mob that had gathered in Rivertown decided to march on the Council. There was considerable breakage of display windows and looting along the way . . ."

The fact that the marchers had walked the more than five milles from Rivertown to a point close to the Council buildings both amazed and concerned Dekkard.

". . . when they reached the barriers set up by the patrollers and the Army, the protestors refused to disperse. More than a score of individuals within the mob then opened fire on the patrollers and the Army. The patrollers and troopers returned fire. They tried to limit fire to the areas from which shots had come, but obviously others in the mob were hurt, at times fatally. After less than a sixth, the mob dispersed in disarray . . . the number of casualties exceeded a hundred, and there are more than twenty deaths . . .

"In addition, while the mob was forming early this morning, the New Meritorists made another raid on the Guldoran Ironway terminal market here in Machtarn using three stolen lorries. The lorries transported stolen produce and other food items to Southtown and Woodlake, where they were abandoned.

"The Army now has a regiment on the streets in Machtarn, and another regiment has been moved here and is being held in reserve."

As Hasheem finished summarizing the follow-up to the morning catastrophe, Dekkard knew that there was something odd about it all, something that linked in to what Avraal had proposed earlier that morning. He forced his concentration back to Hasheem.

"The Navy has no more reports about the *Khuld*'s location. Locating the cruiser has proved difficult largely because of patches of heavy fog along the coast and immediately offshore from Paelart all the way northeast to Machtarn and east from there as far as Ondeliew. The *Resolute* and its battle group have moved closer to Machtarn to deny access to the capital."

When Hasheem finished, he asked, "Are there any questions?"

"Yes, Sr. Chairman," answered Navione. "Is there anything linking the mob's movement toward the Council to the New Meritorists?"

"Why should that matter?" interjected Rikkard. "They're both lawbreakers."

Navione shot a withering glance at Rikkard, who ignored it.

"At present, neither the patrollers nor the Palace Guards are aware of any linkage," replied Hasheem.

"What about any linkage to disturbances in Woodlake, Easthill, or Southtown?" asked Navione.

"So far there appear to be none," Hasheem said calmly.

"Thank you, Sr. Chairman."

"Have any of the New Meritorist demonstrations involved looting?" asked Breffyn Haastar.

"Not that we're aware of, although there might be minor incidents that were never brought to the attention of the Ministry of Public Safety."

Dekkard saw what the two Landor councilors were establishing, but since neither one seemed to want to ask the last question, he cleared his throat and then said, "So this is the only time that crowds from a disturbance have left the general area of the disturbance?"

"To date," replied Hasheem.

"Thank you, Sr. Chairman." Dekkard didn't need any more questions, because he now knew why he'd felt there was something missing from Avraal's earlier suggestion.

"When will we know more about that cruiser?" asked Rikkard.

"Given the weather, we don't know," Hasheem replied.

"And we're supposed to accept that?"

"Councilor," replied Hasheem wearily, "the Council controls neither the weather nor the mutineers. There being no more relevant questions, the committee is recessed until further notice." He rapped the gavel once, then stood and strode from the committee chamber.

"He wasn't happy with Rikkard," said Pajiin quietly as he rose from his seat beside Dekkard.

"Would you be?" asked Dekkard wryly.

"Not when he has to deal with unhappy angry poor workers on one hand and smart-assed rebels on the other and Rikkard can't tell the difference between the two." Pajiin shook his head. "I'll see you on the floor."

"Until then."

When Dekkard left the committee chamber, Avraal looked at him inquiringly.

"I'll tell you most of what Hasheem said on the way to the councilors' lobby." Dekkard mentioned what Hasheem said about the morning demonstration, except for the last few questions. He did not mention the *Khuld*. When they reached the lobby entrance, he finished by saying, "I'll tell you the rest later. The session won't be long, and we can have an early lunch, if that's all right."

"What if I meet you in the dining room?"

"I'll be there," agreed Dekkard.

A handful of councilors lingered in the lobby, including three Crafters that Dekkard barely knew—Lewell Contiago from Devult, Leister Milyaard from Nuile, and Paarkyn Noyell from Oost. Milyaard and Noyell had backed Mardosh for premier. Contiago hadn't, and Dekkard had wondered why. He smiled and nodded politely before making his way to the floor, where he found Ingrella Obreduur already at her desk.

"Good morning, Steffan."

"The same to you. Did you come in early this morning or did you have to avoid the demonstrators?"

"Neither. I don't like taking Imperial Boulevard, but I did come in a bit earlier. There's still so much that I have to catch up on."

"Your instincts are good. You missed an accident on Jacquez that happened as we left, not to mention the mobs that blocked Imperial Boulevard, as well as Justiciary and Council Avenues."

"So I heard."

"Are you free for an early lunch?"

"You're kind to ask, Steffan, but I already agreed to lunch with Erskine Mardosh."

Dekkard raised his eyebrows.

"I'm well aware of your concerns, and I share them, but the lunch will be pleasant, and I might even learn something."

"You might," Dekkard agreed pleasantly.

Ingrella smiled. "We'll see."

Moments later, the chime rang, and the lieutenant-at-arms thumped his staff, announcing the beginning of the session.

Hasheem only waited until the chamber quieted before beginning to speak. What he said about the mob was almost identical to what he had said before the Security Committee. Then he said, "The other matter of which you should be aware is the situation involving the light cruiser *Khuld*. The newssheets have reported that the cruiser is missing at sea and may be lost. That might be true. Unfortunately what initially occurred aboard the *Khuld* was somewhat different. On Unadi the thirteenth of Winterend, after the ship docked in Port Reale and half the crew and officers were given leave, the remaining crew mutinied and took over the vessel. The mutineers immediately put to sea, stopping only at a civilian coaling station outside the port of Zeiryn. The last confirmed sighting of the *Khuld* was offshore of Surpunta. The Admiralty has deployed a battle group headed by the dreadnought *Resolute* to deal with the *Khuld,* should it approach Machtarn."

To Dekkard, Hasheem's announcement in open session of the Council meant that the newssheets already knew the story and that there was little point in further attempts at suppression.

"The Admiralty believes, but cannot confirm, agents of the New Meritorists led the mutineers. Both the Admiralty and the Ministry of Public Safety have launched even wider investigations of the New Meritorists. In the meantime, the Council will resume its normal order of business." Hasheem paused. "The Council will be informed of any new developments as they can be verified." Hasheem looked to Haarsfel, who moved to the lectern.

"There being no other business, the Council is hereby recessed until further notice, but no later than Quindi the twenty-ninth of Winterend."

Dekkard stood and looked to Ingrella. "Do you think he should have said more?"

"He didn't have to. Everyone will know the rest in a bell."

In short, he should have. Dekkard smiled. "You didn't answer my question."

"You know the answer as well as I do, Steffan. Each premier has to do as he believes is the most practical and useful."

Whether it really is right or the best for Guldor.

The muttered conversations scattered across the chamber floor also told Dekkard that Hasheem had withheld the information about the *Khuld* far too long, but after Hasheem had cut Dekkard off earlier on that matter, Dekkard had been reluctant to bring it up again. He also had the feeling, based on his earlier conversation with Eyril Konnigsburg, that Hasheem had deferred, unwisely, to First Marshal Bernotte.

Dekkard eased his way to the councilors' dining room by the passage off the floor that led directly there.

Avraal was alone at a table when Dekkard appeared and sat down across from her.

"What happened?"

Dekkard told her, including Ingrella's response and her lunch meeting with Mardosh.

"You don't have to worry about how she handles herself with Mardosh," said Avraal.

"I still worry, and you know why."

"The last thing Mardosh wants to talk about is anything involving Siincleer Shipbuilding, and Ingrella won't talk about it unless it would have him admitting bribery and treason."

Dekkard thought as much, but that didn't lessen his worry.

"What else is on your mind?—Hold that thought for a moment." Avraal smiled pleasantly as a server arrived, then said, "The onion soup, with café, please."

"I'll have the same," added Dekkard, since he wasn't that hungry, and the onion soup was the least filling item on the menu, even with the melted cheese.

Once the server departed, Avraal asked, "What were you about to say?"

"During the committee meeting, I realized something that had been gnawing at me, but I hadn't quite put it together. As Tomas put it after the meeting, we have on one hand poor, starving, and angry people in dismal areas and, on the other hand, smart-ass rebels who are better off and clearly better educated. Two totally different groups. And, until this morning, none of the unrest in Easthill and the other places left those areas. Why, suddenly, did all those people march almost five milles to the Council? In this cold? I don't think it was coincidence."

"You think that the New Meritorists brought in some empies and a handful of armed men, and used the empies to channel that anger, and then the armed Meritorists shot at the patrollers and Army troopers?"

"I do, and I'll bet that they shot from shielded places to the sides or farther back."

"And in a while, they'll do it again," suggested Avraal.

"You can't have a revolution without more angry people than the Meritorists have, even with the expanded capabilities that Ulrich and Minz provided. That also means that in our little scheme I need to talk in places where New Meritorists can be found, squares and corners near café shops and bistros."

"You still think we should?"

"We need to do something before the New Meritorists can create too many more opportunities for massacres." Dekkard paused as he saw Ingrella and Erskine Mardosh enter the dining room. "We can talk about details later."

Avraal just nodded. "It's a little warmer out now. I checked while you were in Council."

"That's still colder than usual." Dekkard lowered his voice. "Speaking of cold, Zenya Onswyrth's weekly report said that Jens Seigryn has been missing since the big storm."

"I don't mind that he's missing," replied Avraal, "but if he turns up dead, that could pose a definite problem."

"Exactly. A little more than three weeks since we left Gaarlak, after Jens's attempts to undermine me, he vanishes. Especially since he wanted to be selected as councilor, and too many people are suspicious about how I was chosen."

"No matter how it turns out, you didn't do whatever happened."

"But some people will think that, and it will be another unlikely event connected to the questionable Councilor Dekkard, one that *The Machtarn Tribune* will certainly find a way to publicize."

The rest of lunch, and, indeed, the rest of the day in Dekkard's office, was, at least, uneventful.

27

D EKKARD did not bring up his other concerns to Avraal until well after dinner that evening and once they had retired to their rather chilly second-floor bedroom.

"You've been preoccupied all evening," said Avraal.

"I've been thinking about your idea," said Dekkard. "Wouldn't Carlos have a good idea of café shops and tavernas that disgruntled university graduates and others who can't get positions they think they should have might frequent? You could ask him, couldn't you?"

"I thought of that. He probably does." Avraal's tone conveyed a certain concern. "What plausible reason would I give him?"

"Tell him that neither the Ministry of Public Safety nor the Justiciary Ministry is having any luck in uncovering any New Meritorists, and that your dear husband is under a certain amount of pressure to offer suggestions because of my past semi-successes. Also tell him he doesn't have to offer judgments on which establishments might be most likely."

"I suppose . . ."

"Dear, we don't have a lot of time, and researching that on our own increases the chances of being discovered. Emrelda will know the ones near her station, but we can't confine our efforts to an area near us."

"That's true." Avraal paused. "We'll have to borrow his undercover Ferrum, too. Either of the Gresynts would be far too conspicuous. He'll be suspicious, but I can tell him that we'll be doing some scouting and that the Gresynt is too obvious."

"That's the best we can do with that," agreed Dekkard. "What about clothing? I'd thought of wearing old, almost worn-out grays, with that beat-up jacket I use for dirty outside chores, and I certainly have plenty of old gloves."

"You'll need more of a disguise than that."

"How about a red wig and beard? Blond would be too obviously a disguise."

Avraal smiled. "Red, even mahogany, would be better."

"We'll also need a hand-painted sign with a simple message."

"That's your job," she said with a smile. "That, and whatever simplistic patter you intend to prate."

"Simplistic, but it has to mean something to people, and it also needs to annoy the New Meritorists."

"That sounds like you want to make yourself a target."

"If I'm not regarded as at least a minor threat, they won't even bother to investigate," Dekkard pointed out.

"And when they do?"

"That's when you signal for us to vanish before they get there."

"If we don't see them, how will we be able to identify them or track them?"

"We can't afford to get involved directly too soon. I'm hoping we can get some mention in the newssheets first."

"If you don't want to get shot, we'll have to bring Gaaroll in. I can't sense a shooter from that far."

"You're right, but I'd like to try out what we're doing once or twice before that, to test what we're trying before we work in a third person."

"Once. Only once."

"Once," Dekkard agreed.

"I'll take care of the wig and beard. No one thinks about women shopping for hair accessories."

Dekkard had to agree with that.

28

DUADI dawned slightly warmer than previous days, and the slight warming brought even more haze, although the smoke seemed less severe to Dekkard. The *Gestirn* article about Unadi's disturbance was moderately restrained, suggesting that the unrest had been stirred up by agitators not from the Rivertown community and that the Ministry of Public Safety was investigating.

With the city seemingly quieter, Dekkard turned the Gresynt over to Avraal at the Council Office Building, and she headed back south to work. Dekkard and Gaaroll walked swiftly to the office, but there was only one message—from Hasheem as chairman of the Security Committee announcing that a hearing on port security had been rescheduled for Furdi at the fourth morning bell. Dekkard didn't recall such a hearing ever being scheduled, and when he checked the message file, he couldn't find any record, except for one back in Fallend where the security director of the Treasury Ministry testified about foreign powers' attempts to use vessels from other countries to smuggle spies into Guldoran ports.

Had Hasheem promised to hold a hearing and forgotten to schedule it? Or is something else going on?

Since Dekkard couldn't do anything about it, he made sure the hearing was on his calendar and went to work reading the incoming mail, finding nothing unusual. *But then most people's concerns and problems with government tend to be predictable after a while.*

If they weren't, Dekkard had discovered, that meant larger issues were at stake.

After dealing with the incoming mail, he spent some time trying to write phrases and slogans he could use in his coming evening "appearances" across Machtarn. The remainder of the day was routine, although Dekkard kept wondering where the *Khuld* might be, and whether he'd been totally mistaken when he'd suggested to Hasheem that the cruiser might target the Council buildings or the Palace of the Imperador.

Avraal walked into Dekkard's personal office at a third past fourth bell, offering a warm and cheerful smile.

"You look happy," said Dekkard.

"I've been shopping for us. How has your day been?"

"Quietly routine. Which my days will likely be until, suddenly, they aren't."

"How long before that happens?"

"I have no idea. I'd guess we have a few weeks, but that might just be wistful thinking. Or it could be longer."

"Various additional disturbances will start shortly. Major disruptions will come later." Avraal paused. "Are you ready to leave?"

"Absolutely." Dekkard stood and went to get his overcoat, donned it, picked up his leather folder, and turned off the wall lamp before following Avraal out of his personal office.

Dekkard could tell that Roostof and Margrit were both ready to close the office, because Roostof had everything shut down and locked up almost as soon as Margrit, Gaaroll, Avraal, and Dekkard were out in the main corridor.

Dekkard refrained from asking Roostof if his haste had anything to do with Bettina Safaell, although he did smile at the thought. Avraal had also smiled when Roostof had hurried out the door, offered a pleasant, "Have a good evening," and then hurried toward the central staircase.

When Dekkard, Avraal, and Gaaroll reached the Gresynt, Gaaroll settled into the second seat, then looked behind her at the bags and packages in the rear seat. "What's all this stuff for?"

"Steffan and I need to do some reconnaissance of sorts," replied Avraal, "and he's far too distinctive in his normal attire."

"What about you? You're not invisible."

"You're right. That's why I'll be wearing what looks like it once might have been a messenger boy's uniform—without identifying patches."

"What about me?"

"After the first trial reconnaissance, you'll be coming too, but you'll need to wear some of your old clothes."

"I only kept the best ones."

"They'll do fine, especially with that old cap. I'd wager you kept it."

"Had it a long time." After a pause, Gaaroll asked warily, "What kind of reconnaissance?"

"You'll see," replied Avraal cheerfully. "Once we're ready."

"Last time you said that someone died."

"We're not planning on anything like that," said Dekkard.

"Unless someone attacks you, you mean?"

"The idea is to use disguises so that no one feels the need to attack," replied Dekkard.

"Been real successful at that, haven't you, sir?" asked Gaaroll sarcastically.

"That's why you'll be with us after the first trial."

Gaaroll snorted quietly.

Dekkard was pleasantly surprised to see that Emrelda was actually home when he headed up the drive, and relieved, because that suggested matters in Southtown hadn't gotten any worse.

Dekkard and Gaaroll helped Avraal carry in the various packages from the rear seat of the Gresynt and put them on the desk in the study, then washed up and got ready for dinner, which turned out to be chicken milanesia. Dekkard enjoyed every bite.

Once the three cleaned up after dinner, Emrelda said, "I saw you carrying packages into the study."

"You don't miss much," said Avraal, "even when you're not looking. You never did, though."

Emrelda laughed softly. "That's not an answer."

"Some items to help disguise us. Steffan has to do some reconnaissance and deliver a few messages."

"No one else can do it?"

Avraal shook her head. "Not this time, but I'd hoped you'd help with the disguises."

"So long as I don't have to be the one disguised."

Avraal led the way into the study. "Steffan graduated from the Military Institute, no matter what clothes he wears. So I thought these might help." As Avraal spoke, she extracted a reddish mahogany wig and beard from one of the bags. "Most of the other beard shades would have looked too false."

And mahogany doesn't? Dekkard decided not to voice that thought.

"You should try them on." Avraal's words were not a suggestion.

Dekkard had to struggle some with the wig, but did get it on correctly, or so he thought.

Avraal shook her head. "The idea is *not* to look like you're wearing a wig."

In the end, both Emrelda and Avraal worked on adapting the wig so that it fit snugly.

"That looks much better," declared Emrelda. "Now let's see how the beard looks."

"How does it attach?" asked Dekkard.

"With spirit gum adhesive," said Emrelda. "For right now, just hold it in place, Avraal."

Avraal did so.

Emrelda looked at Dekkard, then shook her head. "Your skin tone doesn't quite go with the hair and beard. We'll have to adjust that. I'll be back in just a moment."

In less than three minutes, Emrelda appeared with a small case, which she set on the side of the desk. She studied whatever was in the case, then nodded. "I think this foundation will do. It's got a matte finish. He'll need a touch of red in his eyebrows, too. Turn your head a bit, Steffan. I'm just going to apply a bit to your cheek to see how it looks."

Dekkard just followed directions, for what seemed a good bell but turned out to be little more than a sixth when Avraal looked to her sister and said, "That works."

"That's the number two for the foundation."

Dekkard listened carefully as Emrelda went over the procedure with Avraal, but hoped he didn't have to remember the steps.

Then Avraal turned to him. "Tonight, you can just wipe that bit off your cheek, and wash it, but when we do your full face you'll need to wipe it all off with a damp cloth, and then go over it with oil before washing your face. Otherwise, you'll have problems with your skin, and you'll be uncomfortable. Also, the wrong people might ask questions."

"I'll keep that very much in mind." Dekkard knew that if he didn't Avraal certainly would.

Emrelda replaced everything in the case and turned to Avraal. "You might as well keep this for now."

"Thank you. We'll be needing it for a while. Can we put everything in the top of the study closet?"

"That's as good a place as any," said Emrelda. "I'll see you all in the morning. The last week has been long."

"Good night," added Gaaroll, following Emrelda out of the study.

After Dekkard and Avraal stored everything in the closet, and they were alone in the study, he smiled and said, "I didn't ask when you showed up with that theatrical kohl. I won't ask now, but it would be nice to know."

"You ask without asking so carefully, dear."

"You told me not to ask. So I didn't."

"A statement can still be a question," said Avraal, if with the hint of a smile. "So I'll give you a question that you can answer for yourself . . . silently . . . and only to yourself. That will be as much as I feel comfortable revealing."

"You don't have to—"

"With your complex mind, you could easily imagine far worse. Now, for that question." Avraal frowned.

Dekkard waited.

"Has it not occurred to you that there might be occasions where a woman patroller might be required to pose as a different type of professional in order to apprehend a criminal in a fashion that involved far less danger to other patrollers, and that it might take a certain presence to do so without personal compromise?" As she finished speaking, Avraal laid her finger across his lips. "Not a word about it, please."

Dekkard nodded, then smiled wryly. "You both continue to amaze me."

She smiled warmly. "Good."

29

TRIDI wasn't that much different from Duadi, as far as Dekkard's day went, except that there was a pro forma Council session, and a long afternoon hearing before the Workplace Administration Committee, where guild officials from Guldoran Ironworks testified about the various shortcomings in machinery and safety procedures.

Dekkard initially wondered why Haarsfel had requested testimony from guilds at Guldoran Ironworks, rather than Kathaar Iron & Steel, but then decided that at least part of Haarsfel's rationale was to avoid unduly antagonizing Councilor Vhiola Sandegarde, who was the principal heir to Kathaar Iron & Steel.

As the hearing progressed, Dekkard had a nagging feeling that he'd already heard something about Guldoran Ironworks, but he couldn't recall what.

Once the hearing was over, and Dekkard started to leave, Eduardo Nortak approached. Although Nortak was the other Craft councilor on the committee besides Dekkard and Haarsfel, he seldom said much, either to Dekkard or others. "Do you have a moment, Steffan?"

"Of course."

"Let's wait a minute, until everyone else leaves the chamber. By the way, how is your charming wife? I noticed that you have a new security aide."

"Technically, Nincya's just a clerk. She's only partially trained and not certified, but she can handle duties within the Council buildings. Avraal is just fine. What about Adryann?"

"She's well, except she hates winter here in Machtarn."

"It's definitely colder than Encora."

"She reminds me of that often." Nortak paused, then said, "You're on the Security Committee. Have you heard any more about that cruiser?"

"The *Khuld*? Not a word. Has Mardosh said anything in the Military Affairs Committee?"

Nortak shook his head. "You're a Military Institute type, and I've seen you lunch with Admiral Konnigsburg. Has he said anything?"

"We've met once or twice. There's no real secret about what we discussed. The *Khuld* could be close to Machtarn by now, but since there haven't been any sightings, she's either taken her time to save coal, gone elsewhere, or is using the mist and fog to keep the *Resolute* from finding her. Neither of us knows which it might be." That was true. Dekkard didn't *know.*

"You have good instincts for this sort of thing. What do you think?"

"I think the mutineers have a definite goal in mind, some sort of strike against the government, but what that strike might be? That's more of a guess. It could be another attempt at the Council or the Imperador, or it could be something else entirely."

"What about all three?" pressed Nortak.

"That might be harder. Once the *Khuld* uses her guns on one target, those in the other possible targets will have time to escape."

"They could still destroy the Palace or the Council Hall," Nortak pointed out.

"The councilors are the power, not the Council Hall. The Imperador, not the Palace."

After a pause, Nortak said, "I see your point. If they start shelling the Council Hall, then what?"

"Get away from the buildings. As far away as you can and as fast as possible."

"You went to the basement when the Meritorists shelled the building."

"Those were tiny charges compared to the guns of even a light cruiser. While the Council buildings are made of stone—it doesn't matter. Continuing successful salvos could effectively destroy either building and pile rubble over the basement."

"You're not exactly encouraging, Steffan."

"You asked, Eduardo. That's why I earnestly hope that the *Resolute* is successful in finding and destroying the *Khuld.*"

"How could they . . . ?" Nortak broke off his words.

"Everyone," *including me,* "has underestimated them. Certain Commercers tried to use them and got used instead."

"Commercers?"

"Jaime Minz, the one who was charged with assassinating the head legalist of Siincleer Shipbuilding, was a former Commercer security aide who obtained the dunnite for the New Meritorists and funded the terrorists who shelled the Council Office Building."

"Why would any Commercer support them?"

"It's been suggested that it was part of an effort to get the Council to strengthen the powers of the Security Ministry to be used against Crafters and uncooperative Landors."

"I can believe that." Nortak shook his head. "Thank you, Steffan. I hope you'll share any other insights you might have. Until later."

Dekkard let Nortak leave the committee chamber first, then followed.

He and Gaaroll were walking across the courtyard on the way back to the office when he finally recalled what had been nagging him during the committee meeting. It had been a single sentence Obreduur had uttered well before he'd become premier and Dekkard had become a councilor—Dekkard just shook his head.

Once he was back in his office, Dekkard immediately asked Teitryn to join him.

The engineering aide looked concerned when he entered Dekkard's personal office, but Dekkard smiled. "You didn't do anything. I did. I just recalled something I should have remembered much sooner, and I'd like you to track it down, that is, if you haven't already. Last year, I overheard a conversation where Councilor Obreduur mentioned Guldoran Ironworks. In some fashion the ironworks financially destroyed a business that had developed a better punch-card lathe and gained control of the equipment. At the time, I had no idea that I'd be looking into such matters. Frankly, it skipped my mind until this afternoon at the hearing."

"The Guldoran Ironworks? In Storz?"

"I know their headquarters and their main facility is there," replied Dekkard. "I don't even know exactly what they make."

"All sorts of machine tools. They're the largest machine tool corporacion in Guldor. They have other plants as well. There's one in Uldwyrk, I know." Teitryn paused. "They'd definitely be interested in a better or more precise lathe."

"If you can find out anything, I'd appreciate it. As always, without revealing anything you don't have to."

"It might take a while, sir."

"Everything does," replied Dekkard dryly. "Just do what you can."

Once Teitryn left, Dekkard walked to the window and looked to the north, not that he could make out much more than the bare outlines of the Imperador's Palace through the smoke and haze. He couldn't help but wonder how soon it would be before the *Khuld* would be close enough to open fire on the city. If, indeed, that was what the mutineers had in mind. He doubted that they could wait too long, since the *Khuld* couldn't have been fully provisioned when it was headed into Port Reale for a refit.

Dekkard turned and walked back to the desk and the waiting stack of responses he had to read and sign—or revise.

Avraal arrived in the office a good sixth before fourth bell.

"You're early," Dekkard said cheerfully. "Did you manage to pry out a list of possible café shops and tavernas from Carlos?"

"I did. He doesn't think we'll have much fortune. He's had people watching most of those places without much success. The ones who talk haven't ever done anything, and the ones who may be involved with the New Meritorists don't talk. His only request is that we share anything that we can. Oh . . . we can have the old Ferrum any night for the next week, and probably after that."

"Tonight?"

Avraal shook her head. "Tonight is for maps and planning. Tomorrow night at the earliest, depending on the weather."

Dekkard wasn't happy with any delay, but Avraal made sense, as usual. "Then, tomorrow."

"If possible," said Avraal.

30

FURDI morning was slightly clearer and colder than Tridi had been, and Dekkard wondered if another storm might be coming, but realized that the cold might be because the air was clearer.

Gestirn had a short article on the New Meritorists' raids on the terminal market adjoining Guldoran Ironway's Machtarn station. The newssheet also ran a story about the *Khuld*, the first time it had mentioned the light cruiser by name. The story cited unnamed and reliable sources saying that the cruiser might have been taken over by disgruntled sailors, but that the Admiralty had refused comment.

After finishing her first mug of café and reading the story, Avraal said to Dekkard, "The Navy is gambling that they can find and stop the *Khuld* before it does any damage."

"They don't think it's a gamble. That's obvious," replied Dekkard sourly.

"You're not that positive about our great Imperial Navy, are you? As if I didn't already know."

"A great Imperial Navy that let itself buy coal semi-legally stolen from its own Naval Coal Reserve—and at inflated prices, no less. A Navy that accepted contracts so flawed and disadvantageous that it ended up financing Siincleer Shipbuilding's various dubious acquisition tactics. A Navy so unperceptive that it just experienced the first warship mutiny in at least more than a century, if not ever, a Navy—"

"I do believe you've made your point. Has Councilor Konnigsburg ventured anything?"

"Only that such policies will continue so long as Bernotte remains as First Marshal and if the current Fleet Marshal succeeds him, but I told you that earlier."

"He really say that?" asked Gaaroll.

"He did, but keep it to yourself," said Dekkard.

"Why isn't he First Marshal?" asked Gaaroll.

"Because he's too perceptive and too honest," said Avraal before Dekkard could reply.

"Figures," snorted Gaaroll.

Before long, the three were in the Gresynt headed for the Council Office Building, taking one of the routes Dekkard used to avoid assassins.

He turned the Gresynt over to Avraal outside the building, and he and Gaaroll walked to his office. He didn't encounter any other councilors along the way. The only message Margrit gave him was a reminder from Hasheem about the committee meeting.

Once in his office, Dekkard sat down to go through the mail. The first envelope was on Guldoran Ironway stationery, if postmarked from Gaarlak. Dekkard smiled, knowing that Margrit had put it on top. He also was fairly sure it had to be from the ironway's district manager. After extracting the letter, he began to read, almost ignoring the polite and courteous opening.

> . . . *The recent unprecedented level of snow has created a difficult situation in regard to maintaining the rails and right-of-way here in the Gaarlak district. Because snowfall is seldom this deep and the cold so unrelenting, what plow engines we have are operating non-stop. This is creating far more stress on the rails and railbed. The conditions are worse farther north.*
>
> *As I wrote earlier, we had great concerns about the lack of adequate supplemental funds for ironway right-of-way and track maintenance. With the restrictions on the last reallocation legislation, Guldoran Ironway's ability to maintain the track in the Gaarlak district will be even more greatly diminished over the coming year, a matter of import and concern for both the ironway and your district . . .*

As Dekkard had known, the signature was that of Waaltar Haelkoch, District Manager.

At the dinner where Dekkard had met Haelkoch's wife, she had been intelligent and perceptive. *But that doesn't mean Guldoran should get the lion's share of supplemental funds.* He smiled wryly, set the letter aside for Roostof to draft a response, and picked up the next one.

At a third before fourth bell, Dekkard and Gaaroll left the office and made their way down the center staircase and then to the bronze doors to the courtyard, where someone called, "Steffan!"

Dekkard turned to see Villem Baar walking toward him.

"Might I join you?"

"Of course, Villem."

Without a word, Gaaroll dropped back as the three stepped out into the courtyard.

"If you don't mind," began Baar, "do you recall if there was any mention of this hearing before Duadi?"

Dekkard laughed, but not loudly, then said, "I had that same question. I checked my files, but the only other hearing on port security was back in Fallend."

"I recall that—about foreign-flagged vessels being used to smuggle spies into Guldoran ports. So I was right about this not being rescheduled. Do you think Hasheem put it that way so that the newssheets wouldn't think he'd just scheduled it in response to a problem?"

"That very well could be. Also, the subject was rather vague, and there was no mention of what kind of port security. We'll just have to see."

The two arrived in the committee chamber just after Haastar and Navione, but by the time Dekkard had seated himself, Pajiin and Rikkard entered.

Less than two minutes later, Hasheem gaveled the committee to order. "This morning's hearing is more of a briefing. Some of you may recall Eldeyn Haarlsyn, the security director of the Treasury Ministry. He testified several months ago before the committee. This time, Director Haarlsyn has some pertinent and disturbing information. This is restricted to Security Committee members." Hasheem nodded to the man at the witness table, whose black hair showed streaks of gray, and whose dark eyes had faint dark circles around them. "Director, please begin."

"Thank you, Sr. Chairman." Haarlsyn paused and cleared his throat. "This past Quindi evening, the S.V. *Autarch* ported here in Machtarn. As I testified before this committee earlier, we've noted that Noldaran vessels, such as the *Autarch*, have been observed to carry individuals of dubious provenance."

A delicate way of saying "spies." Dekkard managed not to smile.

"One individual stood out to customs, and when they moved to confront him, he used Atacaman pepper spray to escape. Our agents managed to seize one of the two cases in his possession. The case concealed more than a quarter million in mark notes of various denominations. All the notes were real and had been circulated . . ."

Lots of marks being smuggled from Noldar . . . where the Banque of Oersynt has recently established a subsidiary, where Guldoran Ironway has set up a textile manufactory, not to mention several other Guldoran corporacions. And where one of the men involved in Markell's disappearance had fled, most likely to work for a Siincleer Shipbuilding facility there.

"We do not know the true identity of the individual. He booked passage under the name Syoll Thearl, which was later determined to be an alias. His passport appeared to be genuine or a forgery so good that it could not be detected as such—unfortunately, 'Thearl' managed to retain it. We do not know for whom the marks were intended, but we do have reason to believe that this was not the first such delivery."

For the next third of a bell, Director Haarlsyn provided more specifics on the S.V. *Autarch,* its ports of call before Machtarn, but little more on the courier of the marks clearly intended for an unsavory purpose.

When Haarlsyn finished his prepared briefing, Hasheem said, "Thank you, Director," then turned to Navione. "Do you have any questions?"

"I do, Sr. Chairman." Navione looked to Haarlsyn. "What alerted your observers?"

"A number of factors, Councilor, small in themselves. While he took second-class passage, as befit a fabric salesman seeking markets for new Noldaran manufactories—that was his cover—he was too young for his supposed experience. His clothes were less . . . tasteful . . . than they should have been for his profession. Other small items just didn't fit."

"Do you have any idea for whom the marks were intended?"

"Only that the purpose could not have been legal. It would have been much easier and safer to use a commercial bond or letter of credit for legitimate transactions. Also, the marks were concealed behind a false lining of the case walls."

In turn, Haastar asked several questions about the customs procedures.

Rikkard was blunt in his first question. "How did you let him escape?"

"He'd been searched for weapons and found to be unarmed. He seemed compliant. Then, suddenly, he sprayed the two customs officers with Atacaman pepper dust. He sprinted through a line of disembarking passengers and was gone, before anyone else quite knew what had happened."

"No one could catch him?"

"No one could find him. He may have had a confederate waiting."

"That's how you protect us against foreign agents?" asked Rikkard sarcastically. Before Haarlsyn could answer, Rikkard added, "Don't bother."

"Councilor Pajiin?"

"My question is somewhat like Councilor Rikkard's inquiry. Two years ago, Treasury investigators shot two loggers who refused to leave the Eshbruk river pier because they hadn't finished unloading a work lorry. They were Guldoran citizens. Yet customs agents who suspected a foreigner of being a problem couldn't manage to keep their hands on him?"

"It was a most regrettable failure," returned Haarlsyn.

"I have no further questions," declared Pajiin.

"Councilor Dekkard?"

"Thank you, Sr. Chairman." Dekkard looked to Haarlsyn. "Under the provisions of the Security and Public Safety Reorganization Act, a number of Special Agents were transferred to the Treasury Ministry. Have any of them been assigned to assist customs officers?"

"I'm not aware of any such transfers, not to Treasury Security."

"In that event, would you look into the matter and inform the committee as to why no Special Agents from the former Security Ministry were transferred to Treasury Security since it would appear that they would certainly be qualified for such duties?"

"That would not lie in my area of responsibility."

"Director Haarlsyn," said Hasheem coldly. "It may not have been within your purview to determine where the Special Agents were assigned. It is certainly within your responsibility to provide information on the matter. The committee looks forward to your reporting at your earliest convenience."

"Yes, Sr. Chairman."

"I have no further questions," said Dekkard.

Villem Baar had a single question. "Which Noldaran corporacion or corporacions was this individual purporting to represent? Were any of them associated with Guldoran corporacions?"

"That is a detail on which I was not briefed. I'll be happy to provide whatever information the customs officers obtained."

"Please do," said Hasheem. "There being no other questions, you may go, Director Haarlsyn."

Once the committee was dismissed, Dekkard walked over to Baar. "That was a very good question. What made you think of it?"

"I had a thought." Baar paused and waited until the two were alone at the committee table. "Someone here in Guldor is funding the New Meritorists. They're aware that large financial transactions might come to the attention of banque officials and the Treasury Ministry. So they're bringing in funds indirectly, but it would be difficult for a corporacion that doesn't have operations both in Guldor and Noldar to obtain that much in mark notes without notice. That former Council security aide— the one who hired the men who attacked the Council Office Building—he didn't get his position with Northwest Industrial Chemical early enough to have obtained dunnite. He also would have had to have gotten funds to pay those men from someone with greater access." Baar smiled almost sadly. "You knew that, didn't you?"

"I suspected it, but never could prove it."

"The manslaughter charge was because he was behind the Atacaman red pepper attack on you, wasn't it?"

"Again, I'd thought that all along, but once more, I had no proof."

"Do you know who found the proof?"

"It had to be Council Guard and the Justiciary Ministry."

"I got the impression that Guard Captain Trujillo is very thorough."

"So did I. I don't think he ever gives up."

"Do you think the top people in Suvion Industries are involved?"

"*Someone* has to be. At the same time, I don't know of any proof."

"You're sounding remarkably like a legalist again," said Baar with a smile.

"Which I'm definitely not," returned Dekkard.

"With what I know, and what I know about you, Steffan, I'm very glad I'm a councilor and no longer a legalist whose firm is linked to Suvion Industries." Baar paused. "What do you think will happen next?"

"The *Khuld* is waiting for something else to occur. Or the New Meritorists are waiting for the *Khuld* to attack before they do something else. I wish I knew what." *Or maybe you don't.*

"You're saying that we're in the calm before the storm," Baar said evenly. "I have the same feeling. I wish I didn't."

"How is Gretina doing?"

"She's preparing to go position-seeking and not particularly enthused about it." Baar's lips curled into a sardonic expression.

"She's too good not to get offers."

"We'll see." Baar gestured toward the door.

The two, accompanied by Gaaroll, walked back to the Council Office Building, their conversation centered on mundane matters, including the weather and whether Machtarn might get another large storm before spring, technically only three weeks away, not that anyone expected warming temperatures until at least the second week of Springfirst.

The remainder of the day was thankfully uneventful, and Dekkard felt more than ready to leave the office when Avraal arrived at just past fourth bell.

"Did anything interesting happen today?" she asked.

"Only the hearing where the Treasury's security director admitted that they let a foreign infiltrator of some sort escape. They did manage to hold on to the quarter-million marks he had hidden in one of his cases." Dekkard quickly explained.

"Do you think Ulrich is behind it?"

"In some fashion. Even Villem Baar thinks someone in Suvion Industries has to be involved, although he has no idea who. He did say he was glad to be a councilor rather than remaining with the legalist firm." After a slight hesitation, Dekkard asked, "What about your day?"

"Everything's arranged. Carlos avoided asking any questions."

"It's better for him that way."

Avraal nodded. "And for us." She walked around the desk, bent down and kissed his cheek, then stepped back.

Dekkard grinned. "That was the best part of the whole day." Then he stood and went to retrieve his overcoat, gloves, and leather folder.

When Dekkard, Avraal, and Gaaroll stepped outside the Council Office Building, he could immediately tell that it was definitely warmer, if still below freezing. *That might help in drawing a few more people.*

On the drive home, as Dekkard turned south on Jacquez, Gaaroll said, "More scattered strong feelings to the east. Might be something in East-hill."

"A fire or another disturbance?" asked Avraal. "It's too far for me to sense."

"Can't tell," replied Gaaroll. "Not near as strong as what came out of Rivertown."

"Let's hope it stays that way," said Dekkard. "Let us know if it gets stronger."

Gaaroll was silent for the rest of the way home.

Emrelda met them in the hallway. "Are you two still going to do this 'reconnaissance' tonight?"

Dekkard looked to Avraal, who said, "We are."

"That's what I thought," replied Emrelda. "Dinner's just about ready. Nothing fancy, gramajo scramble."

"We haven't had that in a long time," said Avraal.

That was fine with me. Dekkard didn't voice the thought, even though he'd never cared much for the combination of scrambled eggs, fried ham and potatoes, and *peas,* especially peas.

In the end, as the four ate around the breakfast table, he minimized his intake of peas and swallowed them quickly.

After that, he changed into the old grays, the worn boots, and set the old winter jacket aside while Avraal and Emrelda helped him with the mahogany wig and beard, especially with the spirit gum. Then came the makeup. When he looked in the hall mirror, he didn't see much of a trace of the well-groomed and fashionably attired councilor. Even his throwing knives were well-hidden, which meant he'd have less time to react to danger.

"That will definitely do," said Emrelda. "You now look like you'd fit in at Fernando's."

That wasn't exactly a compliment, but it also meant that they'd accomplished what he and Avraal had in mind.

"Don't forget the sign," said Emrelda as Dekkard and Avraal left the house.

"We won't. It's in the garage," replied Dekkard.

After slipping the sign into the back seat, Dekkard eased the Gresynt down the drive and then along back streets to the office of Carlos Baartol. Once there, they got out, removed the sign, locked the Gresynt, and got into the nondescript brown Ferrum, which took far longer to light off and reach operating pressure than did the Gresynt, something Dekkard expected, but which he still found mildly irritating.

You've already gotten too used to being a councilor.

Several minutes later, they headed back northwest. Slightly more than a sixth later, Dekkard eased the brown Ferrum into a space between a battered Realto that had seen better days, and another, slightly newer Ferrum.

When they got out, in the fading light filtering through the winter haze, Dekkard removed the hand-lettered sign attached to two narrow poles from the Ferrum and glanced around, but didn't see any patrollers. A block up the side street was the Setting Sun, a tavern frequented by iron-way workers, not surprisingly, since Guldoran Ironway's works lay three blocks to the west. A block south was the Chequered Board, catering more to locals, who tended to work in service positions in the west part of the city, a neighborhood with only a few tough back alleys.

While Avraal locked the steamer, he took a quick look at the message on the sign.

FAIR WAGES

SAFE WORK.

"Let's see how you look," said Avraal.

Dekkard turned.

"You're definitely ready for the square."

"Is anyone there?" he asked. Seasprite Square was one of the many small squares scattered throughout Machtarn, generally occupying the middle section of a block, and roughly fifty yards on a side with some sort of central fountain or statue and paths surrounded by low boxwood hedges, with benches and occasional evergreens, spread far enough apart so as not to provide cover for mayhem or worse.

"When we drove past, there were two couples, a man with a dog on a leash, a few others on benches, likely off work but too poor to go to a tavern. It can't have changed much. You go first. I'll follow."

Carrying the sign, Dekkard walked past the three-story buildings that largely held flats rented by working-class families until he reached the iron gateposts that marked the south entry to the square.

He glanced around, but the older couple seated at a bench on the walk-way to his right barely gave him a glance, as they continued talking, a blanket wrapped around their legs. He walked to the center of the small parklike square and propped the hand-lettered sign against the empty basin of the fountain that featured a marble rendition of a sea nymph, whose visage lacked any character.

"Fair wages?" called out an older man with a small dog. "Not likely."

"But there should be," replied Dekkard. "Fair wages and safe work. That's what built Guldor. We're losing that."

"You one of those Meritorists?"

"Not me," declared Dekkard. "They're no better than the Commer-cers. Commercers control everything with their marks. Meritorists want to run the country by who's popular and who can give away the most marks."

"At least we'd get something," said another voice.

Dekkard turned to face the white-bearded man with a cane. "For a little while, maybe. Meritorists blew up buildings all over Guldor. They attacked the Council. They killed a few councilors. But who were most of the folks who got killed? Working folks. Secretaries, messengers, typists, guards."

"So what's the sign for? You a Crafter sort?"

"My family are all crafters and worked with their hands. I did, too. Till I lost my last job." Which was technically true. "I'm not shilling for Craft-ers. I'm just saying that working folks deserve fair wages and safe work. Talking about who voted for what doesn't make wages fair. Neither does blowing up government buildings and killing more workers."

"What does?" asked a younger man in a patched and worn jacket, who limped slightly as he came to a stop.

"Getting the Council to pass laws does. Getting the newssheets to print stories about unfair wages and unsafe workplaces does."

"That doesn't work," said the man in the worn jacket.

"We got the first Craft government in more than a century," answered Dekkard. "They pushed through Security reform in weeks. Then a Com-mercer type gave money and explosives to the New Meritorists, and they killed the Premier who got those reforms. What does that tell you?"

"Never heard that."

"It was in both newssheets. Someone shot the Commercer type when he was being taken to trial. Makes you think. Or it should."

"Who are you?" demanded the younger man.

"If you want a name, call me the Contrarian. Contrary to the Com-mercers and the Meritorists. My name doesn't matter. What I stand for does." Dekkard realized that there were now almost twenty people loosely gathered near him.

"You're all talk," declared the younger man. "Power is what matters. The New Meritorists understand that."

"Laws matter," countered Dekkard. "If the laws allow us to be abused, power doesn't matter. Premier Obreduur—the one who got assassinated—he understood that. That's why the Meritorists killed him. They just want power. He wanted fair wages and safe work. Without laws requiring fair wages and safe workplaces, what good is power? Commercers had power for generations. Did it help us? Landors had it before them. Did they help us? New Meritorists are trying to grab power, just like the Commercers grabbed it from the Landors. Will that help us?"

Despite the cold of the growing evening, Dekkard was sweating. He also knew he was getting too complicated. "It's simple. Fair wages for safe work. Get that, and you get a better life."

"You're just an old Crafter," snapped the young man.

"And you're a shill for power-grabbers," countered Dekkard. "Destroy everything and call it progress. Explode buildings and call it success. We need to make the Council work for us. Security reforms are just a start."

Dekkard knew he wasn't doing that well with the words, but he saw people nodding, and he could see frustration in the face of the Meritorist supporter. He almost smiled, realizing, belatedly, that he was getting some needed assistance from Avraal, who now stood beyond the back of the group and to one side.

"We've got a new councilor here in Machtarn. Emile Hebersyn. That's right, Emile Hebersyn. Write him. Demand that he support fair wages and safe work. Demand that workers be treated fairly! If you don't tell him what you think, what you need, who will? You know other councilors? Write them! Write the Premier! Let them know! You deserve fair wages and safe work!" Dekkard glanced in Avraal's direction. She drew her finger across her throat, indicating it was time to cut his speaking short, and pointing to the north gate to the small square.

"Just remember! Be a Contrarian! Stand for Fair Wages . . . Safe Work." With that Dekkard stepped back and picked up the sign, brandishing it, not quite like a lance, before turning and walking swiftly toward the north gate. No one seemed to follow him, but he realized that was because Avraal had obviously created some sort of emotional distraction.

He was almost thirty yards east of the gate before she caught up to him.

"What happened?" he asked.

"A patroller lorry pulled up on the street. You had some people listening even by the south gate. The patrollers were getting worried."

"I wouldn't have gotten anywhere without you."

"I wouldn't say that. It takes both of us."

Dekkard didn't breathe easily until they were safely in the Ferrum and well on their way back to Carlos Baartol's to drop off the Ferrum and reclaim the Gresynt.

No one was in Baartol's building or nearby, and Dekkard and Avraal locked the Ferrum and moved to the Gresynt. Dekkard was still tense even after he pulled up in front of the garage at the house. After garaging the Gresynt, he stowed the sign beside the shelves that held the toolbox and a few other items, then closed up the garage, and walked with Avraal to the portico door.

Both Emrelda and Gaaroll were in the hallway waiting when Dekkard and Avraal walked through the portico door.

"How did it go?" asked Emrelda.

"Acceptably, I think," said Dekkard.

"Better than that," Avraal chided.

"Not much," countered Dekkard, "but I did come up with a name for our nonexistent movement or for me. I'm now the Contrarian."

Emrelda frowned.

"I like it," said Gaaroll.

"So do I," added Avraal. "It's one word. We should put it on the sign."

"Then it should be plural," said Dekkard. "To suggest there are more of us. Now can we get this makeup and beard off?"

"I think we can manage that," said Emrelda dryly.

31

O N Quindi morning, as soon as he'd given Avraal her café, Dekkard skimmed through the morning edition of *Gestirn* to see if there was anything more about the *Khuld* or anything that might have related to what Gaaroll had sensed the afternoon before.

A small front-page story stated that "reliable sources" had confirmed that the light cruiser I.S. *Khuld* had been seized by mutinous sailors, but that the Admiralty had refused to comment.

Idiots! How are they going to explain it if shells start dropping on Machtarn? And why has it taken so long for much to appear in the news-sheets? Dekkard shook his head.

"What are you shaking your head about?" asked Avraal.

"The Admiralty is refusing to comment on the *Khuld*."

"That's not only a big gamble, but a bad wager," replied Avraal. "It's to be expected, unfortunately, given what the admiral told you."

Dekkard nodded and turned to the other story of interest. It was short, but noted that the unruly crowds in Easthill had gathered around the fires in a partially abandoned section of row houses, and that two men had been killed and a number of others injured. To Dekkard, "partially abandoned" meant that poor people were trying to get shelter in nearly uninhabitable buildings.

"There was a disturbance in Easthill," he said after taking a sip of his café.

"It must have been fairly violent, in addition to the deaths," said Emrelda as she rose to leave. "Those are the only disturbances that the newssheets ever cover."

"If nothing else violent or untoward occurs," said Dekkard, "we need to go out again tonight. I have the feeling we don't have that much time. You'll come, too, Nincya. I think we ought to be in the north, at Detruro Square." He grinned as he named the square.

"You would pick that square," said Avraal. "No one else will know why."

"I would have picked a Scarlet Square, except there isn't one."

"Whatever square it is," said Emrelda, "make it after services. It's a Quindi night, and people will be out and about later. Besides, you haven't been to services as often as you should have been. Also, you can claim you were at services." She smiled. "Not that the times will match, but it will disarm people."

"Most of all," said Dekkard dryly, "for some reason you feel we should be at services."

The two sisters exchanged glances.

Dekkard shrugged. "After services, then. That will give me some time to add 'Contrarians' to the sign."

"Just make it 'Contrarian,'" suggested Avraal. "I can't tell you why, but I like the singular better."

"So do I," said Emrelda.

"Then it will be the singular." Dekkard took a bite of his croissant, followed by café.

"I'll see you later." Emrelda turned and left the breakfast room.

A little more than two thirds later, Dekkard headed out to the garage to ready the Gresynt. A few minutes later, once everyone was in the steamer, he crossed Jacquez heading east for several blocks, before turning north. He said to Gaaroll, "When we reach Justiciary Avenue, or before, if you can, see if you can still sense strong feelings to the east."

Just after Dekkard crossed Justiciary Avenue, Gaaroll said, "Still strong feelings there. Tops of the piles aren't as high. More piles, though."

"That sounds like more people are angry or upset, but individually they're not quite as angry. That's not good. If something else sets them off, though . . ."

"You think the same thing could happen there that did in Rivertown?" asked Avraal.

"It would be harder. Easthill's farther from the Council. It wouldn't be good, though." *And that's an understatement.*

The traffic on Council Avenue was normal and the iron gates were drawn back, for which Dekkard was grateful as he turned the Gresynt over to Avraal.

When he entered the Council Office Building, he almost bumped into another councilor and quickly said, "I'm sorry. My thoughts were elsewhere."

In return, Elyncya Duforgue said, "I can imagine, Steffan. You've had more than enough to handle. You seem to get punished for surviving and doing what a councilor should." She gestured, and the two of them resumed walking toward the central staircase.

"I'm certain you've dealt with far more than I have, with far less recognition of the fact."

"My office didn't get shelled, Steffan," she said pleasantly.

"Other than that, then," he returned.

"The Commercers dislike me on principle," said Duforgue. "The twisted principle that women really shouldn't hold high office or be in positions of authority. A number of them, however, seem to actively hate you. Do you know why?"

"I don't *know.* I can only surmise it's because I upset their plans for turning the former Security Ministry into a tool for permanent Commercer control of the Council and government."

"You proposed the law. The Council passed it, and Premier Obreduur implemented it. You weren't the only one involved."

"No. But he's dead, and they've certainly tried to kill me." Dekkard gestured toward the stairs. "Are you headed up?"

"Not right now. I'll see you later."

"Until then," he replied cheerfully.

When Dekkard and Gaaroll reached the second level, Gaaroll said quietly, "She was concerned. About you, I think. That's still hard for me to tell."

"Thank you for telling me. You're doing better, you know. In time, you'll be certified."

"Like what I'm doing."

"I like what you're doing, too. *But* I could pay you more."

Theoretically, he could anyway, but Dekkard felt he should stay close to the normal pay ranges for qualifications and expertise, as did most councilors.

He also wondered at Elyncya Duforgue's words, almost as if she had been alluding to something more than what they had briefly discussed. Then, when he entered the office and saw Roostof, an expression of concern on his face and with something in his hand, Dekkard was fairly certain he wouldn't like what the senior legalist was about to tell him.

"Good morning, sir."

"Good morning, Svard. What is it that I'm not going to like?"

"There was another editorial about you in *The Machtarn Tribune.*" Roostof handed the newssheet to Dekkard, folded back to the editorial page, a page that did not exist in *Gestirn,* which prided itself on factual reporting.

Dekkard began to read.

MORE ON THE QUESTIONABLE COUNCILOR DEKKARD

Remember the questionable Councilor Steffan Dekkard? The Military Institute graduate who never really served out his service obligation? The short-term former security aide who got himself appointed a councilor for a district in which he never lived? Who immediately masterminded the passage of so-called Security reform that destroyed the Security Ministry, and disarmed Special Agents and the ability of the government to deal with the so-called New Meritorists. And who miraculously survived the shelling of the Council that killed the Premier who had been his champion, and then had the nerve to press, successfully, the new Premier to select the late Premier Obreduur's widow to fill her husband's seat, overriding suggestions from the Craft Party of Oersynt.

Since then, the questionable councilor has bought a lovely and quite spacious dwelling in Gaarlak, and in a fashionable district, to fulfill the residency requirement, without borrowing a single mark, most amazingly, given that he's never earned more than seven hundred marks a year. Not only that, but just yesterday the distinguished councilor had the nerve to question the security director of the Treasury Ministry on the failure of customs officers to apprehend a foreign national caught smuggling marks into Guldor, apparently to aid the New Meritorists. Why did the councilor even need to question the poor director, since Councilor Dekkard was the one responsible for gutting the Security Ministry? And then, he had the nerve to blame someone else?

But it's all the same to the questionable Councilor Dekkard.

Dekkard managed not to flinch and handed the newssheet back to Roostof. "Most of it's true, but partial truths presented in a most unflattering and false way. If I point out that the marks for the house came from Ritten Ysella-Dekkard, then they'll assert that I married her for her nonexistent wealth. The house was an unexpected wedding present that came well after we married, and it's all she has. I did question the security director, and so did most of the others on the committee, but I never blamed him."

"It's unfair and wrong," said Roostof. "There have always been rumors and gossip, but I've never seen them go after anyone like this before. The Kraffeist Affair was illegal and corrupt, and so was that bastard Minz, but the *Tribune* barely said a word."

"That's because they were all Commercers. The old rules don't apply to Crafters. What the *Tribune* prints will likely only get worse." Dekkard managed not to take a deep breath.

"How did the *Tribune* get the story about what happened in the Security Committee?" asked Roostof. "Those hearings aren't open to the newssheets."

"Obviously, someone leaked the information." Dekkard had a very good idea who that had been, given the particular slant of the *Tribune* editorial. What he wondered more about was how the newssheet had obtained the information about the house in Gaarlak. Since no one had mentioned the repairs to the kitchen, which could have been characterized as "extensive renovations"—and certainly would have been had the newssheet known—the information had likely been pieced together. *By Jens Seigryn, perhaps?* Had that been the reason he disappeared? Dekkard doubted that he'd ever know, as was turning out to be the case in so many instances.

"It had to be one of the Commercer councilors," said Roostof.

"I doubt it was Villem Baar," said Dekkard.

"Rikkard, then."

"Most likely, but don't say anything."

"Do you think he might be tied to the New Meritorists?"

"Not in any way he might recognize. He detests them. But there has to be some corporacion linkage to the New Meritorists. Otherwise, the Meritorists wouldn't have gotten the dunnite."

"Wouldn't Councilor Rikkard know that?"

"He's often too angry to think clearly. Anger does that. Put the story in the file with the first one. There will be others. I'm too good a target to pass up."

Once he was in his office, he immediately began reading the incoming mail. When he finished and handed it over to Roostof, he went back to his office and looked out the window. The view hadn't changed, although the outline of the Imperador's Palace was slightly clearer. Then he sat down and began to write, trying to find shorter phrases for the Contrarian "message."

During the course of the day, he checked with Teitryn to see if the engineering aide had been able to find out more about the punch-card lathe and Guldoran Ironworks, but Teitryn hadn't yet come up with anything.

Avraal appeared in his office at a third past fourth afternoon bell as Dekkard turned from the window from where he'd been looking out over the snow and the grayness of winter.

With a smile, he walked to her and held one gloved hand and kissed her cheek. "You definitely brighten a dismal day."

"I was afraid you might feel that way. Carlos showed me that nasty editorial in the *Tribune*. Incomplete but true facts in a misleading context. It had to be Rikkard who told about the Security Committee, didn't it?"

Dekkard stepped back slightly and said, "I don't see how it could have been anyone else. The *Tribune* must have sent someone to Gaarlak to see what they could dig up. The house information was comparatively impersonal, what they could have gotten from registry records."

"If someone told them where to look," Avraal pointed out.

"It could have been the Commercer candidate who ran against Decaro, Elvann Wheiter. His father is the presidente of the Banque of Gaarlak."

"Or it could have been Jens Seigryn."

"We won't find out any time soon, and it won't change anything," said Dekkard tiredly. "So we might as well leave, get an early dinner, go to services, and then try to boost the Contrarian cause at Detruro Square."

"There were two squares equidistant from the Swan and the Black Pillar—"

"Somehow, I just couldn't see speaking at Bluffsyn Square. Besides, Detruro has a certain meaning."

"If you're looking for that kind of meaning, I'm just glad there's not a Delehya Square."

"There should be. She's why the Council and the Great Charter exist as they do." Dekkard smiled.

"Only because of her excesses." Avraal shook her head. "We should go."

"We should," agreed Dekkard.

Only about two thirds passed before Dekkard, Avraal, and Gaaroll reached home and stepped through the portico door to the definite and near-overpowering odor of onions.

"Khasaaran goulash," said Avraal, continuing toward the kitchen. "Emrelda definitely wants you to have the aura of a working man. I'll even bet she's hung your grays in the kitchen."

"In this cold, no one will smell anything," said Dekkard.

"You'd be surprised," replied Emrelda from the kitchen, "but I didn't think about your grays. The onions were cheap, and I wanted goulash."

Dekkard did note that she wore an old jacket and trousers and not her uniform.

While Avraal and Gaaroll helped get dinner on the table, Dekkard returned to the garage, where he got out the paint and added the word "Contrarian" to the sign, which he then carried into the house and laid out in the study for the paint to dry.

The goulash turned out to be tasty, with more than enough left for another meal. After the four cleaned up the kitchen, Emrelda changed into a tasteful dark maroon suit, but one that featured trousers, and they all left for the Hillside Trinitarian Chapel.

In his homily, Presider Buusen focused on winter, and how necessary warmth was for survival, not only physical warmth, but the warmth of feelings for others, yet how an excess of physical warmth led to uncontrolled fires and damage, and how raging-hot emotions could be even more destructive. Dekkard agreed, but couldn't immediately think of how he might work such thoughts into Contrarianism, only that there ought to be a way.

When the four returned to the house, Dekkard, Avraal, and Gaaroll all changed into their far less distinguished "reconnaissance" garb, and Emrelda applied Dekkard's makeup.

As the three prepared to leave, Emrelda said, "Be careful. The way you're dressed, if you get in any sort of scuffle, patrollers won't be gentle."

"He looks tough," said Gaaroll. "Not like a swell now."

"He's always been tough," said Avraal.

Dekkard reclaimed the sign and led the way to the garage. Once the three were in the Gresynt, he looked to Gaaroll. "Any strong feelings nearby?"

"No, sir."

Dekkard eased the steamer down the drive, absently noting that the snow that he'd shoveled to each side was markedly lower although the temperature had remained below freezing, then turned east on Florinda Way. Traffic wasn't that heavy on the way to Baartol's office, even on Imperial Boulevard. After they locked the Gresynt and moved to the Ferrum, Dekkard glanced around.

"There's no one nearby," said Gaaroll.

"Thank you." Dekkard slipped behind the wheel, lit the steamer off, and made sure Avraal and Gaaroll were secure while the pressure built. Then he drove out of the parking area.

Detruro Square was roughly five milles east-northeast from where Dekkard turned back onto Imperial Boulevard. Somewhat less than a third of a bell later, as he neared the square, he asked again, "Any strong feelings anywhere?"

"Piles of feelings, not real strong, maybe two blocks ahead."

"That should be the Swan," said Avraal.

Because the Black Pillar was at the east end of the block holding the square, Dekkard decided to park the Ferrum closer to the west end because he didn't want to have to walk too near the tavern when the three left the square after he finished speaking.

In the end, he parked across the street from the west end, simply because that was the closest open space. In the early-evening darkness, Dekkard removed the now-modified sign from the nondescript brown Ferrum, parked behind a small and battered Ferrum lorry, and turned to Gaaroll.

"You stay close to Avraal. Let her know if you sense *anything* out of sorts."

"Yes, sir."

"Now . . . let's see what we can do." *Hopefully better than last time.*

He waited until a Realto drove past before striding swiftly across the street and then heading east toward the north gates of the small square. Ahead, he saw two men talking as they walked toward the Black Pillar, not much different from the Setting Sun, he surmised, except for where its patrons worked. *But you'll see if those who come to listen—if anyone does—are any different.*

"Who's in the square?"

"Just two people," said Gaaroll.

Dekkard had hoped for a few more, but others might show once he started talking. He kept walking past the buildings that had once been town houses for well-off professionals, but which had been converted into rental flats decades earlier.

As he neared Detruro Square, he could see that its design was essentially the same as that of Seasprite Square, positioned in the middle of the block. The most immediate difference was the more elaborate wrought-iron gatework, suggesting the area had once been more fashionable, and the fountain statue was larger—that of a man in early Imperial attire, presumably Iustaan Detruro, and doubtless looking more dignified and handsome than he had in life. The varnished oak benches looked relatively recent against the low, raggedly trimmed boxwood hedges.

Still carrying the sign, Dekkard walked through the iron gateposts that marked the north entry to the square, while Avraal and Gaaroll remained just outside the gate. He could only see the two older men, each on a separate bench facing the dry fountain. The one on the east side of the fountain appeared to be dozing, a ragged blanket wrapped around his legs, while the man on the west side immediately turned his head to watch Dekkard.

He propped the hand-lettered sign against the empty basin of the fountain, not directly in front of the older man who watched him, then turned to face the sole onlooker.

"Safe workplace. Not that I ever saw." The man lifted an arm with a cloth-wrapped stump that ended just above where his wrist should have been.

"There should be. That would be better for everyone."

"You ever really work with your hands?"

"Decorative plasterer until I couldn't do it anymore."

"Dust?"

"It got bad. Then I did security stuff."

"Was that any better?"

"Until the Meritorists killed my boss."

"Take it you don't care for them."

"They've got it all wrong," declared Dekkard. "They're no better than the Commercers. Commercers control everything with their marks. Meritorists want to run the country by who's popular and who can give away the most marks. We need fair wages and safe workplaces, not handouts." From the corner of his eye, Dekkard saw another figure approaching, but not Avraal or Gaaroll.

"No Council'll do anything about that," said the newcomer in a raspy voice.

"That new premier tried," said the one-handed man. "They killed him."

"That's what I meant."

"The Meritorists killed him," the one-handed man went on. "Doesn't say much for them."

"What do you expect?" asked Dekkard. "They blew up buildings all over Guldor. They attacked the Council. They killed a few councilors. But who were most of the folks who got killed? Working folks . . . secretaries, messengers, typists, guards."

"What's a Contaarian?" asked the newcomer, a blocky figure in faded browns, wearing a scarred brown leather jacket.

"Contrarian," replied Dekkard. "It means I'm contrary toward the Commercers, the Landors, and the Meritorists. The Crafters mean well, but they haven't done much besides get rid of the Security thugs."

"That's something."

"They need to do more," declared Dekkard. "Working folks deserve fair wages and safe work. Talking about who voted for what doesn't make wages fair. Neither does blowing up government buildings and killing more workers. First premier to do anything for working people, and the Meritorists killed him."

"That's just what the newsies say," interjected a third man, younger, accompanied by another person, who looked to be more youth than man. "Had to be the Commercers. Meritorists'd never do that."

"Meritorists blew up buildings all over Guldor," interjected the one-handed man. "Blew up the Craft Guildhall, too."

"We got the first Craft government in more than a century," answered Dekkard. "They pushed through Security reform in weeks. Then a Commercer type gave money and explosives to the New Meritorists and they killed the premier who got those reforms. What does that tell you? Commercers and Meritorists—neither one cares about working folks. Commercers only want marks. Meritorists want power. Neither one's out for fair wages and safe work. Fair wages and safe work—that's what Contrarians want. No more blood on the shop floor. No more millions to the corporacions while men can't find work, and the corporacions bring in cheap goods from Noldar—"

"You think you're the friggin' Almighty?" declared the younger man with the companion.

"Do I look like the Almighty?" countered Dekkard. "Almighty'd be in a big chapel somewhere. I'm just tired of having the Commercers and the Meritorists fighting and not giving a frig about the working folks."

"You're just talk," declared the raspy-voiced man.

"That's right," said Dekkard. "I haven't got much else. But talk changes things. If you talk about what's wrong, you can change 'em. Talk to enough people and they vote different."

"What does that do?"

"It changes laws. Laws matter. Commercers don't want change. Landors don't, either. Better laws can get us fair wages and safe work. Commercers had power for generations. Did it help us? Landors had it before them. Did they help us? New Meritorists are trying to grab power, just like the Commercers grabbed it from the Landors. Will that help us?"

In the dimness of the square, Dekkard couldn't tell how many people had gathered, although he thought there might be a half score, and a half score was better than none. He couldn't help wondering how long it would take before his talks came to the attention of the Meritorists . . . or if they ever would.

"Talk doesn't help."

"Talk is what I've got. It's simple. Fair wages for safe work. Get that, and you get a better life. Commercers don't care about either. Meritorists just want power."

"You're talking like an old Crafter," snapped the younger man. "Times are different now."

"You young ones, you think times are different," retorted Dekkard. "They're not. The Landors grabbed power. The Commercers grabbed power from them. The Crafters barely got power, and now the Meritorists are trying to grab it from them. They'll destroy everything and call it progress. Explode buildings and call it success. We need to make the Council work for us. Not them."

Dekkard felt he was doing a shade better than he had the night before, but he still felt awkward. But the one-handed man was nodding, and so were a pair of gray-haired and stocky women he hadn't noticed before, likely the result of Avraal's empathic talents.

Avraal had moved into the square, and she and Gaaroll stood to the rear and closer to the south entrance to the square.

"You've got power. Tell people not to fall for Meritorist deception or corporacion pressure. We've got a new councilor here in Machtarn. Emile Hebersyn. That's right, Emile Hebersyn. Write him. Demand that he support fair wages and safe work. Demand that workers be treated fairly! If you don't tell him what you think, what you need, who will?"

"What's in it for you?" demanded the younger man. "Who bought you?"

"No one bought me. I'm a Contrarian. I'm saying we all deserve fair wages and safe work." Dekkard jabbed a finger toward the man. "You don't think we deserve that? Go ahead. Tell everyone you're for unfair wages and unsafe work."

"Shill," growled the younger man before he turned and walked toward the south entrance gates, his even younger companion hanging on his arm.

"If I'm a shill," said Dekkard, "then I'm a shill for fair wages and safe work. We still don't have either, and the time for both is long overdue."

Dekkard's eyes flitted to Avraal, who gave the slightest nod. Then he said, "Just remember! Fair Wages . . . Safe Work. And the Contrarians!" He turned, picked up the sign, raising it like a battle ensign for a long moment, before turning and walking swiftly to the north gate.

Once more, no one seemed to follow him, and he slowed his steps, glancing around to make sure. He was halfway to the Ferrum before Gaaroll and Avraal joined him.

"Did you distract them when I left?" he asked.

"I didn't have to," Avraal replied.

"No patrollers tonight?"

"No sign of them," said Gaaroll.

"There was one thing," Avraal said quietly. "You were actually projecting some of what you felt."

"You can sense what I feel?" asked Dekkard uncertainly, because isolates—were isolates. They didn't project or receive emotion.

"No," replied Avraal firmly. "Not a single thing. But your words, when you were speaking to those people, they had feeling beyond your voice in them. I've never sensed anything like that before. It's . . . disconcerting."

"Did you sense that?" Dekkard asked Gaaroll.

"Not that way." Gaaroll gave a thoughtful pause. "More like each word carried a little pile of feeling."

"I can't believe . . ." Dekkard's muttered words were more to himself.

"You'd better," said Avraal. "We both sensed it."

Dekkard was still trying to figure out what he'd done differently when they reached the brown Ferrum. He was especially careful on the drive to Baartol's office to return the Ferrum and then on the way back to the house.

"How did it go?" asked Emrelda as she met them in the side hall.

"Steffan enticed a small crowd into listening," said Avraal. "He seems to be able to put actual feeling into his words . . . not just by tone. It's a little disconcerting."

"But . . . he's an isolate."

"He's still an isolate," replied Avraal. "I can't sense him at all . . . just the emotional content of the words."

"That's . . . it's more than strange." After a moment, Emrelda asked, "Have you ever heard of that before?"

Avraal shook her head. "Please don't mention it . . . not that you would. I think it only happens when he feels strongly."

"Did anyone notice?"

"No. Only an empath who focused on the words would notice, and the crowd was small."

"How small?" asked Emrelda.

"Twenty-three, not counting us."

"That's big enough to get patrollers interested, even if they didn't notice anything about the words."

"We left before they got interested," said Dekkard. "I spoke, and Avraal enticed them, while Nincya watched out for trouble. Fortunately, there wasn't any."

"There won't be, not until someone is looking for you," said Emrelda. "That could be a while if you don't speak for a long time. Machtarn is not a small city, and there are scores of small squares."

"Only about a score near where we're likely to find New Meritorists," replied Dekkard. "Now, can we get this makeup off?" He paused. "I'm sorry. I didn't mean to be abrupt. It just feels . . . sticky."

"Does it itch?" asked Avraal.

"No."

"Good."

Dekkard felt better once he had removed the spirit gum holding the beard in place and after he had the makeup off. Both Emrelda and Gaaroll went to their rooms, and Dekkard and Avraal were alone in the sitting room.

"You're sure I was tying emotions to the words?"

Avraal raised her eyebrows. "I know what I sensed. So did Gaaroll."

"But isolates can't be empaths. They just can't be."

"We don't know that. There's no record of that, but if it's something really rare there wouldn't be. *But* you're not an empath. It's not the same. I can project feelings. Just feelings. Not words. Somehow, you've linked emotion to the words. Everyone else radiates emotion, and I can sense their feelings behind the words, but your words, tonight . . . the words had the feelings. Not you, but the words. I couldn't feel anything else you were feeling. Neither could Nincya."

"Have I ever done that before?"

"You must have, but I never sensed it before."

"But . . . how?"

"You sense death when you cause it, except you describe it as 'seeing' an image, rather than feeling it. Somehow . . . you're a little different from most isolates."

A little different?

Dekkard shivered, just slightly. He hadn't had trouble accepting that he was an isolate. But discovering he had the ability to imbue words with emotion, something that he'd never heard of, or read about . . . that was . . . disconcerting, to say the least.

32

DEKKARD woke on Findi morning pondering whether his "Contrarian" plan was a fool's game.

The New Meritorists could ignore you, and the corporacion types could attempt another assassination. But neither Trujillo nor the Ministry of Public Safety had gotten anywhere in finding out much about the New Meritorists. The Treasury and Justiciary Ministries hadn't done any better, and Dekkard had been personally attacked for pointing out the shortcomings of the Treasury Ministry.

He was still worrying about it when Avraal joined him in the breakfast room. Surprisingly, they were the first two up. He got *Gestirn* from the front porch box and read it while she sipped her café. The only story of more than passing interest noted that the current frigid weather was the longest unbroken stretch of freezing weather since accurate daily records had been kept—more than fifty years.

Finally, Avraal said, "What's bothering you? You're never this quiet in the morning."

"I worry about doing these Contrarian appearances." He briefly explained his misgivings.

"When you were just being a councilor," she replied quietly, "you were worried that you weren't doing enough and that no one else was, either. Now you're doing something, and that worries you? Two appearances aren't enough to prove or disprove anything." She offered a brief wry smile. "Besides, if you didn't try something, you'd worry even more."

"Friggin' right," offered Gaaroll as she entered the breakfast room, followed by Emrelda.

"You can't start a movement overnight," said Emrelda. "Or even the impression of one."

"No, but the more appearances I make, the sooner I'll get an idea of whether it might work or whether it's a dead end," said Dekkard. "I thought we could do two today."

"You mentioned that last night," replied Avraal. "What areas do you have in mind?"

"We did one on the west side and one in the northeast. South and southeast?"

"If you do one in the south, don't make it near Fernando's," said Emrelda.

"You think the patrollers would recognize us?" asked Dekkard.

"That's not the problem. The street toughs there are looking for a fight. Any excuse will do. You'll either maim or kill someone or get killed or maimed. Go farther west and south, maybe near the White Cougar. More university types there."

"Thank you," said Dekkard. "We'll do that. Would late afternoon or evening be better for the White Cougar area?"

"Late afternoon would be better, but that's just a guess."

"Your guess over mine," replied Dekkard, taking a bite of his croissant.

After breakfast, Dekkard and Avraal retreated to the study with Emrelda's street maps of Machtarn.

After several minutes, he said, "Anaatol Square is the closest to the White Cougar. Do you know who Anaatol was? I feel like I should know."

"He was a cynical poet in the nine hundreds."

"That explains it. My literary education definitely has gaps in it. I picked up some at the Institute, but only the minimum. Did he write anything I should know?"

"You aren't missing much. That's why he's almost forgotten these days."

"But you know him."

"That's because Father was always quoting a few of his lines. There's one couplet that goes something like this:

> *"There is more wisdom in a bistro's pot*
> *Than sixty-six councilors all have got."*

"From what I've seen of some councilors, there's some truth in that." Dekkard frowned, then smiled wryly. "But as a councilor, I might not be considered objective."

"Father was always quoting that line . . . and another one."

"Do I want to ask about the other one?"

"You won't like it, but you'll understand where I came from a little better."

"Go ahead," Dekkard said warily.

"You asked," said Avraal.

> *"While they can make a Crafter a Ritter*
> *It doesn't make him any fitter . . ."*

She added, "It goes on from there, but I don't recall the rest. Father usually only quoted the first lines. Just so you know, Cliven quotes Anaatol as well, but only when Fleur's not around."

"I might like Fleur."

"You will. You'll like Cliven, too, so long as you don't talk politics or history."

"Or the Silent Revolution," suggested Dekkard.

"Definitely not that." Avraal paused, then said, "Where should we try this evening?"

"Did you ask Carlos about bistros or tavernas nearer the harbor? I don't think we want to be near Rabool's. I can't see disgruntled professionals and intellectuals frequenting it."

"There's a place that's half bistro, half tavern about four blocks from there. It's called 'Colorado.'"

"Odd name for a bistro."

"The original owner fled Atacama."

"I suppose that makes as much sense as anything. Where is it on the map?"

Avraal pointed.

"I don't think I've ever been there," said Dekkard. "Not that I recall. At least we're learning a bit more about Machtarn." *Not that I ever planned to learn it this way.*

"There's a patrol station west of Colorado," said Avraal. "Emrelda marked them all with triangles. The closest square to the east is Raadhym. Here."

"That will have to do. That's another name I've never heard."

"I haven't, either. That's not surprising. With all the small squares in the older parts of the city, they likely used some obscure names."

"Or names that were once better known. I wouldn't have known about Iustaan Detruro if Ingrella hadn't given me that history to read."

"Do you want to plan out somewhere for tomorrow night?" asked Avraal.

"We probably should try something closer to Imperial Boulevard, but let's see how today goes." Dekkard replaced the map in the leather case, still silently questioning whether his efforts would be effective in the slightest.

Just after second bell, Dekkard began getting himself ready, starting with the mahogany wig and beard. Almost two thirds passed before the three were on their way to pick up the brown Ferrum, and three bells were ringing out across the city when Dekkard drove past the White Cougar in the Ferrum.

As Dekkard circled the block, looking for a place to park, he could see that there were definitely more people out and about. He finally found a parking space a half block farther west. When the three of them got out of the Ferrum, Dekkard glanced around, noticing that the air was slightly above freezing, possibly due to the weak sunlight struggling through a haze that wasn't quite so thick as on recent days.

As the three began to walk toward the south entrance to Anaatol Square, most people on the street gave the sign Dekkard carried little more than a passing glance, as if such signs were common, or at least not uncommon.

As the three neared the gate, Dekkard asked, "How many in the square?"

"More than a score. Mostly singles or couples. Likely on the benches. One small group at the west end," said Gaaroll.

"We'll aim for the east end, then. What about feelings?"

"Nothing real strong," replied Gaaroll.

Avraal and Gaaroll slowed as Dekkard neared the gates, then halted as he passed through the black ironwork.

Anaatol Square, unlike the previous two squares where Dekkard had spoken, was actually an oblong with an extended oval basin around the fountain, which featured a statue of a man in tights and a jacket, with a quill pen in one hand and a scroll in the other. The statue's mouth was open, and Dekkard realized that had to be so that water could flow out.

His words flow like water, thirst-quenching, yet without lasting meaning. That was Dekkard's immediate interpretation, and that of the sculptor might have been considerably more charitable.

The speaker at the west end of the fountain basin was a man with short black hair but a well-trimmed spade beard who wore a plain black cassock, a garment Dekkard associated with the Solidan priesthood. Dekkard could only pick up snatches of his moderately strong light baritone:

". . . immaterialism denies the reality of the world . . . dematerialism denies . . . what people are . . . Trinitarianism . . . arbitrary division . . ."

Dekkard smiled wryly as he moved to the east end of the dry fountain basin, deciding to prop the sign against the side of a vacant bench and to face the fountain, since there was ample space for onlookers, and he wanted to see if what he said had any effect elsewhere in the square.

He propped up the sign, turned to face the older-looking couple wrapped in blankets on the closest bench, but said nothing for several long moments.

The man laughed heartily. "Do you think your sign says it all?"

"Not all," returned Dekkard. "It's a good place to start, though. Most wages aren't fair, and most workplaces aren't safe. Especially large workplaces. The lower corporacions can keep wages, the more marks the corporacion makes."

"The corporacions would say that allows them to hire more men," replied the older man, "and stay in business. If they can't stay in business, there wouldn't be any jobs at all."

"All of the big corporacions could raise wages at current prices and still make a profit."

"Then their competitors would undercut them."

Dekkard laughed harshly. "That can't happen because they've all bought up and driven out smaller competitors."

"Then how come there are different corporacions producing steamers and not one corporacion?"

"Each steamer corporacion produces for a different price range," countered Dekkard. "Besides, not that many people can afford steamers. More could if wages were fairer."

"Do you even know what 'Contrarian' means?" asked a younger man who sauntered toward Dekkard almost contemptuously. His not quite ragged beard and the scuffed reddish leather jacket suggested he was or had been a student.

"Looking at things differently from others," replied Dekkard. "Different from Commercers, Landors, New Meritorists, or most Crafters."

The bearded young man angled toward Dekkard, then backed off when Dekkard faced him, as if he realized that Dekkard was considerably taller and broader across the shoulders.

"Don't like it when you can't outtalk or intimidate a square speaker, do you?" said the older man.

The bearded man lunged toward the seated older man, but Dekkard intercepted him and used a side kick to drop him to the stone pavement, before kicking the knife from his hand.

"Schoolboy," snapped Dekkard, "get your bearded ass out of the square. Now."

The bearded man's hand then went toward his belt, but Dekkard had anticipated that as well, and the pistol skittered across the stone.

At that point, the "older" man stood, throwing aside the blankets, revealing a patroller's uniform. The "woman" turned out to be a youthful male patroller, once his wig vanished.

Dekkard just kicked the knife farther from the bearded man and stepped back.

The bearded man scrambled to his feet, looking like he wanted to run, but then slumped as the two patrollers approached and cuffed him. "Could have gotten clear," he snarled as he glared at Dekkard.

"Stealing isn't a way to get fair wages," Dekkard said. "Killing isn't, either."

The older patroller looked at Dekkard. "Military training?"

"A while back."

"Patrol could always use a good man."

"I thought about it, but right now, I need to deliver a message."

"Just avoid the Southtown squares. They shoot first."

Dekkard inclined his head. "Much obliged for the warning. Expect they wouldn't care about the message there."

"Hardly," said the younger patroller.

Dekkard watched as the two patrollers marched the bearded man away, the younger one carrying the old blankets. *At least you didn't have to disable that bastard.*

At that point, the preacher in the cassock appeared. "Did you have to disrupt everything? You scared everyone away."

"Just kept that little bastard from knifing me. You have a problem with that?" Dekkard glared at the preacher.

"No . . . not at all."

After the preacher turned away, Dekkard glanced to Avraal, who had moved closer and gestured that he should stay.

So he turned and walked back to stand beside the sign, waiting.

He didn't have to wait that long, almost certainly because Avraal was emp-enticing some passersby into the square.

Several people moved toward him, expressions suggesting they wondered why they were there.

Dekkard smiled and pointed to the sign. "Fair wages . . . safe work. Sounds simple, doesn't it? So why is it so hard for so many working men and women to get either?"

Despite the semi-blank looks, Dekkard went on. "Because corporacions make sure that good jobs are hard to come by and that workers have to take what they offer. How many little businesses have you seen vanish? One day they're doing well and paying better, and the next they're gone. Bought out or beaten down by the big corporacions. The smart smaller businesses sell out because they know they'll be destroyed one way or another if they don't."

"That's absurd, isn't it?" asked one man.

"My brother's dead, and so's his boss," said Dekkard, misstating slightly because he wanted to be truthful, but not too truthful, "because his boss's business cut into the profits of a huge corporacion. Look around. Look close. You can see it if you look.

"How many workers die on the job, or get so used up that they can't work any longer and then die? The Commercers don't care. Neither do the New Meritorists. The Meritorists just want to change the way the Council votes so they can get power. The Landors just want their old power back."

For the next bell, Dekkard did his best, but he was getting hoarse by the time he said, "Just think about it. Think how everything affects you. Think Contrarian." He lifted the sign. "Contrarian! The way to get fair wages and safe work." Then he turned and marched out of Anaatol Square, hoping his words had more effect than those of the long-dead poet.

Once the three were in the steamer, with the sign in the small rear seat with Gaaroll, Avraal handed Dekkard a bottle from which she'd removed the cork. "Lager. Cold, but a little flat."

Dekkard took a swallow, then another before handing the bottle back. "That helps."

"Why didn't the bearded guy go after the square preacher?" asked Gaaroll as they drove from Anaatol Square.

"Solidan street or square preachers never carry marks." Dekkard looked to Avraal. "You blunted the patrollers' curiosity about me, didn't you?"

"I couldn't do much until you said you'd had military training. Then I could project the feeling that it all made sense, and another feeling that there wasn't any reason to drag you into it."

"Thank you. Again."

"You did a lot of that, with your words, in the way that you have."

Dekkard nodded, understanding what she meant. At the same time, the fact that he applied some weight of feeling to his words definitely concerned him. He didn't think that made him an empath, but others might not see it that way. *And empaths can't be councilors.*

Dekkard forced his thoughts back to his driving as he guided the Ferrum to the riverside and parked beside one of the older and empty piers gradually abandoned with the growth of ironway freight. He sipped more of the ale and let his voice rest. Almost a bell later, he started the Ferrum, and headed north toward Raadhym Square.

As he'd suspected, as the darkness settled over the square, fewer and fewer people stopped to listen, even with the encouragement provided by Avraal's emping, and after two-thirds of a bell, Dekkard decided that there was little point in remaining.

The one good aspect of ending up at Raadhym Square was that it was only six blocks or so from Carlos Baartol's office, and that made returning the brown Ferrum much easier and quicker.

When they finally returned to the house, Emrelda emerged from the kitchen and met them in the hall. "Dinner isn't quite ready. You're back earlier than I thought."

"There weren't many near Raadhym Square," said Dekkard. "At Anaatol Square . . . we had some . . . unexpected experiences." He went on to recount briefly what had happened.

"I should have warned you about that," said Emrelda. "When there have been reports of repeated thefts or assaults in a square, sometimes we set up watchers. I hadn't heard of any station doing that lately. Usually it isn't necessary in winter."

"Well," said Dekkard wryly, "maybe those patrollers will spread the word about the Contrarians."

"Then we'll have to worry about watching even more for patrollers, in addition to New Meritorists," Avraal pointed out.

"Everything has its complications." Dekkard shrugged. *Always.* "At least I'll have time to get out of the wig and makeup before we eat."

33

ON Unadi morning, Dekkard read *Gestirn* thoroughly, relieved to find that there was no mention of the incident at Anaatol Square.

When he mentioned that at breakfast, Emrelda just shook her head. "No one got killed, and no patrollers got hurt. Even the idiot you disarmed wasn't more than bruised. I'm sure the patrollers at the University Station were more than happy with the way you handled the situation. They thought you didn't want any fuss, and neither did they."

Dekkard could see that and turned his attention to his café and croissants.

After he finished breakfast and walked out to the garage, he felt that the day was a shade colder, and slightly hazier, than Findi had been and wondered if another storm might be heading down from the north toward Machtarn. His fingers briefly touched his personal truncheon. While he doubted he'd need it at the Council buildings, Avraal had insisted that he carry it, since it was possible that something could happen on the way to and from the Council Office Building.

Once Avraal dropped him and Gaaroll off outside the Council Office Building, Dekkard took a moment to survey the area, noting that Guard Captain Trujillo still had extra guards posted on the rooftop emplacements, but that there were fewer guards around the sturdy iron gates.

When Dekkard reached his office, Roostof stood beside Margrit, who immediately handed Dekkard a message.

"This just arrived a few minutes ago, sir. The messenger said it was urgent."

"Thank you." Dekkard immediately opened the missive, which was from Premier Hasheem. The text was simple.

Steffan—
I'd appreciate your meeting me at the Premier's floor office at third bell, earlier if you can make it.

Fredrich

Dekkard looked to Gaaroll. "Keep your jacket on." Then he looked to Roostof. "We're headed to the Council Hall. The Premier wants to see me."

"That doesn't sound good, sir." Roostof offered an inquiring look.

"He didn't say why." Dekkard turned to Margrit. "I'll keep the message for now." *Just in case the Council Guard outside the office wants to know why.*

Dekkard walked swiftly out of the Council Office Building, through the courtyard, and along the main corridor of the Council Hall to the Premier's floor office. Gaaroll had to trot to keep up with Dekkard's longer steps.

The Council Guard outside the door didn't even ask, but opened the door and motioned the two to enter.

The door to the inner office was closed, but the secretary simply said, "You're to go right in, Councilor."

Dekkard still rapped on the door as he opened it, stepped inside, and said, "I came as soon as I got the message." Then he closed the door.

Hasheem looked up from his desk, the dark circles under his eyes clearly visible. "You obviously hurried. I do appreciate it." He extended a single sheet of paper to Dekkard. "This has to remain between us. You'll see why when you read it. It's actually a copy of a message that was delivered to the Palace of the Imperador late yesterday afternoon by a messenger from Guldoran Heliograph. The return address on the outside of the routing envelope indicated it was from the Admiral of the Southern Fleet. The priority routing codes were correct, and it went directly to the Imperador's private secretary."

Dekkard took the sheet and began to read.

Your Imperial Mightiness—

The Council of Sixty-Six has continued to ignore our request that all votes on legislative matters be recorded in a manner that discloses how each councilor voted on each and every measure. There has been no attempt to modify the Great Charter to make such a change. Nor has the Council moved to change the party composition of the Council to allow a political party to elect a majority of councilors so that the people of Guldor can have a truly representative government.

Since the Council has not seen fit to undertake either of these necessary reforms, we request the dissolution of the current Council and call for elections. If you do not take such a step in the next two days, we will make the same request of your successor and what remains of the current Council.

There was no signature, only the typed words "The New Meritorists of Guldor."

Dekkard read it again, then returned the sheet. "That threat isn't even veiled."

"As you might imagine, I didn't get much sleep last night, and I was at the Palace again early this morning. First Marshal Bernotte is quite confident that his battle group can deal with the *Khuld,* which is an outdated light cruiser. The Imperador has every confidence in him. This is, however, unfortunately not a matter I can bring before the Security Committee at present. I assume you understand why?"

"I would judge that the editorial published by *The Machtarn Tribune* about the questionable Councilor Dekkard has something to do with that."

"Precisely. Who do you think provided that information to the *Tribune*?"

"The information about the briefing most likely came from the most honorable Jaradd Rikkard, since he dislikes me, and no other councilor on the committee would have anything to gain by providing such information."

"Why not the other Commercer councilor?"

Dekkard found it interesting that Hasheem didn't want to refer to Baar by name. "We don't share the same set of beliefs, but he's honest, and I don't think he sees any future in going back to Suvion."

"Is that your judgment?"

"It's also my wife's judgment, and she's one of the best empaths in Guldor."

"What about the Landors?"

"Haastar wouldn't do that, and I doubt that Navione would see any purpose in doing so. Also, the other interesting fact is that the information in the *Tribune* editorial about our house purchase in Gaarlak was extremely limited, which suggests it was obtained from the Banque of Gaarlak."

Hasheem frowned. "The Banque of Gaarlak? Why?"

"That's a considered guess. The property was held by the Lakaan Valley Banque, and everyone involved there knew much more than was reported, but nothing personal showed up in the *Tribune* editorial. The information only revealed what would be entered in the district land registry, information readily available to a banque. The son of the presidente of the Banque of Gaarlak was second in the balloting for councilor in the last election."

"That's a little thin, Steffan."

Dekkard smiled politely. "I said it was a considered guess."

"What do you think the New Meritorists have planned?"

"As I told you earlier, I believe they intend for the *Khuld* to shell the Council buildings and the Imperial Palace. Without spotters, even excellent gunners would have a hard time hitting specific targets. My guess, and it is a guess, is that when those shells start exploding across Machtarn, the New Meritorists will have teams with explosive devices that they'll plant and detonate. Certainly, some will target the Council buildings and the Palace of the Imperador, possibly the ironways. They may also position snipers to target councilors who attempt to leave the buildings."

"What would you tell the Imperador?"

"I'd tell him what I told you. I'd also suggest that, in the meantime, he move to a secure location unknown to the Meritorists that is more than fifteen milles from the harbor until the attacks pass, which they will. He shouldn't go to any place he habitually visits or along usual routes. They could easily plant assassins there."

"Why do you say that?"

"The Navy is having great difficulty locating a near-obsolete light cruiser with a partial crew. If the *Khuld* succeeds in evading the First Marshal's battle group and starts shelling the city, and I still believe that is possible, despite First Marshal Bernotte's assurances to the contrary, that will reveal her location and make her a target—unless the mutineers quickly fire salvos and depart. Either the *Khuld* will fire until she's sunk or she'll retreat. Likewise, the New Meritorists have a limited supply of dunnite, but there are likely enough guns to make it difficult for patrollers alone to bring them under control. The Meritorist tactics are to create chaos that the Council seems unable to control. They've already struck at the ironway terminal markets. There could be more attacks of that nature. They might also try to damage the ironways in some fashion."

"The ironways? Why?"

"Because that could cut off the rapid movement of troops to Machtarn. Several weeks ago, they attacked a coaling tower. There was some damage, but no coal was taken. I have to wonder if that might have been a test of some sort. You might consider pointing that out to the Imperador." When Hasheem did not immediately reply, Dekkard added, "To keep control of Machtarn and maintain order, force will be necessary. Too much force, and people will want the Commercers back. Too little force, and the Council will give the impression of lack of control."

"You're suggesting that it's better to err on the side of too much force," said Hasheem.

"It's better to show force and not use it than not have sufficient force ready to act. I also think that the Security Committee should know about the possible danger, and, if the *Khuld* is sighted anywhere near Machtarn, the entire Council should be told." Dekkard waited.

Hasheem smiled, wanly. "I appreciate your thoughts. I've already ordered the Marshal of the Army to bring in additional troopers to deal with the New Meritorists here in Machtarn. Perhaps we should add some more. There will be a brief Security Committee meeting at first bell. It will include the possible danger from the *Khuld,* but not the ultimatum to the Imperador." The Premier stood. "Thank you, Steffan."

Dekkard inclined his head. "I wish you the best in dealing with all of this."

Hasheem merely nodded.

Dekkard turned and left the inner office, opening and then closing the door behind himself. He smiled at the secretary and said, "Have the best day you can."

"Thank you, Councilor. We appreciate your coming so quickly."

Dekkard thought about her words as he and Gaaroll walked across the courtyard and back to the Council Office Building. Those words hadn't sounded perfunctory, but had she been speaking for Hasheem? Or for the Premier's staff? Both?

"Were you paying attention to the Premier's secretary, Nincya?"

"About what, sir?"

"Her words suggested . . ." Dekkard broke off what he was saying, since he wasn't certain what those words had suggested.

"She and the clerks had strong feelings when we came. They weren't as strong when we left."

"Were they relieved? Or resigned? What do you think?" Dekkard thought it might have been relief, but he didn't want to deceive himself. Also, if his presence relieved the staff, that meant they were concerned about Hasheem, and that wasn't good.

"Their feelings were more reddish gray when we got there. When we left they were blacker and lower."

"More like relief, then?"

"I'd say so, sir."

I was afraid of that. But all Dekkard said was, "Thank you."

As Dekkard expected, as soon as he stepped through the office door, Roostof hurried out of the staff office, but Dekkard looked to Margrit. "Any more messages?"

"No, sir."

"The Premier wanted my thoughts on what the New Meritorists might do next. I suggested that they'll do their best to create a sense of chaos, one way or another. I outlined some of the possibilities. He thanked me and dismissed me. I suspect he'll be meeting with the Imperador before long."

Roostof tried to hide a frown.

"Svard," said Dekkard, "right now, I can't say more. I will say that I'm worried about that missing cruiser mentioned in the newssheets because it's likely in New Meritorist hands. That may be the reason why there's a naval battle group patrolling the waters south of Machtarn—and both those points *are* more than I should say. So please keep them to yourselves for now."

"Things aren't good, then, are they, sir?" asked Margrit.

"Let's just say they could be much better. I'll let you know more as I can." He offered a wry smile. "In the meantime, the mail awaits me."

"And your weekly report from Zenya Onswyrth," added Margrit.

Once Dekkard had hung up his overcoat and seated himself behind his desk, he picked up the report from Gaarlak and began to read.

The entry for Duadi the twentieth of Winterend definitely caught his attention.

A patroller first came to the office. He said that Jens Seigryn was still missing. He asked when I had last seen Sr. Seigryn. I told him that it had been on the fifteenth of Winterend. He wanted to know how I remembered the date. I told him it was because Sr. Seigryn was a Craft political coordinator, and I had reported his visit to you. I suggested he confirm that with Legalist Desharra. He went to see her. He did not question me again.

The remainder of Onswyrth's report was unremarkable, relaying concerns about levees when the ice melted and the spring runoff began, the "exorbitant" ironway charges for produce, and the failure of the Council to deal with the New Meritorists.

Dekkard then turned to the mail. Most of it was as he had come to expect, except that four different letters espoused various aspects of the New Meritorist proposals. At least one of those return addresses had to be false, because, after his and Avraal's house-hunting in Gaarlak, Dekkard knew that such an address did not exist. Two of the letters had handwriting that appeared remarkably similar.

So how many New Meritorists are there outside of Machtarn? A few hundred spread out to create the impression of thousands? Or thousands afraid to reveal themselves? Or something in between? How much is illusion and how much reality?

Dekkard had to admit that he had no idea.

As Hasheem had indicated to Dekkard, by fourth bell there was a notice of the Security Committee meeting.

Dekkard entered the committee chamber just before first bell and took his seat beside Tomas Pajiin.

After gaveling the committee to order, Hasheem began. "The Admiralty has no further word on the location or the activities of the I.S. *Khuld*. Because there is always the possibility that the mutineers might attempt to use the *Khuld*'s guns against ports or cities, or for some other purpose the New Meritorists deem as necessary for their interests, the battle group headed by the I.S. *Resolute* continues to patrol the offshore waters to the south of Machtarn."

Hasheem continued for several minutes, providing only general details about the battle group before gaveling the meeting to a halt and quickly departing.

"He's not saying anything, and he's worried," said Pajiin quietly. "What do you know, Steffan?"

"It's more than a little worrisome that a battle group can't find a near-obsolete cruiser crewed by fanatical New Meritorist mutineers. There's something else going on."

"He almost said that they were aiming at Machtarn, maybe at the Council. Is that possible?"

"The *Khuld* has eight-digit guns. From just outside the harbor they could reach as far as the Imperador's Palace, and a light cruiser can fire a shell a minute from each gun. The *Khuld* has three two-gun turrets. But they wouldn't have spotters, and even with good fire control and spotters, they'd be fortunate to have one shell out of twenty hit near a target. The problem is that they could just keep firing and create a lot of damage." *And they could get lucky and actually hit the Council or the Palace.*

"Why didn't he say that?"

"He honestly may not know that. Also, possibly because he doesn't want to get people worried when the Admiralty believes they can sink the *Khuld* before it does any damage."

Pajiin shook his head. "I don't like it."

"For what it's worth, neither do I," replied Dekkard.

Pajiin left the chamber in a hurry. Dekkard was slightly slower, and found Villem Baar waiting for him just inside the doorway to the main corridor.

"Was that as bad as I think it was, Steffan?"

"Probably worse. The committee's not being told everything. That may be because too much has been leaked. But when people hide things, even for what they think are the best of reasons, after a while people don't trust them. Often, the distrust is misplaced."

"Misplaced?"

"For example, if a committee chair is continually constrained from informing the councilors on a committee about various matters, the chair is placed in a position of losing trust or disobeying the Premier."

Baar frowned. "But Fredrich is both chair and Premier."

"The principle applies at various levels," said Dekkard dryly.

After a moment, Baar said worriedly, "So it is worse. How much worse?"

"It's hard to say. There's too much we don't know. How many empies do the Meritorists have to push disturbances into riots against the Council? How much dunnite do they still have? How good are the gunners on the *Khuld*? How incompetent is the First Marshal? Are there still corporacion types feeding marks and information to the Meritorists?" Dekkard smiled sourly and looked directly at Baar. "Those are just a few of the questions I have that neither the Premier nor a certain other committee chair wants to look into. Right now, so far as I can tell, no one has answers to those questions. There is one thing I *do* know that bothers me. Any group organized enough to take over a Navy ship and keep it out of sight even with the obvious destination of Machtarn is not to be underestimated. I worry that the First Marshal is doing just that."

"You ought to be Security Committee chair."

Dekkard laughed softly. "Right now, I don't think it would make much difference."

Baar paused, then said, "I see what you mean." Then he smiled sadly. "Thank you."

As he walked silently back to his office with Gaaroll, Dekkard worried about what he'd said to both Pajiin and Baar. He'd tried to direct their thoughts to the possible attack on Machtarn without specifically revealing the ultimatum, but it still bothered him. Yet, with Rikkard on the Security Committee . . . ?

He shook his head.

Once back in his office, Dekkard did his best to deal with the routine matters. He talked to Teitryn, but the engineering aide hadn't yet been able to find out about the punch-card lathe. He signed and revised more letters.

He worried.

Avraal arrived at slightly past fourth bell. Once the door to his personal office was securely closed, Dekkard immediately told her about his meeting with Hasheem, as well as the later Security Committee meeting and his conversations with Pajiin and Baar.

Her eyes didn't even widen. When he finished, she asked, "Do you think it's possible the Meritorists are bluffing?"

"They may be overestimating their capabilities, but it's not a bluff. The timing of the message and the accurate routing codes suggests that the *Khuld* is somewhere close to Machtarn. They can't possibly be sure that their gunnery will be accurate enough to take out both the Council buildings and the Palace, but I'd judge that they'll use the damage and confusion that the shells will cause as cover to plant other explosives. They also warned the Imperador to induce him to leave the security of the Palace for one of his other properties, where I suspect they have assassins or explosives in readiness, either en route or in place." He paused, then added, "There's also the possibility that the note is a ruse, and when the *Khuld* doesn't show up and nothing happens, everyone will let down their guard, and the *Khuld* will move in and strike."

"Is that more likely?" asked Avraal.

"I'd wager on the first, because the Meritorists like to create the impression of control. Also, because the Admiralty is saying nothing about the *Khuld*, most people will be totally shocked and unprepared when shells start falling on Machtarn."

"You said 'when,' not 'if.'"

"I have more confidence in the abilities of the New Meritorists than in the First Marshal."

"Let us hope you're wrong. Do you have any more encouraging news?"

"Not really. Zenya Onswyrth's report said that Jens Seigryn was still missing and Gaarlak patrollers questioned her and Namoor Desharra."

"That's not good, either."

"No, it's not, but they didn't bother Zenya after Namoor talked to them," replied Dekkard. "What about you?"

"The day was quiet. I asked Carlos if we could keep using the Ferrum in the evening. He said yes and didn't ask for details."

"Then we'd better get moving." Dekkard stood and retrieved his overcoat and his folder.

When he, Avraal, and Gaaroll stepped outside the Council Office Building less than a sixth of a bell later, the air felt warmer than it had for days, if not weeks, but the haze and coal smoke were heavier. The drive home was uneventful, except for a detour because Gaaroll noted strong feelings near Jacquez.

Dekkard left the Gresynt under the portico, since they planned to make another attempt at creating the image of a Contrarian movement later that evening.

When he stepped through the portico door, Avraal walked toward him, smiling. "We got a letter from Hrald Iglis."

"How is he coming on rebuilding the kitchen?"

"He thinks he'll be done in another two weeks. He also sent the proposed costs for the new stove and the coal-gas cooler."

"For which we'll need to pay him before he procures them . . . and the balance due?"

"The total for the stove and cooler—the ones we decided on—will be two hundred ninety marks. He wrote that he wouldn't know the balance due until he's finished, but he thinks it will be around six hundred marks."

"That's a little less than he estimated," said Dekkard, hanging up his overcoat.

"The stove and cooler are a bit higher, though."

"The way things are going here," said Dekkard ironically, "having a house in Gaarlak sounds better and better."

"I wouldn't go that far yet," replied Avraal.

"Do we need to help Emrelda with dinner?"

"She says it's under control. Pork milanesia. She said we should plan out the evening 'reconnaissance,' and not anywhere near Southtown."

"Disturbances there, again?"

"She didn't say, but I imagine so." Avraal turned toward the study.

Dekkard followed. So did Emrelda and Gaaroll.

Once Dekkard had the maps laid out on the desk, Avraal said, "Let's try the area to the east of the Council. It used to be fashionable a long time ago." She grinned. "Formerly fashionable areas often have a few disgruntled professionals and intellectuals."

"Is Hillside formerly fashionable?" asked Gaaroll.

"Hillside has yet to *become* fashionable," replied Emrelda. "But with two councilors residing here, that might change."

"I doubt it. We're both about as junior as possible."

"Not any longer," said Avraal. "If I've recalled correctly, there are now five councilors junior to you, and another handful that are only a few days senior to you."

Dekkard paused. Avraal was right, but he hadn't thought of it that way. That was likely more turnover in less than a year than since the time of the Silent Revolution. *And if the* Resolute *doesn't sink the* Khuld . . . He pushed that thought away. "Do you have a tavern in mind?"

"The Roaring Bull."

"Bulls don't roar."

"That's probably why someone picked that name. The closest of the squares nearby is Ilspieth Square."

Dekkard frowned. The name sounded familiar. "Ilspieth? I should know that name."

"You should, dear. Princess Ilspieth was the Imperador's daughter rumored to be one of the unnamed conspirators behind the Silent Revolution. After Obreduur mentioned her, I did some research. Some think she was also an empath, but that was never confirmed. She never married and spent most of her life writing a history of the early Imperadors." Avraal smiled. "The history is not known to have been published."

Dekkard looked at Avraal. "You think . . . the rare history book Ingrella had me read?"

"It's possible. It couldn't have been published under her name, and the copy didn't have an author listed, unlike *The City of Truth,* which is much older."

"Have you asked Ingrella?"

"At the times we've been with her, there have been more 'pressing' matters."

Dekkard nodded. That had been all too true. He looked at the map, finally locating the square. "It's a larger square, set off by itself."

"That's likely why it was named for a princess. Most likely renamed, since that part of the city predates Ilspieth. It was a token gesture, about as little as they could do. There's nothing else that bears her name."

Dekkard was still mulling that over long after he'd donned the wig, beard, and makeup and changed into the decidedly grubby grays.

By a third before sixth bell, Dekkard had brought the Gresynt to a stop in the parking area that served Carlos Baartol's office. Unlike previous evenings, there were several steamers parked in the lot besides the brown Ferrum, and there were lamps on inside the building. Dekkard glanced up, but no one seemed to be looking. So he quickly got out of the Gresynt, locked it, and moved to the Ferrum, as did Avraal and Gaaroll.

Once they were all well away from the building, Dekkard asked, "Do you have any idea what might have kept Carlos working late?"

"He didn't mention anything, but I don't know everything he's working on. He is spending a great deal of time trying to find out who is behind the removal of so many investigators."

"Ulrich. Or his associates or superiors. Not that there's going to be much proof." *If any.*

"What about del Larrano?" asked Avraal.

"That's likely, given the connections between Ulrich and Siincleer Shipbuilding." Dekkard turned north on Imperial Boulevard.

While it wasn't absolutely necessary, he drove by the Roaring Bull on the way to Ilspieth Square. He wanted to see what the outside of the tavern looked like, but the exterior was unremarkable, the façade appearing to be that of a converted town house—with just a single wide black door lit by two lamps and flanked on each side by a narrow window. The sign-board above the door and between lamps showed a rearing horned white bull with a beaker inexplicably grasped in one hoof.

Parking spaces were infrequent, but Dekkard found one on a side street leading to the square, which turned out to be a narrow oblong between Treasury Avenue and Chelles Street. He suspected that the square—only thirty yards wide, if almost seventy long—had been created around the turn of the century when Treasury Avenue had been widened and extended, simply because the strip was too narrow for decent housing and unsuited for commercial buildings.

A chest-high stone wall surrounded Ilspieth Square except at the four entrances. The square also held two small fountains, one near the east end and the other near the west. Carrying his sign, Dekkard walked toward the east end, slightly closer to the Roaring Bull. As before, as he neared the east entrance, Avraal and Gaaroll lagged behind. Dekkard could see people walking or standing and talking in the square, but spied an empty stone bench on the west side of the fountain, which featured an elegantly dressed woman, presumably the princess.

Four youngish men looked at Dekkard's sign as he propped it up behind the bench. Then one, square-shouldered and blocky, stepped forward. "Contrarian? What's that?"

"Someone contrary to the way things are today. We're also contrary to the ways people like the New Meritorists want to change things . . . because those changes will make things worse."

"That's not contrary—it's reactionary," declared the blocky man, who wore a heavy brown jacket.

"Are you for anything?" demanded one of the others.

"Like the sign says, we're for fair wages and safe work."

The first man moved closer to Dekkard, just slightly, and laughed. "Simplistic slogans."

"Most good principles are simplistic," replied Dekkard. "Do no harm—that's a good principle for people and governments. It's not always possible, but it's a good place to start." He could see Avraal easing closer, but she looked interested, not worried.

"You can't run Guldor like that," said the second man.

"Why not?" riposted Dekkard.

"Some people . . . especially swells with marks . . . are already doing harm."

"You're right," agreed Dekkard. "But that's because for a half century or more those swells controlled the Council and they didn't follow that rule."

"That's because they weren't held personally accountable."

Dekkard snorted loudly. "Everyone knew what the Commercers were doing. Did you hold them accountable? Did you persuade your friends to persuade their friends to vote differently?"

"Right now, voting doesn't make any difference."

"Tell that to all the corrupt Special Agents who lost their jobs. Or the corrupt Security minister who was tried, found guilty of treason, and executed."

"That'll change," declared the blocky man. "The Crafters will get as corrupt as the Commercers were. Without personal accountability for every vote, we'll see the same old, same old."

"With so-called personal accountability, things will get worse," declared Dekkard. "You'll make it easier for any councilor to be bought by popularity or by marks. The Council votes on scores of measures every year. Nothing pleases everyone. Those with marks can represent those votes any way they choose, and who will stop that misrepresentation?"

Dekkard belatedly realized that there were already close to twenty people gathered behind the four who faced him. *Where did they come from? Avraal's doing? Or are square speaker debates more usual here?*

"We know nothing about each councilor," declared the second man. "They're never held personally accountable."

"You can vote them out in every election, and you know where each party stands on each matter," said Dekkard. "You can make a party accountable. If every councilor has to worry about every vote in order to be reelected, whatever's popular will be enacted, and whatever's not won't be. Taxes aren't popular, so taxes will be reduced, but that will mean that there won't be funds for roads, bridges, ports . . . or patrollers . . ."

"Those are just scare tactics. You're sounding like a Commercer shill. People aren't that stupid."

Oh yes they are. Dekkard laughed, loudly. "You require personal accountability, and in a decade most councilors, regardless of party, will be owned by the Commercers. Unless, of course, you confiscate all their marks, and then all the councilors will be doing whatever's popular at the moment. Party accountability isn't perfect, but it's frigging better than plutocracy or mob rule."

"You claim to be a Contrarian, but that sounds like the same old crap." The second man spat to the side.

"The people deserve more power," declared the blocky man.

"That's been the claim of every despot in history. Look what happened to Teknar. Not that you care about history. Everyone talks about the lessons of history, and then fails to learn them. Politics is always about power. Despots want to concentrate power in themselves. So do most revolutionaries, no matter what they say."

"That's not true!" shouted someone.

"More power to one person or one group means less power to everyone else," Dekkard retorted. "The Great Charter split up power so that wouldn't happen. But the New Meritorists want to change that. They say that they want personal accountability. That ends up concentrating power in the hands of those who are the most popular."

The blocky man glowered, but said nothing.

Dekkard kept talking, and more people appeared.

After a time, another man called out, "More power to the people!"

"No one deserves more power," Dekkard replied. "Everyone deserves a government that applies the laws fairly to everyone. Right now, there's no difference between the Commercers and the New Meritorists. They both want more. More power over the Council. The Commercers did it with marks. The New Meritorists would do it with popular pressure on individual councilors."

By now there were close to forty people in the square. Dekkard glanced to Avraal, who drew a finger across her throat.

Dekkard managed a broad smile. "You've heard what I had to say. You can agree or disagree. But remember: Concentrating power takes it away from you, and that's what Contrarianism is all about. We're contrary to concentrating power. Have a pleasant evening."

Dekkard stepped back.

The blocky man moved forward. "You're not welcome here, whoever you are."

Dekkard smiled pleasantly. "The laws say that the squares are open to all speakers who don't espouse violence. I do hope you're not threatening violence."

"You're not welcome here," repeated the blocky man.

"I heard you the first time." Dekkard's smile turned sardonic. "I'm wearing my old security grays."

The second man murmured, "He is. Let it go, Hamaar."

Without a word, the blocky man turned, and the other three followed him.

Dekkard turned and retrieved his sign, but as he started to leave, a pudgy young man eased closer.

"Sr. Contrarian? Be careful. Hamaar's a mean one."

"Hamaar who? Or does he just go by Hamaar?"

"Hamaar Dykstraan. He thinks the square is his."

"I'll keep that in mind. Thank you." Dekkard inclined his head.

"You're welcome. You gave me a lot to think about." The pudgy young man eased away.

Dekkard let him move farther away before he began to walk toward the east entrance, watching carefully to see if Hamaar Dykstraan or his followers waited for him.

Avraal joined him before he reached the gates. "Those four were really angry with you, even before you said a word."

"The last young man to speak to me said the one regarded the square as his private speaking site. He also told me that the troublemaker's name was Hamaar Dykstraan."

"I'll see if Carlos can find anything about him."

Gaaroll appeared out of the shadows. "Those four are gone, headed toward the tavern. No strong feelings going our way."

For that Dekkard was glad.

34

A COLD wind was rattling the shutters when Dekkard woke on Duadi, but when he peered out through the window, the sky appeared clearer than it had in days, which suggested that the wind might be preceding a snowstorm. He hurried through shaving, showering, and dressing.

He took a quick look at *Gestirn,* noting that there was a small frontpage story about the "disappearance" of the I.S. *Khuld,* which stated that the Admiralty had refused to confirm a mutiny and would only say that the situation was under investigation.

Dekkard shook his head, set the newssheet on the side table, and went to prepare cafés.

Avraal arrived in the breakfast room only a few minutes later, where Dekkard had her café waiting. After she had taken several sips, she said, "I made out the cheque to Hrald Iglis for the stove and cooler. I can post it from the office."

"Thank you . . . again."

"Without you, I wouldn't have the marks to send."

"I'm still grateful." Dekkard didn't mention that he remained angry about how Avraal had gotten any inheritance at all.

Avraal offered a brief sad smile, then took another sip of café.

Dekkard finally said, "I've been thinking about that Meritorist last night. Even if the name is correct, will one name lead to something?"

"What do you think?" replied Avraal with an amused smile.

"Very improbable, even if it is his name, but you were right about that being a location drawing New Meritorists. Could you get Carlos to pass that on, since . . . ?"

"Someone just might ask what you happened to be doing there?" said Emrelda as she stood to leave. "I could have Captain Narryt pass it on as well."

"Everything will help," said Dekkard. *If it's not already too late.*

"You can only do what you can," added Emrelda. "You're not the Premier or the Imperador." Then she headed toward the portico door.

Dekkard looked across the table at his wife. "I'm not sure I'd want to be either right now."

Avraal raised her eyebrows and asked sardonically, "You're not sure?"

Gaaroll snorted.

"You're both right. I wouldn't want to be either."

"They're both idiots," added Gaaroll.

"Hasheem isn't an idiot," replied Dekkard. "He's just too traditional."

"Same thing," said Gaaroll.

"Now, anyway," added Avraal.

With that, Dekkard reluctantly agreed, picking up one of his croissants.

Once everyone finished eating and cleaning up, Dekkard went out to get the Gresynt, thinking, as he opened the garage door, that everything looked so normal. *Superficially, at least.*

As he drove from the house toward the Council Office Building, he studied everything along the way, but nothing had changed, and that left him with a surrealistic feeling that he couldn't shake, even after he'd turned over the steamer to Avraal, and he and Gaaroll walked to his office.

There, Margrit offered a cheerful "Good morning," followed by a warm smile, and Dekkard had an urge to scream out the question, *Why is everyone acting so normal?!!!* At any moment, shells could come through the roof, and Meritorists could be charging through the streets.

He refrained, realizing that he'd contributed to the impression that everything was normal. He managed a pleasant "Good morning to you," even as he wondered what else he could do, since talking about shells that might never come would sound almost unhinged.

"You have two messages, sir. One from Chairman Haarsfel and one from Councilor Konnigsburg." Margrit handed the envelopes to Dekkard.

"Nothing from the Premier?"

"No, sir."

"Thank you."

Dekkard retreated to his private office, hanging up his coat, and setting his leather folder on the side table before walking back to his desk and opening the message from Haarsfel, which was simply a reminder about the hearing at first bell with the officers of the Uldwyrk Machinists Guild. He set that aside and opened the message from Konnigsburg, which turned out to be an invitation to lunch at a sixth before noon.

He immediately wrote an acceptance and dispatched Gaaroll to deliver it. Then he returned to his private office and walked to the window, where he looked out at another unremarkable gray winter day, recalling all too well another unremarkable gray day, and a brown stake lorry and its steam cannon that had resulted in death and destruction.

Unlike those small handmade shells, if a shell from the Khuld *hits this part of the Council Office Building, you won't even know it. You'll be dead before you can realize anything.*

Knowing that the odds of such a hit were extremely low didn't help his mood much, not when all that meant was that some other part of the city would suffer.

But since he couldn't very well flee—to Gaarlak or anywhere else—because of what *might* happen, he seated himself behind his desk and began to read the incoming letters. While there were more than a few, all addressed issues or matters he'd seen before, if in different contexts. He was pondering that over when Margrit rapped on his door and opened it.

"Sir . . . Councilor Baar is here to see you."

Dekkard immediately stood. "Have him come in."

Baar entered the office, and Margrit discreetly shut the door behind him.

"Villem, what brings you here?" Dekkard walked around the desk and gestured to one of the chairs there, then turned the one adjacent to it and seated himself.

Baar took the proffered chair. "I didn't see you around, and since there's no Security Committee meetings scheduled for the rest of the week, I thought I'd just see if you were available."

"Right now, I have the feeling we're all available," replied Dekkard dryly. "What do you have in mind?"

"I wanted to thank you, on Gretina's behalf—and mine. She's gotten requests for interviews from several legalist firms. One looks very promising. That's a firm called Chaensyl and Charboneau." Baar smiled. "It used to be called Chaensyl and Obreduur. They mentioned a referral from a former partner. They're discussing terms with Gretina this morning."

"That's wonderful!" Dekkard didn't have to counterfeit enthusiasm. "I'm so happy for her. For both of you."

"That was your doing, wasn't it?"

"Avraal and I mentioned Gretina's qualifications to Ingrella," Dekkard admitted, "and we asked if she'd spread the word. That's all. Whatever happens, it's all because of Gretina's qualifications."

"It wouldn't have happened, certainly not so quickly, without your assistance. We both can't tell you how much it means. Once it's firmly set, then she'll tell her uncle Haarden."

"Not quite gleefully?" asked Dekkard.

"The glee will not be exhibited to Haarden. There will be just a quiet note thanking him for his assistance in getting us settled and a paragraph informing him of her new position."

"That's probably for the best."

Baar did not immediately speak, then asked, "What do you really think about what will happen with the New Meritorists?"

"I don't *know* what will happen. I'm afraid that the mutineers on the

Khuld will evade the *Resolute* and will manage to fire shells at the Council. Most of the shells won't hit their intended targets, but they'll cause great damage. The Meritorists will emerge and create more chaos, trying to break down civil order and to destroy the Council. I've shared those fears with Hasheem and Guard Captain Trujillo, and I believe that Hasheem has shared them with the Imperador, although I don't know that for certain. Hasheem has ordered more Army troops into Machtarn just in case."

Baar looked at Dekkard. "I'm glad you spoke to him. I'm not sure he'd listen to anyone else."

"I'm sure others have spoken."

"They may have," replied Baar, "but you're one of the few to whom he listens. I think he fears you."

"I'm rather junior to be feared." Dekkard made his tone light.

"Things happen to people who strike at you, and you seem to be able to avoid or survive attacks. Councilor Bassaana cautioned me about you. She said you were the most dangerous man in the Council, but also the most trustworthy. From what I've seen, she's correct."

For a moment, Dekkard was silent. "I don't know what to say to that."

"You don't have to." Baar smiled. "I won't take any more of your time. I appreciate your honesty about the New Meritorists."

Dekkard stood. "I appreciate your coming. I just hope I'm not that accurate."

"So do I. But until things go otherwise, I'm assuming that you are." With a last smile, Baar turned and made his way out of Dekkard's personal office, closing the door as he left.

For several moments, Dekkard just stood there.

Then he returned the straight-backed chair to its previous position, walked around the desk, and seated himself behind it.

When noon approached, Dekkard was more than ready to leave the stack of responses that Margrit had delivered for his signature or revision, knowing that, even though he'd dealt with those, there would be even more waiting when he returned. Recalling the cold morning wind, he donned his overcoat before heading out.

As he and Gaaroll walked toward the center staircase, he said, "I'll likely be about a bell at the councilors' dining room. I'm having lunch with Councilor Konnigsburg. You can get something to eat at the staff cafeteria or wait. Just be back by a sixth before first bell so you can escort me to the Workplace Administration Committee hearing."

"I'll be there."

When Dekkard stepped out into the courtyard, the wind almost ripped the heavy bronze door out of his gloved hand. He eased the door shut and looked to the north. The green-tinged sky showed a hint of haze, but no sign of clouds.

Several figures farther east walked swiftly to the Council Hall, but Dekkard saw no one else. He walked quickly as well, given the bitter wind chill. By the time he reached the Council Hall, his face felt numb.

As soon as they were inside, Gaaroll muttered, "Colder than iced iron."

"I agree, but we'll have time to warm up."

When Dekkard reached the dining room, leaving Gaaroll near the door, Konnigsburg waited just inside.

"Steffan, I'm glad you could join me."

"I appreciate the invitation."

Konnigsburg laughed quietly. "You may not after we talk."

Dekkard stepped to the side and handed his overcoat to an attendant. "I doubt that."

Konnigsburg gestured to the maître d'hôtel. "Two, please."

In moments, the two were seated.

Clearly waiting for their server, Konnigsburg asked, "How was your endday?"

"Busier than I anticipated, but I imagine you're finding that out after moving."

"It's not so bad for us as for Villem Baar. We've leased a smaller furnished place." Konnigsburg looked up to the server who had appeared. "Café and the hearty vegetable soup."

"Do they have that?" asked Dekkard. "It's not on the menu."

"I asked. They do, but only in the winter."

Dekkard still opted for the white bean soup and café.

Once the server left, Konnigsburg smiled and said, "I enjoy your company, Steffan, but that's not why I asked you for lunch."

"I thought you might have something else in mind."

"There haven't been any recent meetings of the Military Affairs Committee. Chairman Mardosh has yet to schedule any hearings on procurement requirements. There hasn't been a briefing about the *Khuld* mutiny in more than a week. There's been nothing about the New Meritorists, but the Premier has ordered at least three additional Army battalions to be relocated in and around Machtarn." Konnigsburg smiled. "What did you have to do with that?"

Dekkard largely repeated what he'd told Hasheem.

Konnigsburg nodded. "I thought it must have been you. No one else has even mentioned the ironways. I did say you'd have made an outstanding intelligence officer. When do you think this will happen?"

Dekkard shrugged and smiled ruefully. "I don't know. My best guess is when the weather changes enough that the *Khuld* has a chance of getting past the *Resolute* and reaching the outer harbor."

"Did you tell the Premier that?"

Dekkard shook his head. "Just that I thought the *Khuld* could evade the *Resolute*. Better to get the basic message through than to have it rejected because I got too detailed."

"Very good tactic as well." Konnigsburg inclined his head toward the server approaching with their soups and café.

Neither said more until after they'd been served and the server had departed.

"I've told you what I know," said Dekkard. "What *don't* I know?"

"I understand that the Marshal of the Army is far more concerned than the First Marshal. The First Marshal seems more irritated than concerned about the inability of the *Resolute* to locate the *Khuld*." Konnigsburg lowered his voice. "After an investigation, the Admiralty found that two officers from the *Khuld* are unaccounted for. One is a senior lieutenant who came up through the ranks and who is considered an outstanding navigator and ship handler. He was denied promotion to lieutenant commander because of his lack of formal higher education, although he is reputed to be more educated than most of his superiors."

Dekkard shook his head sadly. "That doesn't surprise me. Who is the other, a gunnery officer?"

"A gunnery officer who requested duty on the *Khuld*, and who came on board four months ago. Since few officers wanted to serve there, he was accommodated. The First Marshal knows about both, but has said nothing."

"After this is all over, looking into that might provide an interesting hearing."

"I imagine you also have some interesting ideas for hearings. I believe you mentioned the possibility of investigating, shall we say, mislaid dunnite."

"As a beginning."

"When that time comes, let me know. I might know more by then."

Dekkard had no doubt that Konnigsburg already knew more, but just said, "Thank you. I can do that."

The remainder of their lunch dealt more with comparing occurrences and aspects of their respective times at the Military Institute.

The Workplace Administration Committee hearing was similar to all of the others Haarsfel had conducted recently, with various officers of the Uldwyrk Machinists Guild outlining how Uldwyrk Systems avoided complying with various safety rules.

As he left the hearing, Dekkard managed to appear pleasant. *But*

what's the point of all this if we aren't going to come up with a solution?
He paused. *Or is Haarsfel setting you up to be the one to draft them? The
same way Axel Obreduur and Hasheem did?*

The bitter wind still blew when Dekkard and Gaaroll headed back to
the Council Office Building. There were no messages waiting.

Once in his personal office, Dekkard shed his overcoat and walked to
the window, feeling the chill radiating from the glass. He took a long look
at the now-gated service road before settling behind his desk.

After dealing with several responses, he walked out to the staff office to
Teitryn's desk. "Shuryn, have you had any success in tracking down that
punch-card lathe?"

"The industrial machinery section of the proprietary device registry is
looking into it. It will be several days before they can address the request.
I haven't been able to find any other information."

Dekkard nodded. "Let me know." Then he walked back to his office to
deal with more responses.

Avraal did not step into Dekkard's personal office until close to a third
before fifth bell.

"A long day in the consulting business?" he asked.

"Very long. Carlos also wanted to know the details about Hamaar
Dykstraan. He's never heard anything about Dykstraan. He wasn't too
hopeful, but he'll try."

"Did Carlos say anything about why someone was working late last
night?"

"He did say that he noticed our Gresynt was there when he finally left
and the Ferrum wasn't, *and* that he was relieved to see it was there this
morning." She paused, then asked, "How was your day?"

"I had a surprise visit from Villem Baar." Dekkard briefly explained.

"That's excellent. I'd like to think that would tell her uncle something,
but it won't. What else?"

Dekkard related his luncheon conversation with Eyril Konnigsburg,
ending by saying, "I think he's even more worried than he's saying about
incompetence in the Admiralty."

"It sounds that way." She looked directly at her husband. "What do we
do if shells do start falling on the city?"

"Don't panic. The *Khuld* doesn't have the best fire-control system, and
I doubt it has a full gun crew, but the mutineers could still loose a fair
number of shells. If you're not near where they hit, stay put. If shells are
falling near you, get farther away—in whatever direction are the fewest
tall buildings, and stay well clear of the Council and Palace . . . or the
ironway station."

"That's all?"

"The only defense against that sort of attack is to sink the *Khuld* or to get where the shells can't reach. That means getting at least five milles north of the Palace or an equivalent distance to the east. Trying that during a bombardment would be more dangerous than just going a short distance to where shells obviously aren't falling. If I'm right, they'll concentrate on the Council, the Palace, and the ironway station as long as they can."

"Can you avoid coming to work?"

"For something that apparently only I think is possible? We'll just have to be very aware from now on. Even if I'm right, the Meritorists will want to claim that they gave the Imperador and the Council every chance to be 'reasonable.'" Dekkard's final words were sardonic as he rose to get his overcoat.

When the three stepped out of the Council Office Building, Dekkard was amazed, because the wind had vanished, and the late-afternoon air felt warmer than it had in days.

"I was thinking about not going out tonight," he said to Avraal, "but it's not that bad now. Not at all."

"Let's see what it's like in two bells."

"Friggin' straight," muttered Gaaroll.

Dekkard glanced across the drive to the covered parking and then to his left at Council Avenue, where a modest stream of steamers and lorries was headed in each direction, as normal, then started across the pavement.

After settling into the Gresynt, pulling out of the parking area, and heading east on Council Avenue, roughly a third of a bell later, he parked the Gresynt under the portico, where Avraal looked at him.

"If we don't go out, I'll garage it after we eat."

Her second look was at least neutral.

Dinner was warmed-up and leftover pork milanesia, accompanied by canned pears and flatbread. As Dekkard finished his last sliver of pears, he glanced in the direction of the study.

"You're really thinking about going out tonight?" Emrelda paused, then asked, "Where? I hope not near Ilspieth Square."

"Maybe west of there and a bit northeast from the Guldoran Ironway station."

"Do you want more trouble?" asked Emrelda. "Even Captain Narryt doesn't have much influence in the northwest part of the city."

"I'm not looking for trouble, just names or hints."

"Sometimes, that's trouble," Emrelda pointed out.

"I won't dispute that," replied Dekkard in a slightly amused tone.

"If you're set on doing this," said Avraal, her voice between accepting and resigned, "we need to get on with it."

"Gaaroll and I will do the dishes," said Emrelda.

"Thank you," returned Dekkard as he stood and turned toward the study.

In minutes, he and Avraal were studying one of the maps.

"The tavern most likely frequented by the ironway workers would be, obviously, East Station," said Avraal. "It's a block west of Kurkwyl Square."

Another third passed before the three left the house, headed toward Imperial Boulevard and Baartol's office in the Gresynt. Yet another third passed, after switching to the brown Ferrum, before Dekkard parked and then led the way to Kurkwyl Square, which was trapezoidal, with the west end slightly narrower than the east end. When he entered the square through the north gate, he noticed that the south gate lay farther west rather than directly across from the north gate, as had been the case in other squares. A statue of a man in late Imperial garb, with bloused trousers and knee boots and a short jacket above a wide belt, held sway above the circular and dry fountain basin. The angular and predatory face of the statue, presumably of Sr. Kurkwyl, was the only statue Dekkard could remember that hinted so directly that the figure represented in stone had been less than pleasant.

A young man strumming a mandolin sat on the westernmost edge of the fountain basin, the mandolin case open at his feet. Carrying his sign, Dekkard walked by the singer and dropped a coin—a third of a mark—in the case. The singer did not seem to look up as Dekkard walked around the fountain basin and back to the eastern end of the square, where he propped the sign against the back of a bench.

He stood waiting for someone to arrive, hoping that Avraal could stir up some interest. After a time, an older, almost grizzled, woman in a long shapeless coat, also wearing a heavy scarf wrapped around her hair and ears, appeared and looked at Dekkard, then at the sign, and then back to Dekkard.

"It's simple," he said. "Fair wages and safe work will make Guldor a better place."

"Easier to drink water with a knife than get fair wages." Her rough voice was sarcastic.

"Why do you think that?"

"Where you been living? With seasprites?"

"That's why I'm here. Contrarian means contrary to what's happening. Contrary to Commercers who only care about marks. Contrary to

Landors who can't forget when they ruled. Contrary to Crafters who only think about guilds. Contrary to New Meritorists who peddle popularity as a way to get power."

"Sounds like you don't like anybody very much," replied the woman dismissively.

"I like the few smaller businesses who pay fair—until they get squashed by the corporacions. I liked the last premier—until the Meritorists blew him up. I liked the engineering company that hired the sons of working folk—until the corporacions killed the top two people. Those are all reasons why we need Contrarians."

"Never heard of you."

"We have to start somewhere before it's too late."

"What's too late?" asked the older man who stopped well short of Dekkard and the woman.

"It's not too late," said Dekkard, "to change things." He gestured to the sign. "To get fair wages and safe work. To move away from Commercers who only think about marks, and Meritorists who think electing popular people will solve everything."

"Better that than faceless politicians," said a third voice, which came from a thin younger man.

"Their names are all out there," replied Dekkard. "When you don't know them, you make them faceless."

"Who's our councilor, then?" asked the thin man. "Do you even know?" His tone was patronizing.

"Was Marryat Osmond," replied Dekkard. "He got killed when the Meritorists blew up part of that Council building. New councilor is Emile Hebersyn. Write him. Tell him you want fair wages and safe work. That's what counts."

"Making the councilors listen to us is what counts," said the younger man. "Making each vote public so they can't hide."

"Right," said Dekkard sardonically. "That'll teach each one to listen to what's popular in his district, *or* to whoever has the most marks. You can't do that now, but you make each vote public, that's what you'll get. Getting people together for fair wages and making the whole Council listen is what counts. Otherwise, each councilor will just listen to the loudest voices or the ones with the most marks."

"I'd like some of those marks!" called another voice.

"Wouldn't we all?" returned Dekkard. "Wouldn't we all? Except it doesn't work that way, not so long as Commercers have the marks and we're grubbing for coins."

"You ever grubbed?" called someone else.

"Through more plaster dust than you'll ever see," retorted Dekkard.

Dekkard kept talking and throwing back the questions and gibes for close to two thirds before Avraal signaled to him.

"I've said what I had to say," Dekkard concluded. "You can take it. You can leave it, but remember that Commercer marks, guild preferences, endless lands tied up by Landors, and false promises of salvation through popularity contests won't give us fair wages or safe work." Then he took the sign and raised it high. "For Contrarians and the future!"

Most of those who'd been listening, not quite a score, began to drift away, one or two heading in the direction of East Station.

The older woman, who'd remained from the start, said, "I'd vote for you if it were possible." Then she turned.

That left the young thin man, who moved closer to Dekkard. "Who the frig are you? Who sent you to stir up things?"

"No one sent me," Dekkard said firmly, his voice full of conviction. "I came because it's necessary."

For a moment, the young man froze, then abruptly turned and hurried away.

Dekkard caught a muttered fragment of a comment.

". . . almost like . . . frigging empie . . ."

Dekkard lowered the sign slightly and turned back toward the north gate to the square, where Avraal and then Gaaroll joined him.

"What did you say to the last one?"

Dekkard told her, word for word.

"Scared the piss out of him," said Gaaroll.

"I didn't even raise my voice," replied Dekkard.

"Sometimes," said Avraal, "you don't have to."

35

ON Tridi morning, Dekkard quickly read *Gestirn* before fixing cafés for Avraal, Gaaroll, and himself, but there were no stories about New Meritorists or about the *Khuld*. There was a short front-page story about the snowstorm in the north effectively shutting down various heliograph lines and slowing and disrupting some scheduled expresses, but not creating any significant ironway route closures.

So far. Still thinking that, Dekkard continued with breakfast preparations.

Almost a bell later, when Dekkard left the portico and walked toward the garage to ready the Gresynt, he looked to the northeast, where, in the distant sky, he could barely make out greenish-black clouds. He watched for several moments, but he couldn't see any obvious movement, suggesting that the clouds were either much farther away than he thought or not advancing quickly on Machtarn, if not both. He turned and looked south. There was definitely a haze or mist over the ocean, but that didn't matter, not at present. It could matter a great deal by Furdi.

Unless Hasheem had changed his mind, the Council was not meeting, and by the end of the day that lack of action would effectively signal to the New Meritorists that neither the Imperador nor the Council intended to change the Great Charter to allow the recording of votes by individual councilors.

Dekkard returned his attention to getting the steamer ready and out of the garage. Shortly, he had the Gresynt under the portico. He didn't have long to wait because, minutes later, both Avraal and Gaaroll were seated, and he eased the steamer down the drive, still bordered with reduced piles of previously shoveled snow, and out onto Florinda Way, heading west.

"You've been awfully quiet this morning," said Avraal.

"Just thinking."

"Do you think the Premier will call the Council into session today?"

"Only if he can announce the *Khuld* has been located and is no longer a danger."

"No longer a danger? Is that a euphemism for sunk or destroyed?"

"It is," he replied with a brief smile, "but it's along the lines of what Hasheem would say."

"You're probably right."

"Still say he's not all that impressive," murmured Gaaroll.

"He's better than the possible alternatives," replied Dekkard, thinking of what a disaster Mardosh would have been.

"You'd be better," said Gaaroll firmly.

"I'm barely ready to be a councilor. I'm not ready for that." *And, more important, the Council's definitely not ready for an isolate premier . . . and may never be.*

No one said much on the remainder of the drive to the Council Office Building, where Dekkard relinquished the Gresynt to Avraal, and he and Gaaroll walked up to the office.

As he walked toward Margrit, Dekkard asked, "Any messages this morning?"

"Just one from Chairman Haarsfel." She handed him the envelope.

"Something about hearings, I imagine. Thank you."

"You're welcome, sir."

Dekkard took the unopened message into his office and laid it on the desk, leaving it until he hung up his overcoat. When he opened it, he smiled wryly at the announcement of a Workplace Administration Committee hearing for the next Tridi, the third of Springfirst, not that spring would appear anytime soon. The committee would be hearing from the Ironworkers Guild about practices at Kathaar Stove Works, a hearing previously scheduled for 9 Winterfirst.

The day after the Council Office Building was shelled.

Dekkard had to admit that, once Haarsfel got something in his mind, he never let go of it. He took the message back out to Margrit. "If you'd please put this on my schedule."

"Yes, sir." She did smile, possibly at his wry tone.

After returning to his desk, he began to read the incoming letters and petitions, which contained pleas and complaints that were not at all unfamiliar.

About a third before noon, Dekkard, though not particularly hungry, decided to walk over to the councilors' dining room to see who might be there and if anyone asked him to join them. If not, to take a table and see if there was anyone he wanted to have lunch with.

After he donned his overcoat and stepped out into the main office, Dekkard caught the momentary resigned expression on Gaaroll's face as she quickly donned her winter jacket and gloves. With a smile, he said cheerfully, "It's not that bad, Nincya."

"It's getting colder and grayer out, sir. Every minute. I could see that from the staff office windows."

"Practicing your typing?"

"Yes, sir. If I can't get certified as an empie, I could make more as a typist."

"That's a good thought, but I think you have a good chance at certification." He gestured toward the door to the main corridor.

Gaaroll turned and then opened the door.

When they reached the courtyard door and stepped outside, the cold was like a slap to Dekkard's face, and he said to Gaaroll, "You were definitely right about the weather."

Gaaroll just grinned, if briefly.

After they reached the councilors' dining room, Dekkard handed Gaaroll two marks. "I'll be a little over a bell. Go have a hot meal on me." He smiled. "That's an order."

She smiled back. "Yes, sir."

Dekkard entered the dining room, divested himself of his coat, and then walked toward the maître d'hôtel.

"Councilor, I believe your party is already here and seated. If you'll follow me?"

My party? Dekkard shrugged and followed. He wasn't exactly surprised to find Kaliara Bassaana alone at a table for two, smiling as Dekkard approached. "How did you know? Did you have Amelya or Elyssa looking for me?"

"Almighty, no. I just told Brycen that if you came in alone to escort you to my table."

Dekkard laughed as he sat down. "How many names did you give him?"

"Enough, but I really was hoping I might see you here."

"I'm not sure that's exactly a compliment, Kaliara." Dekkard had no doubt that she knew something and wanted him to either confirm it, speculate on it, or refute it.

"We can talk about that after we order. What do you think about this weather?"

"It's colder than any winter since I've been here, not that I've been in Machtarn nearly so long as you have."

"Do you think it's helping or hindering the New Meritorists?" She added quickly, "Here comes our server. Hold that thought until after we order."

She ordered a cup of the white bean soup with café. Dekkard chose a bowl of the onion soup with the cheese-covered toast squares, along with café. His face was still cool from the brief trip across the courtyard, and a warm but not too heavy soup sounded perfect.

"Your thoughts on the weather and the New Meritorists?" she prompted once the server was well away from the table.

"It keeps them out of the streets, but that makes it harder for patrollers and Justiciary investigators to keep track of them. I doubt that it changes their plans that much. It might slow their ability to mount whatever new tactics or schemes they have in mind." Pausing as the server brought their cafés, Dekkard then took a sip, grateful for the warmth.

"What new tactics do you anticipate?"

"I have no real idea, except that the *Khuld* will figure into them." Dekkard had no reason not to say that, given that Hasheem had announced the disappearance to the entire Council, but he didn't want to go beyond that.

"Your words convey a certain doubt that the First Marshal's plans will be as effective as Fredrich believes."

"There's a very old saying that no battle plan survives contact with the enemy. So far, no plan has survived contact with the New Meritorists. Why would this time be any different?"

"You make a good point, Steffan. But then, you usually do." Bassaana smiled pleasantly. "Here come our soups."

Dekkard waited for Bassaana to sample her soup before he did the same.

After two small swallows of her soup, the older councilor went on, her voice conversational, although Dekkard knew she was after something, since she always was. "While there have been recent disturbances around Machtarn, most don't seem to have had much connection to the New Meritorists. Your thoughts?"

"More people are out of work. Food is scarcer and more costly, and the winter is much colder than usual, freezing the water lines in some less . . . fortunate areas. All that has created more unrest. The New Meritorists will try to channel that unrest against the Council."

"I had the definite impression that someone did that already with the last demonstration in Rivertown."

"It's likely it was the Meritorists," agreed Dekkard, "but I don't *know* that, and I think we'd know if there were evidence to link the two."

"What if it happened to be another group?"

"Another group?"

"I do have a few sources," admitted Bassaana, "and there are at least two other groups proselytizing in the city."

"Two others?" asked Dekkard, letting his real surprise show through.

"One is the Solidan Front. They're mostly Argenti immigrants or their children, and they want legal protection for freedom of religion in the Great Charter."

"The Charter already says that people can worship as they please."

"But there are no effective sanctions against those who disrupt worship."

"That's never been a problem before," said Dekkard.

"Apparently, it is now," replied Bassaana dryly.

"And the other group?"

"It's just come to light in the last few days. Something called Contrarianism. It won't go anywhere, I'm sure, but we've never had so many different groups being so loud at the same time."

"I see your point," said Dekkard, managing not to show surprise. "That indicates there's more discontent that the Meritorists can exploit."

"I thought you might see that." She paused, then said slowly, "There is one other aspect of all this."

"There's probably more than just one."

"This is more concerning. There's a rumor—a well-grounded one—that the New Meritorists have presented the Imperador and the Premier with an ultimatum. What do you know about that?"

"I'm not surprised. I've gotten more than a few demands, in some form or another, to change the Great Charter to require every vote be recorded with every councilor being identified as to how he or she voted. Every councilor has likely received something like that. Why wouldn't the Premier and the Imperador?"

"This ultimatum is reputed to suggest that if the Council does not act, councilors and the Imperador will be killed."

Dekkard nodded. "That has to tie in with the *Khuld*. While she's an older light cruiser, her shells could reach the Council buildings and even the Palace. That's why the First Marshal has a battle group patrolling the ocean south of Machtarn. That also may be why additional Army troops have been moved into Machtarn."

"Steffan." Bassaana's voice hardened, even as she spoke more quietly. "What are *you* going to do?" She smiled coolly. "Please don't tell me you know nothing about this."

"I told the Premier about the possible danger. I've mentioned it to more than a few people. I understand that the First Marshal believes his forces can deal with the *Khuld*. That's assuming that the mutineers behave like well-trained rational sailors. They're not. They're likely well-trained, highly motivated, and fanatical sailors with a cause. I passed that on as well."

"He seems to have done nothing." Bassaana's tone was icy.

"What can he do? Evacuate the entire city for something that might not even happen? Even announcing the possibility might cause more unrest and deaths, given that most people would have nowhere to go, not in the middle of winter."

"You make it sound so cold."

"What else would you have me do? Shout it down the Council corridors? Or from the housetops? Especially since nothing has been made known to the Council except a cruiser crew has mutinied and disappeared with the ship?"

"Even so, Fredrich is saying nothing. Wouldn't you say more?"

"If I were Premier, I would, but I'm not."

Bassaana shook her head. "By the Almighty, I wish you were. Or even Axel."

"Kaliara . . . I don't have the experience or the talents." Dekkard took a long slow sip of his cooled café. He knew he had taken an enormous risk in what he'd revealed, but to have lied or denied would have been an even greater risk, since he knew he wasn't that opaque. *And you revealed nothing about the ultimatum.*

She looked at him directly. "Why did you let me know?"

"Because not doing so would have been worse. I've evaded you in the past. I've not revealed information that wasn't mine to divulge, but I haven't lied."

"No, you haven't." She smiled ruefully. "Now what?"

"We wait. If the worst happens, we hope the steps Fredrich has taken will mitigate the damage and control the New Meritorists. And . . . if you hear lots of huge explosions, get yourself and your staff out of the buildings and a long way away—at an angle. Northeast or northwest or southeast or southwest—except if there's been a hit in one of those directions. That's all I have. Unless you have a better idea?"

"Even practical advice," Bassaana said dryly.

"I hope it's unnecessary." Dekkard lifted his café, then set it down without drinking.

"So do I." After a moment, she shook her head. "If we spread the information widely, that will create panic."

"And if we don't, we can be accused of hiding information and killing people. Also, if we spread it, and nothing happens, we could cause needless deaths."

Neither spoke for a time.

Then Bassaana offered a sardonic smile. "There's no good answer, is there?"

"I haven't found one."

"Whatever I do, I won't mention your name. That would be a waste." Then she stood. "Shall we go?"

Minutes later, Dekkard walked back across the courtyard with Gaaroll. The wind had died down, but not stopped. The leading edge of the greenish-black clouds just north of the Imperador's Palace shed a whitish-gray curtain beneath. Before long the clouds would be over the city, with more snow to add to the problems.

Dekkard took a long and slow breath and kept walking.

There were no messages when he returned to the office, but the typed responses awaited his signature or revisions.

By the third afternoon bell, snow was falling. Dekkard put aside the remaining revisions and stood, walking to the window to get a better look. The fine, dry snow fell from comparatively higher clouds, the kind of storm that wouldn't pass quickly and wouldn't be affected much by the ocean close to Machtarn. After watching for several minutes more, he sat down and penned a simple note, signed it, and then read it over.

Ingrella—
    Because of the snow and other factors, I'm sending my staff home at fourth bell and telling them not to come in until noon, or later, if the snow continues. I respectfully suggest that you do the same.

He nodded and sealed it, then walked out to the front office and handed the note to Gaaroll. "Please take this to Councilor Obreduur. You're to hand it to her personally, and no one else. Wait if you have to. Tell her that I need no response. Is that clear?"

"Yes, sir."

"And let me know when you return."

After Gaaroll left, Dekkard peered into the staff office and beckoned to Roostof.

Once the two were in Dekkard's personal office, he turned and said, "Svard, this snowstorm could be like the last one. I want you to close the office at fourth bell, and I don't want anyone coming in to work until noon tomorrow, and that includes you. And if it's still snowing no one is to come in the afternoon, either."

"Sir, the snow's not that heavy, and what if there's a Council meeting?"

"There's nothing scheduled, and I don't see the Premier calling the Council into session in the middle of a snowstorm." *If not for that precise reason.*

"Sir—"

Dekkard smiled. "Svard, that's an order. If something comes up, I'm perfectly able to get to the Council."

"Sir, is there something . . . ?"

"Yes, there is. No"—he held up a hand as Svard started to speak again—

"I'm not at liberty to say, and neither are you, especially since I could be wrong. Just tell everyone and have them follow those directions. That includes you. That's all I have for you right now."

"Yes, sir."

After Roostof left, Dekkard walked to the window and looked out, not really seeing the snow. He knew Roostof was disturbed, and at least slightly angry at what Dekkard wasn't saying. *But the whole situation is impossible. If you overtly tell everyone and nothing happens, you'll have created a needless panic. Not to mention directly disobeying an order from the Premier. If you say nothing, and the worst happens . . .*

He shook his head.

A third later Gaaroll returned and knocked at his door.

"Come in."

"I delivered it. She said, 'Thank you.' She didn't open it, but she took it into her office."

"Excellent. And thank you."

Gaaroll smiled, then left his office, closing the door.

Avraal arrived at a third past fourth bell to an office where only Roostof, Gaaroll, and Dekkard remained.

At her arrival, Dekkard turned to Roostof. "Svard, you can go now. We won't be far behind. I'll see you either tomorrow at noon or first thing on Quindi, depending on the snow. If it's really deep, then on Unadi."

"Yes, sir." Roostof stiffened.

"Svard, it's not you. I'm wrestling with a great deal. You've done more than anyone could possibly expect. We'll talk about it later."

"Sir—"

"One way or another, we'll work it out. Be careful on the way home."

Avraal frowned momentarily, then said gently and warmly, "Please be careful, Svard. It's already slick out there."

Roostof smiled, if briefly. "Thank you, Ritten. I will be."

Once Roostof left, Dekkard turned to Gaaroll. "We'll only be a few minutes, Nincya." He gestured, and then followed Avraal back into his office, closing the door.

"What was that all about?"

"First, thank you for helping with Svard." Then Dekkard told her. When he finished the summary, he added, "I know I'm giving my staff special treatment, but I was ordered not to mention the ultimatum, and I can claim that I worried about the snow. I'm not breaking any laws or requirements by adjusting their working bells because of the snow." He paused. "I also wrote a note to Ingrella recommending she follow my snow precautions."

"She'll understand, I'm sure."

"At lunch, I found myself escorted to Kaliara Bassaana's table."

"Of course," declared Avraal coolly. "That doesn't surprise me. What did she want?"

"Information." Dekkard went on to explain, then waited for Avraal's reaction.

She said nothing for close to a minute. Neither did Dekkard.

Finally, Avraal said, "I don't like it, but . . ."

"But?"

"Under the circumstances, the way you handled it was the least of the terrible alternatives. If either Hasheem or the First Marshal had just been open about everything with the *Khuld*, it would have been much easier."

"It still could be, if the *Resolute* can find and sink the *Khuld*."

"You really don't think that's going to happen, do you?"

"No. It should, by all rights. The Navy has more ships with better equipment and guns, but the Meritorists have outthought or outmaneuvered us so often that I have the feeling it's going to happen again. They don't even have to hit the Council or the Palace. They can drop shells anywhere in Machtarn, and that will undermine the Council, if not more."

"Will it help the Meritorists?"

"It'll anger thousands, and that will benefit them."

"Can we do anything more here?" asked Avraal quietly.

"No."

"Then we should head home. We can think as well there as here. Besides, I'm hungry."

"We can do that." Dekkard offered a faint smile.

36

D EKKARD did not sleep well and woke early on an eerily silent Furdi morning. He immediately eased back the curtains a touch and discovered that it was still snowing.

"Still snowing?" mumbled Avraal from beneath the blankets.

"Just lightly. I can't tell how deep it is."

"Are we going anywhere this morning?"

"I'd thought I might stop and have a talk with Carlos. If nothing happens by fifth bell, it's less likely anything will happen today."

"Why fifth bell?"

"They'll want to shell the Council and the Palace when councilors are likely to be there, and that would be anytime after third bell."

"What about the snow?"

"I'll need to see. If it's light, and the clouds aren't that low, they'll be able to get close to their targets, if they haven't already. They really don't have to hit the Council. In fact, it might be better from their viewpoint if they didn't. The damage would be greater for others, and the Council would be blamed."

"You are cynical. Go take your shower."

Dekkard did so, and then dressed quickly, making sure that his throwing knives and personal truncheon were securely in place.

Emrelda was heading out the door when he came down the stairs.

"Just be careful," he said.

"Do you really think those mutineers will attack today? It's snowing."

While Dekkard personally thought that made it more likely, he only said, "I haven't been that accurate lately at predicting when and where the Meritorists will strike, but I have the feeling it won't be that long."

"Why do you think that?"

"People are hungry and cold, and the *Khuld* can't keep evading the Imperial Navy forever. The ship's likely short on provisions, and I doubt they had time to fill the coal bunkers when they made a coaling stop."

"You and Avraal are the ones who need to take care. If the mutineers even show up, they won't be wasting shells on Erslaan and Southtown."

"I wouldn't wager against you on that." Although the eight-digit guns might not be that accurate firing through a light snow, Dekkard doubted that they'd be off by three to five milles.

After Emrelda left, Dekkard made his way to the kitchen and began fixing cafés and refilling Gaaroll's mug as well. He didn't see a newssheet.

"No *Gestirn*?" he asked Gaaroll.

"Not yet. Don't see why. Snow's only four, maybe five digits. If that." Gaaroll paused, then asked, "Are we going somewhere this morning?"

"We are, but not to the Council. That will be later. We'll leave a little before third bell."

Neither Dekkard nor Avraal said much at breakfast, but then there wasn't much either could have added, and no point in further worrying Gaaroll.

Just before third bell, Dekkard went out to ready the Gresynt, but stopped to look south. He couldn't see the ocean, but he could see the tops of buildings in the Erslaan area. He had the feeling that the hazy visibility was perfect for allowing the *Khuld* to reach a point just outside the harbor without being observed from a distance, but wouldn't stop the mutineers from firing uphill into the city. But he was no gunnery officer, or anywhere close. He only knew that the light snow and haze would restrict the range of even the new naval heliographs and make it harder for the *Resolute* to communicate with other ships.

A few minutes later, after Avraal and Gaaroll joined him, he started the steamer down the drive, turning east on Florinda and then south on Jacquez. When he reached Camelia Avenue, he turned west. There were fewer steamers on Camelia Avenue, and Dekkard even saw students on the sidewalks, sidewalks that had been shoveled earlier, but looked to have several digits of recently fallen snow.

When the three reached Baartol's office on the Avenue of the Guilds and stepped out in the clearly diminishing snow, Dekkard motioned for Gaaroll to accompany them, then led the way into the building, with its polished gray stone floor, and up the wide gray stone staircase, with its brass bannister, and into the second-floor anteroom.

Carlos Baartol stood outside his office talking to his secretary, then turned. His eyes widened, if but for an instant, as he saw Gaaroll, Dekkard, and Avraal. "You look quite stylish, Nincya."

"Comes with the job, sir."

"It obviously agrees with you," replied Baartol.

"She's also improved her empath abilities," said Dekkard. "Do you have a few moments?"

"For a third, maybe a little longer." Baartol gestured to his office door.

As Dekkard passed Baartol's secretary, he smiled and said, "A good if snowy morning to you, Elicya."

"And to you, Councilor."

Dekkard closed the door behind himself, then took the remaining chair in front of the desk.

"I must admit I didn't expect to see you today," said Baartol.

"I gave the staff the morning off because of the snow. I heard it would be deeper. So, when it wasn't, I thought I'd come over, since I haven't seen you in a while. I assume you haven't made much headway in discovering who is behind the missing investigators."

Baartol smiled ironically. "That couldn't have been much of a surprise to you."

"Not really, but my suspicions would center on Suvion Industries and Siincleer Shipbuilding."

"They're certainly among the usual suspects, but why would you pick them?"

"Because Oskaar Ulrich is now vice-presidente for political affairs at Suvion Industries, which most probably supplied the dunnite to the New Meritorists, something that Suvion Industries would scarcely appreciate coming to light. Juan del Larrano is ruthless and unprincipled, and he has to be worried that a Crafter government just might look too closely into how Siincleer Shipbuilding and its subsidiaries obtained certain government contracts and forced competitors out of business. He's also doubtless seething over the death of Pietro Venburg, since Venburg's death removed 'insulation' between him and dubious business practices." *And because he strongly suspects that Jaime Minz did not kill Venburg, not when Minz worked for Ulrich and possibly on matters for Siincleer as well.* That unspoken thought was not something that Dekkard would ever voice.

"But you don't have any proof of that, either, I take it," said Baartol.

"If I did there might be some interesting hearings taking place. What more can you tell me about del Larrano?"

"He's secretive about his private life. More so than most corporacion presidentes."

"My staff has discovered that. Possibly because he worries about people wanting to get back at him?"

"You're not the first to suggest that, but there's nothing public."

"Anything else?"

"He's also not ostentatious, not for a corporacion presidente. He's reputed to have a very modest mansion on secluded and well-guarded grounds on the coast south of Siincleer."

"No extravagances?"

"Nothing's ever come out. So I'd expect not. Well . . . there is one thing. He has a yacht."

"He's presidente of a shipbuilding concern," said Dekkard matter-of-factly.

"It's not the usual yacht. He had it built to test the newer turbines from Uldwyrk Systems. I heard that it looks more like a smaller version of a corvette. That's just hearsay, though."

"Anything else?"

Baartol offered an amused smile. "About del Larrano? Even hearsay is dangerous to repeat."

"Have you discovered anything about Hamaar Dykstraan?"

Baartol shook his head.

"I recalled something else," said Dekkard, "about Guldoran Ironworks and how they took over a smaller business that had developed a unique punch-card lathe."

Baartol frowned for a moment, then nodded. "Axel was interested in that."

"Do you have anything you might be able to share there? It would tie in well to a legislative proposal I have my staff working on."

"There's not a great deal there, but I can certainly have Elicya make a copy in the next few days and give it to Avraal—"

Baartol stopped as what sounded like a low roll of thunder rumbled through the building, which, less than a minute later, was followed by another.

"Frig!" Dekkard turned to the north-facing window, his eyes looking for something besides the scattered flurries of snow and the buildings across the Avenue of the Guilds. He waited, hoping he wouldn't hear anything else, but, after another half minute, the building vibrated just slightly with the arrival of another growling roll of thunder.

Then beyond the buildings, to the northeast and in the general direction of the Council buildings, he could make out, just barely, what appeared to be yellowish-gray smoke from the impact and explosion of the *Khuld*'s shells. Then, coming from the south, was a slightly higher-pitched thundering sound.

From the south?

Dekkard turned back to the clearly disconcerted Baartol. "They're firing on both the Council and the ships in the harbor!" Seeing Baartol's lack of immediate comprehension, he added, "The *Khuld*, the light cruiser that Meritorist mutineers captured. She got around the battle group patrolling south of here. Her smaller guns are likely sinking ships in the harbor to block it, and the bigger eight-digit guns look like they're aimed at the Council buildings or possibly the Palace."

"Shelling the Council and the Palace? Shouldn't we go someplace safer?" asked Baartol.

"We're as safe here as anywhere, and this can't last too long. The *Khuld* is only a single ship. Her rate of fire and her shells are likely limited. Also, by now the *Resolute* should be moving in." *You hope.*

"We're just supposed to sit here and watch?" asked Baartol.

"Listen, mostly," replied Dekkard, hoping fervently that his analysis was correct. "Just a moment." He hurried to the office door and opened it. "Elicya, Nincya, just stay put here. Those thundering sounds are naval guns. The mutineers on the missing light cruiser appear to be shelling the Council and the harbor. Before long, they'll be getting shelled in return. We're as safe here as anyplace else that we could get to." He left the door ajar as he turned and walked back toward the north window.

"Are you sure it's the Meritorist mutineers?" asked Baartol.

"That's my best guess. They already attacked the Council Office Building when Axel didn't give them what they wanted. Fredrich Hasheem didn't, either, and they seem to have stepped up their attacks."

"None of that makes sense," said Baartol.

"It does," said Dekkard, pausing as another rumble of thunder passed over the office building. "It does if the larger corporacions quietly support the Meritorists in order to discredit the Crafters and force the Imperador to dissolve the Council and call new elections."

"They're ruthless," admitted Baartol, "but that verges on ruthlessness to the point of stupidity."

"Not if they pull it off. They'll reinstate the old Security Ministry and use Security agents against anyone who opposes them. They were already doing that, but Axel stopped it, which was why Minz hired malcontents to attack the Council Office Building. The first shells hit Axel's office. I'm not so sure that the later shells weren't covering the fact that it was an assassination." To the north-northwest Dekkard could now see the yellowish-white smoke slowly rising.

"Have you brought this up to the Premier?"

"Only that it was an assassination and that the dunnite had to come from either Suvion Industries or Northwest Industrial Chemical. I suggested looking into it. He wasn't interested unless there was proof."

"He's too traditional and conservative." Baartol flinched as more of the muted thunder reached his ears.

A third of a bell—or longer—passed before a deeper and more forceful thunder rolled from the direction of the harbor, a thunder that was almost continuous.

Avraal looked to Dekkard. "That sounds different."

"Larger shells. Twelve-digit from the *Resolute*. She's got the *Khuld* in her sights. If the gunners are any good, there will soon be a much larger explosion from the harbor."

"How do you know all this, Steffan?" asked Baartol.

"Remember? I was a Military Institute graduate, but I went security instead of line."

"You ought to be the one heading the Security Committee."

"I'm too junior."

"How can you be that calm?" asked Baartol, shifting his weight in his chair.

"I'm not. I just look calm. I talk more when I'm worried. I also know that staying here is safer than moving now that we know we're not in the target area. That's until the shelling stops. Then Avraal and I will have a lot to do."

Dekkard hadn't the faintest idea of exactly what that might be, but he *knew* they had to get to the Council as soon as it appeared safe to do so.

Roughly five minutes later, in fact, the explosion Dekkard had predicted occurred, one loud enough to shake the building with enough volume to dwarf the previous detonations. Dekkard had a strong feeling that a good chunk of the harbor was in ruins. Then, over the next few minutes, all of the thunder-like sounds vanished.

At that point, Dekkard turned to Baartol. "Thank you for your hospitality, Carlos. We need to be heading to the Council buildings."

"Is if safe for you to be doing that?" asked Baartol.

"Probably not," admitted Dekkard, "but at least an attempt is necessary." *For more than a few reasons.*

As Dekkard, Avraal, and Gaaroll left the building, he heard the screaming of patroller steam whistles, coming from the south—almost certainly from the harbor area. "Nincya, what do you sense? From where?"

"Strong feelings. Everywhere."

What else would you expect? Dekkard's wry smile at the stupidity of his question faded immediately as he lit off the Gresynt. "I'd judge most of them are from the harbor. I'd guess that the shells from the *Resolute* finally got to the magazines of the *Khuld*. The *Khuld*'s smaller guns were probably already targeting all the ships docked at the piers as well as anything else they could destroy. Then, the explosion of the *Khuld* compounded the danger. All that's a guess, but I'd wager something like that occurred."

Just as he finished speaking, another explosion rumbled from the direction of the harbor.

"What do you think that was?" asked Avraal.

"A ship or building exploded, probably from a fire caused by the *Khuld* shelling the harbor." Dekkard drove out of the parking area and east on the Avenue of the Guilds, then turned north on Imperial Boulevard. "We need to hurry. Once people realize the shelling's over, it will be even harder to get anywhere."

As Dekkard neared Justiciary Avenue he saw steamers backed up to the north and smoke rising through the scattered snow flurries near Council Avenue. He also heard more steam whistles ahead. He immediately turned right at the next side street, but only traveled a block before having to turn again because of fire lorries blocking the street. Beyond them, he saw a building in flames and a mass of rubble that must have been a building.

More than two-thirds of a bell passed before Dekkard neared the Council Hall from the west, after having to wind through alleys and side streets to avoid blocked thoroughfares—one by a large shell crater, two steamers piled into each other, and patrollers waving him away. When he finally neared the Council Hall, the west end appeared largely untouched. But smoke rose from the east end of the Council Office Building, and it appeared that at least one shell had struck the northeast corner of the building, where it was now a combination of partial outside walls and rubble.

Just about where your office is—or was. How were they so accurate? They had no spotters, and the visibility wasn't all that good.

Dekkard looked again. Firefighters wrestling with a canvas hose played a stream of water over part of the collapsed section. From the line of thin smoke rising behind the courtyard wall, Dekkard thought another shell had hit and exploded perhaps fifteen yards to the southeast. The walls bordering the southeast corner of the courtyard had been reduced to rubble.

In addition to the Council Guards, at least two companies of Army troopers were posted along just that part of the iron fence Dekkard could see from the steamer.

Dekkard shuddered as he slowed the Gresynt to a stop in front of the gates.

A Council Guard walked toward the steamer, and Dekkard lowered the window.

"Councilor?"

"Councilor Dekkard. I was at a meeting." Dekkard partly drew back his overcoat to display his pin.

"Sir, the Premier has asked any councilors to meet near the Council chamber. They just reopened the building a sixth ago. There's going to be a briefing. We'll open the gates for you. Just park at the curb in front of the Council Hall, where the other steamers are. You'll have to enter by the side service door where the guards are posted."

"Thank you."

"Just glad you're safe, sir." The guard stepped back and gestured toward the two other guards at the gates.

Dekkard eased the Gresynt slowly forward and through the gates that the guards immediately closed as he passed and turned the Gresynt toward the curb, parking it beside a dark blue Gresynt, a high-end but older model also bearing the councilor insignia. *Eyril Konnigsburg's steamer?*

As he got out of the Gresynt, he looked to his left and saw a familiar gray Gresynt—Ingrella's smaller steamer. For a moment, he smiled, glad that she'd taken his recommendation.

Then he looked to the west end of the Council Office Building, which had also sustained some damage, although he couldn't discern the extent.

"Friggin' Meritorist bastards," muttered Gaaroll.

And a few others. "I quite agree, Nincya," said Dekkard as he led the way to the service door into the Council Hall, still wondering how the mutineer gunners had been so accurate.

The two guards flanking the service door each nodded as Dekkard approached. Once inside, Dekkard was immediately struck by how dim the main corridor was, but then realized that the coal gas had obviously been shut off, possibly within minutes, although that could also have been accomplished by mechanical pressure shutoff valves. The hall was crowded, mainly with staffers.

Dekkard didn't see any other councilors as he neared the councilors' lobby, but then realized they were likely in the chamber itself, waiting for what Hasheem might say. "I need to see Premier Hasheem first, if he's not already speaking."

When he reached the door to the Premier's floor office, the guard looked at him.

"He'll see me," Dekkard said, then added to Avraal and Gaaroll, "It might be best if you waited here." Then he opened the door and stepped inside, closing the door and looking to the secretary. "Is he in or already on the floor?"

"He's still here, sir."

"I didn't ask for permission," said Dekkard wryly, "but he needs to see me." With that he opened the door, stepped inside the small office, and closed the door.

Hasheem, who was standing beside his desk, turned and his mouth dropped open. "How did you escape?"

"I wasn't here. I had a meeting in the city. Last night, I gave my staff the morning off because of the snow—"

"You knew!"

"No. I didn't. But I thought it likely, told you as much, and you ordered me not to say anything. But you seem to have matters in hand," said Dekkard. "Army troopers and firefighters in position. Coal gas turned off."

"Thanks to Guard Captain Trujillo, not to you," said Hasheem angrily.

"Did they hit the Palace and the ironway station?"

"How did you know that?" demanded the Premier.

"I didn't. It was logical. I told you that I thought they'd try. From what I heard and the locations of the explosions, they also did their best to make the harbor unusable with their smaller guns. I didn't think they'd get close enough for that."

Hasheem's mouth opened.

"How many did we lose?"

"I *thought* we'd lost you. I should have known better."

"How many?" repeated Dekkard.

"Three councilors . . . so far. Ellus Fader, Julian Andros, and Gerhard Safaell."

Dekkard swallowed at the names of Andros and Safaell.

"Gerhard was in Julian's office when the shells hit the west end of the building. Most of their staffs were killed, except for Gerhard's. Maximillian Connard's office was across from yours, and was totally destroyed, like yours. We don't yet know about him and his staff, but it doesn't look good . . ."

All that made sense, unhappily, because Fader's office was next to Dekkard's.

"How could you just leave your staff?" Hasheem paused, then demanded, "Where were you? What about your staff?"

"I just told you." Dekkard said calmly, "Last night I told my staff they didn't have to come in until noon, or later, if the snow was heavy. I had a meeting with Carlos Baartol this morning. Partway through the meeting the shells started falling—they were from the *Khuld,* I presume. As soon as they stopped falling, I headed here. With all the damage, it took a while."

"You *knew* this was going to happen." Hasheem's voice was low, hard, and angry.

Dekkard ignored the angry repetition. "No, I didn't. I *thought* it would. I *told* you that. You ordered me not to say anything. I didn't. I warned you that the *Resolute* might not be able to stop the *Khuld.* You and the First Marshal apparently decided I was mistaken. Don't dare blame me for any of this—*ever.*" Dekkard's last words held cold iron.

Hasheem stepped back, stopped, then opened his mouth.

"Don't say another word of reproach, Fredrich," interjected Dekkard. "I could have been wrong. You could have been right. It didn't turn out that way. I understand that you had to follow what you thought best. Almost any other premier would have done something along the same lines. But don't you dare blame me for not being here. If I had been, I'd likely be dead. I prefer the alternative. So should you. What I said about the snow and my meeting was absolutely true. Knowing what I felt and what you had ordered as Premier, exactly what else could I do?"

"You could have been *here*."

"I draw the line at things that could get me and my staff killed needlessly. You should know that I'll risk it when necessary, but not for nothing . . . or for the sake of appearances." Dekkard forced a pleasant smile. "Now, don't you think we should get on with eliminating these Meritorist bastards and the treacherous corporacion types who funded and supplied them?"

"Just like that? I thought you and Gerhard were friends." Hasheem's tone turned accusatory.

"We were," snapped Dekkard. "I'll miss him, almost as much as Axel, but right now regrets and sorrow have to wait."

"You're a cold bastard, Steffan."

"I'm neither, and you should know that."

Hasheem took a long and deliberate breath, then said, "What do you want?"

"Exactly what I told you. I want to hammer any corporacion type who was behind this, and there are some, even if I can't prove it yet. I want to put an end to this Meritorist nonsense, by rooting out the terrorists and improving the lives of working people. The last thing in the world that I want is the power and responsibility you have."

After a long moment, Hasheem said, "The Council will meet at noon. I'll see you there, and not before. I'm waiting for more information."

"I'll be there." Dekkard inclined his head, turned, and left the small office, closing the door behind him, but being careful not to slam it, much as he felt that way.

Gerhard . . . and Julian . . .

"Thank you for coming, Councilor," said the secretary.

"I came as soon as I could."

"You always do," she replied quietly, barely above a murmur.

"Thank you," said Dekkard equally quietly, then opened the door to the main corridor.

When he came out into the corridor, Dekkard couldn't have said he was surprised to see Roostof with Avraal and Gaaroll. He was surprised to see Villem Baar talking to Avraal.

Dekkard immediately beckoned to Roostof.

"Sir! I *know,* but I couldn't *not* come—"

"Svard, you're fine. That's not why I motioned to you. I think you should do something."

"Sir?"

"Gerhard Safaell was one of the councilors killed by the Meritorists' shells. You can't do anything for me right now, but I think Bettina Safaell might need to find out from someone she knows."

Roostof froze for a moment. "Sir, he's really dead?"

"He was visiting Councilor Andros. Andros's office was destroyed. The Premier is certain he's dead."

Roostof shook his head, as if he couldn't believe it.

"She has no family here, and you're the best one to tell her. She might not find out for a while otherwise. It might be . . . rather harsh . . . from another source. Don't hurry back. You can help her. There's not much you can do here for a while." Dekkard paused, then added quickly, "Later, if you still have addresses for the rest of the staff at your flat, you could send messages saying you'll let them know when and how to return to work."

"I can do that, sir."

"Now . . . go find Bettina Safaell."

Roostof took a deep breath. "Thank you, sir."

After Roostof hurried off, Dekkard turned to Avraal and Villem Baar.

"Safaell?" asked Baar.

"Safaell, Julian Andros, Ellus Fader, and most likely Maximillian Connard. So far."

"You knew, didn't you?" Baar said evenly.

"No. I had absolutely no evidence that the *Khuld* could avoid an entire battle group and aim fifteen-year-old guns even close to targets seven milles away with no real fire control or spotters. I did know that they had to attack before long, and I had a feeling that it might be soon. When I saw how fine the snow was late yesterday afternoon, I thought the *Khuld* might use it for a screen to get close to the harbor. That was only a guess. I should have said more to others, but I didn't." Dekkard shrugged helplessly. "What could I have said? That I have this idea, against what everyone else has said, that a bunch of mutineers with almost no officers on an undermanned, near-obsolete light cruiser will evade the newest and most powerful warships we have and spend twenty-five minutes shelling the capital city of Guldor, in a snowstorm, no less?"

"The snow started yesterday."

"They had to wait until it was dark and visibility was low before they could move closer to Machtarn, and they wanted to attack when there were councilors present," Dekkard said. "That meant after third bell and before the *Resolute* sighted the *Khuld*."

"And you didn't tell the Premier?" Baar's tone was more puzzled than accusatory.

"I warned him twice. He told me that the First Marshal had it well in hand, and ordered me not to say more. I tried to let you know what I could, and by the time the snow was falling, most everyone had left." Dekkard paused. "And I could have been very wrong. I'm sorry. I should have said more, especially to you."

Baar just stood there. Abruptly, he shook his head. "You were in an impossible position. Logic and known facts say it couldn't happen. It did. How can I blame you for not disobeying the order of the Premier in those circumstances? Especially as a junior councilor." He paused. "What did you tell your staff?"

"I didn't. I told them I was worried about the snow and not to come in until after noon, and not then if the snow was still heavy."

After a moment, Baar said, "It's getting close to noon. We need to go to the floor."

Avraal stepped forward. "We'll wait near the lobby."

No councilors were in the lobby, probably because it was dark, the only light coming through the archway to the Council chamber. The high gallery windows dimly lighted the Council chamber itself.

Several councilors Dekkard barely knew looked his way as he and Baar entered, but returned to their conversations after a glance.

"Do you see Eyril Konnigsburg?" Dekkard asked Baar.

"Not yet. Oh . . . he's over there talking to Erich Kuuresoh." Baar gestured.

Dekkard turned in that direction. After a moment, Baar joined him.

Konnigsburg turned immediately. "Steffan! Villem! I'm glad to see you're both all right." He looked to Dekkard. "Apparently, your judgment of the abilities of the mutineers was far more accurate than the First Marshal's."

"I did mention that to the Premier," said Dekkard.

"As did I," replied Konnigsburg.

Kuuresoh shook his head. "An admiral and a security tech, who actually know something, and the Premier doesn't listen to either."

"Too often people defer to position, rather than actual expertise," observed Konnigsburg. "People think that because they know one field well they're equally versed in all fields—and so do their subordinates. That's always been a problem with the Admiralty."

Someone tapped Dekkard on the shoulder, and he turned to see Ingrella, who took his hand and squeezed it.

"I'm so glad you're all right, Steffan. How did you escape?"

Dekkard managed a wry smile and murmured, "By not being there. I worried about the snow. So I was late, and I'd already given the staff the morning off." Ingrella already knew that, but Dekkard needed to play out the semi-charade.

"Good. We'll talk later." She squeezed his hand again, then released it and turned away.

Dekkard felt his eyes burning, and he didn't know why. He blinked, blotted them with his sleeve, and turned back to the others.

At that moment, Kaliara Bassaana joined the group, her eyes going to Dekkard. "I saw your office. What's left of it."

Dekkard simply said, "Fortunate enough to have a meeting in the city. Told the staff late yesterday to take the morning off because of the snow."

Konnigsburg smiled wryly at Dekkard, but said nothing.

Kuuresoh frowned. "That's the second time."

"I'd rather there weren't a third," said Dekkard sardonically.

"Steffan would have made a great intelligence officer," said Konnigsburg quickly but smoothly. "He learns everything, and he has a great sense of impending danger, even when others disregard his warnings."

For just an instant, Bassaana seemed to freeze, but she quickly said, "That's indeed a pity . . . for all of us." Her words held more than a trace of sarcasm.

Baar gestured toward the speaker's dais, where the lieutenant-at-arms had appeared and began to thump his heavy staff.

Dekkard moved away from the others to his small desk, set between those of Ingrella and Tomas Pajiin, both of whom were already seated.

Pajiin leaned toward Dekkard. "Glad to see you made it through. You nailed it better than Hasheem."

"I'm more cynical," replied Dekkard, who turned back to watch as Hasheem stepped to the lectern.

The Premier cleared his throat, then said, "As is obvious, the city of Machtarn has been shelled. That danger is past, and we are dealing with the surviving insurrectionists. I will get to that in a minute. How did this occur? The mutineers who captured the light cruiser *Khuld* used the current snowstorm to momentarily evade the naval battle group patrolling just to the south of the city. They traveled in water barely deep enough to keep the cruiser from going aground, then moved into position around third bell this morning, where they anchored and opened fire at roughly a third past third bell."

Anchored?

Abruptly, the accuracy of the gunners made far more sense. While Dekkard couldn't prove it, he would have bet that the anchorage had been decided far earlier, and that the distance and exact bearings to the Council buildings, the Palace, and the Guldoran Ironway station had been measured and determined well before the mutiny. With accurate tables for powder charges and distance, the gunners had an excellent chance of at least getting close to their targets, and, if they fired enough shells, some were likely to hit—and that was what had happened.

Dekkard quickly calculated. With each two-gun turret releasing six shells every two minutes, the three turrets could have fired a maximum of two hundred twenty-five shells in the twenty-five minutes before the *Resolute* reached a point near enough to destroy the light cruiser. They probably hadn't loosed that many, but could easily have exceeded a hundred. He focused his attention back on Hasheem.

"The *Khuld*'s eight-digit guns focused on the Palace, the Council, and the Guldoran Ironway station. The Palace suffered the greatest damage, but the Imperador, his family, and a majority of the staff were not present . . . most shells appeared to be directed at the Council, but the damage spread over a five-square-block area . . . ironway station had the least physical damage but it will be a week if not longer before that section of the ironway is usable . . . fires raging in all the ironway coal towers near Machtarn . . . possibly because of subsequent actions by the New Meritorists . . . the mutineers directed the *Khuld*'s smaller guns at ships and structures in the harbor area . . . number of vessels and buildings still burning . . . some of that damage, regrettably, may have been incurred from the initial shells fired by the *Resolute* attempting to destroy the *Khuld* as quickly as possible . . ."

And the Imperial gunnery under time pressure wasn't all that accurate to begin with possibly because the battle group was too far offshore?

". . . direct hits on the *Khuld* caused the cruiser's magazines to explode, regretfully causing more damage to the harbor area . . . witnesses reported seeing several boats leaving the *Khuld* sometime after the cruiser fired its first shells and before the final explosion . . ."

Leaving just the gunnery crews firing shells? Dekkard frowned at that, but continued to listen to Hasheem.

". . . groups of New Meritorist terrorists appeared immediately after the shelling stopped, but most of them were either routed, captured, or killed by patrollers and Army troopers . . . more than fifty killed, some thirty captured so far and undergoing interrogation by Justiciary Ministry empaths and investigators. I will be working with the First Marshal and informing the Imperador of all developments.

"Once this session is over, Council will be recessed until noon on Unadi to allow for repairs. That session will be short. If matters change, you will each be notified by messenger. That is all."

The lieutenant-at-arms thumped his staff, and Hasheem turned and walked off the dais, without looking at anyone, presumably to his floor office.

Dekkard turned to Ingrella.

She motioned for him to move closer.

"You warned him, and he didn't listen."

"I also told him to get the Imperador out of the Palace and not in any of his usual retreats until the *Khuld* was located and destroyed. He's not happy with me, because I arrived here after the shelling."

"So did I, thanks to a certain note."

"I couldn't warn everyone—" *That would have been almost a different form of mutiny.*

"From what I overheard, and what Tomas told me, you made it clear to a number of councilors that there was more danger than Fredrich wanted known. There are limits, and . . . Steffan? Axel would have understood that. Fredrich *won't.*"

"He won't forgive, and he won't forget."

"That's true. He also won't forget that people respect you, and that the Council is a very small world."

Dekkard hoped that would be enough.

"We might as well walk out together," said Ingrella. "I'd like to see Avraal."

"We can do that."

37

A FTER Dekkard drove past or around several shell craters to the
west of the Council Hall and next to or actually in the Avenue of
the Guilds, the rest of the way home looked to be uneventful, except for
the faint wail of steam whistles coming from all parts of Machtarn. As he
turned and headed south on Jacquez, Dekkard explained how the attack
had been planned and had actually occurred and why he thought the
Khuld had been anchored where it had been.

"That means the mutiny was planned months ago," said Avraal.

"Longer than that. The gunnery officer had to request a transfer a long
time in advance." Dekkard paused. "That raises even more questions
about why Ulrich would ever want to give dunnite to the Meritorists."

"Unless he had no idea just how organized they were," replied Avraal.

"Everyone has been underestimating everyone else," said Dekkard
sourly.

"That surprises you? The only surprise in that is that you're one of the
few who aren't and who see it."

"There's a lot I didn't see," Dekkard pointed out. *And really should
have.*

"But you've never underestimated anyone."

"Except the New Meritorists. Anyway, that's a distinction that doesn't
mean much right now," he replied, thinking about how he hadn't considered that the *Khuld*'s three-digit guns could wreak havoc on unarmored
ships and buildings around the harbor. "We're going to see food shortages
for a while, too. Or at least of some foods, and prices will be higher."

"Food shortages?" asked Gaaroll.

"The harbor likely isn't going to be immediately usable, and the ironway around the station isn't. I don't know if the ironway freight yards
were damaged as well, but I'd suspect so. None of the coaling towers are
operable, either. The Meritorists set fire to them. I did think that the Meritorists would target them, and I told Hasheem that was likely."

"Which he'll have forgotten," said Avraal acidly, pausing for a moment
and then saying, "We should go shopping now. Most people won't think
about food immediately, and we should lay in some tinned meats as well.
They'll keep."

Dekkard nodded and continued south on Jacquez toward the shops around Erslaan.

As they neared the grocer's, Avraal said firmly, "You and Gaaroll stay with the Gresynt. I'll be quick as I can."

Dekkard almost frowned, then said, "It's probably better that way. Gaaroll can sense danger outside." He knew that wasn't the reason, but that a councilor stocking up on food immediately after a disaster might be faulted far more than a councilor's wife. "But don't take too long."

"I'll be quick and careful."

Avraal was as good as her word, at both the grocer's and the butcher shop, and in little less than a bell, Dekkard was driving back to the house.

"Did anyone say anything about the explosions?" he asked.

"All anyone here knows is that there were lots of explosions from the harbor. It won't be long before everyone in the city will know. No one recognized me."

"You had something to do with that, I take it?"

"A little. It didn't take much."

When Dekkard reached the house, he temporarily parked the Gresynt under the portico roof while the three unloaded what Avraal had bought. Then, while Avraal and Gaaroll started putting all of that away, Dekkard garaged the Gresynt, checked it over, and refilled the tanks before returning to the house.

It was close to sixth bell when Emrelda finally arrived home and hurried to the kitchen, her eyes going from Avraal to Dekkard to Gaaroll. "You're all safe, thank the Almighty. When I heard the Council buildings had been shelled . . ." She shook her head.

"Steffan was right," Avraal said quietly. "His office was one of those destroyed. If he and his staff had been there . . ."

Emrelda frowned, then said, "You said you'd told the staff not to come in, but it looked like you were going to work before noon."

"We went to meet with Carlos Baartol," said Dekkard. "The shelling started while we were there." He gave her a quick summary of what he knew, had heard, and had seen. "What else do you know?"

"According to Captain Narryt, the harbor is a disaster. Only a few ships were destroyed, but everything was damaged, and the fires that followed caused explosions in warehouses—he didn't know how many. The waterfront had more damage than the piers. The river piers were scarcely damaged at all, but getting to them won't be easy for the next few days."

At the sound of a muffled bell, Dekkard held up a hand. "Someone rang the front bell." He looked to Avraal. "Can you tell anything?"

"I think it's a woman . . ."

"I'll get it," said Emrelda, turning and walking toward the front door. Avraal and Dekkard followed.

When Emrelda opened the front door, the dark-haired young empath nanny from next door stood there.

"Sra. Waaldwud sent me. I'm Sigourna Miletus. Might I come in, Sra. Markell?"

Emrelda stepped back and allowed the young woman into the front foyer, closing the door.

"Thank you . . . it's just . . . it's cold . . . she's so upset. I can't be gone long." The words tumbled out.

"What is it you need?" asked Emrelda.

"You're a patroller. Do you know anything about what's happened? There were explosions from the direction of the harbor . . . and the steam whistles keep screeching. Sr. Waaldwud works for the Shipping Authority. He should have been home over a bell ago. He has the only steamer . . . and Sra. Waaldwud is so worried. So is Tomas. When I saw you drive up, we thought you might know."

Emrelda looked to Avraal, then Dekkard.

"You know as much about the harbor as we do," said Dekkard. "If we can add anything, we will."

"Matters around the harbor aren't good, Sigourna," said Emrelda gently. "The crew of a Navy cruiser mutinied. The mutineers fired on the harbor area, and at the Imperador's Palace, the Council, and the ironway station. Right now, the harbor's cordoned off because of the fires caused by those shells hitting warehouses and other buildings. Quite a few people were injured or killed, and there are likely others who are all right, but who can't move from where they are because of the fires. Even my patrol captain didn't know any more than that when I left the station a little while ago."

The young woman did not speak, but just looked from face to face.

Avraal finally said, "We don't know, Sigourna. Right now, no one knows for sure what happened to whom in the harbor. We don't want to mislead you or Sra. Waaldwud. People have died. Sr. Waaldwud might be home tonight or tomorrow. He might be injured. He might be dead."

"When things like this happen," added Dekkard, "usually more people survive than die or are injured, but there's no way to tell right now. Do you know exactly where he worked?"

"No, sir. Only that he is a logistics manager for the Shipping Authority. He never talked about work."

"I'll go back to your house with you," said Avraal.

"So will I," added Emrelda.

"Would you?" asked the nanny.

"We will."

In minutes, the three left, and Dekkard returned to the kitchen to watch over the almost-ready-to-serve dinner.

Almost a third passed before Avraal and Emrelda returned.

"How did it go?" asked Dekkard.

"She's upset, obviously," said Avraal. "She doesn't know what to do. I got the impression he made all the decisions. We calmed her down. We also told her to talk things over with Sigourna, and that we're here, at least in the evenings."

"This long after the attack," said Dekkard, "the odds are that Waaldwud is either injured or dead."

"I'd agree," said Emrelda, "but the captain said the situation was still chaotic."

"The situation everywhere in Machtarn is chaotic to some extent," said Dekkard, "and will be for several days." *At the very least.*

A sixth later, everyone sat down to eat the Jeeroh-style pork roast with fried julienned potatoes and roasted red cabbage.

No one spoke for several minutes.

Finally, Emrelda said, "You know that once it gets out that Steffan's entire office was destroyed—again—and that he wasn't there, and neither was his staff . . ."

"*The Machtarn Tribune* is going to write some more frigging shit about how questionable a councilor I am," interjected Dekkard in a tone both angry and sardonic. "It's as though the only way I could be honorable would be to sit in my office and get blown up. Or to publicly speak out with information that shouldn't be made public and then argue openly and violently with the Craft Party leadership, which just might result in new elections that the Commercers and the old-line Landors could win."

"That may be true, but it's still going to be a problem," said Emrelda calmly.

"You don't think I haven't thought about it? My real problem is that I'm intelligent enough to see what could happen, but not soon enough, and even when I do warn them, they remain skeptical. So I have to act alone, and that makes them even more wary of me." Dekkard shook his head. "If I'd only followed up more on that frigging brown stake lorry . . . then maybe Obreduur would still be premier."

"There wasn't anything to follow up on when we first saw that lorry," said Avraal. "It was empty, remember? And you told Guard Captain Trujillo immediately. What else could you have done?"

"That's what's so frustrating," returned Dekkard. "I have to rely on other people, and they have to rely on yet more people, and it takes time and sometimes . . . nothing gets done."

"You've known about that for a good while," Avraal pointed out evenly. "Or was it easier to accept when Obreduur was the one responsible?"

After a moment, Dekkard said, "Like the *Tribune* editorials about me being questionable, your words are true, but not complete. At least as premier, Obreduur had more power to accomplish things than I do."

"Steffan," snapped Avraal. "That's indulgent self-pity. For years he didn't have that kind of power. You've been a councilor for three months, and you have far more power as a junior councilor than he ever did."

Gaaroll's mouth dropped open, but she clamped it shut immediately, her eyes wide.

Avraal went on, "You *chose* not to oppose Hasheem's order not to tell anyone about the Meritorists' ultimatum. You also chose not to bring it up publicly. That was a judgment call. If you had brought it up, that wouldn't have changed much. The New Meritorists would still have shelled the city. Hasheem still might not have closed down the Council. If he had, the *Khuld* would still have shelled the Council buildings. But you deferred to Hasheem, as required, and that resulted in the death of four councilors and their staffers. That was *his* choice, *not* yours. Even if you'd protested publicly, he still might not have closed the Council. We don't know. But you were trying to avoid a direct conflict with the Premier and not to pay too high a price. That meant you didn't offend and anger the Premier and that you and your staff lived. Others didn't." Avraal looked directly across the table at him. "I'm selfish, and I'm glad you're alive. I'm glad your staff is alive. But stop feeling sorry for yourself. *Everything* has a price, Steffan. *Everything.*"

And part of that price is being publicly labeled as questionable. Dekkard swallowed. Finally, he said, "You're right."

"At some point, you may have to call out the Premier," said Avraal. "He isn't going to change."

"Not him," murmured Gaaroll.

"*But* do it when you've lined up allies or when it's obvious to the poorest street sweeper in Gaarlak."

"That makes sense," Dekkard managed to say evenly, glad that Avraal hadn't said what she had every right to say—that he hadn't turned down the chance to be a councilor and that unpleasant situations came with the position.

Cleaning up after dinner was a quiet affair, and Dekkard didn't say much until later, when he and Avraal were alone in their room.

Then, his first words were, "I'm sorry. I should have talked it over more with you."

Avraal shook her head. "I'm sorry, too. People, especially newsies and those who know nothing about government and politics, always make things much simpler than they are."

"And they also say that politicians make them more complicated when what makes it complicated is the fact that every solution to a problem hurts someone."

Avraal took a deep breath. "We've said enough about all this for now. We need to get our minds off what's happened over the last week. Especially today."

"I think you're suggesting we read a certain antique tome about a city that may or may not have existed."

Avraal offered a slightly strained smile. "I am."

"That's a better suggestion than the none that I have."

38

At almost any street market, whether in Teknar or Aloor, Cuipremaan or Cimaguile—or even here in Averra—one can find street magicians or illusionists—men or women, sometimes girls or boys—who make coins vanish and reappear or who take a pastecard from a deck and yet have it reappear where it seemingly could not possibly be. Magic like that does not exist. We know this to be true, but street illusionists work to convey the impression that their magic does.

Most of us are drawn in by such, even though we know it does not reflect reality. Unless we are illusionists ourselves or have had a particular illusion explained to us, most of us are still captivated and struggle to discern how the effect was accomplished. One key to seeing through illusions is to realize that the illusionist has misdirected the watcher's attention. The second key is to understand that most people want to believe in what they think they see. All successful illusions combine misdirection with an appeal to what those watching the illusion wish to believe.

Illusions, for better or worse, are not confined to marketplace magicians or entertainers in other venues. They occur in the fields of performance and visual art, and in the building of structures and monuments, where they often enhance the artistry, but also in other fields, from medicine, law, commerce, and politics, where most, especially those not experienced in a particular field, would not expect illusions, often with the result that blame is placed upon the innocent. Seldom do the adverse effects of such negative illusions fall upon the guilty, for they are usually the ones creating such illusions for their own benefit.

In all such instances, what we think we see or perceive is seldom what we think it is or what has actually occurred, particularly since too many fail to understand that the most dangerous illusions occur far from the street markets.

AVERRA
The City of Truth
Johan Eschbach
377 TE

39

DEKKARD woke at his normal time on Quindi to another quiet morning, without the faintest hint of steam whistles. He shaved and showered quickly, but dressed in one of his older gray suits, and headed downstairs while Avraal was still dressing. Emrelda was finishing her café as he entered the breakfast room and glanced at the morning edition of *Gestirn* on the side table.

"There's not much there that we didn't know or suspect," said Emrelda. "The harbor's still burning in places. When I got the newssheet from the dropbox, the air smelled and tasted of all sorts of burnt . . . stuff. That has to be because the wind's shifted, and it's coming from the southwest."

"Burning or off-gassing," said Dekkard. "Maybe both."

"Stunk," added Gaaroll.

Knowing he had a few minutes before Avraal came down to breakfast, Dekkard picked up the newssheet and began to read. The front page was entirely about the *Khuld*'s attack on the city. The first story dealt with the attack and the damage, and the fact that it might be days before the fates of all those working in the harbor and adjoining buildings were known. The second focused on the failure of the Navy to prevent the attack, including the disclosure that the First Marshal had no statement or explanation on the attack and going on from there to point out that the mutineers had apparently lightened the cruiser enough that the warship had been able to use a barge channel shielded by foliage for most of its approach to the attack location.

Planned carefully and then some.

The third story summed up the areas damaged by the shells and stated that schools, shops, and most commercial enterprises were expected to continue as usual, except for the ironway station and freight depot, the harbor area, the Council buildings, and any structure suffering damage.

The brief statement from Premier Hasheem basically stated that the I.S. *Khuld* had been effectively destroyed with no signs of survivors. Given what Hasheem had said to the Council the day before, Dekkard wondered about that, but perhaps the shells from the *Resolute* had sunk the boats initially reported to have left the cruiser before its demise. Hasheem was quoted as saying that a number of New Meritorist insurgents had been captured and incarcerated, in addition to those killed by patrollers and Army troopers. His last words were that the Council would be using emergency funds to assist in the rebuilding.

Rather vague there, Fredrich.

Dekkard finished reading, set the newssheet aside, and went to fix cafés. He'd barely set Avraal's on the breakfast table before she arrived.

"You two are dressed for work," said Emrelda as she stood to leave. "I thought the Council buildings were closed."

"They are, but Carlos isn't, and we never finished our last conversation," said Dekkard ruefully. "So I thought I'd do that, at least if he isn't too busy."

"As if he wouldn't see you," said Avraal as she sat down and reached for her café.

"Do you think you'll be late tonight?" Dekkard asked Emrelda.

"Count on it. If I'm not, we'll all be pleasantly surprised. Try not to get into any more trouble," said Emrelda, adding, "Contrarian or otherwise."

"For the moment, anyway," replied Dekkard, "the Contrarians are lying low."

"Very wise of them," replied Emrelda dryly, before leaving the breakfast room.

Dekkard thought he saw a momentary grin from Gaaroll before she looked away from him and toward Avraal.

"What is it, Nincya?" asked Avraal.

"Will you be needing me?"

"Definitely," said Dekkard. "There may be Meritorists running around . . . or even Contrarians."

Both women just looked at him.

Dekkard smiled sheepishly and decided to go get the croissants from the cooler. He returned several minutes later and slipped one onto Avraal's plate and two onto his own.

She looked up with a twinkle in her eye and murmured, "I love how you can admit you were thoughtless without ever saying a word."

He smiled again and replied, "And I love the way you can tell me that without a word."

Less than a bell passed before Avraal and Gaaroll joined Dekkard in the Gresynt.

Because he doubted that the patrollers and Army troopers had dealt with anywhere near all the New Meritorists in Machtarn, although he also had doubts there would be any in the Hillside area, he still asked Gaaroll, "Are there any strong emotions around?"

"Only next door, sir."

"Poor woman." While Dekkard could feel sorry for her and Tomas, he didn't feel at all sorry about Sr. Waaldwud, except for the grief and possible privation his death might cause the others. "It might be days before she knows." He pulled out of the drive and turned east on Florinda Way, then turned south on Jacquez.

After turning west on Camelia Avenue, he said, "Let me know if you sense anything at all out of the ordinary near the university."

"Yes, sir."

Dekkard's own mention of the university got him thinking about Gerhard Safaell—and Bettina and Svard Roostof. *Too often, the good people suffer, and even when the not-so-good ones are killed, that affects innocents.*

As he approached Imperial University, all he saw were scattered groups of students, perhaps a few more than on other occasions, but no signs of disorder.

When he turned south on Imperial Boulevard, he wondered how much of the harbor area was closed off. Once he reached the Avenue of the Guilds, he could see barricades across the boulevard—several blocks from the piers. He wondered about Rabool's, the bistro that Carlos Baartol often frequented, but there was no way to tell whether it had been damaged.

He parked the Gresynt in a visitor's spot in the parking area beside Baartol's building and let Avraal lead the way.

As Avraal, Dekkard, and Gaaroll came up the steps and stepped into Baartol's anteroom, Elicya looked up from her desk. "We thought we might see you today after your departure yesterday."

"Everyone here is all right?" asked Avraal.

"We were all fortunate," replied Elicya.

"What about Rabool's?" asked Dekkard.

Elicya smiled. "He had a little roof damage from fragments, but no one there was hurt."

Baartol stepped out of his inner office. "I thought I heard familiar voices. I'm glad to see you're unharmed." He paused, then said, "I assume you didn't come just to let us know that."

"Since I can't do much for Steffan," said Avraal, "I thought there might be a few things I could do here."

"We never quite finished our conversation yesterday," added Dekkard, "and if you have a few moments, now might be as good a time as any."

"I can manage that," replied Baartol, "but let me talk to Avraal first about a situation I want her to look into. She can read the file while we're talking."

After Avraal entered Baartol's inner office and closed the door, Dekkard turned to Elicya. "Do you know any more about the damage to the harbor than was in the newssheets?"

"Not much, Councilor. Most of the warehouses adjoining the piers are a total loss. We heard that two of Transoceanic's ships were badly damaged and a third sank right next to the pier. One of the packet ships of Noldaran Lines isn't even worth salvaging. Most of the ships moored at piers farther west only had minor damage, but the Transoceanic ship that sank was trying to leave port when the attack happened and the wreck mostly blocks the main deepwater channel."

She went on for several minutes before saying, "That's all I know."

"That's a great deal more than not much," said Dekkard cheerfully.

"What happened to the Council?" asked Elicya.

By the time Dekkard had finished explaining that, Avraal walked out of Baartol's private office carrying a file.

"Your turn," she said cheerfully.

Dekkard walked into the private office.

Baartol motioned for him to shut the door.

Dekkard did so, then sat down in one of the straight-backed chairs. "We were talking about Guldoran Ironworks and how they obtained the rights to a unique punch-card lathe."

"There's not much more than what's in the file. Elicya has a copy waiting for you."

"Thank you. You've been of great assistance in many ways, and I do appreciate it."

Baartol nodded, then leaned back slightly in his chair. "You know, Steffan, that premiers get very wary of junior councilors who are usually correct in their surmises and recommendations, and who uncannily seem to avoid disasters."

"I've become increasingly aware of that, but a particular premier ignores or minimizes my observations and recommendations with the result that the steps I take to avoid becoming a casualty only seem uncanny."

"I understand that the Imperador and his family were nowhere near the Palace. Might I ask how that occurred?"

"I did suggest that the Imperador not be within range of a cruiser's guns nor in any of his usual known retreats. Apparently, *that* recommendation was passed on."

"That suggests that whoever passed it along felt that councilors were more expendable than the Imperador."

"I confess that I had not thought of it in quite that light."

"You're young for a councilor and more cynical than most men your age."

"Meaning that I'm not cynical enough."

Baartol smiled warmly. "I didn't say that."

"You made the point without saying it, and that's an ability I need to perfect," Dekkard admitted willingly.

"I'm quite sure that it's more a question of realizing that those in power almost always appreciate indirection. Except, of course, when seeking praise."

"I can see that, but indirection also enables deniability."

"For both parties," Baartol observed.

"True," agreed Dekkard. "What do you think about the Meritorist threat?"

"If the Council acts decisively and quickly, the Meritorists are finished."

Dekkard couldn't help frowning. "Why do you say that?"

"They moved too soon, and there aren't enough of them. They don't have a wide enough base among the rabble, and spring is almost here. Don't get me wrong. Hasheem still has the chance to botch it all. That's what the Commercers want him to do."

"In your view, how could the Crafters botch it?"

"By either executing all the Meritorists or letting them go. Lots of executions will make the Crafters seem as bad as the old Landors. If you let them go with slaps on their wrists, they'll be back at it in less than a year, and the Commercers will be pressing the Imperador to call new elections."

"What about varying-length sentences in work camps followed by involuntary exile?"

"It might be better to exile immediately most of those who can be determined to have been actively guilty of insurrection, while sentencing any higher-ups actually caught to work camps for a while."

Dekkard nodded. "That way you break communication between the planners and the actual foot soldiers and ignore those who were either cautious or half-hearted followers."

"That would be the hope."

"That still leaves the First Marshal and the Fleet Marshal."

"It does, doesn't it?" said Baartol.

Under the Great Charter, as Dekkard well knew, the Premier could remove one of the two immediately, but the selection of his replacement was up to the Imperador, and the Premier could not make a second removal until two months passed. Then he nodded, realizing what Baartol had indirectly suggested. "That might prove interesting."

"It might, indeed." Baartol leaned forward in his chair. "I don't know that I can add much to what we've discussed. Not now, anyway."

Dekkard got the message and stood. "I appreciate your giving me the time and your insights."

Baartol stood as well. "You're welcome here, any time."

"I appreciate that as well."

Baartol accompanied Dekkard into the outer office, where he turned and said, "Elicya, that file for Councilor Dekkard?"

Elicya lifted a large brown envelope from the corner of the desk. "It's right here."

In turn, Baartol took the envelope and handed it to Dekkard. "Here you go."

Dekkard inclined his head. "Thank you. Again."

"It was my pleasure."

Once Dekkard, Avraal, and Gaaroll were back in the Gresynt, Avraal asked, "Did you have a good talk with Carlos?"

"Let's say it was both pleasant and useful. Now I'd thought we'd take a long drive around Machtarn to get a feel for the extent of the damage."

"That's a good idea," replied Avraal. "The Council will be held responsible for paying to repair some if not all of it."

"While this Council is only partly responsible," said Dekkard as he lit off the Gresynt, "we will be considered fully responsible, although I'd like to extend that responsibility." *And outright blame to certain corporacions and former councilors and to the Imperador.*

After leaving the parking area and driving east on the Avenue of the Guilds, he turned south on Imperial Boulevard, but came to the barricades two blocks north of Harbor Way. He stopped there and got out to look in the direction of the harbor. While he could see the blackened roofless structures on each side of the boulevard on the north side of Harbor Way, the intervening buildings east and west blocked his view of other structures farther away. He could make out the sunken ship that partially blocked the deepwater channel, but the superstructure protruding above the water was so blackened that he couldn't discern details, and the untouched buildings north of Harbor Way blocked his view of the piers.

"Sir?" said an approaching patroller. "You can't stop here."

Dekkard turned. "I understand. I was just trying to get an idea of the damage."

The patroller's eyes dropped to the Council bumper emblem. "You're a councilor?"

"I am." Dekkard opened his overcoat enough to show the Council badge. "I wanted to see personally how bad it was."

"We're under orders to keep anyone out who doesn't live or work here. Otherwise . . ."

"I do understand. How bad is it?"

"Most of the buildings on Harbor Way were totally destroyed, except for their walls. About half those working there got out before the fires took over."

If the law hadn't required brick or stone exterior walls, Dekkard suspected that the fire damage could have been much greater, but all he said was, "Do you know where they took the injured? My neighbor here in Machtarn works at the Shipping Authority."

"No, sir, I don't. I usually patrol in West Quarter."

"Thank you. I won't impose on you any longer."

"Can I have your name, sir?"

Dekkard fumbled in his suit coat pocket and managed to come up with a card, which he handed to the patroller.

"Thank you, sir."

"You're welcome." Dekkard got back into the Gresynt and carefully maneuvered it around so that it was heading back north. He glanced in the rearview mirror. The patroller was still looking at the card. "He wanted my name. I hope that's because they're hoping to catch Meritorists admiring their so-called handiwork."

As he drove, Dekkard relayed what the patroller had said. There were more steamers on the boulevard once Dekkard passed the Avenue of the Guilds on the way to the Guldoran Ironway station, until he turned off Imperial Boulevard. The closest he could get to the station was about a block away. Even from that distance, he could see men working everywhere, unlike near the harbor.

Except they might have been working on Harbor Way or at the piers you couldn't see.

After that, he made his way to Council Avenue and drove east. The section to the west of Imperial Boulevard appeared to have escaped the shells from the *Khuld,* and there were more than a few steamers on that part of the avenue. Most of them turned south on Imperial Boulevard, while Dekkard headed north toward the Square of Heroes, initially heartened when he saw that the square wasn't blocked off. As he reached the square, because of the gradual way the ground rose on the north side of the Way of Gold, Dekkard immediately saw craters ripped out of the manicured grounds flanking the long white stone drive to the pale golden marble edifice that was the Palace. Several of the gardens, all of which Dekkard had previously marveled at, had suffered from shell impacts, in several cases destroying elaborate topiary hedges as well. A section of the white stone drive was missing with a crater in its place, and it appeared to Dekkard that part of the east side of the Palace had also been damaged.

"That's even worse than around the Council," said Gaaroll.

"It's hard to tell how badly the Palace itself was damaged, but the grounds certainly took a beating," said Dekkard as he guided the Gresynt around the square and back south on Imperial Boulevard. "I'd guess we saw most of the damage, though."

"Why do you think that?" asked Avraal.

"Because the craters run mostly east to west, and they only had so much time and so many shells. Now, that's a guess. If I'm wrong, I'll certainly find out in tomorrow's newssheet."

Once Dekkard reached Council Avenue, he turned east and almost immediately saw several areas where the shells had destroyed small buildings or sections of larger ones. The few craters in Council Avenue had all been filled in and were surrounded by construction sawhorses, but had not been re-bitumened.

The iron gates blocking off the Council buildings were closed and guarded, but Dekkard saw lorries lined up in the west drive and workmen swarming around the west end of the Council Office Building.

"Hasheem's not wasting any time," Dekkard said, his voice flat, as he turned south toward Justiciary Avenue.

"Not on repairs," agreed Avraal.

"Shoulda listened to you," growled Gaaroll.

"The buildings still would have been damaged," said Dekkard. "That responsibility rests on the First Marshal."

"Do you think Hasheem will remove him?" asked Avraal.

"We'll have to see," Dekkard replied evenly, turning west. He didn't bother to turn north to get back on Council Avenue, but continued east on Justiciary Avenue until he reached Jacquez and headed south.

A sixth later, he pulled into the drive.

"Just go to the garage," said Avraal. "I'll get the doors."

Dekkard followed her directions, but after he garaged the Gresynt, he was the one who closed the doors.

The three were about to enter the house when Sigourna Miletus hurried across time-compressed snow toward them. Dekkard turned, wondering whether to dread what she said.

"Councilor, Ritten . . . I just wanted you to know that Sr. Waaldwud is home."

"How is he?" asked Dekkard.

"He'll be all right in time. He has a broken right arm, a sprained left wrist, lots of bruises, and a few burns. Sra. Waaldwud wanted you to know because you were so good yesterday."

"That is very kind of you," said Avraal. "Is there anything—"

"I don't think so." The nanny smiled ruefully. "It might be interesting. We got a message that he was hurt but ready to come home. I had to walk down to Erslaan to get a steamhack to take us to the Ritten Alorsana Hospital to get Sr. Waaldwud . . . and the steamer."

"If the steamer was all right . . ." began Dekkard.

"Someone at work drove him to the hospital, but they got to him later because of the more serious injuries. He can't drive for a while, and Sra. Waaldwud never learned."

"So you're now both nanny and chauffeur?" said Avraal.

"For a while." Miletus smiled ruefully once more. "I need to go, but thank you again."

Then she hurried back to the Waaldwud house.

"Matters there are going to be interesting," said Dekkard.

"Especially after Sr. Waaldwud starts feeling better and still can't drive," added Avraal.

"He won't get any nicer," said Gaaroll. "That kind never does."

Dekkard found himself relieved that Waaldwud had survived. He also felt sorry for both Gaaroll and the nanny because he had no doubt there would be many strong feelings from the adjoining house over the coming weeks.

While Avraal and Gaaroll headed to the kitchen to begin work on fixing dinner, Dekkard retreated to the study to consider Baartol's words and to plan how he intended to work with Hasheem on Unadi.

He was still working on that when Emrelda stepped through the portico door earlier than any of the three expected, at a third past fourth bell.

"We didn't expect you so soon," said Avraal.

"That's the good news," replied Emrelda. "The bad news is that I'm duty dispatcher tomorrow for the morning-to-midafternoon shift. At least I wasn't one of the patrollers seconded to help those at the harbor station."

"We went there after we met with Carlos Baartol," said Dekkard. "From what I saw, there's not much left south of Harbor Way."

"That's what the captain said."

"What about dinner?" asked Avraal. "I can have it ready in a third."

"I'd like that," replied Emrelda. "We all need to go to services tonight. Offering thanks is in order." Emrelda looked at Dekkard and added, "Even if you're skeptical about the existence of an Almighty, it can't hurt." Then she looked at Avraal. "And no, I'm not changing. People need to see me in uniform. Especially now."

Avraal just laughed.

Then, so did Emrelda.

Dinner was moderately quiet, although Avraal and Dekkard told Emrelda what they'd seen and learned at Baartol's office . . . and about Sr. Waaldwud, at which news Emrelda just shook her head.

Later, when the four reached the Hillside Trinitarian Chapel, Dekkard immediately saw that the parking area held more steamers than usual. *And we're a bit early.* He kept both thoughts to himself as Emrelda led the way inside.

As Dekkard stood at the end of the pew, while Gaaroll, Emrelda, and Avraal seated themselves, he looked to the rear of the other side of the chapel, where he was slightly surprised to see Villem and Gretina Baar, as well as Karlotta and Matteus. He wondered who there had suggested giving thanks, but suspected it had been Gretina.

Villem looked in his direction, offering a smile both amused and resigned, and Dekkard inclined his head in return before sitting down.

The harmonium soon ended the prelude and began the short processional, while the slender Presider Buusen, clad in a plain green cassock, moved to the front of the sanctuary.

When the music ended and the congregation stood, Presider Buusen intoned, "In this time of unexpected trials and suffering, let us still offer thanks to the Almighty for his support and guidance for the day that has been and for the nights and days to come, through his love, power, and mercy.

"Thanks be to the Almighty, for his love, power, and mercy."

Dekkard wasn't all that sure about support and guidance, but he understood what the presider was trying to do, and he listened more intently when Buusen began his homily.

"Although we all attempt to establish certainty and regularity in our lives, as everyone in Machtarn discovered in some fashion yesterday, the certainty of our everyday routines can be shattered in an instant. One moment, everything is as expected. The next moment, we can be faced with the unexpected. The unexpected can come from nature, as in a violent spoutstorm, or from other human beings, as happened with the naval gunfire dropping shells across the city. No matter how we prepare, there is always the possibility of the unexpected."

That is certainly true. Dekkard nodded and continued to listen.

40

FOR Dekkard, Avraal, and Gaaroll, Findi was remarkably uneventful, although Dekkard heard a few more steam whistles than usual on an endday. When Emrelda got off duty, she confirmed that was in fact so, although she had no idea why, since little out of the ordinary had happened involving her station.

Unadi morning dawned with high clouds and continued light winds from the southwest, which suggested to Dekkard that spring might actually arrive, although not immediately.

Once downstairs, he checked *Gestirn* and found that the newssheet held a modest story about how patrollers and Army units had rounded up more armed Meritorist insurgents, which he mentioned as he set the newssheet aside.

"How come they can find all those Meritorists now?" asked Gaaroll, before starting on her second mug of café. "No one could find any of them before."

"Because once they captured a few known to be Meritorists, they could use empies and interrogation to discover more," replied Avraal. "More leads to more. That's also the reason why someone, most likely Ulrich, had Minz killed before he could be questioned by a skilled empie interrogator."

"That was why the New Meritorists were so careful before," said Dekkard. "They never exposed anyone who knew anything."

"Why now?" pressed Gaaroll.

Dekkard shrugged. "I don't know. Maybe the patrollers or the Army finally caught someone who knew too much. Maybe Guard Captain Trujillo did. At that point, if the Meritorists didn't move, they'd lose too much of their leadership and wouldn't be effective for years. Maybe they thought they had more support than they really did. Maybe they thought that people in Rivertown or Southtown would riot when the shells started falling." He looked across the table to Avraal. "Can you think of any other possibilities?"

"Could they have expected the shells to be more effective against the Council and the Imperador? So that there wasn't much of a government left?"

"That could be. Also, maybe they didn't anticipate that so many troops would be moved in. That reduced the effectiveness of the armed insurgents." Dekkard shook his head. "The way things have gone, I'm not sure we'll ever know."

"I do know one thing," said Avraal. "After breakfast, we need to get to the Council, and you need to talk to the Premier."

Dekkard didn't argue about that, but he did notice that she did pick up *Gestirn,* and scan through the pages until she reached the last pages. *For the food and wine column.*

By a little after second bell, the three were on their way. There were fewer steamers on Jacquez than usual, and Council Avenue was again open, although there were definitely guards and workmen around the Council buildings. The covered parking was open to councilors, but the guard at the entrance did ask to see Dekkard's badge and passcard.

From there the three had to walk along the south side of the Council Office Building, since the west doors were blocked because of the shell damage to the northwest corner of the building, and from there through a side gate to the courtyard—a gate Dekkard had never seen unlocked or open.

Once inside the Council Hall, Dekkard noted the unlit wall lamps, suggesting that repairs to the coal-gas lines had not been completed, and that the corridor was mostly empty . . . and very chilly. Two Council Guards stood outside the unmarked door to the Premier's floor office.

"Councilor, the Premier isn't seeing anyone," declared the taller guard.

"Anyone?" asked Dekkard. "Are you certain about that?"

As he spoke, Avraal stepped forward and opened the door.

Stepping past the confused guards, Dekkard followed her in and closed the door behind himself, noticing, once he was inside, that the outer office was dimly lit by two kerosene lamps.

The secretary's look of surprise was followed by a smile that was half resignation, half amusement. Then she said, "He won't want to see you, but he's in his office. There's no one with him."

Dekkard didn't bother to knock. He just opened the door and walked in, closing the door firmly.

"I said I wasn't—" Hasheem looked up from the paper he was reading in the dim light of the single kerosene lamp, and his look of annoyance turned to something darker. "How dare you."

"Let's not talk about that right now, Fredrich. You can't wall yourself off from this mess."

"Exactly why are you here?" asked Hasheem, ignoring what Dekkard had said. "The Council isn't in session. It will be another week before the main part of the Council Hall is usable, and several weeks or longer before the damage to the Council Office Building and the end of the west end of the Hall can be repaired."

"That's good to know, but it's not exactly relevant right now," said Dekkard calmly as he took the chair across the desk from the Premier. "I thought we might talk about what is."

"Talk? Talk won't do anything. Matters are not for the best, as you must know. I'm also not exactly pleased that you come and go as you please. I wonder what might happen if other members were reminded how you avoided danger while they were subjected to it."

"We were all subjected to it, but I think that they might be more concerned if they discovered that the Imperador was warned and moved out of danger but they weren't told, because of other considerations."

"They might consider the source, first," said Hasheem smoothly.

"You mean, from a junior councilor already known for 'questionable' behavior?"

"I never said that."

"Of course not, but you thought it." Dekkard let the silence draw out before asking gently, "Do you want to gamble on that, Fredrich? It could be a costly wager for the Craft Party—and for you."

"As I recall, you said you didn't want anything. Or were you dissembling?"

"No . . . I said I didn't want your power and responsibility. I still don't. But it might be better for both of us if we worked together, rather than your listening to me only when you feel you must. I'm not always right. I've made mistakes. So have you. I'm likely too impetuous. You're likely too cautious. Together we might do a great deal better. You want the Craft Party to remain in power. So do I, and I don't want any more avoidable casualties. So should you."

"There was no way—"

Dekkard snorted. "What's done is done. That's not the question."

"And what is the question, pray tell, most knowledgeable councilor?"

Dekkard ignored the cynical sarcasm. "Where the Council goes from here, and what needs to be done immediately."

"Haven't you done enough?"

Dekkard took a long slow breath, then said quietly and firmly, as intently as he could, letting his feeling infuse his words, "I did nothing, except try not to be killed by your decisions. You took my information and made the decisions. I made no decisions for anyone else but me and my staff. You did. Some of them weren't good. Don't blame me."

The paper slipped from Hasheem's fingers. Then he gave the smallest of headshakes and moistened his lips. "I . . . haven't blamed you."

Dekkard managed a pleasant expression, then said, "All I'm asking is for you to listen seriously in private and then to have an honest discussion where I don't have to tread lightly or to defer blindly to your position. In turn, you can tell me why you think what I'm proposing or concerned about is foolish, dangerous, or impractical. Right now is not the time for indirection and deferral."

"Was that the way you operated with Premier Obreduur? Much good it did him."

Dekkard ignored Hasheem's cutting last words. "He asked for my advice, but he also told me to warn him about things he might not have taken into account." That wasn't quite the way it had been, Dekkard knew, because there had been more nuances, but it was close enough, and Dekkard wanted to make sure the basics of what he was proposing—or insisting on—were clear.

"I did warn him that the New Meritorists would attack councilors and not the Council Hall. I just wasn't omniscient enough to predict a frigging steam cannon. I even described the stake lorry they used to Guard Captain Trujillo—unfortunately before they loaded the steam cannon into it. Or didn't the Guard captain mention that to you?"

"He did," said Hasheem, almost grudgingly.

"Is there any other councilor who's been as accurate? Even close?"

Hasheem did not meet Dekkard's eyes.

Dekkard spoke, his voice quiet but again intensely earnest. "I don't want to be premier, certainly not any time soon, and maybe never. I want the Craft Party to remain in power, especially long enough to accomplish the reforms necessary to preclude another insurgency, which there will be if we don't make some reforms." Then he waited.

And waited.

Dekkard forced himself to sit looking at Hasheem without saying a word.

While it felt like five minutes passed, it was likely closer to two.

Abruptly, Hasheem offered a rueful smile. "You should talk like that more often."

"I haven't had the experience or practice that you have," replied Dekkard.

"Axel told me that you would either save Guldor or destroy it. I thought he was overstating matters. Now, I'm not so sure. The way you speak . . . at times . . ." Hasheem paused. "Before I agree or disagree, beyond rhetoric about cooperating, tell me what you would recommend that the Council do in the present situation—as concretely as you can."

"The most immediate need is absolute firmness with the New Meritorists, firmness without excessive executions or brutality. I'd suggest immediate exile for those Meritorists carrying arms but who cannot be determined to have used them. The highest placed of those who actually plotted the insurrection should be executed. Lower-level plotters and those leading bands of Meritorists should be put in work camps for two years, then exiled, a few at a time."

Hasheem frowned. "Why bother with the work camps?"

"To maximize the separation of plotters and followers and to disrupt communications among them as much as possible. Also immediately remove the First Marshal and appoint a Council group to investigate the mutiny and the failure of the Admiralty to intercept the *Khuld*. Councilor . . . Admiral Konnigsburg should head it."

Hasheem nodded at the mention of Konnigsburg, but asked, "What else besides the New Meritorists?"

Dekkard went through his list of proposals—including the repeal of tariffs on swampgrass rice, the restructuring of freight rates on produce combined with one-time funding for ironway repair, creation of a worker safety office with power to fine and sanction corporacions for unsafe workplace conditions or practices, removal of enrollment caps on university entrance with acceptance through competitive examinations similar to those used for the Military Institute.

"You have thought this through, Steffan."

"There's one other matter. The Security Committee needs to make a thorough investigation of how corporacion dunnite ended up in the hands of the New Meritorists."

"We don't know that for certain."

"We know that all dunnite comes from one of two corporacions. We know that the man who paid the team that shelled the Council Office Building was in the pay of one of those corporacions, and we have evidence that his business was set up by a current vice-presidente of the other. That's enough to hold hearings."

"Steffan . . . if I do that as chair of the Security Committee . . ."

"Perhaps you should recuse yourself as chair on the grounds that you need to devote your full attention to the rebuilding and reforms necessary to deal with the damage caused to the Council and the people of Machtarn and Guldor . . . and appoint a Craft councilor with security experience as acting chair . . ."

"You don't want to be chair?" asked Hasheem in a tone half sarcastic and half ironic.

"Almighty, no. I'm too junior, and if I'm just an acting chair, you can remove me more easily, if necessary. That way you show you're still in control." Dekkard paused. "If I'm right, you'll get pressure to remove me, but only if I don't make any glaring mistakes."

"If you *don't*?"

"If I do, you'll have to remove me and appoint someone else, and they won't need to pressure you."

Abruptly, Hasheem asked, "Why are you pushing me so hard?"

"Because Axel Obreduur was right. If the Craft Party doesn't make the most of this Council, and enact significant reforms, Guldor will go the way of Teknar, likely sooner than later. There's more technology today, and things happen faster. Obreduur spent almost his entire life getting a Craft government, and that effort shouldn't go to waste. The second reason is because I don't want a government determined by personal popularity or one bought by marks."

"The New Meritorists failed."

"This time. The problems are still here. We've had riots because people are hungry and because there aren't enough jobs. The guilds are unhappy because workers don't have safe workplaces. The government is paying too much for goods and services from large corporacions. I could go on, but you know the other problems." *Or you should.*

"The Council can't do all that at once."

"Not all, but it can start on much of it. Give a top priority to each committee. Then keep pressing them to get on with it."

Hasheem smiled sardonically. "You said you wanted to work together. Perhaps I should give them the priority we agree on, once we can use the Council buildings, and then tell them that you'll be following up and keeping me informed."

Which will make me less than well-liked, unless I'm very careful, but . . . "That has certain drawbacks, but I agree. Removing the First Marshal should be an immediate priority, though."

"I was reading the draft of his removal when you entered." Hasheem paused. "It might be easier on everyone if we met regularly. Say . . . every morning at third bell until the buildings are usable. Then we can reschedule."

"With the exception of information that could have an immediate and severe adverse impact."

Hasheem frowned for a moment, then nodded.

Dekkard understood well enough. Hasheem felt he couldn't easily stop Dekkard from getting to him and wanted to manage the situation. The Premier also thought that using Dekkard to press committee chairs and committees would make senior members wary of Dekkard while increasing Hasheem's control.

You'll have to live with that.

"Is there anything else we need to discuss?" asked Hasheem.

"I'd suggest you talk with Councilor Konnigsburg and get a list of admirals who would be good candidates for Fleet Marshal."

"Oh?"

"The current Fleet Marshal is apparently similar to the present First Marshal. It might be better not to replace First Marshals every two months. With a list in hand, you might be able to offer a name acceptable to the Imperador."

"You don't have such a list?" Hasheem's tone was gently ironic.

"I'd trust a former admiral who was the head of Naval Intelligence far more than me, Fredrich."

"Even a Commerce councilor?"

"That Commerce councilor."

"What does your wife think? As an empath, that is?"

"He's honest and truthful. We may not agree on some political issues, but I'd trust his insights on able and trustworthy naval officers over those of Councilor Mardosh."

"Unfortunately, so would I," replied Hasheem. "What else?"

"Make the policy for dealing with the New Meritorists clear to Justiciary Minister Kuta, the acting Minister of Public Safety, and the Marshal of the Army. Then talk to someone at *Gestirn* and say the same thing, and then *The Machtarn Tribune*. People need to see and hear that you're in control."

"Anything else?"

"Not at the moment."

"Then I'll see you tomorrow at third bell." Hasheem stood.

So did Dekkard. "Thank you, Fredrich."

Hasheem merely nodded.

Dekkard inclined his head in return, then left the inner office, closing the door quietly.

Avraal rose from the side chair where she had been waiting, then turned to the secretary. "Thank you, Meldra. I appreciated your thoughts."

"Our pleasure, Ritten. It's always good to see you, Councilor."

"Thank you," replied Dekkard.

Once the three were back in the main corridor and more than a few yards from the floor office and the two guards, Avraal asked, "Where to, now?"

"In a few minutes, I want to see if Guard Captain Trujillo is anywhere around." Dekkard looked to Gaaroll. "Do you sense any strong emotions anywhere nearby?"

"No, sir."

"Let's walk over to the councilors' lobby, then."

When they reached the entrance to the councilors' lobby, Avraal said, "There's no one here."

"Good." Dekkard motioned. "Nincya, I need a few words with Avraal. While we're talking, I'd like you to stay right here and concentrate on the Premier's office and the Guard captain's office. If you sense any strong emotions, let us know." Dekkard led Avraal to one of the staff waiting benches, where they sat down.

"What did you sense from Fredrich?" asked Dekkard quietly.

"He was furious when you first came in," replied Avraal in a low voice. "He stayed that way for several minutes."

"Did he lie about anything?"

"Not that I could tell."

"How was he just before I left?"

"A bit of resignation, a little of what I'd call cautious hope, along with a bit of residual anger."

"That's about what I'd expect."

"You know . . . there is one thing . . . I think you did it again."

"Did what?"

"Whatever you said at first stunned him. There was an emotional impact to your words."

"You said I'm not an empath."

"You're not, but somehow, when you feel strongly, you can put emotional force in your words. It's not from you. It's in the words, but only, I think, when you believe what you're saying. Later on, somehow you convinced him of something."

Dekkard quickly summarized the conversation. "Do you think he was just agreeing to get rid of me?"

"It didn't feel that way. It was more like he decided he might as well go along with what you suggested. I get the impression that he's not very creative."

"Let's hope he feels that way for the next few weeks, preferably for the next few months."

"He doesn't have much choice if he wants to remain premier. No one else seems to have an actual plan. So far as I've heard," said Avraal dryly, "Obreduur and you were the only Crafters who did."

"Haarsfel has a plan for his committee, and so does Harleona Zerlyon."

"I should have said an overall plan or strategy." Avraal's voice held a touch of testiness.

"You're right," agreed Dekkard. "There's a difference." After a moment, he asked, "What did you find out from Meldra?"

"She didn't say that much, except that she was glad to see us. She murmured that you seemed to give the Premier energy."

"Focused anger is more like it."

"If it works . . ." An amused half smile vanished from her face as she added, "You are a Contrarian, you know, if not in quite the way you've played it in public."

"Does that really surprise you?"

"No. I think it's more of a surprise to you."

Dekkard was still thinking about that when she asked, "What do you want to do now?"

"See if the good Guard Captain Trujillo is anywhere around." Dekkard stood and walked over to Gaaroll.

"No one's got strong emotions." Gaaroll grinned. "Not even in the Premier's office."

"Let's go see if the Guard captain is in."

A quick walk to Trujillo's office revealed that the door was locked, and neither Avraal nor Gaaroll could sense anyone. The door to the stairs down to the lower level was unlocked, but the staircase was pitch-black, and Gaaroll couldn't sense anyone on the lower level.

"So what do you want to do now?" asked Avraal.

"Take another tour of Machtarn to see what's happened, and then head home. You're going to help me work out that detailed plan for the Council so that I can present it to Hasheem tomorrow morning at third bell."

41

O N Duadi morning, Dekkard and Avraal rose only slightly later than usual. After shaving, showering, and dressing, Dekkard hurried downstairs just as Emrelda was leaving.

She looked at him and smiled. "Don't be too hard on the Premier. He's not used to working with you." Before Dekkard could reply, she held up a hand and added, "Not a word, Steffan. I'll see you tonight."

Dekkard was still shaking his head as he entered the kitchen to fix cafés. Once he had the cafés at his place and Avraal's, he went back to the cooler for the croissants. Then he picked up the morning edition of *Gestirn*. The first story to catch his eye had the headline BETTER LATE THAN NEVER. The crux of the story was contained in a few sentences . . .

> . . . First Marshal Bernotte not only misjudged the capabilities of the mutineers aboard the I.S. *Khuld*. He failed to take the threat seriously enough and also did not convey the severity of the potential consequences to the Council, which became real and deadly . . . In turn, Premier Hasheem failed to act swiftly enough to remove Bernotte, but the removal was necessary, if better late than never . . .

The second story featured an update on the capture of New Meritorists and a statement by Hasheem that the leaders of the New Meritorist movement, some of whom were already incarcerated, would face charges of high treason, and the others would face charges that could land them in work camps or in exile, if not both. "All those found guilty of carrying firearms will at the least be subject to statelessness, and, if they attempt to return to Guldor, to death sentences."

As he set the newssheet on the side table, Dekkard hoped that more severe measures did not turn out to be necessary.

When Avraal entered the breakfast room, she picked up the newssheet, scanned it briefly, and replaced it. "It appears that Hasheem took your advice."

"He would have removed Bernotte anyway, but I do hope he meets with Konnigsburg before he discusses any appointments with the Imperador."

Avraal took several sips of café before she spoke again. "Now that you've slept on it, how do you feel about your plan?"

"It's our plan, even if Hasheem doesn't know that. It's the best we could do in the time we have, and the Council needs to act quickly. We need a good plan now more than a perfect one at some undefined point in the future." Dekkard shrugged. "If Hasheem can make it better, then that's fine with me . . . so long as better doesn't significantly delay any of the objectives. I worry about Mardosh and possibly Leister Milyaard."

"Why Milyaard?"

"He became chair of the Transportation Committee after Waarfel's death, and he was with the councilors who backed Mardosh for premier."

"I can see why that's a worry."

"I also have the feeling that I need to visit with a few councilors, as I can." Dekkard almost said "those who are still here," but realized that most councilors would have to stay in Machtarn, since there wouldn't be any ironway service in or out of Machtarn for several days. "That means I'll have to drop you off at your office."

"Except when you visit Mardosh and Milyaard."

"Point taken," replied Dekkard. *If I know about it in advance.*

Gaaroll smiled.

In less than a bell, Dekkard was driving the back way to Imperial Boulevard, just because he didn't want to ever be too predictable. After letting Avraal off at the entrance to Baartol's office, he turned the Gresynt north on Imperial and made his way to Council Avenue. The few shell craters in the avenue remained blocked off and had not been resurfaced with bitumen. Dekkard had to stop at the entrance to covered parking, where a Council Guard again checked his pin and passcard.

As he and Gaaroll walked toward the Council Office Building, Dekkard saw even more workers than the day before. *Even so, it's going to be a while before everything's back together, especially if there's another big snowstorm.*

More likely, now that spring was approaching, would be an ice-cold drenching rain that melted the remaining snow and flooded all the low spots or places where the storm sewers had iced up or clogged.

Just before third bell, Dekkard and Gaaroll arrived at the main-corridor door to the Premier's office. In his gray leather folder were two copies of the plan he and Avraal had worked out, as well as other papers with supporting details, papers he hoped he wouldn't need. *If your memory is good enough.*

Dekkard didn't recognize either Council Guard posted there. "Councilor Dekkard, for a third-bell appointment with the Premier."

"Yes, sir. You're expected."

Dekkard motioned for Gaaroll to enter, then followed her inside, noting that the outer office was still lighted by the kerosene lamps.

"Meldra, I don't believe I've ever introduced you to Nincya Gaaroll. She's my empath-in-training. Nincya, this is Meldra."

"I'm pleased to meet you, Nincya." Meldra nodded to Dekkard. "He's expecting you."

"Thank you." Dekkard inclined his head and then entered the small private office, also still lit by a single kerosene lamp. "Good morning, Fredrich."

"Good morning, Steffan. I assume you saw a newssheet this morning."

"I saw the stories in *Gestirn*."

"The article about the First Marshal wasn't entirely accurate. He had submitted his resignation to the Imperador before my dismissal reached him."

"Does that still count as a removal?"

"A resignation to avoid dismissal does."

"Then it's better that *Gestirn* got it wrong."

Hasheem offered a fleeting smile. "We agree on that. Former Fleet Marshal Harraaf is now First Marshal. I'll be meeting with the Imperador tomorrow afternoon to discuss the appointment of a new Fleet Marshal. I'll be meeting here with Councilor Konnigsburg at fifth bell. Do you intend to be here?"

"I hadn't thought to. You don't need me for that, and it would show that you're reaching out to Commercers based on their expertise."

"Have you talked to him about the First Marshal?"

"After the mutiny and after the Military Affairs Committee was briefed, we shared concerns that the First Marshal didn't understand how well the mutiny had been planned and the expertise of the two officers who were apparently involved. One was an outstanding navigator and shiphandler and the other was an experienced gunnery officer who'd come up through the ranks and been denied further promotion because of that. He requested a transfer to the *Khuld* some considerable time before the mutiny."

"He told you all that?"

"He did. We do share a certain common background." At Hasheem's quizzical look, Dekkard added, "We're both Military Institute graduates." Dekkard was surprised that Hasheem didn't know that, but while it had come out with other councilors in a few conversations, Dekkard had never mentioned it to Hasheem. *But Vhiola Sandegarde and a few others whom you never told knew as well.* The fact that Hasheem didn't bothered him, but Dekkard had always had a feeling that Hasheem wasn't excessively curious. "The only comment Councilor Konnigsburg made about the Fleet Marshal, whose name he never even mentioned, was that he was much like the First Marshal. We never talked about other officers, and I know none of the senior officers in the Admiralty, or even any junior officers."

Hasheem nodded. "Do you have anything else you feel I should know?"

"You asked me about possible priorities yesterday. I thought it might be helpful if I presented those in a more orderly fashion." Dekkard opened the leather folder and handed Hasheem the ten pages that he and Avraal had worked on. "I tried to keep it short, roughly a page for each committee that I mentioned."

Hasheem looked at the front page, then asked, "Who wrote this out? Your wife?"

Dekkard shook his head. "I did. I have a readable hand, and I don't have a typewriter, let alone the ability to type."

"If you write like this you don't need a typewriter." Hasheem went through each sheet, at least half reading each, before he looked up. "You write well and succinctly. I'm going to have to give these some thought on how and where we should go with them. My initial thought is that it might be helpful for me to meet with the various chairs over the next few days and then we'll see to what degree you need to be involved. I suspect you're more . . . persuasive . . . than I am."

"I doubt that. I'm likely more able to convey the intensity of the need to accomplish these goals. It may take both of us."

"The intensity of the need," mused Hasheem. "That's a good and more political way of putting it." He laid the papers on the desk in front of him. "What else do you have in mind?"

"I'd thought to talk to Guard Captain Trujillo. I did some analytical work for him before all this happened."

"About what?" Hasheem's voice sharpened slightly.

"The financial transactions used by Jaime Minz and the Meritorists. We'd talked about it because Minz was the one who set up that Council clerk with Atacaman pepper spray. The Guard captain was kind enough to let me know about it after Minz was taken into custody."

Hasheem seemed to relax. "You think financial transactions will lead anywhere?"

"The Guard captain seemed to think so, but I never quite finished the analysis before . . ."

Dekkard left the words hanging. The *Khuld*'s shelling wasn't the only reason Dekkard hadn't finished, but it was definitely the reason Trujillo hadn't been able to pursue the matter of identifying the sources of the various banque drafts and cheques.

"I can see why you might have a certain . . . interest in that. I'd appreciate it if that didn't hamper other matters . . . or take much of the Guard captain's time."

"I won't impose on him in any way to take him away from his pressing duties."

"Good." Hasheem stood, then gestured to the short stack of paper Dekkard had delivered. "That will be very helpful. I'll see you tomorrow morning."

Dekkard stood and inclined his head. "Until then."

From the Premier's floor office Dekkard and Gaaroll walked to Guard Captain Trujillo's office, where the door was open, presumably to provide some light. Dekkard peered in and saw Trujillo behind his desk, apparently sifting through papers. "Do you have a few moments?"

"For you, Councilor, I can spare some time."

Dekkard turned to Gaaroll. "Just stay out here." Then he stepped into the small office, leaving the door half open, since the room had no other light, and sat down in the single chair across the desk from Trujillo.

"What can I do for you, Councilor?"

"How did you and the Council Guards fare as a result of the attack by the mutineers?"

"We lost six roof guards to the naval guns, and another three to gunfire in the streets. Another eight were wounded and will recover."

"I'm sorry for them and their families."

"You did what you could, Councilor. I know you can't always do what you'd like, but you've shared more information with me directly than any other councilor."

He knows or is guessing that I knew more than I said, but was ordered not to mention the ultimatum.

"I intend to make sure you know as much as I do in the future." Dekkard smiled wryly. "Right now, I suspect you know everything I do about the New Meritorists and their possible Commercer allies, and a great deal more. I've always appreciated your straightforwardness."

Trujillo uttered a sound between a cough and a laugh, but said nothing.

"I was wondering," said Dekkard, "if any of the captured New Meritorists have any links to the missing dunnite, or to anyone who might have supplied it?"

"The Justiciary Ministry is conducting the interviews and interrogation. They have a staff of empaths trained for that. The Council Guard only has two, and they're both working with the Justiciary Ministry right now. I did talk with the chief investigator and provided her with a number of questions pertinent to the Council. Several dealt with dunnite, Jaime Minz, former Premier Ulrich, and Capitol Services. It might be several days, or longer, before I hear anything. They have over four hundred New Meritorists in custody."

"That many?"

"That few," replied Trujillo. "The Army troopers are excellent shots, and they shot to kill. Also, with so many New Meritorists in the streets, many of the wounded died before anyone could tend to them."

"You're suggesting hundreds of deaths."

"Over twelve hundred . . . that's what we've been able to confirm. The chief investigator thinks they'll have leads to more than that once all the interrogations are completed." Trujillo offered a crooked smile. "The damage to the harbor and port facilities and to the ironway station will make it harder for some of them to escape."

"So . . ." said Dekkard slowly, "between the dead and captured, there are at least sixteen hundred known Meritorists."

"Some of the dead likely aren't New Meritorists. The Army and the patrollers shot looters, possibly several hundred."

"Even so . . . with those that weren't shot or captured, that's easily several thousand people." *In winter, no less.*

"The best estimates we have are that over five thousand people were involved in the three locations. One indication that they were New Meritorists is that they moved into those areas from elsewhere after the shelling."

"So at least someone in the Meritorist hierarchy knew where the shells would be aimed."

"It would seem so. The interrogations will clear that up, but they'll take time."

Dekkard understood that. Sensing emotional clues and following up on them was a painstaking and time-consuming process—and hard on the empath as well after a while. "If the interrogations lead to another thousand, you'd have found half of those on the streets, and those on the streets might have amounted to . . . what . . . half of those believing strongly in the Meritorist cause?"

"There's no way of knowing that, sir. I'd be inclined to think those on the streets might have been a third or a fifth of those calling themselves New Meritorists. Those on the streets would have been more committed."

"Except for the top plotters."

"The Justiciary's chief investigator has some strong leads there."

"How much damage has all this done to the New Meritorists, do you think?" asked Dekkard.

"I wouldn't want to guess, Councilor. I doubt they could put that many people on the streets anytime soon, but until the investigations are over I don't think anyone could make an accurate judgment."

"You're very cautious, Guard Captain, but that's for the best." Dekkard paused. "I assume you haven't had the chance to follow up on those banque transactions?"

"There are still some inquiries in progress. If anything new turns up, I'll let you know."

"I'd appreciate that . . . and if I discover anything you might not know, I'll be in touch."

"You've always been helpful, sir."

"I've tried, Guard Captain." *If not always as much as I should have.* Dekkard stood. "I wish you well with all you have to handle."

"Thank you, sir."

After Dekkard left Trujillo's small office, he didn't say anything to Gaaroll until they were in the courtyard, heading back to the covered parking.

"Did you sense anything out of the ordinary with the Guard captain?"

"Only strong feeling was when you walked in. Not real strong, though."

"Could you tell if he was lying at any time?"

"I'm not as good as the Ritten, but I don't think so. He might have been hiding something near the end. There's a waver to the piles, sometimes, when people do that."

"Thank you. That's helpful." Dekkard paused. "You are getting better."

"I think so. It's slow, though."

"Learning or improving skills is always slow."

When they reached the covered parking and got into the Gresynt, Dekkard said, "We're going to take a drive around before we go see Ritten Obreduur."

"Does she know you're coming?"

"No, but if she's not there, I'll leave a card and a note and try later."

Dekkard's first destination was the Square of Heroes, from where he could see what looked to be a small army of gardeners filling in the shell craters that dotted the Palace grounds. The gates were open, but guarded, and lorries were coming and going, even in the short time Dekkard watched.

There were also scores of workers near the Guldoran Ironway station, and a bitumen roller paving over shell craters around the station, unlike on Council Avenue. Dekkard wondered about that, but supposed that since the temperature was above freezing and the ground wasn't wet, it might work. If not, then Guldoran Ironway would just have to repave in late spring or summer. He didn't feel particularly charitable toward any of the ironways, not after all he'd seen, heard, and read over the previous year.

From there, Dekkard headed south on Imperial Boulevard, but had to stop at the same barricades he'd encountered before, which limited what he could see. There were several barges around the visible superstructure of the sunken Transoceanic steamship, but Dekkard couldn't tell what they were doing. He didn't stay long enough to attract a patroller, and then headed back north on Imperial Boulevard, until he reached Altarama Drive, where he turned east. When he reached Ingrella's house, he made a U-turn and parked on the street, then used the pedestrian gate, and motioned for Gaaroll to precede him up the walk.

Dekkard knocked at the front door and waited for more than a minute.

Rhosali, wearing her usual white apron and blue dress, opened the door . . . and just stared for a moment. "Steffan . . . I mean, Councilor. We didn't expect . . ."

Dekkard just laughed. "I'm still Steffan. Is she in?"

"Come in. I'll tell her. I'm sure she'll want to see you."

"Rhosali . . . this is Nincya Gaaroll. She's an empath-in-training. Nincya, this is Rhosali Mantero. She's been with the Obreduur family much longer than I was."

"Not that much longer. Ritten Ysella was here longer." Abruptly, Rhosali stepped back and opened the door wide. "You shouldn't be standing there in cold. Just wait here in the foyer, and I'll tell her."

After they entered, Dekkard closed the door, while Rhosali hurried off in the direction of the study.

Ingrella appeared almost immediately, trailed by Rhosali.

"Steffan! What a pleasant surprise."

"Since we can't meet at the Council and I'd just driven to take a look at the harbor . . . well, as close as I could get . . . I thought I'd take a chance on your being here."

"I'm so glad you did."

Dekkard turned slightly. "Ingrella, you recall Nincya Gaaroll. She's getting close to where she can apply for provisional certification as an empath."

"Of course, I remember. She's also delivered messages you didn't trust to Council messengers." The older councilor looked to Gaaroll. "I saw that doubtful expression. If Steffan says you're close, then you're close." Ingrella smiled, then said to Rhosali, "Why don't you two have some refreshments while I talk to Steffan."

After Rhosali guided Gaaroll toward the staff room, Dekkard had no doubt that there would be some conversation, the details of which he wasn't certain he'd want to know.

Ingrella led the way to the study, where, after entering, she motioned for Dekkard to close the door, then seated herself behind the desk and waited for him to sit down. "I thought I might be seeing you before long. How are you coming with Fredrich? He said you brushed aside his guards and walked into his office yesterday."

"I take it he came to see you?"

Ingrella offered a smile both amused and somehow sympathetic. "He wanted to know everything I could tell him about you. In particular, how trustworthy you were and how loyal. I was honest. I told him you were trustworthy and loyal, but that your trust and loyalty wasn't blind and didn't extend to illegalities or acts not in the best interests of the Council or Guldor. That didn't reassure him. So I asked him why he expected blind loyalty from you when he hadn't given it to Axel."

Dekkard kept the smile to himself. "What was his reaction?"

"After a moment—a long moment—he laughed."

"Is there anything else you'd like to tell me?"

"You're being deferential, Steffan."

Dekkard laughed. "Practical. If I'd asked if there was anything else I needed to know, you might have had to evade or say more than you wished. I might do that to Kaliara Bassaana or Vhiola Sandegarde, but not to you. I trust you and your judgment."

"That's a very great compliment, and I appreciate it." She paused. "As I told you before, Fredrich is a nice man. He will try to do the right thing, but only if he's convinced that it's the right thing, and that he won't have to fight too hard for it. Without saying that, I told him that he should turn to one of us before making hard decisions if he perceived difficulties because, between us, we might be able to ease such difficulties."

"You're likely to be the one easing the difficulties. I seem to be more inclined to . . . confront them."

"Or remove them," Ingrella added. "Sometimes, the hint of removal is equally effective."

"Two other people have offered similar advice. That suggests that I take it."

"Avraal and Carlos?"

"Who else?

"That's not surprising. Very few others want to confront you, Steffan. Don't make them, unless it's absolutely necessary."

Dekkard frowned. "I've only been that . . . insistent with a very few people."

"That's been enough. The Council is a very small world."

"I'll definitely keep that in mind."

"That would be good."

"This morning I gave Fredrich the outline of what committee priorities I recommended and why. Was that pushing him too much?"

"If your language was advisory—even if you think it's the only rational approach—Fredrich can accept that."

For the next third of a bell, Dekkard largely listened to Ingrella.

Then she smiled warmly and stood. "I think I've overdone the advice, but you've been such a good listener."

Dekkard immediately stood as well. "I just wish I'd asked and listened earlier."

She offered a smile that was both rueful and amused, then shook her head.

Dekkard raised his eyebrows, but didn't actually ask what she was thinking.

After a moment, she said, "In some ways, you're very much like Axel. I think he saw that in you from the beginning."

Dekkard swallowed silently. "You both have taught me a great deal."

Ingrella smiled brightly. "We can reminisce more after all this is past." She gestured to the study door.

Dekkard opened it, but waited for her to leave the study first.

Rhosali and Gaaroll appeared in moments, most likely because Gaaroll had sensed Dekkard and Ingrella leaving the study.

At the front door Ingrella said, "I trust I'll see you and Avraal before too long."

"We'll do our best," Dekkard promised.

Once he and Gaaroll were in the Gresynt, he thought for a moment, then decided to head back to see how Avraal was doing.

As he drove west on Altarama, he asked Gaaroll, "Did you learn anything interesting from Rhosali?"

"Some. She wanted to know what working for you was like. She said everything was quieter in the house since you and the Ritten left."

"It wasn't just us. Gustoff left about that time to join his older brother at the Military Institute."

"Don't think that was what she meant, sir."

Dekkard chuckled. "Probably not."

42

THE remainder of Duadi was quietly uneventful, as were all of Tridi and Furdi, which were also slightly warmer, if grayer, than Duadi. Each day *Gestirn* reported small updates on the damage and that the various authorities were continuing with arrests and charges of known New Meritorists. Emrelda had nothing to add, except that the patrol was busy enough that she'd be working late on Quindi, until after fifth bell.

Avraal spent most of each day at Baartol's office, while Dekkard met Hasheem each morning at third bell, and Hasheem questioned Dekkard on the priorities the younger councilor had given him. Hasheem offered few suggestions, but did ask for more details on several of the areas, and finding the information and addressing those details took up most of Dekkard's time. He finished the last revision, the one on ironway freight charge restructuring, by Furdi afternoon, before he went to pick up Avraal.

At breakfast on Quindi, Avraal had several sips of café before asking, "Do you know when Hasheem plans to reconvene the Council?"

"I don't. I'd guess it will be soon, but not until the Council Hall has lights and heat. They've walled off the upper level of the east wing, the area past the Security Committee and Military Affairs Committee rooms. Hasheem told me that the lower level would also be usable once they restore the gas and heat."

"I thought the main systems weren't damaged," said Emrelda.

"They weren't, but they have to cap or repair all the lines going into the damaged sections of both buildings, and then they have to test them."

"Makes sense," observed Gaaroll.

"How is your project going?" Dekkard asked Avraal, knowing that she'd been asked to evaluate the latest possible replacements for the staff members of the Guilds' Advisory Committee who had been killed by the Meritorist bomb at the annual Yearend reception.

"I'll be tied up with the final interviews for the top staff positions today and possibly Unadi."

"You want me to plan to pick you up at fourth bell?"

"Make it a third after." Avraal looked to Emrelda. "Services tonight? You're working late."

"We can go to services and then to Elfredo's," replied Emrelda, as she stood to leave for her patrol station. "Don't you think that's for the best?"

"For many reasons," replied Avraal. "I was just checking."

Less than two-thirds of a bell passed before Dekkard, Avraal, and Gaaroll headed south on Jacquez, but he continued past Camelia Avenue and turned west on Wisteria, which led him to Imperial Boulevard, if more slowly. After dropping off Avraal, Dekkard got back on Imperial Boulevard. When he turned onto Council Avenue, he could see a crew working on repaving the filled shell crater holes in the avenue and had to slow in making his way around the work crews.

He and Gaaroll reached the covered parking west of the Council Office Building at close to a half before third bell. When they walked into the Council Hall from the courtyard, Dekkard immediately noticed that the coal-gas lamps were on and the main corridor definitely felt warmer.

The guards outside the corridor door to the Premier's floor office just nodded as Dekkard and Gaaroll entered.

"He's expecting you, Councilor," said Meldra cheerfully.

Dekkard entered the small inner office and closed the door. Even before seating himself, he opened the gray leather folder and extracted the material that Hasheem had requested, carefully placing it on the desk facing the Premier. Then he sat down and said, "That's what you asked for."

"Thank you, Steffan."

"I see that the Council Hall now has lights and heat."

"So does the Council Office Building—except for the damaged sections. The Council was fortunate that the mutineers weren't that accurate. It could have been much worse."

"Sir, given the circumstances, the mutineers' gunnery was unfortunately outstanding. What kept the situation from being worse was that the *Resolute*'s heavier shells destroyed the *Khuld* as soon as they did. The shelling lasted about twenty-five minutes. The greatest number of shells the *Khuld* could have fired was slightly over two hundred. I'd guess the number was closer to a hundred and eighty. The eight-digit guns had three targets, roughly sixty shells being aimed at each. Four shells hit the Council buildings or the courtyard, another six hit within a hundred yards of the Council Hall. That's an accuracy of sixteen percent at almost ten milles. Most ships would be below ten percent at that distance, and the *Khuld* did it without spotters and in poor visibility." Dekkard went on to explain how the mutineers had to have measured distances and bearings in advance and why the *Khuld* had been anchored.

Hasheem was silent for almost a minute after Dekkard finished. "You don't have any proof of this, do you?"

"Only that the *Khuld* was lightened so she could use the barge canal to get into position, that she anchored in a specific position with barely enough water beneath her keel, that she had an outstanding navigator and an outstanding gunnery officer, and that I know of no other way that the gunners could have been that accurate under those conditions. You can tell Councilor Konnigsburg of my conclusions and rationale."

"I'll do that. I have the feeling he'll agree to a large extent." Hasheem smiled sourly. "On another matter . . . I'll be sending messages out to all councilors this afternoon notifying them of a brief session of the Council on Unadi at first afternoon bell. At that time, I should be able to announce when the occupancy of the Council Office Building will be possible."

"Do you have any idea yet?"

"I'm hoping on a week from Unadi. I don't want to open the Council Office Building until there are usable offices for everyone. Some of you may have to work around the finish work and painting. The rebuilding of the east end of the Council Hall will take another month, possibly two."

Dekkard nodded and waited.

"You have a way with words. If you're amenable, I'd appreciate it if you could draft something that emphasizes in a solid way the severity of the damage and deaths the New Meritorists have caused the Council and the people of Guldor. Just bring it with you on Unadi morning."

"I can do that."

"I've been meeting with committee chairs over the past few days, to inform them about the New Meritorists and to get their thoughts. When we're closer to normal, we'll need to start pressing—gently—for those objectives necessary to defuse the appeal of the New Meritorists. With some of the chairs, I may bring you in. We'll have to see."

"Some of them will be resistant to any change, I suspect, but you certainly know that." Dekkard paused briefly, then asked, "Do you know if the Justiciary has found out any more about the leadership of the New Meritorists?"

"Yes, but it's still tentative, and I'm not about to say more until it's confirmed. I'm hoping we'll have a confirmation by Unadi."

Confirmation of what? Names of leaders? Meritorist plans and objectives? Ties with corporacions? From the way Hasheem's jaw was set, Dekkard decided not to press and merely said, "I hope it goes well."

"So do we all, Steffan. I don't have any more for you, but I'll be looking through what you brought." Hasheem didn't stand.

Because Dekkard knew the meeting was over, he stood. "Then I'll see you on Unadi morning."

After leaving Hasheem, Dekkard, accompanied by Gaaroll, walked to

Guard Captain Trujillo's office. The Guard captain wasn't there, as had been the case when Dekkard had checked on the previous two days. That wasn't exactly unexpected, given that Trujillo worked with the Ministry of Public Safety and the Justiciary Ministry, and Dekkard could have waited bells and Trujillo wouldn't necessarily have shown up.

Dekkard turned from the closed and locked doors and said, "We can't do anything else here. So we'll check how the repairs are coming elsewhere and then head back to the house. I've got some more work to do for the Premier."

"You ought to be premier."

Dekkard shook his head. "I don't know enough, both about rules and precedents, and about the histories of other members and where the bodies are buried. I'm also too junior, and too many of the senior councilors would be upset and wouldn't listen. All told, it would be a disaster. It's better that I give Hasheem advice and strengthen his position."

"What about your position, sir?"

"I'm working on that," replied Dekkard dryly. "Let's go make our various inspections." When they were out of the Council Hall and on the way to the covered parking, he said, "Now you can tell me what you sensed from the Premier."

"He's still afraid of you. One time, he was surprised and annoyed."

"That was probably when I told him how accurate the mutineers' gunnery was."

"He felt better near the end. He was relieved when you left."

Dekkard couldn't help worrying about Hasheem's fears of him. *Fearful men with power are dangerous. You're going to have to work on reassuring him that you want him to remain as premier.* Dekkard definitely wanted Hasheem as premier, especially given the alternatives.

From the covered parking, Dekkard drove to the Square of Heroes, where he saw that the stone drive from the gates to the Palace had been repaired, and all the craters in the Palace grounds had been filled in. Replacing the grass and hedges would likely have to wait for spring.

The next stop was the Guldoran Ironway station, and Dekkard was actually able to drive to within a block. The *Khuld*'s shells had destroyed the old terminal market. The site had been leveled and a beam and post building had taken shape, and the pallets of bricks suggested that the new structure would be permanent. He could make out the smoke of a locomotive to the northwest, less than a third of a mille away, indicating that the track had been rebuilt or repaired that far, and that the station would likely be in limited operation within a few days. Still, it would be weeks before the ironway was back to normal operation.

Absently, Dekkard wondered why the *Khuld* hadn't targeted the main ironway bridge across the Rio Azulete, because that would have cut off easy access to all the produce from the south. *Except that the bridge was beyond the range of eight-digit guns.*

From the station, Dekkard drove back to Imperial Boulevard, where he turned south. The barricades had been moved to just north of Harbor Way, where Dekkard stopped to study the waterfront and the harbor.

The semi-sunken Transoceanic steamship had apparently been refloated or removed, because the deepwater channel was clear, and Dekkard could get a glimpse of the bow of the *Khuld,* but what little he could make out was a twisted mass of metal. Several smaller naval craft surrounded the wreckage. There didn't appear to be any intact buildings on Harbor Way, but there might have been some farther west.

He studied the harbor for a few minutes more, then eased the Gresynt away from the barricades back up Imperial Boulevard, heading to the house and what he knew would be considerable time and effort in writing out what Hasheem had requested.

After returning to the house, he immediately set to work on the summary of New Meritorist destruction over the past year. First, he had to sketch out the timeline and then add the details. Then came putting it together in a form Hasheem could either read or send to councilors. By the time he'd written a second draft, it was time to pick up Avraal.

When they reached Baartol's office, Dekkard waited for several minutes outside, then shut down the Gresynt and went inside, leaving Gaaroll with the steamer.

Elicya looked up as he entered the office. "Good afternoon, Councilor. The interviews were over a while ago. They've been reviewing the candidates. I wouldn't imagine it will be long before they're done."

"Have there been any new events not in the newssheets?"

"I don't think so." Elicya smiled. "Except that Rabool has completed the repairs, and the bistro reopened this afternoon."

"That's good."

"You've been there, I hear."

"Only once."

"You should go more often."

"We probably should."

At that moment, the door to the inner office opened, and Avraal stepped out.

"I'm sorry. It took a little longer—"

"I understand," replied Dekkard. "I've only been here a few minutes. I was talking to Elicya. Are you finished, or do you need more time?"

"No, we're finished for today."

Baartol appeared in the doorway to the inner office. "Steffan, do you know when the Council will reconvene?"

"The Premier has announced a brief session on Unadi. Other than that, I have no idea. Most of the Council Hall is functional, and the repairs are proceeding on the Council Office Building. Have you heard anything that I don't know?"

"I haven't heard much of anything, except that the Justiciary Ministry is running out of space for all the New Meritorists they've incarcerated."

"That might continue awhile," replied Dekkard. "They're interrogating every one of them with empaths."

Baartol frowned. "Is that allowed under the Great Charter? I know it is for capital crimes, but just for demonstrating?"

"Being part of an insurrection against the Council likely qualifies as treason, and it's allowed there," Dekkard pointed out.

"Hmmmm." Baartol cocked his head to the side. "I suspect the New Meritorists didn't consider that. Some legalists may contest it."

"I couldn't say," replied Dekkard. "I suspect that won't get very far, but that's up to the legalists."

Baartol nodded. "You're right about that."

Dekkard could see that Baartol was concerned, if not disturbed, by the idea that empaths were being used to interrogate everyone incarcerated in the attacks and demonstrations following the shelling of the city.

"Both of you, have a good endday," Baartol added, more cheerfully.

"Thank you," replied Avraal.

After Dekkard and Avraal went down the steps and were outside, Avraal asked, "Why did you tell Carlos that an appeal against using empaths on everyone won't get very far?"

"Because, if they're not guilty of treason, there's likely enough physical evidence to convict them on lesser charges, in which case, what was discovered by an empath isn't necessary, and if they are found guilty of treason—"

"What's discovered by an empath is allowable," finished Avraal.

Dekkard opened the passenger-side door for her, then closed it after she was seated, before walking around the Gresynt and seating himself behind the wheel.

Once he was headed north on Imperial Boulevard, he said, "Hasheem asked me to write a statement on what the Meritorists have done to the Council and people of Guldor. If you wouldn't mind, I'd like you to read what I've drafted. We should have some time before Emrelda arrives and we leave for services."

"You're worried about it, aren't you?"

"Why do you think that?"

"Because it's the first thing you've said to me about today," she replied with a smile.

"You're right, but since you implied I should tell you about the rest of the day, I will." For the rest of the drive home, Dekkard filled her in on what Hasheem had said and what he'd observed on his "inspection tour."

Then once they were home, they went to the study, where he handed her what he'd written, and watched as she read through it.

When Avraal finished reading, she handed the sheets back to Dekkard and said, "There's no conclusion."

"I know, but he just asked for a strong factual statement of what happened. I don't know how he wants to use this, even in a general sense."

"Have you thought about writing a conclusion separately? Or even two? Then you could tell him that he didn't specify a purpose and you have some possible conclusions that might fit, depending on what he has in mind."

"You don't think he knows what he wants to do, and he asked me to write this to spur his thoughts?"

"From what you've said and what I've seen, it's possible."

Dekkard slowly nodded. "You could be right. Thank you. I'll have to be very careful, and I'd appreciate it if you'd go over what I write." He paused. "One conclusion might be the need to deal firmly but fairly with the New Meritorists."

"And with any allies that may be turned up by the Justiciary Ministry," added Avraal.

"Another might be that the Council understands that times change and that the Council must address the changed needs of the people of Guldor, but that such changes should not destroy a system that has worked longer and better than any government in the world." Dekkard smiled wryly. "I'll have to work on that."

"We'll have tomorrow," said Avraal. "You can think about it in the meantime."

Less than a third of a bell later, Emrelda arrived and joined them in the study.

"Anything interesting happen today?" asked Dekkard.

"Nothing out of the ordinary," said Emrelda in a way that suggested she had more to say.

When she didn't volunteer more, Dekkard said, "That means there's something else out of the ordinary."

"There is. We're losing Captain Narryt."

"Is that bad or good?" asked Avraal, concern in her voice.

"Good . . . sort of. He's been selected to be the Civic Patrol's deputy chief inspector for the entire Machtarn district. The acting Minister of Public Safely picked him over several more senior captains. I think it was because of the way he handled the attack on the house. They were looking for someone who would do what needs to be done."

"That's good," said Avraal, "but it sounds like you have reservations about who will replace him."

"Who will replace him?" asked Dekkard almost simultaneously.

"Lieutenant Kunskyn," replied Emrelda. "He's one of the most senior lieutenants, and he's very good."

For several moments, Dekkard didn't quite see why Emrelda was concerned, until he remembered when he'd met the lieutenant at Elfredo's several months before.

Avraal understood immediately and asked, "Do you think that will be a problem . . . the fact that he's strongly attracted to you?"

"He's never been anything but completely professional . . . but it does worry me a little. They usually rotate lieutenants who are promoted to captain, but there wasn't anyone else being promoted, and they didn't want any unnecessary disruption, not right now. He's been very effective in dealing with Southtown in a way that hasn't created more violence, and there's no one else with that experience who isn't already dealing with it somewhere else."

"That makes sense," said Dekkard, "but it could be awkward for you."

"Not if the lieutenant remains professional," said Emrelda, "but I still worry."

"I could help . . . if you want," said Avraal.

"I'll keep that in mind," replied Emrelda, "but I hope that won't be necessary."

"I'd thought we'd leave for services in a bit less than a third," said Avraal.

That statement, Dekkard knew, was a veiled question as to whether Emrelda would change out of her uniform.

Emrelda smiled. "I'll stay in uniform. We're only going to Elfredo's after services. How were your days?"

"Nothing new to tell," said Dekkard. "Repairs are proceeding. More Meritorists are being ensnared, one way or another, and I keep writing reports for the Premier."

"I just participated in interviews and weeded out one applicant for blatant falsehoods," added Avraal.

"Just watched for strong feelings," added Gaaroll, who had quietly joined the other three. "Glad I didn't sense any . . . except next door. Sr. Waaldwud got angry, I'd guess. The new nanny wasn't having any. She's gotten stronger. She damped his feelings. I think."

"Good!" declared Avraal.

Emrelda just smiled.

Before all that long, it was time to leave for services.

When Dekkard went out to get the Gresynt, he could feel a light and warmer wind from the southwest. He glanced in that direction and saw in the distance grayish-green clouds, far enough away that, if it did rain, it would fall much later. If the rain turned out to be heavy, though, and melted the remaining snow, parts of Machtarn would be filled with mud and standing water, possibly for days. He shook his head and finished getting the Gresynt ready and driving it under the portico, where the three women waited. Then he headed down the drive.

When Dekkard pulled into the parking area of the chapel, he saw four people just getting out of an older Gresynt, and as he took an open space two steamers over, he realized that the four had to be Villem and Gretina Baar and their children. Dekkard saw, as he got out of the steamer, that the Baars were waiting at the end of the walk that led to the chapel.

"Until last week," said Villem as Dekkard and Avraal neared, "I didn't realize we'd be seeing you at services until I saw you all."

Dekkard smiled. "I could say the same. How are you finding this chapel?"

"Presider Buusen gives a far better homily than we've endured before."

Gretina offered a smile that combined tolerance and amusement, while Matteus's unspoken comment was a definitive nod. Karlotta seemed to be studying the chapel building.

"He generally gives a good homily," replied Dekkard. "He's also a thoughtful and charitable man."

Before anyone else could say anything more, Emrelda looked to Gretina and said, "We keep meaning to ask you two to dinner. What about tomorrow, an early dinner, say at fourth bell?"

Gretina looked to Villem, who just smiled, after which Gretina said, "We'd be delighted." Then she looked to Karlotta and said, "You get to plan and cook dinner for the two of you, tomorrow."

Karlotta looked surprised, but not exactly displeased.

Gretina then looked to Matteus. "You'll help, as Karlotta tells you, and you both clean up." After the slightest pause, she turned back to Emrelda and added, "We can catch up on things tomorrow, when we'll have a chance to talk without hurrying. Now . . . I suppose we should think about getting into the chapel."

Dekkard gestured for the Baars to lead the way.

Both families were seated for several minutes before the harmonium shifted from prelude music to the processional. Dekkard's thoughts were elsewhere as the service proceeded, until Presider Buusen was a few sentences into his homily.

"I do not usually touch upon politics, because the Almighty should be above politics, but occasionally our everyday world offers a blatant example of why the precepts of faith can matter so much. The worthy Trelliand once wrote, 'Do not aspire to perfection if that aspiration stifles the good and the worthy.' How can the aspiration toward perfection stifle good?

"Perfection is an ideal . . . and as an ideal, it is a worthy goal . . . but too often when people cannot attain perfection, they do nothing. Sometimes, they don't even try. And sometimes, at the other extreme, we have those who destroy an imperfect good because it is less than perfect in their eyes. As we have seen in the past year all across Guldor, would-be perfectionists have done their best to destroy a good and working government. The Great Charter is far from perfect, but Councils over the years have improved it, and it is good enough that people from surrounding lands come here for the opportunity they do not have in their own country. Yet this futile quest for political perfection has killed thousands across Guldor and marred our capital city."

Dekkard definitely agreed with much of what Buusen said, although Dekkard hadn't thought of the New Meritorists exactly as perfectionists. Yet, they did have a vision of perfection. The only problem was that their vision hadn't worked before, and there was no indication that it would ever work.

He was still thinking about the homily well after the service was over and he was driving toward Elfredo's.

"You're quiet, dear," said Avraal. "Are you all right?"

"I'm fine. I was just thinking about the homily. I'd never thought of the Meritorists as misguided perfectionists."

"Aren't most revolutionaries misguided perfectionists?" asked Emrelda dryly. "The practical idealists try to fix what's wrong in the system, rather than throwing everything out."

"But revolution is likely what we'll get if we don't fix the problems."

"Exactly," said Avraal firmly. "That can be one of your conclusions. Now . . . what are we going to fix for dinner tomorrow?"

"There's still a leg of lamb in the cooler," replied Emrelda. "I'd thought we could start with that . . ."

Dekkard just listened the rest of the way to Elfredo's. He wondered if they'd find a place at the taverna, a simple square building constructed of gray brick with black shutters, given that it was Quindi evening, but the moment Emrelda walked into the crowded taverna, one of the servers hurried over.

"Give me a moment and I'll have a table for you."

"Thank you, Chellara. It's been a long week."

Chellara? The name was familiar. Then Dekkard remembered. She was Elfredo's niece and had served them once before.

While they waited, Dekkard's eyes went from table to table, catching sight of uniformed patrollers at three different tables, although not everyone looked to be a patroller. He eased closer to Emrelda so he wouldn't have to raise his voice. "You know all the patrollers here?"

"Yes. Some better than others."

"Are there any here I've met?"

"At the third table from the corner, with the four patrollers? The two with their backs half to the wall? Georg and Sammel."

"Georg's the one who got his arm broken in the early Southtown disturbances?"

Emrelda nodded.

Then Chellara reappeared and led the four to a wall table between two shuttered and draped windows. On the way, Dekkard looked at the wall chalkboard that held the specials—veal Jeeroh and the crayfish and mushroom ravioli.

"Take a look at the specials," said Chellara. "I'll be back in minute."

As Chellara left, Dekkard didn't miss that Emrelda slipped her a mark note, but all he said was, "I wonder if someone's going to have the crayfish and mushroom ravioli."

"I can't imagine who you're talking about," said Emrelda.

"Or chicken piccata," added Dekkard.

"Just for that," said Avraal, "I think I'll see if they have chicken rosara."

In the end, Emrelda ordered the ravioli, Avraal and Gaaroll chicken rosara, and Dekkard decided to try the veal Jeeroh. The sisters ordered white wine, and Dekkard and Gaaroll pale lager. The four had barely gotten their drinks when Dekkard saw that Georg and Sammel had gotten up from their table and were walking toward them. As the pair neared, Dekkard could see that Georg wore a heavy brace over his left forearm.

As Sammel and Georg reached the table, Dekkard started to stand, but Sammel gestured for Dekkard to remain seated and said good-naturedly, grinning, "We ought to be standing for you, but since we already are . . ." Then he said to Emrelda, still grinning, "We're glad to see you haven't forsaken us."

Emrelda shook her head, then said, "Maybe that roof tile should have hit your arm."

Sammel offered a doleful face. "Then the bastard who threw it would have gotten away. Georg's a lousy shot." Then he gestured to Avraal and Dekkard. "They ever tell you that they took down a pair of armed thieves without even getting mussed? Nasty pair, but they're both in the Nolaan work camp. Will be for years."

"All they said was they had a little difficulty, but you were kind enough to clean up the mess."

Sammel's laugh was almost a bellow. "The only one who had difficulty was that slime Eskraff. We knew he'd done several slash-and-grabs. Never could find him. When Snaelyn heard about it, he gave us a little crap. Said we couldn't get him, but a Ritter and Ritten could. The lieutenant asked Snaelyn if he'd rather face Eskraff or the Ritter and Ritten . . . considering that they were considered the best security team in Guldor."

"So . . . that was what that was all about," said Emrelda.

"We had a good time with Snaelyn. Almost hated to see him go, but he'll learn. Have to, now that he's in the harbor district. Anyway, really just wanted to wish you well."

"The same to you," said Emrelda. "We'll all hate to see you go, but you deserve that promotion."

Promotion? Dekkard was certain that Emrelda had never mentioned that Sammel had been promoted. "Congratulations! Where are they posting you?"

"Woodlake. Better than Easthill or Rivertown."

"I'm sure you'll do well there," said Dekkard. "You two have been through quite a bit, I heard—and I can see."

"So have you, I heard."

"It's usually rare for councilors," demurred Dekkard. "You have to deal with it all the time."

"You can almost make me believe that." Sammel grinned, then said, "We won't spoil your dinner anymore." Then the two patrollers walked back to their table.

"You never mentioned that Sammel was promoted," said Avraal.

"I promised I wouldn't say anything until it was posted. It wasn't when I left the station."

"Promoted to what?" asked Gaaroll.

"Sublieutenant," replied Emrelda. "It's probationary for four months. If he does well, he becomes permanent lieutenant. If not, he reverts to sergeant and is transferred elsewhere."

"Trial by fire," said Dekkard.

"Isn't everything these days?" asked Emrelda dryly, if with an underlying hint of bitterness.

Considering all she'd been through, Dekkard was often amazed at how seldom she revealed anger and bitterness.

"Here comes your food!" called out Chellara, arriving at the table with a large tray, from which she unloaded four platters and a basket of bread, so gracefully she made it seem effortless.

"Thank you!" said Emrelda.

Chellara flashed a smile and was gone.

Dekkard looked at his platter. He could feel his mouth water. *But then, you've had almost nothing to eat since breakfast.*

43

B Y midmorning on Findi, Dekkard was in the study working on possible statements that Hasheem could use as conclusions to Dekkard's factual presentation about the damage and deaths caused by the New Meritorists.

Less than a bell later, he heard the post bell and went to the front door. A single envelope was in the box, addressed to Ritten Avraal Ysella-Dekkard. Then he saw the name above the return address—GAARLAK CABINETRY—and smiled. He turned and handed the envelope to Avraal, who had obviously heard the post bell and followed him to the front door. "It's for you."

She looked at the envelope and said, "I hope it's just the bill, and everything's all right."

"So do I, but I think we would have heard earlier if there was a problem." Dekkard closed the front door and followed her to the study, where she opened the envelope.

She offered a smile, clearly of relief, and said, "It's just a letter, saying that it's all done, with an invoice for five hundred and eighty marks."

"That's just about what he estimated, even a little less."

"Some things do work out."

"Once in a while."

"Go back to your writing. I'll need your help in the kitchen later." She slipped the letter into the desk drawer that was theirs and left the study.

Dekkard settled down at the desk. By a little before noon, he had written two different conclusions. After he proofread them, he got up and eased into the kitchen, where Emrelda, Avraal, and Gaaroll were engaged in various efforts toward the afternoon dinner.

"What is it?" asked Avraal.

"I'd like you to read what I have . . . please?"

"Now?"

"Now. Because if what I wrote is awful, and I don't have time to rewrite it, we'll all suffer."

"That important?" asked Emrelda.

"The Premier might read one of them to the entire Council," said Dekkard.

"You'd better read it," said Emrelda.

"They're not long. Not like the last one," promised Dekkard.

Avraal washed her hands in the kitchen sink, then dried them, and followed Dekkard to the study.

He handed her the one he liked the least. "Just read it out loud, if you would."

Avraal took the single sheet and began to read. "'While the New Meritorists have inflicted great damage upon Guldor, we can and must do more than repair that damage. We must build back better and stronger, and we must work together in that effort . . .'"

When she finished, Dekkard handed her the second sheet.

Once more, she read. "'The New Meritorists saw problems in Guldor, but rather than addressing those problems, they tried to destroy a good and working system because they claimed it's not perfect. We did not let them do that, and we cannot allow anyone else such a chance again. That means we cannot ignore the fact that the Council faces problems . . .'"

When she finished, she returned both sheets to him and said, "You like the second one better, don't you?"

"I do." He paused, then asked, "Do I need to write another possible conclusion?"

Avraal shook her head. "A third will just confuse him." Her words were dry. "Either one is likely better than he or his staff could come up with."

"You've never heard him talk much."

"I was on the floor when he gave the eulogy for Obreduur. Sensing him as he spoke was enough to give me a very good feel for his abilities."

Dekkard winced.

"That's why he needs you."

"And why I need him," said Dekkard quietly.

"That, too, dear." Then she smiled. "Let him choose. He's political enough to determine which one best fits what he has in mind, and they're different enough that it's a real choice."

"I hope he sees it that way."

"You've done what you can, and I need some herbs minced."

Dekkard offered a rueful smile, set aside the two drafts, and followed her back to the kitchen and the cutting board that was clearly waiting for him.

By just before third bell, everything that could be done in advance for dinner had been completed, and Dekkard and Avraal cleaned up and dressed in "winter casual."

For a modest additional fee, Gaaroll had more than happily agreed to serve for the dinner. Although she had protested that she didn't need to be paid, Dekkard told her, "You're paid by the Council for security and other official duties, not for serving dinners. If anyone ever asks you, you can honestly say that you were paid separately and personally for these kinds of work."

At just a few minutes past fourth bell, Villem and Gretina drove up. Dekkard waved them up the drive to the portico, and then ushered them into the house.

"Your floor plan is familiar," said Villem, "if in a mirror-image way."

"They were likely built or designed by the same person," said Emrelda as everyone moved to the front parlor.

"This was so kind of you," said Gretina as she seated herself. "After everything . . ."

"It was our pleasure," replied Emrelda.

"You hinted that you had some news . . ." ventured Avraal cheerfully.

"She does, indeed," said Villem with a broad smile.

Gretina looked down for a moment. "I can't thank you enough. I was offered a position with Chaensyl and Charboneau. It was an excellent offer, and I accepted it. I started last Unadi, and it's already so much better than I anticipated."

"That's wonderful!" exclaimed Avraal. "We're so glad for you."

"It wouldn't have happened without you," said Gretina.

"You would have gotten a good position sooner or later," said Dekkard. "We might have made it a little quicker, but that firm wouldn't have hired you if they hadn't thought you were right for the position."

"There might be some truth in that," admitted Gretina. "They had several cases that they handed me immediately. Nothing that I wasn't familiar with."

Dekkard smiled wickedly. "Have you told your uncle?"

"I thought I'd wait a little." Gretina's smile held a hint of mischief. "Until I'm established and he asks, if he does, how my position search is coming."

Dekkard could see Villem's beaming face, but the other councilor didn't say anything; then he realized he hadn't done his hosting duties. "That was such good news that I forgot to ask what everyone would like to drink."

In minutes Dekkard was in the pantry, getting Silverhills reds for Avraal, Emrelda, and Villem, and Kuhrs for Gretina and himself. After Dekkard returned and served everyone, he seated himself, while Gretina talked about the legalists at the firm—all women.

When a lull occurred in the conversation, Villem turned to Dekkard. "What do you think the Premier will say tomorrow?"

"I have no idea. I *hope* he'll say that the Meritorists need to be handled severely but justly, and that the Council needs to address the fundamental problems in Guldor that created the unrest." After a slight hesitation, Dekkard asked, "What do you think he'll say, or should say?"

Villem fingered his chin. "That's a good question. He should deal strongly with the insurgents. He can't avoid the mutiny, either. *But* most of the Commercers and Landors don't want any radical change in the way things are."

"I've suspected that for a long time," said Dekkard. "The problem is that some change is necessary, or we'll have another uprising. That might be put down as well, but the problems will get worse. On the other hand, if we address the problems now, we can do it more gradually."

"That way," said Gretina, "the Council might not need to change things as much."

"Many of the Commercers and most Landors don't want any change at all," said Villem.

"I'm so glad you're not one of them," replied Gretina sweetly.

Dekkard smothered a grin.

"How could I be?" returned Villem in an amused tone. "I'm married to you."

"Now that you've been in Machtarn for a few months," said Emrelda, clearly steering the conversation off politics, "how are you finding it?"

"Much warmer," said Villem, "among other things."

"I wasn't sure I'd like it at all," admitted Gretina, "but it's been a pleasant surprise, especially occupationally. I had several other inquiries, and they were serious. Far more interest here than in Suvion."

"You even found a spirits shop that carries Riverfall," said Dekkard, "a discovery I never made in over two years."

"You didn't have to," said Avraal. "Until we were married, you weren't the one buying the lager."

From what Avraal and Emrelda had said so far, Dekkard could tell that there would be no more discussion of politics, and that if either he or Villem mentioned anything along those lines, it wouldn't last long.

That was fine with Dekkard. He was looking forward to the lamb with the rosemary cream sauce, the potato soufflé, and the green beans with sautéed mushrooms, not to mention the apple tarts.

44

WELL after the apple tarts, and the departure of Villem and Gretina, and the cleaning up, Dekkard and Avraal found themselves alone in the sitting room.

"That went well," he observed.

"Without politics."

"You and Emrelda saw to that," he pointed out.

"And Gretina," added Avraal. "But you and Villem were good about it." Dekkard smiled. *As if we had that much choice.*

Avraal laughed softly. "I saw that smile."

"I didn't say a word."

"You didn't have to." She tilted her head slightly, then said, "I have the feeling that the Baars won't be going back to Suvion any time soon."

"Not if she has anything to say about it, and there's no doubt she has a lot to say. As does someone else I know, although you often say it without uttering a word."

"Gretina must have felt very constricted in Suvion."

"You mean as the wife of the semi-important legalist and as a mere woman who doubtless had to defer to legalists superior in position to her husband, when she was often brighter than any of them?"

"When both of them were," replied Avraal. "Sometimes, it's harder to be quiet when someone you love is belittled than when you're the target."

"It was likely hard on him, too. He's pretty direct about how intelligent she is. That might be another reason why he accepted the selection as councilor, even if the Commercers push him out in the next election."

"You think they will, don't you?"

"It's not a certainty, but he's in a much more precarious position than I am—politically, I mean. His district is much more Commercer, and with Ulrich working for Suvion Industries, if there's any hint that Villem's not a good Commercer, they'll put someone else up in the next election." Dekkard smiled sardonically. "That sort of attitude is another reason why we can't let the Meritorists win. Under the Great Charter as it now stands, Villem or any other councilor can at least occasionally vote for what he or she thinks is best, against what the Commercer floor leader wants. Under a system where every vote is known, if you wanted to keep your seat, the choice would be between the party line or what's popular. Too often, neither is the right choice."

"People would say that's elitist or snobbish, as if the popular choice is always wrong or bad."

"That's not the problem. What people want is often what they need or deserve. The problem is that the Council can't provide all those needs without increasing taxes, and taxes aren't popular." Dekkard shook his head. "You know where that goes, and we've talked about that before. There's no point in going over it again."

"A year ago, I would have heard the whole explanation." She leaned forward and took his hand. "It was a good and enjoyable day, and it's time to go upstairs." She stood.

So did Dekkard. He definitely liked the words she'd used.

45

DEKKARD, Avraal, and Gaaroll were out of the house early on Unadi morning under a cloudy sky, with warmer air coming from the south and clouds that suggested rain. Dekkard carried his leather folder, and Avraal had an envelope containing a cheque for Gaarlak Cabinetry.

He immediately drove Avraal to Baartol's office, after which he headed for the Council Hall, where he left the Gresynt in the covered parking. As he and Gaaroll walked past the west end of the Council Office Building, he could see that the stonemasons appeared to be close to finishing the repairs to the walls and façade of the northwest corner of the building.

But then, the stonework is often the easiest part. At least, if it didn't have to be custom sculpted, which wasn't required for the Council Office Building.

The west doors were still blocked off, and he and Gaaroll walked along the south side of the building and to the usually locked, but now open, south gate into the courtyard, and from there into the Council Hall, and then to the Premier's floor office, where the guards nodded as he and Gaaroll entered.

"Good morning, Meldra," said Dekkard warmly.

"Good morning, Councilor. The Premier said you'd be early and for you to go right in."

After taking off his overcoat, and with his gray leather folder in hand, Dekkard entered the small inner office, closing the door behind himself. "Good morning, Fredrich."

"Good morning, Steffan." Hasheem did not stand and gestured to the chairs.

Dekkard opened his folder and took out the papers, setting them separately on the desk facing Hasheem. "I have three items for you. The three sheets at the end are the factual summary you requested. When I completed writing and revising, it felt . . . unfinished . . . as if it needed a conclusion. So I wrote two different versions. They may not be what you had in mind, but they're yours to use, adapt, or discard . . . as you see fit." Dekkard seated himself and waited.

"Let me read the factual one first. Then, if I have any questions, you'll be handy." Hasheem picked up the sheets and began to read, occasionally nodding as he continued. When he finished, he set the sheets on the desk. "That's an excellent factual summary. No overstatement, no embellishment, just the facts." The Premier paused. "I do see what you mean, though. It does seem to need a conclusion. Let's see what you have here."

Dekkard watched as Hasheem picked up the slightly harsher conclusion and began to read. Dekkard noticed several frowns, but managed to keep a pleasant expression on his face.

Without saying a word, Hasheem set down the first and started on the second, again frowning upon occasion. When he finished, he set it down and looked at Dekkard. "You have some good words and thoughts here. I trust you won't mind if I rearrange them somewhat."

"They're yours to use as you see fit. As I said earlier, I just felt a factual recounting needed a conclusion. I thought you already might have something in mind, but I wrote those to possibly add to what you had."

"I appreciate that, Steffan."

While Dekkard wanted to ask what might be new, he merely said, "Is there anything else you need?"

Hasheem smiled pleasantly, but not effusively. "Not right now. I'll see you tomorrow morning as usual."

"I look forward to hearing what you have to say to the Council." Dekkard offered an equally pleasant smile and stood.

"Thank you again, Steffan."

"I'm glad I could help."

Dekkard made his way out, gently closing the door. Then he picked up his overcoat and turned to the secretary. "We'll see you again tomorrow, Meldra."

"Take care, Councilor."

"You, too."

Once Dekkard and Gaaroll were in the main corridor, he walked to Guard Captain Trujillo's office, wondering if he should even knock.

"Someone's in there," said Gaaroll.

Dekkard knocked.

Trujillo opened the door. "I thought it might be you, Councilor."

"Do you have a minute or two?"

"Of course."

"Thank you." Dekkard looked to Gaaroll. "If you'd just wait nearby."

"Yes, sir."

The Guard captain stepped back, and Dekkard entered the small office, now lit by a functioning brass wall lamp, closed the door, and seated himself across the narrow desk from Trujillo, his overcoat and folder in his lap.

"What did you have in mind, Councilor?"

"Obtaining some information that might be useful to the Security Committee."

Trujillo merely nodded.

So Dekkard asked, "Do you have any idea how much of the leadership of the New Meritorists has been apprehended?"

"I doubt anyone on our side knows that for certain," replied Trujillo. "Justiciary Minister Kuta believes that we have at least close to half of those involved in planning and organizing their various activities. We have names for perhaps another quarter of that group, but those individuals have fled. We also discovered a hidden print and bindery establishment here in Machtarn."

"And a substantial armory of firearms as well?"

"That, too. How did you surmise that? Or did you know it already?"

"Last summer, as I recall, I heard a report of a barge washed up on our side of the Rio Doro containing cases of new pistols and possibly rifles. Since there was no subsequent mention of the matter, I didn't give it much thought, not until more and more firearms appeared in the hands of the New Meritorists . . . and a few others." *With a few aimed at me.* "Might this armory have also contained patroller, STF, and Special Agent uniforms?" That was a guess.

"There were a few. Not enough to account for the false patrollers who shot into the demonstration. There were also sanitation uniforms and Nordstar uniforms."

Nordstar, the coal-gas utility corporacion! "Which just might have something to do with some or all of the explosions at Security buildings."

"Justiciary Minister Kuta made a similar observation."

"Was any dunnite recovered?" Dekkard watched Trujillo closely.

"Only a little. About five pounds of powder, roughly."

Enough to kill anyone within five yards, depending on the device. "What color was it?" asked Dekkard.

"Color?"

"Bright yellow or slightly orangish bright yellow?"

"I was told it was a bright yellow."

The brighter yellow would be from Suvion Industries, unless they've changed the formulation recently. "Who has custody of it?"

"The Security section of the Justiciary Ministry."

"Why didn't you mention this earlier?"

"You haven't asked about it, Councilor." Trujillo offered an amused smile.

"What about ties to other corporacions?" asked Dekkard.

"You seem to have uncovered as much as any of the ministries. That is not something they happen to be pursuing." Trujillo's tone of voice was almost idle, but Dekkard doubted that was how the Guard captain really felt.

"What about banque accounts? Or have their financial transactions been strictly with mark notes?"

"From what I've heard, that was the prevalent practice."

"So they had uniforms, weapons, signs, thousands upon thousands of pages of broadsheets, and the marks to post them to the entire Council on numerous occasions, their own printing press and bindery, and the tools and expertise to destroy buildings, coal-gas piping, and sewer systems. Where did they get the financial support to accomplish this? Has anyone investigated the finances of those apprehended?"

"I've been told that is ongoing."

"By whom?"

"Investigators from both the Treasury Ministry and the Justiciary Ministry. It's not considered to be a matter directly relevant to the Council Guard."

"You don't agree with that assessment?"

"It's not my position to participate in such a determination."

Meaning that Trujillo disagrees, but doesn't have Hasheem's backing. Dekkard had to wonder, but he merely said, "I see. That might be an interesting area for the Security Committee to look into."

"As always, the Council Guard will support whatever the Security Committee determines is necessary and proper."

"Is there any line of inquiry that you or others in the Council Guard feel should be pursued?"

"That has to be a matter for the Security Committee to decide, Councilor."

"Is there any area that you or others feel has been neglected or overlooked?"

"While almost all areas have received some attention, some, such as those in which you have expressed interest, have received less attention than perhaps they might."

That was about as much as Dekkard was going to get, not that he'd expected otherwise, given that Trujillo would be questioned by Hasheem.

"How are the Council Guards doing after all this?" asked Dekkard sympathetically. "It's been a long and trying year for them."

"They've done well. I'm proud of them. They'll be pleased that you asked. A number of them think of you almost as one of them."

"I've experienced a bit of what they go through. I'd like to think that I understand, at least a little."

Trujillo laughed, softly, yet sardonically. "More than a bit, and some of them know that." He paused. "Is there anything else, sir?"

"Not right now." Dekkard stood. "If I come across anything that might be of use or interest to you, I'll definitely let you know."

Trujillo stood. "All of us appreciate that."

Dekkard smiled warmly. "Until later, whenever that may be."

Once he was out in the main corridor and well away from the Guard captain's office, still carrying his folder and overcoat, he asked Gaaroll, "Did the Guard captain seem angry or upset at any time?"

"No, sir. He felt quite composed. No strong feelings."

"Thank you." While Dekkard thought that was for the best, he wasn't entirely certain, because at times, upsetting people led to finding out more. *And, at times, it's led to people wanting to remove you.*

"Nincya, for the next bell or so, we're just going to wander around the Council buildings . . . where we can, anyway. If you sense anything unusual, please let me know."

"Yes, sir."

Dekkard hoped to get inside the Council Office Building to see how repair or reconstruction was coming on his office, but while the Council Guards let him into the main level, the staff stairways were locked, and the guards at the main central staircase politely insisted that the second and third levels weren't open to anyone. The remainder of what he saw looked to be in decent shape, except for an excessive amount of dust from the repairs.

Sometime after fifth bell, Dekkard headed back to the Council Hall to see if the councilors' dining room was open. It was. So he and Gaaroll walked down the main corridor to the staff cafeteria, which was open, although Dekkard only saw one staffer present at the tables.

He turned to Gaaroll. "I'm going to eat in the dining room, and you can eat here. I'll go straight to the floor after I eat. Meet me outside the councilors' lobby at two thirds past first bell. I'm guessing, but that's about when the Council session is likely to end."

The two walked back to the dining room, where Dekkard entered, and Gaaroll departed, presumably for the cafeteria.

"Just one?" asked the server acting as maître d'hôtel when Dekkard appeared and hung up his overcoat. "Or will someone be joining you, sir?"

"It's possible," said Dekkard with a smile, "but not certain."

Once Dekkard entered the dining area, he saw Hasheem and Craft Party Floor Leader Guilhohn Haarsfel seated at a corner table, doubtless conversing about the forthcoming session. The server seated Dekkard well away from the pair, but left two menus on the table, not that Dekkard had any need for either, then asked, "Would you like anything to drink, sir?"

"Café, please."

The server departed and returned almost immediately with the café.

"I'd like a few minutes before ordering," Dekkard said.

"Of course, sir." The server returned to his temporary post at the entrance.

Several minutes later, three councilors appeared—Saandaar Vonauer, the Landor floor leader, along with Felix Quellar and Elskar Halljen. Dekkard doubted that the lunch meeting was entirely social, but had no idea what it might involve, since all three were on different committees.

Dekkard was still pondering how long to wait before a single councilor peered into the dining room and, catching sight of Dekkard, immediately walked toward him. Dekkard maintained a pleasant expression, despite his surprise at seeing Erich Kuuresoh headed his way.

"Steffan . . . would you mind if I joined you?"

"Not at all. I'd be pleased." Dekkard gestured toward the seat across from him.

Kuuresoh took the chair, then said, "I know I must have surprised you."

"In fact, you did," replied Dekkard with an amused smile.

"I was talking with Eyril Konnigsburg the other day. He was most complimentary about you . . . and how the two of you had similar backgrounds. He suggested it might be a good idea if we got together. Even shared some information." Kuuresoh paused as the server approached, then said, "Café and the duck cassoulet."

"The white bean soup," added Dekkard. Once the server was well away from the table, he looked to Kuuresoh. "You were saying?"

"According to Eyril, both of you share certain concerns about matters before the Security and Military Affairs Committees."

"That's true. We're both convinced that the so-called mutiny on the *Khuld* was anything but spontaneous, and we both had a strong feeling that the *Khuld* would be able to avoid the *Resolute*'s battle group."

"Eyril mentioned that. He also said you had concerns that there might be more dunnite in the hands of the Meritorists, *and* that it might have come from an . . . unexpected source."

"Not exactly," replied Dekkard. "The source had to be either Northwest Industrial Chemical or Suvion Industries. They're the only manufacturers, and the Navy would have noticed the theft. The Security Committee did discover a forged report in the Security Ministry files saying that a Navy lorry carrying dunnite had been hijacked. Senior Navy officials told the Premier, before an empath, that the report was fraudulent."

Kuuresoh frowned. "Then how did they obtain the dunnite?"

"That has not been determined." Dekkard went on to summarize what he'd told other councilors about Minz, Capitol Services, and the connection to Oskaar Ulrich.

Kuuresoh nodded slowly. "Eyril did not put it quite so succinctly."

"Likely he phrased it more elegantly. Did you ever talk to Minz?"

"Twice, as I recall, after he became an influencer. He was concerned that the Council might enact unworkable additional regulations on chemical plants. He wasn't terribly specific about what they might be. I told him that if he had specifics he should give them to my legalist. He never did, but then, I suppose he couldn't," said Kuuresoh ironically.

Dekkard managed a knowing nod, surprised as he was by Kuuresoh's lie about the number of times he'd met with Minz. "A sniper assassinated Minz minutes before he was due to appear before the Justiciary to be charged."

"Someone didn't want him to reveal anything, or they wanted to create that impression."

"I'd tend to go with the first. The Council Guard wanted to learn what Minz knew. So did the Premier and the Justiciary Ministry. As a member of the Security Committee, I knew he'd been apprehended and would be charged, but I had no idea when or where that would be. The assassin had to know in advance."

Kuuresoh pursed his lips. "Someone inside, then."

"More likely someone inside on the hidden payroll of someone outside. Minz didn't know that many people, if any, in the Justiciary Ministry." Dekkard paused as the server returned with their orders. Then he took a sip of café and followed it with a spoonful of the white bean soup. He looked up as Harleona Zerlyon, Elyncya Duforgue, and Ingrella Obreduur were escorted to a table equidistant from him and Hasheem.

Kuuresoh took several mouthfuls of the cassoulet before speaking. "On the surface that doesn't make sense."

"There's the fact that Lukkyn Wyath had been the director of security for Suvion Industries before he became Security minister."

Kuuresoh frowned. "I vaguely remember that. But why would Suvion Industries or Northwest want to get involved with the New Meritorists? That doesn't seem to make sense."

"That's exactly the problem that the Security Committee faces," said Dekkard. "All that seems like more than coincidence, but the committee has yet to find hard evidence. The Military Affairs Committee may be facing the same problem in regard to finding the real causes and power behind the mutiny and takeover of the *Khuld*."

"Eyril Konnigsburg is convinced he knows the names of the officers behind the mutiny," Kuuresoh pointed out.

"He doubtless does, but did they survive the *Resolute*'s shells? He mentioned their ranks and positions, but they were junior enough that it's going to be difficult to trace any contacts. People don't pay much attention to junior officers." *Far less than they do to junior councilors.*

"There's always someone who knows," said Kuuresoh.

"I'd agree, but sometimes it's difficult to find them. The New Meritorists have been causing trouble for close to a year, and it's only recently that there have been any significant breakthroughs in identifying anyone who knows much of anything. I'll be very surprised if the Navy makes much progress in tracking Meritorist contacts with them."

Kuuresoh frowned. "Eyril Konnigsburg said the same thing. Did he mention that to you?"

"No. We never talked about that."

"What do you think will happen next?"

"That all depends on what the Premier decides."

"I can't believe you have no idea what he has in mind," said Kuuresoh skeptically.

"I've made recommendations, but he hasn't said what he thinks about them. I know he's also met with Eyril Konnigsburg, but the Premier's said nothing to me except that they've met."

"Well, at least that was a good idea."

"Premier Hasheem has only held the position a little more than a month, and he never expected to be premier. I do know that he likes to talk to a number of people, including Commercers and Landors"—*if only a few*—"before making up his mind. He doesn't say much. He just does it."

"That's good to know."

"What do you think the Council should do?" asked Dekkard.

"The plotters all should be executed. So should any proved to have severely injured or killed anyone."

"What about the others?"

"Work camps or exile if they actively took part in the violence."

Dekkard nodded, then said, "What do you think the Council should do beyond that?"

"Does the Council need to do anything more?"

"Well . . . we have more than a few men without jobs. We have workers protesting unsafe workplaces. Young girls are walking the streets in the poorer areas of Machtarn in numbers that haven't been seen in decades."

"There will always be poor people. A lot of them are just lazy."

"But there are a lot who worked hard and well, and lost their jobs because the manufactories where they worked closed. Guldoran Ironway shut its textile manufactory in Oersynt and opened one in Noldar staffed largely by underpaid susceptibles."

"Do you know that for a fact?"

"Premier Obreduur verified it. They aren't the only one, either." Dekkard paused. "I could see it if workers in Noldar were paid fairly, but using susceptibles as slave labor? That's not even legal here. Guldoran wasn't exactly losing marks, and the textiles were used for their ironway carriages."

"You're sounding like you want the Council to dictate where corporacions can buy or produce goods."

"Any government does that, Erich, one way or another. I happen to think that workplaces should be safe and workers paid enough to live on. Guldor's prosperous enough for that."

"What else?" asked Kuuresoh dryly.

"The number of smaller businesses that have been destroyed or driven out of business by unethical and sometimes illegal practices."

"People have been claiming that for years. There's never any proof."

"Oh, there's plenty of proof," replied Dekkard, "but it's difficult to get dead men who died in strange ways or disappeared to document what happened to them. You might want to look into what happened to the small corporacion that designed and built the first of the new and improved night heliographs for the Navy. You don't have to take my word for it. Talk to Eyril Konnigsburg."

"There was a huge cost overrun. I know that."

"Just talk to him." Dekkard smiled pleasantly. "How was your duck?"

"About as usual," replied Kuuresoh. "And your white bean soup?"

"About the same," replied Dekkard. "I never heard how you became a councilor."

"There's not much to tell. After I graduated from Imperial University, I obtained a position as a cost accountant at Nordstar. I worked my way up to regional vice-presidente, and then the Commercer Party of Whulte asked if I'd consider running for the Council. I likely wasn't going to go much higher in the corporacion, and we didn't have children to consider. So I said yes, and was fortunate enough to get elected." Kuuresoh offered an amiable smile. "Much less exciting or interesting than your background."

"That may be a matter of perspective," replied Dekkard. "Being a security aide consists largely of keeping yourself aware and alert through long stretches of boredom. I was fortunate that Axel Obreduur decided not to waste those interludes and gave me work that trained other abilities when I wasn't actively guarding him."

"Axel struck me as a very perceptive man. I've wondered what might have happened if the Commercers had a premier like him."

Dekkard didn't point out that it was unlikely anyone with Obreduur's characteristics would ever have been a Commercer and only said, "That would have changed everything."

The remaining minutes of the lunch were filled with pleasantries, after which the two made their way to the floor, where they went in different directions.

When Dekkard neared his desk, Tomas Pajiin looked up from the adjacent desk. "Do you know what he's going to say?"

Dekkard offered a ragged smile. "I know what I hope."

Just before first bell rang, Ingrella Obreduur slipped behind her desk. "How was your lunch, Steffan?"

"Pleasant. Less informative than it might have been. What about yours?"

"Mostly legalist talk." She stopped as the single chime rang out and the lieutenant-at-arms appeared and thumped his staff.

Then Guilhohn Haarsfel announced, "The Council is now in session."

Hasheem walked to the lectern, cleared his throat, and surveyed the watching councilors. "To begin with, I have a few announcements. First, for those of you who do not know, the Council lost another four councilors to the attack on the Council—Julian Andros, Maximillian Connard, Ellus Fader, and Gerhard Safaell. To date, the Council has not received the recommended selectees from the respective district party committees.

"The remaining announcements are about the status of the Council and Council buildings. There will be another short session of the Council on Tridi at the first bell of the afternoon. There may be another session on Quindi as well. That will be announced on Tridi.

"Except for the sealed-off eastern main level, the Council Hall will be open from now on. The Military Affairs Committee and the Security Committee will be meeting later this week, beginning on Tridi. Meeting times will be posted in the councilors' lobby. The Council Office Building will open next Unadi. Some individual offices may need special arrangements, and I will meet with those councilors on Unadi morning. The councilors' dining room will be open every day but Findi from fifth bell to third bell. Updates on these and other matters will be posted in the councilors' lobby."

After Hasheem finished with the announcements, he cleared his throat several times and surveyed the Council Hall before continuing. "Now it is time to address what faces the Council. The New Meritorists inflicted great damage upon Guldor, but we can and must do more than repair that damage. We must build back better and stronger, and we must work together in that effort. We must also acknowledge that the New Meritorists acted because they saw problems in Guldor. Rather than acting through the Council, however, they tried to destroy a good and working system because they claimed it wasn't perfect. We cannot allow anyone else such a chance again. We cannot ignore the fact that the Council faces problems. So we face three challenges. The first is to shut down the Meritorists and to put an end to the simplistic belief that electing councilors on the basis of their personal popularity will solve everything. The second challenge is to investigate the circumstances that allowed a well-planned mutiny to take place on a naval vessel, a mutiny that should never have occurred. The third, and most daunting, challenge is to address the problems that fed popular belief in the Meritorists.

"The third challenge is the hardest, and the most important, because, if the Council does not address those problems, the New Meritorists or some other simplistic reformer will arise and claim that the Council has failed . . . as we will, if we do not find a way to create more jobs for those who do not have them, to assure that the working people of Guldor can afford the food to feed themselves and their children, and that all those children with intelligence and ability have the opportunity to better themselves. Make no mistake about it. Merely removing the New Meritorists will only buy a little time before more unrest appears.

"For this reason, I have been meeting with the chairs of Council committees to establish the framework for addressing these problems . . ."

Dekkard managed not to nod as Hasheem laid out a general framework for what he planned for the Council.

When Hasheem finished speaking and recessed the Council until Tridi, Ingrella turned to look at Dekkard and raised her eyebrows.

Dekkard nodded and said, "Some."

She replied quietly. "Most."

Dekkard looked to Pajiin. "What do you think?"

"It might work. Didn't think he had it in him to go that far. Sounded a bit like Premier Obreduur. What do you think, Steffan?"

"He's got his work cut out. If he can make it work . . . then we'll have a good chance to shut down the Meritorists and improve life for the people who turned to the Meritorists for hope." Dekkard stood. "Talk to any

Landor or Commercer acquaintances you have. We'll need some help before it's all over."

Dekkard turned toward the councilors' lobby, but before he reached it, Erskine Mardosh joined him.

"Quite a speech Hasheem gave," said the older councilor. "Never heard him talk like that before."

"He's never been Premier before," replied Dekkard. "Or not long, I should say."

"He sounded more like Obreduur, don't you think?"

"Somewhat, but it's natural that Craft premiers should have similar interests. Besides, I was under the impression that he and Obreduur worked closely for a while."

"Not that closely, from what I saw."

"What else could he have said, Erskine? Especially as a Craft premier?"

Mardosh smiled genially, an expression Dekkard mistrusted, and said, "That's what I meant, Steffan. He's sounding and acting like a Craft premier. He hasn't been before."

"I'm glad he is," replied Dekkard. "Sometimes, it takes a crisis to bring out the best in people."

"Sometimes, it's more the people around them who bring out the best . . . or the worst. Good speech, though, I have to say. I'm sure we'll be talking more later." After another genial smile, Mardosh turned and headed toward the floor entrance to the councilors' dining room.

Dekkard was still thinking over the not-so-hidden implications of Mardosh's words and the fact that the Military Affairs Committee chairman had clearly sought out Dekkard when Elyncya Duforgue appeared.

"Do you have a moment, Steffan?"

"For you, distinguished legalist, always."

"Flattery, yet." She offered a momentary smile, then nodded toward the back of the chamber.

Dekkard followed her, then waited.

"Hasheem gave a good speech, Steffan. He's seldom that focused."

"I thought it was a good speech."

"The wording and style seemed familiar to me. How did you manage it?"

Dekkard could tell that evasion would be folly. "I offered to help. He was reluctant. I persevered. I'd prefer that not be widely known." *Not that more councilors than you'd like already know or suspect.*

She nodded. "I can respect that. I won't mention it." She smiled again. "Keep persevering." Then she turned and left.

By the time Dekkard got to the councilors' lobby, it was almost empty, except for Gerard Schmidtz and Pohl Palafaux, who were talking. Schmidtz nodded to Dekkard, but Palafaux didn't even look in Dekkard's direction.

When Dekkard stepped out of the councilors' lobby, he saw Svard Roostof talking to Gaaroll. Both immediately moved to him.

"Good afternoon, Svard. How did you know?"

"The Premier sent a notice to all staff directors or senior legalists about the session today. The notice said that the Council Office Building wouldn't be open until next Unadi, but I thought this would be a good time to check with you."

"I do appreciate that. Very much." Dekkard paused. "Bettina Safaell? How is she?"

"She's still a bit stunned. Very composed, though . . . now. Under that composure, she's still distraught."

"I hope you spent some time with her. From what Gerhard told me, none of her siblings live anywhere close."

"In Enke, but her sister arrived yesterday, and her brother will be here tomorrow. Her sister is a surgeon. She's . . . reserved, but seems very nice. I'm glad I could spend the time with Bettina. Mostly, I just listened."

"I didn't mean to impose on you, but I thought a great deal of Gerhard, and I didn't know anyone else who'd be better to break the news to her."

"Sir . . . I know that. I appreciate that trust, and so does Bettina. She asked me to thank you for your thoughtfulness and kindness. So did her sister."

"Is there anything else I should know?" asked Dekkard.

"I don't think so. Do you know when we can open the office?"

"It won't be before Unadi. The Premier said some offices would need special arrangements. We might fall into that group. Plan for you and Margrit to be here on Unadi."

"In the meantime, when should I meet you again?" asked Roostof.

"Right here, on Tridi after the Council session. I may know more. I may not. Right now, there's not any more you can do than what you have been doing. Give my best to Bettina."

"I will, sir." Roostof paused. "Until Tridi, then?"

"Until Tridi."

Dekkard watched for a moment as Roostof strode away, then turned to Gaaroll.

"Wager there's a wedding there . . . sooner or later," said Gaaroll.

"Not too soon, I hope," said Dekkard, thinking about how long it had taken him to truly appreciate Avraal. *But then, Svard's a few years older than you.* "I need to retrieve my overcoat from the dining room. Then we're going to do a little shopping before we go pick up Avraal." He checked his jacket pocket to make sure he still had the list she'd made out.

46

FOR Dekkard, the rest of the afternoon was largely consumed by shopping, putting away the results of the shopping in the pantry or coalgas cooler, picking up Avraal, returning to the house, and then helping Avraal and Emrelda prepare dinner. Because Emrelda had had an interesting day in dealing with a squabble and a possible assault on two "working women" and wanted to talk about it, Dekkard didn't have a chance to talk privately to Avraal until they retired to their bedroom.

Then he asked, "Did anything interesting happen today that you didn't mention at dinner?"

"Apparently, some of the members of the Guilds' Advisory Committee questioned my expertise in finding that one of the favored candidates lied about several matters. Carlos knew that would happen. So he looked further into the situation and found a few documents to confirm that the applicant had lied. Several guildmeisters were most unhappy with the second-ranked applicant. That led to a decision not to immediately fill the position."

"Would I know the applicant?"

"Probably not, although you might have met him in passing. I certainly didn't."

"Anything else?"

"Not a thing." Avraal offered a mischievous smile. "You've been dying to tell me something . . . or somethings. What might they be?"

"First, after meeting with Hasheem, who didn't have much to say except that he liked the factual summary, I finally caught up with Guard Captain Trujillo." Dekkard summarized what Trujillo had told him.

"They found some dunnite, and he didn't tell you?"

"I made a bad assumption. I assumed he'd tell me, knowing of my interest."

"Why wouldn't he tell you?"

"He can't refuse to divulge information if asked by a councilor on the Security Committee, but he can be ordered not to volunteer certain information."

"Why would Hasheem order that?"

"Because he doesn't want me looking into the dunnite question . . . or not yet."

Avraal shook her head. "What else?"

"Erich Kuuresoh sought me out for lunch . . ." Dekkard related the conversation as closely as he could remember, then ended by saying, "I don't see how he could have met just twice with Minz. You don't give access to someone described the way Kuuresoh described Minz."

"Unless Schmidtz persuaded Kuuresoh to put Minz on the list," said Avraal.

"Even so, Kuuresoh was either outright lying or minimizing his contacts with Minz."

"Wouldn't you, in his position? If he was involved with Minz, he certainly doesn't want it known, and he knows he can't totally deny meeting with Minz because there are records. If he didn't do more than meet with Minz, he'd still want to minimize the number of times."

"What are your thoughts?" asked Dekkard.

"I suspect he knows more than he wants to say, but that he wasn't actually involved in the plot. From what you've learned, Minz and Ulrich liked to keep matters tight."

"And why did Kuuresoh want to have lunch?"

"He wants to know what you know and suspect," said Avraal, "and he's worried because Konnigsburg is looking into possibilities that might involve Commercers and corporacions."

"I wish I knew more about what corporacions have headquarters or significant operations in Whulte besides Nordstar."

"I can ask Carlos tomorrow. He might know or know someone who does." After a moment, Avraal added, "When you started, you said, 'First.' Second was Kuuresoh. What else?"

"Hasheem addressed the Council. He mostly followed what I drafted." Dekkard went on to give details, including the reactions of Ingrella Obreduur, Elyncya Duforgue, and Erskine Mardosh. Then he asked, "How should I handle it?"

"You can't do much else besides what you did. Just say you offered suggestions to Hasheem and like any good premier, he accepted some and rejected others."

"I worry about Mardosh."

"You'll just have to be very careful with him. You ought to talk to Eyril Konnigsburg before too long as well."

"I'd thought about that. He's more interested in resolving the problems with the Navy than in covering up corporacion corruption."

"Just be careful."

"I will." Dekkard paused. "What about Elyncya Duforgue?"

"She'll listen to Ingrella and Harleona Zerlyon, and those three don't want anything to happen to you."

"Because I'm proposing legislation that benefits women?"

"No, dear. It's because you're the kind of man who not only proposes, but follows through on what you propose."

Dekkard grinned. "I did with you."

She leaned toward him and kissed his cheek. "I know . . . and so did I."

"For which I'm very glad."

"And I think we've talked enough tonight." She took his hands and drew him toward her.

47

O N Duadi, Avraal took the Gresynt, while Dekkard spent most of the day in the study, planning out the Security Committee hearings that he wanted to hold, including possible witnesses and lines of questioning, assuming that Hasheem agreed to his proposal about the Security Committee. Even if Hasheem didn't agree, Dekkard intended to push for hearings.

On Tridi morning, he and Gaaroll dropped Avraal off at Baartol's office again and made their way to the covered parking west of the Council Office Building, from where they walked to the front courtyard gate and then to the Council Hall.

Dekkard and Gaaroll walked past the two Council Guards outside the corridor door and into the Premier's floor office at a sixth before third bell.

"Good morning, Councilor," said Meldra even before Dekkard could greet her.

"Good morning, Meldra."

She offered a pleasant smile and gestured to the door to the inner office. In moments, Dekkard had his overcoat off and was seated and waiting to hear what Hasheem might have to say, his leather folder in his lap.

"Erskine Mardosh congratulated me on what I said to the Council on Unadi," said Hasheem blandly.

"He made a point of telling me that you gave quite a speech."

"I'm certain he said more than that," replied Hasheem dryly. "He always hints at something."

"He said you sounded a bit like Obreduur. I said that it was natural for a Craft premier to share some of the same priorities as his predecessor."

"He knows you've made recommendations."

"Isn't that normal? Councilors offer ideas and recommendations, and the Premier chooses what he feels are the best and the most appropriate."

Hasheem laughed softly. "Sometimes, I think you have some of the empath in you. That's what I told Erskine."

"No empath here. My wife has been quite clear about that. But isn't that the way it should be? Councilors recommending and you weighing the evidence and political situation?"

"Obreduur was the first to actually do that in a long time."

"Then, if anyone brings it up again, just say that Craft premiers are more willing to listen. That doesn't commit you to accepting everything that's offered."

"Does that include you?" Hasheem's tone was pleasant, but his eyes were hard.

"If you have a good reason, yes." *But not just because it makes you uncomfortable.*

"I can see why Axel might have had mixed feelings about your becoming a councilor."

Dekkard managed an ironic laugh. "*I* had very mixed feelings about becoming a councilor."

Hasheem looked puzzled, for a moment. "Why?"

"You might recall that by the time I was selected, four councilors had been killed, five if you count Freust, as had three district councilors, and there had been three attempts on Obreduur, and one on me. That didn't count the destruction at the regional Security headquarters buildings."

"One actually on you? Before you were a councilor?"

"You can ask Guard Captain Trujillo."

"Why you?"

"I doubt it was anything to do with me personally. Someone likely thought it would be easier to get to Obreduur if they removed me. Avraal would have had to train a new isolate, even if one qualified could have been found quickly."

"Why did you accept, then?"

"I'd met the other candidates. I doubted they'd have been as good. The one who was murdered before the election would have been a good councilor, but he never got the chance."

"I imagine your wife had something to do with your accepting."

"Everything."

Hasheem was silent for several moments, then said, "The Security Committee will be meeting at second bell this afternoon. I've thought over your suggestion about giving you authority to hold hearings, and I've decided on a slightly different way of dealing with the situation from what you suggested. There's a precedent, although it hasn't been employed for quite some time. I'll announce that a number of issues have been raised by the acquisition of dunnite and weapons used by the New Meritorists. To deal with that most effectively, as chairman, I am creating a special investigatory subcommittee to look into the matter. In view of your extensive security expertise you will be the chair of that subcommittee with the power to issue orders for witnesses to appear."

Dekkard hadn't thought of that possibility, but then, he'd never heard of it and didn't know many of the obscure and seldom-used precedents. "That makes perfect sense."

"Who would you suggest as the other subcommittee members, besides Tomas Pajiin, since there will need to be two Craft councilors?"

"I'd prefer Breffyn Haastar and Villem Baar."

"Then that will be the subcommittee. Do you have any idea of what hearings and witnesses you intend to call?"

"I've been working on that. I can give you a proposed schedule and listing for the first set of hearings tomorrow morning."

"Did you plan to force this, even if I didn't agree?"

"I wouldn't have forced it, Fredrich, but I would have suggested it before the committee. You could have rejected it or asked for a vote."

Hasheem offered a smile both amused and cool. "Under the circumstances, I'd likely have lost such a vote, and rejecting it under those circumstances would have been less than helpful—as you well know."

"Fredrich," said Dekkard quietly and warmly, "I'm not out to undermine you. I am out to make sure that the corporacions—or those in certain corporacions—who helped the New Meritorists are uncovered and brought to justice."

"Will that help the Craft Party?"

"I believe so. I also believe that if we don't succeed in that, the Commercers will be back in power in less than two years, and we'll have another uprising in five years or less. Remember, some corporacion interest funneled as much as a tonne of dunnite, if not more, to the New Meritorists without the great majority of the previous Council even knowing about it."

"Are you using the phrase 'the great majority' knowingly?"

"I referred to the previous Council, advisedly," returned Dekkard. "Do you really believe that Johan Grieg's house caught fire accidentally, especially after the 'incident' at our house?"

"You do have a point, Steffan." Hasheem sighed. "But then, you always have a point, usually a rather sharp one." After a moment, he rose from behind the narrow desk. "I'll expect a preliminary outline of what you plan tomorrow morning."

Dekkard stood. "You'll have it."

"With you, Steffan, I never doubt it."

Once Dekkard had left the inner office, and closed the door, he turned to the Premier's secretary. "Meldra, could you spare some sheets of paper? Perhaps twenty sheets?"

"Paper we can spare. I have an old pen you can borrow, if you need it."

"I appreciate the paper, but I have a pen."

After Meldra handed him the paper and he slipped it into his gray leather folder, Dekkard inclined his head. "Thank you. I do appreciate it."

Dekkard gestured for Gaaroll to leave first, then followed her out into the main corridor, overcoat over his arm carrying the folder. He thought about seeing whether Guard Captain Trujillo was in his office, but since he had nothing new to impart and no pressing questions, he decided against that and turned toward the councilors' dining room.

"Nincya, I'm afraid you're going to have a boring next two bells."

"Sir?"

"I need to write up some notes from my meeting with the Premier, and the only place where I can do that in quiet will be the councilors' dining room. I'd like you to wait outside and make certain nothing dangerous is headed my way. With what I'll be thinking about, I won't be as vigilant as I should be. If someone like that appears, don't worry about going into the dining room to find me. They won't be officially open until fifth bell. You can also practice sensing. After fifth bell, you can go eat, and I'll see you outside the councilors' lobby after the Council session." He handed her two mark notes. "As partial compensation for that boredom, I'll pay for your lunch."

"Sir, you don't have to—"

"I can't afford it all the time, but the peace of mind is worth it at the moment."

"Thank you, sir."

Dekkard then made his way into the dining room, opening the closed archway door that was usually open.

Within moments, a server appeared. "Sir, we're not open until fifth bell."

"I know that. I need to write up some things for the Premier. Since the Council Office Building is closed, I just need a quiet table."

"Sir—"

Dekkard concentrated on trying to convey the urgency of his next words. "The work is most important. I won't bother anyone, and I won't ask for anything except the space until after fifth bell."

The server glanced at Dekkard's councilor's pin, then backed away a step or so. "If you say so, sir."

"Thank you. Let me hang up my overcoat, and just point out a table where I'll be out of the way."

Less than a minute later Dekkard was seated at a table near a wall lamp. He folded back the table linens to get a firmer surface and laid out the stack of paper. For the next bell and two thirds, he wrote, almost continuously, crossing out more than a few lines and rewriting them. First, he concentrated on witnesses, either by name, when he knew the name, or by position when he didn't. Then he began to draft questions, not that he was about to show all of what he worked on to Hasheem immediately. The first witnesses would be from Naval Logistics, including the admiral who had confirmed to Obreduur that the naval dunnite theft report in the Security Ministry files had been a forgery. Offhand, Dekkard couldn't remember his name, but that shouldn't be hard to discover. Then the next witnesses would be from Northwest Industrial Chemical.

Just before fifth bell, another server appeared. "Councilor? We're about to open, and this table . . ."

"Isn't ready," Dekkard said cheerfully. "I appreciate your letting me work here. Can I just take another table? I'll be ready to order in just a bit."

"Take any other table you prefer, sir."

"Thank you."

Dekkard moved to a nearby table, but seated himself facing the entrance.

Almost a third passed before any councilors appeared, and that first group consisted of Ingrella Obreduur, Harleona Zerlyon, and Elyncya Duforgue. The three exchanged glances, and then Duforgue said, "Would you like to join us, Steffan?"

"I'd be delighted," replied Dekkard, meaning very word.

As he rose, he slipped the papers he'd been studying into the leather folder, then joined the three as a server led them to a table for four.

"It looks like you've been working," said Zerlyon.

"Steffan usually is," added Ingrella Obreduur.

"So, I suspect, are you three," he replied genially. "I think of you as the legal reformists."

"There's a little truth in that," agreed Zerlyon as she seated herself beside Duforgue.

Dekkard sat directly across from Zerlyon, with Ingrella to his right.

"Why did you use the term 'reformist'?" asked Ingrella.

"Because you want to make quiet legal structural changes, rather than merely tinkering with how the system functions. Also, people tend to be leery of reformers. They likely would have to think about someone who insisted on being termed a reformist. Personally, I think the idea of legal reformism sounds more distinguished."

"Café for everyone?" asked Zerlyon as a server approached.

The other three at the table nodded.

"Café for all of us," Zerlyon told the server. "You can take everyone's order now."

Since Dekkard wasn't that hungry, he ordered the onion soup with the melted cheese over toast squares, as did Ingrella. Zerlyon ordered a half-sized duck cassoulet, and Elyncya the three-cheese chicken.

Once the server departed, Duforgue asked, "Steffan, do you know if anything survived in your office?"

"I tried to find out the other day, but the Council Guards were most insistent about keeping anyone from that part of the Council Office Building. What about your office?"

"Unless there was later damage, I don't think we lost anything."

"I just might be asking for copies of what I originally sent you on working women, again." He did his best to make the last word sound dolefully resigned. "You'd think that the New Meritorists had something against women, or anyone trying to improve matters for them."

"They likely do," replied Zerlyon, "not that I think they targeted your office for that reason. I spent a little time with Justiciary Minister Kuta the other day. Some of the captured Meritorists are actually would-be legalists, men who couldn't get certified. They resented being questioned by women legalists, so much so that the legalists, or rather the assisting empaths, had to take breaks because of the strong feelings of hatred."

"Were they from a Landor background?" asked Dekkard.

"Mixed Commercer and Landor . . . spoiled third and fourth sons or something similar. Not enough family marks to support them all."

There's something . . . women legalists . . . "Are there quite a number of women legalists, career legalists, I mean, at the Justiciary Ministry?"

"About half, I'd say," answered Ingrella. "More in the recent hires."

"There's an examination for career legalists, isn't there?" asked Dekkard. All three women smiled, but coolly.

"And until recently, the results were biased or ignored?" Dekkard pressed.

"Until a certain lower Justiciary ruling in a case pressed by a certain guild legalist was overturned by the High Justiciary," replied Ingrella.

"Which of you two?" asked Dekkard, looking from Zerlyon to Duforgue.

"Harleona," said Elyncya Duforgue. "She was the number three graduate from the legalist program at Ondeliew University, and she applied for an entry-level legalist position in the Justiciary Ministry. She was rejected."

"Three years running," added Zerlyon. "So I filed a motion against the ministry, noting that the one graduate of Ondeliew that they hired was a man in the bottom quarter of the graduating class a year later. I had to open my own office, because no one wanted to hire me, and once I filed the motion, I lost most of the clients I had. So I took the position as the legalist for the Working Women Guild."

"When was that?" asked Dekkard.

"Twelve years ago. It took almost two years for the case to reach the High Justiciary, and by then I was making more than I would have at the ministry, and I didn't want to work in a situation where everyone I worked for would have been male and angry. So I insisted that the remedy be that all legalist hires be based on the test results—without names—and by a board with equal numbers of male and female legalists who didn't work at the ministry. That took another two years to work out. About then, I started working toward getting elected as a councilor." She looked across the table. "Ingrella was one of the first women on the hiring board."

"Axel was successful in getting a similar system adopted in all the ministries," added Ingrella.

Dekkard nodded slowly. That had to be the reason for the number of junior women legalists in the Justiciary Ministry—because the pay was by ministry grade, and women could get paid more fairly by the ministries than by corporacions. *And legalist positions that had once been handed out to less qualified third sons became much harder for those less qualified third sons to obtain.* "The one thing I'm sure of was that it was far longer, more tedious, and more difficult than you made it sound." He smiled ruefully. "In what little I'm working on, I'll try to uphold the standard you three have set. That won't be easy."

"Just keep convincing people," said Elyncya Duforgue. "Legal reasoning by itself doesn't persuade people. Too many councilors who are initially convincing fail because they don't know what they're talking about. You make sure you know what you're talking about before you open your mouth, and most councilors have come to realize it."

Dekkard laughed softly. "One thing that Axel made certain of was never to say anything I couldn't back with facts. It's much easier to be convincing when you know the facts, especially the ones that matter."

"You'd make a good legalist," said Elyncya.

"Don't tempt him," said Ingrella dryly. "He's a better councilor."

From what he'd seen and learned, Dekkard wasn't in the slightest tempted, but he saw no point in saying so. Instead, he looked to Zerlyon. "Did you learn anything from the Justiciary minister that you can tell us?"

"Not really. What was surprising to her was the amount of marks the investigators found."

"That makes sense," said Dekkard. "It's harder to track where it came from and what they used it for."

"What are you working on, Steffan?" asked Duforgue.

"I have some ideas, but I'll know more after the Security Committee meeting this afternoon."

"The meeting was posted in the councilors' lobby," said Ingrella. "The notice didn't give a subject."

"I believe the meeting will discuss what steps the Security Committee needs to take to look into the various factors behind the New Meritorists' abilities to do what they did." After a brief hesitation, Dekkard asked, "What will the Justiciary Committee be considering once it's able to meet?"

"Nothing compared to what you'll be doing," replied Zerlyon.

"What about investigating the shooting of Jaime Minz? I barely knew he'd been taken into custody, and certainly not where and when he'd be charged. But someone in the Justiciary Ministry had to have passed that information to the assassin, or to someone else, who then hired the assassin. It might be very informative to find out who, considering that Minz was an influencer for one manufacturer of dunnite and had worked for Oskaar Ulrich."

"That is a *possible* subject for a hearing and an investigation," said Zerlyon evenly.

"Possible?" pressed Dekkard ironically.

Elyncya Duforgue grinned. "She'll never admit it, Steffan, but there's no way she can't look into that."

"Was that one reason for meeting with Minister Kuta?" asked Dekkard cheerfully.

"You asked if there was anything I was able to tell you," replied Zerlyon. "At present, I'm not able to comment on that."

In short, you applied pressure and are waiting for the results. "I understand."

"I'm sure you do." Zerlyon's smile was cheerfully amused.

At that moment, Dekkard saw the server approaching the table with a tray, presumably holding their orders.

"After we're served, Steffan," said Ingrella, "I'd like to hear when you think you might have that working women's legislation ready to bring before the Workplace Administration Committee . . . and what you plan after that."

Dekkard smiled. *Meaning that you will be working with all three of them on both.* Not that he minded that in the slightest. But it also meant he wouldn't find out any more about the Meritorists from Zerlyon, at least not at the moment.

He enjoyed the onion soup, and mentally filed some of their suggestions about his workplace proposals and how to approach their introduction.

All too soon, lunch was over, and the three women excused themselves and Dekkard made his way to the Council chamber, even though it was close to a third before first bell.

The chamber was almost empty, and Dekkard sat down at his desk, thinking, but within minutes he heard footsteps. He looked up to see Kaliara Bassaana headed toward him. He stood and waited.

"Steffan, I thought you might be in the dining room, but one of the servers said you looked to be heading here."

"What can I do for you?" he asked cheerfully.

"You could tell me what Fredrich intends to do with the Security Committee in dealing with the New Meritorist scum."

"He hasn't said. I imagine he'll announce what he has in mind this afternoon. He has been studying the factual background of the situation, and he has met with me and with Eyril Konnigsburg and others."

"And what did he convey?"

"He didn't convey anything about what he intends. He was much more interested in factual answers to a number of questions. At least he was with me. I imagine, but do not know, that his meetings with Eyril were the same."

"You know more than that, Steffan."

Dekkard smiled warmly. "I could guess, but guessing what a committee chair who is also premier *might* do is not something I'm inclined to do. I will say that it's fairly clear that he's quietly angry, if not furious, at how matters came to be."

"He's the Premier. He should have known."

"Did Premier Ulrich know about the Summerend demonstrations before they occurred?" asked Dekkard, his voice pleasant. "And before him, Premier Grieg apparently didn't know that his own Minister of Public Resources had illegally leased a Naval Coal Reserve to Eastern Ironway. Isn't that a bit of a double standard, Kaliara?"

"Isn't the minority party allowed a little leeway?" Bassaana smiled coolly.

"Kaliara, you're a lovely and intelligent woman, but that's a bit disingenuous."

"It's worth the attempt." She paused. "The word is that you warned Fredrich that the *Khuld* was more dangerous than the First Marshal believed."

"That's true. So did Eyril Konnigsburg."

"Did Fredrich advise the Imperador to leave the Palace?"

"I have no idea what he said to the Imperador. Nor would I presume to suggest what he might say." *And that's definitely true.*

Bassaana laughed quietly. "You're treading a narrow and dangerous path, Steffan."

"Right now, all paths are dangerous, from what I can see."

"Yours is far more dangerous." She glanced toward the entry from the councilors' lobby, then looked back to Dekkard. "I won't keep you further." With an amused smile, she turned and walked toward the desks of the Commercer councilors.

Bassaana had only taken a few steps before Ingrella Obreduur appeared and made her way toward her desk. Dekkard remained standing.

Ingrella paused beside her desk. "I saw Kaliara Bassaana walking away from your desk. Did she have anything interesting to say?"

"She wanted to know how Fredrich intends to use the Security Committee to deal with the Meritorists. I told her that he hasn't said, but likely would at this afternoon's meeting."

"You phrased it that way, didn't you?"

"Of course."

"So she knows you know or have a good idea, but won't say."

"I suspect so."

"Will she like what Fredrich has in mind, or what you think he has in mind?"

"I have no idea."

"That means you, or you and Fredrich, came up with something that isn't on anyone else's mind, at least at present."

"I had an idea. He didn't like it, but came up with something else workable as a possibility. Until this afternoon, I won't know what he'll do. Which is another reason why I didn't appease Kaliara's curiosity."

"Or mine?" asked Ingrella gently.

"Or yours."

"Then whatever you're doing is going to disconcert a number of councilors." Ingrella smiled mischievously. "I do believe I'll enjoy watching."

As other councilors began to fill the chamber, Dekkard and Ingrella took their seats behind their desks.

Once the lieutenant-at-arms thumped his staff, Hasheem took the lectern. "Good afternoon. I have some information for the Council. First, the Imperador is still considering who he will recommend for Fleet Marshal, now that former Fleet Marshal Harraaf has become First Marshal. Second, the Premier's nominees for Treasury Minister and Minister of Public Safety will be presented to the Council on Unadi for a vote. Third, there will be no session of the Council on Quindi."

Hasheem's remaining announcements were largely procedural, including a scheduled vote on a supplemental appropriations measure on Unadi to cover damages to government buildings from the attack. He also confirmed that the Council would return to the usual bells and business on Unadi.

In less than a third, Hasheem recessed the Council until Unadi.

Dekkard turned to Ingrella. "For some of us, it won't quite be business as usual. I don't even know if any of my files survived, except for the few I had in my folder. I just hope Svard, Luara, and Shuryn have excellent memories." He shook his head.

Ingrella smiled wryly. "I'm sure they do. Now, go and see if Hasheem does what you hope. He likely will. His other options aren't that good."

"First, I have to talk to Svard."

"How is he doing?"

Dekkard gave her a quick summary of Roostof's organizational skills as well as his involvement with Bettina Safaell.

When he finished, Ingrella just said, "Give him my best and be careful."

As Dekkard stood, Tomas Pajiin, who had been waiting, stepped forward.

"Are you going to the committee room?"

"Not for a few minutes. I need to meet with my senior legalist. If you want to talk, we can walk there after I finish."

"That'd be fine. I'll wait in the councilors' lobby."

The two crossed the chamber floor to the lobby, where Pajiin took a chair, and Dekkard continued out to the main corridor.

Roostof and Gaaroll were seated on one of the benches outside the councilors' lobby, but both stood as Dekkard appeared.

"How are you doing, Svard?"

"Well enough, sir."

"And with Bettina's siblings?"

"They're good people. All three of them are still stunned and subdued. I get the feeling that they thought the councilor would be there forever."

"I can see that. He had a quiet sort of strength, the enduring kind," said Dekkard, thinking that he still thought of his parents always being around. *Even when you've had a few reminders that life can be uncertain . . . and sometimes fragile.* Did all children think that about their parents, or was it only those children who were fortunate enough to have strong and caring parents?

"I didn't know him, sir, but that's the impression I've gotten from Bettina." After a long moment, Roostof said, "About the office, sir?"

"The Premier says the Council Office Building will be open on Unadi. How do you want to handle it so far as the rest of the staff is concerned?"

"I'd like Margrit and Bretta in there at second bell, the others around fourth bell."

"Then message them all to that effect. Keep track of the charges, and make sure to put in a reimbursement form for *all* of the messages you've sent. They shouldn't come out of your wallet."

"Yes, sir."

"I might need your help, and possibly Shuryn's, on another new project, but I won't know for sure until later today. But we can talk about that on Unadi. Now, is there anything I should know?"

"No, sir. I'll check with administration on Unadi once I see about what we need in the office."

"Excellent. There's nothing more you can do until then. Enjoy the days off, and give my best to Bettina if you see her."

"I certainly will, sir."

After Roostof left, Dekkard turned. "Nincya, I'm going to walk to the committee room and talk on the way to Councilor Pajiin. Give us a bit of space, if you would, but keep sensing. He's waiting in the councilors' lobby. I'll be back in a moment."

Dekkard no sooner entered the councilors' lobby than Pajiin was on his feet.

"Shall we go?" asked Dekkard.

"You didn't take that long."

"Right now, what he can do is limited."

"What any of us can do is limited," replied Pajiin.

"You had something on your mind," prompted Dekkard as he and Pajiin left the lobby and turned left. Gaaroll dropped back.

"When Hasheem first briefed the committee about the *Khuld,* what you said could happen was very close to what did."

"I was wrong about one thing." Dekkard went on to explain why he thought the cruiser had been anchored and what that had meant for the accuracy of the gunnery.

"Then they had that planned out for months, maybe longer."

"The timing of the mutiny would support that. The accuracy of the gunnery is still a supposition on my part."

Pajiin snorted. "Supposition, my ass! Your suppositions were better than the First Marshal's battle group plans."

"They're still suppositions. There's no proof, except the circumstantial evidence provided by the accuracy of the gunnery."

"So what's Hasheem going to do? He gave a fair speech, but speeches aren't acts."

"I made some recommendations for the Security Committee. He wasn't pleased with them, but he said he'd address the problem in his own way. I suspect we'll hear what he has in mind this afternoon."

"You think Rikkard and Baar are going to support it? Or even the Landors?"

"We'll see before long," said Dekkard dryly.

Dekkard and Pajiin were the first into the committee room, but were followed almost immediately by Haastar and Navione. Then, slightly before second bell, Hasheem appeared, then Villem Baar. Rikkard sauntered into the chamber as the two bells echoed through the main corridor.

Hasheem thumped the gavel even before Rikkard was seated. "The committee will come to order. That includes you, Councilor Rikkard."

"My apologies, Sr. Chairman." Rikkard's tone was coolly pleasant, but without a hint of apology.

"In order to investigate and determine what remedies are necessary to deal with the New Meritorists, I have been meeting with the chairs of every committee to work out a comprehensive approach in all areas. Given the importance of making sure everything is properly coordinated, it has become apparent that I cannot devote full attention to the details of further investigation and remediation by the Security Committee. Therefore, I am hereby establishing a special investigatory subcommittee. The subcommittee will have full delegated powers, but with their use being first approved by the chairman. The subcommittee will consist of Councilors Haastar, Pajiin, Dekkard, and Baar. The acting chair of that committee, by virtue of his extensive experience and success in security, will be Councilor Dekkard."

"Sr. Chairman, I must protest and offer a point of order," said Rikkard belligerently. "This so-called subcommittee is nothing more than the unlawful delegation of authority to the most junior members of the Security Committee."

Hasheem rapped the gavel. "Councilor, the subcommittee consists of the most senior Craft councilors beside the chair, as well as a senior Landor councilor. Councilor Baar was included on the subcommittee, rather than you, because he is a qualified legalist, and you are not. Neither of the Landor councilors is a legalist, and there is little difference in seniority among any of the subcommittee members and you, with the exception of Councilor Haastar, who is definitely senior. Under the precedents of the Council, the composition of special subcommittees is the prerogative of the chair. The acting chair of the subcommittee must present all proposed hearings and witnesses to the chair before such hearings are announced and witnesses called. I can assure you that I will scrutinize those most carefully. Your point of order is overruled. Are there any other questions?"

"What is the specific purpose of this subcommittee?" asked Kharl Navione.

"The purpose is to investigate known breaches in Imperial security, including the unexplained acquisition of restricted explosives by the New Meritorists, the ability of the insurgents to gain access to sixteen Security buildings, the known linkages of former Council employees to the New Meritorists, and any other matters that these investigations may uncover, as approved by the chairman of the full Security Committee."

"Thank you, Sr. Chairman."

"There have been other groups advocating change," said Breffyn Haastar, "such as Foothill Freedom and, more recently, a small group calling themselves Contrarians. Will this subcommittee be looking into those groups?"

"No, it will not," declared Hasheem. "The subcommittee's scope of action is limited to the New Meritorists and to anyone through which or by which they obtained dunnite or other materials or acts relating to the recent attacks."

Dekkard couldn't help wondering where Haastar had learned about the Contrarians. From Kaliara Bassaana, although that seemed unlikely? Perhaps in *The Machtarn Tribune*? Either way, he wasn't about to ask.

"To whom will the findings of the committee be revealed?" asked Baar.

"To the chair and Premier, and, as necessary, to the Justiciary minister, the Minister of Public Safety, and the Council Guard captain. Once any required legal action is taken and completed, the subcommittee will make a full report to the full committee."

"Will this 'subcommittee' have the power to order the appearance of non-governmental witnesses?" asked Rikkard.

"The subcommittee, as approved by the committee chair or the Premier, will have the power to require the presence of any individual in the Imperium. In cases of possible criminal activity, the subcommittee chair may also request the assistance of certified empaths."

"That seems exceedingly excessive," stated Rikkard.

"Two shellings of the Council buildings, and one of the Imperial Palace and the ironway system in Machtarn, are far more excessive than requiring the verification of truth by witnesses. Are there any other questions?" Hasheem glanced to one side and then the other, then said, "The first meeting of the special subcommittee will be at second afternoon bell on Unadi, or immediately after the Council session, whichever comes later.

Subsequent meetings and hearings will be announced by the subcommittee chair, after approval by the full committee chairman." Hasheem paused, studied the committee, then declared, "The committee is adjourned."

Rikkard stalked out of the committee chamber almost before the echo of Hasheem's gavel died away.

Pajiin leaned toward Dekkard and said quietly, "Never seen Rikkard that pissed, and he's always pissed."

That's because he knows where the subcommittee is heading. "Apparently, he doesn't want anyone looking into how all that dunnite ended up in the hands of the New Meritorists."

"I wouldn't either, not if I were a Commercer." Pajiin glanced around, then lowered his voice and asked, "How'd you get Hasheem to agree to that?"

"I told him that the committee had to do *something*. The subcommittee was his idea. I didn't even know that possibility existed."

"That way he can say the committee's acting, but you're the target."

Is that so new? "When you agitate for action, sometimes you get more than you anticipated."

"Just tell me anything you need."

"I'd appreciate your contacting any guild members or officers who might know of corporacion marks funneled to past Commercer committee chairs."

Pajiin frowned. "You hear things all the time, but details are harder to come by."

"Or smaller businesses with military contracts forced under and then acquired by big corporacions."

Pajiin nodded. "I'll see what I can do."

By the time Dekkard gathered himself together, the only other councilor in the chamber was Villem Baar, who was clearly waiting. Dekkard walked to where Baar stood. "What is it, Villem?"

"I don't think I've ever seen Jaradd that angry," said Baar, "and that's saying something."

"Do you know why? Is it because he's slightly senior to Pajiin, me, and you?"

"He's always annoyed about that, but not furious."

"I thought he was all in favor of going after the Meritorists and those who helped them."

"After the New Meritorists, yes."

"That suggests that he knows something—or fears it."

"Fears it, I think," mused Baar. "He's in political debt to . . . a number of supporters who have strong corporacion ties. He knows that you believe some corporacions are involved. He also knows you can be effective."

"We've already had one corporacion employee with hard evidence of involvement, who was killed just before being charged. That's a bit more than belief," Dekkard pointed out.

"There's more than that, isn't there?"

"Yes."

"I thought so. Hasheem set up that subcommittee because he knows that, and he doesn't want to be the target. He also knows that information won't stay hidden. Jaradd knows he can't stop it from coming out. If it does, then he'll lose support he doesn't think he can afford to lose."

"It might not matter if there isn't an election for a while," said Dekkard.

"That's not the best possible wager, Steffan."

"But it's the only one that makes sense."

Baar raised his eyebrows.

"Any other outcome will result in more unrest and violence." Dekkard paused, then asked, "How is it likely to affect you?"

"Thanks to you, we don't have to worry quite so much. Although I've discovered that some aspects to being a councilor can be . . . rewarding." Baar then added quickly, "I don't mean financially."

"I understood before the qualification," replied Dekkard. "I'm going to need your counsel and assistance, you know?"

"I thought that might be a factor . . . in addition to Jaradd's . . . inflexibility. Do you have a schedule of hearings yet?"

"I had a list that I was going to propose for the full committee. I'll have to rework that and submit it to Hasheem before I dare share it."

"I can see that."

"If you have any ideas about possible witnesses or corporacions who might shed any light on these matters, I'd appreciate them, particularly anyone in Suvion Industries."

"Let me think about that."

"Of course. How is Gretina coming?"

"She's enjoying working there."

"Has she told her uncle?"

"Not yet, but he may find out before long. There's some possible land inheritance litigation that might involve the Imperial Banque." Baar grinned.

Dekkard laughed, if quietly. "I'll see you on Unadi, if not sooner." He let Baar lead the way out of the committee chamber.

Once he had recovered his overcoat from the councilors' dining room and he and Gaaroll were outside in the courtyard, walking toward the covered parking, he said, "Nincya, Chairman Hasheem just put something in motion that's going to focus the anger of certain corporacion interests on me. From now on, I'd like you to be especially watchful."

"Can I ask what you did, sir?"

"I got appointed chair of a subcommittee looking into how the New Meritorists got all their dunnite and weapons."

"About frigging time."

"I thought so, too, but the Council is often not known for speed." *Or impartiality.* "On the way to pick up Avraal, we'll stop by a new spirits shop and buy a keg of Riverfall, although it's not exactly on the way home."

"Riverfall?"

"A lager that's as good as, if not better than, Kuhrs. We're running low on lager, and I've been meaning to do that for weeks. That way we'll only be a little early, if that."

48

ON Tridi night after dinner Dekkard worked for another two bells refining the draft of the first set of proposed hearings for the investigatory subcommittee, in all too many places using descriptive titles for the witnesses he had in mind, because he had no idea who the director of security or the shipping manager were at Northwest Industrial Chemical. He did finally recall the name of the admiral who headed Naval Logistics—Admiral Jingao—whom he intended to call on initially to explain how the Navy handled the transportation and security of dunnite and other explosives, as well as discuss the matter of the forged dunnite theft report.

A cold misty rain enshrouded Machtarn on Furdi morning as Dekkard headed down the steps to the main floor and breakfast. If the rain continued, Dekkard knew that what remained of the snow would become a sooty slush before collecting into dark puddles and pools that would flood the storm sewers. The air would be less acrid, however.

The mixed joys of early spring. Not that Dekkard had ever been that fond of the time that mixed snow, rain, and mud.

"Miserable morning," he said to Emrelda as he entered the breakfast room.

"The rest of the day won't be any better," she replied.

Gaaroll only nodded, then picked up her mug and had more café.

Dekkard reached for the newssheet on the side table.

"*Gestirn* isn't any better," added Emrelda.

"Thanks for the warning." Dekkard scanned the front page, his eyes going to the secondary headline—COUNCIL SLOW TO ACT. He read further, deciding that the bulk of the story was in the first few lines.

> . . . without dispute that the damage to the Council Hall and other buildings has hampered the Council in carrying out its duties, but to date the Premier has announced no real action against the New Meritorists who were behind the destruction . . .

"What the frig do they want?" Dekkard dropped the newssheet on the side table. "The Justiciary and patrollers find and incarcerate more

Meritorists every day. Repairs to the streets and buildings started the day after the attacks. The First Marshal was removed—"

"They want the Premier to announce that everything is well under control," said Avraal as she walked into the breakfast room. "Hasheem doesn't want to say that because things are only temporarily under control."

"He needs to say something," said Emrelda.

Although he agreed with Emrelda, Dekkard decided not to comment and went to fix cafés.

A bell later, Dekkard drove toward Baartol's office through the misty rain, more slowly than was his wont because the misty rain, in addition to the soot and muddy water thrown up by other steamers, further reduced the already limited effectiveness of the windscreen wipers.

When he stopped next to the office door to let Avraal off, he asked, "Half past fourth bell?"

"That should be fine."

"More interviews?"

She shook her head. "A negotiation session between a guild and a small manufactory. The guild doesn't trust the manufactory owner or his empath."

"That could prove interesting."

"I hope not. Good fortune with the Premier."

Dekkard arrived at the covered parking at a third past second bell. When he and Gaaroll crossed the drive, he saw that the scaffolding had been removed from the west end of the Council Office Building, although the west doors were still blocked. After he reached the open courtyard gate, he saw that the scaffolds had vanished from the east end of the Council Office Building as well. *That doesn't mean you'll have a usable office on Unadi.*

Once he and Gaaroll entered the Premier's floor office, Meldra just motioned for Dekkard to go into the inner office. After shedding his overcoat, Dekkard did so, closing the door.

"Good day, Steffan."

"The same to you, Fredrich. Did you read *Gestirn* this morning?" Dekkard seated himself in front of the desk, still holding his leather folder.

"That and the *Tribune*," replied Hasheem. "The *Tribune* was worse. I'll have to make a statement. If those print-lice don't have something new every few days, or sometimes every day, they start fomenting mis-statements. The *Tribune,* especially. But then, you know all about the *Tribune.*"

Dekkard deliberately ignored the reference. "You know what to say. Tell them how well all the repairs are coming, and that the Justiciary has incarcerated however many Meritorists it now happens to be, and that giving details is premature."

"What else would *you* say?"

"Not much. Just that the Council, through its various committees, is setting up investigations and hearings to look into the underlying factors, including organizations and individuals, that may have supported the insurgency, either deliberately or inadvertently, and that those hearings, if held properly, will take time and care in order to assure that something similar doesn't recur."

"They'll want something shorter," said Hasheem, not concealing his distaste for the newsies.

"The insurgency was created over years, and ensuring that it doesn't recur can't be accomplished overnight."

"Starting with something along those lines might be best."

"You've had more experience with them than I ever hope to have," said Dekkard dryly.

"You'll have your share," said Hasheem. "Once you start holding hearings, you'll be the one talking to the newsies." He paused, then asked, "What do you have for me on the proposed hearings?"

Dekkard open the folder and withdrew the small stack of papers. "These are the hearings I propose for the first two weeks along with the rationale for each and for the order in which I propose they occur." He handed the papers across the desk.

Hasheem took them, immediately setting them to one side without even a glance. "You're starting with the dunnite, I assume?"

"Not directly. I thought we should start with Naval Logistics. Have them explain how explosives are ordered, delivered, recorded, and safeguarded at every step. Then Admiral Jingao can explain about the false theft report created in the office of the former Minister of Security."

Dekkard continued with a brief summary and waited for Hasheem's response.

"For the most part, all that sounds feasible, but I'll need to go over your proposal and see what I think, whether it needs changes or additions. We'll talk about that tomorrow morning."

Before Hasheem could stand or dismiss him, Dekkard asked, "Are you aware if the Justiciary Ministry has uncovered anything new or significant about the New Meritorists?"

"I've not been informed of any significant changes, but it will be another week before the interrogations of the New Meritorists in custody will be complete."

"And the matter of the Fleet Marshal?"

"The Imperador is still considering his options."

"Meaning that the officers he favors are too much like the previous First Marshal?"

"He is considering his options," said Hasheem evenly as he stood. "I'll see you tomorrow morning, Steffan."

"I'll be here, Fredrich." Dekkard stood and inclined his head politely.

After leaving the inner office, recovering his overcoat, and exchanging pleasantries with Meldra, Dekkard stepped out into the main corridor, where he saw a number of staffers, suggesting that the Council Hall was at least partly open.

"We'll see if Guard Captain Trujillo is around," Dekkard said to Gaaroll. "If he is, I'd like you to stay close and keep track of his feelings."

"Yes, sir."

Trujillo's door was barely ajar, and Dekkard knocked. "Guard Captain?"

"You can come in, Councilor."

Dekkard entered and shut the door, then took the chair in front of the desk.

"What can I do for you, Councilor?"

"In case you already didn't know," began Dekkard, "the Security Committee has established a special investigatory subcommittee to look into how the New Meritorists obtained dunnite and other matters. I was tasked with being chair of the subcommittee."

Trujillo nodded knowingly. "The Premier informed me of that yesterday afternoon. The Council Guard and I will provide whatever information and assistance we can."

"Besides the small amount of dunnite found in the Meritorist armory, has anything else turned up that might bear on how the Meritorists obtained dunnite?"

"That depends on how you define it. The Suvion Commerce Banque will not provide the name of the individual or individuals who bought the large banque drafts deposited in the account of Capitol Services without an order from the Council. I imagine an order from the Security Committee would meet that requirement."

Dekkard wasn't totally surprised that Trujillo had followed up with the Suvion Commerce Banque, given that the small amount of dunnite found had to have come from Suvion Industries. He also knew that Trujillo often couldn't volunteer information. "What about the others—the Banque of

Siincleer, the Northwest Banque of Chuive, the Banque of Uldwyrk, or the Neewyrk Imperial Banque?"

"The Northwest Banque of Chuive declined to offer a name without a Council order. The others were not contacted because there was no physical evidence that might have been created in those cities."

"Once the subcommittee hearings have been approved by the chairman, I assume that information will be available to the subcommittee."

"Any security-related evidence or information in the possession of the Council Guard or known by guards is always available upon an official request." Trujillo offered a smile that Dekkard could only have called enigmatic.

The problem there, as Dekkard well knew, was that one had to know enough to know what to ask for, and to keep asking, because there was always more information. *Until suddenly there isn't.*

"Have any government investigators or law enforcement personnel located the empath that lured the rioters from Rivertown toward the Council?"

For the first time in weeks, if not months, for just an instant, Trujillo showed a hint of surprise. "I'm not aware of anything along those lines, but it might be worth inquiring. I appreciate your mentioning that possibility." He leaned back slightly in his chair. "Is there anything else you need?"

"Not at present, Guard Captain. I do appreciate all you and the Council Guards have done." *I just wish I'd known more sooner.*

"We all have done the best we could manage, Councilor, as have you."

"You're kind." Dekkard stood. "Once the subcommittee schedule is firmed up, I'll be in touch—or if I come across anything else of mutual interest." He inclined his head, then left Trujillo's office, leaving the door the way he had found it, just slightly ajar.

Gaaroll was outside in the main corridor only about a yard away.

Dekkard motioned for her to join him as he walked in the direction of the west doors to the courtyard. "What did you sense?"

"No strong feelings . . . maybe caution. I'm not sure."

"Could you tell what he felt just before I left?"

"His feelings didn't change."

"Then it's likely that he didn't feel relieved or upset, and that's good." As they neared the entrance to the councilors' dining room, Dekkard thought about waiting around to have lunch and seeing who, if anyone, might show up, then decided against it. He thought about taking another tour of the city and dismissed that as well.

What you really need to do is go home and work more on the hearings and what specifics you want each one to accomplish.

That was going to be hard, because he'd just been searching for anything, and just anything wasn't going to accomplish what was necessary.

He took a deep breath and kept walking.

49

WHEN Dekkard rose on Quindi morning, he could tell that the clouds and gloom had cleared. That meant that the air would be far less acrid, at least for a day or two, and that the sun might make some progress in drying up the mud remaining from the now-melted snow. As he shaved, showered, and dressed, he still worried about what sort of changes Hasheem might insist upon before approving the proposed hearings and the schedule.

When he entered the breakfast room, both Emrelda and Gaaroll had finished eating and sat sipping the last of their second cafés.

"I didn't ask last night," said Dekkard to Emrelda, "but how are things in Southtown?"

"Quiet for now. There have been more smash-and-grabs, and even some slash-and-grabs."

"Not enough food? Or marks for food?" asked Dekkard.

"It's the same either way," replied Emrelda.

"Guldoran Ironway is rebuilding the terminal market, and the ironway repairs should be complete very shortly."

"That won't help in Southtown or Rivertown."

"Not directly, but when more food can be shipped into Machtarn, prices should drop, or at least stop increasing." At Emrelda's expression, which clearly indicated that Dekkard didn't really understand, he added, "I know. When they don't have any marks to buy food, the fact that prices aren't increasing is meaningless, but any improvement is better than none."

Dekkard hurried into the kitchen, and then to the pantry, where he got three croissants from the cooler and set them on the kitchen counter. After fixing two cafés, he carried those to the breakfast room and set them on the table, then went back and got the croissants. "Is there anything of interest in *Gestirn*?"

"Not really. The Premier pointed out the obvious—that the damage caused by the New Meritorists couldn't be rebuilt overnight, and that while destruction was instantaneous, rebuilding took longer. I got the feeling that he was losing patience with the newsies."

"He did call them print-lice yesterday when we talked."

"Sometimes they are," said Avraal as she entered the breakfast room and took her seat, immediately reaching for her café. "And sometimes they're helpful."

"Not often," said Gaaroll. "Not to most folks."

Dekkard took a quick look at the story, but, as Emrelda had said, there was little beyond Hasheem's words and a few lines about the challenge facing the Council. He put aside the newssheet, sat down at the table, and took a sip of café.

He could understand Gaaroll's point. Most of what was in the news-sheets concerned those who weren't struggling for a few marks just to avoid going hungry. When the newssheets did have stories about the less fortunate, the stories were usually about riots, fires, and crime. But then, most of the stories about those better off were about crime or what officials, corporacions, councilors, or others weren't doing or weren't doing the way the newsies thought it should be done. Or about questionable councilors.

When Dekkard left the house to get the Gresynt, the morning air was the warmest in weeks, if not months, not quite springlike, but he could actually feel the heat of the white sun, possibly because the sky was the clear pale green that was so infrequent, given the usual omnipresent haze. Still, it wasn't warm enough that he was ready to do without his overcoat.

By a third after second bell, Dekkard had dropped off Avraal, traveled Imperial Boulevard without incident, and was guiding the Gresynt to a stop in his spot in the covered parking. On the walk to the Council Hall, he saw only a handful of workers on the roof of the Council Office Building.

When Dekkard and Gaaroll entered the Premier's floor office, Meldra said, "You'll have to wait, Councilor. He's meeting with Guard Captain Trujillo. It shouldn't be long."

"Thank you. Is there any news you can share?" Dekkard took off his overcoat and laid it on a side chair, thinking the bother of the overcoat was another reason he hoped true spring came before long.

Meldra smiled. "The workers will have most of the damaged councilors' offices ready by Unadi. The paint might be barely dry."

"That's encouraging. Anything else?"

"The eastern committee rooms will take longer." She looked past Dekkard. "Here comes the Guard captain."

Dekkard turned as Trujillo stepped out of the inner office. "Good morning."

"Good morning, Councilor. If you have a moment after your meeting, you might stop by."

"I don't know how long this meeting will last, but I'll come by afterward."

"If I'm not there, you might check in the records room."

"I will, thank you."

After Trujillo left, Meldra said, "You can go in now."

Dekkard nodded to Gaaroll, then entered the small inner office and closed the door. "Good morning, Fredrich."

Without speaking, Hasheem gestured for Dekkard to sit down.

Dekkard did, and waited for the Premier to speak.

Hasheem fingered his chin, then finally said, "In terms of background and content, I didn't find anything lacking in your rationale and choice of witnesses. In one case, I was able to add the actual name of the proper witness. There is a standard format for announcing each hearing and recording it, but you wouldn't have known that, and the committee staff takes care of it. You did a solid job."

"I tried to follow your example."

"There is, however, one other aspect to this, Steffan."

"What have I overlooked?"

Hasheem actually offered an amused smile. "In some ways, working with you is refreshing. I would suggest that the hearing appearance orders be typed up, authorized, and sent before the schedule is made available to the subcommittee and the full committee." Hasheem paused for a moment. "Meldra can type them up this morning, and I'll sign and seal them, and Meldra can dispatch them today."

Dekkard nodded, then asked, "How soon will it be before Northwest Industrial Chemical and Suvion Industries direct complaints and protests to you?"

"They will likely ask for more time, which you and I will deny. Then they'll claim that it would be most inconvenient for those witnesses at that time. How would you handle that?"

"I'd be tempted to say that we'd be happy to accommodate them at an earlier date, and that the delay in scheduling was caused by the New Meritorist attack on Machtarn."

"That would suffice, but don't elaborate. Except for something as momentous as the attack on the city, don't explain. It implies a weaker position or uncertainty, and, especially in dealing with corporacion functionaries or officers, the Council should never do that."

"There is one other aspect to this," said Dekkard.

"Oh?" Hasheem's voice was immediately wary.

"You may recall that the bulk of the funds received by Capitol Services were in the form of drafts on various banques, which concealed the source of those funds."

"I take it that you also want to send Council orders to those banques requiring that they divulge the purchaser."

"I do. That information will narrow who was behind that funding and will indicate who might be involved and who is likely not."

Hasheem nodded. "That's not unreasonable. Those funds were involved in a high crime. Have Guard Captain Trujillo make out the disclosure orders and submit them to me this afternoon." Hasheem then asked, "Do you intend to hold hearings continuously?"

"I'd thought to do so every week for the first few weeks, then assess the situation." *That way, I just might be able to keep Ulrich and possibly del Larrano off balance.* "Unless there's some pressing or procedural reason not to follow that kind of schedule."

Hasheem smiled. "The only reason for not doing so is that it will take a great deal of effort on your part—and from your staff and the committee staff. I have to admit that it could reduce the amount of attention that the newsies have been paying me."

"You could give them something else," suggested Dekkard.

"Oh? What might that be?" Hasheem's tone turned skeptical.

"Repeal the tariff on swampgrass rice. That won't require extensive hearings, although some Landors might insist as a delaying tactic. But repealing the tariff will make cheaper rice available to the poor by late spring. That's when food supplies will really get tight and prices will go up."

"That might have some merit. How do the farmworkers' guilds feel about that?"

"Those in my district don't have a problem. I doubt most of them would care, especially if you point out to the Advisory Committee that rice is only grown in great amounts in three districts. The Landors have been the big supporters of the tariff."

"What three districts? Or do you know?"

"Khasaar, Khuld, and Daal."

Hasheem fingered his chin again, thinking. Then he said, "Olaaf Sturmsyn votes mostly with the Commercers, so does Juurgan Presswyth. Jareem Saarh . . . Who knows? It might work."

"I do know that Saarh doesn't grow rice," Dekkard added.

"Let me think about it."

Dekkard knew that was the best he'd get out of Hasheem for the moment, but he did say, "I suggested it because it should have been done years ago. It's also something immediate and tangible that you can point to. From what I've overheard, a number of Commercers have been in favor of that for years."

"It has possibilities," Hasheem said evenly, then straightened in his chair. "I'll have Meldra type up those orders. Come back after lunch. You can proof them, and then we'll both sign them and have them sealed."

"I'll be here." Dekkard stood and inclined his head, then turned and left. He wasn't sure whether Hasheem approved or had just decided to let Dekkard investigate and become a corporacion target. But then, Hasheem could approve and still be happy Dekkard was the target.

Once in the outer office, Dekkard picked up his coat and nodded to Meldra, saying, "Thank you . . . in advance." He didn't say more until he and Gaaroll were in the main corridor. "After you tell me what you sensed, we'll head to the Guard captain's office." Not that the door to Trujillo's office was even ten yards away.

"No strong feelings. Just short black piles."

"No anger or worry?"

"Didn't sense anything like that."

"Thank you." *Is he resigned—or does he think that the hearings are a good idea?* Dekkard didn't know what to think, since Hasheem had been angry when Dekkard had first pushed for hearings on the dunnite.

Dekkard turned and walked up to the Guard captain's closed door.

Gaaroll said, "Someone's inside. Just one person."

"Then I'll knock. Stay close by. I'd really like to know what he's feeling."

"Can't always tell that. Not like the Ritten."

"You're getting much better."

"Doubt I'll ever be that good."

"You two are different. She'll never be able to sense as far as you can." Dekkard knocked, then eased the door ajar. "Guard Captain?"

"Come on in, Councilor."

Dekkard stepped inside and closed the door before taking the chair in front of the desk. "You suggested that I stop by."

"I did. The other day you mentioned an empath luring rioters from Rivertown. How did you come to that conclusion?"

"Because there didn't seem to be any other reason rioters would go in that direction. There aren't many shops and places for easy looting, and the distance is considerable. There was also the empath who killed Councilor Aashtaan."

"As I recall, she had personal motives," said Trujillo.

"She did," agreed Dekkard. "But who supplied her with the Council messenger's uniform and briefed her on how to find Councilor Aashtaan?

There was the Atacaman pepper dust. I doubt she came up with that on her own. That suggests the Meritorists had someone who works in the Council Hall—or did—as a sympathizer or informer, if not an actual Meritorist. I'm sure you already knew that." He looked directly at Trujillo.

"We surmised as much, but it wouldn't have been practical, and certainly not politically feasible, to interview, with an empath, every person who worked in the Council Hall or the Council Office Building. There wasn't any evidence that would have narrowed the number of people to interview, either."

"Especially since there are a score of isolates among staff, as well."

"Exactly," replied Trujillo.

"Someone had to have given the empath assassin the training necessary to deliver a death blast—and that someone had to be another empath, if not more than one. The Meritorists also used what appeared to be municipal steamers or lorries, and apparently no one ever questioned them. That's odd, unless they were accompanied by a skilled empath." Dekkard smiled easily. "I should have realized some of this earlier, as I'm sure you already did, but my training was more along the lines of preventing and countering direct physical threats."

"You've been more effective than anyone expected," said Trujillo. "That's why many are convinced you're more than a former security aide and a happenstance junior councilor."

"Someone at *The Machtarn Tribune* certainly thinks so."

"Is all of it true?"

"Each fragment is accurate, but taken out of context and pasted together to present an inaccurate depiction."

"How so?"

"I didn't seek to avoid sea duty out of the Institute. They encouraged me to take security training and later sent my name to the Council as a possible security aide. I didn't even know that was a way to fulfill the service obligation. A guild official in Gaarlak, whom I'd met exactly once, insisted on my being the recommended replacement councilor."

"What about the house in Gaarlak?"

"My wife bought it for us with the marks she received from her parents as a wedding gift. That's all the inheritance she'll ever have."

Trujillo shook his head. "I can see why you're not saying much. No one would believe that an heiress, even a disinherited one, would marry a mere security aide."

"She borrowed from her sister to pay for her empath training and started out as a parole screener."

"Where, might I ask?"

"At the prison in Siincleer."

Trujillo flinched almost imperceptibly, then said, "Councilor Schmidtz inquired whether any Council aides—or councilors—had permission to carry firearms. I told him that permission had never been granted to any aide or councilor. Then he asked if I'd dealt much with you."

"Implied association," replied Dekkard. "He's good at that, in his pseudo-genial way."

"Would you care to tell me why you think he made that approach?"

"He was on the Military Affairs Committee and has remained close to Councilor Palafaux, who remains on that committee and who is closely tied to Siincleer Shipbuilding. Both of them have to know that I have serious concerns about the ethical—or lack of ethical behavior on the part of that particular corporacion."

"You and everyone else. There's never been proof," said Trujillo mildly.

"It might be better said that witnesses and proof have largely and continually vanished. After Pietro Venburg was killed, Juan del Larrano issued a public statement that nothing would change. I see that as a warning. Unless the Council does something, I believe that witnesses and proof will continue to be hard to come by."

"What does all that have to do with Councilor Schmidtz and you?"

"Schmidtz was on the Military Affairs Committee, and about a month after I became a councilor, out of nowhere, Councilor Schmidtz introduced himself to me in the councilors' lobby. He said he had nothing in mind except to meet me. But he did so right after I saw Schmidtz with one of his former legalists in the main corridor of the Council Office Building, and my empath-in-training said that the legalist immediately manifested strong feelings. Schmidtz and the legalist must have talked, because less than a third later Schmidtz made his introduction. What makes that interesting is I'd seen Jaime Minz and the legalist—Fernand Stoltz—in the Council Office Building together earlier, without escorts. Stoltz is now a legalist for a firm that represents Eastern Ironway."

"While it all might be coincidence," said Trujillo, "I'm skeptical of a confluence of coincidences."

"So am I," replied Dekkard.

"Is there anything else?"

"The Premier approved the hearings and witnesses for the special investigatory subcommittee. He also approved my request to order disclosure of the purchasers of the large banque drafts to Capitol Services. He told me to convey to you that he would like your orders for them this afternoon for his signature and seal."

Trujillo smiled. "That won't be a problem at all. Knowing you,

Councilor, I had an idea that would be coming. The orders are ready for his signature. All I have to do is sign, date, and seal them and hand them to him."

"I appreciate your foresight, Guard Captain."

"The Council Guard appreciates your diligence, Councilor."

"There's one other request I'll be making of you and the Council Guard, and that is to provide an empath for the subcommittee hearings."

Trujillo raised his eyebrows as part of a questioning look.

"Someone—possibly several someones—has been lying about the dunnite and other matters, matters that have resulted in the death of fifteen councilors so far. That's the most since the times of the Silent Revolution. Don't you think the hearings merit an empath, possibly two?"

"The Guard can and will supply one empath."

"I appreciate that, Guard Captain. I believe I'll be able to obtain a second highly qualified empath. With two, there should be no question about their determinations."

"I can see where these hearings might present a heightened risk to the subcommittee chair. I assume you've also prepared for that?"

"As well as we can. Has the Justiciary Ministry made any progress in finding a possible Meritorist empath?"

"I suggested that they pursue that possibility."

"Then we'll just have to see." Since it was clear that Trujillo didn't have more to say, Dekkard smiled pleasantly and stood. "Thank you for keeping me informed."

"You're more than welcome, Councilor. Do be careful."

"We're working on that as well."

Once Dekkard was out in the corridor and well away from the Guard captain's office, he stopped and turned to Gaaroll. "What did you sense?"

"Not much, sir, except a sixth before you came out. His feelings got stronger then."

That had to be the ties between Minz, Stoltz, and Schmidtz. "Thank you. That's very helpful. Could you tell more than that?"

"Be a guess, sir."

"Guess," said Dekkard cheerfully.

"Worried, maybe."

"Now, since neither of us can eat for almost another bell, we'll walk around, and anyone we encounter, you try to sense not only how strong their feelings are, but what they're feeling. Don't guess. If you can't tell, say you can't tell. But if you have a hint, say what the hint is."

Gaaroll just nodded.

For the next two-thirds of a bell, the two walked back and forth along the open part of the main corridor of the Council Hall, while Gaaroll worked on trying to refine her sensing skills.

Then they returned to the entrance to the councilors' dining room, where Dekkard entered, and Gaaroll headed for the staff cafeteria.

Since it was Quindi, with the Council not in session and no committee hearings scheduled for the afternoon, Dekkard didn't expect to see many councilors in the dining room, but, as the server escorted him into the dining area, he did see a solitary councilor—Guilhohn Haarsfel. What surprised him more was that Haarsfel beckoned to him.

"Steffan . . . unless you have other plans, would you care to join me?"

"I have no other plans, not until later this afternoon, and I'd be happy to."

"Excellent. We haven't talked in quite some time."

"No, we haven't." *Not since Obreduur's death and Ingrella's selection as his replacement.* Dekkard took the chair across from Haarsfel. "Have you ordered?"

"I just did."

Dekkard looked to the server. "Café and the white bean soup."

The server took Dekkard's order, departing and almost immediately returning with the café. Then he headed for the kitchen.

Once the server was out of earshot, Dekkard said, "I really didn't expect to see many, if any, councilors here today."

"I just finished going over the floor schedule for Unadi's session with Fredrich. He told me you'll be heading an investigatory subcommittee dealing with the situation."

"That keeps the Premier out of the direct line of fire," replied Dekkard, "which will be particularly helpful if the subcommittee discovers corporacion mishandling or actual additional involvement with the New Meritorists by corporacion workers."

"Additional involvement?" Haarsfel frowned.

"Jaime Minz, the Northwest Industrial Chemical influencer," said Dekkard.

"That's right. Do you think there really might be others?"

"I seriously doubt that Minz personally loaded or stole the dunnite used to destroy the Security buildings and employed in the steam cannon shells."

"I meant at a higher level."

"That's what the subcommittee will be investigating."

"You'll need to proceed carefully, Steffan."

"I've been cautioned about that. The first hearings will be to look into how that much dunnite could have been obtained without it coming to anyone's attention, as well as how or why the late Security minister felt it necessary to insert in Security records a forged Navy report about a dunnite theft that the Navy has denied ever occurred."

"Axel mentioned that." Haarsfel paused. "You know . . . it's possible that you may never be able to resolve everything."

"The subcommittee will be able to discover how the dunnite could have been obtained and from where. Whether we can ever discover those who enabled it is another question."

"Quite so." Haarsfel paused as the server arrived with their orders, Haarsfel's being what had to be the hearty vegetable soup. He did not say more until he and Dekkard had sampled their lunch.

"I read that you have bought a house in Gaarlak. Was that an accurate report?"

"I assume you read the editorial in the *Tribune*. The purchase was accurate. The rest of what was printed was less accurate."

"Do you think . . . perhaps . . . ?" Haarsfel lifted his eyebrows rather than finish the implied question.

"That buying a house was too precipitous for a junior councilor? We asked each other that question, but the final decision was Ritten Ysella-Dekkard's, since she was the one who actually purchased it. We spent almost two weeks in Gaarlak, mostly meeting people, especially the key Crafters. We also opened banque accounts there."

"I hope the house wasn't just a token."

"It's a modest dwelling in a good area of Gaarlak. It needed work, and we hired an old friend of Axel's who's a very skilled cabinetmaker to make the repairs. He just finished, and we furnished the house enough so that it's habitable for the next time we go to Gaarlak."

"You're acting as if you'll be a councilor for a while."

Dekkard shook his head. "I'll be a councilor as long as people will vote for me, but I have to show that I have a stake in Gaarlak, and we had to make that commitment firmly and quickly."

Haarsfel chuckled. "I've never seen you do anything that hasn't been done firmly and quickly." He added, "Every once in a while, there are times *not* to act firmly and quickly."

"Do you think this is one of those times?"

The Craft floor leader's smile turned wry. "I've found that most of those times are recognized soon after one has acted quickly and decisively. If only foresight were as accurate as hindsight."

Dekkard laughed quietly. "If only . . ."

"If you were premier, Steffan . . ."

"If I were premier right now, Guilhohn, there wouldn't be anything

I could do that would work. I suspect that Fredrich is the only hope we have."

"That's an interesting observation."

"Fredrich is known to be cautious and careful. Some think possibly too cautious. The times require bolder action than he's comfortable with. I think, but don't know, that if various committee chairs press for a great deal more than he's comfortable with, and he reins them in, he *might* be able to guide the Council to do the bare minimum of what's necessary."

"And that would be?"

"Getting as many Meritorists as possible into work camps while executing those few who were the leaders . . ." From there Dekkard gave a quick summary, ending with, "Reforming military procurement to stop the massive cost overruns incurred over the past several years—"

"Why is that a priority?"

"Because it siphons off millions of marks from other needs. That means that those needs go unfunded or the Council has to raise taxes and tariffs, and that makes everyone unhappy, except for the few corporacions making excessive profits." Dekkard shrugged. "Those are what immediately come to mind."

"You'll pardon me if I doubt that those just came to mind, Steffan." Haarsfel's wry smile reappeared.

"I'm not that experienced yet. I need to think carefully."

"Would that some of your colleagues felt that way." Haarsfel took a sip of café, then said, "How did you and your wife find Gaarlak in the winter?"

"Colder than Machtarn," replied Dekkard, understanding that Haarsfel had learned what he wanted to know. Dekkard hoped what he said would lead Haarsfel in the direction that Dekkard felt was necessary. *You can't deceive him, and you can't force him. But you can try to guide him.*

The remainder of lunch dealt with comparisons of their respective districts, which Dekkard found interesting, because Haarsfel represented Kathaar, the headquarters of Kathaar Iron & Steel, to which Vhiola Sandegarde was the heiress, except Sandegarde represented Nolaan. *Because Sandegarde's family chose a less "industrial" city in which to live or because it was easier to get elected from Nolaan.* But then it could have been either, or something else.

As the two left the dining room, Haarsfel said kindly, "Don't let the *Tribune* get to you. They're attacking because you're effective and because you don't have powerful allies."

Because I passed one major piece of legislation I'm effective? "Do any Craft councilors have powerful allies?" Dekkard kept his voice wry.

Haarsfel chuckled. "None that I've ever heard of."

Gaaroll waited outside the dining room entrance.

"Did you get something to eat?" asked Dekkard.

"Crayfish burrito. Pretty good."

"I never saw that on the menu." And Dekkard certainly wouldn't have ordered it.

"Must be new," returned Gaaroll.

Dekkard began to walk toward the Premier's floor office. "I don't know how long going through all the papers will take, but at least you can sit down inside the office."

Gaaroll smiled. "Not doing anything else, and I'm getting paid."

"And you're learning to be a better empath. Remember, if you get certified, I can pay you more."

She nodded.

When Dekkard and Gaaroll entered the Premier's floor office, Dekkard immediately looked to Meldra.

In response, she lifted a folder and said, "This is the hearing schedule." Then she held up a noticeably thicker folder. "And these are the witness appearance orders that you and the Premier have to sign. The Premier said you need to proofread everything before the two of you sign them. You can sit at Baldemar's desk. He's out this afternoon."

"You typed all of that up already?"

She offered an amused smile. "That's what I'm paid for."

"It's still impressive," replied Dekkard as he took both folders and moved to the temporarily vacant desk.

A little more than a third later he'd proofread the contents of both folders and hadn't found a single mistake. *Meldra's paid not only to type, but to type well.* "I'm finished proofreading."

"He said for you to take them in when you finished."

Dekkard picked up the two folders and then opened the door to the inner office.

"Come in, Steffan. Shut the door."

Dekkard did so, then set the two folders on the desk.

"Guard Captain Trujillo already provided the disclosure orders, and I've signed and sealed them. We'll sign and seal all of these before we talk," said Hasheem. "You sign first, and I'll sign next and affix the Security Committee seal."

Dekkard got out his pen and opened the first folder.

By the time all the signing and sealing was complete, and the necessary documents turned over to Meldra for dispatching, a little more than a bell had passed.

Only then did Hasheem lean back slightly in his chair and say, "Guard Captain Trujillo told me about your insight concerning empaths."

"I wish I'd put those pieces together sooner."

"It wouldn't have changed anything. The New Meritorists have been most effective at concealing their capabilities."

"So have certain Commercers and corporacions," replied Dekkard dryly.

"Proving that will be even harder, Steffan, and possibly more dangerous." Hasheem's tone turned bleak with his last words.

At Hasheem's words, Dekkard had an idea. "There's one way we might make it easier."

"What do you have in mind?" Hasheem sounded interested, rather than cautious.

"What if you let it be known that, in response to any inquiries, while the investigatory subcommittee is an absolute necessity, politically, you'd like to resolve matters as quickly as possible and get on with rebuilding Machtarn?" Dekkard knew there was a definite possibility that that was what Hasheem might have in mind, if only as a fallback position.

"Implying that I'm letting you hold hearings to show that the Council means business, but that I'm inclined not to go too deeply?"

"More like letting them infer that," replied Dekkard.

"Certain corporacions are likely to say that I have the power to shut down such hearings and should."

"You might ask them how well that worked for Premier Ulrich, and point out that the *Khuld* mutiny was planned well before the elections, as were the destruction of fifteen Security buildings and the fire in Security headquarters."

Hasheem frowned.

"One of the key officers involved in the mutiny requested a transfer to the *Khuld* and received it. He arrived on board four months ago. I doubt that the Navy could process a transfer request in less than a month."

"You found that out from Councilor Konnigsburg? Interesting."

Dekkard found it more than interesting, but just sat and waited.

After a time, Hasheem said, "All that bears some thought."

"I understand."

"I believe you do, Steffan. I'll see you on Unadi morning. Enjoy your endday."

"We'll do our best, Fredrich." Dekkard stood and inclined his head, then left the inner office. Before leaving the outer office with Gaaroll, he said to Meldra, "Thank you for typing up everything so perfectly. I do appreciate it, and I hope you have a pleasant endday."

"Thank you, Councilor."

Once he and Gaaroll left the Council Hall and walked through the not-quite-springlike air of the courtyard and toward the covered parking, Dekkard asked, "Did the Premier have strong feelings any time while I was in with him?"

"No, sir. His feelings stayed the same. Short black piles."

"Thank you." Dekkard didn't know whether to be pleased or concerned, although he still worried that Hasheem would slowly choke off the hearings as they progressed. *But you'll just have to see.* Hasheem definitely understood that the Council had to at least appear to take some action, but how far Hasheem wanted to go was definitely uncertain.

"Sir? What are we doing next?"

"Oh, we're going to drive around Machtarn and see how the repairs are coming."

On the drive, Dekkard took his time, heading first for the Square of Heroes. From there he could see that the Palace gardeners had re-sodded the filled shell craters, and replaced some of the damaged hedges around the ornamental flower beds. Then he drove to the Guldoran Ironway station, which appeared to be operating normally. The outer brick wall of the new terminal market was about two-thirds completed, and a good score of masons were at work.

Then he took Imperial Boulevard to the harbor rotary. While Harbor Way itself was open, a good half of the structures on the north side for the first two blocks were gone. The others were either being taken down or being rebuilt, depending on the damage from the *Khuld*'s guns. Beyond the first two blocks the damage was scattered, almost random. All of the piers appeared usable, and vessels were docked at all the piers to the west of the first three. Dekkard assumed that the first three piers were vacant because utilities had not been restored and because common support items, such as gangways and steam cranes, had yet to be replaced.

Service barges remained around the grounded mass of twisted metal that had been the *Khuld*, with workers armed with cutting torches dismantling the wreckage.

By the time he finished his informal inspection tour, it was close to fourth bell, and he turned the Gresynt toward Baartol's office, not that he had that far to go.

When he and Gaaroll walked up the steps and into the outer office, the door to the inner office opened, and Avraal immediately walked out, followed by Baartol.

"I'm actually ready," she said with a smile.

"That you are," replied Dekkard with a smile of his own.

Baartol looked to Avraal. "Now that Harbor Way is open, why don't you two and your sister join Talenna and me for an early dinner at Rabool's. Say at fourth bell tomorrow?"

Avraal looked to Dekkard, who nodded, and then said, "We'd love to."

As she spoke, Dekkard realized that in the almost-year since he'd first met Baartol, he'd never known whether Baartol was married—let alone the name of his wife, assuming Talenna was indeed his spouse.

"Then we'll see you there," replied Baartol.

Dekkard didn't say anything until the three were in the Gresynt heading north on Imperial Boulevard. "How was your day?"

"Quiet. I set up a meeting for a business that needs to improve security for its owner."

"Competing against larger corporacions?"

"Not yet, but it might be possible before long. Carlos pointed out that they need to think about that before the fact."

It's an indictment of the Imperium that smaller businesses have to consider founder security in addition to better products and services. Dekkard didn't bother to say that because both Gaaroll and Avraal already knew it.

"How was your day?"

"I met with Hasheem." Dekkard gave a concise summary of his day, without revealing certain details he'd go over later with Avraal. Then he added, "Services tonight?"

"Of course. You need to be a dutiful councilor." She added with a smile, "Even if you're a bit of a Contrarian."

While not quite shaking his head, Dekkard just hoped that Presider Buusen's homily was good.

50

BY early afternoon on Findi, the air was almost spring-warm, but a haze had begun to dim the formerly clear green sky, possibly because there was no wind whatsoever. Dekkard had gotten out the target and was practicing with his throwing knives. Before long, the three women joined him.

While Dekkard's blades hit the target, they weren't always hitting close enough to where he'd aimed—almost certainly because of his recent lack of practice.

"I'm going to have to be more diligent about practicing," he said, to no one in particular. *Especially since it won't be long before word of the Security subcommittee hearings reaches certain corporacions.*

"We all are," replied Avraal.

"Least it's not freezing out now," muttered Gaaroll.

Emrelda looked sharply at Gaaroll, but didn't say a word.

"Is there anything new at the station that you haven't mentioned?" asked Dekkard.

"It's the same as always. Everyone's wondering when something will flare up in Southtown. I'd guess another few weeks, but that's more of a feeling than anything."

"How are things working out with Captain Kunskyn?" asked Dekkard, ignoring the sharp glance from Avraal.

"So far, so good. I have the feeling that Captain Narryt—Deputy Chief Inspector Narryt, now—had a talk with him before he left. Captain Kunskyn's always pleasant, but never more than that. I have the feeling that's the way it will be."

"Unless you encourage him," said Gaaroll.

Emrelda laughed cheerfully. "I like working with him, but that's it."

Dekkard couldn't help but think his relationship with Avraal had started exactly the same way, but he wasn't about to say that. What he did say was, "It's better that way. When are you going to become head dispatcher?"

"Who have you been talking to?" demanded Emrelda.

"No one. That's a total guess, but you didn't tell even Avraal when you made patroller first."

"You're going to be head dispatcher?" asked Avraal.

"It's not certain," said Emrelda almost reluctantly. "I've passed all the tests, and Roberto Kirchner is transferring to the Point Larmat district next month. There's no one else qualified at our station, but they could transfer someone else in from another station. That's why I didn't want to say anything."

"I'm sorry," said Dekkard. "I was just teasing."

Emrelda offered a smile that was part rueful and part amused. "You see so much, and you usually don't tease that way. So I assumed you'd found out somehow."

"It really was meant in jest," replied Dekkard.

"With you, Steffan, sometimes it's hard to know," said Emrelda.

As Dekkard was about to suggest ending practice, he saw someone walking under the portico toward them. Then he realized it was the Waaldwuds' nanny. "Here comes Sigourna Miletus."

Gaaroll said quietly, "Hope she's not quitting. That boy's so much better off with her."

"She's not upset," murmured Avraal, "but she is shielding her feelings. She wasn't doing that earlier, or couldn't."

"How are things going?" asked Dekkard as Sigourna neared.

"Tomas is doing much better. He's quite bright, and not just for a susceptible. In another year, he could go to the Susceptible Academy."

If you keep working with him. But Dekkard only said, "That sounds very promising."

"I think so. That wasn't why I came over. I wanted to thank all of you for being here. You helped so much with Sra. Waaldwud." Sigourna's eyes turned to Avraal, Gaaroll, and finally Emrelda. "And you showed me, just by being who you are, how much more is possible."

"Are you leaving, then?" asked Emrelda.

"Not any time soon. I have too much to learn. I'm working, as I can, with the Machtarn Empath Association to improve my skills. They think I might be able to learn enough to be probationer in a year, perhaps sooner."

"And the Waaldwuds?" asked Emrelda.

Sigourna smiled. "What little I've already learned has helped. Sra. Waaldwud insisted that I should be paid a little more, and Sr. Waaldwud agreed. His arm doesn't hurt so much now, and he's calmer. Anyway, I just wanted to thank you, and to let you know how everything is going."

"I'm very glad," said Avraal. "I hope you keep us informed of your progress. There are always opportunities for well-trained empaths."

"I will, but I have a lot to learn." Sigourna smiled again. "I need to get back, but I wanted to let you know." Then she turned and walked swiftly back the way she had come.

Once Sigourna was out of earshot, Dekkard asked Avraal, "What do you think?"

"If she keeps making progress, she could probably get a decent position in a number of areas. But she'll need to keep working."

"She will," said Dekkard. "All she needed were a few good examples of strong women."

"We'll see," replied Avraal, but Dekkard thought he glimpsed a hint of a smile.

After the four finished practicing, Dekkard put away the target and sharpened both his practice blades and the ones he carried all the time, while Emrelda and Avraal got ready for the early dinner with Carlos and Talenna Baartol.

Dekkard, Avraal, and Emrelda left the house at half before fourth bell, heading down Jacquez to Camelia Avenue, and west past Imperial University, where some students strolled about. When they reached Rabool's, situated on West River Avenue, a block north of and parallel to Harbor Way, Dekkard found a parking space less than forty yards from the door.

As the three walked toward the yellow brick structure with the polished brass double doors, a brawny figure wearing a brilliant green vest over a yellow shirt stepped forward, the same bouncer/greeter Dekkard recalled from his and Avraal's previous visit.

"Welcome to Rabool's," offered the greeter as he opened the door. "You're the Rittens and the councilor, right? With Sr. Baartol?"

"We are," said Dekkard.

"He just arrived. Enjoy your dinner."

Belatedly, Dekkard slipped two marks to the greeter.

"Thank you, sir. The gray Gresynt behind the dark green one, right?"

"That's right."

When Dekkard and Avraal stepped inside the bistro, he saw that the main dining area was about half full, but he didn't see the Baartols anywhere.

A server appeared. "You're looking for Sr. Baartol? He's in the side room."

"Thank you." Dekkard glanced in the direction she pointed, taking in the archway that he vaguely remembered. Then he, Avraal, and Emrelda made their way past several tables and through the archway to the smaller dining area beyond.

Carlos stood by a circular corner table in the side room talking to Rabool, a short muscular man with slicked-back gray hair in a silver-gray jacket.

Carlos turned and said, "Rabool, you might recall Steffan and Avraal. They used to be—"

"I remember. They tried to blow you up, too. How come they got Axel and not you?"

"Because they fired at him and three others first."

"They're still after you, I hear."

"They are," said Avraal coolly. "It's cost them dearly."

"Make 'em pay more," said Rabool. "Axel was worth a thousand of them." He turned to Carlos. "We'll talk later."

Once the bistro's proprietor walked away, Carlos gestured to the dark-haired woman with silver streaks in her hair. "Steffan, Avraal, Emrelda . . . my wife Talenna."

"It's good to meet you," replied Talenna. "I've heard about you all for years. It's a pleasure to actually meet you."

"We're pleased to meet you," returned Avraal.

Once everyone was seated, Carlos looked to Dekkard, then to Avraal. "Rabool was a little . . . stiff."

"The last time we were here, he told us to keep Axel safe," replied Dekkard. "We didn't." *Not that we could have.*

"He's angry," said Avraal. "He wants to blame us for not protecting Axel, but he has to know that it wasn't our duty once Steffan became a councilor."

"Besides," said Emrelda coldly, "if Steffan had refused to become a councilor, you two would likely be dead, and things would be even worse. Not that people are rational when they're hurt and angry."

Dekkard could have said that Emrelda knew that in a deep and personal way. He didn't.

"Rabool thought Axel was special," said Carlos.

"He was," agreed Avraal, "but he was also human. He didn't take Steffan's warnings seriously enough."

"From what I've heard from Carlos and others," said Talenna, "almost no one did. Why do you think they didn't, Steffan?"

"No one believed that the New Meritorists were well-organized. While Axel knew that certain Commercer factions tried to use the Meritorists to gain greater power over the Landor and Craft Parties, he didn't know, and none of us knew at the time, that the Meritorists were using them to obtain dunnite and weapons." Dekkard stopped, partly because he didn't want to say more and partly because he saw a server approaching.

"What would you like to drink?" asked a stocky woman possibly a decade older than Dekkard with hair too black to be natural and a pleasant voice.

Dekkard had Kuhrs; everyone else had wine, Silverhills white for Avraal, Emrelda, and Carlos, Giltridge red for Talenna.

In minutes, the server returned with their beverages.

"To an excellent meal," said Carlos, lifting his wineglass.

"To an excellent meal," returned the others.

Then everyone drank.

"What's the Giltridge like?" asked Avraal.

"It's heavier than Silverhills red," replied Talenna, "but without oakiness."

Avraal frowned, then said, "You're Talenna Torchio, or, rather T. Torchio, aren't you?"

"As a matter of fact," said Carlos, with a smile, "she is."

Dekkard was struggling to puzzle out who Talenna, or "T. Torchio," happened to be, when Avraal said, for Dekkard's benefit, since she clearly knew and Emrelda had nodded, "*Gestirn*'s food and wine critic."

Dekkard shook his head sheepishly. "I have to confess that I don't usually read that section of the newssheets."

Talenna offered a gentle and amused laugh. "Most men don't. Carlos reads it only because I'm writing it. I took over the column for my father, Tomas Torchio, but I'd been helping him for several years before he died. Even before that, the newssheet changed his byline from 'Tomas Torchio' to 'T. Torchio.'"

Meaning that the column was popular and that the editors knew she was writing most of it for her father near the end, and planned in advance for her to continue.

"That was some time ago," said Emrelda.

"A little over six years."

"Well," said Dekkard, "one of your columns led to my being able to find Riverfall lager here in Machtarn."

"Secondhand," said Avraal mischievously.

"Better than not at all," Dekkard archly replied.

"I liked the story about the Northcoast vineyards," said Emrelda, "and the shipping feud between Laanar and Gilthills."

"That one gave the editors heartburn, and there was a threat of legalist action by Laanar, but that died away when the Kastenaro family realized the more they threatened, the more sales they lost to Gilthills."

There was another pause when the server returned, a delay longer than it might have been because no one had looked at the menu, but Dekkard settled on the special, a chicken supreme with mushrooms and artichoke hearts, accompanied by truffled risotto, as did Avraal. Baartol opted for lamb chops with a mint-garlic-pepper glaze, while Emrelda and Talenna chose veal medallions in a mushroom and red wine reduction.

"That's quite a menu," said Dekkard after the server had taken their order and departed.

"It is," agreed Carlos, with a smile, "but Rabool makes an effort to keep the good food largely secret, except by word of mouth. Most people who haven't been here have no idea. He told me he wouldn't serve me ever again if Talenna ever mentioned or alluded to the bistro."

"I never have," confirmed Talenna.

"Steffan," said Carlos cautiously, "there have been some rather nasty editorials in *The Machtarn Tribune*. I know that they have to be scurrilous, but the facts . . . ?"

"The facts are largely correct, but what the editorials omit distorts the actual situation." Dekkard explained, ending with, "The problem is that it would take a full page of the newssheet to lay it out properly, and people would *still* get the wrong impression because they'd believe anything that convoluted was a fabrication or they'd take the facts that supported the editorial and discard the rest, and *then* they'd attack me for marrying into a wealthy Landor family."

"Which isn't true," interjected Emrelda. "Old and distinguished, but not wealthy."

Dekkard added calmly, "The next editorial, and there will be one, will be just as bad, if not worse."

For a moment, Carlos looked puzzled. Then he said, "You weren't in the Council buildings during the shelling. You were with me, and you said you'd given your staff the morning off."

"And my office was in that part of the Council Office Building that was hit. The Premier believed that the Admiralty would successfully intercept the *Khuld*. I didn't, and I thought the mutineers would use the light snowstorm as cover to get into position. I said as much to the Premier and hinted at it to the few other councilors I could trust. I'd be dead if I'd been in my office. How do you explain that? I'm either a coward or incompetent because I couldn't make the Premier understand."

"Why didn't you go to the press?" asked Talenna.

"I had no proof. Just calculations as to when the *Khuld* could arrive, what her guns could do, and my own belief that mutinous New Meritorists were superior in tactics and seamanship to the newest and best dreadnought in the fleet. Also, I would have revealed restricted information."

Carlos and Talenna exchanged glances.

"If what you say and what Carlos has told me are true," Talenna said, "the Commercers and the corporacions want you dead, and have made several attempts on your life—"

"Six," said Avraal. "That doesn't include the times where Steffan avoided assassins."

"Apparently the Premier was reluctant to listen," concluded Talenna.

"Until recently," said Dekkard. *Mostly.* "He just made me chair of a special Security Committee subcommittee investigating how dunnite from either Suvion Industries or Northwest Industrial Chemical ended up in the hands of the New Meritorists."

"Is that public yet?" asked Talenna.

"Not until after second bell tomorrow." Dekkard's voice was sardonic. "Unless *The Machtarn Tribune* publishes a snarky version earlier."

"Oh?" Talenna didn't sound that surprised.

"I'm fairly certain that Councilor Rikkard will make sure of that. If he hasn't already."

"That seems a rather obvious tactic," said Talenna.

"I'm not sure that the Commercers have other options, besides assassinations, right now," said Dekkard. "The deaths of Ivaan Maendaan and Erik Marrak and the removal of Oskaar Ulrich by the Imperador resulted in a lack of Commercer seniority on the Security Committee, and the Craft election victory precluded quiet Council action to stop an investigation. It wasn't planned that way. Marrak was transferred to Security in the last Council, and Ulrich stepped aside and made him chair. If the Commercers had won control of the Council, he would have continued as chair."

"That might have been why he was so upset when Hasheem allowed you to introduce the Security reform bill," said Carlos. "Hasheem is good behind the scenes. He's less effective when he has to be out front, although I've been surprised at his recent public statements."

Dekkard merely said, "So have I."

"Do you think he'll be able to maintain a strong public presence?" asked Talenna.

"It's been a change for him, but I don't see why not," replied Dekkard. "What do the newsies at *Gestirn* think?"

"They're skeptical."

"Aren't most newsies?" countered Dekkard. "About everything?"

"They wouldn't be newsies if they weren't," returned Talenna. "Not good ones, anyway."

Dekkard was about to speak when he saw a server approaching with a large tray. "That must be our food." Even as he spoke, he realized they were the only party in the side room, and he quickly added, "And sometimes I announce the all-too-obvious."

Talenna laughed, if quietly.

Once everyone had been served and sampled their fare, Carlos asked, "What do you think?"

"Excellent," declared Dekkard. "Tender and flavorful."

"I'm usually more of a pasta person," said Emrelda, "but these veal medallions are superb."

"They always are," said Talenna. "I won't have them anyplace else."

"What do you do," asked Dekkard, "if you eat in a bistro or restaurant, and it's terrible?"

"I don't write about it. People are more interested in where to go than where not. Besides, why would I waste a column on a place that I can't recommend and that will only make the people who own or like that bistro mad?"

Since no one else mentioned the Council or politics for the remainder of the dinner, Dekkard didn't, either, although he kept wondering why Talenna had wanted her husband to invite them to dinner. Talenna was a food and wine critic, and writing something about Dekkard wouldn't be in his or Carlos's interest at the moment. Since Dekkard couldn't see Talenna writing something that could rebound to hurt her husband, he knew he was missing something, especially since, even in questioning him, she had been warm and friendly. *But then good interviewers are that way and can still write viciously.*

After the main course, Carlos ordered Rabool's special marzipan flan for everyone. Dekkard had to agree that it was special, and not nearly so sweet as he'd thought it might be. Even so, although the dinner had been leisurely, Dekkard knew it wouldn't be a good idea to go to bed early.

After the two groups parted at the door to Rabool's, Dekkard didn't say anything until he, Avraal, and Emrelda were in the Gresynt and he was driving north on Imperial Boulevard. "Can either of you tell me what that was all about?"

"Carlos wanted you to eat at Rabool's, and Talenna wanted to meet you," said Avraal sweetly.

"That much was obvious. Why?"

"Maybe she was just curious. Carlos respects you. *The Machtarn Tribune* has taken a position that suggests they detest you. She could have wanted to see for herself. I could be wrong, but I didn't sense either calculation or anything dark."

"You're almost always right," replied Dekkard, "but I still worry."

"I do, too, a bit," admitted Avraal, "but Carlos has always been trustworthy, both for Obreduur and for us."

Dekkard nodded. "Talenna explains another thing. She's likely how

Obreduur managed to plant a few things in *Gestirn*." He paused. "Do you think he knew about her, or did he just send the information through Carlos?"

"He never mentioned her. He'd mentioned Carlos to me, but I never met him until we both went to Rabool's with Obreduur."

"Talenna has to be one of Carlos's sources. I'd wager that she's very sociable with the other newsies, and that she never mentions her husband's last name."

"It wouldn't make any difference," replied Avraal. "Carlos is a consultant, mainly to Craft interests and businesses other than major corporacions. Those aren't the people the newsies follow, unless there's a gory death or sensational scandal. I doubt if most of the newsies would even know about what he does."

"You have a good point there," said Dekkard.

"Sometimes I do, dear."

"More than sometimes," Dekkard conceded. "That's why I listen to you."

"Unlike so many men," said Emrelda.

"I think more men listen than you think," said Dekkard dryly. "They just don't admit it."

"And claim their wife's ideas and insights as their own," added Emrelda.

"I do use both of your insights," said Dekkard, "and sometimes I don't credit you. But I'm very aware that I wouldn't be where I am without all that Avraal has taught me." *I wouldn't even be alive in all probability.* "Anyway, we'll just have to see about Talenna."

51

The low walls of Averra are ancient, among the oldest in the world. They still possess a simple beauty of well-set stone that I cannot but appreciate every time I behold them. The granite has been polished by time, its color bleached from dark gray to a shade so slight that they seem white in a certain light. While they have been maintained, they have not been strengthened or reinforced in all the centuries since they were first constructed, and now the city proper extends far beyond those walls. That is as it should be, because walls embody an illusion.

Think of the massive edifices that enclosed Argorn. Did they in the end protect the Autarchs? Or were those walls so high and massive that the Autarchs could not see beyond them to discern that their collapse lay not in force of arms, or seemingly impregnable fortifications, but in their failure to understand that war is the most costly and visible form of conquest, whereas the most effective tool is the skillful management of commerce over time, so that triumph is scarcely noticed by the victor and seems inevitable to the loser because the loss occurs so gradually. When one cannot afford to train and maintain an army or a navy, walls are merely an empty reflection of past strength.

Yet Teknar's mercantilist monarchs still built walls to ring their city, before they were dispossessed by their own barons of commerce who, in turn, now build walled pleasure gardens to hold against those they have ensnared in their wage-slavery.

Walls, for various reasons, cannot long hold against enemies from without. Their effect is not so much to forestall invasion or thwart attacks, but to subjugate and subordinate those within such walls. Those who build walls create an illusion of power, because true power lies in those with the skill and strength to circumvent or crush those walls . . . as shown by the long and sordid history of Sudlynd and, to a lesser degree, of Aloor and the other barbarian domains of Nordum.

AVERRA
The City of Truth
Johan Eschbach
377 TE

52

O N Unadi morning, a light but pervasive haze hung over Machtarn, but the air was definitely springlike. Dekkard wore one of his heavier gray suits, and was glad he didn't need to wear an overcoat. On the way to drop Avraal off, he took a slight detour, heading west on Altarama Drive and passing the Obreduur house on the way to Imperial Boulevard.

After Dekkard brought the Gresynt to a stop outside Baartol's office, he said, "I should be here at half after fourth bell, but it could be a little later, depending on how long the Council session lasts. I can't start the subcommittee hearing until the Council is recessed."

"That's not a problem. I'm sure there will be something for me to deal with, and you've had to wait on me often enough." She leaned over and kissed his cheek before getting out of the steamer.

Dekkard waited until she entered the building before easing the Gresynt out of the parking area and heading for Imperial Boulevard. Once he approached the covered parking, he saw the Council was clearly back at work, with Council Guards in position both at the west doors to the Council Office Building and in their rooftop posts as well. The guards scrutinized Dekkard's and Gaaroll's lapel pins as they passed but said nothing.

Dekkard wasn't sure what to expect when he reached the top of the central staircase and turned east toward his office. As he neared the east end of the corridor, he could see that the walls above the chair railing had been recently painted. Still, the door to his office looked the same, as did the bronze wall plaque beside the door and bearing his name. When he opened the door, he smelled the strong, but not overpowering, odor of fresh paint.

"Good morning, sir," said Margrit cheerfully, seated behind a desk that seemed oddly off, and it took Dekkard a moment to realize that it was slightly lower.

"Good morning. I see you actually have a typewriter."

"We all do. Svard got here very early and took care of that, and basic supplies. The typewriters in the main staff office just needed cleaning and new ribbons. Our file cabinets were tossed around, but we didn't lose anything. Most of the damage was to your office and where my old desk was. Administration delivered new stationery less than a sixth ago." After a pause, she added apologetically, "Your old desk and everything in it was destroyed."

"There wasn't anything vital in it."

Roostof hurried out of the side office. "Good morning, sir."

"So . . . did you work here on Quindi and Findi?" asked Dekkard.

"Just Findi. They wouldn't let me in on Quindi. They were still painting."

"I did tell you . . ."

"I knew it would be easier." Roostof grinned. "I have a friend in administration. He gave me a pass. Have you seen your office?"

"No," admitted Dekkard.

"You should."

Dekkard looked at his senior legalist. "You've been up to something."

"Just look."

Dekkard opened the door and stepped inside. Immediately, he noticed the black-walnut desk, clearly in the modest but almost classic turn-of-the-century style. The three straight-backed chairs in front of the desk matched as well, as did the side table. "Where did you find this?"

"Buried in the back, spare furniture rooms in the lowest levels. Bettina and I had to do a little polishing."

"You didn't have to—" protested Dekkard.

"Sir," said Roostof gently, "you've saved my life twice, possibly three times, *and* you introduced the two of us. This only took us a few bells, and the staff porters would have had to bring up some furniture anyway." He paused. "The desk chair isn't quite a match, but it's close."

For a moment, Dekkard couldn't say anything. "It's beautiful, and so much more . . ."

". . . impressive," finished Roostof. "You deserve it."

"I can't thank you enough. Any of my colleagues who see it . . ." Then Dekkard shook his head. "Most likely won't even notice or understand just how good a piece it is." *Villem Baar might . . . possibly Konnigsburg.*

After a long moment of silence, Dekkard finally said, "I need to tell you both something. You'll have to keep it quiet until this afternoon." He explained about heading the special subcommittee, then said, "That was the possible special project I mentioned last week. The first meeting is this afternoon after the Council session."

"Chairing that subcommittee could be dangerous for you," said Roostof, immediately adding, "More dangerous, I mean."

"That's likely," replied Dekkard, "but this may be the last chance to catch those responsible for a deadly insurgency and put them before the

Justiciary. They're at least partly responsible for the death of Bettina's father." After a slight hesitation, he asked warily, "You didn't see anything about the special subcommittee in *The Machtarn Tribune*, did you?"

"No. I didn't see anything, but they might not want to print it, if you think about it."

"Oh . . . Because it would show that the Craft councilors are serious about getting to the bottom of matters?"

Roostof nodded. "Then, later—when you do something they think is a mistake, or could embarrass you—they'll point out why you shouldn't have been picked to head the subcommittee."

"That sounds more like the *Tribune*."

"The *Tribune* can be gratuitously vicious. We've seen that."

"Indeed we have. Is there anything else you need from me?"

"There are some papers you need to sign, basically affirming the replacement office furniture and supplies. We weren't charged, but you need to certify what we received. I haven't quite finished checking everything against the listing. I'll bring the papers in when I do."

"Then don't let me keep you, but . . . thank you, again, for this magnificent desk."

Roostof grinned. "The property superintendent was happy to let me take it. No one wants the older furniture. I don't think the desk was ever used. It was stored down there as a replacement, and just forgotten. It was still wrapped in kraft paper."

"I do appreciate the extra effort."

Roostof nodded, seemingly embarrassed. "I need to finish that inventory before the others arrive."

"Go." Smiling, Dekkard gestured. Then he turned to Margrit. "Have you gotten a huge stack of letters and petitions? Or has that stack yet to descend upon you?"

"It arrived just after I did. I'll bring it in when you're ready. There are two reports from Zenya Onswyrth—one for last week, and one for the week before. The only notice was from the Premier, but he also sent a message."

"I'll read the message and notice first, and then the reports from Zenya." Dekkard definitely wanted to know if there was any word about Jens Seigryn.

When Margrit left the inner office to get the mail, Dekkard studied the desk again, taking in the clean lines and the inlaid white oak corners. Then he walked to the side table and set down his leather folder before moving back to the again-replaced window and looking to the north, through the haze at the Palace. His eyes dropped to the serviceway just north of the building, now blocked off by a sturdy gate. *If only you'd known . . .* But as Haarsfel had said, hindsight was always so much clearer than foresight.

He turned and moved behind the desk, easing himself into the surprisingly comfortable chair, then checked the desk drawers, empty except for the stationery drawer, which held full-sized Council letterhead, notepaper, and note cards, along with the matching envelopes.

Margrit stepped through the door and walked to the desk. "Here is the message from the Premier, the notice, and Zenya's reports, along with the mail she sent from Gaarlak"—she laid a neat stack to the left side, before placing another next to that—"and here is the first stack of letters and petitions. I'll be back in a moment with the other three stacks."

The message from Hasheem was simple. He saw no point in meeting until Duadi morning, when Dekkard could report on the subcommittee meeting. The notice just gave the legislative schedule for the day, beginning with swearing in the four new councilors, and stated that a more complete calendar for the week would be sent out on Duadi. That made sense, since much of that would be scheduled later in the day.

He decided to read the reports from Zenya Onswyrth in the order in which she'd written them. The light snow that had concealed the *Khuld* from the *Resolute* and its battle group had been far heavier in Gaarlak and had dropped a half yard of snow, so that on that Furdi, Zenya hadn't made it to the office until noon, but since no one had come by even in the afternoon, she felt her absence hadn't been too negative. The sun was so bright that half the snow melted by endday. The day after the snow Josiah Arkham, a lieutenant at the main Gaarlak patroller station, came by and spent almost a bell talking to Zenya, wanting to know about Dekkard, before asking when she'd last seen Jens Seigryn. Zenya wrote that she repeated exactly what she said before and referred Arkham to Namoor Desharra. Arkham spent half a bell with the legalist. Dekkard shook his head. The rest of the first report consisted of what a handful of people who had come by the office had either asked or complained about.

Dekkard turned to the second report. The first part dealt with the people who'd visited the office, and the fact that a number had asked about Dekkard, and the fact that the weather was warming up and that the snow was melting. The next lines were what Dekkard had feared.

> . . . this morning's *Gaarlak Times* had a story. I've enclosed the clipping. Someone found a frozen body in the melting snow piled in the alley beside the Red Onion. It was Jens Seigryn. No one has come to see me. I talked to Legalist Desharra, and no one has come to see her, either.

Dekkard turned to the clipping. The story didn't say much more than Zenya had written, except that there were no marks or wounds . . .

No marks or wounds? To Dekkard, that sounded like someone had drugged Seigryn and buried him in the snow in a place where an intoxicated man might have fallen and where they knew no one would find him until spring. *Which is exactly what happened.* Dekkard wondered who might have been the one behind it. *Myshella Degriff? Gretna Haarl? Or someone else? Jens wasn't exactly without enemies.*

Unfortunately, Dekkard had no doubt that sooner or later that information would make its way to a certain newssheet and become part of another editorial about a questionable councilor. He took a deep breath, stood, and walked out into the side office, where Roostof was organizing papers on his desk. No one else had arrived yet, but Dekkard expected that, since Roostof had told the rest of the staff to arrive later.

"Svard?"

"Yes, sir?"

"I just got a disturbing bit of news from Zenya Onswyrth. Jens Seigryn was found frozen to death in the snow beside a tavern in Gaarlak. He's been missing for close to four weeks."

Roostof offered a puzzled frown.

"The questionable councilor," said Dekkard.

"Frig," said Roostof, if quietly.

"It's not as though he didn't have a fair number of enemies," said Dekkard, "but I thought you should know. Zenya found out from the *Gaarlak Times.* When she wrote the report last Quindi no one had contacted her, and that was several days after the story was in the newssheet."

"That sounds like the patrollers there think he drank too much and froze."

"Or they want everyone to think that while they investigate further. They might never find out what happened, but that won't stop a certain newssheet from implying a connection. Anyway, I wanted you to know." Dekkard paused, then asked, "How much of the files did we lose?"

"Almost none—except whatever was in your office and part of the entry office. Some files were rather dusty."

"So the only things we'll be behind on are letters and petitions, and whatever I add to the workload from the Security special subcommittee?"

"Unless there's something we're both missing."

"Which is likely, the way things have been going." Dekkard's tone was sardonic. Then he walked back to his office and extracted several sheets from the folder, containing the approved hearing schedule and the witnesses ordered to appear, and took them to Margrit. "I'm sorry to drop these on you, but I'll need five copies of each before I leave for lunch and the Council session."

"That's no problem, sir. I've almost finished sorting the mail and petitions."

Dekkard returned to his office. He finished reading Zenya's second report and more than half of the mail by the time the rest of the staff appeared and he went out to greet each one personally. After that, he read through the rest of the mail and turned it all over to Roostof by half before noon. Then he gathered together all the schedules and witness lists that Margrit had typed up for the subcommittee meeting and slipped them into his gray leather folder.

Minutes after that, he and Gaaroll walked down the main corridor to the center staircase. At the top of the staircase, he saw Breffyn Haastar with a trimly muscular and graying man in a charcoal suit without a security or staff pin, whom Dekkard did not recognize.

"Good morning, Breffyn."

"The same to you, Steffan. I'd like you to meet Arturo Escalante, the councilor-select from Silverhills. Arturo, this is Steffan Dekkard."

"I'm pleased to meet you," replied Dekkard immediately.

"And I, you," replied Escalante. "Breffyn has told me about you."

"If what he said is favorable, remember that Breffyn is kind at heart."

"Not when it comes to character. I've known him long enough to understand when he's polite and when he means it."

"We're going to meet Kharl in his office before lunch," said Haastar, "but I wanted to introduce you two."

"I likely wouldn't be here," said Escalante, "if you hadn't been selected first."

The charcoal suit and Escalante's words cued Dekkard. "I have to confess that I've never met a Landor isolate, although I'm married to a Landor empath."

"I can't match you on that," replied Escalante, returning the smile.

"We'll see you later," said Haastar cheerfully.

Dekkard was halfway down the central staircase before he said, "That was interesting. Did you sense anything unusual from Councilor Haastar?"

"He felt as pleasant as he sounded," said Gaaroll. "The isolate councilor . . . got the feeling he's not near as strong as you."

"You can tell that?"

"Sort of. With you, it's like there's a wall. No feeling, nothing except you're there. With him, it's like . . . I can't say, except there's something . . . just can't tell what."

"So you might actually be able to identify individual isolates by their barrier characteristics?"

Gaaroll shook her head, then said, "Didn't think there were any Landor isolates."

"Landors don't regard either empaths or isolates that highly," replied Dekkard, knowing that Escalante's selection suggested that he came from a powerful family. "He might have been selected because few other qualified Landors in Silverhills wanted to be a councilor after the deaths of the Fader brothers, one right after the other."

Gaaroll snorted.

While he saw several councilors at a distance on the way to the Council Hall, including Villem Baar and Eyril Konnigsburg, none were close enough to exchange greetings.

He had just given Gaaroll instructions on when and where to meet him and was about to enter the councilors' dining room when Gaaroll said quietly, "Sir . . ."

"Steffan . . ." came an unfamiliar voice from behind.

Dekkard turned to see an older councilor hurrying toward him, hampered slightly by a limp.

"Leister Milyaard, in case you don't recall."

"We haven't officially met, but I do recall," replied Dekkard, who knew very little about Milyaard, except that he was from Nuile, had been a guild steward for the mineworkers, and had supported Mardosh as the Craft candidate for premier. That last fact made Dekkard wary.

"You never can tell. I was here a year and didn't recognize Paarkyn Noyell." Milyaard offered a crooked grin and brushed back a few strands of his thinning black hair. "Don't know as he's ever forgotten, but you can't tell with him. Since you're alone, I was hoping we could have lunch."

"Of course." Dekkard gestured to the maître d'hôtel and said, "Two, please."

"This way, Councilors."

As Dekkard entered the dining area, he saw Ingrella, in a quietly animated conversation with Elyncya Duforgue and Traelyna Treshaam. He also saw Baar and Konnigsburg together at a table, as well as several other Commercers and Landors.

Once he and Milyaard were seated and had ordered, the older councilor said, "I wanted to have lunch with you because Gerard Schmidtz has been inquiring about you, and because you've definitely pissed off the *Tribune*." Milyaard chuckled and added, "There must be something else about you beyond the fact that you're the first isolate councilor and were behind the

Security reform bill." He held up a hand. "I got your biography from Tomas Pajiin. He finds you impressive, but couldn't or wouldn't explain."

"Tomas is a good man," said Dekkard. "We're on the Security Committee together."

"I know. That's why I asked him."

Dekkard shrugged. "It might be that I'm such a new councilor that I look into assumptions that are taken for granted by more experienced councilors."

"Such as?"

"There wasn't any statutory basis for the Security Ministry's Special Agents." That had come up in Dekkard's research, and it addressed the point without giving anything newer away.

"Tomas said you were worried about that light cruiser when no one else was."

"That's not quite true. Eyril Konnigsburg was also worried. We're both Military Institute graduates, although as a former admiral he has much greater expertise."

"You avoid danger in an almost uncanny fashion, at least according to the *Tribune*."

"That's what I was trained to do, before I became a councilor." Dekkard smiled. "You're now chair of the Transportation Committee. How is that going?"

"We were just getting organized and setting up hearings when the last attack on the Council occurred."

Dekkard had wondered, given that Haarsfel had briefly been chair before leaving the committee and handing the position to Tedor Waarfel, who'd died in the first shelling of the Council Office Building. Dekkard couldn't imagine Waarfel standing up to the senior Landor, Saandaar Vonauer, or to Kaliara Bassaana, who would have been chair if the Commercers had won the election. "You don't have many experienced Craft members."

"Traelyna Treshaam's a sharp woman."

Dekkard noted that Milyaard didn't mention the other Crafter on the committee, Wilhelm Ghossaan, from Storz, who was also chair of the Commerce and Treasury Committee.

"I understand that you know Kaliara Bassaana," said Milyaard.

"She and I are both on the Workplace Administration Committee. We've had several conversations, most of them initiated by her."

"No fragile fern there," replied Milyaard. "Has she ever mentioned anything about transportation?"

"She once intimated that she wasn't exactly pleased with Eastern Iron-way," replied Dekkard.

"I understand there's a long history there, but I have no idea what it is, and no one else seems to know . . . or if they do, they won't talk about it. I asked her what she thought of you."

"And?"

"She said you were bright, personable, and knowledgeable. Able to carry on an intelligent conservation while revealing nothing, if that suited you. What do you think of her?"

"I could make the same observation, except she's better at it, and far more experienced." Dekkard paused, then said, "You mentioned Gerard Schmidtz. Exactly what was he interested in?"

"Here comes our server. I'll tell you in a minute."

Dekkard ordered the duck cassoulet, while Milyaard chose the three-cheese chicken. Both had café.

Once the server departed, Milyaard began, "We were talking about Gerard Schmidtz. After the elections he lost his seat on the Military Affairs Committee, and Kuuresoh kept his seat because he was entitled to a major committee and Gerard was ranking Commercer on Public Resources."

"That didn't set well with Gerard?"

"Who knows? He's always genial, unless he doesn't think anyone is looking. We talk in passing, but he never says much. That's why I was surprised when he asked if I knew you in more than passing."

Dekkard just nodded, although he got the impression that Milyaard and Schmidtz were closer than Milyaard was admitting, then took a bite of the cassoulet. "You know one of Schmidtz's former legalists on the Public Resources Committee was quite close to Jaime Minz?"

Milyaard frowned, then said, "Minz? That name is familiar, but I can't place it."

"Minz was a security aide for the Security Committee when Ulrich was chair and premier. After the election Minz became an assistant director of security here in Machtarn for Northwest Industrial Chemical, effectively an influencer. Does that chime with anything?"

"Probably should, but I can't say it does."

Dekkard quickly summarized the background on Minz, then added, "I saw Schmidtz several times with the former committee legalist, and the legalist several times with Minz in the Council Office Building."

"Interesting, but it doesn't prove anything."

"No, it doesn't. Oh . . . and the legalist is now working for the firm that represents Eastern Ironway, which might be of interest to you."

"Would I know the legalist?"

"I have no idea. Fernand Stoltz. He was the chief legalist for the Public Resources Committee, and he's now with Paarsens and Alvara."

"That name is sort of familiar." Milyaard took several bites of his meal.

Dekkard wished Avraal were nearby, because he had a hard time believing Milyaard was that clueless. Wishing didn't make it so, and he asked, "How is your chicken?"

"About the same as always. Good, not great. Your duck?"

"Better than usual, but not great. Maybe that's because I haven't had it in a while."

"That could be." Milyaard took a sip of café, then said, "Can you think of any reason why Gerard would be interested in the Security Committee?"

Dekkard could immediately think of several, but replied, "Indirectly, Security affects every district, and certain districts more directly. Offhand, I can't think of anything we have on the schedule or even on proposed schedules that would affect Obaan." *Possibly Schmidtz personally, but that remains to be seen.*

"He seemed more interested in you, not the committee."

"Outside of exchanging greetings, I've only talked to him once, very briefly, and that was over a month ago. The only legislative proposal I've been involved with was Security reform, and that affected everyone, but his district less than most."

"That does seem odd. Gerard has always seemed focused on what's best for him or his district."

"Did he mention anything in particular or even in general?" Dekkard tried to express puzzled curiosity.

"He seldom does that, unless he knows you already know something. He just talks in generalities."

"Maybe I upset him that one time. I asked him if he had been disconcerted when Ulrich decided that Military Affairs would hold hearings over the Kraffeist Affair, rather than Public Resources, since the Naval Coal Reserve was under his committee's jurisdiction."

"He didn't mention it." Milyaard paused. "He *did* say it was unusual for a junior councilor to present a major reform bill. I'd wondered that myself."

Dekkard laughed. "That was simple enough. I drafted a bill, or rather my legalists put my ideas in the proper language and form, and offered it in committee. It just happened to fit in with what the Premier wanted, although we'd never talked about the proposal. No one else wanted to take the lead. It was an odd situation that likely won't occur again."

"That was it," said Milyaard. "He said that odd things always happened around you, and asked if I knew anything about why."

While Dekkard doubted that Milyaard had suddenly recalled what Schmidtz had said, he replied, "There have been lots of odd occurrences lately. Two councilors—brothers—died in two separate shellings on the Council Office Building. And how likely was it that an almost obsolete light cruiser escaped the newest dreadnought in the Navy to create so much damage?"

"When you put it that way . . . But there's still those editorials in the *Tribune*."

"The *Tribune* left out all the boring details that would have explained everything, like the fact that the Council was so short of security aides that it contacted the Military Institute and asked for the names of recent graduates. I didn't push for it; the Navy strongly encouraged me to interview." Dekkard smiled and added, "And when the Navy strongly encourages a very junior lieutenant to do something, any junior lieutenant with a dram of brains responds positively to that encouragement. I'm not going to go into all the other boring details because we'd be here until second bell at the least."

Milyaard smiled pleasantly. "That makes a great deal of sense."

"It's also true. Ask Councilor Konnigsburg, if you like. He's a former admiral."

"I'd heard that."

The last few minutes of the luncheon dealt with speculation about what Hasheem might say at the beginning of the Council session.

Then Dekkard excused himself to use the facilities before going to the Council chamber. Although he'd definitely had enough of Leister Milyaard for a good while, he still found himself puzzled by the conversation and wondering exactly what the relationship between Milyaard and Schmidtz might be. There were a few people he could trust who might know.

The first was Ingrella Obreduur, and since her desk on the floor was next to his, and since she, Elyncya Duforgue, and Traelyna Treshaam had left the councilors' dining room before he had, Dekkard decided to start with her.

Although it was more than a sixth before first bell, Ingrella was already seated, except the nameplates had been moved to reflect the changes in seniority as a result of the deaths of Safaell and Andros and she sat at Pajiin's former desk with Dekkard seated, again, to her right.

Dekkard smiled and asked, "Are you creating a Craft women's caucus?"

"No, but it might not be a bad idea."

"Possibly overdue," replied Dekkard. "How was your lunch?"

"Very pleasant. How was yours?"

"Puzzling. Leister Milyaard asked to join me. I still can't figure why. He told me he wanted to have a chance to talk because of the editorials about me in the *Tribune* and because Gerard Schmidtz had asked about me. Why would Schmidtz ask Milyaard about me?"

"Leister is a very nice man, and he likes to be pleasant to everyone, but his curiosity and his willingness to share what he knows are not always circumscribed by prudence."

"So, you think Schmidtz . . . ?"

"That would be my guess, and I'm fairly certain it would have been Axel's as well."

"What are your thoughts about Pohl Palafaux?"

"What are yours, Steffan?"

"I know him even less than Schmidtz, but I don't think I'd ever want to rely upon him."

"Trust those feelings." She paused, then said, "Hasheem told me about your special subcommittee."

"And?"

"He doesn't want you to go as far as you'll need to. I didn't tell him that. Neither should you." She looked up past Dekkard and said, "Here comes Tomas."

As Pajiin approached, when he saw both Ingrella and Dekkard he offered a puzzled glance, then abruptly nodded and moved to take the desk bearing his name. "Do you think this will be a long session?"

"Not too long, but more than a bell. There will be at least three votes."

"You have any surprises planned for the subcommittee meeting?"

"I wouldn't think anyone would be surprised. I've made no secret of my concerns."

"When he finds out, Rikkard won't be happy."

"That's a change?" asked Dekkard sardonically. He didn't say more because the lieutenant-at-arms appeared on the dais and, as first bell chimed, thumped his heavy ceremonial staff.

"The Council will be in order," declared Hasheem, pausing for silence, then continuing. "I have a few announcements for the Council before we proceed with the swearing in of new councilors and the scheduled legislative business. Beginning immediately after this Council session, various committees will hold meetings to discuss forthcoming hearings investigating the recent insurgency. They will also investigate possible links within Guldor to the New Meritorists. A complete calendar for the remainder of this week will be available no later than second bell tomorrow morning."

Having finished the more routine announcements, Hasheem cleared his throat. "Would the lieutenant-at-arms escort the councilors-select to the front of the chamber."

Dekkard watched as the four lined up in front of the dais. According to the Premier's earlier notice, the four councilors were: Gaaston Caarvera, the Craft replacement for Julian Andros; Arturo Escalante, the Landor replacing Ellus Fader; Elias Mhuraan, the Craft replacement for Gerhard Safaell; and Deityr Waeltyr, the Commercer replacement for Maximillian Connard.

Of the four, Dekkard only knew Escalante, and only because of the introduction earlier that morning by Breffyn Haastar.

The swearing in was brief, and the four left the front of the chamber to go to their desks.

Then Haarsfel, as majority floor leader, took the lectern. "The next matter is a vote on the acceptance of the Premier's nomination of Hans Tauryn as Minister of the Treasury." The final tally on the vote was forty votes for, twenty-six against, with all the Craft councilors voting for, all the Commercers against, and eleven Landors for and seven opposed.

The second vote was on the nomination of Kaastor Perez as Minister of Public Safety. Before receiving the material circulated to all councilors, Dekkard had never heard of Perez, although he'd been the regional administrator of Security and then of Public Safety for northeast Guldor. The vote totals were the same for Perez as they had been for Tauryn.

After the votes for the two nominees, it was almost second bell, and the last legislative business for the day was the vote on the supplemental appropriations measure to cover damages to government buildings from the *Khuld* attack. Since the details of the comparatively limited funding had been worked out between the three floor leaders, the proposal was presented on a straight up-or-down vote, without debate and without allowance for amendments. The final vote was sixty in favor, and six opposed. All those opposed were Landors.

Having announced the results of the supplemental appropriations, Hasheem took the lectern again. "There being no further business, the Council is recessed until first afternoon bell on Furdi."

Dekkard stood and looked to Ingrella. "Military Affairs Committee meeting?"

She nodded.

"Best of fortune."

"Thank you. I'd say the same, but fortune alone won't suffice."

"I think you're saying I've got a more than difficult task in front of me."

Ingrella just smiled before she turned.

Gaaroll waited for Dekkard outside the councilors' lobby.

"Have you sensed any strong feelings from councilors leaving the chamber?" asked Dekkard.

"No, sir. Councilor Obreduur said, 'Good day,' and called me by name, though."

"She's a good legalist, a good councilor, and a good person."

"Can't sense much from her. Keeps her feelings under control."

That didn't surprise Dekkard.

He was the first one to the committee room, where he told Gaaroll to wait outside and sense the feelings in the chamber. He didn't see Hasheem, who, as chair, had the right to observe the meeting. But then, Dekkard had the feeling that Hasheem wanted to keep as much distance from the subcommittee as possible, at least for a while. Since no one else had arrived, Dekkard put copies of the schedule and witnesses at the place of each subcommittee member. He debated taking his normal seat, but decided against it, and set his folder down on the curved desk at Hasheem's usual place. *You are the chair of the special subcommittee.*

The next councilor to arrive was Breffyn Haastar, followed quickly by Villem Baar and Pajiin.

Once everyone was seated, Dekkard said, "The subcommittee will come to order." *Not that it's in the slightest disordered.* "You each have a copy of the first set of hearings and the witnesses that have been scheduled. Please take a few minutes to read through them. Then you can ask questions or make observations or suggestions."

Dekkard said nothing as the other three councilors studied the papers. When all three had clearly finished reading, he turned to the most senior member of the subcommittee and asked, "Do you have any questions, Councilor Haastar?"

"There are only two corporacions who produce dunnite. Is there a specific reason why you have naval witnesses scheduled before witnesses from either corporacion?"

"I felt the subcommittee should have the full background on the procurement and shipping procedures required by the Navy before hearing from corporacion witnesses."

"You've scheduled Guard Captain Trujillo. What does he have to do with the matter?"

"The Council Guards were the ones who observed the attack and who gathered evidence afterward," replied Dekkard, which was true, but not the only reason for Trujillo's appearance, if later in the schedule.

"I have no further questions."

"Councilor Pajiin?"

"I notice there aren't any witnesses from the Ministry of Public Safety. Is there a reason for that omission?"

"At present, there's no indication that any are pertinent to the sub-committee's purpose. If testimony from those ordered to appear reveals relevance of specific patrollers or Public Safety officials, then the subcommittee can order them to appear."

"Thank you. That's all I have."

"Councilor Baar?"

"The subcommittee has ordered the appearance of various officials from both Suvion Industries and Northwest Industrial Chemical. I understand the rationale for making inquiries of those in charge of production, transportation, storage, and maintaining physical security of dunnite. But you also have ordered the vice-presidente of political affairs of Suvion Industries to appear as well. Can you explain your reasoning?"

"That rationale is restricted information. I will be happy to reveal that, provided that all members of the subcommittee recognize and agree not to disclose that information to anyone outside the subcommittee—except for the chair of the full committee—until after the testimony of the witness. Premature disclosure of that information can result in discipline by the full Council. Is that understood?" Dekkard looked at each Councilor, ending with Baar.

"Yes, Sr. Chairman," replied Baar, almost simultaneously with the others.

Dekkard paused, then said, "The vice-presidente of political affairs is one Oskaar Ulrich, formerly premier of the Council. While he was chair of the Military Affairs Committee and before he became premier he established a business called Capitol Services. That business was operated by one Jaime Minz. Capitol Services funded and organized the group that built the steam cannon and projectiles used in the first shelling of the Council Office Building. The explosive in those projectiles was dunnite. A sniper assassinated Minz outside the District Justiciary Courthouse before he was officially charged. After the last election, Minz was hired by Northwest Industrial Chemical as an assistant director of security, although all indications are that he was effectively an influencer. Prior to that, Minz was a security aide who also accompanied Chairman Ulrich on several official inspection trips—*after* Ivaan Maendaan was killed in the Summerend riots, and Ulrich became senior on the Security Committee." Dekkard looked to Baar. "Does that address your question, Councilor?"

"It does, Sr. Chairman."

Dekkard thought Baar looked uneasy, but he couldn't be sure. "Do you have any other questions?"

"I do. Can you tell us how long the Premier has known that information?"

"I don't know precisely. The information about Capitol Services was discovered in stages. Premier Obreduur knew that former Premier Ulrich had founded Capitol Services and that Jaime Minz was operating it. The information linking the group who did the shelling to Capitol Services was discovered through the investigations led by the Justiciary Ministry, the Ministry of Public Safety, and the Council Guard. I'm under the impression that much of that was discovered by the Council Guard soon after the first attack, but that is something that I cannot absolutely confirm."

"How did you come to know this?" pressed Baar.

"It seemed prudent to ask Guard Captain Trujillo what he knew before making the hearing and witness schedule. I knew about Minz's connection with Oskaar Ulrich when we were both security aides, but, at that time, I knew nothing about Capitol Services, or that it even existed. Minz sent me a letter when he went to work for Northwest Industrial Chemical."

"Did you inform Premier Hasheem?"

"I informed him of what I knew before he became premier. He told me, at that time, the committee could not investigate without more evidence. The investigations following the second attack on the Council convinced him that hearings were warranted."

"Thank you, Sr. Chairman."

Dekkard had the feeling that all three councilors were a bit stunned by the totality of what he'd revealed, although he'd shared some of it with Pajiin and Baar. *But you've lived with all of this for months, and it's sometimes easy to forget that there's a lot most councilors don't know at all. The few Commercers—and Mardosh—who know don't want anything to come out.*

Dekkard paused, then said, "As you may have seen on the schedule, the first hearing is scheduled for Quindi, the second for next Unadi. The subcommittee will meet again on Tridi morning at fourth bell. This will give everyone time to think over the issues and what specific information you believe is necessary." He paused again. "Are there any other questions or matters anyone would like to bring up?"

The other three councilors all shook their heads.

"Then the subcommittee is recessed until Tridi morning."

Dekkard remained seated for several moments.

Haastar leaned toward him and said quietly, "When this gets out you'll need both your wife and the other empath around you all the time. Be *very* careful." Then he nodded and stood, saying in a louder tone, "Until Tridi."

Dekkard gathered his papers together and stood.

Pajiin gave him a rueful smile and said, "Better you than me, Steffan," before he turned and left the chamber.

As Dekkard had suspected would be the case, Villem Baar waited at the back of the chamber. Dekkard joined him.

"Steffan, I'm beginning to see why you didn't say more to me. I should have put some of those pieces together, but . . ."

"Villem, you weren't here when some events happened, but I tried to give you as much insight as I was allowed, given the restrictions placed on me."

"You've been trying to get to the bottom of this since you became a councilor, haven't you?"

"Even before that," Dekkard admitted.

"The facts suggest that Oskaar Ulrich and others . . ." Baar shook his head, then continued, "But how could they even conceive of something like that?"

"Would you want to be the first Commercer premier in generations to lose power, not to the Landors, but to Crafters? I'd wager that it wasn't just about power, but about pride, and a belief that anything justified stopping the Crafters from gaining control of the Council."

"I suppose that makes sense to some people. I just wouldn't have thought that way."

"Do you think Jaradd Rikkard might?"

"It's possible."

More than possible. But Dekkard only said, "It's pretty clear that some Commercers did, like Lukkyn Wyath and Isomer Munchyn."

"Munchyn?"

"The former Treasury minister who tried to kill Premier Obreduur instead of turning in his resignation."

"Oh. I knew about the attempt, but I didn't recall his name."

"When that happened," said Dekkard, "you were likely being a diligent legalist far less interested in government intrigue."

"You're right. I was trying to finish a brief on a case dealing with asset misrepresentation. I did wonder why—Munchyn, was it?—would go to such extremes."

"Because he would probably end up stateless, without assets, or in a work camp, if not worse, for abusing his office by ordering tariff inspectors to make false assessments to benefit a Commercer trading company."

Baar nodded. "I will keep everything that transpired in the committee room to myself."

"You can tell Gretina the purpose of the hearings, that we're looking into how all that dunnite ended up in the hands of the New Meritorists, and that Minz was involved. That's public, although not that widely known."

"I think you specialize in assembling public information that's not widely known."

"Eyril Konnigsburg has said something similar," replied Dekkard.

"He's right. I'll see you on Tridi . . . if not before."

"Until then." Dekkard let Baar precede him out of the committee room, then followed, but stopped where Gaaroll waited.

"Sir?"

"In the last few minutes, did Councilor Baar have strong or strange feelings?"

Gaaroll shook her head. "About a third ago, though, all of them but you got really stronger feelings."

"All of them?"

"Yes, sir."

"Good, and thank you. Now, we need to head back to the office. Keep looking for strong feelings or danger."

A sixth later, when Dekkard stepped into his office, he saw two stacks on his desk. The larger stack was responses. The smaller stack looked to hold perhaps five sheets of paper. Dekkard settled himself behind the desk and immediately looked at the shorter pile, then smiled as he realized it was the listing of furniture and office equipment Roostof had mentioned earlier. He immediately read through the inventory methodically, noting that his desk was described as "old desk, value negligible," with a similar description for the three straight-backed chairs in front of the desk.

Once he signed the list, he returned it to Roostof, saying, "Apparently, my desk has no value. At first, I thought that might be useful, but with my luck, if we ever said anything, someone would appraise it and find it a priceless antique."

Roostof smiled. "I thought somewhat the same when I saw the description."

"So, I think I'll just enjoy my currently undervalued desk. Tomorrow morning, at some time, I want to talk to you and Shuryn about the subcommittee hearings." Dekkard paused. "Don't forget to put in a voucher for all the messages you had to send."

"I'll have it on your desk first thing tomorrow."

"Don't count on my forgetting," replied Dekkard, grinning.

Roostof offered an embarrassed smile. "No, sir."

Once back in his personal office, Dekkard turned to reading the responses, signing most of them, adding handwritten notes to a few, and making major revisions to only a handful. When he finished, it was only a sixth after fourth bell.

He took the stack out to Margrit and set it on her desk. "I know you won't listen unless I stay here, but don't you, Bretta, or Illana stay beyond half past. They won't go out any sooner."

"Svard told us the same thing."

Dekkard just looked at her.

"Not more than a minute later than half past," she said.

Dekkard sighed. Loudly.

"Maybe a sixth later. We all hate coming in to do yesterday's work. We might even finish before that."

Dekkard capitulated. "I'll see you tomorrow morning."

"Good afternoon, sir."

Dekkard turned to Gaaroll, and the two stepped out into the corridor.

53

W HILE Dekkard did tell everyone at dinner about Roostof and Bettina getting and polishing the never-used antique desk, about Arturo Escalante, and about the Council session, he said very little about the subcommittee meeting, except that he'd handed out the schedule and witness list and that he expected that discussions would be livelier during Tridi's meeting.

Only when he and Avraal were alone in their bedroom did he reveal Jen Seigryn's death and what had been in the *Gaarlak Times*.

"No marks or bruises," mused Avraal. "Most likely drugs in his drink, possibly with distraction by an empath."

"That's something else for the *Tribune* to use," said Dekkard.

"You can't do much about it, and if you try . . ."

"It will make matters worse," said Dekkard tiredly. "Still . . ." He shook his head.

After a moment, Avraal asked, "Was there anything else?"

Dekkard relayed the details of his meeting with Leister Milyaard, as well as what Ingrella had said.

"All that confirms is that Schmidtz is what you think he is," replied Avraal, "and that Milyaard is easily swayed."

"Then there was the subcommittee meeting," said Dekkard before telling Avraal what happened, and what Gaaroll had sensed. When he finished, he asked, "What are your thoughts?"

"How long will it be before everyone knows what you told the subcommittee?"

"Eventually, everyone will know."

"More councilors should know it sooner."

"Enough people know it now that it can't be covered up."

"Then the danger is that someone will want to kill you for bringing it out, just the way that Siincleer Shipbuilding has removed witness after witness, to make a point that it's dangerous to reveal corporacion misdeeds."

"So I have to survive long enough to reveal and punish enough corporacion malefactors that they see their tactics won't work any longer."

Avraal shook her head. "Dear, this is Guldor. It won't work that way.

It only works so long as you're alive and have the power to bring things to light and to the law, *and* make sure the law is applied fully. Right now, with Obreduur gone, there isn't anyone else."

"I suppose that's what I meant, but it seems so egocentric to say it that way."

"Even if it's true?" she asked gently.

"I don't know if I have the power to do all that," Dekkard said slowly.

"If you can expose what Ulrich has done, and survive, power won't be a problem. Hasheem doesn't see any other way to stay in power, or he wouldn't have agreed to your heading the subcommittee."

Thinking of what Ulrich had likely already done, in removing Kraffeist, Minz, and Grieg, and what *The Machtarn Tribune* had already begun, Dekkard said, "This is going to get worse, and that's if we succeed."

"It will be even worse for Guldor if we don't. Ulrich and the corporacion presidentes will be able to remove or dictate to every councilor."

"Only until the Meritorists mount a more successful insurgency," said Dekkard.

"That will take years, possibly a generation, and the violence and bloodshed will make what's already happened seem like nothing."

"No," said Dekkard, "the bloodshed will begin within a year and get worse every year."

"Do you want it to happen, either way?" asked Avraal.

"You have a definite point, dear."

"No. I have several. First, you're the only one in a position to stop either possibility. Second, the two of us can't do it alone. You'll need every ally you can find. Third, Hasheem has to remain premier. And fourth, to do all that, *you have to stay alive.*"

"What about staying alive politically, with what's bound to come from *The Machtarn Tribune*?"

"That's the least of your worries. If the *Tribune* is still attacking you when this furor is all over, then you'll have won."

"Just a furor?"

"One way or another, that's all the historians will call it." Avraal's words were gently bitter.

Dekkard lay in their bed, mulling over all Avraal had said long after she had dropped off to sleep.

54

D EKKARD didn't sleep well, having wrestled with nightmares. In the
first, he couldn't save Axel Obreduur, and in the second, he found
himself trapped in the Council Hall with snipers seemingly everywhere.
He woke early and sweating on Duadi, despite the chill in the bedroom,
and slipped out of bed and into the bathroom as soon as Emrelda left it.

He was mostly dressed when Avraal woke and said sleepily, "You were
restless last night."

"Nightmares about not saving Obreduur and then trying to avoid snipers in the Council Hall."

"The second one's definitely metaphorical."

"Metaphorical or not, one way or another, the second one has too
much truth in it to ignore," replied Dekkard. "By the way, there's plenty
of warm water left."

Avraal smiled. "Even when you're stressed, you're thoughtful. Thank
you."

Dekkard couldn't help but return the smile before he left the bedroom.

Once he was downstairs, he reached for the morning edition of *Gestirn*.

"There's nothing about the Council in it," said Emrelda.

Dekkard still looked through the newssheet. While he felt relieved that
there wasn't anything, he worried whether that meant there would be
something worse later.

Breakfast was quiet.

Dekkard took another indirect route to Baartol's office, and neither
Avraal nor Gaaroll sensed anything indicating possible trouble.

When Dekkard entered his office, Margrit greeted him cheerfully, then
handed him two notices and a message. The first notice was a reminder
from Hasheem as chair of the Security Committee of the special subcommittee hearing on Tridi morning. The second notice was the master
schedule of Council hearings for the week. The special Security subcommittee hearings were listed simply as "New Meritorist Investigation and
Oversight."

The message envelope contained a note from Eyril Konnigsburg inquiring whether Dekkard would be free for lunch. Dekkard immediately
wrote out an acceptance, and had Margrit dispatch it by messenger.

After that Dekkard approved the voucher to reimburse Roostof for all the messages he'd sent to staff while the Council Office Building had been closed. Then he turned to the mail.

Dekkard and Gaaroll left his office at less than a third before third bell. As they crossed the courtyard he noticed traces of green in the gardens and that the cool air was getting close to springlike, even if it held a hint of the acridity of burning coal.

He entered Hasheem's floor office just before third bell.

As Dekkard sat down, Hasheem asked, "How did yesterday's meeting go?"

Dekkard replied with a quick summary, then waited for Hasheem's response.

"I've come to realize that you have a forceful personality, Steffan, but the fact that nothing you said yesterday has found its way to the newssheets is another indication of that."

"It's more that the subcommittee members realize the seriousness of the situation."

"I suspect your presentation of the situation conveyed that. However you managed it, that's for the best."

"Have there been any requests for delays?" asked Dekkard.

"It's early for that. The witnesses from the Navy won't have any reason to delay, and I doubt that the witnesses from Northwest Industrial Chemical or Suvion Industries even got their orders to appear until yesterday." Hasheem didn't mention Guard Captain Trujillo, but there was no doubt Trujillo and his specialists would report.

"There's another aspect of the hearings I'd like to bring up," said Dekkard. "We already agreed that a Council Guard empath would be present for all witness testimony. I'd like to add an empath with criminal experience as well."

Hasheem frowned. "I don't know that's a good idea, with restricted information."

"I know a fully certified empath with additional certification as a criminal parole screener. She was a Council employee for over five years. She does not have to be paid."

Hasheem's frown deepened. Then he asked, "Are you talking about Ritten Ysella-Dekkard?"

"I am."

"She really was a criminal parole screener?"

"At the main prison in Siincleer."

Hasheem nodded slowly, then said, "While that's not technically nepotism, since she gains nothing and the subcommittee receives useful services, once it becomes known, you and the Council will face considerable criticism."

"You can turn that against them. First, she won't be the only empath. Second, the people who will complain are the ones testifying in an instance of possible malfeasance, if not worse. Third, what do they have against a high-level empath with both Council security experience and criminal experience?"

"You make a powerful argument. Then, you always do."

"I also want the power to confine a recalcitrant witness, even one who was a premier."

"You're asking for a lot, Steffan." Hasheem shook his head. "I don't know . . ."

"I'm asking for the tools to determine whether corporacion Commercers cooperated with the New Meritorists in multiple attacks on the Council and an attack on the Imperador. Why should a former councilor and premier be exempt from the same measures as any other witness in a proceeding that may uncover high crimes or treason?"

"Technically, they shouldn't, but politically? That's another matter."

"If we fail to look thoroughly into the matter, and don't look deeply, once that gets out, and it will, we'll be the ones to suffer."

Hasheem took a slightly deeper breath that wasn't quite a sigh. Then he said, "Axel told me that halfway measures weren't in your nature."

Dekkard managed a rueful smile. "Sometimes they are. Just not when what we do or don't do might well determine whether the Guldor of the Great Charter survives."

"That's an interesting phrasing."

"Guldor will survive, at least for a few decades, but by the end of that time, it won't be the Guldor that was, or still is right now." Dekkard held up a hand to forestall any immediate response. "Guldor's changed for the better over the years—until recently. Granting women suffrage didn't change the basics. Neither did repealing the harsher provisions of the sections of the Great Charter dealing with susceptibles. What the New Meritorists want will. So will a Guldor with the kind of Security Ministry that Lukkyn Wyath and Oskaar Ulrich almost succeeded in creating."

Hasheem's smile was wan. "I tend to be more cautious, but, as you pointed out, at least twelve councilors have been killed in the past year, possibly as many as fifteen. You're one of the few who has a plan that's something besides a version of 'kill all the Meritorists and go back to what we were doing.' Just be polite and courteous. Once each witness appears, you'd best warn them that their testimony must be truthful and complete and that the subcommittee is investigating matters that could well involve high crimes and possible treason. You should refresh yourself on the procedures necessary if any witness reveals material or events that appear clearly criminal in nature."

"The way you dealt with Intelligence Director Mangele?"

"If your concerns are realized, there could be more situations like that. That's why I suggest you review the procedures."

"Thank you. I appreciate the suggestion." *Even if it is more of a warning.* "Is there anything else I should know?"

"I can't think of anything. Do you have any questions?"

"Has the Imperador settled on a new Fleet Marshal."

"Not yet. He has two months before the Council can preempt his choice and choose one for him."

"The delay suggests he might be facing some difficult choices or waiting for something to happen. If it's the second, it would be useful to know. Has he given you any indication?"

"Not directly. He has said that he hopes the Council will concentrate on rooting out all the New Meritorists."

"In short, don't dig into all the Commercer abuses."

"Don't you think that digging into personal abuses of Commercers would be counterproductive right now, Steffan?"

"In terms of petty graft, abuse of favors, and those kinds of abuses, I'd agree. I don't think that hiring snipers to kill potential witnesses falls into that category. Nor does diverting dunnite to New Meritorists."

Hasheem offered a sour smile. "I did point out that the diversion of dunnite to insurgents was far more than a personal abuse. The Imperador agreed."

"But he implied that anything less should have lower priority than dealing with the New Meritorists?"

"I think that's an accurate reading of his feelings." Hasheem barely paused before he said, "Tomorrow morning? At a third past second bell?"

"I'll be here."

After Dekkard left Hasheem's office, he returned to his own, where he asked Roostof and Shuryn Teitryn to join him.

Once the two were seated, Dekkard said, "As I've already told Svard, I've been appointed chair of the Security Committee's special investigatory subcommittee." He went on to explain the purpose of the subcommittee in general terms, then handed each of them a copy of the witness list for Quindi's hearing. "What I need from you two are questions that will draw out more information, preferably information not known to the Council. I want every question you can think of dealing with how the Navy procedures work or might not, and every question about what the Council

Guard uncovered about the first shelling of the Council Office Building. Even if you think a question may be stupid, ask it. No one will see your questions but me." He paused, "Your thoughts?"

"Sir," began Teitryn, "you know far more than I do, so . . . ?"

"Why am I asking you two? Because I've lived and thought about this for months, and I need some smart aides who haven't to ask questions that I haven't thought about. Don't hesitate to ask other questions that come to mind. They could be useful in later hearings." Dekkard looked at his engineering aide. "If you could come up with some technical or chemical questions regarding dunnite, especially dealing with manufacturing, transport, storage, or security, that would be particularly useful."

Teitryn frowned. "Dunnite is ammonium picrate. That's stable except at high temperatures, but it's made from picric acid, and that can be nasty."

"Do what you can," said Dekkard. "That's all I have for now."

After Roostof and Teitryn left the office, Dekkard went to work reading and signing responses to earlier correspondence. He didn't finish before it was time to leave for his lunch with Konnigsburg. Gaaroll didn't detect any strong feelings on the walk to the councilors' dining room, but Dekkard thought he might have a day or two before any corporacion effort against him surfaced, assuming someone acted directly, rather than indirectly, but he had no real feel which course of action might be more likely. *That's if they don't try both.*

Konnigsburg waited for Dekkard at the entrance to the dining room, even though Dekkard arrived there almost a sixth before noon. The maître d'hôtel seated them immediately.

"I'm glad this worked out," said Konnigsburg after their server had taken their order.

"So am I," replied Dekkard. "Are there any interesting hearings coming before the Military Affairs Committee?"

"The next hearing is scheduled a week from tomorrow. It's a follow-up to one held in the last Council." Konnigsburg gave a sardonic smile. "The subject is pricing procedures for the acquisition of coal for naval vessels."

"That would have been useful two years ago," said Dekkard.

"It might have been," agreed the older councilor. "Chairman Mardosh has pointed out that the Admiralty has yet to review or change the procedures that led to the Navy's buying overpriced coal from Eastern Ironway."

"Coal illegally obtained from the Eshbruk Naval Coal Reserve," added Dekkard, "although that issue doesn't fall under the committee's jurisdiction, does it?"

"I don't believe so."

"But it is an interesting choice for a hearing, given that Guldor just saw the first successful mutiny on a warship in centuries, if not longer."

"That will be the next series of hearings, I understand," said Konnigsburg. "After the coal procurement procedures are thoroughly reviewed."

"And after that?"

"What follows those hasn't been announced."

Dekkard waited until the server delivered his pork empanadas, with verde sauce, an infrequent special that he'd never tried, while Konnigsburg received the hearty vegetable soup.

After taking a sip of his café, and some of his soup, Konnigsburg said, "Villem Baar stopped by late after a subcommittee meeting. I didn't know there were subcommittees."

"As I understand it, there are no standing subcommittees, but a committee chair can create a special subcommittee for a specific purpose."

"He said you were chair of the subcommittee. Can you tell me its specific purpose?"

"The purpose isn't a secret. It's an inquiry into how the New Meritorists managed to obtain all that dunnite without anyone knowing until they damaged or destroyed fifteen regional security buildings."

"All that dunnite?" asked Konnigsburg skeptically.

"You'd have a better idea than I, but it had to take a considerable amount of dunnite to inflict the damage I saw to the Security building in Oersynt. For fifteen buildings, that would work out to at least a tonne, but they also used it for the steam cannon shells and to destroy part of the Machtarn water system. It might have been as much as two tonnes, possibly more."

"That amount would easily fit in a lorry with good springs."

"That's still enough that I'd think it would be missed," replied Dekkard.

"It's almost certain that the New Meritorists obtained the dunnite before it reached the Navy," Konnigsburg pointed out. "The Navy receives the dunnite in fifteen-decem kegs. That's almost thirty sizable kegs." Konnigsburg stopped. "You have the strangest look, Steffan."

"I'd always thought that they'd put the dunnite into hollow or counterfeit bricks, or possibly just put the powder in sacks between the walls."

Konnigsburg offered a rueful expression and shook his head. "The sacks would be easier, but you'd still have to detonate it."

"A modified compression lighter to a lead azide fuse." After the slightest pause, Dekkard said, "Go on about the process. I assume that the naval munitions works logs in and verifies every shipment of dunnite."

"The Navy logs in and verifies even shipments of jams and jellies," replied the former admiral dryly.

"You've made it clear it's more likely that the dunnite got diverted before it reached the Navy or was simply shipped illegally, but is there any possible way it could have been removed from the munitions plant before it was turned into the projectile's explosive charge?"

"Steffan, there's always a possibility. I'd just say that it's lower with regard to the Navy. Once the dunnite is received and logged into inventory, the numbers won't balance if it's subsequently removed."

"So I could ask if the number of projectiles manufactured, and the dunnite employed, plus the dunnite in inventory match closely, and request the inventory and projectile numbers for the last three years?"

"Admiral Jingao won't be happy."

"Even if I make the point that the excellence of Navy records will help resolve from where the dunnite was diverted?"

"That would help."

"On a related subject, we'd talked previously about Siincleer Shipbuilding."

"I recall that. We shared certain concerns." Konnigsburg's voice verged on wariness.

"I heard something the other day that surprised me. The person who informed me said that it was more gossip than verified fact. He said that Juan del Larrano has a comparatively modest mansion on the coast south of Siincleer, but an unusual yacht—"

Konnigsburg managed to stifle what sounded like it might have been a rueful laugh, then shook his head. "An unusual yacht? That might be one of the great understatements."

"Something about how it was built like a small corvette? And moored near the modest mansion?" The last was a guess on Dekkard's part, but he couldn't imagine someone like del Larrano wanting to travel to use his yacht.

"So it's said. Del Larrano had it built with the latest turbines from Uldwyrk Systems as well as the newest evaporators. He attempted to include some of the development costs in the construction budget for the *Defiant*. Most of them were disallowed. Interesting enough, the final budget for the *Resolute* contained an 'unavoidable' cost overrun equal to those disallowed costs."

"How could he get away with that? How could the Navy allow it? Even if the Navy did, that's effectively shifting corporacion funds to private use."

Konnigsburg shook his head. "That yacht—I believe the name is *Ultima*—technically belongs to the corporacion as a development project, even if it is moored offshore of his grounds. And yes, it is very much like a high-speed small corvette, without obvious guns, of course. And with greater range. The Navy disallowed most of the cost overrun."

"So the corporacion paid for it in the end, and since Siincleer is a family-run corporacion, I suppose no one is going to call him on that," said Dekkard.

"If you worked there, would you?" asked Konnigsburg sardonically.

"Not if I wanted to keep my job." Dekkard paused, then asked, "Have you heard anything about a new Fleet Marshal?"

"Not a thing. I suspect the Imperador doesn't like the flag officers the Premier proposed, and the Premier is reluctant to press at this point."

Hasheem's almost always reluctant to press. "Is that because the Imperador may have already hinted about whom he prefers and wants to force the Council to make a choice so that he doesn't have to?"

"That's possible, but I wouldn't be surprised if the Imperador feels the Council is usurping one of the few powers remaining to him."

Dekkard hadn't seen it that way, but he saw Konnigsburg's point. "Telling him that the Council will likely remove a certain kind of officer as soon as it can usurps his power? He can still appoint such an officer. Or does saying that remind him of the limits on his power and that's not good?"

"I think you've grasped the difficulty," Konnigsburg dryly observed.

Dekkard shook his head, mostly at his own failure to see how the Imperador would take the suggestion. *It's not as though the Fleet Marshal is the one who makes the final decisions. But to have three senior officers in a row with the same shortcomings?* "Sometimes all the available choices are bad."

"Guldor is at one of those points in history, I fear," replied Konnigsburg. "When any choice is bad, too many of those faced with decisions opt to make none, and circumstances choose for them. Or others step up and force decisions, which is often hard, if not fatal, for those who do. But if someone doesn't decide, it's usually worse for everyone." Konnigsburg took a sip of café and set his mug down. "I don't envy you, Steffan."

"I don't envy you, either, Eyril. You know more than anyone on the Military Affairs Committee, and you're a Commercer who's not trusted by many Commercers, and the only other Commercer is . . . often less than reliable."

"It's one of those situations that are called 'interesting.' All we can do is our best, because doing anything else will be even worse."

"Aren't we optimistic this afternoon?" said Dekkard cheerfully.

"We've had a useful and filling lunch. There's something to be said for that."

"There is," agreed Dekkard.

Within minutes, the two stood and left the councilors' dining room.

As Dekkard and Gaaroll walked back to the Council Office Building, Dekkard thought over the lunch, and the fact that Konnigsburg had effectively told him that Mardosh wasn't about to do anything meaningful with the Military Affairs Committee any time soon, if ever. While that was scarcely a surprise, it was disappointing. Konnigsburg also intimated that Dekkard was one of the few seriously working to improve matters in Guldor, and that any more missteps, like the one with replacing the Fleet Marshal, could be dangerous, if not deadly.

He would have shaken his head, but there wasn't any point in doing so.

55

WHILE Dekkard went over his day during dinner at the house on Duadi evening, he didn't go into details. Nor, he noticed, did Avraal.

Once they retired to their bedroom, he asked, "What happened today that you didn't want to share with everyone?"

"What about you?" she replied. "You were exceptionally quiet."

"You first. I have quite a few things you should know."

"There was a reason why Carlos had trouble finding out about large corporacions in Whulte. There aren't any. There are several modest brick and ceramic corporacions, and several regional offices of larger corporacions. As regional vice-presidente, Kuuresoh was the top person at Nordstar's regional office, but Nordstar has nine regional offices, and Whulte is the smallest."

"So Kuuresoh was telling the truth about there being little chance of advancement with Nordstar?"

"He may not have had a choice. Nordstar limits the terms of regional vice-presidentes to six years."

Dekkard nodded. "What else?"

"Carlos received several messages this afternoon. One of them was about Wheitz and Groebel."

"That was the firm that represented the Special Agents who attacked the house. What about them?"

"Someone from Barthow, Juarez and Whittsyn visited them," said Avraal.

"That's Villem Baar's old firm."

"It's more interesting than that. That legalist had lunch with your old friend Fernand Stoltz, who's with Paarsens and Alvara. Think about that."

Dekkard did, and it still didn't make that much sense. "But Paarsens and Alvara are also local counsel for Barthow, Juarez and Whittsyn, at least for matters coming before the High Justiciary. Villem said most of the work representing Lukkyn Wyath was handled by Paarsens and Alvara. If Suvion Industries' corporacion officials want legalist counsel before the subcommittee, they'd want someone from Paarsens and Alvara. They wouldn't want Wheitz and Groebel doing it, because they handle criminal matters, usually involving people hired indirectly to accomplish criminal acts that no one wants traced back to a corporacion. It sounds like someone has already been charged who might be tied to Suvion Industries . . . or to Ulrich."

"If that's so, then Fernand has to know who that is," Avraal pointed out.

"Neither the court nor the subcommittee can require Fernand to divulge what client was referred to Wheitz and Groebel, not unless we can tie it to a crime or to the New Meritorists. Whatever it is, if both Paarsens and Alvara and Barthow, Juarez and Whittsyn are involved, it's either embarrassing or important. I'd wager it has to do with the New Meritorists or Capitol Services in some way or another, but how I can't figure out. Villem might be able to add something, but I'm not sure I want to share that without knowing more."

"I'd have to agree. Carlos is following it as well as his people can, but that's all I know. Now, what's your news?"

"First, as of last Quindi, there's nothing new about Jens Seigryn's death. The fact that there's only been one not very large newssheet article suggests there's more there. Sooner or later, that's going to come up in the *Tribune,* along with a few other matters."

"You'll just have to deal with it then," said Avraal. "Anything you try now will make matters worse. You said that yourself."

"I know. It doesn't make me any happier, though." Dekkard paused, then said, "Second, I got Hasheem to agree that you would be present at all the hearings as an official empath in addition to the Council Guard empath."

"How did you manage that?"

"With my nonexistent personal charm," replied Dekkard.

"You know that will come to the attention of the *Tribune*? No newsie could possibly ignore it."

"Since nothing we do will ever please the *Tribune,* there's little additional risk in that regard. Since the hearings are closed, and Jaradd Rikkard isn't on the subcommittee, it will be a while before your presence as an empath comes to light."

"Is the risk worth it, since I might not sense any more than the Guard empath?"

"The Guard empath is doubtless quite good, but you have more ability than most other empaths, and I need those extra abilities." *And even they may not be enough.* "Hasheem also agreed I had the power to incarcerate reluctant witnesses, but cautioned me to act according to all procedures."

"I can't imagine he'd do otherwise. What else?"

"Eyril Konnigsburg asked me to lunch." Dekkard summarized the conversation.

When he finished, Avraal said, "Mardosh is turning out to be an even greater problem, and there's no way Hasheem can remove him from the Council unless Mardosh is actually implicated in something illegal, which delaying or avoiding holding hearings isn't."

"If he were doing something illegal," Dekkard replied, "Hasheem would still be reluctant because that would cost the Craft Party the seat, at least until the next election. He could remove him as chair, but that might make Craft councilors angry enough to make a motion to replace Hasheem with Mardosh."

"From what you said, Konnigsburg was saying that your subcommittee is the only part of the Council really looking into who supported the New Meritorists. Was that what he meant, or am I reading more into his words?"

"I got that impression."

"Ingrella's on the Military Affairs Committee," said Avraal.

"But Kuuresoh will agree with Mardosh, and so could Chiram Ghohal, possibly even Eduardo Nortak and both Landors. That leaves Ingrella and Konnigsburg. The only other committee that will really look into matters is the Justiciary Committee, but the Justiciary Committee doesn't have much jurisdiction beyond the laws and the courts."

"That makes you and your subcommittee the main target for Ulrich," said Avraal, "but we've known that was likely all along."

"Eyril Konnigsburg was kind enough to confirm it," said Dekkard sardonically.

"Why is he letting you know all this? Surely not just because you're both graduates of the Military Institute?"

"That helps, because it proves to him that I'm intelligent and competent, but it's also because he's very displeased with the leadership of the Admiralty. That's been clear all along. I've gotten the impression he's concerned about the growth and the power of the largest corporacions, and the way they're grossly overcharging the Navy, as well as how they're overcharging everyone else and abusing their power. His willingness to discuss del Larrano's use of corporacion funds for what amounts to a personal yacht is another indication of that."

"Why is he helping you?"

"I'd like to say that it's because it's the right thing to do, but it's also because I got Hasheem to consult with him about who the next Fleet Marshal will be. Better officers leading the Admiralty is in everyone's interest."

"He *seems* trustworthy in that he won't lie to you or imply support that he won't give," said Avraal.

"I think he's better than that, but we'll have to see. He's far better than Mardosh," replied Dekkard, "and, unfortunately, Mardosh is probably better than any Commercer that could be elected from Siincleer."

"That's deplorable, but I can certainly see that." Avraal stopped, then yawned. "Anything else?"

"Not that I can recall, and I think that it's more than enough."

56

ON Tridi morning, Dekkard stepped into Hasheem's inner floor office at precisely a third past second bell.

Hasheem looked up and said dryly, "You're always punctual, Steffan. I must say I appreciate it." He gestured in the direction of the two chairs in front of the desk.

"I respect your time. People who habitually don't respect others' time usually don't respect them in other ways." Dekkard sat down, his gray leather folder in his lap.

"That was carefully phrased, but then you choose your words well." Hasheem leaned forward just a bit. "What do you expect from the subcommittee meeting this morning?"

"I'll go over the differences between a usual hearing and one with potential criminal implications. Then I'll ask each councilor if he has particular concerns. After that, I'll open the meeting to discussion and questions. As for the questions, I don't know what to expect, except that it will be polite. Councilor Haastar will have some valid inquiries, possibly some of which I haven't considered. So will Councilor Baar. Councilor Pajiin will have at least one question."

"That's what I'd expect," said Hasheem. "The subcommittee meeting this morning and the hearings on Quindi and Unadi aren't my greatest concern. The Navy will be most professional, and those witnesses will provide massive documentation. Later corporacion witnesses might not prove so accommodating, except superficially and procedurally."

"The subcommittee will thank them all for their care and documentation, but will reserve the right to recall any witness necessary to clarify any points that examination of such material and other information might reveal." *And what the Council Guard reveals, if it comes to that.*

"So long as you make the same point to each entity, I see no problem with that. Do you intend to make it clear to the subcommittee that you intend to use two empaths for the hearings?"

"Anything else would be deceptive, and neither the subcommittee nor I nor you need to deal with charges of deception."

"What will you do if you're unable to come up with enough proof to determine beyond a doubt how and where the New Meritorists obtained the dunnite?"

"It's highly likely that the subcommittee will be able to determine the source of the dunnite. What may be difficult will be discovering who was involved and to what extent. One way or another, it would seem useful to issue a public report on what we find."

"I have no problem with that as long as the findings are supported factually and are not conjectures."

The remainder of the conversation dealt with procedural points that Hasheem wanted to make clear. Dekkard was more than happy to listen.

After leaving the Premier's floor office, Dekkard took his time making his way to the committee chamber. Before he entered, he looked toward the temporary wooden wall some twenty yards away that blocked the corridor. He thought he could hear the sounds of continuing rebuilding, but that might have been his imagination. Then he turned to Gaaroll. "I'd like you to remain close by and sense what you can as the meeting proceeds. It should be good practice for you, and it might prove helpful."

"I'll try, sir. That's not my strongest ability."

"Maybe practice will help, and maybe not, but you can't tell unless you work at it."

"What if I can't?"

"Then we think of another way you could use your abilities and see if that works. You can't tell if you don't try, and I mean really try. But if you work hard, and you don't get results, you need to consider another way to get to that point, or some other use of your talents. Your talents are even rarer than those of the usual empath, and it would be a shame to waste or fail to develop them as much as possible." Dekkard paused, then said, "You'll see each councilor enter the chamber. See if you can sense what makes each one unique in a way that you might be able to identify each without seeing him."

"Never thought about that."

"Now you have. I'll see you after the meeting." Dekkard turned and opened the door to the empty committee chamber.

He'd barely settled himself in the center position when Villem Baar appeared. "Good morning."

"Good morning to you. I was just thinking, Steffan. If you don't have other plans, how about an early lunch after the subcommittee meeting?"

"I don't have other plans, and I think that's a very good idea."

The next councilor to arrive was Breffyn Haastar, quickly followed by Tomas Pajiin.

As soon as Pajiin took his seat, Dekkard said, "The subcommittee will come to order." After the briefest of pauses, Dekkard continued, "This subcommittee is tasked with determining how so much dunnite ended up in the hands of the New Meritorists and, if possible, who was responsible. Given that the dunnite was used to commit high crimes and possibly treason, the subcommittee will follow the procedures required in such instances." From there he quickly laid out the procedural requirements, ending with, "While such procedures require at least one empath be present to advise the subcommittee of possible untruths or evasion, because what these hearings may reveal bears directly on the killings of four councilors and is directly associated with the killing of seven others and the attempted assassination of the Imperador, there will be at least one highly qualified empath present for all testimony by witnesses, and in most instances two such empaths." Dekkard paused, then asked, "Are there any questions about the subcommittee procedures for the forthcoming hearings?"

"Sr. Chairman," said Breffyn Haastar, "some might claim that having empaths present is perhaps excessive. Would you address such a possible contention?"

"I'm certain that some might feel that way, particularly those who were involved in transferring two tonnes of dunnite to the New Meritorists, or those who merely facilitated it. The fact remains that the Council Hall was successfully attacked twice and twelve councilors and thousands of Guldorans definitely died from Meritorist efforts in less than a year. As I already noted, empaths are mandated in the instances of high crimes and treason, and attacks against the Council. Because both corporacions producing dunnite have extensive political ties, the subcommittee needs certainty in all matters, including findings by empaths."

"Thank you, Sr. Chairman. I do have one other question. Guard Captain Trujillo is not included in the first set of hearings. Might I ask why?"

"There are several reasons. First is that the Council Guard is attempting to obtain some information from elsewhere in Guldor that will not be available until later. Second, the chairman and I made the determination that the evidence and materials uncovered by the Council Guard would be more useful to the subcommittee after hearing from the Navy and the two corporacions." *And presenting them early risks problems with a later Justiciary prosecution.*

"Thank you."

"Will questioning be limited if it appears that a witness has committed an offense?" asked Pajiin.

"Only about the possible offense," replied Dekkard. "Other questions will be permitted. This is not a Justiciary proceeding."

After another sixth of questions and discussion about the procedural side of the hearings, Dekkard then asked, "Are there any other questions?"

"Do you expect any information from the Navy officers who will be testifying that conflicts with what we know?" asked Haastar.

"I doubt that, but it's certainly possible. We don't know exactly what the hearings will reveal," replied Dekkard, "and there are a number of technical issues that we need to cover before the witnesses from either Northwest Industrial Chemical or Suvion Industries testify."

"What if a witness doesn't know the answer to a question and promises to provide it, but then doesn't?"

"The Premier confirmed that we can recall witnesses as often as necessary to obtain information."

The next third of a bell was filled with similar speculative questions, but Dekkard answered with variations on what he had previously confirmed with Hasheem.

Finally, Dekkard was able to say, "There being no other questions, the subcommittee is recessed until third bell on Quindi."

Haastar looked to Dekkard. "The hearings could be very interesting."

"On Quindi, I suspect they'll appear very routine."

"And next week?"

"That remains to be seen."

"So it does." Haastar smiled and rose from his seat, then turned toward the chamber door.

Dekkard stood and gathered his papers into the gray folder.

Pajiin waited just in front of the desk, then asked, "Do you really think the Navy is going to be happy to answer all the questions?"

"They should be grateful to have the chance to show that they weren't responsible for allowing the dunnite into the hands of the New Meritorists. That is, of course, assuming that they weren't the ones responsible. Quindi's hearing will shed light on that."

"Don't you already know, Steffan?"

"What I think I know means nothing without proof that's acceptable to the majority of the full Security Committee. I'm hoping that the hearings will provide that, or at least provide enough information that the Justiciary Ministry can fully investigate."

"Fair enough." Pajiin nodded, then turned and left the chamber.

Villem Baar was waiting outside in the main corridor. "Shall we go?"

"We should." Dekkard looked to Gaaroll. "We'll talk later. Do you sense anything?"

"No, sir."

"Good." He smiled at her. "Thank you."

As Dekkard and Baar began to walk toward the councilors' dining room, Baar said, "I still think you'd have made a good legalist."

"I appreciate the kind words, but I think I would have been a very unhappy legalist."

Baar laughed. "Good legalists are often unhappy."

"And you think I should be one?"

"I didn't say that. I said you'd be good at it."

"So why are good legalists often unhappy?"

"Because so often their job is to resolve situations where no one will be completely satisfied, and they often get paid more for winning litigation that they know isn't just."

"The first part of that sounds like being a councilor," replied Dekkard dryly.

"Why do you think I said you'd make a good legalist?"

Dekkard shook his head.

Once they reached the entry to the dining room, Dekkard said to Gaaroll, "I'll see you here at first bell."

"Yes, sir." Gaaroll nodded, but continued to scan the corridor as the two councilors walked through the entry archway.

When Dekkard and Baar followed the maître d'hôtel to a table they were the first into the dining area, since it was little more than a third past fifth bell. But then, Dekkard suspected that Villem just might have wanted it that way.

Dekkard ended up ordering the white bean soup, while Villem chose the three-cheese chicken.

Once the server took their orders, returned with their cafés, and then moved away, Baar said pleasantly, "Gerryt Baarna stopped by to see me yesterday."

"Gerryt Baarna?" Dekkard had never heard that name. "That doesn't strike a chime."

"I thought you might have recognized his name. He's one of the two legalists that my old firm has in Machtarn. He wanted to know about you." Baar paused. "It wasn't a casual inquiry. I asked him why the firm was so interested in a junior councilor. He said he didn't know, but the assignment came from a very senior member of the firm. That meant it was for a client."

Dekkard nodded.

"Steffan, we both know that client has to be Suvion Industries."

"Might I ask what you told him?"

"That you were intelligent and diligent and that the Premier had put you in charge of finding out how the New Meritorists had gotten hold of so much dunnite, and that from the hearings scheduled, the subcommittee would be looking into the security, transport, and storage of dunnite for Northwest Industrial Chemical, Suvion Industries, and the Navy." After a moment, Baar added, "I also told him that any Council would have to hold hearings on that after all the damage caused by dunnite explosions. He wasn't happy when I said that. His reaction suggested that he knew very well who the client is. I didn't think I was giving away anything since the first hearing was listed on the weekly schedule released by the Premier yesterday, and Suvion Industries already knows they have to testify." Baar paused as the server returned with their meals.

Neither said anything for several minutes as they ate.

Then Dekkard said, "Villem, did Baarna say any more . . . that you're able to tell me?"

"He kept asking personal questions about you. I just told him that I knew you were married, and that I'd met your wife at the Yearend Ball. That you'd been put on the Security Committee because that was your expertise, and the former premier had recognized that. He asked about that scurrilous editorial in *The Machtarn Tribune*—how true and accurate it was. I told him that the facts were likely true, but totally misrepresentative, and, in any other context, might well be found libelous. He wasn't exactly pleased when he left."

"I appreciate what you said, and your letting me know. In turn," said Dekkard, "I'd better tell you something I just found out last night. A legalist from the Machtarn office of your former firm visited a legalist firm of, shall we say, dubious provenance, a firm that represented the Special Agents convicted of attempting the arson of Emrelda's house, with the intent to murder. After that visit, the legalist met with one Fernand Stoltz, a legalist with another firm you know, Paarsens and Alvara. That meeting wouldn't concern me so much if I hadn't seen and verified that Stoltz was a working acquaintance, if not more, of Jaime Minz. Stoltz also used to be legalist for the Public Resources Committee."

Baar nodded slowly. "I'm glad I didn't say more to Sr. Baarna, and I'm very glad I never worked on any matters dealing with Suvion Industries." He offered a rueful expression. "Gretina was more glad, and that was before this came up."

"What do you think is behind the firm's interest in me?"

"Either the dunnite came from Suvion Industries, or someone there fears the Security Committee will place blame on them, possibly both."

"Both?"

"I can't believe that most of upper management would be that stupid or reckless. My first thought was that someone just high enough to authorize a shipment did so and that it went to a front for the New Meritorists."

"There's already evidence to indicate that Capitol Services was involved," Dekkard pointed out.

"But it has to be more than Oskaar Ulrich," said Baar, "because the dunnite was used long before Suvion Industries hired him, and it had to have been obtained *before* he became premier."

"Exactly, but that's why he has to testify. It's likely that he persuaded whoever was responsible to hire him when the Imperador demanded his resignation as premier and councilor. When the evidence about Minz surfaced, someone clearly arranged Minz's death, and I see someone at Suvion Industries as most likely, and, if so, it had to be someone high enough to authorize hiring a vice-presidente."

"Only most likely?" asked Baar.

"A number of entities provided significant funds through banque drafts made out to Capitol Services. It is possible, if less likely, that one of those entities would not like its identity revealed. Or perhaps, one of those entities persuaded—"

"Blackmailed, you mean?"

"Either way," replied Dekkard.

"Do you know who purchased those drafts?"

"No. Pursuant to the subcommittee's hearings, the Council Guard is attempting to determine that."

"The Council Guard? Not Public Safety or Justiciary?"

"The Council Guard discovered Minz's role and his financial dealings."

"How are you so privy to the Council Guard?"

"For better or worse, I've had to deal with Guard Captain Trujillo on a number of occasions." Dekkard quickly summarized the various attacks on him that required his dealing with the Council Guard, as well as the times he'd officially reported matters. He did not mention his more private conversations with Trujillo, but he did mention being allowed to look at the evidence gathered on Minz.

Baar shook his head. "You could even qualify as a prosecuting legalist—if you weren't an isolate. The more I learn about you, the more I see why Chairman Hasheem essentially delegated the investigation to you."

"I pushed for it," Dekkard said. "I didn't think he really wanted to do what's necessary."

"What *do* you think is necessary?" Baar leaned forward just a trace.

"For the subcommittee to investigate as far as the facts will take us, and then make those facts known, either publicly, if we cannot trace actual criminal conduct, or to the Justiciary, if we can. Is there any other responsible alternative?"

"Not as long as you use the term 'responsible alternative,'" replied Baar. "The only problem is that if anything happens to you, the whole investigation could just quietly die away after several inconclusive hearings."

"Knowing what you now know, would you let it die away?"

"Steffan, I'm even junior to you and in the wrong party. Tomas Pajiin doesn't have much power, and both Landors on the full committee seem reluctant to lead anything."

"But they'll support."

"No. They'll support you." Baar looked directly at Dekkard. "Just be careful." Then he offered a forced smile. "That's all I had."

"I appreciate the information—enormously."

"I thought you should know."

"I appreciate that even more," replied Dekkard, adding after a long moment, "How's Gretina doing?"

"She's very happy with the position. I haven't seen her that cheerful professionally, maybe ever."

"I'm very glad to hear that."

The remainder of the conversation was on a variety of subjects, none of which dealt with the Council.

Gaaroll waited outside the councilors' dining room when Dekkard looked out slightly before first bell. Dekkard immediately joined her. "Did you get something to eat?"

"Fish jalapeño empanadas."

Dekkard managed not to wince as they started to walk toward the courtyard doors. "Any strong feelings around now?"

"Not one."

"Did you sense any during the subcommittee meeting?"

"Not in your meeting. Couple of real strong feelings in the committee room across the hall."

The Military Affairs Committee. "Did you have any sense of who it might have been?"

"No, sir."

"Well, that's the Military Affairs Committee, and with all they're considering"—*and all they're not considering*—"I can't say that's surprising. When we step out into the courtyard, try to sense more distant strong feelings."

"Sniper-type?"

"Yes, unfortunately."

"Yes, sir."

Neither Dekkard nor Gaaroll said anything more on the walk back to the office, where Dekkard immediately walked into the staff office and to Roostof's desk. "Svard, have you and Shuryn come up with any questions for the Navy for Quindi's hearing?"

"We have a few. I'll bring them right in, if that's all right?"

"That would be good, thank you." Dekkard then walked to Margrit's desk. "Are there any messages?"

"No, sir."

"Excellent!" Dekkard smiled, because more often than not messages meant either trouble or more work.

The rest of the afternoon Dekkard spent going over the questions suggested by Roostof and Teitryn, reading the incoming letters and petitions, and signing or revising responses.

He and Gaaroll didn't leave the office until a third past fourth bell. Even so, he'd left a small stack of responses unread and unsigned, but he'd have time in the morning to catch up, and if he'd stayed longer, Margrit would have insisted on staying even later to "finish up."

Even though he was somewhat later in arriving at Baartol's office, he still had to wait a sixth before Avraal appeared.

Once she was in the steamer, she asked cheerfully, "How did your day go?"

"My meeting with Hasheem wasn't that long," replied Dekkard as he eased the Gresynt out of the parking area and headed toward Imperial Boulevard. "He's still worried. The subcommittee meeting went about as I thought, with questions about procedure, all very civil. Then I had a pleasant lunch with Villem Baar, and a long afternoon going over questions for Quindi's hearing and dealing with letters. What about your day?"

"Very legalistic and boring." Avraal half turned toward the rear. "Nincya, did he do anything I would have frowned at?"

"Not today, Ritten," replied Gaaroll with a smile in her voice.

"Excellent."

The drive home was as uneventful as the dinner and the conversations that followed.

Once they had retired to their bedroom, Dekkard related his luncheon conversation with Villem Baar, then waited for Avraal's response.

"We knew this would happen."

"Do you think the smear campaign will precede the physical attack or follow?"

"Follow, but only if the physical attacks are unsuccessful. They've already planted two nasty editorials, and you and Hasheem have ignored them. Those were warnings. We'll have to be more careful. From now on, both Gaaroll and I need to be with you every minute."

"Except in the bedroom, I hope," replied Dekkard with a grin.

"There and the bathroom," countered Avraal. "You need to talk to Guard Captain Trujillo about making sure any package sent to your office is inspected."

"I'd already thought about that. What about Hasheem?"

"Minimize what you tell Hasheem, and tell him that you've alerted Trujillo. Trujillo is the head of Council security. I'll tell Carlos in the morning about your need for greater security and the legalist from Villem's former firm."

"I'm sure he'll find the legalist intriguing."

"More like chilling, I suspect, but we'll see." Avraal yawned. "We both need some sleep." After a brief pause, she said, again, "Sleep."

57

WHEN Dekkard brought the Gresynt to a stop outside Baartol's office on Furdi morning, he immediately said, "I should come in with you."

"No, you shouldn't. It's my job and my choice. I can always get another job. I'll never find another you, and I don't want to. I'm just going to ask for a leave of absence until this gets resolved. I'm sure Carlos will agree to that." With those words, Avraal left the steamer and went inside the building.

Dekkard waited behind the steering wheel for what seemed to be an entire bell, but turned out to be just a little over a sixth before Avraal returned, her face pleasantly non-expressive. Once she was seated, he asked, "Did he agree?"

"Halfway. I get the leave of absence, but he insisted that I get half pay."

"He wants to keep you."

Avraal shook her head. "That's only part of it. He wants to keep me, even if something happens to you, but he's wagering that you'll survive whatever happens."

"Does he know something we don't?"

"I don't think so. I can sense he's not hiding anything from me. He does have great confidence in you."

"No. He has great confidence in us. All four of us."

Avraal laughed softly. "That's probably more accurate."

"Four?" asked Nincya.

"You and Emrelda," replied Dekkard. "And it will take all of us." *And then some.*

Once Dekkard parked the steamer in the covered parking, the three walked to his office, where he checked for any urgent messages—there were none—before Avraal and Gaaroll escorted him to Guard Captain Trujillo's small office in the Council Hall.

When the Guard captain opened his door, his eyes widened at the sight of Avraal in her tailored security-gray jacket and trousers. "All of you?"

"Just the councilor," said Avraal. "We'll stay out here."

Trujillo stepped back, and Dekkard entered the small office, closing the door and taking the single chair before the desk.

"Who or what is threatening you now?" asked the Guard captain as he seated himself behind the desk.

"Let's just say that the situation has become more interesting. Two legalists from different firms, but both representing Suvion Industries, are now inquiring into my personal life and background."

"Did you expect any less?"

"No, but it was slightly concerning that one of them visited the same law firm that represented the Special Agents who attempted to set fire to our home, or rather the house owned by my wife's sister. That wasn't why I stopped by. I wanted to know if the Council's internal mail and package delivery system still screens packages being sent to councilors."

"As a matter of fact, it does. After the events of the last year, that screening never stopped."

"I thought that might be so, but I wanted to make certain."

Trujillo smiled wryly. "I'll reemphasize to the Council's delivery personnel that, with several oversight hearings, a certain amount of additional care in screening packages would be advisable. It would appear that some individuals may not share your interest in discovering how a large amount of dunnite ended up in the hands of the New Meritorists."

"They're even less interested in the subcommittee discovering who made it possible."

"I doubt it's possible to discover how it got to the New Meritorists without revealing, at least indirectly, who made it possible," replied Trujillo in a tone both sardonic and amused. "You obviously have considered that likelihood."

"Any one of a few people near the top of a corporacion could have done so."

"Not without others finding out, if after the fact," pointed out Trujillo. "That means testifying before a subcommittee monitored by empaths presents considerable danger to corporacion officials, and, in turn, especially to the subcommittee chair."

"As well as some danger to Council Guards."

"Unless you request preventive detention by the Council Guard, based on testimony before your subcommittee," said Trujillo. "It's seldom used, but in investigatory hearings concerning high crimes or treason, it is available."

"Is that in the Great Charter?"

"Indirectly. The Charter allows protective detention within the Council buildings of any person suspected of enabling or committing high crimes or treason until the Justiciary can present a recommendation before the High Court, but for no longer than two weeks, after which normal pretrial procedures apply."

"Is the Premier aware of this provision?"

"He may be. We have not discussed it. Since you are the chair of the investigatory committee, I'm just responding to your inquiries."

In short, you're worried, too, and want me to know about that provision.

"I appreciate your providing full and complete answers to my questions." *Especially to questions I haven't asked and should have.*

"The Council Guard would be remiss in our duties if we failed to consider all eventualities, especially after recent events."

"Have there been any responses to the orders for the names of the purchasers of the banque drafts made out to Capitol Services?"

"All the banques promised that information will be provided no later than this coming Unadi. I suspect that every purchaser is a clerk of some sort."

"Who someone else ordered to take a corporacion cheque to the banque and to convert it into a banque draft? And then send it to Capitol Services?"

"Would you think it would be otherwise, Councilor?"

Dekkard could see where that would lead. Tracing the responsibility for deciding to send funds to Capitol Services could take days, if not weeks. *And, all the while, you're a target.* "Is there anything else I should know?"

"I can't think of anything, but you know where to find me." Trujillo smiled pleasantly.

"Thank you." Dekkard stood. "I'm sure we'll be seeing each other more than occasionally in the weeks ahead."

"I'd be surprised if we didn't, Councilor."

After Dekkard left Trujillo's office, Avraal looked to him.

"Good and bad, but too complicated to discuss here."

In minutes, the three were inside Hasheem's floor office.

Meldra looked to Avraal and nodded. "It's good to see both of you with him."

"It's going to be like that for a while," replied Avraal.

Meldra said to Dekkard, "You can go on in."

"Thank you." Dekkard made his way into the smaller office and, at Hasheem's gesture, seated himself. "Good morning, Fredrich. Have you heard anything from any of the witnesses or their corporacions?"

"Not a word, and there aren't any letters or correspondence in the committee offices, either for you or me." Hasheem paused, then added, "Since you're now a subcommittee chair, you should check in there every morning."

"I'll do that after I leave here."

"Have you heard anything that might relate to the hearings?" asked Hasheem.

"I've discovered that legalists from Paarsens and Alvara, and from the Machtarn office of Barthow, Juarez and Whittsyn, have been meeting and asking questions about my background."

"No doubt prompted by those misleading editorials in *The Machtarn Tribune*."

"That's definitely possible," agreed Dekkard.

"What did you do to get Councilor Rikkard so upset with you? Some of that information had to come from him."

"Besides drafting a Security reform proposal? I have no idea." Dekkard shrugged. "Perhaps he and Marrak were supposed to stop any reform measure."

"Do you think he blames you for Councilor Marrak's death?"

"I have no idea. At the time, as you may recall, I was more concerned with the Special Agents who attempted to destroy the house where Avraal and I were living."

"For such a polite and talented young councilor, Steffan, you certainly have created enemies more along the lines of those acquired by a far more senior and seasoned councilor."

"That may be because we're in a time where the Council must change, either to strengthen the old principles or to abandon them. Those with marks and power wish to abandon the old principles because those principles restrict their ability to gain more marks and power, and those with neither seek to make popularity the basis of the Council."

"And you, Steffan?"

"I stand contrary to both marks and power and to abandoning principle to popularity, as I suspect you do as well."

"Why do you think you're the subcommittee chair?" replied Hasheem ironically. "What you've set out to do is going to be difficult, if not impossible."

"Every day, I discover another difficulty, but that just underscores the necessity of succeeding."

Hasheem just nodded, then said, "No need to meet tomorrow morning. I would like you to stop by tomorrow after the hearing is concluded for the day."

"I'll be happy to do that."

From Hasheem's floor office, the three walked to the Security Committee offices adjoining the committee hearing chamber, but there were no messages or letters for Dekkard. From there they made their way back to

Dekkard's office. Once he and Avraal were alone in his personal office, he related what had happened in both meetings.

When he finished, Avraal said, "Trujillo wants you to succeed. Hasheem's still not sure. I'd guess he wants you to succeed, *if* it's not too costly."

Dekkard shook his head. "The more I learn, the more I discover I need to know. But first, I need to find out precisely what that preventive-detention section of the Great Charter says and how it might affect the hearings."

Dekkard left the inner office and quickly returned with Roostof, closing the door and then turning to the senior legalist. "Svard, I need you to research the complete Great Charter. I don't want anyone else doing it, or even knowing exactly what you're looking for. I've been led to believe that there's a provision that allows limited protective detention of witnesses or others suspected of enabling or committing high crimes or treason. I need to know if that is in fact true and, if so, exactly what it requires."

"I recall something about that, but I'd rather check it exactly before saying anything."

Dekkard smiled. "I'd rather you did as well."

Once Roostof left, Dekkard turned his attention, first, to the incoming letters, and after reading those and turning them over to Roostof, then to reading and signing, or rewriting, the stack of responses he hadn't finished the night before.

"I assume we're doing lunch," said Avraal at close to a third before noon.

"We are. There's always the possibility of finding out something."

Less than a sixth later, Dekkard, Avraal, and Gaaroll headed down the central staircase, when Avraal said, "I take it that the gray-haired man in the charcoal suit at the bottom of the stairs is Arturo Escalante."

"It is. Can you tell that he's an isolate?"

"He's not as strong as you are. A really powerful empath could make him a touch uncomfortable."

"One like you?"

"Possibly, but there wouldn't be much point in it."

The three followed Escalante, who was joined by Kharl Navione and Elskar Halljen at the entrance to the councilors' dining room, suggesting to Dekkard that Escalante was one of the Landors more likely to vote with the Crafters.

Dekkard and Avraal had barely stepped into the dining area when Ingrella Obreduur motioned for them to join her and Traelyna Treshaam. Dekkard ended up sitting beside Ingrella and across from Treshaam.

The auburn-haired Treshaam immediately said, "I've so wanted to have a chance to talk to both of you. From what I've read and what Councilor Obreduur has said—"

"Ingrella, please."

"That comes hard to me. I've respected you and your husband for so long."

"It took us a while to get used to using her first name," said Dekkard.

"It makes me feel younger," said Ingrella.

Treshaam offered a rueful smile and said, "From what Ingrella has said, you two are an amazing pair."

"Neither one of us would be here if it hadn't been for Axel and Ingrella," said Dekkard, "and all that they taught us."

"Mostly what Axel taught you," said Ingrella.

"But much of what he taught us," said Dekkard, with a smile, "was because of what he learned from you. And he said so." *If not in quite those words.*

"Steffan, you give me too much credit."

"No. You're not taking enough. Just as Axel wouldn't have accomplished all he did without you, I wouldn't be anywhere without all I learned from Avraal." *And I also wouldn't be alive.*

At that moment a server approached to take their order. Ingrella and Avraal had onion soup, Dekkard a half order of the duck cassoulet, and Treshaam a half order of the three-cheese chicken. All had café.

Once the server departed, Ingrella said, "Traelyna, did you know that Steffan has been appointed as chair of a special Security subcommittee investigating how the New Meritorists obtained all the dunnite they used?"

"As a matter of fact, Kaliara Bassaana asked me if that happened to be true." Treshaam laughed. "I told her that was news to me, which it was at the time. She did ask what I thought of you, Steffan."

"And?"

"I said that I didn't know you personally, but that any councilor that junior who managed to persuade the Council to pass any reform, especially Security reform, was someone to watch. She said you were definitely someone to watch—carefully. I got the feeling that she has a wary respect for you. What do you think of her?"

"She's very able," replied Dekkard. "She's also irritated at the lack of competence among male Commercer councilors, and she'll support Crafter initiatives to some degree, if they make sense and they suit her purposes. I'd never trust her to be the deciding vote, although she might well be."

"That sounds like you've talked to her more than a little."

"One of her security aides was very helpful in conveying messages to

Axel, and when I became a councilor I introduced myself. We talked in walks to the floor, and we had lunch several times. She's since approached me asking what the Premier would do with the Security Committee. I didn't know, and I told her that."

"Although you had a good idea?" asked Treshaam.

"I'd made some recommendations. The Premier didn't take them, and instead came up with a better approach."

"Which he would not have," said Avraal, "if you hadn't made the recommendations."

"I don't know that," replied Dekkard. "I prefer to give him full credit."

"And that is the way it should be," said Ingrella.

The conversation paused while the server delivered their meals.

Once the server departed, Dekkard asked Treshaam, "How did you become a councilor?"

"The short version is that I was the director of accounting for municipal transportation services in Jeeroh, and I kept pointing out ways to improve the system, only to find out that there was some rule or some administrator that precluded improvements. So I ran for Council in the previous election and lost. I ran again in the last election and won."

"That's more of a Commercer background," said Avraal.

"I could never be a Commercer. Besides, my husband is the guild steward for the ironway workers."

The remaining conversation dealt with sharing of personal backgrounds and anecdotes.

After lunch Ingrella and Dekkard went directly to the Council chamber, and Avraal went to the spouses' gallery to watch.

The Council session lasted only a little more than a bell, the sole business being consideration of provisions to reorganize the River Patrol and authorize an increase in the number of allowable patrollers in response to the surge in Atacaman refugees, as well as an increase in the smuggling of various illicit substances.

In the end, the legislation passed by a vote of fifty to sixteen.

By half past second bell, Dekkard, Avraal, and Gaaroll were back in Dekkard's office, where Dekkard worked on reading and signing responses until Roostof knocked on the door.

"Sir? I have the answer to your question."

"Have Avraal join us. Then come on in and close the door."

Once the three were seated, Roostof said, "That provision you asked about?"

"It doesn't exist?" asked Dekkard.

"No . . . it exists. It's a bit more convoluted than you stated, and from the way it's written, right now, only the Premier or you can exercise it."

Avraal raised her eyebrows.

"The exact wording reads"—Roostof looked down at the sheet he held—"'In the event of occurrences that jeopardize the Council and the Great Charter whereupon the Chairman of the Security Committee or a member of that Committee vested with the authority of the Chairman, in the course of investigating probable High Crimes or Treason, discovers probable cause that a witness acted to commit or enable the commission of such High Crimes or Treason, the Chairman or a councilor acting with the full authority of the Chairman may impose protective custody upon that individual or individuals immediately under the direct authority of the Council, said custody to last no longer than either a determination by the High Court that such custody is unwarranted or that it is warranted under the mandates of the Justiciary Ministry, whereby such individual or individuals shall be released, if custody is not warranted, or retained in pretrial custody under the provisions of the law. In no case, however, shall custody under Council authority exceed two weeks.'"

"So, apparently I have that authority."

"Until it's revoked," replied Roostof. "In the course of researching the hearings, I was reminded of another situation that you may face, sir. It's the doctrine of collective knowledge, otherwise known to legalists as effective personal denial."

"I have no idea what that means legally, Svard, but I don't like what it sounds like."

"I'll do my best to explain. No one would question that shipping dunnite to someone who isn't authorized to use it is a crime. *But* within the corporacion, that action requires several people. The shipping clerk is ordered to prepare the documents to ship dunnite to Capitol Services. He's told it's all right. The legalist knows that Capitol Services can receive up to a decem, but has to report it. However, he doesn't know that two hundred decems were shipped. The person who tells the clerk assumes the order from higher authority is correct. The higher authority will claim he was following orders. So the corporacion as a whole has the collective knowledge that what was done was against the law, and therefore the corporacion can be charged with illegal shipping, but unless you can prove intent and knowledge of what the dunnite was to be used for on the part of a specific higher authority, the Justiciary Ministry is likely only to be able to prosecute the corporacion, rather than individuals, and only for violations of shipping limitations and enabling excessive possession of explosives."

"So we have to prove that, first, dunnite went to Capitol Services, second, that whoever ordered the shipping knew that the dunnite would be used criminally, and third, that it would be used against Security buildings, and against the Council?"

"Roughly . . . yes."

"Can we just order the presidente of either corporacion to appear and testify?"

"You can, but without building a case from lower-level employees, the High Court may well disallow even empath-verified testimony."

"What about testimony from other senior officers?"

"That would suffice if a lower-level employee testified that he or she had been ordered to ship the dunnite."

"If not," Avraal asked quietly, "could Steffan make the point that memory blockage by empaths can be used, and therefore higher-level employees need to testify?"

"The Council has that power. Whether information discovered in that fashion would be accepted in a case of high crimes by the High Court is another question."

"Could you look into that?" asked Dekkard. "Quietly."

"Yes, sir. I'll see what I can find."

Once Roostof left, Dekkard looked to Avraal. "You know, neither you nor Nincya have sensed any dangers. I'm beginning to see why Suvion Industries isn't worried."

"Not yet," replied Avraal, "but once you start getting Suvion Industries personnel to testify, that could change quickly."

"If that's what we have to do, then we'll figure out how to do it. If we don't . . . ?" *The Imperium of Guldor as we know it will inevitably, if slowly, and inexorably, vanish, and we'll follow the path of the Grand Democracy of Teknold.*

Dekkard looked at the remaining responses that he needed to read and sign or revise. He took a deep breath and picked up his pen.

58

AT a third past second bell on Quindi morning, Dekkard, Avraal, and Gaaroll were in the staff offices of the Security Committee, where Dekkard had made sure that there were no messages, and that the clerk taking down the testimony had the current witness list.

Then he said to Gaaroll, "You'll have to wait here until the hearing is over for the day. We should finish before noon." Personally, Dekkard thought the hearing would be shorter, but that depended on how many questions others on the subcommittee asked and how verbose the witnesses might be.

Then he turned to Avraal and to Larelli Daespaan, the Council Guard empath. "As I understand the procedures, if a witness remains truthful, you do nothing. If you lift a hand, I should ask the witness to repeat the statement, and if you raise your hand again, I'm to suggest to the witness that there's some doubt as to the veracity of the statement. Is that correct?"

"Yes, Councilor," replied Daespaan, clad in the formal uniform of a Council Guard.

Avraal, in a severe but tailored security-gray jacket and trousers, and wearing the small gold pin with a red stone in the center, also nodded.

Several minutes before third bell, Dekkard, the two empaths, and the recording clerk entered the main Security Committee room. Breffyn Haastar, Tomas Pajiin, and Villem Baar were already seated. Dekkard and those accompanying him took their places.

The Navy witnesses were seated at a table facing the subcommittee, while Avraal and Larelli Daespaan sat at a small table set in front of the inside wall midway between the committee desk on the low dais and the witness table. The clerk taking down the testimony sat at another small table under the outside wall and across from the empaths' table.

As the three bells died away, Dekkard tapped the gavel once. "The special investigatory subcommittee of the Security Committee is now in session. The subcommittee appreciates the presence of Admiral Draavyn Jingao, chief of Naval Logistics, and Commodore Chymyn Triaste, chief of Naval Munitions, as well as those of you accompanying them. The purpose of the subcommittee is to investigate the circumstances surrounding the possession of an estimated two tonnes of dunnite by the insurgent group known as the New Meritorists. Because the dunnite was used against more than fifteen Security buildings or structures, as well as against the Council and its buildings, all hearings by the subcommittee are being conducted under the procedures required in the investigation of high crimes and treason, with two certified empaths in attendance for all testimony, even for witnesses providing background and supporting information. Disclosure of information revealed in this hearing to unauthorized persons is prohibited."

Dekkard paused, then said, "Admiral Jingao, the subcommittee appreciates your appearance. While the subcommittee has a number of questions for you and Commodore Triaste, would you care to offer any opening remarks?"

"Thank you, Sr. Chairman. I do not have any prepared remarks, but we do appreciate the opportunity to provide useful information to the subcommittee and to work with the subcommittee to assure that there are no misconceptions about the careful fashion in which the Navy, and particularly the Naval Logistics Command, manages the logistics of weapons, especially projectiles employing high explosives. Since the establishment of the Naval Munitions Command more than thirty years ago, there has not been a single fatality in either the manufacture or transportation of naval munitions. There has also never been a documented instance of the diversion of explosives from any naval facility or vessel. We are, I believe, justifiably proud of that record, and we intend to maintain and improve the procedures which have established that success in safe manufacturing and transportation of all types of naval munitions. Also, we are more than willing to work with the Council and the subcommittee to improve the handling and transport of high explosives before they reach the Naval Munitions facility."

"Again, we appreciate the benefit of your presence and your expertise," said Dekkard. "I apologize in advance for the simplicity of the initial questions, but they're necessary to establish the factual background."

Both the commodore and the admiral nodded.

"For what applications does the Navy employ dunnite?"

Jingao nodded to Triaste, who cleared his throat, then replied, "For the past ten years, the only military use of dunnite has been as the primary explosive in naval munitions, exclusively in gun projectiles, often referred to as shells. All dunnite is shipped to the naval munitions works in Plaatz. The Navy does not take possession of the dunnite until it is logged in at the works." Triaste went on to describe the log-in procedures in detail.

When the commodore finished, Dekkard asked, "These procedures apply equally to the dunnite provided by Northwest Industrial Chemical and Suvion Industries?"

"They do, Sr. Chairman."

"I understand that, while the chemical composition of the dunnite provided is exactly the same, the color varies depending on the manufacturer? Is that correct?"

"It is. The dunnite provided by Northwest Industrial Chemical is yellow, but several shades darker than that provided by Suvion Industries. That way we can be sure not to mix batches in individual projectiles."

"But if they're chemically identical?"

"The differentiation is a precaution required by the Legalist of the Navy."

"Thank you. In what form is dunnite shipped?"

"Dunnite is shipped in standard fifteen-decem kegs, designed to be watertight and with no metal or metal surfaces on the interior surface of the kegs."

"So . . . two tonnes of dunnite would take almost thirty kegs, which would require at least a small lorry to transport."

"If you were transporting them all at once. We use smaller carts at the Plaatz munitions facility."

"What procedures does the plant use to track the dunnite once it is logged in?" asked Dekkard.

"Each keg is weighed and numbered, then transported to the explosives warehouse, where it's entered into the warehouse inventory. When dunnite is needed for projectiles, the kegs are again weighed and transferred to the munitions works' inventory. At the end of each production run, the number of projectiles and the weight of their explosives content are cross-checked against the dunnite input. There is some slight loss in the production process. But it runs less than a percent."

"Is there a cross-check on how much dunnite is used for projectiles, by for example noting how many projectiles of what size have been produced and added to the inventory?"

"As I noted earlier, that is part of the inventory and record-keeping process." Triaste went on to explain further.

Dekkard then looked to Haastar. "Councilor?"

Haastar smiled pleasantly, then asked, "Why exactly was the Naval Munitions Command established?"

Triaste offered a wry smile. "That was considerably before my time, but my understanding is that there was considerable variability in the tolerances for gun projectiles produced by various civilian munitions facilities.

Some were unable to be loaded into guns. Some fitted too loosely in the barrel, and that meant range and impact velocity were adversely affected."

"So the Navy was forced to manufacture its own munitions because of excessive costs and low quality of civilian facilities?"

"I believe that to be the case."

"Thank you," said Haastar. "How then does the Navy assure that the quality of the dunnite produced by civilian sources meets Navy standards?"

"The munitions works takes random samples from each incoming batch. The works also notes which batches go in what projectiles. We can theoretically trace a malfunction in a projectile back to a batch and manufacturer."

As Triaste explained, Dekkard got the distinct feeling that the Naval Munitions Command didn't fully trust either Northwest Industrial Chemical or Suvion Industries with anything that couldn't be tested and verified. *Which leads to another question.*

That was Haastar's next inquiry. "Given the efforts your command makes to assure quality, has the Navy ever considered simply producing its own dunnite?"

Triaste did not reply, but nodded to Admiral Jingao.

"Councilor," said Jingao, "that course of action was proposed three times in the decade following the creation of the Naval Munitions Command. On each occasion, the Council passed legislation denying the Navy's request. The Council made the point that while manufacturing the actual munitions was in the interests of the Navy and the Imperium as a whole, if the Navy manufactured dunnite, the Council would be subsidizing a competitor to the domestic blasting industry," but as Jingao continued his voice turned sardonic, "even though other explosives are far better suited to domestic blasting and mining use."

"Thank you very much, Admiral," replied Haastar.

Dekkard turned to Pajiin. "Councilor?"

"No questions at present, Sr. Chairman."

"Councilor Baar?"

"Commodore Triaste, you mentioned quality testing. Is there any statistical difference between the success or failure rates of the dunnite produced by the two suppliers of dunnite to the Naval Munitions Command?"

"Councilor, in recent years, only three batches of dunnite have been rejected. None in the past year, but two from Suvion Industries in 1265, and one from Northwest Industrial Chemical in late 1264."

"What about in prior years?" asked Baar.

"I'd have to check the records, Councilor. I've only been in my present posting the past several months, and I haven't had a chance to review all of the older records. I'd be happy to send any information we have since 1257. We don't keep testing records more than ten years."

"If you would," said Dekkard, "the subcommittee would appreciate that."

"No further questions," said Baar.

"Admiral Jingao," said Dekkard pleasantly, "there is one other matter that bears on the misdirection of dunnite to the New Meritorists. The former acting Minister of Security, Deputy Security Minister Maartyn Manwaeren, stated before the full committee that the Navy had reported the theft of a considerable amount of dunnite. The Premier later recovered that letter from Security Ministry files. I realize that you later spoke with Premier Obreduur about that letter. For the record, and the information of the subcommittee, would you clarify that situation?"

"The letter to which you refer is a forgery. While the letterhead is correct, and the signature is purported to be that of Admiral Gorral, my predecessor, the signature is only a rough approximation of the admiral's actual signature. More to the point, the body of the letter is replete with inaccuracies. It referenced the transportation of dunnite by lorry. Such transport is only by ironway. It also referenced Navy guards. As Commodore Triaste previously stated, the Navy does not even take possession of the dunnite until it is unloaded at the Navy ironway freight depot at Plaatz. Furthermore, the letter referred to lost barrels. Dunnite is shipped in kegs."

When Jingao finished, Dekkard said, "Thank you, very much, Admiral. While I doubt seriously that the Navy would ever lose or misplace dunnite, how would the Navy report, say, even a mishap with a loading cart that resulted in even a single keg breaking?"

"The officer in charge of that section of the plant would file a report. That report would be reviewed by a board of inquiry, which would issue a finding of cause."

"Would such a report be sent to the former Security Ministry or the present Ministry of Public Safety?"

"That would be highly unlikely." Jingao's tone was even. "Unless there happened to be a crime committed or an explosion with injuries, the reports would remain on file with the Navy."

"Sr. Chairman?" asked Baar.

Dekkard nodded.

"Admiral," Baar continued, "are there any such reports on file covering the last three years?"

"There have been no mishaps and no reports over that period."

Dekkard glanced to Avraal and the Council Guard empath. Neither lifted a hand. Dekkard then looked to Jingao. "Is there any other information that you feel is relevant to this investigation which the subcommittee has not raised or of which the subcommittee is unaware?"

"I would not presume to pass judgment on the awareness of the subcommittee, or the lack thereof," said Jingao, with the hint of a smile, "but I would like to thank the subcommittee for the open-ended questions that focused entirely on the matter at hand. We will provide the testing records within the week."

"Thank you, Admiral, Commodore." Dekkard scanned the faces of the other councilors, then said, "While it appears unlikely, I must inform you that, if other questions arise that are critical to the subcommittee's mission, there is always the possibility that we may require additional information or testimony."

"We understand that possibility," replied Jingao.

"There being no other questions, the subcommittee is adjourned until third morning bell on Unadi." Dekkard tapped the gavel once.

As the other councilors and the witnesses stood, Dekkard was surprised to see Admiral Jingao moving toward the dais. Wondering what the admiral might have to say, Dekkard moved around the desk and off the dais.

"Councilor," said Jingao, with a pleasant easy smile, "I just wanted to thank you for keeping the hearing short and to the point. If you need any more information of this nature, we'll be more than happy to provide it."

"I appreciate that, Admiral. If we do, I'll let you know."

"It's a pity that Minister Wyath didn't live to be ordered to testify. One way or another, he could have provided a great deal of information."

"I'm certain he could have, as could have a few others."

"That's true, but assassinations often leave other traces. In any event, we wish you success in tracking down the origin of the dunnite." Jingao smiled pleasantly once more, then turned and walked to join Commodore Triaste.

Dekkard turned immediately to Breffyn Haastar. "Thank you for your questions."

"The admiral seemed to want to answer them."

"That's good for us."

Dekkard looked around for Pajiin and Baar, but both had already left the committee chamber. So he walked over to where Avraal stood alone beside the empath table. "Were there any revealing feelings?"

"Only that the admiral was pleased to answer Breffyn's question."

"I suspect it was something he couldn't volunteer."

"No doubt of that," said Avraal dryly.

"Now, I need to report to Hasheem. Then we can have lunch, and see if anyone wants to join us."

While Dekkard was wary on the short walk to Hasheem's floor office, neither Avraal nor Gaaroll sensed anything out of the ordinary.

Once Dekkard was seated in the small office, Hasheem asked, in a tone of mild surprise, "Is the hearing over already?"

"It is."

"What did you accomplish?"

"We obtained the background information we'll need, plus a bit more, including some testimony that suggests that both Suvion Industries and Northwest Industrial Chemical are likely making excess profits on the production and sale of dunnite to the Navy and are sloppy enough in their production that the Navy has to conduct continual quality checks. That, of course, wasn't the point of the hearing, but it might come in useful at some point."

"That's on the record?"

"It is, thanks to questions by Breffyn Haastar and Villem Baar."

"Even so, it might be difficult to prove what you're after."

"We likely have enough information to put Suvion Industries in an unpleasant position, and we'll find out next week whether there's circumstantial evidence against others."

"Circumstantial evidence is hardly enough, Steffan."

"Not for a Justiciary charge and trial." *But the newssheets would love it.* "We'll just have to see what else the rest of the hearings reveal."

Hasheem nodded, dubiously. "There's no need to meet on Unadi morning, not unless you discover something new and profound. Stop by after the hearing."

"I'll do that. Enjoy your endday."

"As I can, Steffan."

"I'll see you on Unadi, then," said Dekkard as he stood.

Neither Dekkard nor Avraal spoke until he, Avraal, and Gaaroll were out in the main corridor, walking toward the councilors' dining room.

"That was short," said Avraal.

"There wasn't much to say. He's still dubious about how much new the subcommittee will discover."

Gaaroll offered a muffled snort.

"He has been dubious about a great deal," said Avraal, if with a smile.

"But he has supported you, even if he likely feels that he doesn't have much choice."

"So we just have to disprove his doubt, again."

"Of course. Each time you do, you gain power. Power means you can do more to rein in the corporacions and Commercers. But you know that."

"Sometimes, I like a little reassurance."

"At times, we all do."

Dekkard understood. *She's telling you to stop complaining, and she's right.*

He didn't say much more until they were seated at a table for four in the councilors' dining room and had ordered.

"What was your general reaction to the hearing?" he asked.

"You did what you needed to do."

"What about the commodore and the admiral? What were they feeling?"

"The commodore was there to do his duty, effectively and professionally. So was the admiral, but beneath that professional surface and those calm and even words, he despises both Northwest Industrial Chemical and Suvion Industries. I couldn't say which he detests more."

"What feeling did you get from Larelli Daespaan?"

"She was mildly interested, and felt it was better than doing nothing."

"It might get more interesting over the coming weeks, but not as soon as I'd originally thought."

"Because of what Svard told you about the collective knowledge of corporacions?"

"That's my feeling," replied Dekkard. "We can likely prove that Suvion Industries broke more than a few laws, but if we don't come up with a way to pin responsibility on someone of import, the corporacion will pay heavy penalties, but none of those really behind sending dunnite to Capitol Services, and nothing will change."

"Except you and I will likely perish in an 'accident' or a fire or some other disaster, sooner or later, just like Kraffeist and the Griegs."

"It's also looking like pinning responsibility on anyone of import is going to be difficult *and* take longer."

"Doesn't everything take longer?" asked Avraal.

"Unless it's a disaster, and then we won't have enough time to react effectively," replied Dekkard.

As he slowly ate the mixed green salad topped with chicken, he kept thinking about the legal doctrine of collective knowledge, and wondered if there might be some way to employ it with all the banque drafts most likely originating from various corporacions to show a pattern of corporate linkage to Capitol Services and thus to the New Meritorists, even though Dekkard was almost certain that hadn't been the original purpose of much of the funding.

After lunch and for much of Findi he also needed to put in more work on the questions for the officials that were presumably coming from Northwest Industrial Chemical for Unadi's subcommittee hearings.

59

DEKKARD woke early on Findi, but just lay in bed thinking for a time about Presider Buusen's homily on the need to carry on and trust the Almighty, with which Dekkard definitely disagreed. His disagreement wasn't about carrying on, but about blind trust in the Almighty. That led to running various ideas and strategies through his mind before Avraal woke. When they finally rose and went down to breakfast, each wore old security grays.

Emrelda looked up from her café and grinned. "It's about time, and don't tell me you were tired."

Dekkard looked back at her and said, deadpan, "We're tired now."

Avraal gave him a gentle elbow in the gut, but smiled.

Dekkard escaped to the kitchen, while Avraal seated herself at the table. Dekkard returned shortly with two mugs of café, one of which he set carefully before his wife.

"Thank you, dear."

"How long before I have to start really worrying again?" asked Emrelda.

"I'm worried now," replied Dekkard. "It all depends on whether certain corporacions decide to rely on legalists or assassins."

"Assassins are surer," said Avraal, "but can leave a trail. Legalists obliterate the trail, but sometimes aren't as effective."

"That means you have to worry about both. How soon?"

"Maybe now," said Dekkard. "Certainly after the hearings on Unadi."

"Why then?" asked Gaaroll as she entered the breakfast room.

"Because it will be obvious to the witnesses testifying that the hearings are not a mere formality and that the subcommittee intends to pursue the matter fully," said Dekkard.

"It will be even more obvious that the subcommittee *chairman* intends to pursue the matter," added Avraal, "and it's not exactly unknown that he can be very effective."

"I thought you said that revealing the testimony is prohibited," said Emrelda. "Or is a little matter like the law irrelevant to corporacions?"

Dekkard thought the acid in Emrelda's voice could have etched the words in stone. "Apparently, it has been for quite some time, as we all know. The corporacions who transferred marks to Capitol Services are all in this together, at least to some extent."

"Can't the Justiciary prosecute them?" asked Emrelda.

"Not without more evidence," replied Dekkard, "and the Justiciary is rather overwhelmed with the numbers of New Meritorists and looters at the moment. If we wait until all those dockets are processed, individuals and evidence may not be available—one way or another."

"Why would the Justiciary take up anything you discover any sooner?"

"Because the Great Charter requires it." Dekkard went on to explain.

"That suggests Guard Captain Trujillo doesn't trust the Premier to act in a timely fashion."

"Couldn't act in a timely fashion if you strapped a clock to his neck," muttered Gaaroll.

"Guard Captain Trujillo lost a number of Council Guards," said Dekkard. "I suspect he doesn't want a recurrence. That could easily happen if we don't put away those behind it."

"What's to keep that from happening again?" asked Emrelda.

"If the Council doesn't change a few laws and practices, then nothing. But putting away some of those involved—if we're successful—just might buy us enough time and support to make those changes."

"Provided nothing happens to you," said Emrelda.

"*If* we can get through the first part of the hearings, and *if* we can bring to light enough evidence, it may not matter, and at that point, removing me might just make matters worse for the corporacions involved."

"Until that time . . ." offered Emrelda.

"From now on, and especially after Unadi, we're going to have to be very careful." Dekkard took a sip of café, then asked, "What do you have planned for the day?"

"You work on your questions for the hearing," said Avraal. "Emrelda and I will do some shopping, and later you can help with dinner." Her eyes went to Gaaroll. "Your job, Nincya, is to stay here and make sure no strong emotions approach the house undetected while Steffan is working."

Gaaroll nodded.

60

WHILE Dekkard spent much of Findi formulating and reformulating questions for the coming hearing, he also spent a good bell, with the others, practicing throwing knives, a practice complicated by a brisk wind out of the northeast. He slept moderately well, at least until he woke in the middle of the night with another nightmare where he failed to save Obreduur. After that, his sleep was troubled, but he woke at his usual time. The morning routine was uninterrupted by any untoward occurrences, as was the drive to the covered parking for councilors.

After walking to his office and spending less than a sixth there, just to make certain there were no urgent messages, since the mail hadn't yet arrived, Dekkard set out for the Council Hall, escorted by Avraal and Gaaroll.

Once they were in the Council Hall and walking past the councilors' lobby toward the committee rooms, Gaaroll said, "Strong feelings ahead, sir."

"From the Security Committee chamber or staff offices?"

"No, sir. Across the hall from there."

From the Military Affairs Committee? "Dangerous feelings? Or just strong?"

"Real strong. They're fading now."

Dekkard looked to Avraal.

"I could only sense a touch of that. We're a bit far for me, but it felt like an outburst of anger."

When Dekkard, Avraal, and Gaaroll stepped into the Security Committee offices, Mario deCaastro, the Security Committee staff director, hurried toward Dekkard. "Sir, the Premier asked that you stop by his floor office as soon as you arrived."

"Did he say why?"

"No, sir."

Now what? Dekkard refrained from shaking his head and gestured for Avraal and Gaaroll to accompany him back to Hasheem's floor office. *Has some witness failed to show up? Is the Imperador getting involved?*

Once he stepped inside the outer part of the floor office, Meldra immediately gestured for Dekkard to go into the inner office. Dekkard did so, closing the door.

Hasheem looked up, but didn't gesture for Dekkard to sit. "Steffan, although you did not request his presence, Ansel Gutarez, the vice-presidente of operations for Northwest Industrial Chemical, has requested to be included as a possible witness. Do you have any objection to including him?"

So he can make sure that no one strays from the corporacion line, no doubt. "So long as he doesn't interrupt the scheduled witnesses." *Or attempt to intimidate or coerce them, except he's likely already done that.*

"I'll leave it to you to make that explanation, then. I just didn't want you to be surprised."

"I appreciate the notice, Fredrich. Thank you. Is that all?"

"It is, except for letting me know the results of the hearing."

"Then I'll let the rest of the subcommittee know about the change." Dekkard smiled pleasantly, then nodded and left the inner office.

Only after Dekkard, Avraal, and Gaaroll headed back to the Security Committee staff offices through the main corridor did Avraal speak. "Can I ask?"

"Ansel Gutarez, the vice-presidente of operations for Northwest Industrial Chemical, has requested to be included in the hearings. I'd like you to let me know if you sense anything out of the ordinary. Just say you have a technical question and walk up to the center of the committee desk. I hope it won't be necessary. Also, tell Larelli Daespaan that you may have to do that."

"She won't object," said Avraal.

"Good."

As soon as Dekkard reached the staff offices, he gestured to deCaastro. "Mario, please have someone tell each councilor to join me here before entering the main committee room."

"Yes, sir." The staff director immediately moved away and began to talk to one of the clerks.

Given that deCaastro didn't seem in the slightest surprised by the order, Dekkard had no doubt that Hasheem had already told the staff director, but had asked for Dekkard to see him in order not to put deCaastro in the position of ordering a councilor to do something, because, despite Fredrich's politeness, it had been an order. *Will something similar happen with Suvion Industries?*

The first subcommittee member to arrive was Breffyn Haastar, followed by Villem Baar, and then Tomas Pajiin.

"The reason I asked you all to join me here first is that the Premier decided to make an accommodation for Northwest Industrial Chemical. The corporacion's vice-presidente of operations asked to be included in the hearings. The Premier agreed."

"That's . . . unusual," said Haastar, frowning.

"Can he do that?" asked Pajiin.

"He's the Premier and the chair of the full committee," said Dekkard dryly. "I'd rather not object over including another witness. I've already asked the empaths to inform me if something unusual is going on."

"I'm beginning to see why you wanted Ritten Ysella-Dekkard as an additional empath," said Baar. "Did you have any idea this might occur?"

"Not this in particular, but I thought something out of the ordinary might occur." Dekkard paused. "We'll enter by the staff entrance. Shall we go?"

Dekkard led the way into the main committee room. The chamber was set up as it had been on Quindi, with the four witnesses already seated at the table facing the dais. He noticed that the vice-presidente as well as the other three witnesses each had a nameplate, and he wondered how long Hasheem had known. When all the councilors on the committee were seated, Dekkard waited for the three chimes to sound before he gaveled the subcommittee to order.

As the three bells died away, Dekkard tapped the gavel once. "The special investigatory subcommittee of the Security Committee is now in session. The subcommittee appreciates the presence of Ansel Gutarez, vice-presidente of operations for Northwest Industrial Chemical; Heilbart Marcuse, production manager; Kastor Guufrey, shipping and transportation manager; and Claytaan Shoull, director of security." From there Dekkard gave precisely the same explanation and cautions as he had on the previous Quindi. Then he paused before saying, "Sr. Gutarez, the subcommittee appreciates your appearance, and the appearance of Sr. Shoull, Sr. Marcuse, and Sr. Guufrey. While the subcommittee has a number of questions for each of you, would you care to offer any opening remarks on behalf of Northwest Industrial Chemical?"

"Thank you, Sr. Chairman. I would." Gutarez smiled warmly and effusively, the kind of smile Dekkard instinctively distrusted. "Northwest Industrial Chemical would like to assure the investigatory subcommittee and, by extension, the full Security Committee and the Council of Sixty-Six, that the corporacion fully supports the subcommittee's efforts to discover the source of the dunnite used by the insurgency calling itself the New Meritorists. Any person or organization that would willingly enable an insurgency by providing high explosives to a group obsessed with the destruction of the longest-standing and fairest government in the world has indeed committed a high crime and should face the consequences. We are willing to assist in this effort by providing whatever information the subcommittee requires."

As Gutarez spoke, Dekkard's eyes flicked to the table where Avraal and Larelli Daespaan sat, but neither indicated any sign of sensing untruths.

"Thank you, Sr. Gutarez, the subcommittee appreciates your statement of support. We will initially concentrate on Northwest's production process. Sr. Marcuse, will you briefly explain how your facility produces dunnite? It would be helpful if you could also explain to the subcommittee the measures the facility takes to assure that finished dunnite is not removed in the final stages of production."

"Sr. Chairman, Northwest Industrial Chemical produces a wide range of chemicals and products based on coal tar obtained largely as a by-product of coking furnaces. To manufacture dunnite, the coal tar is processed to obtain phenol, and the phenol is further processed to obtain picric acid, which is also highly explosive, particularly when its crystalline form remains in contact with a range of metals for any length of time. Picric acid is too sensitive and too hazardous for military or commercial blasting, but by processing the picric acid with ammonia, we obtain a solution which, when dewatered and cooled, forms crystals of ammonium picrate, otherwise known as dunnite. Until the final crystals are dried, there is no way to divert any of the dunnite. From that point onward, strict inventory-control measures are in place, including comparing gross batch output to the weight contained in the shipping kegs of that batch. Each keg is sealed and numbered."

Dekkard listened closely as Marcuse detailed the rest of the process. When the production manager finished, he said, "Thank you. Sr. Marcuse. Are there any questions?"

"Yes, Sr. Chairman," said Tomas Pajiin.

"Go ahead, Councilor."

"This might be slightly off-track, but what sorts of impurities and residues result from the dewatering process?"

"Given the nature of the process, there are few solids left in the wastewater, and the amount of ammonium picrate in the wastewater is minuscule. The wastewater is discharged into evaporation lagoons, which are rotated. The excess ammonia is released as a gas during evaporation. We don't discharge the wastewater into any nearby streams."

Several questions later, including several about quality control, Dekkard rapped the gavel gently. "Perhaps we should hear from Sr. Guufrey about the shipping and transportation procedures used by Northwest Industrial

Chemical. Sr. Guufrey, at present, or for the last five years, has North-west shipped dunnite to anyone other than the Navy, and if so, have you brought the invoices and shipping documents for such sales, as requested by the subcommittee?"

"Sir, the only customer we have for dunnite is the Navy. Other explosives are better for mining or construction blasting."

"Would you be so kind as to describe the basic procedures for shipping kegs of dunnite?"

"Yes, sir. All the shipping is by ironway, and with special locked freight carriages. There's an inventory locked in the carriages, and a separate and identical inventory dispatched by secure message service to the Naval Munitions Plant in Plaatz." From there, Guufrey described, in excruciating detail over the next half bell, the shipping and inventory process.

Even though Dekkard had a less than favorable opinion of the deceased Jaime Minz, after listening to Kastor Guufrey, Dekkard could see why Minz had declared that every bit of dunnite from Northwest Industrial Chemical would be fully documented and that no one would find otherwise. *Whether the documentation is accurate is another question.*

"Sr. Guufrey," said Dekkard, "you said that you sent an inventory to the Navy for each shipment. Has the Navy ever disputed an inventory?"

"Not in the six years I've been shipping manager."

"Do you contract out any of the handling of dunnite?" asked Villem Baar.

"Only the ironway transportation, sir, and the freight carriages are sealed and locked. Only our people and the Navy have the combination lock numbers. They're changed for each shipment."

When the questions for Guufrey ended, Dekkard turned to Claytaan Shoull. "Sr. Shoull, would you please describe the scope of your duties as director of security and tell us how long you've held that position?"

"I've been the director of security for the past three years and three months. Before that I was the deputy director of security for close to five years. My duties include overseeing physical security at all Northwest Industrial Chemical facilities as well as investigating any possible compromise of proprietary production or research materials."

"Do your duties include monitoring the security of shipments of dunnite to the Navy?" asked Dekkard.

"The actual security monitoring of all shipments is carried out by the manager of shipping security, who reports to me."

"How many breaches of shipping security have occurred in the last two years?"

"Three," replied Shoull. "All of them involved thefts or attempted thefts of tolite."

Dekkard was familiar with tolite, the blasting explosive that was sold in sticks of waxed cardboard more suited to mining or commercial blasting. "What were those instances?"

"In one instance, the thief was caught inside one of our transport lorries. In the second, working with local patrollers, we tracked down the thieves who had forced their way into one of our regional warehouses. We recovered all but one stick of the tolite. We're still working on the third instance, which occurred two weeks ago, when one of our lorries was caught in heavy snow near Caylaan. A decem case of tolite was taken."

"But you've had no instances of thefts of dunnite or missing dunnite?"

"No, Councilor, we have not. Not during my time as director or deputy director."

Dekkard looked to the other members of the subcommittee. "Are there any other questions? Councilor Haastar?"

"Thank you, Sr. Chairman." The Landor councilor looked to Shoull. "I'm fairly certain that Northwest Industrial Chemical has more than a few proprietary processing methods and equipment. Is a portion of your duties devoted to assuring that competitors do not gain access to such methods and equipment?"

"The chemical production facilities can be very dangerous for anyone unfamiliar with them. Part of physical security is also to make certain that anyone not authorized to be in a given area is kept from that area, for various reasons, but primarily to assure a safe workplace. Obviously, that would include unauthorized outsiders."

"What about protecting access to engineering designs or drawings?" pressed Haastar.

"Our job is to protect physical intrusion. It's up to the engineers to keep their plans and processes locked away."

"Thank you for the clarification, Director Shoull. I have no further questions at this time."

"Councilor Pajiin?" asked Dekkard.

"Director Shoull, in the case of workplace disputes, are you responsible for the security of both inventory and facilities?"

"We are, as I already indicated. We also haven't had any workplace disputes in the time I've been director."

But he was talking about his time as director and deputy director when he answered your question about losses and thefts of dunnite. Interesting.

"Are all your duties related to physical and production security?"

"And to the protection, if necessary, of all personnel, as I said before."

"Have you ever had anyone break into the dunnite production facilities?" asked Pajiin.

"In my time in security, we've had no break-ins at the production facilities."

After several more questions about facility security, when it appeared the other councilors had no additional questions, Dekkard said, "I have a slightly different question for you, Director Shoull. A former security aide for the Security Committee in the last Council was employed by Northwest Industrial Chemical as an assistant director of security, with an office here in Machtarn. His name was Jaime Minz. What can you tell me about him?"

Dekkard could see the slight stiffening of both Gutarez and Shoull, but just waited.

Gutarez murmured something to Shoull, and the director of security cleared his throat, then said, "I did not know Sr. Minz. In fact, I never met him. I have no knowledge of what his duties were or to whom he reported. It is my understanding that he was hired as an influencer, but listed as an assistant director of security because he was not a trained legalist."

"From where did you gain that 'understanding'?" asked Dekkard.

"When Sr. Minz's name and salary came up on my payroll, I went to the director of accounting to inquire. That was what I was told. I was also told that the amount of his salary had been transferred to my budget from the budget of the legalist department. I said that it was highly irregular. I was told that the matter was settled, and not to inquire further."

"The director of accounting told you that?"

"Yes, sir."

"Do you know who made the decision to hire Sr. Minz?"

"I do not."

Dekkard looked to the empaths' table. Neither raised a hand.

"Sr. Gutarez, as a vice-presidente, do you know who made that decision?"

"I do not know."

"I'll phrase that in a different way, then. Could you, as a vice-presidente, hire someone and pay them through another department without seeking authorization or approval?"

Gutarez did not speak for several moments, but finally said, "I don't know. I never even considered doing anything like that."

"Who could?"

"I don't know."

Both empaths raised their hands.

"Would you like to reconsider that answer, Sr. Gutarez?" asked Dekkard coolly.

"I'd rather not, Sr. Chairman."

"You have a choice," said Dekkard. "You can answer the question honestly, or you can spend whatever time it takes for you to do so in detention here in the Council Hall. This is an investigation involving high crimes and possible treason. No appeal to the High Justiciary will release you. Only an honest answer will."

"You would do that?"

Dekkard concentrated on his words as he looked intently at Gutarez. "I've had to kill people in the line of duty, Sr. Gutarez. People have tried to kill me. Your answer?"

At the impact of Dekkard's words, Gutarez swallowed, once, twice. Finally, he said, "I don't know absolutely. This is the only instance I've heard about. I suppose one could get the approval of the corporacion vicepresidente, or the vice-presidente for legal affairs, but I wouldn't even consider anything like that without the approval of Presidente Chassont."

Neither Avraal nor Larelli Daespaan lifted a hand.

"Director Shoull, who paid for the Machtarn office expenses of Sr. Minz?"

"I don't know, sir. I do know that any expenses did not come from my budget."

"Sr. Gutarez?" asked Dekkard.

"I also do not know. To my knowledge, none of Sr. Minz's expenses came from any facility operations budget."

"Thank you, Sr. Gutarez. Just a few more questions. Sr. Guufrey, have you ever seen or heard the name 'Capitol Services'?"

Guufrey looked puzzled, then frowned as if trying to see if he could place the name. Finally, he said, "We ship to several hundred people and corporacions, but I don't recall that name."

"What about the rest of you?" asked Dekkard. "Sr. Shoull?"

"No, sir."

"Sr. Marcuse?"

"No, sir."

"Sr. Gutarez?"

"No, Sr. Chairman."

"Does any other member of the subcommittee have any last questions?"

"I do, Sr. Chairman," said Tomas Pajiin.

Dekkard nodded to Pajiin.

"Sr. Gutarez, you were not ordered to appear as a witness, but you requested to be included. Would you tell the subcommittee why you made that request? Also, who, if anyone, in the corporacion requested or suggested you appear?"

Gutarez glanced at Dekkard, moistened his lips, then said, "An order to appear before a Council committee always goes to the vice-presidente for legal affairs, Kurtois Hadenaur, for legal review, as well as to those ordered to appear. Legalist Hadenaur suggested I might wish to accompany the witnesses and ask to be included, in order to see if any of the questions dealt with proprietary matters . . ."

Hadenaur? Any relation to the Sanitation guildmeister? Dekkard doubted it, although it was possible, but with the size of the Imperium, similarities in surnames often came up.

". . . I was relieved that they did not, since in the past, some hearings have tended in that direction."

"Did anyone else have comments or give you direction about the hearing?" asked Pajiin.

"No one else even spoke to me about the hearing," replied Gutarez.

"Thank you, Sr. Gutarez."

Dekkard looked to Baar, who shook his head, then to Haastar, who did the same. "The witnesses are excused, as are empaths and committee staff. The subcommittee will remain for a brief executive session."

Once the chamber was clear except for the subcommittee members, Dekkard simply asked, "Thoughts?"

"From what I heard," said Pajiin, "they're cold bastards. But it'd surprise me if they had anything to do with getting dunnite to the New Meritorists. That business with Minz stinks, though."

"It would seem that way," replied Dekkard. "Councilor Baar, you're the practicing legalist. What do you make of that hiring arrangement for Jaime Minz?"

Baar frowned. "I'd say that Legalist Hadenaur didn't want Sr. Minz to appear on his department's payroll. There's certainly no legal reason that they couldn't have a security type on the payroll. Some legalist firms routinely have a few isolates and empaths as part of their permanent staff."

"Do you have any thoughts on why Hadenaur might feel that way?"

"Minz was tied to a former premier. Hadenaur might have felt it was better to emphasize Minz's position to senior professionals in the corporacion as security, rather than as political."

"But influencers are by nature and profession political," pointed out Haastar.

"Maybe Hadenaur was ordered to hire Minz," said Dekkard, "and felt he was a danger. By disassociating Minz from the legalists, he might have felt that the legalists wouldn't be tarred by association."

"That's shaky," replied Baar, "but if Hadenaur was given no choice, it could be that was the best of bad choices."

"He could have quit," said Haastar.

"For a legalist to quit a senior corporacion position over principle would make it difficult if not impossible to get another job of comparable pay or stature, especially in a city as small as Chuive," countered Baar dryly.

"I do believe we're going to have to order the presidente and vice-presidente for legal affairs to appear before the subcommittee," said Dekkard.

"Will Premier Hasheem even agree to that?" asked Haastar.

"He won't like it," said Dekkard, "but if I point out that what we've discovered will eventually get out, and that it won't look good for the Craft Party if it appears we covered up that a corporacion presidente or head legalist ordered an irregular hiring of a man assassinated before he could be tried for high crimes and possibly treason."

"This is going to get worse," said Pajiin. "Much worse, and we've barely started." He paused, then added, "The bastards deserve it."

While Dekkard agreed, he just said, "Does anyone want to add anything before we recess until Tridi morning?"

The other three each shook their heads.

"Then the subcommittee stands recessed."

Haastar leaned toward Dekkard and said quietly, "You know what you've started?"

"After Obreduur's death, there wasn't any choice, not if we want Guldor to survive as anything close to what it's supposed to be."

"Some would say it's too late for that."

"We'll have to see, won't we, Breffyn?"

"I just hope we all will, especially you." Haastar offered a smile that held a touch of sadness, then stood.

Dekkard gathered together his papers, stood, and walked to the back of the committee room, where Villem Baar stood waiting.

"You'll be fortunate to get out of this alive, Steffan."

"Why do you think we're pursuing this through an investigatory subcommittee and why I brought out the Minz connection and problem so quickly?"

"I can see that you're hoping to get enough evidence and information in enough hands that even Suvion Industries can't hush it all up, but there's something else you should know. There's one other legal link I didn't mention to you the other day. Paarsens and Alvara is also the Machtarn counsel for Siincleer Shipbuilding."

"I didn't know that, but I can't say it surprises me, given the ties Pohl Palafaux has to Siincleer and that he was able to get a position for Fernand Stoltz with Paarsens and Alvara."

"You realize that Juan del Larrano is not only very intelligent, but also powerful and incredibly vindictive? And that he has allies in the Council, even among Crafters?"

"I've been aware of that for some time. That's one reason why, if we're unsuccessful, there will be no military contracting reform, among other things." Dekkard looked at Baar. "If we're not successful, we'll both be single-term councilors." *If I'm fortunate enough to be alive to see it.*

"Steffan, when you made that statement about having to kill in the line of duty . . . I had the feeling that you could have killed Gutarez at that moment. So did he. He went from being almost arrogantly flippant to being . . . well . . . frightened, especially of you."

"I just told him the truth."

"But the way you told it felt so real. You chilled the whole committee room."

"I thought isolates were supposed to be chill," said Dekkard, trying to put a touch of humor in his voice.

With a rueful expression, Baar shook his head, then asked, "Do you want to be premier? Someday, I mean."

"No. I have no desire to be premier. Not now, and not later. I don't have those skills, and I don't have that kind of patience." Dekkard smiled wryly. "I once asked Guilhohn Haarsfel why he didn't want to be premier instead of Axel. He told me he didn't have the right skills, and that he'd be a terrible premier. I understand that better now. I'd be a terrible premier, if for different reasons. You'd be much better at it than I would be."

"Sometimes, Steffan, you mystify me."

"Sometimes, I mystify myself, unfortunately."

After a moment, Baar asked, "How do you think Tridi's hearings will go?"

"I suspect they'll be longer, and politely more contentious. Beyond that, who knows?"

"You don't have any idea?"

"I have several ideas, but whether the hearings will turn out that way remains to be seen."

"Do you think any of the witnesses will refuse to show up?"

"And risk a Council warrant for contempt and immediate incarceration in the Council Hall?"

"That hasn't been used in years," Baar pointed out.

"When the government and the corporacion sector had the same interests, it wasn't needed. It was used more in the time of Landor governments, and against Landors in the first Commercer governments."

"That makes sense. I hadn't thought of it that way." Baar paused, then said, "I'll see you on Tridi morning . . . if not sooner." He turned and hurried out of the committee chamber.

Dekkard followed.

Gaaroll was outside the door in the main corridor. "The Ritten is in the committee staff offices."

"Then we should join her." Dekkard turned and began to walk toward the corridor door to the staff offices.

They were still several yards away when Avraal stepped out into the corridor.

"Did you sense something?" asked Dekkard.

Avraal shook her head. "I just wanted to compare what I sensed with what Larelli did. There weren't any discrepancies."

"That's good, then, isn't it?"

"It is. Where to, now?"

"Now I have to report to Hasheem, after we make a quick stop to see if Guard Captain Trujillo is available." Dekkard turned back in the direction of the Council chamber, and Gaaroll stepped back, letting Dekkard and Avraal lead the way.

"What will you tell Hasheem?"

"What happened, and Vice-Presidente Gutarez's attempt not to point at Presidente Cloys Chassont as the only one who could have approved an unorthodox and strange hiring arrangement that makes no sense whatsoever."

"Dear, it makes perfect sense. Gutarez explained it. There's nothing so inflexible as a corporacion policy. Presidente Chassont doubtless told Legalist Hadenaur to hire Minz, and to just get it done, whatever it took. That's what Hadenaur did. The real question is why Chassont felt that he had to hire Minz."

As they neared Trujillo's office, Gaaroll said, "Sir, he's not there."

Dekkard still knocked, but there was no response. "We'll check back after I brief Hasheem."

In less than three minutes, Dekkard was in the Premier's floor office, and Hasheem's eyes fixed on Dekkard as he entered the inner office. "What did the subcommittee discover?"

"As far as the dunnite went, it's highly unlikely, and practically close to impossible, for anyone at Northwest Industrial Chemical to have diverted two tonnes of dunnite, especially since the Navy is the only customer, and there wasn't the slightest hint of dishonesty or evasion concerning the dunnite." Dekkard gave a concise summary of the questioning and the responses, then said, "But there was a new development regarding Sr. Jaime Minz." He then explained.

"Why would Presidente Chassont demand that Jaime Minz be hired? That makes no sense. He was a Commercer aide."

"He can be very persuasive," replied Dekkard, "but I don't think that was why he was hired. Capitol Services is the link there." Dekkard went back over the matter of the banque drafts. "Guard Captain Trujillo should have the responses from the banques by now. If the responses are what the Guard captain and I suspect, every one of those corporacions can at least be charged as accessories to high crimes. That also allows the subcommittee to order each of the presidentes and their head legalist to testify under empath scrutiny."

Hasheem shook his head. "I was afraid it would come to this." He handed a single sheet of paper to Dekkard. The letterhead was that of the presidente of Suvion Industries.

My dear Premier—

I understand that a special investigatory subcommittee of the Council's Security Committee is looking into the matter of how the terrorists calling themselves New Meritorists purportedly obtained dunnite in quantities sufficient to destroy Security buildings and serve as the explosive agent for shells purportedly fabricated from such dunnite and which are rumored to have been used in the first attack against the Council.

To the best of my knowledge, any factual information that would support such highly speculative and possibly dubious conclusions has not been made publicly available, and to hold hearings so quickly bears the mark of deciding on a finding without evidence and using the hearings to fabricate such evidence, a point that the corporacion will certainly make public if you allow this charade, which cannot even be called a pretense of justice, to continue.

If you choose this course, we will be forced to protest in all forums and manner about the high-handed conduct of this Council.

We look forward to your canceling the forthcoming hearings until more evidence is presented in a more suitable fashion.

The signature was that of Johann Daenyld.

"He's threatening because he's scared," said Dekkard. "Patrollers don't have to make evidence public except at a trial."

"You realize that, if you continue the investigation, you risk the same fate as Axel," said Hasheem.

"I've known that from the beginning, but it isn't going away, and I doubt it will go away even if I'm murdered. It will just take longer to play out."

"That's why you wanted a separate investigation, wasn't it?"

That wasn't the real question, Dekkard knew. Hasheem was suggesting that Dekkard had pushed for an investigation that Hasheem couldn't hush up. "You know I thought it necessary. I never made any secret of that."

"How would you suggest I handle this?"

"Send back a very polite letter saying that the subcommittee has already held two hearings about the mechanics, security, and shipping of dunnite, and that those hearings, pending the arrival of certain naval testing data, revealed no improprieties in the handling of dunnite by either the Navy or by Northwest Industrial Chemical. The third hearing, involving Suvion Industries and the same issues, will be held on schedule on Tridi. Point out that the first three hearings have already been announced publicly, and that it would reflect badly on both the Council and Suvion Industries if the third hearing were canceled. Then suggest that he come to Machtarn to discuss the matter with you before any more hearings are announced on, say, next Unadi, telling him that you certainly wouldn't want to have the subcommittee engage in any sort of rush to summary judgment."

"What if he refuses?"

"Then we serve him with an order to appear, but if you appear concerned he might just come."

"And?"

"If Tridi's hearing reveals what I think it will, he gets served right then and there. If it doesn't, then you agree to a more deliberate pace in terms of the hearings."

"You think he's guilty."

"That's not the question. The question before the committee, and, if necessary, before the High Court, is whether any guilt can be proved."

"Pohl Palafaux and—"

"Gerard Schmidtz have both made inquiries or complained about the speed of the subcommittee's acts?"

"As a matter of fact, they have."

"That's because the other influential corporacion likely involved in this is Siincleer Shipbuilding."

"How involved?"

"If . . . *if* the seventeen banque drafts drawn on the Banque of Siincleer and deposited in the account of Capitol Services all come from Siincleer

Shipbuilding, that would represent the largest number of drafts and the greatest amount of funds."

"You've actually seen the copies of those drafts?"

"I have."

"If you're right, Steffan, and I have no reason to believe you're not . . ." Hasheem shook his head. "I'll write Johann Daenyld the kind of letter you suggested. For the next few weeks, you need to be very careful."

"I know."

"Plan on seeing me tomorrow morning and before the hearing on Tridi."

"I'll be here."

When Dekkard, Avraal, and Gaaroll left the Premier's floor office and began to walk toward Guard Captain Trujillo's office, Avraal looked to him.

"Later," he said quietly.

Avraal just nodded.

Trujillo wasn't in his office, and the three turned back toward the councilors' dining room.

As Dekkard and Avraal entered the dining room, a councilor immediately stood up and walked toward them. After an instant, Dekkard recognized Felix Quellar, who had been seated with Elskar Halljen.

"Steffan. Ritten, might I beg your indulgence for a few quick words with your husband?"

Avraal smiled warmly, although Dekkard noticed that she looked directly at Quellar. "Certainly." She looked to Dekkard. "Would you like me to order for you?"

"Please. The white bean soup and café." Then Dekkard followed the Commercer councilor to the passageway leading to the Council chamber.

Quellar stopped beyond the door to the men's lavatory and said, "Steffan, you know I have the highest respect for you."

"I take it that Sr. Gutarez visited you after this morning's hearing."

"He did. He wouldn't discuss the particulars, but he said you threatened to incarcerate him if he failed to answer a question. Might I ask what was so important that you insisted on that?"

"I'll tell you, Felix, with the understanding that the question concerned an aspect of the subcommittee's investigation of various corporacion ties to the New Meritorists. Revealing those details until the subcommittee's investigations are complete would not be wise."

"Is it that bad?"

"Do you recall Jaime Minz?"

Quellar frowned, then asked, "The influencer who was shot just before he was to be charged? What does that have to do with threatening Sr. Gutarez?"

"At the hearing, the director of security at Northwest Industrial Chemical . . ." Dekkard went on to quickly relate the details about Minz. "I only wanted to know who had the authority to hire Minz, given his ties to the New Meritorists."

Quellar didn't say anything for a minute. "That's all true?"

"It is. We're trying to find out more."

"Sr. Gutarez said you threatened his life, if without words."

"He asked me if I'd incarcerate him over such a matter. I told him that people had tried to kill me in the line of duty, and that I'd been forced to kill some of them, and that I wanted an honest answer. My only threat was simple. If he didn't give an honest answer, he'd be incarcerated until he did. The fact that he didn't want to answer such a simple question should tell you why the subcommittee investigation is so important to the future of the Council. There are two other facts you should know, and both of them are open knowledge. Minz was a security aide to Oskaar Ulrich, and Ulrich is now the vice-presidente of political affairs for Suvion Industries, which is the only other manufacturer of dunnite. I think you can put the pieces together."

Quellar shook his head. "I think I'll just write Sr. Gutarez that I'm looking into the matter and will be in touch when I know more."

"That might be for the best."

"Thank you for being direct, Steffan. I apologize for intruding."

"No apology is necessary. If someone from my district had told me what Sr. Gutarez told you, I'd want to know as well."

Dekkard could see that Quellar was disturbed, but he had no idea what had upset him—the possible New Meritorist ties to Northwest or Dekkard's handling of the matter. *Most likely both.*

He let Quellar lead the way back to the dining area.

"Might I ask?" said Avraal as Dekkard seated himself across from her. "Councilor Quellar came back feeling very worried."

"Quellar is the councilor from Chuive. Gutarez complained about my high-handed manner." Dekkard gave a short, bitter laugh. "I didn't complain about Gutarez's arrogance. I did give Felix the basics of the situation, but nothing that was revealed in the hearing."

"Sooner or later, the entire Council will know, or is that your plan?"

"I don't need the entire Council. I just need enough councilors so that it can't be hushed up, and if anyone tries, *Gestirn* and other reputable newssheets will keep asking questions."

"I notice you're not mentioning the *Tribune*."

"I did say reputable," replied Dekkard dryly.

"What did Hasheem say?"

Dekkard told her, including the letter from Presidente Daenyld, and the barely veiled threat.

"That's the way they've operated for years," replied Avraal. "It's always worked. They've done it for so long that they may not realize that much of what they've done is against the law and even against the Great Charter."

"In some ways, the Council is the law, but that's a blade that cuts two ways. They're beginning to realize that this Council's not in their wallet, and they don't like it."

"People with political power believe that it should always belong to them, even when they lose the votes behind that power." Avraal stopped as the server arrived with their orders.

When the server left, Dekkard said, "After we finish eating, I want to see Guard Captain Trujillo."

"You're worried about the banque drafts?"

"One way or another, they'll show something."

Dekkard was still wondering what they'd show when he entered Trujillo's office almost a bell later. "I came by earlier." He sat down opposite the Guard captain.

"I thought you might, but I needed to take care of something. What's on your mind, Councilor?"

"Have you received any replies on the origin of those various banque drafts?"

"We have. I've shared all of them with the Justiciary minister. That was where I was this morning."

"I take it that they trace back to specific corporacions?"

"To the same corporacions you suggested in your notes file."

Dekkard wasn't surprised. In fact, he would have been astonished if Trujillo hadn't read the notes he'd written for the file kept in the records room.

"In each case," Trujillo continued, "a corporacion accounting clerk presented a corporacion cheque and an authorization for the banque draft. In each case, the banque sent a separate confirmation of the transaction to the corporacion. All the banques were kind enough to provide a copy of that as well."

"Did the Justiciary minister say anything?"

"Of course not. She just thanked me and had copies made before returning the original replies to me. She was kind enough to make a second copy for the records room. I've put the copies with the files. She did tell me to keep the originals safe. They are."

"That would seem to make it difficult for the corporacions to deny sending marks to a corporacion tied to the New Meritorists."

"I've seen many instances where corporate guilt didn't result in individual guilt, Councilor," replied Trujillo. "Even the corporate guilt was waived after a year or two on the grounds of the best interests of the Imperium. Some of them may claim they didn't know about the ties between Capitol Services and the New Meritorists."

In other words, the subcommittee still has a long way to go. "I appreciate the observation, Guard Captain, and all you and the Council Guard have done."

"In the end, the Council Guard must answer to the Great Charter." Trujillo laughed softly and mirthlessly. "That's the way I see it. Other previous Guard captains have been somewhat more 'flexible.'"

Dekkard realized that observation was also a warning—that this might be the only time in his life where returning the Council to the basic principles was possible. "Thank you."

"I haven't had a chance to inform the Premier, but I will inform him that you requested and received that information."

"I appreciate that." Dekkard stood. "I'd appreciate it if Council Guards were immediately available during the hearing on Tridi."

"During hearings bearing on possible high crimes, guards will always be available. That is a standing order."

Dekkard shook his head. "There's still so much I don't know."

"That's true of all of us."

"Until later, Guard Captain." Dekkard inclined his head and left, closing the door to the corridor quietly.

Neither Avraal nor Gaaroll said anything as the three walked toward the courtyard doors.

Dekkard couldn't help but think about the proof of involvement of the five corporacions, but particularly Siincleer Shipbuilding, and the fact that all seventeen cheques the corporacion had sent to Capitol Services had likely been authorized by the late Pietro Venburg, and that there were likely no ties whatsoever to Juan del Larrano. Then he recalled something he'd discovered in trying to find out more about military contracting, although he didn't recall all the particulars.

When the three neared the courtyard doors, Dekkard looked to Gaaroll. "Is there anything that's even remotely dangerous anywhere close by?"

"I can't sense anything."

"Neither can I," said Avraal.

Even as he'd asked, Dekkard realized that the greatest danger would likely come from something that neither Gaaroll nor Avraal could sense.

That realization made him feel even more vulnerable, and he quickly crossed the courtyard to the Council Office Building.

As soon as Dekkard and Avraal returned to his office, he immediately asked Roostof to join him and Avraal in his personal office. Dekkard was still standing when the senior legalist entered.

"Sir?"

"If you'd have someone pick up the afternoon editions of *Gestirn* and the *Tribune* when they come out, I'd appreciate it. I'd like to know if anyone revealed anything about the subcommittee hearings. Nincya can do it, if that works for you. I'm not going anywhere for a while." He paused. "There's one other legal item. As I recall, unfair competition or fraud in military contracts can bar a corporacion from obtaining future contracts for up to ten years. Could you or Shuryn look into what other actions can trigger exclusion from obtaining contracts?"

"How soon do you need that, sir?"

"The sooner the better, but not if it means letting anyone outside the office know. I don't need it today, but before the office closes tomorrow would be very helpful."

"Yes, sir. We should be able to run that down by then."

"Thank you, Svard."

After Roostof left, as well as Avraal, who said she'd help Margrit, Dekkard settled behind his desk and immediately picked up the weekly report from Zenya Onswyrth and began to read. Most of what he read was similar to what seemed to happen weekly, except for two matters. The first was that the snow was melting fast and the Lakaan River was already at flood stage and might near its all-time high. The second was definitely disturbing.

Legalist Desharra stopped by the office on Furdi. She said that an examination of Sr. Seigryn's body showed no wounds or bruises. There was no sign of poison . . . she also mentioned strangers in town were asking about how you became councilor . . .

Dekkard wondered if Jens had really just drunk too much or his drinking had been supplemented in some way—and by whom. Several people had suggested that Jens had more than a few enemies, but his death couldn't have come at a less opportune time, especially with inquiries at nearly the same time. *But then, death is almost always inopportune.*

Somewhat more than a bell later, Dekkard had read through the incoming letters and was reading and signing responses when Avraal slipped into his office and closed the door.

Dekkard looked up.

She laid the afternoon editions of *Gestirn* and the *Tribune* on the side of the desk. "There's nothing about the subcommittee in *Gestirn*. The *Tribune* handled it differently. It's on the editorial page."

"Another editorial on the questionable Councilor Dekkard?"

Avraal nodded. "It's about what you'd expect."

Dekkard picked up the *Tribune,* leafed back to the editorial page, and began to read.

THE HIGHLY QUESTIONABLE COUNCILOR DEKKARD

Remember the questionable Councilor Steffan Dekkard? How could anyone forget? The Military Institute graduate who never really served out his service obligation? The short-term former security aide who got himself appointed a councilor for a district in which he never lived? And who bought a house there that no one on his pay could possibly afford, in solid marks, no less? Who miraculously survived the shelling of the Council that killed the Premier who had been his champion?

Those questionable deeds are hardly the end of his dubious exploits. More recently, the most questionable councilor was conveniently at a meeting away from the Council Hall the morning that the New Meritorists' captured cruiser rained shells down on Machtarn. His office was again targeted, but he and his staff weren't there. Was it fortuitous because of a light snow, as he claims, or does the councilor possess knowledge he's hidden from others? And there's yet another dubious death, that of Jens Seigryn. Seigryn reputedly had been the choice of former Premier Obreduur to fill the seat Dekkard now holds, the seat of Haasan Decaro, who died mysteriously before he could be sworn in. But several weeks ago, Seigryn was reported missing. His frozen body was recently found when the snows melted in Gaarlak. Interestingly enough, just before his disappearance, Seigryn had talked about how Dekkard had manipulated key members of the Gaarlak Craft Party to gain appointment to the Council.

But the latest exploit of the questionable Councilor Dekkard is even more astonishing. Despite being the second most junior member of the Council's Security Committee, he has managed to get himself appointed as the chairman of a special investigatory subcommittee ostensibly looking into how the New Meritorist terrorists obtained the explosives they used. Without evidence, or at least without evidence known to this newssheet, Councilor Dekkard has apparently decided that the explosives were military dunnite and has launched an investigation apparently focused on discrediting reputable and long-established Guldoran manufacturing corporacions.

Does Guldor really need politicians of dubious intent and even more dubious background?

Dekkard put the newssheet back on the desk. "It's more of the same, except that the last part could have been written by the presidente of Suvion Industries."

"Then it probably was . . . or by one of his legalists."

"Did you show it to Svard?"

Avraal shook her head.

"If you wouldn't mind asking him to come in?"

Avraal smiled. "I can do that."

"And come back with him. I want to know how he really feels."

Avraal returned in moments with Roostof.

Dekkard stood and handed the *Tribune* to the senior legalist. "Our friends are at it again. I'd like you to read the latest editorial on the questionable councilor and give me your honest opinion."

Roostof turned to the editorial. When he finished, he shook his head. "A legalist drafted that . . . or at least reviewed it. There's only one outright wrong statement, and that's about evidence, but even that's hedged. It does suggest that someone is very worried about you."

"And since it doesn't mention votes and the facts are correct, if misrepresented, any attempt I might make to set things straight would just make them worse."

"You're a better councilor than I'd ever be, sir, but that would be my judgment."

Dekkard smiled. "I agree with your judgment about the *Tribune* editorial, but not about how good a councilor you'd make. One other thing. I've been so involved with the subcommittee work, and a few other matters, that I haven't had a chance to talk with Luara about putting together a legislative package on legalist representation of working women for the Workplace Administration Committee."

"We've gone over that, and she should have something ready for your review in a week or so."

"Thank you."

When Roostof left, Dekkard asked, "His reaction?"

"He was angry . . . a little depressed, too." She paused, then said, "I'd like to say I'm beyond anger, but it's beyond anger into cold fury. These bastards backed a group that never really could have succeeded at changing government—and actually gave them a shot at it—all in an effort to get more power and to kept the Crafters out . . . and they *still* might be able to get away with it, especially if they can get you off the Council."

Or remove me in some less legitimate way.

"You look . . . distracted . . . distant," said Avraal quietly. "What are you thinking?"

"I'm wondering what new form of removal Ulrich and Presidente Daenyld might come up with. Something that we haven't thought of, something hard to predict or foresee."

"More likely something simple and direct in an unexpected setting."

"Like a men's room?"

"It was effective. But that's why I concentrated on Felix Quellar—to make certain there was no malign intent."

Dekkard nodded, then looked at the stack of responses he needed to sign, something that he doubted his predecessor had been all that diligent about, at least not in the last year of his term. "I need to finish these before we go."

In the end, he did finish signing or revising the responses quickly enough that it was only a few minutes past fourth bell when he, Avraal, and Gaaroll left the office.

The walk to the covered parking and the drive home were both uneventful, and neither Avraal nor Gaaroll sensed any danger that felt focused anywhere close to Dekkard. Even so, he felt uneasy the whole time, and that feeling didn't subside after he garaged the Gresynt and was in the kitchen, where Avraal and Gaaroll were already helping Emrelda with dinner.

Emrelda half turned from the stove. "Captain Kunskyn sends his condolences. Over the newssheet article. He said you must be doing something right to make the *Tribune* that mad."

"He isn't a great supporter of the *Tribune,* I take it?"

"Not for years, and not after the way they savaged the patrol last year."

"You mean when the *Tribune* supported the STF's shooting all the unarmed demonstrators in the back, and condemned the patrollers for not doing the same?" asked Gaaroll.

"The station patrol captains across the city threatened to shoot the STFs or Specials who fired on unarmed demonstrators," Avraal said to Gaaroll. "That was before the New Meritorists took up arms—" She stopped as the front bell rang.

"It's the nanny from next door, I think," said Gaaroll. "Feels like an empie."

Avraal frowned, then nodded.

"Avraal, you and Steffan see what she wants," said Emrelda. "Nincya and I can finish up here."

Dekkard followed Avraal to the front door, where she opened it.

Sigourna Miletus stood there, a look of concern on her face.

"Are you all right?" asked Avraal.

"I'm fine, Ritten. I'm worried. There's been a blue Realto. It's been by here three or four times this afternoon. It isn't just the steamer. There are Realtos everywhere, but this one has a different feel. There are always two men in it. They feel cold. Not like patrollers."

"You can sense all that?" asked Avraal, stepping back and motioning for the empath/nanny to come in before closing the door.

"Not all at once," admitted Miletus. "The second time they drove by, I was outside with Tomas. I got a better feel then. They didn't even look at me or Tomas. I could sense they were studying your house. The last time they came by was maybe a sixth before the Ritten—she's a Ritten, too, isn't she? A sixth before she got home."

"Was it an old Realto or a new one?" asked Dekkard.

"It wasn't either. Not new, but no rust or scratches."

"Did you see either of the men?"

"Not that close. They were both dark-haired and wore dark jackets. Brown, maybe."

"Was there anything else that stood out?"

"I can't think of anything, sir."

"Thank you so much," said Avraal. "We appreciate that. If you notice anything else, please let us know."

"I will, Ritten."

"You've been practicing, haven't you?" asked Avraal.

"As much as I can. Quietly . . . and carefully. It's made things around the house much calmer." Miletus offered an amused smile, an expression that made her look older.

"We should talk," said Avraal. "Perhaps this endday?"

"I'd like that very much. I'd better go now. I told Sra. Waaldwud I'd only be a few minutes."

"Thank you . . . again," said Dekkard.

"You're welcome, Ritter." Miletus turned and left through the door that Avraal opened, then closed behind the nanny.

"Very interesting in a definitely sinister way," said Dekkard.

"We need to tell Emrelda and Gaaroll."

When they entered the kitchen, Emrelda said, "We're serving. Just sit down."

Dekkard exchanged glances with Avraal, and then they seated themselves.

Once everyone was seated and helped themselves to the veal and mushrooms and the potato cakes and pickled beets, Emrelda asked, "What did the nanny want?"

"To warn us," said Dekkard, nodding to Avraal to continue.

After Avraal finished explaining, Emrelda said, "That sounds like they're scouting. Making several trips more than a bell apart so that they don't have to stop. People notice when strange steamers stop. Most likely, they won't do anything tonight. I'll talk to Captain Kunskyn in the morning to see what he might be able to do."

"We'll stop by Carlos's office in the morning and let him know as well," added Avraal.

"Nincya," said Dekkard, "in addition to everything else, you now also have the duty of watching and sensing for blue Realtos driven by cold-feeling men."

"Fewer blue Realtos than cold-feeling men," countered Gaaroll sarcastically.

"More like a toss-up," replied Emrelda. "What else happened today?"

Avraal looked to Dekkard.

"We had the hearing for Northwest Industrial Chemical. It turns out that there were some irregularities in the way they hired Jaime Minz." Dekkard gave a brief summary of the day, but left out anything concerning Suvion Industries or the banque drafts, but ended by mentioning that Namoor Desharra had told Zenya Onswyrth about strangers in Gaarlak asking about him.

Emrelda shook her head. "As Captain Kunskyn said, you must be doing something right to have half the major corporacions in Guldor wanting your head."

"Only about a quarter," replied Dekkard. "I'm both honored and really, really worried."

"That's sensible," said Emrelda. "Being worried, that is. But you do have three empaths and a few patrollers looking out for you."

"If I didn't," answered Dekkard, "I wouldn't be worried; I'd be terrified." *And maybe you still ought to be terrified.*

"Now that we've covered that," said Avraal, not quite tartly, "could we change the subject for a while?"

"The veal is very good," said Dekkard cheerfully. "I know it would be a step down, but I wish you two were the ones cooking for the councilors' dining room."

"Dream on, dear," said Avraal.

Even Gaaroll smiled.

Once Dekkard and Avraal retired to their room, he went over in detail what he'd found out from Trujillo about the banque drafts.

"None of that is surprising," said Avraal, "except possibly the arrogance and the belief that they'll never be called to answer for it."

"We've discovered it, but we don't have much proof that would identify the specific individuals actually behind it all. So . . ." said Dekkard, drawing out the word, "who's the mastermind? Ulrich or Daenyld? Or del Larrano?"

"Juan del Larrano," suggested Avraal. "Haven't most of those banque drafts come from Siincleer?"

"Well, from what Shuryn and Svard have dug up, that's certainly possible. Proving more than supporting Capitol Services will be close to impossible, especially since del Larrano can blame everything on Pietro Venburg, and possibly do so without lying."

"What about Markell and Engaard Engineering?"

"We might be able to bring that up as subsidiary evidence under collective corporacion knowledge. It could be a stretch, but with other evidence . . ."

"You think you can do something with what you asked Svard to research?"

"I'm hoping, but I don't know."

Avraal paused, then lifted a small book. "I need to get my mind on something else, and so do you."

Dekkard certainly wasn't about to argue.

61

The white cougar of Sudlynd can kill a red deer with a single slash of claws so strong and sharp that they can etch glass. So silent is it when it stalks that even a smoky owl cannot hear it approach. A female bears but a single cub every other year, but every cub lives to become an adult. The white cougar is the most fearsome predator anywhere, as well as a perfect parent. It does not deceive, and pairs mate for life.

For these admirable qualities, over the centuries, certain aristocratic families in Sudlynd have taken the white cougar as an emblem, a symbol of strength and virtue.

The aristocratic emblem and the image of the predator are in fact widely accepted illusions. The Family Daenyld claims the earliest use of the white cougar in its family crest, yet the Counts of Daenyld have broken more pledges than any aristocratic family in Sudlynd, and historians have documented thrice as many fratricides and patricides in the Daenyld lineage compared to the Family Cleonid, the clan closest in intra-familial violence. Other families who have adopted the white cougar have not fared much better.

Nor has the white cougar. There remain but a few thousand in all of Sudlynd, because fearsome as they are to a single hunter, they are solitary creatures, and no solitary cougar is a match for a well-equipped hunting party. They now only exist in the wildest and most inaccessible mountain areas. That inaccessibility, paradoxically, protects them—and their fearsome image.

The white cougar remains, for now, even as its numbers are declining. Those who use its likeness to create an illusion of strength have also seen their power dwindle, but that correlation is yet another illusion.

AVERRA
The City of Truth
Johan Eschbach
377 TE

62

ALTHOUGH Gaaroll kept sensing the few steamers that drove past the house early on Duadi morning, none fit the description or the feel of the one Sigourna Miletus had described the night before. Nor did either Avraal or Gaaroll sense anything out of the ordinary on the drive to Carlos Baartol's office. Once there, Dekkard had Gaaroll watch the Gresynt from just inside the doorway, while he and Avraal walked up the single flight of stairs.

"You're both here," said Baartol cheerily when the two entered his personal office. "That must mean more trouble."

"The presidente of Suvion Industries doesn't like the hearings my investigatory subcommittee is conducting and has issued barely veiled threats. Neither does the presidente of Northwest Industrial Chemical, and yesterday an empath detected a blue Realto with two emotionally cold individuals periodically driving past the house when no one was there."

"An empath? Not either you or Nincya Gaaroll?" Baartol asked, looking at Avraal.

"A late-emerging empath working as a nanny next door," she explained.

"Avraal and Emrelda helped her with certain matters," added Dekkard.

"Is this just about the subcommittee?" asked Baartol.

"The hearings may reveal a widespread pattern of influence and corruption," said Dekkard. "I wouldn't be surprised if the disappearances and deaths of some of your trackers and investigators might be part of that pattern, but that's just a guess."

"Your guesses, Steffan, have a consistently higher probability of accuracy than they should. I'll have some of my people look into it."

"We appreciate it."

"It's part of the job. Besides, I'd like to have Avraal back working full-time, and that won't happen until this whole mess gets cleaned up."

And I'll owe you . . . and then some. But Dekkard only said, "I'm afraid that's true."

"Can I do anything else?"

"Not right now, but if there's something you can do, we'll let you know."

"Don't hesitate to ask . . . and take care of yourselves."

"We're doing our best," replied Dekkard.

When Dekkard and Avraal reached the door to the parking area, Gaaroll said, "No signs of anything."

Neither empath noted anything out of the ordinary on the way to the Council covered parking either, and Dekkard wondered if his senses were off or if the corporacion operatives were holding back for the moment, or something else entirely was underway.

As he, Avraal, and Gaaroll walked toward his office, he tried to study the area around him with a fresh eye. The Council Park was on the south side of Council Avenue directly opposite the Council Hall, the Council Office Building, the low-walled courtyard and gardens connecting them, and the covered parking. The north side of the service road was bordered by grassy stretches. All that effectively removed any hidden location from which a sniper could target any councilor walking from the covered parking to the Council Office Building.

When Dekkard reached the office, Margrit handed Dekkard a large thick envelope. "That's a notice from the Premier." Then she gave him two smaller envelopes. "One's from the Premier, and the other's a message from Councilor Konnigsburg. I'll have the mail to you in a few minutes. It was a little late this morning. The Council post messenger said it's because they have to check everything now."

"I'll look at these in my office," replied Dekkard. "Bring the mail when you can."

"Yes, sir."

The notice was a reminder of the Council session beginning at the first afternoon bell to deal with legislation addressing the death and injury claims against the Navy as a result of the *Khuld* mutiny. Attached was a copy of the proposed legislation. Dekkard couldn't help wondering what might be hidden in it.

Hasheem's message was simple, saying that since nothing had changed since their last meeting, he would see Dekkard before Tridi's hearing.

The message from Eyril Konnigsburg suggested that they meet for lunch at a third before noon. Dekkard showed the note to Avraal.

"I don't like you being there alone. Not now. Let me see if I can persuade Ingrella to have lunch with me at the same time. If not, I'll work something else out."

"I'm sure you'll manage that better than I will this legislation. I never heard anything about it, and I at least need to read through it to see if I can make any sense of it."

"Then, I'll see you shortly," said Avraal. "I hope." She offered a brief smile before departing.

After sending off a quick message to Eyril Konnigsburg agreeing to lunch, Dekkard began to read the proposed legislation, which was close to impenetrable because it consisted entirely of amendments to the Military Tort Claims Act, inserting numbers in place of others and changing phrases. After about a third of a bell, he *thought* he understood the gist of the proposal and asked Roostof to join him.

"Svard, you got a copy of the bill coming up on the floor today, didn't you?"

Roostof nodded. "Just like every other senior legalist."

"Good. Now, if I understand this," Dekkard said, lifting his copy, "it raises the limit on allowable damages under the Military Tort Claims Act, and authorizes and appropriates additional funds to cover the damages to individuals and their properties in Machtarn as a result of the shelling from the *Khuld*. I thought we already passed appropriations for that."

"The Council did," replied Roostof, "but that only applied to direct damages to publicly owned properties where liability is not an issue, because it's based on an agreement between levels of government. Claims affecting individuals and private property have to be paid under the Military Tort Claims Act, and the current cap hasn't been changed in fifty years."

Dekkard thought for a moment. "This bill was reported out of both the Military Affairs Committee and the Transportation Committee. Was part of it written by the Transportation Committee because the existing cap wouldn't cover the damages suffered by Guldoran Ironway?"

Roostof smiled wryly. "I don't know that for a fact, but that's most likely the case."

"Why should I support it?"

"The committees couldn't very well compensate Guldoran for its damages without raising the limits for individuals. Guldoran could likely afford the repairs, but the costs would put a huge dent in their funds and reserves. Many people in the city could not afford any of the costs, and the old limit on compensation for the loss of income from a breadwinner would hardly be sufficient these days."

"Is there a downside to this?"

"The Council might have to raise taxes or tariffs. I'd also guess that the committees have underfunded it, and that another supplemental will be necessary."

Dekkard shook his head. He was still thinking about what Roostof had said as he read through the mail, when Avraal returned.

"Did you have any success?" he asked.

"Ingrella is having lunch with Harleona Zerlyon, but she's included me, along with Elyncya Duforgue. They're meeting at half before noon, so that will work out very well."

"Good."

Dekkard finished with the mail and spent a bit more time studying the proposed amendments to the Military Tort Claims Act, before it was time to leave for the Council Hall with Avraal and Gaaroll.

Ingrella already stood inside the entry to the councilors' dining room, and inclined her head. "As always, you two look so composed and professional."

"The composure is more external than internal," replied Dekkard.

"Good. Too much internal composure leads to arrogance and thoughtless pride, both of which are the occupational hazards of legalists and politicians." Ingrella turned. "Here come Harleona and Elyncya. Have a productive lunch, Steffan."

"You, too," replied Dekkard.

Less than a sixth passed before Eyril Konnigsburg arrived. "I'm glad you were able to accommodate my request, Steffan."

"My pleasure. I always learn something new when I talk with you."

Konnigsburg turned to the maître d'hôtel. "Two, please."

"This way, Councilors."

As he entered the dining area, Dekkard noticed that Kaliara Bassaana sat with Vhiola Sandegarde, obviously a pairing for political ends, because, from what Dekkard had gathered, the two were anything but personally close. He couldn't help wondering what they were plotting.

After Dekkard and Konnigsburg ordered, Konnigsburg said, "I see your wife over there with Ingrella Obreduur, Elyncya Duforgue, and Harleona Zerlyon."

"She was fortunate to be invited to join them. If you hadn't asked me to lunch, I might well have been alone in my office."

"You wouldn't have lunched here anyway?"

Dekkard managed a grin. "I might have."

Konnigsburg grinned in return. "More than might, I think." Then the grin vanished. "Obviously, I invited you for a purpose. We talked about your subcommittee the last time we met. Have you done much more than you indicated, if I might ask?"

"We haven't even finished the first round of hearings. Admiral Jingao didn't seem displeased and was very helpful. From what he and the head of the Naval Munitions Command provided, it appears that the diversion occurred before anything got to the Navy."

"That's what I heard, indirectly, of course."

"We had the first hearing with Northwest Industrial Chemical yesterday, and it would appear that, between the Navy's testimony and that of Northwest, it's unlikely the dunnite came from Northwest, but we still have the preliminary hearing with Suvion Industries tomorrow. Then the subcommittee will determine where we go from there."

"Erich Kuuresoh is concerned about the hearings. Do you know why that might be?"

"You may recall Jaime Minz?"

"Of course. The influencer and former aide for Premier Ulrich."

"He provided at least some of the dunnite for the first Council shelling, most likely through a business called Capitol Services." Dekkard paused, then said, "Oskaar Ulrich created Capitol Services."

"Is that verified or another rumor?"

"The existence of Capitol Services is well-documented, and Minz had more than a few meetings with Erich," said Dekkard.

"That's what influencers are supposed to do."

"But Erich put him on his access list. Of course, that was before anything appeared about Minz being connected to the New Meritorists."

"About some things, Erich is too trusting. Adding a known influencer to an access list isn't a good idea." Konnigsburg shook his head. "I can see why he's nervous. Is there more about Capitol Services?"

"Whatever other services Minz provided—except for getting the dunnite and making shells—haven't surfaced. A fair amount of marks passed through the Capitol Services banque account from various corporacions, but his secretary has vanished, and the only documentary records are banque records."

Konnigsburg said nothing more for a moment. "You're sitting on the equivalent of a tonne of dunnite. Large sums of marks from corporacions, a possible tie to a former premier, and dunnite going to insurgents. Is there more you can tell me?"

"I don't know of anything else so far as Erich is concerned." And, except for Kuuresoh's lies about not meeting much with Minz, that was true. Dekkard had suspicions that Kuuresoh had ties with Schmidtz and Palafaux, and possibly Siincleer Shipbuilding, but he certainly didn't know.

Both councilors waited for the server to deliver their meals—a duck cassoulet for Dekkard and the onion soup for Konnigsburg—and withdraw.

Then the former admiral said, "You think Suvion Industries is involved, don't you?"

"If the amount of funding received by Capitol Services is any indication, and it might not be, the most likely corporacions to be involved are Suvion and Siincleer Shipbuilding."

"Was that one of the reasons you asked about Juan del Larrano's so-called yacht?"

"I was particularly interested in its speed and armor," said Dekkard, "given the years of unsavory rumors about the corporacion, and, now, with the information about funds paid . . ."

"I can't believe del Larrano would send corporacion cheques to a shadowy business like Capitol Services."

"He or whoever it was didn't send a corporacion cheque. The cheques were issued by the Banque of Siincleer, but paid for with a corporacion cheque." Dekkard knew that revealing that to Konnigsburg was danger-ous, but the information would be out before long. "I suspect they were authorized by Venburg, but I can't believe del Larrano didn't know."

Konnigsburg was silent for almost a minute. "Do you honestly think Juan del Larrano planned that yacht . . . just in case?"

"I have no idea, but a great deal of scattered evidence exists about the less than scrupulous behavior of Siincleer Shipbuilding. There's also the fact that Siincleer Engineering is quite active in Noldar. If the parent cor-poracion turns out to be implicated in funding, even indirectly, the New Meritorists . . . ?" Dekkard wasn't about to finish that statement. "As we were talking, it occurred to me that the Admiralty might wish to know about the possibilities. In any event, I'm hoping the hearings will make things clear."

"You'll make them clear, and quite a number of important individuals won't be pleased."

"That's likely, but what are you basing that upon?"

"Because the Premier made you chair of the subcommittee. If he'd named Pajiin, it would have been an indication that he didn't think the investigation could go anywhere."

"That remains to be seen. A great deal will depend on what we find out—or don't find out—tomorrow." Dekkard paused. "Do you think the Imperador will choose one of the admirals you recommended?"

"I don't know, but it's unlikely." Konnigsburg took several spoonfuls of soup.

While he waited to see if the former admiral had more to say, Dekkard addressed his attentions to the duck cassoulet, discovering that he was actually hungry.

Finally, Konnigsburg spoke. "You know, people think that admirals and other military professionals always look to use weapons to prove a point or gain an advantage. Most good senior officers don't go looking for ways to create conflict. The optimal way to win a war is not to fight it and to obtain the objective by other means. If you have to fight a war, it's best to act decisively and quickly, but remember to keep a little more in reserve than your enemy thinks you have. It seems to me that politics is very much the same."

"Isn't there a saying that politics is war waged with different weapons?"

"Politics and war are both waged to seek or maintain power, but the weapons differ." Konnigsburg paused, then added, "Except that in war, mercy is often honorable. In politics, it can be fatal. At least from the little I've seen." He laughed softly and ironically.

Dekkard felt a chill, but managed not to shiver. "I haven't seen that much more than you have, but I tend to agree."

"But too many politicians think that admirals are the bloodthirsty ones."

"Except those who've been both," replied Dekkard.

"Or those who've actually had to take a life in the line of duty." Konnigsburg smiled ruefully. "I think that's enough of aphorisms for now. Have you managed to get your office back together—again?"

"This time wasn't as bad. We didn't lose as much in the way of records. Most of the damage was to my personal office. There wasn't any damage to yours, was there?"

"Just dust and more dust."

The remainder of the lunch was pleasant and superficial, and when Konnigsburg left at a sixth before first bell, Dekkard found Avraal in the entry lobby.

"Well?" he asked.

"We can talk later," said Avraal, keeping her voice low, "but he was worried, mostly about you. Just before you got off the serious talk, he was really worried, but it wasn't as much concentrated on you."

"That was after I hinted that Juan del Larrano might use the high-speed armored small corvette that he calls a yacht to leave Guldor if the hearings go badly."

"Do you really think del Larrano would do that?"

"I have my doubts, but why else would he build it?" Dekkard shrugged. "How did Konnigsburg feel?"

"He seemed a little less worried when he left. I get the sense that he likes and respects you." Avraal turned to face Kaliara Bassaana, who walked toward them.

"Good afternoon, Avraal, Steffan. Splitting your forces, I see."

"But staying close enough to reinforce each other, if necessary," replied Dekkard. "Did you and Vhiola have a productive lunch?"

"All lunches with other councilors are productive, in one way or another, as you've obviously grasped."

"I've only followed your example," replied Dekkard cheerfully.

"You've been conducting some hearings, Steffan. Explosive, some might say."

"It's no secret that we're trying to discover how the New Meritorists got their hands on so much dunnite."

Bassaana turned to Avraal. "Steffan always focuses on the important issues. He's quite good at it. Right now, I need to hurry, but I hope we'll have some time in the future to have a leisurely lunch." She looked back to Dekkard and smiled pleasantly. "I'll see you on the floor."

"Until then," replied Dekkard, fearing that he understood the message behind her earlier words.

Once Bassaana was well out of earshot, Avraal said, "We definitely need to talk later. Right now, I'm going to observe from the spouses' gallery. Just in case someone might pass a few words with you. Then I'll be at the councilors' lobby after the session."

"I'll see you there. Can you tell Nincya?"

"I'll take care of it."

Dekkard took the passageway from the dining room to the Council floor, thinking about Pietro Venburg and ready to use his knives, unlikely as that seemed. *But then Venburg didn't expect an armed female security aide in a ball gown to slice through his throat.*

No one else used the narrow hallway while he was in it, and he reached the floor without incident. Both Ingrella and Tomas Pajiin were already at their small desks.

Pajiin looked to Dekkard. "How are you doing?"

"So far, so good. What about you?"

"About the same, but I'm not the subcommittee chair."

"If anything happens to me, you will be," Dekkard pointed out.

"I'd appreciate it, Steffan, if you took good care of yourself."

"We're doing what we can."

"Do more," suggested Pajiin.

Dekkard had thought about not staying in the house, but with some surveillance by Emrelda's patrollers and Baartol's people, he and Avraal might be more vulnerable somewhere else. Besides, the first round of hearings was mostly done, and that suggested that the corporacion strategy might be punitive—eliminating him after the first round and then pressing for an inconclusive report to end the inquiry. That way Hasheem could claim that the Council had done what it could.

Immediately after first bell rang out, the lieutenant-at-arms thumped his ceremonial staff, and Haarsfel called the Council to order for the consideration of the amendments to the Military Tort Claims Act and the authorization and appropriation of the necessary supplemental funds.

The debate wasn't so much a debate as a series of statements by each party's floor leader declaring why the legislation and the associated appropriations were necessary, followed by the vote. The legislative-appropriations package passed by a vote of fifty-nine to seven. Dekkard suspected all the negative votes came from Landors.

Once the vote was over, Hasheem recessed the Council until Furdi at first afternoon bell, noting that several pending matters might be added to the agenda at a later date.

Pajiin left the floor even while Hasheem was in the process of recessing the Council.

Dekkard had just stood when Erskine Mardosh approached. "Rather a short session, wouldn't you say, Steffan? That's the way the Council should operate. Get agreement before something comes to the floor. Briefly explain why it's a good idea, and then get the vote taken with an overwhelming majority."

"Some things work well that way." Dekkard tried not to express the wariness he felt.

"I understand you have some interesting hearings underway. Something about what explosives the New Meritorists used and where they came from."

"The Ministry of Public Safety and the Council Guard have verified that the explosives were all dunnite, but apparently certain newssheets are ignoring that."

"Often the most obvious facts are ignored when someone with great power wants them ignored."

"I understand that can happen. Would you happen to know which person with great power might be dictating what to ignore in this case?"

Mardosh chuckled. "Really, Steffan, I could pick almost any corporacion presidente, and I'd likely be correct."

"Don't you find that disturbing?" asked Dekkard.

"It is what it is."

"I don't doubt that, Erskine. What I asked was whether *you* found it disturbing."

"Great power is disturbing to those who don't have it, and useful to those who do."

Dekkard smiled. "I don't find all power disturbing, just power misused or abused."

"I've found whether power is used wisely or misused is a matter of opinion."

"I'd have to agree with you there," replied Dekkard. *And those who have no doubts about how they use power are most likely to be the ones abusing it.*

"Yet you're holding hearings that will likely change nothing and anger those better not angered?"

"Erskine, after what the New Meritorists did, if we don't at least hold hearings, it won't be long before we don't hold power."

"That suggests that you might be holding more hearings. How far will you press?"

"The last of the preliminary hearings is tomorrow. After all the information requested is returned, then I'll make a recommendation to the chairman of the full committee, and he'll decide whether additional hearings are necessary."

"Very wise of you to take matters one step at a time."

"That's what the Premier wants," replied Dekkard.

"What do you want, Steffan?"

"What I want doesn't matter if the Premier doesn't feel it's wise."

"I hadn't realized you were that cautious."

"Recognizing the position and power of the Premier is a practical necessity, particularly for junior councilors."

"So why did you push for the hearings?"

"Because we can't afford just to pay for the damages and execute New Meritorist followers or throw them into work camps and totally ignore the source of the dunnite that killed councilors. That's my feeling, but the Premier will have the final say."

Mardosh nodded. "Very wise of you. He should have a good idea if there are too many unanswered questions for the subcommittee to proceed. When will a report be available to the Council as a whole?"

"After the chairman decides when to end the hearings. He emphatically insisted that we follow established precedents and procedures."

"That's good to know. It would be helpful, and this is just a personal opinion, if all the legislative aspects of dealing with the insurrection were tied up neatly and quickly."

"I definitely agree," replied Dekkard. *Except I want to tie them up quickly and in a very different fashion from what you have in mind.*

Mardosh smiled pleasantly. "Do have a good afternoon." Then he slipped away.

Ingrella was waiting in the councilors' lobby. "I couldn't help but overhear some of what Erskine was saying."

"The only question is which presidente or presidentes got to him—or their surrogates. It might be interesting to see who's visited him recently, except he's too careful for that."

"From what I heard, he already knew," said Ingrella, "possibly days ago."

"Most likely from someone at Siincleer Shipbuilding."

"Siincleer doesn't have anything to do with dunnite, does it?" asked Ingrella.

"Not that I know of, but they appear to have funneled the most marks to Capitol Services."

"Do you know why?"

"I have suspicions I'm not ready to voice, but no proof," replied Dekkard.

"Then there's more about Capitol Services," said Ingrella dryly.

"I'm sure there is. Whether we'll discover it all is another question."

"Is there enough to refer it to the Justiciary Ministry?" she asked.

"I'll have a better idea after tomorrow's hearing."

"Don't wait too long, Steffan. The Justiciary Ministry can't prosecute on what's in your head."

"I know, but right now there's no proof of what's in my head." *Or not enough to do what you need to do.* Dekkard had the feeling that there was more than enough in Trujillo's files and what the subcommittee had turned up to get a prosecution, but not necessarily a conviction of those responsible, and without that nothing would really change.

"Be careful of wanting too much," said Ingrella quietly. "And be careful." She offered a smile that held sadness as she turned and left.

Both Avraal and Gaaroll waited outside the councilors' lobby.

As the three left the Council Hall and walked swiftly across the courtyard, Dekkard kept wondering why someone hadn't attacked. Was it that an attack would be worse for Suvion Industries, given how much information was already known? Or because an attack would widen the investigation? If that was the case, the greatest danger to Dekkard would be later, and he could easily suffer the same fate as Kraffeist or Grieg.

Once he and Avraal were alone in his private office, he immediately asked, "Could you discern anything off-key from Konnigsburg?"

"No. There was a sadness and concern toward the end, but I couldn't sense more."

"He's either sad about Kuuresoh or me, or possibly both." Dekkard summarized the luncheon conversation as well as he could recall it.

"He wasn't deceiving you. It's more of a guess, but I don't think he likes the way things are heading."

"That makes sense. At the least, Kuuresoh is misleading him, if not lying. He's aware that someone in Suvion Industries apparently funneled dunnite to the New Meritorists and that Siincleer Shipbuilding has more undiscovered bodies. On top of that, the Imperador appears set on appointing another military politician as Fleet Marshal."

"That would fit," she replied. "Could there be another reason?"

"If there is, I don't know it." He paused, then asked, "Could you sense much from my conversation with Mardosh?"

"Not much. Just a certain greasy satisfaction."

Dekkard summarized what Mardosh had said as well, including the "unanswered questions" phrase.

"He almost sounds like a Commercer with that kind of snide remark."

"He likes being a councilor better than being a mere guild officer, and he wants to stay in office as long as he can. He's not fond of the Siincleer corporacions, but he also doesn't want to anger them, especially after Pietro Venburg's death."

"Playing both sides."

"That's not exactly unknown," said Dekkard dryly. "Kaliara Bassaana certainly does."

"I don't like her, but she lets you know where she stands. Mardosh makes her look like a picture of virtue."

Dekkard looked at the stack of responses on his desk. They could wait. He walked out to the staff office. "Svard, do you have that information I requested?"

"Yes, sir. Do you want it now?"

"Bring what you have."

Roostof entered in less than a minute.

"What did you find out?" asked Dekkard.

"Corporacions engaging in certain prohibited or illegal activities are unequivocally barred from receiving Council funding, directly or indirectly, whether in the form of grants, loans, payment for services or products, or to enter into subcontracts to other corporacions' government contracts for construction, for any form of building or conveyance, including ships . . . the list is long and specific."

"What are those prohibited activities?"

"Conviction for restraint of trade, bribery, extortion, illegal work practices, maintaining an unsafe workplace. Those are all pretty standard, but there are several older ones. One is participation, either directly or as an active associate, in any attempt to overthrow the government by force. An active associate is essentially an accessory, and that includes any person, corporacion, or organization raising funds for or transferring funds to any group or organization engaged in insurrection or attempted insurrection. The language includes a phrase that, in the case of insurrection, lack of knowledge of the purpose for which the funds were employed does not absolve a corporacion of responsibility."

"Meaning that the corporacion can't get out of responsibility by claiming ignorance?"

"The law is clear on that point. While individuals may claim lack of knowledge, that defense is not open to the corporacion as a whole."

"What about incomplete or falsified records?" Dekkard was thinking about the request for invoices.

"That gets trickier. If there's an ongoing pattern, then it could be used as supporting evidence that the corporacion knowingly engaged in concealing information, but by itself . . . ? It probably wouldn't be enough, not unless someone confessed to altering records."

"Interesting. When were those provisions enacted?" asked Dekkard.

"In 1170."

At the beginning of the Silent Revolution . . . most interesting. "Would funding Capitol Services qualify?"

"I can't see how it wouldn't be applicable. Minz was the manager or director of Capitol Services, and at the very least some of the funds from corporacions that went to Capitol Services were used to pay for vehicles and personnel involved in the attack on the Council Office Building."

"Then I'd like you to write up something stating that so I can go over it tonight. I don't know if I'll be able to use it tomorrow, but it appears that I'll need it sooner or later, and sooner could be tomorrow."

"Yes, sir. I'll have it to you in the next bell."

"Thank you." Dekkard looked at the responses he needed to read and sign, then added, "I'm not going anywhere soon."

Roostof returned with a typed copy of his recommended language in less than a bell, but almost another bell passed before Dekkard finished dealing with all the correspondence, very little, if any, of which would affect Guldor as much as the hearings would, but each one of which would mean more to the recipient in the immediate future than would the hearings.

Although Dekkard had prepared correspondence replies for Obreduur, he'd never really grasped how time-consuming it could be for a councilor. Yet how else could people really bring their concerns to his attention year-round? Despite Obreduur's efforts to meet people in person, Dekkard could see that most councilors would have difficulty spending much more than a month or a month and a half in their district. From what he'd seen, many councilors relied on family, friends, and former associates to keep them informed of local concerns.

But those reports tend to be limited by the background of the coun-cilor.

As Avraal, Gaaroll, and Dekkard walked toward the central staircase, he looked to Avraal and asked, "Do you think we ought to leave early tomorrow? Really early?"

"It can't hurt," replied Avraal evenly.

"But you think the real danger will be later, don't you?"

"That's my feeling, unless you can somehow expose so many of the cor-poracions that not only are you the least of their problems, but anything untoward happening to you would make their situation worse."

Dekkard nodded. That was the objective of his plan, but as he learned from what had happened to Axel Obreduur, even the best plans by the most talented councilors didn't necessarily work out.

63

DEKKARD woke early and uneasily on Tridi. While Sigourna Miletus had not sighted or sensed the blue Realto—or any other steamer
with a similar feel—since she had first told Dekkard and Avraal, her latest
report hadn't reassured Dekkard in the slightest.

The short article on page two of *Gestirn* hadn't allayed his concerns
either, although it had stated only the bare facts—that a special investigatory subcommittee of the Council's Security Committee was holding the
third hearing on the question of how the New Meritorists had obtained
the military explosives. The hearing would involve various officials from
Suvion Industries, the second of only two manufacturers of that explosive.
The story also stated that senior naval officers and officials from the other
manufacturer—Northwest Industrial Chemical—had testified previously.

Avraal, Dekkard, and Gaaroll hurried through breakfast and left the
house roughly two-thirds of a bell earlier than usual. Even so, the air felt
warmer and springlike.

Dekkard took an indirect route that he hadn't used in weeks, and neither
empath sensed anything more than usual. He actually used his own keys
to get into the office, although Roostof showed up and peered into Dekkard's
personal office little more than a sixth later.

"You were here early, sir."

"I have some matters to discuss with Guard Captain Trujillo and the
Premier before the start of the hearings. Thank you again for working
through that language yesterday."

"I hope it proves useful."

"It already has. I'll just have to see what the subcommittee can put
together." Dekkard stood and nodded to Avraal. "I think we should see
if we can find the Guard captain." Not that Trujillo wouldn't be close to
either the Security Committee or the Premier's floor office, given the subject matter and witnesses—or one of them.

"Just let me know if you need anything else, sir."

"You've been more than helpful. Now, it's up to the subcommittee to
see what we can do with what you provided."

After Roostof departed, Dekkard checked his gray leather folder one
last time to make sure that he had all the papers he needed, including the

statement Roostof had given him the day before. Then he, Avraal, and Gaaroll left the office.

As Dekkard and Avraal started down the center staircase, Gaaroll said quietly, "Strong feelings. Moving away, but still strong. Measured. Not fear or anger. Not an empie."

"Someone posted there to tell someone you're coming down the steps," suggested Avraal. "I could only get a hint before they got too far away."

Dekkard quietly checked his knives and studied what he could see of the main level. Early as it was, there were less than a score of people on the stairs and visible in the lower main corridor. They all were likely staffers, given that he didn't see any councilors he recognized.

But then, posing as a staffer would be one of the more likely ways to get close to a councilor, since most Council Guards likely couldn't be expected to recognize all of the thousand or so professional and clerical staff in the Council Office Building and the Council Hall and name badges could be counterfeited . . . if someone wants to put in the time and marks.

Dekkard was almost to the bottom of the staircase when Gaaroll spoke again.

"Same fellow coming back. Feels the same. Someone with him. Odd piles of feelings from him."

After turning in the direction of the courtyard doors, Dekkard maintained the same even pace.

"No sense of physical violence," murmured Avraal. "Smoldering low anger."

As the two drew nearer, the shorter figure slowed and moved to the corridor wall. Dekkard recognized the taller figure as Gerard Schmidtz, largely because of white-streaked black hair and the arrogance embodied in every step.

Schmidtz angled his approach so that Dekkard would have to turn away to avoid him.

Dekkard chose not to back off and stopped a yard or so short of the older councilor, then looked directly into the eyes of the slightly shorter man. "Good morning, Gerard."

"Heading over to preside over your subcommittee hearings, Steffan?" offered Schmidtz in a warm and hardy tone.

"They're not until later this morning."

"What do you intend to prove with these theatrics? Besides emphasizing that the New Meritorists obtained explosives, that is?"

"That part scarcely needs emphasizing, Gerard. What is your particular interest in the hearings? You obviously have one, or you wouldn't be here."

"You know, Steffan, Crafters have always concentrated on the obvious, rather than the real power. I had hopes you'd avoid that. It's what isn't obvious that matters."

Knowing he was being baited, Dekkard smiled pleasantly. "I'd hoped that as well, but sometimes the obvious is necessary, even if, in the long run, it doesn't matter. If Crafters don't hold some hearings on how the New Meritorists obtained those explosives, we'll spend all the months or years to the next election trying to explain why we didn't. Isn't it better just to have a subcommittee headed by a junior Craft councilor doing the investigating?"

"I'm surprised you'd let Hasheem maneuver you into such a position."

"Since it appeared something along these lines would happen, Gerard, I volunteered."

"Volunteering unnecessarily can be chancy, especially when explosives are involved."

"You're doubtless right," Dekkard replied, "but nothing comes without a price, especially when you've been appointed as a councilor."

Schmidtz offered an avuncular and sage expression, one that Dekkard definitely distrusted, and said, "Under the circumstances, perhaps sticking to the bare necessities of obvious action might be the most rewarding course of action for everyone."

"I appreciate your thoughtfulness and advice, Gerard."

"I do trust that the Council can get past all the uproar caused by an ill-thought-out and failed attempt at insurrection."

"I agree. The Council does need to deal with the situation as necessary and get on with its business," *if not in the way you think.*

"I look forward to seeing that." Schmidtz smiled broadly. "Good day, Steffan."

"Good day, Gerard."

Schmidtz turned and headed back in the direction of his office.

Dekkard, Avraal, and Gaaroll resumed their progress toward the courtyard doors.

After several moments, he asked, "Did you sense anything useful?"

"Not much," said Avraal. "He has to know I'm an empath, and he kept his thoughts and feelings on what he was saying. There was a fair amount of insincerity."

"He's feeling pleased, now, I think," said Gaaroll.

"I hope it's for the right reason." Dekkard frowned. "How could he believe that any insurrection that damaged or destroyed sixteen Security buildings, included successful attacks on the port and ironway stations, the first mutiny since before Laureous the Great, two attacks on the Council, the death of a dozen councilors, and thousands of casualties was totally ill-thought-out? Or was that another effort to bait me?"

"It was," said Avraal. "But you didn't take the bait."

"At least, not to him," said Dekkard ruefully. "Was anyone else around watching?"

"Only the aide back against the wall," said Avraal.

"Slippery sort, but not an empath," added Gaaroll.

The three crossed the courtyard quickly and made their way along the main corridor of the Council Hall. He found Guard Captain Trujillo in his office, and closed the door after entering.

"I thought I'd be seeing you early this morning, Councilor. What do you have in mind?"

"There's a possibility that one witness will refuse to answer several questions."

"Just one?" asked Trujillo, with only a hint of irony in his voice.

"For all I know, there could be more," replied Dekkard, "but I'd be very surprised if there's not at least one."

"Would his failure to answer fall in the area of high crimes or treason?"

"If I use the call pull, it will," replied Dekkard. "I've reviewed the definitions with my senior legalist."

"The Premier showed me the witness list," said Trujillo.

"I did tell you who was on it."

"He wanted to make sure I knew."

"He doubtless asked if you'd have any problem incarcerating anyone on the list."

"That was implied, and I don't." Trujillo's tone was matter-of-fact, if hardly casual. But then, the Guard captain had lost at least two score guards to the New Meritorists.

"I don't expect others to refuse to answer," said Dekkard, "but I could be mistaken. Some answers might open them to civil or criminal charges short of high crimes, but in those instances the subcommittee would have to refer the matter to the Justiciary Ministry." Dekkard frowned. "Can't the Council Guard make referrals?"

"If evidence at a hearing is made available to the Council Guard, the Guard can also make that referral . . . *but* only upon request of the Security Committee chair, or a committee councilor with such delegated powers."

Dekkard managed just to nod before asking, "If testimony is referred to the Council Guard by a subcommittee chair with a request for referral, would that meet such a requirement?"

"It would, although I don't believe the matter has come up in recent years."

That suggests that Hasheem may not know that. "Is there anything else I should know?"

"I believe you've covered everything relevant, Councilor. My men and I will be in the Security Committee staff offices for the duration of the hearing."

"Thank you, Guard Captain." Dekkard stood and let himself out.

After he and Avraal had walked away from Trujillo's door, Dekkard looked at her.

"He was both worried and satisfied."

"He briefed me on certain lesser-known procedures. Now, it's time for me to meet with Hasheem."

When Dekkard, Avraal, and Gaaroll entered the outer floor office, Meldra smiled pleasantly. "He was hoping you'd be here early, Councilor."

Dekkard returned the smile. "I thought it might be best."

Once Dekkard was seated across the desk from Hasheem, he asked, "Have you had any response from Johann Daenyld?"

"No, but he might not have gotten my letter until yesterday. He also may wish to see how today's hearing goes before he decides how to respond."

"He may not like the results," said Dekkard evenly.

"How can you say that even before the hearing begins?"

"For several reasons. First, someone will have to explain how several pounds of dunnite manufactured by Suvion Industries was found in the one Meritorist armory. Second, there's the problem that Capitol Services rented the space used by the group that attacked the Council Office Building, bought the stake lorry, and funded the building of the steam cannon and shells, among other things. Third, sixteen banque drafts to Capitol Services came from Suvion Industries."

"Daenyld will claim that they believed Capitol Services was a legitimate business."

"I'm sure that he will, but under existing law, ignorance, feigned or real, does not absolve the corporacion from responsibility. That means a minimum of two years of no procurement contracts, grants, subcontracts, and the like."

Hasheem frowned. "You're sure of that?"

"My legalist is. Obviously, the Justiciary legalists would have to confirm that."

Hasheem frowned.

"There's also the connection between Ulrich and Minz. We'll have to see what Ulrich has to say, and what he knows about Minz's killing."

"He'll protest it's not relevant."

"How can it not be relevant? Suvion Industries paid over forty thousand marks to a business set up by Ulrich, or by Minz under Ulrich's direction, that supported the New Meritorists."

Hasheem nodded slowly. "I think we should meet immediately after you conclude today's hearing. Immediately."

"I'll be here. It's only a suggestion, but . . ."

"If you're suggesting Guard Captain Trujillo be here as well, I'd already planned on that. We'll see you then, Steffan."

Dekkard stood, inclined his head politely, and left. Once in the outer office, he said, "I hope you have a pleasant morning, Meldra." Then he, Avraal, and Gaaroll stepped out into the main corridor headed toward the Security Committee room and the committee staff offices.

"Hasheem seemed disturbed to me," said Dekkard. "Was he?"

"He was," replied Avraal.

"No more than a seasprite in a spout," added Gaaroll.

"I have to meet him immediately after the hearings," said Dekkard.

"Why doesn't he come and watch?" asked Gaaroll. "He's the Premier. He can do that."

"Because, if things go badly," said Avraal, "he can blame Steffan. He won't have that excuse if he's there. Besides, he needs this mess cleaned up by someone else."

"Or to have someone else fail trying," added Dekkard wryly.

Mario deCaastro, the Security Committee staff director, hurried toward Dekkard the moment Dekkard, Avraal, and Gaaroll stepped into the committee offices. "You're early, sir. Is there a problem?"

"Not that I know of. I had some meetings, and they didn't take as long as I thought. No point in walking back to my office, just to turn around and walk back here. Don't let me disturb you in setting up the committee room."

"Thank you, sir."

Dekkard took one of the chairs in the waiting area, sat down, and opened his leather folder to begin reviewing the materials Roostof had prepared.

The first subcommittee member to arrive was Villem Baar, with Haastar and Pajiin almost immediately behind.

"Do you have any surprises planned, Steffan?" asked Baar.

"We're looking for the facts," replied Dekkard. "Any surprises will come from the witnesses."

"Then it might be a long and boring hearing," said Haastar.

"Almost everything in life has long and boring parts," replied Dekkard, "and if we're smart, we enjoy those, because the exciting parts are dangerous, and not everyone survives."

"For a councilor so junior, Steffan," said Baar, "you can be incredibly cynical."

"That comes from being a security aide," said Pajiin.

Haastar smiled.

Just before third bell, as at the previous hearing, Dekkard led the way into the main committee room, set up as it had been before, with the four witnesses seated at the table facing the dais, each with a nameplate. Although Dekkard, while Obreduur's security aide, had seen Ulrich from a distance more than a few times, he'd never seen the former premier close-up or for any length of time, but Ulrich was definitely a presence, with piercing black eyes, smooth honey skin, and iron-gray hair perfectly in place. His security-blue suit, with the cravat of councilor red, added to the impression of confidence and power.

Once the third bell struck, Dekkard tapped the gavel once. "The special investigatory subcommittee of the Security Committee is now in session. The subcommittee appreciates the presence of the noted former Premier Oskaar Ulrich, now vice-presidente of political affairs for Suvion Industries; Alberto Pastaano, director of production; Felix Guthbaert, shipping and transportation manager; and Ferryn Maartel, director of security." From there Dekkard gave precisely the same explanation and cautions as he had at the beginning of each of the previous hearings.

Then he said, "Sr. Ulrich, the subcommittee particularly appreciates your presence here. We also appreciate the appearance of Sr. Pastaano, Sr. Guthbaert, and Sr. Maartel. Before we begin with the technical matters at hand, Sr. Ulrich, the subcommittee would like to offer you the opportunity of presenting any opening remarks on behalf of Suvion Industries, if you would like to do so."

"Thank you, Sr. Chairman. I would." Ulrich offered a warm, almost blinding smile. "With a proud history that goes back almost two centuries, Suvion Industries is among the world leaders in industrial chemical formulation and manufacture. Along with that, Suvion Industries has maintained an outstanding safety record while faithfully supplying the requirements of the greatest Navy the world has ever seen . . ."

A sixth later, Ulrich concluded his opening remarks, designed to make the point, without it being said, that anything that harmed Suvion would bring about the fall of the Imperium.

The entire time Ulrich had been speaking, neither Avraal nor Larelli Daespaan indicated any sign of sensing untruths, but then Ulrich had been careful enough not to utter any, except some rhetorical excesses.

"Thank you, Sr. Ulrich," said Dekkard. "We will initially concentrate on Suvion Industries' production process. Sr. Pastaano, will you briefly explain how your facility produces dunnite."

For the next third of a bell, Pastaano did just that, describing a process nearly identical to that offered by Northwest Industrial Chemical.

Next came an explanation of the basic shipping procedures from Felix Guthbaert.

After that, Dekkard looked at Guthbaert. "The subcommittee requested that you provide the invoices for all sales of dunnite to parties other than the Navy over the past three years. Have you brought those invoices?"

"Yes, we have, Sr. Chairman," replied Guthbaert.

"Please tender them to the committee clerk," said Dekkard.

Guthbaert rose and carried a large kraft paper envelope to the clerk.

"Thank you," said Dekkard. "The subcommittee will meet in executive session for no longer than a third to examine the invoices. Witnesses will leave the chamber at this time."

"That is most unusual, Sr. Chairman," said Ulrich.

"You are correct, Sr. Ulrich," replied Dekkard politely. "But then, having two shellings of the Council in less than a year is also unusual. The clerk will inform you when it is time to resume."

Once the witnesses, the two empaths, and the clerk had left the chamber, Baar asked, "Do you really expect that they'd turn in any invoices that were incorrect or showed improprieties?"

"Of course not, but the invoices might tell us what questions to ask. Then, they might show nothing." Dekkard handed the envelope to Pajiin. "Count them first. Then look them over."

A minute or so later, Pajiin said, "There are forty-nine invoices, and they only go back two and a half years." Several minutes passed before he spoke again. "There aren't any invoice numbers. Never knew any corporacion that didn't number their invoices. There's a square that's a shade darker in the same place on each one."

"Someone blocked off the numbers on the copies, then," said Baar.

"Why didn't they just renumber them?" asked Haastar. "We couldn't tell the difference."

Pajiin shook his head. "Invoices are printed and the numbers are written in or typed in. Sometimes they're preceded by letters. Over time, they'll look different. Trying to duplicate that'd be a bitch."

Baar was the next to look through the invoices. "There's no regularity here. Usually, people order things on a regular basis."

"Make notes on that. You can question Guthbaert about it," said Dekkard.

By the time Dekkard called the subcommittee back into session, he had a very good idea that more than a few invoices were missing, but how many was impossible to tell. *That's why you have empaths.*

"The subcommittee will continue with Sr. Guthbaert," Dekkard announced. "Sr. Guthbaert, outside of the Navy, do these invoices account for all of the dunnite that left Suvion Industries in the past three years?"

"Sr. Chairman, those are all the invoices that are in the shipping records."

"I don't believe that was the question," said Dekkard mildly. "Do these invoices account for all dunnite that did not go to the Imperial Navy?"

"I have no way of knowing that for certain."

"Let me rephrase my question. Are there, or were there, other invoices for dunnite that you did not present to the subcommittee?"

Guthbaert's eyes flicked to Avraal and then to Larelli Daespaan. "There may be."

"The subcommittee requested all the invoices. Did we receive all of them?"

"I can't say absolutely that you did or did not."

Both empaths raised their hands.

"Would you care to reconsider your answer?" asked Dekkard. "The subcommittee is investigating possible high crimes. Failing to answer honestly could make you an accessory to any wrongdoing."

"You did not receive all the invoices. Someone from the corporacion's legal office went through the invoices before we were told to pull out what the subcommittee ordered."

"How many invoices did that person or others remove?"

"I don't know. There were a number, but over three years, I couldn't say."

Dekkard decided on a long shot. "Do you recall if there was an invoice for Capitol Services or any other business in Machtarn?"

"I don't recall anything called Capitol Services, but there were invoices for shipments to be delivered to the explosives warehouse in Machtarn."

Baar looked to Dekkard.

"Councilor Baar, you may proceed."

"Sr. Guthbaert, does this explosives warehouse have a name? And a permit to handle shipments of more than a decem of dunnite?"

"Yes, sir. Noldar, Limited. They had an export permit for explosives to be sent to Noldar. We checked on that."

"But there are no invoices for Noldar, Limited, in those you supplied."

"No, sir."

"Since you remember Noldar, Limited," said Baar, "you must have shipped regularly to them. Is that correct?"

"About once a season, as I recall."

"Then why didn't you supply the invoices?"

"Someone in higher authority removed them from the files we were allowed to copy before we made the copies."

"Who was that?"

"I don't know. The legalists were the ones who removed the files with all the invoices."

"Were you told that invoices were removed?"

"No, Councilor. I noticed the gaps when the invoice files were returned."

"Did you say anything about it?"

"I asked why some invoices were missing. One of the legalists told me it was a management decision and not to ask anything more."

"Sr. Chairman," said Pajiin.

"You may proceed, Councilor Pajiin."

"Sr. Guthbaert, none of the copies of the invoices the subcommittee received have numbers. Why is that?"

"The legalists instructed us to block out the numbers, Councilor."

With that question and response, Dekkard shifted part of his attention to Ulrich. The former premier's face showed some polite interest, but Dekkard doubted that he was as calm as he appeared.

"Was there a particular legalist who issued that order?" pressed Pajiin.

"Yes, Councilor. The junior legalists said it was the vice-presidente of legal affairs, Oswaald Cassius."

"Did the legalist offer any explanation?"

"He said certain information was proprietary and unrelated to the hearing."

"Did he give any other explanation?"

"No, sir."

"Did anyone else issue orders about the invoices or the hearing?"

"Not to my knowledge."

Pajiin looked to Dekkard. "No further questions at this time."

In turn, Dekkard looked to Haastar. "Do you have any questions?"

"I do, Sr. Chairman." Haastar then asked Guthbaert, "All forty-nine invoices indicate dunnite being shipped to port cities. Dunnite cannot be shipped to entities not licensed for manufacture of ordnance, unless it is being shipped for export, which also requires a special permit. Do you know to what countries the dunnite is being shipped?"

"Not accurately, Councilor. I've gathered over the years that most of it goes to Noldar. That's just my impression."

"No further questions."

"The subcommittee will now address security concerns in the transport and storage of dunnite," stated Dekkard. "Sr. Maartel, please briefly explain your role and duties as director of security."

Over the next third of a bell, Maartel outlined the physical security measures, which were similar to those employed by Northwest Industrial Chemical. Questions were limited.

Dekkard smiled pleasantly as he addressed Ulrich. "Sr. Ulrich, you've been vice-presidente for political affairs at Suvion Industries since early last fall. Is that correct?"

"It is."

"When you were a councilor you were chair of the Military Affairs Committee and a member of the Security Committee."

"That's a matter of record."

"On at least one occasion, a Security Committee aide named Jaime Minz accompanied you on official visits to naval installations. Is that not also true?"

"He may have," answered Ulrich almost casually and dismissively.

"Yes or no?"

"Yes."

"Were you aware that Sr. Minz operated a business known as Capitol Services, while he was serving as a Security Committee aide?"

"I was. Sr. Minz was operating the business as a sole proprietor."

"Before his death, Sr. Minz said that you had helped him establish Capitol Services. Is that true?"

"Sr. Chairman," said Ulrich, sarcastically emphasizing the title, "I understood that this hearing was about dunnite, not about former Council aides."

"It is. The question remains. Did you or did you not help Jaime Minz establish Capitol Services?"

"I object to the entire line of questioning."

"You can object all you want, Sr. Ulrich, so long as you answer the questions."

"Why should I?"

"Jaime Minz was about to be charged with high crimes when he was shot. Those crimes involved the use of Capitol Services to obtain dunnite for New Meritorists. Now, again, did you assist Jaime Minz in establishing Capitol Services?"

"That question does not belong in this proceeding. I refuse to answer that."

As Ulrich started to stand, Dekkard smoothly yanked the bellpull to summon Trujillo and his guards, then said, "You can answer the subcommittee's questions or you can be incarcerated."

Ulrich hadn't gotten more than two steps from the witness table when Council Guards appeared at both the entrance from the committee offices and at the door to the main corridor.

Ulrich stopped and turned back to face Dekkard. "You can incarcerate me for the maximum period, but the High Court will free me for this absurdity."

Dekkard looked levelly at Ulrich, and concentrating on his words, replied, "The High Court will rule on the law, on the need for your response, and on the facts, *not* upon your past position or power." Then he looked to Guard Captain Trujillo.

"Guard Captain, Sr. Ulrich has repeatedly refused to answer questions bearing on high crimes and the attack on the Council buildings. Therefore, he is to be incarcerated until the High Court can hear the issue. Counsel may be admitted to see him, but only one legalist, as under the provisions of the Great Charter."

Trujillo inclined his head. "Under the provisions of the Great Charter, so be it." Then he ordered, "Escort Sr. Ulrich to incarceration."

Ulrich looked coldly at Dekkard.

Dekkard said evenly, again concentrating on the words, "You will relate the facts, accurately." As he spoke, he looked directly at Ulrich.

Abruptly, the former premier turned.

Trujillo and the Council Guards escorted Ulrich from the chamber.

Once the doors closed, Dekkard said quietly, but firmly, "Are there any other questions?"

The other three councilors shook their heads.

Dekkard then said, "The witnesses may leave, but you may be recalled for further testimony, given that the subcommittee's investigation involves possible high crimes and treason. The subcommittee is recessed until the next meeting." He tapped the gavel.

After the empaths and the clerk left, Villem Baar was the first to turn to Dekkard. "Did you know how many laws they're breaking? Before the hearing, I meant?"

"I suspected a few, but not quite so many."

"Brazen bastards," said Pajiin.

"That's because they've gotten away with this sort of thing for years," said

Haastar. "Wilhelm Freust looked into some of the abuses, but he couldn't get enough support, especially with everyone being afraid of Wyath and the old Security Ministry. He'd just approached Obreduur when he died."

"He was likely murdered," added Dekkard, standing. "And that reminds me. I need to talk to the Security Committee staff director." He turned toward the staff office.

The other councilors followed.

Mario deCaastro stood waiting. "Sir, from what—"

"You're right, Mario. You need to have a copy of the testimony of Sr. Guthbaert typed up and sent by secure messenger personally and directly to the Justiciary minister. Also that of Sr. Ulrich."

"Yes, sir."

"At the same time, copies should go to the Premier and to Guard Captain Trujillo."

"The Guard captain?"

"He has very secure files."

After a slight hesitation, deCaastro nodded and smiled.

"You intended something like this all along, didn't you?" asked Baar.

"Like this? I didn't plan it all out this way. What I do know is that if enough councilors knew enough, the corporacions would have a hard time keeping it from coming out."

"They'll be really after you now," said Pajiin.

"For a little while," *you hope.* "But they can't stop it from becoming public, and that will make it hard on councilors closely tied to certain corporacions." After a moment, he added, "Not all of them are Commercers." He offered a rueful smile. "And now I have to go report to the Premier on the damage."

As Dekkard headed toward the corridor door, Gaaroll stepped in front of him. "There's a cold feeling out there, isolate-like," said Gaaroll.

"Where?" asked Avraal.

"Toward the Premier's office."

"Take a quick look and see what you can," said Dekkard. "Look the other way, too." Then he turned to the other three councilors. "I'd strongly suggest remaining here for a bit."

Gaaroll went to the door, opened it, glanced around quickly, then came back to Dekkard.

"Two men with a cart mopping the floor up by the door down to the records room. Two more on the other end. Another cart, but they're fiddling with the barricade closing off the part being repaired. Both on the other side of the corridor."

Dekkard walked over to the staff director. "Marco, I need a sheet of stationery and a pen . . . and someone to run a message to Guard Captain Trujillo. He'll likely be in his office or the Premier's floor office."

The staff director looked puzzled. "That's only—"

"Trust me."

In moments, Dekkard had written out what he needed. "It has to go immediately and directly to the Guard captain, and the messenger needs to stay there for a while."

Dekkard was fairly certain that the would-be assassins wouldn't think much of a single staffer on an errand because their goal was to get several councilors, not to reveal themselves by shooting a staffer. But he still worried as the young woman hurried out the door.

Several moments later, Gaaroll said, "She's past the men mopping. The other two are still near the barricade."

Dekkard released the breath he hadn't realized he'd held.

"What is it?" asked Baar.

"A possible team of assassins gunning for the entire subcommittee," replied Dekkard.

"And you sent that girl out?" asked Pajiin.

"If they'd shot at her, they'd have lost the chance to shoot at us. We probably need to step back and keep the door shut and bolted."

"I've already bolted the corridor door to the committee room," said deCaastro as he slid the bolt on the staff office door.

With masonry interior walls and two-and-a-half-digit-thick solid oak doors, Dekkard thought it was unlikely that any weaponry carried by the putative assassins would have much effect.

Almost a third of a bell passed before several volleys of shots rang out, then several others.

"Four people dead," said Gaaroll laconically. "Two by the barrier. Two this side of the down staircase."

Another sixth passed before there was a muffled rap on the door.

"That's Guard Captain Trujillo. There's no one near him," said Avraal calmly.

"You can tell?" asked Haastar.

"I've sensed him enough to recognize him."

Dekkard stepped forward and slid the bolt, then eased the door open.

Trujillo stood there. "It's all over. The corridor's clear. They refused to surrender. We tried to wound them, but they all jabbed themselves with something. Frog poison, I'd judge. They had sanitary workers' passcards, bur no other identification. They had rifles in the utility carts. They likely killed the four men whose uniforms they wore. We'll be looking into that. The Premier's waiting for you, Councilor Dekkard."

"Thank you, Guard Captain. We all appreciate it."

"The Council Guard appreciates the way you handled it, Councilor. You kept the casualties to the absolute minimum." Trujillo paused, then said, "The Premier seemed insistent. I'll join you there in a few moments, after I debrief the other councilors. I personally vetted all the guards in the Council Hall today."

Dekkard picked up his gray leather folder and looked to Avraal and then Gaaroll. "Thank you both. Without you . . ." He shook his head.

"The three of us make a good team," said Avraal, "and we'd better go. There's no danger now, and there are Council Guards everywhere."

Once the three were walking toward the Premier's office, Dekkard said, "Trujillo spoke quietly, but I got the feeling he was angry."

"Furious," said Avraal.

"Maybe more than that," added Gaaroll.

"At me . . . or the subcommittee?"

"No," said Avraal. "It wasn't that. I think he was angry that the assassins got into the Council Hall. If they'd been successful, it might have changed everything. It would have ruined the Guard captain."

"We're still vulnerable," said Dekkard pensively.

"You do have three empaths looking out for you," replied Avraal, "including Sigourna Miletus. I'm paying her. It's worth every mark."

Dekkard couldn't argue that.

When he stepped into the Premier's floor office, followed by Avraal and Gaaroll, Meldra gestured toward the inner office. "You do make life interesting, Councilor."

Dekkard managed a wry smile.

He wasn't totally surprised to see Justiciary Minister Serapha Marler Kuta seated in the single chair in front of the desk.

"Guard Captain Trujillo?" asked Hasheem.

"He'll be here in a few minutes. He had to debrief the other three councilors."

"How did you know they were assassins?" asked Hasheem.

"One of my empaths detected them."

"From that far away?" asked Minister Kuta.

"One excels at recognizing emotional patterns at a distance."

"You have two?"

"I married one and hired the other," replied Dekkard.

"He and his wife were a security team before he became a councilor and they married," said Hasheem tersely.

Dekkard didn't feel like talking, at least not until Guard Captain Trujillo arrived, but less than a sixth passed before Trujillo stepped into the small and now-crowded office.

Hasheem addressed the Guard captain. "If you'd give a quick report."

"Four men impersonated four sanitary employees. We don't know yet about the real employees. They carried the rifles in a broom box, then concealed them in the cleaning carts. They knew that Councilor Dekkard's empaths have greater range than the usual. That's why they planned to use rifles from beyond the range of even a strong empath once the councilors left the hearing. Because of the rebuilding, the councilors could only go one way, and they'd be caught in a cross fire. If the assassins had been able to carry out shooting as planned, no one would have suspected the false sanitary workers until after they escaped. It should have worked." Trujillo looked to Dekkard. "I'd be interested to know why it didn't."

"One of my empaths has much greater range, but lacks fine emotional discrimination. That's why I have two. She picked up on the presence and lack of emotion."

"They were isolates?"

"At least one was. From that and their position it seemed a likely assassination," replied Dekkard. "I worried about sending the clerk, but if they were really after us, I thought it unlikely that they'd shoot at her, because they'd lose all chance at us."

"You could have waited them out," said the Justiciary minister.

"And give them another chance? Also, I'd hoped that the Council Guards might be able to capture one or more."

"They all had suicide needles," said Trujillo. "It may take weeks to discover who they are."

Left unsaid was the possibility that the shooters' identities might never be discovered, a possibility that Dekkard thought most probable.

After a long moment of silence, Hasheem spoke, his voice carrying annoyance, anger, and resignation. "You seem to be the one with all the answers, Steffan. How would you handle it?"

"Call in the press and give them a full briefing about the attempted assassination of the entire investigatory subcommittee. Point out that a senior official of one of the corporacions under investigation refused to answer questions about ties to and possible aid for the New Meritorists, and that he had close ties to Jaime Minz, who was firmly linked to aiding the New Meritorists. Tell them about Capitol Services and that five major Guldoran corporacions made significant payments to Capitol Services, the company directly responsible for the death of a premier and three other councilors." Dekkard looked to Serapha Marler Kuta. "If it meets your approval, Minister

Kuta, I'd suggest that you state that the Justiciary Ministry is also investigating, and that given the laws about supporting insurrections, all five corporacions, as well as their senior officers, likely face a range of charges."

The Justiciary minister offered a sardonic smile. "How would we prove that?"

"High crimes and treason. I can give you a list of related questions requiring an answer under law with empathic verification. Failure to answer requires statelessness at a minimum, as I recall."

"Juan del Larrano and Johann Daenyld will never answer questions," said Hasheem.

"They don't have to in order for the Justiciary Ministry to revoke all their contracts," replied Dekkard. "There's something called collective knowledge . . ."

Minister Kuta smiled. "I wondered if you'd get to that."

"He's right, then?" asked Hasheem.

"He's simplified the process. It will likely take weeks, if not longer, to deal with all aspects of all the actions by all the corporacions involved. But once we actually start investigating and interviewing, there will be some employees who will reveal more, given certain incentives. Because of the size of the funding involved, we've already quietly started to look into Siincleer Shipbuilding."

"Don't neglect Siincleer Engineering," said Dekkard. "They're already operating in Noldar, and that's where Suvion shipped dunnite. We have some supporting evidence involving Engaard Engineering and the Navy's new research facility west of Siincleer and how they illegally took over that contract. A local patroller captain looking into that was also killed by a sniper."

The Justiciary minister nodded. "We'll talk about that later."

That was fine with Dekkard.

"There's another problem, Steffan," said Hasheem. "If corporacions like Siincleer and Suvion aren't allowed to supply the government, who will?"

"The Navy can build and operate its own dunnite-processing facility. They've claimed for years they could do it cheaper. The Council wouldn't let them because it would cut into corporacion profits. The Navy wouldn't have the quality-control problems, and they wouldn't be selling dunnite to Noldar through various fronts."

Hasheem looked stunned.

"That was in today's testimony. You and Minister Kuta will each be getting a copy shortly." Dekkard looked to Trujillo. "So will you." Dekkard went on. "Those fronts are likely how Capitol Services got the dunnite, but we didn't get that far. Ulrich probably arranged for Minz's murder as well, but I didn't get the chance to ask that question, either. Not that Ulrich would have answered it. As for supplying the Admiralty, there are numbers of small companies who could likely do the job better and cheaper, especially once the Justiciary Ministry interrogates, under empath surveillance, the legal department of Siincleer Shipbuilding about all their illegal methods. That should be possible now, as Minister Kuta just indicated, given the amount of contributions from Siincleer to Capitol Services."

Dekkard turned to Minister Kuta. "The subcommittee will also be sending you a copy of the testimony of Unadi's hearing. There is material in that about who at Northwest Industrial Chemical hired Minz and under what conditions. Given the contributions to Capitol Services by Northwest while Minz was an employee, that testimony seems relevant."

"More than merely relevant," replied Kuta, "it's a sad commentary on Guldoran corporacions. They've grown so accustomed to flouting the law and even the Great Charter that they've come to believe it's their right." She stood. "The Justiciary Ministry looks forward to receiving the testimony from the hearings. In the meantime, we need to prepare for the onslaught of corporacion legalists and their protests of ministry overreach, as well as ready a refutation to Sr. Ulrich's baseless claims that he's exempt from the provisions of the Great Charter." Kuta looked to Hasheem. "Thank you for forewarning and briefing me." Then she looked to Dekkard. "As I promised, we'll be in touch." Then she turned and departed.

Hasheem looked to Trujillo. "Is there anything else?"

"Not right now. We're still looking into why they weren't challenged."

"Let me know," said Hasheem.

"If there's nothing more, sir?"

"I won't keep you, Guard Captain. You and your men handled the situation well."

"Councilor Dekkard made it possible, sir."

Even if Councilor Dekkard's actions prompted the assassination attempt. But Dekkard saw no point in raising that issue, since both Hasheem and Trujillo were well aware of that.

"Councilor Dekkard is quite resourceful, as we both know," said Hasheem.

Trujillo said nothing more, just inclined his head and left the small office.

Once the door was shut, Hasheem said, "Steffan, now that the Justiciary Ministry has decided to act, it might be best to hold further hearings in abeyance."

"Announce that the special investigatory subcommittee will hold off on further hearings to avoid conflicts with the Justiciary Ministry's investigations, while the subcommittee works with the ministry, but that the subcommittee will not foreclose the possibility of further hearings?"

Hasheem frowned.

"Leaving the loaded gun or loose cannon ready to fire," said Dekkard, "will certainly serve notice to the corporacions that the Council will no longer tolerate continuing illegalities. It will also strengthen your position."

"How do you see that?"

"Such a statement will suggest that you and the subcommittee know of those illegalities and that the ministry does as well."

"That may not dissuade some from wishing to act against you."

"That's true, but the downside of killing me, or any other councilor, is now much greater, and it won't stop the investigations and prosecutions. The prosecution of Ulrich will make Commercer councilors more wary of getting deeply involved with corporacions."

"You'll pardon me if I don't share your optimism, Steffan," said Hasheem dourly. "While Oskaar wasn't all that well-liked, and it's unlikely most councilors will be that upset at his being incarcerated, you've threatened some of the most powerful corporacions in Guldor."

"There's no doubt they'll be angry, if not furious, but if we can survive the next few weeks . . ."

"You think it will blow over?" Hasheem shook his head.

"No, it won't, but most of the presidentes likely won't be presidentes by then, and they'd be trying to arrange a murder with far less authority and less ability to escape scrutiny. Their successors won't see much point in beginning their tenure doing something like that. So that reduces the odds considerably." *But only after several weeks, or possibly months, and certainly not completely.*

Hasheem said slowly, "I still can't believe Oskaar did all it appears that he did."

"If I had to guess, he and Johann Daenyld wanted to make the Meritorists enough of a threat to increase the powers of the Security Ministry. Then they would have used the Special Agents to selectively remove councilors and pressure others to amend the Great Charter."

"You really think they thought that far ahead?"

"Lukkyn Wyath used to be the director of security at Suvion Industries," Dekkard pointed out. "Earlier today, Breffyn Haastar told me that Wilhelm Freust had been trying to look into corporacion abuses just before his suspicious death. The choice of councilors targeted by the Meritorists in the Summerend uprising was strange—two nonentities, the Commercer chair of the Security Committee and Axel Obreduur. After that Ulrich acted as chair of the Security Committee before making Marrak chair, but I'd wager Marrak did exactly what Ulrich wanted."

"Obreduur and Maendaan," mused Hasheem. "Maendaan certainly wasn't about to bow to Ulrich, and Axel was the only real threat to the Commercers."

"What most people don't know," said Dekkard, "was that two assassins targeted Obreduur at the Oersynt Summerend opening ceremony—and another on election day."

"You know, you and your wife have spoiled quite a few people's plans and schemes. Some of them just might want to take it out on you for spite."

"I do worry about that," replied Dekkard. "Particularly in the cases of Ulrich, Juan del Larrano, and Johann Daenyld. The strange thing about it all is that Ulrich is the only one I've even met, and that was today, and that certainly didn't go well."

"Just so you know, in addition to a statement for the newssheets, I will be sending a message to all councilors about the hearings and the attempted assassination. As for you personally, you have better security than the Council can provide. All I can say is for you to be careful." Hasheem paused. "I'm sure you already know that. I don't see any need to meet tomorrow, but if something comes up, I'm usually here."

"I hope nothing else does, but we'll have to see." Dekkard picked up his folder, inclined his head, and left the inner office.

Both Avraal and Gaaroll immediately stood.

"Shall we go have lunch?" asked Dekkard as cheerfully as he could manage.

"Are you ready for some inquiries?" countered Avraal.

"We'll have to face them sooner or later. Better sooner so that we can limit the inaccuracies."

"Limit's about the best you'll be able to do."

When they were out in the corridor, Avraal said, "Is Minister Kuta going to do anything?"

"She says they're already investigating Siincleer Shipbuilding and believe they can do something there."

"Did she say what?"

"At the least she believes she can use collective knowledge to strip away all their government contracts, possibly more. She also doesn't believe the High Court will release Ulrich."

"I hope she's right."

"Hasheem's decided to hold any more hearings in abeyance and let the Justiciary pursue matters, now that they have a way to do so."

"That might be better for us."

"I think so, but we'll have to see." *As with so many things.* Dekkard also realized he was using that phrase much more than he would prefer.

When they reached the councilors' dining room, Dekkard handed a five-mark note to Gaaroll. "This isn't the bonus you'll get for today, but you also deserve not to pay for your lunch today."

"Don't have to do that."

"I know, but I want to."

Gaaroll grinned. "Since you want to, I'll take it. First bell?"

"That would be good. And keep looking for people with that cold feeling."

"Been doing it the whole way here."

When Avraal and Dekkard entered the dining area, he was mildly surprised to see Breffyn Haastar and Villem Baar seated together.

"We should join them," murmured Avraal.

So, as soon as they neared, Dekkard asked, "Might we join you?"

"Please," replied Haastar.

"Of course," followed Baar.

"We just ordered," added Haastar, beckoning to a server.

Since Dekkard didn't feel as hungry as he'd initially thought, he opted for the onion soup with the melted cheese. Avraal asked for a half order of the three-cheese chicken.

When the server left, Dekkard asked, "How much did Guard Captain Trujillo tell you?"

"Not all that much," replied Baar. "Just that there had been four assassins who wouldn't surrender. Even when wounded, they jabbed themselves with frog-poison needles."

"What do you have on whom?" asked Haastar. "The New Meritorists couldn't have set that up."

"There's concrete evidence that five corporacions paid substantial funding to Capitol Services. Since Capitol Services was supporting the New Meritorists . . ." Dekkard went on to give a concise explanation.

"So they all could be barred from any Council funding?" asked Haastar.

"For from two to ten years," affirmed Dekkard. "Assuming that Minister Kuta follows through."

"If she says she will, she will," said Baar dryly. "Just ask Eastern Ironway, or Nordstar."

"Nordstar?" asked Dekkard. "I knew about her litigation against Eastern, but I hadn't heard about Nordstar."

Baar laughed. "You should have heard what Erich Kuuresoh had to say about her."

"What was that about?" Dekkard recalled that Kuuresoh had been a regional vice-presidente for Nordstar, but in the Whulte district, and he knew Kuta was from Veerlyn, more than fifteen hundred milles to the east.

"She won a judgment against Nordstar for bribing a district councilor to condemn property to allow a shorter pipeline route to avoid paying the landowner the going rate. There was more to it than that, but Erich claimed that the price the landowner wanted was extortionate."

"Was he the reason why the vote for her appointment was so much closer?" asked Dekkard.

Baar nodded. "He got most of the Commercers to oppose her, said she didn't like business."

"It sounds like she just didn't like certain ways of doing business," said Avraal, a touch of tartness in her voice.

"That's about what Gretina said," replied Baar with an amused smile.

"From what you just told us," said Haastar, "that would suggest the subcommittee won't be holding any more hearings."

"I don't think the Premier will make any statement or commitment like that," replied Dekkard. "At the very least not until the mess with the corporacions is resolved."

"How do you know they won't just fine the corporacions, and a few officials will be retired quietly and paid to disappear?" asked Haastar. "That's what happened with Eastern Ironway over illegally leasing the Naval Coal Reserve."

"That was under a Commercer Council," said Avraal, "and there wasn't an armed insurrection supported by the corporacions, with the near-total destruction of part of the harbor and thousands of deaths."

"I hope you three are right," said Haastar. "I really do, but . . ." He shook his head, then said, "If it hadn't been for Steffan, we'd likely all be dead, and the Council would be scrambling to work out an accommodation with those bastards. It was that close, and we're not out of the spoutstorm yet."

"On that note," said Baar as the server approached with their meals, "we should refresh ourselves before continuing such weighty discussions."

The talk over the remainder of lunch consisted of recollections and speculation, but didn't resolve anything, nor did any of the four come up with anything new.

After lunch Dekkard, Avraal, and Gaaroll returned to the Security Committee staff offices, where he arranged for complete copies of all three hearings to be sent to Guard Captain Trujillo and Justiciary Minister Kuta. Then they walked back to the Council Office Building.

Neither Avraal nor Gaaroll sensed any danger, other isolates, or the calculating feel of a sniper. But then, it was unlikely another attempt would follow within bells of the previous effort.

Dekkard had no idea whether there would be another attempt or whether Daenyld, del Larrano, or possibly Chassont would next attempt to block matters through purely legalistic maneuvers.

Once back in the office, Dekkard briefed Roostof on what had occurred and the possible outcomes and their probable timing. Then he started to read through the mail when Margrit brought in an urgent message from the Premier. While Dekkard suspected what the message contained, he immediately opened and read it.

As he'd thought, the message stated that, under the powers of the Security Committee, the special investigatory subcommittee had incarcerated Oskaar Ulrich for failure to answer inquiries involving high crimes and treason and that immediately after the hearing was concluded four professional assassins in sanitary uniforms were precluded from attacking the entire subcommittee. The message concluded by saying that the Council would be briefed more fully on the matter at Furdi's session.

Dekkard handed the message to Avraal, who scanned it and then looked to Dekkard.

"Margrit, you can read it. Then give it to Svard and tell him that I'd like to have all the staff read it as well."

"Yes, sir." Margrit's eyes widened slightly as she neared the end of the message. "They were after you, weren't they?"

"Not just me. The idea was obviously to tell the Council not to take on large Guldoran corporacions, even if they did collude with the New Meritorists."

"That's . . . terrible. It's *wrong*."

"The subcommittee and the Premier feel the same way," said Dekkard. "The next few weeks will be . . . interesting. Now, if you'd pass that on to Svard."

"Yes, sir. I didn't have a chance to mention that there was one other message." Margrit handed him another envelope, one from the Workplace Administration Committee.

"Thank you." Dekkard suspected it was a hearing notice, but waited until Margrit left before opening it, only to discover that it was indeed from Haarsfel as committee chair announcing another hearing on Tridi, the twenty-seventh of Springfirst, at third morning bell. The subject was steamer-production work practices, and the witnesses were from the Machinists and Assembly Guild in Kathaar, which made sense, since Haarsfel represented Kathaar. He set the notice to the side to give to Margrit to add to his calendar and turned to the mail.

He read two letters and was on the third when Avraal said, "I think I sense Ingrella in the outer office." She stood, walked to the door, which she opened, and motioned for Ingrella to join them.

"Were they after you or the entire subcommittee?" asked the older councilor even before seating herself across the desk from Dekkard.

"There's no way of telling, not for certain," replied Dekkard, "but the way they were set up suggests they wanted to take out all four of us."

"Might I ask what question Oskaar refused to answer?"

"You can. It will be in the hearing transcript. I asked him whether he'd helped Jaime Minz set up Capitol Services. I had a progression of questions, but never had a chance to ask more than the first. They're designed to establish not only that Ulrich set up Capitol Services, but that he was behind the assassination of Jaime Minz." Dekkard then summarized the rest of the hearing, including the fact that Ulrich had tried to leave the hearing.

"Axel always worried about Oskaar," replied Ingrella. "He told me about your belief that Commercers used the New Meritorists as a way to increase the power of the Security Ministry. I don't think he was totally convinced, but he worried more . . . toward the end . . . because you tended to be right far too often. But he had trouble believing that any councilor would go to those extremes for power."

"So did I," replied Dekkard. "I thought at first that Wyath and Ulrich only exploited the Meritorists, but I didn't realize how much deeper it went until after Minz's murder when I discovered all the marks from corporacions being funneled through Capitol Services and that the dunnite had to have come from Suvion Industries." *As well as a few more things.* "I have to say that I worry about how much further they'll go to try to hush this up and discredit Craft control of the Council."

"You've done more than you think, Steffan," replied Ingrella.

"After what happened this morning, it may not be enough."

Ingrella offered an impish smile, surprising Dekkard. "We'll just have to see. Just be very careful for the next few days." She looked to Avraal. "I trust you'll keep reminding him of that."

"I definitely will."

"Good. I won't take any more of your time."

Dekkard puzzled over Ingrella's smile, but decided not to wait on informing Minister Kuta and quickly drafted a letter to her, enclosing a copy of the questions he hadn't had the chance to pose to Ulrich. After giving the draft to Margrit to type up, he was about to go back to the mail when Margrit opened the door.

"Councilor Konnigsburg hopes that you can spare him a few moments."

"Of course."

Avraal murmured, "I'll be right outside, but he'll say more if I'm not here." She slipped out of the inner office just before Konnigsburg entered.

"I read the Premier's urgent message. To what degree is it accurate?"

"It's completely accurate, but I imagine he'll include other details when he addresses the Council tomorrow."

"Do you think Suvion Industries was behind this?"

"Right now, there's no evidence. I personally believe Suvion and Siincleer have a great deal to do with it. Both paid tens of thousands of marks to Capitol Services, which supplied and organized the first attack on the Council. Ulrich set up Capitol Services with Jaime Minz. Ulrich refused to answer any questions about Capitol Services. Also, Suvion Industries has been selling dunnite to Noldar through various fronts. What would you conclude?"

"About the same as you, I'm afraid." With a rueful smile, Konnigsburg settled into the center chair facing the desk. "What do you intend to do next with the subcommittee?"

"Nothing for the immediate future. We're turning over the testimony to the Justiciary minister. Former Premier Ulrich will remain in incarceration until the High Court decides what to do with him. I'm reserving the right to hold further hearings if circumstances merit them." Dekkard paused, then asked, "Have you heard anything about a new Fleet Marshal?"

"Not a thing. I have heard that the Imperador is reconsidering his options. That's hopeful, but we'll see."

"You didn't just come here to inquire about my health, Eyril."

"Not just. You're right. I'm glad that you've turned everything over to the Justiciary Ministry."

"I'm not after that kind of power. I just want the use of illegal methods by corporacions stopped, and I want those responsible removed from the corporacions . . . and from Guldor, one way or another."

"Certain corporacions might prefer matters to remain as they are."

"I know. But the Great Charter was written as it was to allow the Council to deal with excesses by any group, with review by the High Court."

Konnigsburg offered a hearty laugh. "You're one of the few that seems to understand that." Then he stood. "That's all I had. Thank you for seeing me."

"I'm glad you came."

"Thank you. Once this all calms down, Emilya and I would like to have you and your wife over for dinner."

"We'd like that."

As soon as Konnigsburg left the main office, Avraal immediately returned, shutting the inner office door.

"Is something wrong?" asked Dekkard.

"Did you promise him anything?

"No. Why?"

"He came in definitely wanting to know something. Once you talked, he was very relieved."

"The only thing I said was that the subcommittee planned to turn everything over to the Justiciary Ministry, but that we reserved the right to hold hearings if necessary. He said he was glad I'd done that, and he and Emilya would like to have us over to dinner once things calmed down."

"He's honest and straightforward," said Avraal. "I didn't sense any subterfuge, either, but he definitely had something in mind."

"Somehow, he's found a way to get the Imperador to reconsider his choice for Fleet Marshal, and it's connected to this mess. He sounded very sure that matters would calm down, but not immediately."

"I'm more worried about the immediate future," said Avraal.

"So am I." Dekkard looked at the growing stacks of mail and responses on his desk. "But those piles aren't getting any smaller."

Dekkard wasn't quite sure how he managed it, but by a third after fourth bell he'd finished signing or revising the correspondence, and he, Avraal, and Gaaroll neared the central staircase when he saw Chiram Ghohal striding quickly toward them.

Dekkard's hand dropped toward his throwing knives, but Avraal quietly said, "No harmful intent."

"Steffan, I'm so glad you're all right. I can't believe anyone would try something like that. Was Ulrich behind it?"

"The Justiciary Ministry's looking into it. I have the feeling that Minister Kuta will get to the bottom of the matter and that several corporacions will be facing serious charges." *And hopefully a lot more.*

"Tomas Pajiin told me you saved everyone."

"Nincya, here, discovered them. After that, we figured out how to have the Council Guard take care of them."

"You always work it out. I just wanted to tell you I'm glad you're all right. Do have a good evening." After a smile, and Dekkard's gesture for the other councilor to precede them, Ghohal hurried down the steps.

"What was that all about?" asked Dekkard several minutes later. "Chiram's scarcely spoken to me since I pressed him to vote for Hasheem as Premier."

"He was definitely sincere," said Avraal, "but I couldn't sense the reason."

Dekkard still couldn't help wondering why.

64

WHETHER it was Dekkard's circuitous route or Gaaroll's sensing range, the three arrived at the house without event. Avraal and Gaaroll had barely gotten out of the steamer under the portico when Sigourna Miletus appeared.

"As far as I could sense, the men in the blue Realto haven't been back."

"That's good to know," replied Avraal. "We really appreciate it."

"You've been good to me." Miletus paused, then said, "When this is all over, would you mind giving me some advice?"

"I'd be happy to, Sigourna."

"Thank you."

After driving from the portico and garaging the gray Gresynt, Dekkard saw that thick dark green clouds were moving in from the southwest, which usually meant heavy rain, sometimes even a spoutstorm.

When Dekkard reached the kitchen, Emrelda stood by the stove in a worn uniform without insignia or patches, as if waiting for him to arrive.

Not knowing what had been said before he arrived, Dekkard just said, "Whatever it is, it smells wonderful."

Emrelda fixed Dekkard with a stern expression, then said in a resigned tone, "How could I ever have thought that you two would settle into the quiet life of a junior councilor and his devoted wife? Mother and Father will be so disappointed." Then she spoiled the impression by laughing ruefully. "Inspiring and then thwarting a mass assassination. When Captain Kunskyn told me about it just before I left the station, I knew it had to involve you two."

"Three," corrected Dekkard. "Without Nincya, we would likely have been shot."

"Four," said Avraal. "Without Emrelda, we'd be struggling and then some."

"So true," agreed Dekkard.

"You never asked if I wanted to be included," said Emrelda.

"You don't have a choice," replied Avraal.

"That's younger siblings for you. They never give you a choice," declared Emrelda in a mock-aggrieved tone.

"Neither do older siblings," returned Dekkard.

Emrelda shook her head. "Go wash up and then sit down. Everything's ready, except for the rolls. You're getting goulash."

No one argued, and in less than a sixth the four sat at the kitchen table, eating, as Dekkard, Avraal, and Gaaroll related the general events of the hearing and attempted assassination.

When they finished, Emrelda said, "The corporacion I'd worry about the most is Siincleer Shipbuilding."

"I do, too," replied Dekkard, "but del Larrano is vulnerable. Pietro Venburg died over two months ago, and del Larrano publicly stated that nothing would change in Siincleer's operations. That's effectively a statement that he knew what was happening, and such a statement will make it much harder to blame the lawbreaking, especially that involving Capitol Services and the New Meritorists, just on Venburg."

"I hadn't thought about that side of matters."

"I also told Minister Kuta that we had some supporting information about the research-facility construction situation," said Dekkard, "and that a patroller station captain had been killed after looking into it. She was definitely interested."

"Do you really think that will lead anywhere?" asked Emrelda.

"I can't say, but she's taken on corporacions successfully before, and she had no hesitation about pressing for Wyath's execution."

"You've done everything you can, Steffan," said Emrelda. "We'll just have to see. It seems like forever . . . since . . ."

Markell's disappearance and likely death. "At times, it feels like what's happened has taken years, if not longer."

"You've been a councilor only four months," said Emrelda. "You've accomplished quite a bit in that time."

Dekkard shook his head. "Obreduur worked for years to get the Craft Party into power. Without that, none of this would have happened, and it still might not change things that much."

"Don't be a Contrarian of that sort," said Avraal. "Things will change. Less than we'd prefer, and more than Ulrich, the Commercers, and the corporacions will like."

"Or possibly," said Dekkard, "there will be more change of a kind we don't like, either."

"Won't be that bad," said Gaaroll firmly. "Councilor types won't want to make you mad. Things happen when you get upset. Premier's frigging scared of you."

"I know he'd prefer to accommodate me—"

"Nincya's right, dear," said Avraal firmly. "But just keep being politely insistent. That will work better with him."

For now ... but how long will that last? Dekkard managed a broad smile. "Is there any more of that goulash?"

"I thought you'd never ask," replied Emrelda.

Both Avraal and Gaaroll smiled.

65

W HEN Dekkard came down to breakfast on Furdi morning, after being awakened early by the heavy rain, Emrelda pointed to the newssheet. "It's all there. More than I expected."

"Friggin' right," mumbled Gaaroll through a mouthful of croissant.

Dekkard picked up the morning edition and began to read the front-page article, concentrating on the main points.

ATTEMPTED ASSASSINATION FOILED

Just before noon yesterday morning, Council Guards shot four armed assassins disguised as Council Hall cleaners. The four were deployed in the Council Hall in an effort to shoot the four councilors serving on a special subcommittee investigating how the New Meritorists obtained military explosives. The New Meritorists used dunnite to destroy Security buildings last Summerend and in the later attack on the Council Office Building that killed three councilors and then-Premier Obreduur, as well as more than a score of staffers . . .

Former Premier Oskaar Ulrich was placed in Council custody for failure to answer questions involving his interactions with Jaime Minz, a former Council security aide, who was discovered to have supplied the dunnite and aided the New Meritorists . . .

According to Justiciary Minister Serapha Marler Kuta, "The chairman of the special investigatory subcommittee did a superb job in uncovering this pattern of corporacion illegality and abuse of power . . . as did the other councilors on the subcommittee . . . various corporacion officials have already expressed outrage at the hearings . . . I can understand why they're outraged. The hearings uncovered a long-standing pattern of corporacion illegality and abuse of power verging on high crimes and possibly treason, not only in supporting the New Meritorists, but also in circumventing laws against supplying military matériel to other nations without the express approval of the Council . . . the Justiciary Ministry will also be investigating possible links between the corporacions under investigation and the assassins . . ."

Dekkard especially appreciated Minister Kuta's remarks about possible linkages, as well as the separate sidebar article on Jaime Minz and his ties to Ulrich and each of their ties to a corporacion manufacturing dunnite.

Dekkard handed Avraal the newssheet as soon as she entered the breakfast room and went to get their cafés and croissants. When he returned and set her café in front of her, he asked, "What do you think?"

"I'm not surprised. *Gestirn*'s been waiting for something like this for a long time, ever since Ulrich had Security Special Agents censoring and shutting them down."

"Not to mention the murder of the night editor for printing the story about military dunnite being used by the New Meritorists," added Dekkard. "I'd wager that there will be stories every day about Ulrich. I worry more about del Larrano."

"Del Larrano might be more careful after the minister's hint about connections between the assassins and corporacions," Avraal pointed out.

"Or he might just try something for spite," said Dekkard. "From his history, he's one mean bastard."

"All of them at Siincleer are mean bastards," said Emrelda as she stood to leave for duty. "And arrogant."

"He's gotten away with more than a few murders," said Avraal. "That kind of power and arrogance might make him think that nothing can touch him."

"It could be easier to get to him with Venburg gone. We'll have to see." Even as Dekkard spoke those last words, he realized how tired he was of saying they had to wait to see how matters turned out, especially since about the only thing he and Avraal—and Gaaroll—could do at present was to watch and be careful.

Just to remain on the cautious side, Dekkard left early. While the heavy rain minimized the chances for a successful attack, he still varied his drive to the Council buildings, although all of the routes he utilized minimized the possibility of open long-range shots by a sniper.

As Dekkard neared the covered parking, Gaaroll said, "Lots more Council Guards . . . everywhere . . . even on the roofs."

"How can you tell they're guards?" asked Dekkard.

"They feel different in the same way." Gaaroll paused, then added, "I . . . we've been practicing."

"She might be able to pass an empath apprentice-level examination," said Avraal.

Dekkard wondered about the increased number of guards, especially those on the roof, but that made sense. So did the increased inspection when they entered the Council Office Building, including a look at their umbrellas.

No messages from the Premier awaited Dekkard once he reached his office, but he hadn't expected any, not since Hasheem could add nothing to what he'd already said or what he might say to the entire Council. But there were polite messages of support from Guilhohn Haarsfel, Eduardo Nortak, and Kaliara Bassaana, which Dekkard read quickly and passed on to Avraal.

After reading them, she said, "Haarsfel's concerned, and Nortak politely so. That phrase of Kaliara's at the end, though . . ."

"About not forgetting Eastern Ironway? She's guessing, or knows, that Eastern was under investigation. She's always felt Eastern was corrupt. She was right. They were one of the five sending funds to Capitol Services."

"I still don't trust her entirely."

"Neither do I, but she's right about Eastern."

While Avraal settled down in the reception area to work with Gaaroll, Dekkard walked into the staff office to Roostof's desk.

Roostof immediately stood. "Sir?"

"Two things. First, with everything that's happened, I've been preoccupied. I don't want to pry, but . . . well . . . I'm still concerned about Bettina Safaell, and I didn't know . . ."

Roostof offered an amused laugh. "You've never pried. Bettina's fine. She passed her certification examination last week, and she's looking at several offers of a position. I've made my feelings known, and so has she, but we'll wait until next year."

Given how close Bettina had been to her father, Dekkard could certainly understand that.

"We hope you and Ritten Ysella-Dekkard will be at the wedding."

"We wouldn't miss it."

"Since you're the one responsible, I'd hope not." Roostof grinned, then said, "You mentioned two things, sir?"

"What was the story, or stories, in the *Tribune*?"

Roostof lifted the newssheet out of one of the boxes on his desk and handed it to Dekkard. "I thought you'd like to see it."

Dekkard took the newssheet and began to read, focusing on the key points.

. . . shooting of four armed men in the Council Hall by Council Guards yesterday morning once again highlights the weaknesses of the current Council. Rather than try to capture the apparent assassins, the guards just killed them . . .

... regretful as the putative attack on the councilors serving on the special investigatory subcommittee might have been, that doesn't excuse the fact that the subcommittee has engaged in a massive overreach in grilling employees of some of the most notable Guldoran corporacions ... Little in the way of evidence has been made public ...

The peremptory and possibly unjustified incarceration of a noted former premier for refusal to answer a single question he termed irrelevant raises more issues about the motivation and purpose of the subcommittee ...

So who leaked that bit of information? Dekkard shook his head. Any of the other three witnesses could have, although Dekkard would have wagered on Ferryn Maartel, the director of security, if only because Lukkyn Wyath had held that position previously, and because individuals like Wyath reflected their background. Dekkard continued to read.

... not to mention that it is chaired by an unelected very junior councilor about whose background numerous questions have been raised ...

Almost entirely by the Tribune.

... and the implication that the purported assassins were in any way connected to Guldoran corporacions is certainly not supported by any information now available to the public ... far more likely that those armed men were agents of the New Meritorists than linked to reputable corporacions ...

How about being linked to corrupt corporacions that have turned out to be less than reputable?
When he finished reading, Dekkard handed the newssheet back to Roostof. "Nothing different there. Factually, close to accurate, but totally misleading."

"That's their specialty."

"The problem is that too many people believe what they read there because they don't know all of the real facts and the context in which they occur."

"Isn't that true of some councilors, sir?"

"Only a few, thankfully." *So far, anyway.* Dekkard paused, then said, "Later today, you and Luara and I need to review where we stand on the legislative proposal dealing with the rights of working women. We've been distracted. But we can't let those distractions continue to keep us from what else we need to do."

"I'll tell Luara, sir. This afternoon, sometime after the Council session?"

"That would be good."

When Dekkard returned to his personal office, he quickly wrote appreciative replies for Margrit to message back to Haarsfel, Nortak, and Bassaana. Then, he started reading the mail.

At a third before noon, as Dekkard, Avraal, and Gaaroll stepped out into the courtyard on the way to the councilors' dining room, Dekkard asked, "Are there still guards everywhere?"

"Same as before, sir."

Dekkard nodded, almost absently, thinking that the attempted shooting had clearly spurred Hasheem and Trujillo into increasing Council security, at least for the present.

Whether it was because of the additional guards or not, the three reached the councilors' dining room without incident. Dekkard couldn't help noting that Eyril Konnigsburg sat at a table with Hansaal Volkaar. From the body positions, Dekkard wondered what Konnigsburg was trying to get across to the Commercer floor leader.

Dekkard and Avraal had just finished ordering when Dekkard saw Saandaar Vonauer, the Landor Party floor leader, walking toward them.

Avraal, whose back was to Vonauer, said, "Whoever's coming is focused on you. Concerns, but no hint of danger."

"Saandaar Vonauer." Dekkard had no idea what the crusty, often sarcastic, councilor wanted with him, but he couldn't imagine it was anything besides the investigatory subcommittee.

Vonauer stopped opposite the middle of the table, equidistant from Avraal and Dekkard. "Ritten, I understand you were one of the empaths monitoring the investigatory subcommittee hearings these past two weeks."

"I was," replied Avraal.

"Thank you. Fredrich was quite impressed with your credentials and expertise. He's not that easily impressed." Vonauer then looked to Dekkard. "Steffan, one question. Fredrich indicated that further investigations by the Justiciary Ministry could involve the most prestigious corporacion in Chuive. What degree of involvement?"

"If we're talking about the same corporacion, it only sent a few thousand marks to Capitol Services, unlike two others who sent tens of thousands. How the Justiciary Ministry will handle that is up to Minister Kuta. There is, however, the associated problem that they hired Jaime Minz."

Vonauer shook his head. "Hiring anyone associated with Ulrich wasn't a good idea. I'm certain Oskaar was involved in Johan Grieg's death. I told Johan not to resign and definitely not to trust Oskaar. Johan claimed he didn't have any choice." Vonauer paused. "I won't press further, but you did well, Steffan." Then he turned to Avraal. "I'm sorry if I was peremptory, but I had to confirm that you already knew. Both of you, enjoy your lunch."

"Thank you, Saandaar," replied Dekkard. "We hope you do as well."

Avraal watched as Vonauer walked toward one of the larger tables, then said, "He's joining three other councilors—Breffyn Haastar, Kharl Navione, and Felix Quellar."

"They have to be meeting on how to handle the repercussions from possible charges against Northwest Industrial Chemical and why Northwest hired Minz."

"Why do you think they hired him and paid marks to Capitol Services?"

"Because the presidente of Northwest was in on the plot to increase the power of the old Security Ministry, and Ulrich applied pressure. That's only a guess, but I can't think of any other reason." Dekkard paused as the server approached with his white bean soup and Avraal's onion soup with melted cheese.

Once they had taken several mouthfuls, Avraal asked, "Where do you think Eastern Ironway fits in?"

"I don't know, but they're definitely involved, given the number of banque drafts they sent to Capitol Services. Their headquarters are in Neewyrk, and that was Grieg's district before he resigned. From that dinner we had with the Obreduurs and the Griegs, I don't think Grieg knew what was happening with the illegal coal-reserve lease, but Ulrich had to be involved because Kraffeist, who signed the lease, and Grieg are both dead under suspicious circumstances."

"Do you have any idea what Hasheem will say this afternoon?" she asked.

"He indicated that the Council will be more fully briefed. That could mean anything."

Later, at a sixth before first bell, when they stood to leave the dining room, Avraal said, "You take the inside way to the floor, and I'll go to the spouses' gallery. Nincya and I will be outside the councilors' lobby after the session."

Dekkard was in the chamber on the way to his desk in the last row of the Craft section of the floor when Kaliara Bassaana approached him, and he said, "Thank you for the note. It was kind and thoughtful."

She laughed softly. "You don't have to thank me twice, Steffan."

"I did appreciate it." He lowered his voice and added, "And I don't think Eastern Ironway will be forgotten, although what happens next isn't up to me."

"You're always a man of your word. Unlike some. We can talk later." She smiled briefly and then turned back toward her own place.

Dekkard continued on to his own desk.

"Do you know what the Premier is going to say?" Pajiin asked from his adjoining floor desk as Dekkard seated himself.

"Other than it will be something about yesterday's events, I have no idea. I haven't talked to him since then."

"You know more than that, Steffan," said Ingrella Obreduur as she took her place.

"I suspect more than I know, but I'm not always right."

She offered an amused smile, then looked to the dais.

Immediately after the lieutenant-at-arms thumped his ceremonial staff, Hasheem gaveled the Council into session.

"Less than eighteen bells ago, in a hearing held by the Security Committee's special investigatory subcommittee, a former councilor refused to answer a question about his ties to a deceased former staffer implicated in funneling the military explosive dunnite to the New Meritorists. He refused to answer on the grounds that the question wasn't relevant. He is being held in Council custody until the High Court rules. I doubt that the High Court will find the question irrelevant.

"While that hearing took place, four men wearing sanitary workers' uniforms waited in the main corridor outside the Security Committee hearing room, ostensibly cleaning, but in fact flanking the entrance. Thankfully, one councilor noted their placement before entering the corridor. The Council Guards were notified and cordoned the area. The guards requested that the four men move away from their carts with empty hands. The four refused and attempted to use rifles hidden in the carts. The guards shot to wound, and were successful in three instances. However, those three men used frog-poison needles on themselves rather than be interrogated. All three died almost immediately.

"Further investigation by the Council Guard discovered that four sanitary workers had been murdered and their name badges and passcards had been taken. The badges and passcards matched those on the bodies of the assassins. A fifth man, a sanitary supervisor, was among those questioned and admitted that he had been coerced by threats against his family to allow the four imposters into the Council Hall. Additional inquiries are ongoing.

"Investigations by the subcommittee, by the Council Guard, and by the Justiciary Ministry have revealed substantial fund transfers from five Guldoran corporacions to Capitol Services, the business confirmed to have funneled dunnite to the New Meritorists. Those corporacions are, in the order of magnitude of the funds involved, Siincleer Shipbuilding, Suvion Industries, Eastern Ironway, Uldwyrk Systems, and Northwest Industrial Chemical. The Justiciary Ministry is in the process of investigating who in those corporacions was involved, and to what extent.

"The attempt to assassinate all four members of the investigatory sub-committee does not appear to be mere coincidence, and, as you may have noticed, security has been tightened. In addition, for now, the Council will rely on the Justiciary Ministry and the Ministry of Public Safety to continue looking into the matter. If there is a connection, any individuals involved will be charged with high crimes and possibly treason. I'll say that once more. Any individuals involved with the New Meritorist attacks on the Council or any councilor will be charged with high crimes and possibly treason."

When he finished, Hasheem surveyed the chamber, then struck one blow with the gavel. "The Council is hereby recessed until first bell of the afternoon on Unadi." Then he turned and left the lectern.

The entire chamber was silent for more than a minute.

As the silence began to fill with low voices, Ingrella turned to Dekkard and asked quietly, "One councilor?"

"Nincya, really. She's gotten much, much better."

"You and Avraal inspire people to do better. Even premiers." She paused. "You still need to be careful."

"I know. Thank you." Dekkard waited for her to stand and leave before he rose and followed her to the councilors' lobby.

Avraal and Gaaroll waited just outside.

"What do you think?" Dekkard asked.

"I didn't expect anything that blunt."

"I'm guessing that Minister Kuta has even more evidence than the Council Guard does." Dekkard began to walk toward the courtyard doors.

"Stuff like that was always there," declared Gaaroll. "Commercers had the power to keep it hushed up. Now they don't."

"Part of the reason they lost power was the removal of the Special Agents," said Avraal. "They intimidated and murdered people who crossed certain councilors or ministers."

"Most people knew they were corrupt, just not how bad they really were."

"Coulda asked me," said Gaaroll.

"At the time, we hadn't met you yet," Dekkard pointed out, "and I'm very glad we did."

"So am I," said Avraal.

"Me, too," added Gaaroll, almost shyly.

The three had barely entered the Council Office Building and neared the central staircase when a broad-shouldered, muscular woman with bobbed brown hair wearing a dark violet suit and a white blouse and scarf headed toward them.

"Vhiola Sandegarde," murmured Dekkard.

"I know," replied Avraal quietly.

"Vhiola, I don't believe you've met my wife, Avraal."

"I have not." Sandegarde focused on Avraal. "But I've heard of your talents, and your family is scarcely unknown. I'm very glad to meet you."

"And I, you," replied Avraal.

Sandegarde turned slightly so that she evenly faced both Dekkard and Avraal. "Steffan, I must congratulate you on successfully surviving an onslaught of enemies."

"Successfully only so far. When we had lunch several months ago, you mentioned that I had enemies out to kill me. I knew of one, possibly two. I didn't realize how many more there were. I thought you might be exaggerating. I'd like to apologize for not weighing your observation heavily enough."

Sandegarde offered a short and amused laugh. "I exaggerated somewhat then. With most new councilors that's often necessary. But, I have to say that I doubt any new councilor has made as many enemies or as quickly as you have."

"That's what happens when you reveal how many of them are going against both law and the Great Charter."

"No," replied Sandegarde quietly, but firmly, "that's what happens when you make such a revelation so successfully."

"Thank you." Dekkard didn't want to take all the credit, but didn't want to seem ungrateful.

"You have the skills and supporters to survive, Steffan. Just continue to be careful. What's your next project? Now that you're a subcommittee chair, that is?"

"My other committee is Workplace Administration. I'm working with my staff on a few modest improvements in that area."

"Modest? Like your modest Security reforms?"

"I never claimed those were modest. I said they were necessary."

"So you did." Sandegarde offered an amused smile, then said, "At some point before long, the three of us should have lunch." As she finished, Sandegarde inclined her head to Avraal.

"We should," agreed Dekkard.

Avraal nodded.

"I'll be in touch," said Sandegarde, then added to Avraal, "A pleasure to meet you."

Once Dekkard and Avraal left Sandegarde and headed up the central staircase, he said, "The lunch offer was genuine, I take it?"

"You think she would have made an insincere one?"

"Not with you, unless she wanted to send a different message. It was also an acknowledgment that you know everything I do," said Dekkard, "and that she knows the danger of cutting you out or going around you."

"She could be every bit as dangerous—or helpful—as Kaliara Bassaana."

"I've had that feeling since the first time I met her, and I believe I said something to that effect."

"You did, and I can confirm that." Avraal grinned, if momentarily.

When Dekkard got back to the office, he immediately called Roostof and Colsbaan into his personal office. Once they were seated, Dekkard looked to Colsbaan. "Svard told me on Unadi that you'd have the package for legal representation of working women who don't belong to the guild ready early next week. Is that about right?"

"We're going through a final check of all the references, and it might even be ready for your review by Unadi."

"Excellent! After we're all agreed on it, I'll start quietly surfacing the idea with some of the other members of the Workplace Administration Committee." As he spoke, Dekkard realized that he'd need to talk to Arturo Escalante again, about anything but the proposal . . . next time. That shouldn't be that hard, since Escalante had replaced Ellus Fader and Escalante's office was next to Dekkard's.

Purely by chance—and two deaths—and the only two isolate councilors end up in adjoining offices.

"After that," Dekkard went on, "we may have to talk about whether we'll need changes in language or how we approach the committee, and who else we might enlist to persuade enough councilors to get it through committee. Now, how much progress have you made on the equal pay and equivalent jobs proposal?"

"I finished all the research on the existing statutory law two weeks ago," said Colsbaan. "I've drafted possible amendments to those provisions in existing law that will need changing, and I'm working on language that acknowledges those provisions that might be applicable and are not."

"To preclude objections?"

Colsbaan and Roostof both nodded.

"How long before you finish that?"

"Another two weeks," said Colsbaan.

"Then we can start on turning the background material into supporting documentation," added Roostof.

"At least you two are working . . ." Dekkard broke off and shook his head.

"Sir?" asked Roostof.

Dekkard laughed sardonically. "I was going to say that you two were working on something constructive, and you are, but, to do that, you two have to undo discriminatory laws and practices. It just seems odd that to improve things we have to undo what was done before."

"Because they were both done," said Roostof, "to maintain power and to exclude others from the benefits of impartial law."

"Except law is almost never as impartial as legalists think," countered Colsbaan. "Those who write and enforce it are seldom impartial because laws are initially designed to protect those with property and power."

The way Colsbaan put it made sense. While Dekkard understood that, he'd never heard it stated quite so succinctly. "Even if the impartiality of law is an illusion, we still need to make that impartiality less illusory and more real . . . as we can." A moment passed, and he added, "Illusions or not, you're doing good work. You need to get back to it, and I suspect Margrit has a stack of responses for me to read and sign."

Dekkard wasn't mistaken, because the moment the legalists left Margrit brought in a short pile of mail and a larger pile of responses.

Dekkard started on the mail. The first three were likely from Commercers, because each complained about the subcommittee investigating good Guldoran corporacions instead of concentrating on probing the New Meritorists and other agitators, such as Foothill Freedom, Workers First, and the Contrarians. While he had heard of Foothill Freedom and *thought* he might have heard about Workers First, he wondered how three people in Gaarlak had come up with the Contrarians.

Shaking his head, he went out to Roostof's desk, taking one of the letters.

"Sir?"

"I just got the latest mail. There's obviously a group of Commercers in Gaarlak who don't like the subcommittee investigations, and they're declaring that we ought to be investigating the New Meritorists, as well as other groups, such as Foothill Freedom, Workers First, and the Contrarians, instead of reputable Guldoran corporacions. Have you ever heard of Workers First and the Contrarians?"

"I read a little about them in the *Tribune* a few weeks ago," replied Roostof. "There wasn't much, a story or two about political movements supposedly inspired or revitalized by the New Meritorists. Workers First was stronger around the turn of the century. All the *Tribune* said about the Contrarians was that a small group had been proselytizing in various Machtarn squares, and that they seemed to be against both the New Meritorists and the Commercers, if not all existing political parties." Roostof paused. "That's about all I know."

"I'm glad you knew. I'm getting the feeling that, like it or not, I'll need to read the *Tribune* regularly, rather than relying on you. But I do appreciate your wading through all the partisan hyperbole."

"I'd thought about getting an office copy," ventured Roostof, "but I know you're not fond of the *Tribune*."

"Go ahead and order it. I should have had you do it earlier." Dekkard handed the letter to Roostof. "I think we'll be getting more of these, until the news reaches Gaarlak about these oh-so-reputable Guldoran corporacions."

As he returned to his personal office, Dekkard hoped he hadn't missed too much from his failure to read and endure the *Tribune*'s partisan press coverage.

"What was that all about?" asked Avraal as Dekkard closed the door to the inner office. "You look both amused and concerned."

Rather than answer directly, he handed her one of the "Contrarian" letters from his district.

Dekkard watched as she read and then laughed.

"You were more successful than you thought."

Dekkard relayed what Roostof had told him, and then said, "What bothers me is how a *Tribune* story got to people in Gaarlak."

"That's simple enough. The hard-core Commercers have editions of the *Tribune* sent to them by post."

"That has to be expensive," said Dekkard.

"It's cheap at the price for those who truly believe."

"That means I can't ever admit to being the first and last Contrarian. Not for years, anyway."

"You might have been the first, but now that the name's out there, you likely won't be the last."

"I just hope there aren't any New Contrarians in the future," said Dekkard dryly, settling behind his desk.

D EKKARD fell asleep with little trouble on Furdi night, despite the heavy rain, but he slept uneasily. If he had nightmares, he did not remember them when he woke on Quindi. He shaved, showered, and dressed quickly, hurrying downstairs to see what had been reported in *Gestirn*.

Without a word, Emrelda handed him the newssheet, and Dekkard began to read, focusing on the key points of the story beneath the bold headline.

FIVE CORPORACIONS FACE POSSIBLE
TREASON CHARGES

Evidence uncovered following the incarceration of former Premier Oskaar Ulrich, currently a vice-presidente at Suvion Industries, revealed that five Guldoran corporacions paid significant funds to Capitol Services, a business implicated in supplying military explosives and other matériel to the New Meritorists . . .

The story listed the corporacions and their presidentes, and went on to point out that Siincleer Shipbuilding had been the center of rumors about unethical and illegal activities for years. While the corporacion had never been charged, many believed that the unsolved murder of Pietro Venburg was the result of such activities.

Dekkard kept reading.

. . . Justiciary minister raised the possibility that the thwarted assassination of all four councilors serving on the Security Committee's special investigatory subcommittee might have been a last-ditch attempt to pressure the Council not to proceed with the investigation . . .

Interestingly, the story did not mention any of the subcommittee councilors by name.

But then, neither did Hasheem.

. . . the amount of funding going to Capitol Services suggests a strong possibility that officials even more highly placed in the five corporacions may be implicated . . .

. . . former Premier Oskaar Ulrich has been incarcerated for failure to reply to a Council inquiry . . . In the cases of high crimes and treason, the restrictions on self-incrimination do not apply . . . would also not apply to corporacion officers questioned by either the Council or the Justiciary Ministry . . .

Dekkard finished reading the article and set down the newssheet. "At least for now, we're all semi-anonymous."

"Only to *Gestirn*," said Emrelda. "The *Tribune* will list all of you and not the names of the corporacion presidentes."

"Because we're misguided and questionable councilors who don't understand that mere working people can't be trusted to govern, even when some of us were mere working people."

"You've never been a mere working person," said Emrelda dryly.

"Just like you've never been an everyday patroller?"

"That's right in both instances," said Avraal as she entered the breakfast room.

Dekkard headed for the kitchen to get cafés and croissants.

In less than two thirds, Dekkard, Avraal, and Gaaroll headed for the Council buildings in the Gresynt, under a clearing sky with the air cleaner than it had been in days, if not weeks. When they arrived at the gate to the covered parking, even Dekkard had to show his passcard, because of increased security. After he parked, and as the three crossed the drive to the Council Office Building, he saw that additional roof guards were still present. Dekkard, Avraal, and Gaaroll again had to show name badges and cards to the guards at the west doors.

As soon as Dekkard reached his office, he found Roostof and asked, "Do you have the morning *Tribune*?"

Roostof smiled. "I do. I also bought one for you." He handed the newssheet to Dekkard. "We won't start getting office copies until Unadi."

Dekkard immediately took in the front-page headline—COUNCIL CONTINUES TRUMPED-UP ATTACK—then continued to read a long story about the fabricated evidence cited by the Justiciary Ministry and the Craft-dominated Council, and that Premier Hasheem continued the unwarranted attacks on Guldoran commerce begun by his predecessor. One Steffan Dekkard, an unelected junior councilor of questionable deeds, largely executed these attacks, and had in some unknown fashion manipulated the other subcommittee councilors into supporting his assault on the backbone of the Imperium's economy. The companies comprising that backbone were not named, and neither were the other subcommittee members.

Confirming that the attack is concentrated on you.

When he finished, Dekkard lowered the newssheet and looked to Roostof. "How does it feel to be working for the most dubious and questionable councilor of the past century or so?"

"I wouldn't have it any other way. For what it's worth, neither would Bettina."

"I liked that young woman from the first." Dekkard grinned and added, "You liked her even more."

"I did. What else can I say?"

"You don't have to say anything," replied Dekkard. "Thank you for the newssheet."

"You're welcome, sir. There's also an article on the inside pages about how the prosecution of those five corporacions could undermine the Navy's mission to protect Guldoran commercial shipping."

"I appreciate your telling me. I'll look at that immediately."

When Dekkard entered his personal office, Avraal already stood at the window, looking out. Standing beside his marvelous desk, Dekkard opened the newssheet and began to read.

The article on the inside pages of the *Tribune* read almost exactly as Dekkard thought it would—a suggestion that the investigatory subcommittee overstated the degree of wrongdoing by the five corporacions and whatever small amount of any corporacion wrongdoing that did exist was the result of workers, New Meritorist sympathizers, illegally bypassing their superiors. That was followed by an explanation of how Council sanctions against the corporacions would greatly weaken the Navy and increase procurement and contracting costs, resulting in worker layoffs, the result of which would, in turn, hurt productive workers as well as require higher year-end taxes.

When he finished that article, he quickly read through the rest of the newssheet to make sure he didn't miss anything else. Then he handed it to Avraal and settled down to look through the messages and mail. On top was a message envelope from the Justiciary Ministry. He cut the envelope open to avoid breaking the ornate seal and began to read.

Councilor Dekkard—
The Ministry received the full transcripts of the testimony before the special investigatory subcommittee of the Security Committee

yesterday. We appreciate the diligence and promptness of the sub-committee and the committee staff . . .

After reviewing the testimony and other evidence, the Justiciary Ministry submitted its brief to the High Court on the issue of the relevancy of the question posed to Sr. Ulrich. Oral arguments before the Court are scheduled for Unadi. According to past practice and precedent, we expect a ruling by the Court no later than Quindi the twenty-ninth of Springfirst, and most probably sooner . . .

A range of charges has been filed against Siincleer Shipbuilding and its subsidiaries, and as well as against Suvion Industries . . . Lesser charges have been filed against Eastern Ironway, Uldwyrk Systems, Northwest Industrial Chemical.

Conviction on the least of the charges as filed would void all existing and future contracts with the government, except for the required completion of the frigate Baarthan, *which would be required at one-fifth below the stipulated cost.*

Our brief stipulates that, in the instance of Siincleer Shipbuilding and Suvion Industries, all senior officers at the level of vice-presidente and above and senior legalists not convicted of charges filed against them personally or not so charged must be dismissed without any further or future compensation. Those convicted of high crimes and/or treason will face the sentence meted out by the High Court . . .

Dekkard finished reading the letter, signed by Serapha Marler Kuta herself, then looked up at Avraal, who had just laid the morning *Tribune* on the side of the desk. "What did you think of the other article?"

"Corporacions can do no wrong, and if they do, it isn't major, and, besides, it's some poor clerk's fault."

"You'll find this letter more interesting." Dekkard gave her the Justiciary letter, then stood. "Svard will need to read it as well. I'll have him come in."

Dekkard and Roostof returned even before Avraal finished reading the letter. When she was done, she passed it to Roostof.

Dekkard said nothing until Roostof returned the letter. "What do you think, Svard?"

"On the surface, it's simply a report of what the ministry has done and will be attempting under the law and the Great Charter."

"And?" pressed Dekkard.

"There's no doubt of corporacion guilt. The funding alone is enough.

Ulrich will refuse to answer any questions. If no more evidence comes to light, he'll still face statelessness and abject poverty as an indentured laborer in some Almighty-forsaken corner of the globe. I don't know if Minister Kuta will be able to force the removal of all those senior officers. That will depend, again, on the evidence and what ministry investigators learn from other employees. But she may not have to. Other corporacions may not wish to deal with such officers."

"Either because they were corrupt or because they were stupid enough to be part of something where the corporacion got caught?"

"Most likely the second," said Avraal acidly.

"I'd have to agree with the Ritten," declared Roostof. "I'd always thought that corporacion officers weren't exactly close friends with ethics, but it's even more disheartening to see them treat ethics as a sworn enemy."

"For people like Ulrich and Juan del Larrano," replied Avraal, "anything or anyone that gets in the way of amassing power or marks is an enemy."

"It's always been that way," said Roostof. "Until Premier Obreduur began to change things. If you don't keep pushing for change, in time, things will go back to where they were."

Dekkard had his doubts about that, but what if Roostof happened to be right? He managed a wry smile. "That's why you and Luara are working on those two legislative packages." He paused, then added, "You might give some thought to what else could use improvement, preferably something so overlooked and yet, when brought up, something councilors will at least think about."

"I can do that, sir." Roostof was smiling when he left the inner office.

Once Roostof departed, Avraal said, "There's nothing I can do in here. I'm going to work with Nincya."

"Good idea. Whatever you're doing is working well." *"Well" is an understatement for saving the lives of four councilors.*

Dekkard first drafted a reply to Minister Kuta before he went through the mail. Amid the pile of letters from Gaarlak he found another telling him to stop persecuting the corporacions and to go after the remnants of the New Meritorists and the other radicals posing a greater threat—like Foothill Freedom and the Contrarians.

Dekkard shook his head. His effort to root out New Meritorists by creating the nonexistent Contrarians had failed to turn up anything and might well be the beginning of yet another disruptive group. *But how could you know that?*

By noon, Dekkard felt more than ready for a break.

Dekkard, Avraal, and Gaaroll walked to the Council Hall and the councilors' dining room, where he and Avraal had lighter fare—the onion soup with melted cheese for him and a green salad with thin slices of ham for Avraal. The dining room was less than a third full, but that made sense—the Council wasn't in session and tomorrow was Findi. He saw Arturo Escalante, eating with Kharl Navione, and Haarsfel with Leister Milyaard. Most of the other councilors he saw were Landors or Commercers he didn't know that well . . . or in the case of Pohl Palafaux, someone with whom he didn't see much point in exchanging pleasantries.

No councilors approached, but since Navione and Escalante were still at their table when Dekkard and Avraal got up to leave, Dekkard said quietly, "I need to introduce you to Arturo."

"Then do," she murmured back with a smile.

Dekkard and Avraal stopped a yard from the table, and Dekkard said, "Kharl, Arturo, I hope you don't mind, but I thought I'd introduce my wife to Arturo."

"I'm glad you came over," said Navione with a smile.

"Arturo Escalante, my wife Avraal Ysella-Dekkard. Avraal, this is Arturo Escalante, the new councilor from Silverhills, and the only other isolate to be a councilor in at least a few centuries."

The gray-haired isolate smiled warmly. "I'm pleased to meet you. While I've heard much about your family, I have to confess that you're the only one of the Ysellas I've ever met."

"I have to confess the same about your family," Avraal returned in a cheerful tone.

"I appear to be the only isolate in my family," said Escalante. "Are there other empaths in your family, or are you one of the rarities like me?"

"The latter," said Avraal, "although there are family rumors about a great-aunt."

"What about you, Steffan?" asked Navione.

"I have one sibling, my older sister. She's a talented portraitist, and an isolate. Neither of my parents are either isolate or empath, and there aren't any known isolates or empaths elsewhere in the family." Not so much not known as not conveyed, but Dekkard wasn't about to get into that, and there weren't any others known to him.

"She didn't want to go into security?" asked Escalante.

"That would have been a terrible waste of her talent," said Avraal. "She and Steffan's mother are considered to be among the very best portraitists in Oersynt."

"I come from a long line of artisans," added Dekkard. "I have the sensibilities, but not the delicacy of touch and control."

Escalante looked puzzled, but before Dekkard could speak, Avraal did. "Steffan won a place at the Military Institute."

"That led to security training and eventually to a position as a security aide to a councilor," Dekkard added.

"That's one of the many reasons Steffan is on the Security Committee," said Navione.

"Might I ask why Ritten Ysella-Dekkard was one of the empaths at the hearings?" asked Escalante.

Dekkard spoke immediately. "Because, in addition to being a fully certified empath, she's a certified parole screener, trained to detect more than most empaths."

Escalante nodded slowly. "That makes great sense. It is very unusual training."

"For a Landor daughter, you mean?" replied Avraal. "I had to go against my father's wishes. I got the parole-screening certification while working at the Siincleer Prison."

Escalante inclined his head to Avraal, then looked to Dekkard. "You're most fortunate, Steffan."

"I know."

Escalante laughed softly. "When I read about you in *The Machtarn Tribune,* I wondered what sort of councilor could have so enraged Commercers so quickly. This conversation has given me great insight."

Navione grinned. "I think Arturo might have been a little skeptical about what I said."

"More than a little," admitted Escalante. "I'm so glad you both stopped to talk. We won't impose longer. But thank you, again."

Once Dekkard and Avraal left the councilors' dining room and were in the main corridor, accompanied by Gaaroll, Dekkard said, "I know he's an isolate, but how genuine do you think he was?"

"From what I saw and from Kharl Navione's feelings and reactions, I'd wager that what we saw was largely what he felt. As an isolate in a Landor family, I'd think he's a bit less traditional. And if he's spending time with Haastar and Navione. . . ."

Just after Dekkard and Avraal returned to the office, Margrit knocked and eased the door slightly open. "Councilor Saarh is here," she said. "He would appreciate a moment in private with you."

Dekkard looked to Avraal.

After a moment, she said, "He's worried and nervous, but he doesn't have any focused intent. Neither does Micah."

Dekkard said, "Show him in after Avraal leaves."

"Yes, sir." Margrit closed the door.

"Stay close to the door." Dekkard knew that Avraal could overpower Micah, Saarh's empath, but Malcolm was a strong isolate, and Dekkard wanted to be close enough to deal with anything, if he had to. While Dekkard doubted that Saarh would attempt any sort of physical assault, he also knew that any attack would come from an unexpected quarter, and an attack by Saarh or his security aides would be improbable enough to qualify.

"I definitely will." Avraal smiled coolly. "I have my knives, and Malcolm doesn't carry them."

She turned and slipped out of the office, leaving the door ajar.

Dekkard stood and moved up beside the desk.

When Saarh entered the office, he said politely, "I appreciate the time, Steffan." His eyes drifted to the desk and chairs, lingering there.

"Just older pieces my staff found in the office-building storage levels after my office was destroyed—the second time. I rather like them. They date back to a time when the Great Charter was largely observed."

"Those pieces are rather expensive for a junior councilor," said Saarh.

"They came out of storage, and no one else wanted them, according to administration, because they were so old."

"They look like they were never used."

"They weren't."

"You know, Steffan, you have a way of obtaining what is valuable without really paying for it." Saarh's tone was slightly ironic and carried an edge.

Dekkard smiled pleasantly. "I'd like to think that I can see value where others don't. Then they get angry when they realize what they missed. They tend to overlook what I've paid in other ways. But I'm sure that isn't what was on your mind."

"Do you think that attacking corporacions and noted former councilors is to the benefit of Guldor or the Council?"

"Jareem, the subcommittee didn't set out to attack anyone. You know that military dunnite was used in multiple New Meritorist attacks. I was asked to chair a subcommittee to look into how they obtained that dunnite. The hearing revealed possible high crimes and even treason. The subcommittee turned all materials over to the Justiciary Ministry. The subcommittee has no further hearings scheduled. Whatever occurs from here on is in the hands of the Justiciary Ministry and the High Court."

"You don't understand."

"Jareem, what exactly are you trying to say? That it's a bad idea for corporacions to be held accountable?"

Saarh's face remained calm, but Dekkard saw the slight movement and momentary change in Saarh's eyes before he said, "Steffan, there's accountability, and there's the larger question of the future of the Imperium. Sometimes, the larger issues have to be considered. That's really all I have to say."

"You know, Jareem, I agree with that general point, but I suspect we disagree on what might be the larger and most important issue."

"I knew you'd say something like that. I just wanted you to know that there are larger issues your subcommittee apparently failed to consider. I sincerely wish you had." Saarh inclined his head, slightly more than perfunctorily, then turned and walked out of the office.

Dekkard moved to the door and watched as Saarh and his aides left, then motioned for Avraal to join him, but she was already moving toward him. He'd barely closed the door when she spoke.

"Was that what I felt it was?" she asked.

"If you felt it was a politely worded and indirect threat, you were right." Dekkard summarized the short conversation, then said, "I imagine Palafaux and Schmidtz put him up to it. They probably threatened him with a stronger Commercer candidate in the next election, and if the figures you and Obreduur put together are correct, without his income as a councilor, in time, he might have to sell off lands, possibly enough to lose his status as a Landor."

"He already sold Maelle's dowry lands to Guldoran Ironway, but the marks from two hundred hectares of cherry orchards won't last forever." Avraal frowned, as if thinking, then finally said, "His visit might be a good sign."

"A veiled threat as a good sign?"

"It just might signify that they've decided any more killings or attempted killings of councilors might not be in their best interests."

"I can see that for Schmidtz and Palafaux," replied Dekkard, "but I have strong doubts that Juan del Larrano feels that way."

"I'd agree with you on del Larrano."

"Could you sense anything else?"

"Just his normal contempt for anyone who's not a Landor, a certain anger when he looked at me, and a sense of relief as he left the office."

"Possibly because he'd discharged an obligation?"

"That's possible, but it's not something I could determine."

Dekkard next needed to look at the legislative calendar for the coming week. On Unadi, the Council would address the need to replenish the reserve funds appropriated by the Council earlier to cover the costs of repairs to piers, streets, and public buildings caused by the shelling from the *Khuld,* not to mention the other harbor repairs.

After reading the proposed legislation, he realized that he'd failed to do something that, while not strictly his responsibility, he should have followed up on, and he went to talk to Roostof.

"Svard, as I understand this, according to the report on the bill, the committee feels that a temporary two-year increase in import tariffs of one percent won't replenish the reserve fund, but that a greater increase will hurt businesses, depending on imports."

"That's the way I read it as well, sir."

Dekkard smiled. "I'd like you to draft an amendment imposing a twenty-five percent additional tariff for all fine art classed as housewares, or anything else besides fine art, and for all decorative items, including paintings, lamps, ceramics, et cetera."

"All those items that the artisans guilds felt were being grossly undervalued?"

"Exactly. That fell between the cracks after Premier Obreduur's death. I really should have followed up with Ingrella Obreduur."

"You've had quite a bit on your mind, sir. Also, there wasn't much you could have done. We discovered that Munchyn destroyed all the material we sent. The only copies were in the office files."

Which didn't survive the attack on the Council Office Building. "I still should have followed up, but this is a chance to deal with it in another way."

"You may have some trouble getting it passed at the last moment."

"At least I'll be bringing up the issue and the problem. Can you have something ready for me by Unadi with enough copies to distribute? It should help the funding problem as well as the artisans."

"That shouldn't be a problem, sir. I can register the amendment with the clerk this afternoon. He won't need the actual language until third bell on Unadi morning."

"Good!"

After a routine remainder of the afternoon, Dekkard finished with all the correspondence replies and revisions. By a third past fourth bell, he, Avraal, and Gaaroll were on the way home.

Still in her uniform, Emrelda greeted them in the hallway from the portico. "Captain Kunskyn sends his congratulations and his sympathy. He's also posting a patrol steamer near the house for the next few days."

Dekkard grinned. "That's as much for your protection as mine."

Emrelda replied cheerfully, but with a touch of rue, "He did say he didn't want to break in another head dispatcher."

"You got it!" Avraal didn't quite yell, but the enthusiasm in her voice was more than evident.

"Do you get paid more?" asked Gaaroll.

"Starting the first of Springend," said Emrelda.

"We should celebrate," declared Avraal. "We'll go to Elfredo's after services, and we're paying."

"Absolutely!" agreed Dekkard.

67

DEKKARD was more than glad when services finished. While he had agreed to some extent with Presider Buusen's homily—at least the part about needing to believe in something greater than one's self, or something beyond what power or wealth one could amass—he had reservations about believing in a mere deity. He also wondered about the Baars, because he hadn't seen them at the chapel. But, as he drove down Jacquez toward Elfredo's, he put aside theological reservations and the Baars' absence and concentrated on driving.

Neither Avraal nor Gaaroll sensed strong feelings, and a sixth later, Dekkard had parked the Gresynt, and the four were seated at a wall table.

Their server was Lizbet, the older woman who had served them the first time Emrelda had taken both Avraal and Dekkard to Elfredo's. After she took their order—Dekkard chose chicken rosara—a single uniformed patroller rose from a table where he'd been sitting with two others and walked toward Emrelda. As the patroller neared, Dekkard saw the brace on his left arm and realized it had to be Georg.

Emrelda half turned and waited.

Georg grinned at her as he stopped beside the table. "Congratulations. I just heard. Sent off a message to Sammel. He thought you ought to have been head dispatcher a long time ago."

"Thank you. How is he doing at Woodlake?"

"We got a message from him the other day. He said he'd been getting the station in shape. Would have helped if he had a better dispatcher."

"I appreciate the thought, even if you made it up."

Georg shook his head. "All his words." He looked to Dekkard. "Captain said you were one of the councilors being targeted. That true?"

"The shooters were after all the councilors on the subcommittee. I was one of them."

"Had to be contract assassins hired by a corporacion," declared Georg. "Street killers use pistols." He paused, then asked, "Why rifles?"

"They didn't want to get close enough for an empath to sense them. They must have felt rifles were more accurate at that distance."

"Might have been former Naval Marines, then," suggested Georg. "About the only thing they're good for. Harbor patrol station hates it when a dreadnought ports. Not because of the sailors, either." Then he shook his head and turned back to Emrelda. "That's all I had. Just wanted to congratulate you. You deserved it. When you're running dispatch, everything goes smoother." Georg smiled again before turning away.

"Interesting how you both ended up in forms of security," said Dekkard. "Both of you are excellent at it as well."

"Not that Father or Cliven will ever understand or acknowledge the value of what we do," said Avraal.

"Is that just publicly, because security isn't something Landors do?" asked Dekkard.

"Especially Landor women," replied Avraal.

"Publicly is what counts," replied Emrelda. "Private recognition without public recognition is saying that we don't matter as much as the vaunted Landor customs and traditions."

"Just screw 'em all," interjected Gaaroll. "They couldn't do a sixth of what you do."

"No, they couldn't," said Emrelda, "especially what Avraal does. But I'd rather do what I do, and if there's any cutting or denying of family ties, let them be the ones doing the cutting."

So, if there's disavowal, Avraal and Emrelda's parents have to do it, which would entail considerable loss of face, especially now.

Emrelda smiled and said, "From your momentary unguarded expression, Steffan, you understand."

"I certainly hope so." Before Dekkard could say more, Lizbet arrived with their orders.

Once she served everyone and left, Avraal looked at her husband. "You were saying, dear?"

Although Dekkard hadn't planned to voice his thoughts, he replied, "Disavowing women who have succeeded in difficult professions and who married successful men would be regarded as petty by most people, even most Landors, I would guess. So, if anyone is going to be unreasonable and petty, it won't be you."

The two sisters exchanged glances, and Dekkard took a bite of the chicken rosara. It was even better than he recalled.

After a minute or so of silence, Avraal said, "The Baars weren't at services. I can't help worrying."

"I worried about that as well," said Dekkard. "We could drive by their house on the way home. See if their lights are on, and Gaaroll could sense if anyone's there."

"Do you really think the Commercers would attack him?" asked Emrelda.

"It's unlikely. Attacking the sole Commercer on the subcommittee might well turn some of the Commercer councilors against the corporacions, and the corporacions can't afford that. If the attack against the entire subcommittee had succeeded, the Commercers could have rationalized it by saying that the subcommittee went too far, and that was because of me and the Craft Party." Dekkard paused. "But the Commercers haven't always been rational."

"Could still say he went against his party," suggested Gaaroll.

"That would imply that the Commercer Party was in favor of treasonous activities," said Avraal. "I doubt they want that perception."

"Even if some of them are," said Emrelda sardonically.

"Enough of that for now," said Dekkard. "We can drive by on the way home. In the meantime, we're supposed to be celebrating a promotion for a patroller who kept insisting that she might not get it."

"Sometimes, you don't want to hope too much," replied Emrelda.

"Now you don't have to worry about that." Dekkard raised his beaker. "To the new head dispatcher!"

68

DEKKARD slept better on Quindi night, since a quick drive by the Baar household revealed they were all present. Even so, while Dekkard and Avraal attempted to sleep late, Avraal was more successful, and Dekkard came downstairs just before Emrelda left, because, regardless of her promotion, she had to work the morning shift on Findi.

Dekkard checked *Gestirn* to see if the newssheet had reported anything new about the dunnite and Capitol Services issues, but he already knew all that appeared in print. So he fixed himself café and spent almost two bells in the study trying to figure out what options were open to the five corporacions other than those Roostof had suggested in general terms. He especially concentrated on Suvion Industries and Siincleer Shipbuilding. He kept going over what he knew about Juan del Larrano, but he had the feeling that he was missing something important, possibly something he already knew and wasn't connecting.

After he and Avraal had a very late breakfast, the rest of the day was quiet. Neither Avraal nor Gaaroll discerned anything unusual, and Sigourna Miletus hadn't sensed or seen the blue Realto or any other suspicious steamer.

There was nothing new in *Gestirn* on Unadi morning. While that bothered Dekkard, he knew that legal and political business almost never took place on enddays, especially so early in the year.

Once he, Avraal, and Gaaroll got to the office, there wasn't anything from the Justiciary minister in the morning deliveries of messages, and there was nothing from the Premier, either about changes in the Council schedule—or anything else.

Dekkard turned to Avraal. "Let me see what Zenya sent before you work with Nincya."

Avraal nodded and followed him into the inner office. She walked to the window and looked out, surveying the area around the north side of the building before taking the chair farthest from the window.

Dekkard quickly read through Onswyrth's weekly report. Among the complaints and issues raised by people visiting the office were ironway freight rates, the leaking levees on the Lakaan River, the failure of the

Council to deal more harshly with the New Meritorists, and the failure of the Council to rein the corporacion abuses. Onswyrth also included two articles from the Furdi edition of the *Gaarlak Times* about the hearings and the involvement of the five corporacions. Most of the main story was similar to what had appeared in *Gestirn,* but the smaller sidebar article was clearly tailored to local interest:

GAARLAK COUNCILOR TARGETED

The chairman of the Security subcommittee that was the assassins' apparent objective is Steffan Dekkard . . . former security aide to the late Premier Axel Obreduur and the present councilor from Gaarlak. Although a junior councilor, Dekkard drafted and then spearheaded the successful reforms that reduced the unchecked powers of Security agents and replaced the Security Ministry with the Ministry of Public Safety. As subcommittee chair, he was investigating how the New Meritorists obtained military dunnite, including the links between former Premier Oskaar Ulrich and Jaime Minz, an influencer for Northwest Industrial Chemical charged with assisting the New Meritorists and attempted murder. Sr. Minz was killed by a sniper as he was escorted to his charging hearing. Sr. Ulrich is currently a vice-presidente of Suvion Industries, the other corporacion besides Northwest that manufactures dunnite . . .

After he finished reading the sidebar article, Dekkard turned to Avraal. "You should read these." He handed her the two articles, and opened the first of the letters Onswyrth had sent with her report, which turned out to be a complaint about Imperial postal rates.

Makes perfect sense. He avoids paying *postage by handing it to Zenya, and then complains about the rates he's not paying.*

Dekkard saw that Avraal had finished reading. "What do you think?"

"The longer article's an accurate summary. The shorter one implies that you're a target because you've stopped Security abuses and tried to rein in the corporacions, and that Ulrich is corrupt, as are Northwest and Suvion. Martenya Oguire definitely sees things the way you do."

"The Almighty help me if I ever get on the wrong side of what she thinks."

"If you're honest about it, it might not be so bad. She can take honest disagreement, just not lying and deceit. Is there anything else in Zenya's report I should know?"

"Nothing unusual." Dekkard then said, "After I finish with the mail, I need to spend time with Svard about the amendment to the reserve fund replenishment bill. If there's time after that, I'll go over any responses that Bretta and Illana have ready, and then I'd like to see if we can find Guard Captain Trujillo before lunch."

"And then be visible at lunch and see if anything happens?"

"Unless you have a better idea."

"Not right now. If you don't have anything else, I'll go work some more with Nincya."

"That will be more productive than listening to me make comments about some letters."

After Avraal left, Dekkard just sat behind the desk that was truly a showpiece, thinking. There were so many pieces, and some had to fit, but he had no idea where, like the false fabric salesman from Noldar who'd been smuggling Guldoran marks into Guldor and who'd escaped the customs officials. There were more than a few links to Noldar . . . as well as facts that didn't make sense. *Why would del Larrano have a "yacht" worth far more than his house? Even if he got the corporacion to pay for it.* To Dekkard it seemed stupid, and del Larrano was anything but stupid.

Then Dekkard swallowed. *Could it possibly be?* He had his doubts, but it wouldn't hurt to lay some groundwork. *Just in case.* He dashed off a quick note to Eyril Konnigsburg and had Gaaroll take it.

After Gaaroll left, Avraal followed Dekkard back into his office.

"I have a few questions I want to ask Eyril in private. I've asked for a few minutes on our way to the Council Hall." Dekkard went on to explain his concerns, then said, "I don't see any other way. Hasheem wouldn't believe it. There's no hard proof of any sort."

"Can Konnigsburg help?"

"I don't know. We'll have to see." Dekkard then asked Roostof to join him.

The senior legalist brought in a small sheaf of papers. "This is for you—several copies of the amendment. It's two pages long, just because there are short additions and cross-references to different sections of the tariff code. There's a one-page explanation for you, as well, and some very rough estimates of the additional revenue that might be raised. The low estimate would result in adding eight percent to the amount projected to be collected. The high estimate would be twenty percent."

"Did you figure in any additional revenue from year-end taxes? Guldoran artisans should make more marks if unfair competition is reduced."

"No, sir. I'm not sure there's any way to quantify that. Not quickly, anyway."

"That's fine. I can just say the amendment should also generate additional revenues."

Dekkard looked at the draft amendment, which consisted of short inserts to the existing tariff code, then read through the explanation slowly and carefully. "You've registered the amendment with the clerk?"

"I did. If you have any changes, I could substitute them."

"Excellent!" Dekkard took the papers and slipped them into the leather folder.

Less than a third after Roostof returned to his desk, Gaaroll returned with a reply from Konnigsburg that said, "Any time prior to a third before noon."

Dekkard spent most of the next two bells on letters and responses, trying to clear those away because the Council session would last more than a bell, and he wanted to have time free after that for Roostof and Colsbaan to brief him on the legislative proposal for legal representation of working women who didn't belong to the guild.

Just after fifth bell, Dekkard, Avraal, and Gaaroll headed out of the office and down to the main level and Konnigsburg's office.

The moment they entered the outer office, Konnigsburg's personal secretary said, "You can go right in, Councilor. He's expecting you."

Konnigsburg smiled and stood as Dekkard entered the inner office and closed the door, moving beside one of the chairs in front of the desk and motioning to the others.

Dekkard appreciated the gesture. He seated himself as Konnigsburg did and said, "I appreciate your seeing me on such short notice."

"It must be serious."

"It could be. Then again, I could be totally wrong. The other night I spoke to an experienced patroller about the four would-be assassins, and he made a rather interesting observation when I pointed out that they had used rifles. He said that street killers always used handguns, and that most assassins and snipers had been trained as Naval Marines. Knowing how much training they go through, that didn't surprise me. What did surprise me was that I hadn't thought of it, and neither has anyone else I've talked to about it."

"I'd have to agree with you," replied Konnigsburg. "But I don't see how that makes discovering who hired them much easier."

"Possibly not," said Dekkard, "but it got me to wondering if there are other aspects of this that we haven't considered."

"That's definitely possible. Have you come up with any?"

"Only questions. You'd mentioned that del Larrano's yacht—"

"The *Ultima* . . ."

". . . Is moored offshore of his house, and that house is quite modest for the presidente of one of the largest corporacions in Guldor. Then there's the fact that the *Ultima* is likely very fast, possibly faster than any warship in the fleet."

"There's no doubt about that."

"There's also the fact that the Siincleer corporacions have significant facilities, investments, and projects in Noldar, and that the Oligarch, as I recall you told me, is less than amenable to requests, as you put it, from Guldor. Then there's the small problem that Siincleer Shipbuilding sent some sixty thousand marks to Capitol Services."

"That much?"

"Seventeen banque cheques for twenty-five hundred marks and one for fifteen thousand marks all traced back to Siincleer. I doubt very seriously that there is any way to link those cheques directly to Juan del Larrano, but the corporacion will certainly be held responsible for nearly sixty thousand marks going to an accessory to the New Meritorists . . . and . . ."

Konnigsburg nodded slowly. "And?"

"After Pietro Venburg was killed, del Larrano publicly said that there would be no change in Siincleer's ways of doing business. Juan del Larrano is anything but a stupid man."

"I can see the implications, Steffan. But right now, the only hard proof is those cheques."

"Which the Judiciary Ministry already has. Oh, and the ministry is insisting on the completion of the frigate *Baarthan* at twenty percent below cost. In addition, that investigation and other evidence will likely reveal a pattern of illegal restraint of trade and commerce. There's one other aspect of this . . ." Dekkard went on to explain about Engaard Engineering and the substituted and erroneous plans on Siincleer's engineering paper, along with the missing construction manager. "What didn't strike me until this morning is that it's likely Siincleer Engineering has the complete building plans for the Navy's new research building west of Siincleer."

Konnigsburg's eyes narrowed. "How did you know about that?"

"Emrelda's husband Markell was in charge of the project. We have his last communication, telling of his suspicions that his plans had been altered. He vanished the night after the package with the altered plans was sent to me." Dekkard smiled sadly. "I know little of this is widely known, but I thought the Admiralty should be aware of it before it is."

Although Konnigsburg maintained a pleasant expression, Dekkard had the impression that what he'd been told had made an impression.

Dekkard waited.

Konnigsburg offered a wry expression. "Of course, because this is in the interests of the Imperium, I will pass the information on. Informally, you understand."

"That's all I had, Eyril."

"I do believe it's more than enough. Who else knows?"

"So far as I'm aware, no one in the Justiciary Ministry presently knows about the *Ultima,* or its capabilities, or understands just how much the Siincleer corporacions have invested in Noldar. The Premier and Guard Captain Trujillo know the basics of the finances, as do all the members of the subcommittee. Erskine Mardosh knows some of what happened with Engaard Engineering, but didn't want to pursue it."

Konnigsburg nodded, then stood. "I think I need to see some old acquaintances. Socially, you understand."

Dekkard stood quickly. "I thought you, particularly, would appreciate the information." He inclined his head politely.

"I do indeed, Steffan. So should the Admiralty."

As Dekkard made his way from the inner office, he had the feeling that what he'd said had disturbed Konnigsburg, although the former admiral had given no obvious outward sign.

Once he and Avraal, and Gaaroll, were out in the main corridor walking toward the courtyard doors, he quietly asked Avraal, "What did you sense?"

"By the time you finished, he was incredibly worried," said Avraal. "That overshadowed everything else."

Dekkard's first thought was that Konnigsburg should be concerned. *But incredibly worried?* "If he's that worried, there's more we don't know." But then, as Dekkard had increasingly come to realize, there was always more he didn't know.

As they neared the courtyard doors, Dekkard caught sight of Pohl Palafaux and Erich Kuuresoh ahead of them and stepping out into the courtyard. "Can either of you sense what's going on with them?"

"Neither one is happy," said Avraal.

"Councilor Kuuresoh, he's angry, too," added Gaaroll.

"It would be interesting to know why," mused Dekkard. "Right now, nothing irrevocable has occurred. The High Justiciary could find for Ulrich, and it's very possible that only the five corporacions, as entities, could be found guilty, without any charges against individuals being successful."

"Even that would be more than any Commercer or Landor government has ever done," said Avraal.

"We'll just have to see," said Dekkard, adding after a moment, "I'm getting very tired of waiting to see."

"Some things," murmured Gaaroll, "I'd rather not see."

Dekkard could definitely agree with that.

Kuuresoh and Palafaux, absorbed in their conversation, didn't look back as they walked through the courtyard and to the councilors' dining room.

While the pair entered the dining room, Dekkard, Avraal, and Gaaroll continued walking past the door to the Premier's floor office until they reached Guard Captain Trujillo's office.

"He's in," said Avraal and Gaaroll almost simultaneously.

Dekkard knocked.

"Come in," replied Trujillo.

Dekkard did just that, alone, and closed the door.

"How can I help you, Councilor?"

"Among other things, I thought I'd pass on something I heard from a patroller. He pointed out that street criminals tend to use handguns, not rifles. Former Naval Marines, on the other hand, have great familiarity with rifles."

"That's a good thought," replied Trujillo. "One of the guards made the same observation."

"Then you're well ahead of me."

"I doubt that, Councilor."

"You're being kind, Guard Captain." Dekkard smiled. "Have you heard anything from the Justiciary Ministry?"

"Not so far, and I don't expect to before late tomorrow at the earliest."

"How is the former premier?"

"He's promised to have my head, and his tone of voice suggests he means that literally, rather than just having me fired."

"I could be very much mistaken, Guard Captain," replied Dekkard, "but I doubt that Sr. Ulrich will ever be in a position to carry out that threat in any form. Nor should he be. While it may be difficult or impossible to prove, it's likely he was behind the murder of Jaime Minz."

"That may indeed be difficult, but comparison of the bullets fired at the guards from one of the rifles used in the failed attempt on your subcommittee strongly suggests that rifle killed Sr. Minz. The rifle is identical to those used by Naval Marines, and it isn't manufactured for anyone else. The Navy will likely have more information about the rifle in the next day or so. My guess is that it went missing some time ago, and no one reported its loss or it was classed as an unexplained loss from a ship's armory."

"Possibly from a ship being decommissioned and scrapped," suggested Dekkard.

"Or one in for overhaul."

"All these pieces," said Dekkard. "Suggestive, but not conclusive."

"Not yet, but we're working on it. Is there anything else, Councilor?"

Dekkard laughed wryly. "I wish I did have something else to share. I'm convinced that the Siincleer corporacions are at least as involved as Suvion Industries, although I have nothing resembling proof, except for their funding Capitol Services, and I wonder if we'll ever find out."

"We don't have to find out everything," replied Trujillo, "just enough to prove some of the charges."

Dekkard nodded, then said, "That's a very good point." He'd almost forgotten that without naval contracts for years, the Siincleer corporacions would be in financial straits, and with those contracts going elsewhere, the costs to the Council would be less, and by the time Siincleer could bid they'd be faced with much stronger competition—as well as stronger oversight, at least if Dekkard had anything to do with it.

After a moment of silence, Dekkard said, "That's all I had."

"Knowing you, Councilor, you'll find more."

"Thank you, Guard Captain. Until later."

As soon as Dekkard was out of Trujillo's office, and the three were headed back toward the councilors' dining room, Avraal asked, "Did you learn anything?"

"One of the assassins' rifles was likely used to kill Minz."

Avraal shivered slightly. "Minz was killed with a single shot from a distance. If Nincya hadn't sensed them . . ."

"It would have been harder in the Council corridor," said Dekkard, "but some of us would have been hit."

"You, for certain," replied Avraal.

Dekkard wasn't about to argue that.

When Avraal and Dekkard entered the councilors' dining room, he said to the maître d'hôtel, "A table for four, please."

"Yes, sir."

As they were being escorted to their table, Dekkard noticed immediately that Palafaux and Kuuresoh sat with Schmidtz and Rikkard. They had to be talking in low voices, because all four of them leaned in.

They hadn't been seated even long enough to order before Dekkard saw Tomas Pajiin enter the dining area, accompanied by Kastyn Heimrich, the new councilor from Aloor who'd been selected to replace Tedor Waarfel after the first shelling of the Council buildings. Dekkard immediately gestured and said, "Tomas, Kastyn, would you like to join us?"

"With the lovely Ritten there," returned Pajiin, "we're not about to turn down that invitation."

"Not at all," added Heimrich.

"Dear," said Dekkard, "this is Kastyn Heimrich, the new councilor from Aloor. Kastyn, my wife, Avraal Ysella-Dekkard."

"A pleasure to meet you," declared the balding dark-haired Heimrich as he seated himself. "I briefly spoke with your husband a month or so ago, but you were not with him." Heimrich turned to Dekkard. "Tomas has been filling me in on some of the public details of the recent subcommittee hearings. I've been concerned for years about the excesses of the Commercer governments, but I had no idea just how excessive they were."

"Premier Obreduur did," replied Dekkard. "But very few others believed him, not until the Kraffeist Affair and what followed."

"Even some councilors who believed him," added Avraal, "feared speaking out."

"That's how Avraal and I met," said Dekkard. "We were security aides for the Premier even when he was a councilor."

"But your background is Landor," said Heimrich. "I understand your family dates well back into the kingdom of Aloor."

Avraal laughed softly. "There were family stories, but I didn't find proof until last year."

At that moment, a server arrived. Once everyone had ordered, Heimrich asked, "How did you end up working for a noted Craft councilor?"

"Because I didn't want to be a Landor broodmare," replied Avraal. "Neither did my older sister. We left. I became a certified empath. She became a patroller."

Heimrich stiffened, as if the bluntness of Avraal's words had surprised him. Finally, he said, "You two don't seem to be the brutally effective security team I've heard about."

Pajiin laughed harshly.

"Apparently, appearances are especially deceiving in your case."

"It's better that way," said Avraal cheerfully.

Heimrich looked closely at Dekkard, then Avraal. "Knives . . . both of you?"

"Throwing knives," replied Avraal.

"After all," added Dekkard, "since the Commercers turned politics into war, we thought it was better to be armed . . . within the laws of the Council and Imperium, of course. And here comes our order, I believe."

Dekkard had opted for the three-cheese chicken, as had Avraal, while Pajiin had the duck cassoulet, and Heimrich the veal milanesia.

From there on the conversation touched more on family and acquaintances.

At a third before first bell, Dekkard said, "I apologize, but I need to go to the floor. I have an amendment I'll be offering . . ." He explained quickly.

Heimrich listened. "That makes sense. Some Commercers might not like it, though."

"That's possible, but not passing it reduces revenues and rewards unscrupulous importers and Atacaman artisans while punishing Guldoran artisans." Dekkard stood. "I do have to go, but I enjoyed lunch."

"So did we," replied Pajiin before Heimrich could speak.

While Dekkard made his way to the Council chamber, Avraal headed for the spouses' gallery.

Dekkard had barely stepped into the chamber when he was joined by Guilhohn Haarsfel.

"I looked at your amendment. You didn't mention it to me."

"I apologize, Guilhohn. I was going to pursue the matter in another way, but realized at the last moment that the amendment, if accepted by the Council, would resolve two issues at once. The first is the practice of Commercer importers buying cheap artworks and importing them as housewares rather than art. The second is adding revenues to the Council reserves. Axel was pursuing the matter through the Treasury Ministry when he was killed, but his death and the destruction of his office and staff made it difficult for Ingrella Obreduur to follow up on it." That was true. Also, while Dekkard had the knowledge of the inquiry, he would have been required to start the process from the beginning because he couldn't request action on something that another councilor had initiated. *But you should have followed up with Ingrella sooner.*

The plain fact was that that issue had totally skipped Dekkard's mind until he'd looked at the schedule the previous Quindi and realized that he'd completely forgotten about the problem and should have brought the matter to Ingrella's attention.

"It's most irregular, Steffan."

"I understand, but this was an issue Axel was pursuing, and . . . honestly, I didn't realize until late on Quindi that there was no way Ingrella could have known."

Haarsfel frowned, then nodded. "You have had your hands full."

"I appreciate your understanding."

Dekkard then hurried to see if Ingrella was at her desk. She was.

"Good afternoon, Steffan."

"I owe you an apology, and I hope you'll forgive me." Dekkard went on to explain, ending up by saying, "I'd like to introduce the amendment by saying it belongs to both Premier Obreduur and the present Councilor Obreduur because it *does*, and because I should have remembered sooner. Then, if you want to, and only if you do, you could say a few words."

Ingrella offered a smile both amused and slightly sad. "You're hard on yourself. Axel said that as well. I'd be pleased if you made that introduction, and I will say a few words."

"If I'd remembered sooner . . ."

"Steffan, you're not trying to take credit that isn't yours. After all, you did much of the work on looking into the problem."

After the chimes struck first bell, and Haarsfel declared the Council in session, Hasheem took the lectern.

"Before we take up the debate and vote on the proposed Reserve Replenishment Act, I wanted to inform the Council that the Justiciary Ministry presented oral arguments to the High Justiciary concerning the refusal of former Premier Oskaar Ulrich to answer questions dealing with the illegal transfer of military dunnite to Capitol Services. As many of you already know, Capitol Services was responsible for setting up the New Meritorist attack on the Council Office Building."

When Hasheem finished, he returned the lectern to Haarsfel, who recognized Wilhelm Ghossaan, the chair of the Commerce and Treasury Committee. Ghossaan immediately summarized the Reserve Replenishment proposal, then noted that three amendments had been registered, one by Councilor Farris to increase the temporary tariff increase to five percent, one by Councilor Quellar to reduce the tariff increase, and one by Councilor Dekkard for a selective and targeted tariff increase. The maximum time for debate on each amendment was one bell, a third to each party, followed by a bell for debate on the final version of the proposal.

Dekkard doubted that there would be much debate on either of the first two amendments, and there wasn't. Both were defeated. Little more than a bell and a third passed before his amendment was called up.

Dekkard offered a brief summary, emphasizing how the misuse of the housewares classification offered unfair competition to Guldoran artisans and how it also reduced tariff revenues. He then granted time to Ingrella.

"I'm grateful to Councilor Dekkard for pursuing this matter. As all of you know, the loss of the entire staff and all records has made following up on many of my husband's initiatives rather difficult. Not only will the amendment help lessen the burden of unfair competition, but it will reduce the shortfall in revenues necessary to replenish Council reserve funds."

When Ingrella finished speaking, Dekkard yielded the floor.

Hansaal Volkaar immediately stood. "Without yielding the floor, I'll grant the councilor from Gaarlak two minutes to explain why he waited until now to bring up the matter."

Haarsfel looked to Dekkard. "You have two minutes to explain."

"The issue of undertariffing artworks as housewares was a matter being handled by the late Premier Obreduur," replied Dekkard. "It is likely the reason why former Treasury Minister Munchyn attempted to kill the Premier. While I was aware of the problem as an aide to the Premier when he was a councilor, I was not involved in drafting a legislative remedy because the Treasury Ministry was still working on a reply to the Premier when I became a councilor. Apparently, the Treasury Ministry neglected to report back on the matter to the Premier's successor. Since I did not become aware of this until last Quindi, offering the amendment was the first opportunity I have had to pursue the matter, and, as should be clear, I am only doing so with the consent of the current Councilor Obreduur. Does the Commerce Party floor leader believe that an attempt by Atacaman traders to game the tariff laws should be allowed to continue just because the Premier was assassinated and unable to follow up on the matter?"

"This is not a matter that should be handled by a last-moment amendment . . ." From there Volkaar went on to cite the need for careful consideration and proper procedures for almost a third of a bell.

When he finished, Haarsfel returned to the lectern. "The councilor from Gaarlak has time remaining."

Dekkard returned to the dais. "The most honorable Commerce Party floor leader has cited the need for procedure and measured diligence. This problem was raised by then Councilor Obreduur close to a year ago. The Treasury Ministry did nothing except stall until the attempted murder of then acting Premier Obreduur by Minister Munchyn. Strangely, all the paperwork held by the Commercer-controlled Treasury Ministry also vanished. Rebuilding that will take months, all the while costing the Council revenue and impoverishing Guldoran artisans."

When Dekkard finished, Haarsfel announced, "The councilor's time has expired. All councilors have a third to register their vote."

Less than a third passed before all councilors finished voting. Once the votes were counted and the tally sheets presented to Haarsfel, he stepped up to the lectern and announced, "The vote on the amendment presented by the councilor from Gaarlak received twenty-nine Craft votes, eight Landor votes, and two Commerce votes. That amendment will be incorporated into the proposal before the Council. Councilors have one third in which to cast their votes on the Reserve Replenishment Act."

In the end, the amended act passed by the same margin as Dekkard's amendment, after which Haarsfel recessed the Council.

Dekkard immediately stood and turned to Ingrella. "Thank you. I'm so sorry I didn't recall the problem sooner."

"Thank you, Steffan. You don't need to apologize." Ingrella smiled, a trace sadly, and added, "In the same kinds of situations, Axel always had to apologize, and I told him the same thing."

"You're kind."

"Not always, but thank you."

Even after Ingrella's words and her departure, Dekkard still felt guilty as he walked toward the councilors' lobby. He couldn't help worrying about what the High Court would decide about Oskaar Ulrich, even though it could be the end of the week before the justicers ruled.

In the meantime, he needed to get back to the office so that Colsbaan and Roostof could brief him on the legislative proposal to give working women greater access to guild legalists, a proposal that would likely be far more difficult to get enacted than it should be.

69

O N Duadi morning the first thing Dekkard did when he got to the breakfast room was to pick up *Gestirn*. The front-page headline predictably read: FORMER PREMIER APPEALS COUNCIL SANCTION. The article stated that while the proceedings before the High Justiciary were closed, what was known was that Ulrich had refused to answer questions by the Security Committee's investigatory subcommittee about his role in how the New Meritorists had obtained military dunnite. The Security Committee had incarcerated him for failing to answer, and Ulrich had appealed the Council action. The remainder of the story was a rehash of previous stories.

"Newssheet didn't say much," offered Gaaroll.

"There isn't anything else to say until the High Court rules." Emrelda looked to Dekkard. "Do you think the High Justicers will support you?"

"I'd hope so, but, one way or another, it will determine the future of Guldor." Dekkard laughed softly but sardonically. "I definitely sound like a politician."

"You are a politician," Emrelda replied. "If they do, what happens next?"

"An immediate trial before the High Justiciary. Ulrich will remain incarcerated except when he appears and refuses to answer."

"You don't think he will?" asked Gaaroll.

"I'd doubt it. Someone will have to pay, and it will be difficult, if not impossible, to prove that the presidentes of five of the largest corporacions were directly and personally involved. Ulrich could incriminate Johann Daenyld, but he won't, for the same reason that Lukkyn Wyath didn't before his execution."

"Family?"

Dekkard nodded.

"That's blackmail," protested Gaaroll.

"Which is nothing compared to what they've already done," replied Avraal, her tone acidic as she entered the breakfast room.

"Then they'll just keep on doing things like that," said Gaaroll.

"Not necessarily, but we'll have to see." Even as Dekkard said the last words, he wanted to shake his head at the phrase he kept finding himself using.

"Can't you do something more?" asked Gaaroll.

"He's done more than enough," said Emrelda tartly. "There are times when someone else has to do their job."

Dekkard understood what Emrelda wasn't saying. If Markell hadn't insisted on doing an investigation all by himself, he might still be alive. "It helps if there are others who can, and, right now, there are some who are good at it." *I just hope they're good enough.* With that thought, he went to get cafés and croissants.

The rest of breakfast and the drive to the Council covered parking were uneventful, and by second bell, Dekkard was in his office.

Although there was a stack of mail on his desk, there was just one message, and the office copy of *The Machtarn Tribune.* Dekkard picked it up, wincing as he saw one of the front-page headlines—CONTINUED ATTACKS ON FORMER PREMIER. Nonetheless, he read the story, which suggested that Ulrich was being pilloried just because he was a Commercer and because a former aide had been so distraught over defeat of the previous Commercer government that he'd turned to the New Meritorists.

The newssheet's small story about the passage of the Reserve Replenishment Act noted the need for building the reserve fund, but deplored the adoption of the amendment offered by Councilor Steffan Dekkard, which would drastically increase the costs of imported housewares and allow Guldoran crafters to maintain excessively high prices for such goods. There was no mention of the illegal undertariffing that had necessitated the amendment.

After making certain that the *Tribune* held no other news about the Council or councilors, Dekkard opened the message envelope to discover a note from Eyril Konnigsburg, suggesting that Dekkard and Avraal both meet him for lunch at noon.

Dekkard immediately informed Avraal, who was working with Gaaroll in the front office, having Gaaroll sense everyone who passed in the corridor outside.

"Both of us? Either his wife will be there, and it's social, or he wants you to know that what he's saying is so."

"That could be good or very bad."

"Conceivably both," suggested Avraal.

After sending an acceptance note back to Konnigsburg, Dekkard quickly read through the mail, wondering as he did how quickly the High Court would rule and what the ruling would be. Near the bottom of the stack were several critical letters, one of which said, in part:

> . . . *any councilor who attacks the corporacions that support the Imperial Navy commits even greater treason than the traitorous New Meritorists* . . .

. . . corporacions provide the goods you use, and without them we would have nothing, something that all you Crafters seem to overlook . . .

And what about all the designs and ideas that corporacions didn't create, that they stole or bought for coppers on the mark, and the skilled workers who operate and maintain them? Dekkard just added the letter to the pile he'd already read. Roostof could certainly adapt one of the standard responses used to reply politely to irate Commercer supporters.

At a third before noon, Dekkard, Avraal, and Gaaroll set out for the councilors' dining room. Even before they were halfway to the central staircase, Dekkard saw another councilor approaching, but for several moments could not identify the man.

"Nothing hostile," murmured Avraal.

Dekkard finally recognized Emile Hebersyn, the latest Commercer councilor from Machtarn, who had replaced Marryat Osmond, after Osmond had perished in the first attack on the Council Office Building. "Good morning, Emile."

"Good morning, Steffan, or what's left of it. I just wanted to say that I appreciated your amendment yesterday."

"I take it that rebuilding the piers, waterlines, and other public structures in the harbor area will take more funds than the Council has allotted?"

"Quite a bit more. Chairman Dholen has been sympathetic, but said that additional funds are limited until reserve funds are rebuilt."

"I don't know how much the amendment will help."

"Anything will help over the next year or so." Hebersyn paused, then added quietly, "I appreciate what you did with that bastard Ulrich. Just take care of yourself." Then he turned to Avraal. "I understand you're quite formidable, Ritten. If you would, keep him safe for the rest of us as well." Hebersyn nodded, smiled warmly, and turned back in the direction he had come.

"Did he mean all that?" asked Dekkard. "I mean, he must have because he obviously knows your abilities."

"He did. From what I sensed, he might have been one of the two Commercers who voted for your amendment."

"Interesting." That didn't totally surprise Dekkard, since the amendment benefitted Hebersyn's district, but he'd only exchanged a few words in passing with Hebersyn in the time since the other had been selected.

Dekkard and Avraal arrived at the councilors' dining room minutes before Eyril Konnigsburg, and the three were immediately seated. Dekkard noticed that Kaliara Bassaana was sitting with Traelyna Treshaam, which wasn't a total surprise, given Bassaana and the fact that both were on the Transportation Committee—and that Leister Milyaard had become the new chair after Tedor Waarfel's death.

"I appreciate your coming," Konnigsburg said to Avraal. "I'm sure you both understand why."

"You don't want any misunderstandings," returned Dekkard.

"Precisely," said Konnigsburg, "but we should order and then talk."

Dekkard wasn't all that hungry and settled for a salad topped with sliced chicken, while Avraal had a half order of the three-cheese chicken. Konnigsburg settled on the white bean soup.

Once the server left, the former admiral took a sip of his café, then cleared his throat. "I think it's fair to say, Steffan, that your information discomfited certain highly placed individuals in the Admiralty, especially what you revealed about the research facility. While the Admiralty was well aware of the difficulties created by the disappearance of Sr. Roemnal and the death of Sr. Engaard, the matter of the missing engineering plans and the missing supervisor had, for some reason, not come to their attention. Neither had the Justiciary minister yet made them aware of the sales of dunnite to Noldar."

"And what about the *Ultima*?"

"They were aware of the potential difficulties, but . . . by itself . . . ?"

"Suspicious, but not sufficient to justify legalistic remedies?" asked Dekkard.

"There are certain difficulties with legalistic remedies," replied Konnigsburg, "or such has been indicated to me, which place the Admiralty in a difficult situation. It would be helpful to know how the investigatory subcommittee might be inclined to proceed from this point."

"The investigatory subcommittee has no present plans to hold additional hearings, provided that the various processes now underway resolve the situation so that the five corporacions currently under investigation do not and cannot continue their past practices."

Dekkard stopped as he saw the server returning with their orders.

Once everyone had been served, and had taken at least a few mouthfuls, Konnigsburg said, "Do you think the legalistic processes underway will prove sufficient to address the situation?"

"From the statements made publicly and privately, on the record," replied Dekkard, "I personally have some doubts that the presidentes of either Suvion Industries or the Siincleer corporacions have any intent of making significant changes in their operations. Frankly, I also worry about the possibility of the Siincleer corporacions shifting their operations, or at least some of them, as well as their financial and other movable assets, to a location, such as Noldar, where they would face less accountability and scrutiny. It would disturb me greatly to have to hold hearings in the future about why something like that occurred."

Konnigsburg nodded slowly, then said, "I also raised those possibilities to the few contacts who have proved trustworthy. They share those concerns. What they can or will do, I do not know."

Dekkard caught the very slight emphasis on the word "know," and replied, "I understand. At the same time, any action that effectively deals with the problems is likely to be . . . disruptive. I can't see how Guldor can afford to pay artificially and unethically, if not illegally, inflated prices for military procurement and shipbuilding. Somehow, that needs to be addressed in a fashion that paves the way for a more competitive and efficient procurement system. I don't see that happening if the violations and excesses of these corporacions continue. I also don't see much change if the senior officials remain unaffected and the only penalties are limited to token financial settlements and sanctions against midlevel managers."

"Do you see any alternatives?" Konnigsburg's voice was even.

Dekkard offered a rueful smile. "More hearings remain an alternative, but they could continue for months, and, as in the instance of Eastern Ironway, the hearings never really addressed the causes or suggested a remedy. In the present instance, corporacions, and even the Imperial Banque of Machtarn, are investing more heavily in Noldar."

"I don't see that you're suggesting much to be hopeful about, Steffan."

Dekkard shrugged. "We're all limited to the tools we have. I can hold hearings and require witnesses to testify honestly. I'm not familiar with all the tools the Navy possesses, but it seems odd that the Admiralty is reluctant to act against corporacions that have effectively contributed funds to an organization that fomented and attempted insurrection against the lawful government. There's also the issue of why the Admiralty hasn't taken a stronger stand against all the 'irregularities' in the procurement process, especially now that the New Meritorists' funding has been revealed. Combining the two, some councilors might even question the correlation between rapidly rising procurement costs, corporacions indirectly funding insurrection, and the apparent unwillingness of the Navy to look into those corporacions and their practices. It might be interesting to hold hearings to discover the impact on the security of the Imperium." Dekkard again smiled ruefully. "As a former very junior naval officer, I'd find that exceedingly painful, but if there's no other resolution . . ."

"I did suggest to certain contacts that you might feel that way, and that other members of the subcommittee might also. I also said, and I hope I was not misspeaking, that I'd gotten the feeling that would be a last resort, but a necessary one."

"Necessary, if no one else acts," confirmed Dekkard, realizing that, if the Admiralty and the Justiciary Ministry didn't or couldn't act decisively enough, then he was committing himself to another round of hearings, if not worse. *But what else can you do? If del Larrano and Daenyld aren't stopped . . .* He managed an amused smile and said, "After all this, it's clear, again, that I would have had a short career as a regular line officer."

"Sometimes," returned Konnigsburg, "we're fortunate enough to make the right choices, if occasionally for the wrong reasons." He paused. "How do you think the High Court will rule on Ulrich's appeal?"

"They *should* deny it, but I really don't know," replied Dekkard.

Konnigsburg looked to Avraal. "What do you think?"

"He's guilty of so much more, but I don't know how the High Court will rule, either."

"Neither of you was asked to testify before the High Court," Konnigsburg pointed out.

"No one testified," Dekkard said. "It's all a matter of law, and whether the question was relevant to high crimes or treason. Not what anyone feels or believes. Not whether the circumstances extenuate or mitigate. The subcommittee cannot try anyone. It can require that information be disclosed and be accurate, and that information can be used in a trial for misfeasance in office and for high crimes and treason. From what I know, Ulrich is guilty in both areas, but the High Court will have to decide that."

"It's hard to believe that he thought there wouldn't be repercussions."

"The Commercers and some of the corporacions have gotten away with offenses almost as bad for years. That may be why Minz helped them attack the Council Office Building and target Premier Obreduur. Last summer, Minz told me that without Obreduur, the Craft Party couldn't hold power for more than a few months. He obviously believed it, and I'd wager Ulrich did as well." Dekkard smiled sardonically. "But that's speculation based on my recollection of what a dead man said. Not exactly the strongest evidence."

"It does provide an interesting context for what happened." Konnigsburg laid his soup spoon on the plate next to the empty bowl.

"Are you willing to speculate on what the Admiralty will or will not do?" asked Dekkard.

"No. I've learned that what I hope seldom happens, and what I fear often does. That clouds my judgment. So I've found it best not to speculate."

"That's an interesting way of looking at it," said Avraal.

"What else can I say?"

"What about hearings before the Military Affairs Committee?"

"At the moment, no hearings have been officially scheduled."

"And they won't be until the situations with the Security subcommittee are resolved?"

"Chairman Mardosh hasn't said, but that would be my guess." Konnigsburg smiled warmly. "I hope that the Admiralty, the Justiciary Ministry, and the High Justiciary manage to obtain some sort of resolution before long, but I suspect we've done all we could for the present. I don't know if this has been entirely productive, but I did enjoy the lunch and hearing some of the background of which I was unaware." He looked to Avraal. "I also appreciate your forbearance with my rambling. Emilya and I do need to have you over for dinner, but for now I suppose we all should get back to work."

"I, for one," said Avraal, "appreciated your 'ramblings.'"

"You're too kind, but I appreciate the thought. Now, if you will excuse me." Konnigsburg eased back his chair and stood.

Dekkard also stood, as did Avraal.

Neither Dekkard nor Avraal uttered more than pleasantries until they were alone back in Dekkard's personal office.

"If I read that correctly," said Dekkard, "Konnigsburg used or will use the threat of more Security hearings to press the Admiralty, and he wanted to make sure that I won't back down."

"That's the way it felt. I also got the impression that this wasn't a new feeling."

"That's been clear from the first time we talked. He's close to dismissive of the abilities and understanding of the First Marshal and those officers being considered for the Fleet Marshal. Right now, all we can do is see where it leads." Dekkard winced as soon as he realized what he'd said with his last words—once again.

"He was also surprised when you mentioned that comment of Minz's."

"I wish I'd recalled that sooner."

"Maybe it's better that you didn't."

Dekkard could see that.

"You have things to do," said Avraal, "and I'd like to work some more with Nincya. She's getting close to being able to pass the probationary test. Part of her problem is that she doesn't sense emotions in the same way as most other empaths, and she needs to know how to describe what she senses in more standard terms."

"'Piles of feelings' isn't standard, I take it?" Dekkard grinned.

Avraal gave him a look of disgust, then grinned back, before leaving his office.

Dekkard had been working on responses for only about a third of a bell when the door opened. Avraal and Margrit both stood in the doorway.

"There's a messenger here from the Justiciary Ministry," said Margrit. "He needs you to sign for it personally."

Avraal added, "No sign of anything malign."

Dekkard rose from behind his desk and walked out to the front office, where the messenger waited.

After Dekkard signed, the messenger said, "Thank you, sir," and tendered an envelope. On the outside was written:

> *Councilor Steffan Delos Dekkard*
> *Chairman, Investigatory Subcommittee*
> *Council Security Committee*

Inside were two sheets of paper. The first was the High Justiciary's denial of the appeal of one Oskaar Ulrich, declaring that the testimony before the investigatory subcommittee required a trial for high crimes.

The second was a note from Minister Kuta saying that the High Court had set the first of Springend as the beginning date for Ulrich's trial, and that the High Court had accepted charges against Suvion Industries and Siincleer Shipbuilding and its subsidiaries. The initial trial date for the Siincleer corporacions was the thirteenth of Springend, with the trial of Suvion Industries to follow immediately. The ministry planned to file charges against Uldwyrk Systems, Eastern Ironways, and Northwest Industrial Chemical in the next day, along with a request for an injunction against granting any purchases or procurements from any of the five corporacions until the conclusion of their respective trials. In addition, custody warrants had been issued for the presidentes and senior legalists of both Siincleer Shipbuilding and Suvion Industries, and the warrants were in the process of being served and enforced by Justiciary agents.

Dekkard immediately asked Avraal and Roostof to join him and had them read both announcements.

Avraal read the documents first.

When Roostof finished reading, he handed the two sheets back to Dekkard. "Sir, what do you think?"

Dekkard smiled wryly. "You're the legalist. You tell me."

"I haven't seen all the evidence, but I don't see how they all won't be found guilty of enough to be prohibited from procurement and sales. At the very least, they should be."

"I'd agree with that," replied Dekkard. "I'd guess that Johann Daenyld will be found guilty of personal involvement at some level, but that's based on Ulrich. They'll ask Daenyld about his relationship with Ulrich. If he refuses to answer or lies, then he'll be declared stateless, and all his personal assets in Guldor will be forfeit. Of course, he's likely got marks squirreled away in Noldar, but getting to them might be a trifle hard because these days, only the disassociated lands in Medarck welcome stateless exiles, and that's for a ten-year indenture."

"Daenyld will have planned how to buy his way out of that," said Avraal.

"Most likely," agreed Dekkard, "but he'll find he won't have much left after it's all over."

"Such a pity." Avraal's words were ice.

"What about Juan del Larrano?" asked Roostof.

"He's smart and ruthless," said Dekkard. "I'd wager that he'll escape to Noldar." *In his high-speed armored yacht.* "He'll likely leave Guldor before that custody warrant even nears Siincleer. He's got far more in the way of assets than Daenyld, since Siincleer is a family firm, and with what he can offer Noldar, they'll ignore any requests for his return to Guldor."

Avraal just shook her head.

Dekkard turned. "Svard, I'd like to see the afternoon editions of both newssheets. There might be something new there."

"They might not have the news by then," ventured Roostof.

"They'll at least have the denial of Ulrich's appeal."

After Roostof left the inner office, Avraal said, "Do you really think del Larrano will walk away from everything?"

"I have to wonder if he's walking away from that much."

Avraal frowned. "That's hard to believe."

"Most of the last year has been hard to believe," replied Dekkard sardonically, looking at the responses he needed to read and sign—or revise.

"I'll leave you to that and go back to working with Nincya." Avraal slipped out of the office, closing the door as she left.

Dekkard looked at the top response, dealing with spring flooding along the Lakaan River, then began to read.

Close to two bells later, accompanied by Avraal, Roostof returned with copies of the afternoon editions of the newssheets.

Dekkard took *Gestirn* first. The story about Ulrich made the front page.

FORMER PREMIER CHARGED WITH HIGH CRIMES

Late this morning, the High Justiciary denied Oskaar Ulrich's appeal of his incarceration by the investigatory subcommittee of the Council's Security Committee. The former Premier, now a vice-presidente of Suvion Industries, contended that questions posed to him by the investigatory subcommittee were not relevant to the scope of the subcommittee's stated inquiry.

In addition, the High Court set a date for Sr. Ulrich's trial on counts of high crimes . . . speed of the decision by the tripartisan body suggests little doubt about the relevance, accuracy, and applicability of the testimony before the subcommittee . . .

. . . that verdict, and the Justiciary Ministry's ongoing investigation, strongly suggests that the five corporacions involved will face a series of charges for acts involving Capitol Services, a business reputedly established by Sr. Ulrich when he was a councilor . . . Capitol Services aided the attackers who shelled the Council Office Building, an attack that killed former Premier Axel Obreduur and three other councilors . . .

When Dekkard finished reading the *Gestirn* story, he handed that newssheet to Avraal and picked up the *Tribune,* concentrating on the differences as he began to read.

HIGH JUSTICIARY BACKS CRAFT-DOMINATED SUBCOMMITTEE

For reasons not stated in its brief decision, the High Court upheld the inexplicable incarceration of former Premier Oskaar Ulrich . . . appears Ulrich may be the scapegoat because the Craft government is seeking to tie powerful corporacions and Commercer political figures to the New Meritorist terrorists who savaged Machtarn . . .

Dekkard shook his head. As usual, the *Tribune* was close enough to the facts for the remainder of the story that the Justiciary Ministry would have been hard-pressed to sanction or censor the newssheet.

When Dekkard laid the *Tribune* on the desk, Roostof looked at him.

"Typical for the *Tribune,*" Dekkard said. "No matter what happens, it won't change."

"They didn't attack you this time," said Avraal.

"For the moment." Dekkard looked to Roostof. "Thank you, Svard."

Once Roostof had left, Avraal said, "No one's been trying to kill you lately. Why not?"

Dekkard shrugged. "I don't know. My guess is that there's no longer a point. The Justiciary Ministry and the High Court are looking into everything. Shooting me now would just make matters worse for the Commercers and the corporacions, because most people would believe they were behind it." He grinned wryly. "Besides, I'm now more valuable to them as a convenient newssheet target."

"I can see that. Fredrich is almost a cipher. Haarsfel's a legislative bu-reaucrat, and you're someone the corporacions can hate."

"Especially after what's happening." Dekkard looked at the few responses left to sign or revise. "Let me finish these, and we can head home. Nothing much of importance is likely to happen this late in the day."

70

EVEN with all his wondering and worrying, Dekkard slept decently and woke close to his regular time on Tridi morning, only to find Avraal already awake and looking at him. After stifling a yawn, he asked, "What's the matter?"

"Should anything be the matter?"

"When you're awake before I am, there often is. Or you've thought of something that I've overlooked." Dekkard failed to stifle a second yawn.

"Well, I was thinking . . ."

"Yes?"

"I was thinking about what else we need for our house."

Dekkard caught the slight emphasis on the word "our," and said, "The Council is scheduled for a recess the last week of Springend. Are you asking if we're going to Gaarlak? I said we would. That way, we could . . ." Dekkard broke off. "Am I missing something?"

"You're definitely not. You just haven't said anything recently, and I wondered."

"There have been a few other matters to occupy us," Dekkard said wryly as he sat up and swung his legs over the side of the bed. "And those aren't settled yet." He paused. "But then, I'm not sure anything is really ever totally settled. Even if Minister Kuta is moderately successful in prosecuting the five corporacions, then something else will happen. Don't ask me what. A year ago, I certainly couldn't have predicted everything that's happened, or that I'd be a councilor, and especially not that I'd be married to you. I didn't even dare think about that."

"I did." Avraal smiled, reached out, and kissed him, but only briefly. "You need to get your shower, and don't take all the warm water like you did yesterday."

Not even close to all of it. But Dekkard wisely did not verbalize the thought. "I'll be more careful." He stood and headed for the bathroom.

When Dekkard came downstairs after getting ready for the day, he immediately scanned *Gestirn,* but the headline story was only an updated version of what the newssheet had printed the afternoon before, the additions being the charges against the five corporacions. There was no mention of the custody warrants, and Dekkard could certainly understand that.

As he set down the newssheet, Emrelda said, "Do you really think that bastard del Larrano will get away?"

"I hope not, but I have strong doubts that a few Justiciary agents will be sufficient to put him in custody. He's always acted as though the laws were an inconvenience to be skirted or avoided, unless there was no other course." Dekkard paused, then added, "I hope I'm wrong."

"So do I," replied Emrelda.

Thinking of all the misery that del Larrano's machinations had cost her, Dekkard said earnestly, "I'm sorry."

"No one could have asked more of you, Steffan. I'm not angry or upset with you. I just wish these corporacion presidentes and corrupt Commercer councilors would suffer even a fraction of the misery they've created."

"Almighty, yes," said Gaaroll quietly.

"It's not over yet," said Avraal as she sat down at the breakfast table.

"Do you know something we don't?" asked Emrelda.

"I don't think so, but I do know that, after the High Court finding against Ulrich, at least some of those bastards will suffer."

"Not enough," said Gaaroll.

While Dekkard nodded as he headed into the kitchen for cafés and croissants, he couldn't help thinking that, while the Ulrichs and del Larranos of the world needed to be removed so that they didn't create more suffering, the real need was to improve systems and laws so that others couldn't do the same in the future.

A bell later, Dekkard eased the Gresynt to a stop in the covered parking, and the three walked quickly through a light spring drizzle across the drive and through the west doors of the Council Office Building.

As soon as Dekkard entered the outer office, he looked to Margrit. "Any messages?"

"Just one, from the Premier's office." She handed him the envelope.

"Thank you, Margrit." Dekkard opened the envelope and began to read. After several moments, he stopped and said, "It's just a notice to all councilors about what's happened. Not even everything that we know. It's good that he's letting everyone know."

"Unlike Ulrich when he was premier," said Avraal.

Dekkard and Avraal walked into the inner office, and he looked at the mail on the desk, then said, "I think we should have lunch with Villem Baar."

"What about Ingrella?" asked Avraal. "She's suffered as much as anyone from all this, and we haven't talked to her about it."

"According to the schedule, there aren't any Justiciary or Military Affairs Committee meetings. Why don't we just walk down to her office and see if she has a few moments? The mail can wait until after we talk to her."

"That's a good idea."

If a bit overdue. "Let me send off a message to Villem, and then we'll go."

Less than a sixth later, Dekkard, Avraal, and Gaaroll walked down the second-level corridor past the grand central staircase. Once they stepped into Ingrella's office, Dekkard didn't even have time to say a word.

"She'll be so glad to see you both," declared Leyala cheerfully, as she stood and opened the door to the inner office. "Councilor Dekkard and Ritten Ysella-Dekkard are here."

Dekkard didn't hear Ingrella's response, but Leyala opened the door wide, then closed it behind Dekkard and Avraal.

"I hope we're not intruding," said Dekkard, "but things have been rather hectic over the past few weeks, and I really meant to have some time to talk, rather than just exchanging brief comments in the Council chamber."

Ingrella gestured to the chairs in front of the desk and offered a warm smile. "I always appreciate your dropping by. From the news-sheet accounts, you have your hands full, but you both have always been thoughtful."

"My hands may not be quite so full now that the subcommittee has referred all the testimony to the Justiciary Ministry."

"From what I saw, you handled that well, Steffan." Ingrella offered a mischievous smile. "Besides hoping for my approval, Steffan, was there another reason for this impromptu visit?"

"One in particular. We wanted you to know that without all Axel and you did, the investigatory subcommittee wouldn't have been successful—"

"Not another word, Steffan. Axel would have been pleased with what you've done. I am."

"Thank you." Dekkard managed a grin. "On a lighter note . . . there was this rare history book you had me read. The one that told about Avraal's regal ancestry. You never mentioned the author, but I couldn't help but wonder if it might have been Princess Ilspieth. There's a square named for her, and Avraal found out that she reputedly spent most of her life writing a history of the early Imperadors. While her biography stated that the history was not known to have been published, from what you said, the biography would say that."

Ingrella burst into laughter, if quietly. After several moments, she said, "Only the two of you would track that down and make the connections. I believe it to be so, because no one else could have known some of the details in that history. My mother would only say that the history was very special . . . and extremely accurate."

"Families can have a way of not wanting to reveal certain matters," said Dekkard dryly, "as we've discovered."

"Particularly Landor families," added Avraal.

"No, dear," said Ingrella gently, "all families with either position or power, because they too often believe that unfavorable information gives others a weapon." She added in an ironic tone, "Sometimes, they're even right."

"Is Nellara still practicing?" asked Dekkard.

"Diligently."

"If you're not too tied up, perhaps we could come by on Findi," said Dekkard, "and see how she's doing."

"She'd like that."

"How are Axeli and Gustoff doing?" asked Dekkard.

"They must be doing well, or at least surviving," replied Ingrella dryly, "because I only get the obligatory twice-a-month letters, with a great deal of white space, so that they can console themselves that they wrote two pages."

For the next sixth or so the conversation turned to families, until there was a gentle knock on the door.

"That must be my third-bell appointment," said Ingrella. "I didn't realize it was that late. It was so good of you to stop by."

As Dekkard stood, he said, "In the next few days, I'd like to send you a draft of a legislative proposal Luara and Svard have been working on for me."

"The one about legalist representation of working women?"

Dekkard nodded. "I'd thought to introduce it in the Workplace Administration Committee, but I wouldn't want to get crossways with the Justiciary Committee."

"I'd be happy to look at it."

"Thank you." Dekkard grinned and added, "And if you see any way to improve it, I'm more than willing to accept help."

Ingrella shook her head, turned to Avraal, and said in a tone of mock resignation, "He could be even more dangerous than he already is."

In moments, Dekkard and Avraal were on their way back to his office.

"Was she as pleased as she seemed to be?"

"More so, I'd say. You've gotten more powerful, but you haven't grown more distant."

"I worry about that."

"You're doing fine," replied Avraal, "but keep worrying about it."

When they returned to the office, Margrit handed Dekkard a message from Villem Baar.

Gretina and I would be more than happy to have you and Avraal join us for lunch at noon, or just you, if she's not available.

Dekkard showed it to Avraal, who smiled.

Dekkard's reply was even shorter—"We'll both be there."

Then he returned to reading the incoming mail while Avraal went to work with Gaaroll.

The three left the office roughly a third before noon. As they started down the center staircase, a lean, dark-haired councilor at the bottom of the staircase glanced up almost casually, then apparently saw Dekkard, and stepped back, clearly waiting for Dekkard and Avraal.

"Lewell Contiago from Devult," murmured Dekkard, "if you didn't know."

"I didn't recognize him, not until you said his name. Axel said he was rather retiring, but straightforward."

When Dekkard reached the main floor, Contiago stepped forward. "Steffan, we've scarcely spoken, but I wanted to congratulate you on what you've done with your subcommittee. You've uncovered things we all suspected, but never could bring to light."

"Lewell, you couldn't bring them to light under a Commercer premier. I was just fortunate to be on the Security Committee under the first Craft government in centuries, and at a time when even some Commercers were concerned about the abuses of the former Ministry of Security. I'm sure you'll see more from other committees as the year goes on."

"That may be, but you've made it easier for the rest of us." Contiago smiled. "That's all I had to say."

"I appreciate it, but I couldn't have done anything without the support of the Premier."

"From what I've heard, you gave him good reason to support you." The older councilor smiled knowingly. "I won't keep you, but I hope we can talk more in the future."

"So do I."

Once Dekkard, Avraal, and Gaaroll were in the courtyard, walking toward the Council Hall, Avraal said, "There will be more of that."

"For now, but councilors are judged on what they've done lately."

"Steffan," said Avraal in an irritated tone of voice, "are you telling me that you're through trying to make things better?"

"Of course not, but—"

"Then other councilors will keep respecting you." She held up an index finger. "*Don't* say another word."

Dekkard glanced around. "The rain has almost stopped."

"So it has," replied Avraal sweetly.

"It actually feels like spring."

"It has for most of the past two weeks."

Dekkard just smiled, but only until Avraal jabbed an elbow into his side and said, even more sweetly, "You may be subcommittee chairman, but you're only my husband to me." Then she grinned and said, "Besides, as you pointed out, I come from a regal lineage."

Dekkard replied, "I do believe, my lady, that you've made your point, and your elbows are sharp."

"Then don't make her use them," muttered Gaaroll.

Dekkard and Avraal both laughed.

While quite a few staffers were in the main corridor of the Council Hall, the only other councilors Dekkard saw were Jaradd Rikkard and Yordan Farris, who entered the councilors' dining room well before Dekkard and Avraal. Neither councilor looked back.

When the maître d'hôtel returned, Dekkard said, "We're meeting Councilor Baar."

"This way, sir, Ritten."

Villem rose from the table as Avraal and Dekkard approached and said, "We're glad you could join us. Now that Gretina's working again, we decided that we'd have lunch together once a week, usually on Tridi, as a treat for us. It's also cheaper that way, and it's not that far from her office."

Avraal immediately said, "We didn't mean to intrude—"

"It's no intrusion, not at all," insisted Gretina. "Everyone's been so busy, and it's good to see you both." She looked to Dekkard as he seated himself beside her. "Thank you. Villem told me how you kept everyone from being shot."

"I had to," replied Dekkard wryly. "It was likely my doing they were there. If I hadn't pushed for the hearings and wanted Villem on the committee, the assassins wouldn't have been there, and neither would Villem."

Gretina turned to Avraal. "Does he worry about everything?"

Before Avraal could reply, Dekkard said, "Not as much as she does."

"Is he right?" Villem asked Avraal.

Avraal flushed slightly, then said, "Most likely."

Dekkard was grateful for the break provided by the server's arrival, and since he hadn't had the duck cassoulet in a while that was what he ordered. Avraal chose the special, a green pepper stuffed with ground lamb and aubergine. Dekkard managed not to shudder at Avraal's choice. Both Villem and Gretina ordered the three-cheese chicken.

Once the server departed, Villem asked, "Have you heard anything more about Ulrich's appeal other than what the Premier sent around this morning?"

"I understand that the Justiciary Ministry has issued some custody warrants for officials at Suvion and Siincleer."

"They wouldn't do that if they didn't have enough evidence to convince the Commercer justicers," said Gretina.

Villem nodded in agreement.

"Steffan," asked Gretina, "what do you think will happen?"

"I doubt that any of those five corporacions will be getting any procurement or construction contracts for at least a few years. Ulrich faces statelessness and exile, if not execution. Beyond that? Who knows?"

"What other corporacions are there who can do what they do?" asked Gretina.

"I imagine there are several willing to bid who are capable," replied Dekkard. "They just didn't dare, not when terrible things happened to anyone who underbid Siincleer and some of the others."

"You're speaking with the sort of conviction that scares me," said Villem. "When you have that tone, you're invariably right."

"It's better than being totally convinced and wrong, Villem," replied Gretina, "like Jaradd Rikkard."

Villem shook his head. "I'm very glad I'm a councilor right now."

"So am I," said Dekkard, adding, "that you are, I mean."

"Why?" asked Villem, his voice sounding honestly curious.

"Because we can talk reasonably, even when we don't agree. I'm not sure that will ever be possible with Jaradd Rikkard." Dekkard paused, then added, "It's hard with some Crafters as well."

"Did you know, Steffan," asked Villem, "that you've talked, honestly talked, not just idle chatter, to more Commerce and Landor councilors than any other junior Craft councilor?"

"That's because I happened to be persuaded into writing and supporting Security reform measures that almost everyone knew were necessary."

"Did anyone persuade you to press Chairman Hasheem into creating the investigatory subcommittee?" Baar smiled broadly, waiting for Dekkard's response.

Dekkard didn't get a chance to reply, because Avraal said quietly, "Stop protesting so much, Steffan. It doesn't become you, and Villem's correct. So let someone else be right, especially since he is."

Gretina choked back a laugh.

Villem smiled and said to Avraal, "You sound very much like someone else I know." Then he turned to Dekkard. "You're fortunate to have her."

Dekkard shook his head, then said, "I know." After a moment, he said, "No matter what anyone says, the subcommittee couldn't have done what it did without everyone. That's why someone wanted us all dead."

"That's fair," said Avraal. "It's also enough of that for lunch." She looked to Gretina. "How are Matteus and Karlotta doing?"

The remainder of the conversation revolved around children and family, and Dekkard even ate all of the duck cassoulet.

71

THE remainder of Tridi afternoon was uneventful, and the late editions of both *Gestirn* and *The Machtarn Tribune* contained no new information from either the Justiciary Ministry or the High Justiciary. Nor were there any messages from the Premier or anyone else. That comparative quiet gave Dekkard time to study the background material on the working women legislative proposal and to deal with correspondence and replies.

For the duration of the drive back to the house, Dekkard wondered what was happening, especially with regard to the Siincleer corporacions and Suvion Industries. He kept telling himself that Justiciary processes took time, and that it might be days before anything new happened, and weeks if not months before the investigations and trials were complete. Dekkard didn't even want to speculate about the eventual outcomes given the number of people that could be involved and what additional information the investigations might turn up.

But then, how much evidence has been destroyed?

When the four sat down to dinner—leftover lamb in a rice casserole—Emrelda said, "You've been quiet, Steffan."

"He's worried about all the investigations and the trials to come," said Avraal.

"More about what might not happen," said Dekkard. "What if all this only results in what amount to slaps on the wrist or seemingly large awards for damages that turn out to be meaningless? So much is in the hands of the High Justiciary."

"The High Justices denied Ulrich's appeal," replied Emrelda.

"Ulrich could just be an appeasement, followed by a host of symbolic but not terribly useful gestures that avoid further necessary reforms," replied Dekkard.

"So you have to go back to work to make sure those reforms happen," said Avraal. "You didn't think reform would be accomplished all at once, did you?"

"No, but it means persuading or quietly threatening Hasheem to hold more hearings, essentially almost starting over again."

"We're always starting over again," said Emrelda. "Even after great successes. That's life. Besides," she added sardonically, "I don't see either of you happy just sitting around in Gaarlak and trading memories of the one big thing you did in life."

Dekkard winced, then smiled ruefully and said, "It would be nice if there weren't quite so many assassination attempts."

"You're already well on the way to stopping them," replied Avraal. "You know that. The more councilors there are who are backing and initiating reforms, the less point there is in assassinating you, and the greater danger to those involved in plotting those attempts. Why do you think we haven't sensed anything since the last attempt in the Council Hall?"

"Partly what you just said and partly because you and Nincya have made it more dangerous for the assassins than for me."

"Nincya, me, *and* you, dear."

"Now that you've all decided you're going to continue upsetting corporacions and Commercers, no matter what happens," said Emrelda, "would you think about eating dinner while it's still warm?"

"Excellent idea," declared Dekkard, picking up his fork.

72

ARLY on Furdi morning Dekkard and Avraal were awakened by a forceful rapping on their bedroom door.

"What is it?"

"You two need to throw on robes or something and come downstairs now," declared Emrelda in a most determined voice. "*Now!*"

Dekkard looked to Avraal.

"*Now!*" repeated Emrelda.

"She's not angry, and she's not worried," murmured Avraal. "More like excited."

"We're coming!" Dekkard called back.

Following Emrelda's instructions, Dekkard pulled on an old shirt and trousers, and Avraal threw on a robe and stuffed her feet into slippers. Dekkard remained barefoot, and the two hurried down the stairs.

Whatever it was, it had certainly had an effect on Emrelda, because only one of the gas lamps in the breakfast room was on, and she hadn't even started any café. She pointed to the newssheet lying on the table. "Read it!"

Dekkard picked up the newssheet and immediately took in the headline.

SIINCLEER SHIPBUILDING PRESIDENTE DIES
IN NAVAL "INCIDENT"

Early on Tridi morning, Imperial Naval Intelligence received a report that a ship of naval appearance would be leaving a private harbor south of Siincleer and those on board carried stolen, classified ship design plans and other military intelligence. The dreadnought *Resolute* was detailed to investigate and hailed the unknown vessel. Rather than heaving to for inspection, the ship, similar to a small corvette, except with considerably greater speed, attempted to outrun the *Resolute*.

The *Resolute*'s captain fired several warning shots, but the corvette ignored them. A second round of warning shots struck the corvette directly, and it sank before either the *Resolute* or its escorts could reach it . . . there were no survivors . . . Later inquiries revealed that the corvette was in fact the yacht of Juan del Larrano, the presidente of Siincleer Shipbuilding.

Witnesses at the private harbor confirmed that they had seen del Larrano board the corvette . . . appeared to be in "a great hurry" . . .

Subsequent inspections of offices at Siincleer Shipbuilding and at the del Larrano residence revealed that a variety of classified materials were missing and that Sr. del Larrano had recently withdrawn "substantial" funds from a variety of accounts, both personal and corporacion . . . Sra. del Larrano and the couple's children are believed to be somewhere in Noldar.

The Admiralty has not yet made additional information public, but the Justiciary Ministry has confirmed that charges have been filed against the Siincleer corporacions in connection with payments channeled through Capitol Services to New Meritorist insurrectionists . . .

Without a word, Dekkard handed the newssheet to Avraal.

She finished reading and laid the newssheet on the table.

"Did you know about this?" demanded Emrelda.

"Not until we read this," said Dekkard. "We suspected del Larrano might try something like this, and I passed on the information to someone who had better contacts. He was appalled, but only said he'd do what he could."

"The councilor who was an admiral? Konnigsburg?"

Dekkard nodded. "He ran for the position because he was unhappy with the Admiralty."

"Good for him." Emrelda shook her head, and her voice trembled as she went on. "It won't bring back Markell. Nothing . . ."

Even in the dim light of the breakfast room, Dekkard could see her tears.

Avraal put her arms around her sister.

After a time, Emrelda stepped back, sniffed, and wiped her eyes. "At least . . . at least, that bastard del Larrano got some of what he deserved. Too bad that the crew died with him, but then they chose to work for him, and what he happened to be wasn't exactly a secret." Emrelda paused, then looked at her sister. "You killed the other one, didn't you?"

Avraal said nothing.

"I didn't realize that immediately," said Emrelda, "but finally something came to me, and then it was all clear. At the Yearend Ball, I realized I didn't remember anything about sitting at the table in the councilors' dining room. I just don't forget like that. You had to have blurred my memory. You did it so that, if I were questioned, I could honestly say that I didn't recall anything unusual."

"I didn't like doing it," said Avraal.

"I'd give up far more than a sixth of a bell of memories for what you did," replied Emrelda.

"What happened?" asked Gaaroll as she walked into the breakfast room, rubbing her eyes. "You two never get up this early."

Avraal pointed to the newssheet on the breakfast table.

Gaaroll began to read. "Frig." She shook her head. "First bent top swell ever got what he deserved . . . first *I* ever heard of, leastwise . . ."

"There might be a few others now," suggested Dekkard.

"Believe it when I see it," said Gaaroll.

"One way or another, it won't happen this morning." Dekkard stifled a yawn. "I could use some café."

"We all could," agreed Avraal.

By a third after the first morning bell, everyone had eaten and dressed, and Dekkard, Avraal, and Gaaroll were in the Gresynt headed for the Council Office Building.

"I still have trouble believing that the Navy just sank del Larrano's yacht," said Avraal.

"The *Ultima* wasn't exactly a yacht," replied Dekkard. "She had the latest turbines, high-speed screws, a hull designed for speed, and just enough armor so she couldn't be stopped or sunk by anything less than a true warship. Initially, I couldn't figure out why del Larrano wanted a yacht like that. He had to have decided to build it a good two or three years ago."

"Why do you think he did?"

"I don't know, not for certain, but he was always thinking ahead. What he did with Engaard Engineering wasn't spur-of-the-moment. Neither was what happened with the night heliographs. What he didn't foresee was a Craft-controlled Council. That changed everything. I'm guessing, but I believe Minz had orders to make sure Obreduur was killed in the first shelling—"

"And Minz added you to the target list on his own. He always did underestimate you."

Dekkard shook his head. "He underestimated you."

"Me?"

"I wouldn't have known enough about anything without you. You encouraged and challenged me—"

"You would have gotten there without me."

"I doubt it, but even if I had, it wouldn't have been soon enough."

For a moment, Avraal remained silent. Then she said, "It took both of us."

"The thinker and the contrarian."

"You think as much as or more than I do."

"Now." Dekkard grinned and added, "And sometimes you can go in a very contrary direction. Just ask your parents and Emrelda—or Cliven."

Avraal jabbed him lightly in the ribs.

When they reached the office, Roostof hurried out to meet them. "Sir, do you know?"

"About Juan del Larrano? It was in *Gestirn*. I assume that the *Tribune* didn't report it in quite the same fashion."

"Not exactly." Roostof handed Dekkard the morning edition of the *Tribune*.

Standing by Margrit's desk, Dekkard began to read.

NAVAL "WARNING" KILLS CORPORACION PRESIDENTE

For as-yet-unsubstantiated reasons, yesterday afternoon, the Navy dreadnought *Resolute* attempted to intercept the private yacht *Ultima*, owned by Juan del Larrano, Presidente of Siincleer Shipbuilding. The Admiralty claims that the yacht disregarded the summons to halt. When the yacht failed to halt, the *Resolute* fired two sets of warning shots. The second salvo struck the yacht, which sank almost immediately, with all aboard being lost, including Sr. del Larrano.

The Navy has further claimed that Sr. del Larrano had stolen classified materials and advanced engineering designs and intended to take them to an unnamed foreign nation . . .

Haarald Juulaan, the Vice-Presidente of Siincleer Shipbuilding, stated that Sr. del Larrano was en route to Noldar for routine business involved with Siincleer's new shipbuilding facility there and that he was unaware of anything that could be remotely construed as to justify the Navy's claim. Sr. Juulaan also stated that the charges filed against the Siincleer corporacions related to minor transgressions by lower-level managers and possibly involved some transactional bookkeeping errors last year by the then Vice-Presidente for Legal Affairs, Pietro Venburg. Sr. Venburg was murdered at the Council's Yearend Ball, purportedly by Sr. Jaime Minz. Sr. Minz was shot by a sniper on his way to his charging hearing . . . "That was most convenient for the current Justiciary minister," said Sr. Juulaan . . .

When he finished reading the *Tribune* story, Dekkard handed the newssheet to Avraal. He said nothing until she finished. "I can tell you which story the Commercers will believe."

"And that's even with the mention of the new shipbuilding facility in Noldar," said Avraal.

"When all the evidence comes out," said Roostof, "Sr. Juulaan will profess that he had no idea and that it's all a terrible mistake, and that the Siincleer corporacions and all their valuable employees should not be penalized for the errors of misguided leadership, or something similar."

"That sounds about right," said Dekkard. "Is there anything else I should know immediately?"

"You do have an urgent message from Councilor Konnigsburg," said Margrit.

"Nothing from the Premier?"

"Just a notice of a short Council session at first bell."

"No subject?"

"I believe the notice just said 'recent developments,'" said Roostof.

That didn't surprise Dekkard. Hasheem wouldn't want to say more until he was certain about as much as possible.

The message from Konnigsburg was simple:

> Lunch. Both of you. A third before noon.
>
> EK

Dekkard immediately wrote a quick reply and had Margrit dispatch it before he and Avraal went into the inner office.

"Do you think the vice-presidente of Siincleer Shipbuilding was lying? Or misquoted?" asked Dekkard.

"I suspect he never knew anything, except for hints and rumors, and that much of the underhanded and illegal dealing that went on was handled by Venburg until his death. Venburg was an isolate, so questioning him with an empath wouldn't reveal anything, and only a charge of high crimes would put del Larrano in front of a justicer or a Council committee with an empath. None of that would happen as long as Ulrich—or any senior Commercer—was Premier."

"All of that suggests why the corporacions threw in temporarily with the New Meritorists," said Dekkard. "They had to remove Obreduur as quickly as possible."

"Except they didn't count on you being so effective."

"Us," corrected Dekkard.

"I'll accept that." Avraal gestured to the stack of mail. "You might as well start on that. If there are any more important messages or developments, Svard or Margrit will let you know in moments. I'm staying here just in case."

Dekkard didn't ask why. They both knew, and with Avraal close by, he could concentrate on the routine duties that never let up and never would.

Although Dekkard occasionally glanced at the door or the window, he finished off both reading incoming mail and signing or revising responses a good bell before they had to leave for lunch, which left him some time to go over Shuryn's latest update on unethical or possibly illegal corporacion activities.

On the walk to the Council Hall, Dekkard saw Jaradd Rikkard, but Rikkard pretended not to see either Dekkard, Avraal, or Gaaroll and stopped for a time, consulting his watch, presumably so that he wouldn't have to get within hailing distance.

When Dekkard and Avraal entered the councilors' dining room, Daffyd Dholen and Leister Milyaard stood waiting for the return of the maître d'hôtel.

Both turned, and Dholen said, "Steffan, your subcommittee certainly discovered an adders' nest in Siincleer Shipbuilding."

"And in several other corporacions, it would appear," returned Dekkard.

"There's more to come?" asked Milyaard, with a slight tone of alarm.

"There's a possibility in transportation as well," said Dekkard cheerfully, knowing that, since Eastern Ironway had sent funds to Capitol Services, Eastern already faced charges, which wouldn't turn out well for the ironway, especially after Eastern's involvement in the Kraffeist Affair.

After the briefest hesitation, Milyaard said, "Thank you. I appreciate the notice."

As the maître d'hôtel guided the two councilors to their table, Avraal said quietly, "They're both snakes . . . not quite as bad as adders."

No party is pure. The Craft Party's just not as bad, possibly because we haven't held power in a long, long time.

When the maître d'hôtel returned, Dekkard said, "We're meeting Councilor Konnigsburg."

"This way, sir, Ritten."

Even though Avraal and Dekkard arrived early, the councilors' dining room was already half full, most likely because of the session beginning at first bell, and possibly because some councilors wanted to compare notes, given the morning headlines in both newssheets.

"I'm glad you could make it," said Konnigsburg as Dekkard and Avraal seated themselves across the table from him. Then he offered a brief smile and added, "I wouldn't have expected otherwise. If you don't mind, I'd like to wait on talking details until after we order."

Dekkard nodded. "Just one general question. Was the story in *Gestirn* accurate?"

"As far as it went."

Dekkard was actually hungry, possibly because he'd been up and eaten earlier than usual, or because he still worried, and he ordered the three-cheese chicken. Avraal opted for the vegetable soup, while Konnigsburg again chose the white bean soup.

Once they ordered, Dekkard looked to the former admiral.

Konnigsburg smiled wryly. "Matters were worse than you suspected. I'm not at liberty to offer precise details at the moment, but it appears that the new Siincleer Shipbuilding facility in Noldar is designed primarily to construct warships of close to dreadnought size and capability, possibly larger. While Uldwyrk Systems' contracts with the Admiralty prohibit the export of the latest steam turbines, apparently the legalists 'forgot' to prohibit the building of facilities to manufacture them elsewhere."

"There's more, isn't there?"

"Quite a bit. There are almost no reserves left in the Guldoran accounts of Siincleer Shipbuilding. They've been shipping mark notes to Noldar for the last three months."

"Since right after the elections?" asked Dekkard.

Konnigsburg nodded.

"What about Suvion Industries and Johann Daenyld?"

"He's in custody, and he's the Justiciary Ministry's problem. Him and the head legalist."

"Oswaald Cassius," supplied Dekkard. "I take it that the second salvo from the *Resolute* weren't warning shots. And that, even with the *Resolute*'s outstanding gunnery, there were more than two salvos."

Konnigsburg offered a satiric grin. "Steffan, they were all warning shots."

"I see. The captain of the *Resolute* wasn't about to be outmaneuvered again."

"The *Ultima* was considerably faster than anyone knew, but they were *officially* still warning shots." Konnigsburg added, "The Admiralty is considering conducting gunnery practice in new locales. Well offshore. That remains to be determined."

Dekkard nodded, then said, "I assume that you might find the new Fleet Marshal, whoever he may be, slightly more to your liking."

"It's a stronger possibility."

Much more than that, Dekkard suspected, given that Konnigsburg's conveyance of information had prevented a much more embarrassing situation.

"You, and that includes your sister," said Konnigsburg, looking at Avraal, "will be receiving an invitation to dinner from us, in the next day or so. It's something that we've put off too long." He looked up as the server approached with their orders. "I believe I timed that rather well. Now, we can enjoy the rest of our meal. I'm looking forward to hearing what the Premier has to say."

"So are we," replied Dekkard as the server delivered his three-cheese chicken, understanding that Konnigsburg had conveyed what he felt free to say about Navy actions at the moment.

Once the server had left, Dekkard said, "One last question. What does the Premier know?"

"Roughly what I said, and whatever you and the Justiciary Ministry told him."

"Then it will be interesting to hear what he says."

"It may be more interesting to watch the faces of some councilors," said Avraal.

"Speaking of watching," said Konnigsburg, "the Premier is headed this way, and he's looking in our direction, most likely at you, Steffan."

"Worried but not angry," murmured Avraal.

As Konnigsburg predicted, Hasheem stopped at the table. "I hoped you might be here, Steffan. We need to go over a few things. Might I have a moment just before the afternoon session, in the floor office?"

"I'll be there."

"Excellent." Hasheem looked to Konnigsburg and said, "I apologize for interrupting your lunch. I'd also like to thank you and Steffan for your actions in keeping a bad situation from turning into a disaster. I won't forget it." A fleeting smile and a nod followed his words before he turned and walked from the dining room.

Konnigsburg looked to Avraal.

"There wasn't any hint of dread or malice when he said he wanted to talk to Steffan."

"He wants something," said Dekkard. "We'll have to see what it is."

The conversation for the rest of lunch was mainly speculation about how much more the Justiciary Ministry would find and where. Dekkard didn't quite eat all his chicken, but he was comfortably full when he left Avraal to make her way to the spouses' gallery.

As soon as Dekkard walked into the small inner office, Hasheem smiled. "Thank you for being prompt."

"There isn't anything new from the Justiciary Ministry, is there?"

"I'm not aware of any new developments other than Johann Daenyld and Oswaald Cassius being in custody and on their way to Machtarn, but from what Minister Kuta has said, there will be more charges and trials over the next few months. So each week will see some new developments." Hasheem paused, then said, "I've decided to take one of your earlier suggestions."

"Oh?" Dekkard thought that was the safest response.

"Now that your subcommittee hearings have turned into a massive Justiciary investigation, I'm afraid a great deal of my time is going to be taken up in dealing with both the legalist and political implications. So, I've decided to name you as acting chair of the Security Committee." Hasheem smiled wryly. "If you do as well as I expect, some months hence, you'll likely be the chair. You've already proved to be very good at it, and that will take a great burden off my back, and allow me more time for oversight of certain other committees, which I fear will be more than necessary."

Especially Military Affairs, Commerce/Treasury, and Transportation. "I'm honored, Fredrich."

"It's no honor, and we both know it, but your presence in that position will provide assurance that the committee will continue to do its duty."

In other words, keep the corporacions worried and careful.

"And now . . ." said Hasheem.

"I'll leave you to get ready to make a few Commercers very unhappy." Dekkard stood, keeping his tone wry and light.

When he entered the Council chamber from the floor office several heads turned, but the only one who actually approached Dekkard was Eduardo Nortak.

"Steffan, do you know what's going to happen?"

"I don't. I assume that the Premier will give some details about events connected to the subcommittee hearings, this morning's rather lurid headlines, and the Justiciary Ministry's investigation of the five corporacions who sent significant funds to Capitol Services. But I don't know."

"You came from his office."

"That was about Security Committee matters. As a subcommittee chair I am accountable to him. I'm certainly going to be as interested as everyone else when he speaks."

"I'd hoped . . ."

"Even if I did know, Eduardo, I wouldn't say. That's his duty."

Nortak offered a faint smile as he nodded and then headed in the direction of his desk.

Dekkard had only taken a few more steps when Erich Kuuresoh joined him. "Steffan, this is all so improbable. Why would the presidente of one of the most powerful corporacions in Guldor, if not the world, just throw it all away by trying to flee to a second-rate power?"

"Erich, I don't know that he had many options. From what I know, and I certainly don't know it all, he'd broken too many laws to escape some sort of conviction." *And with Venburg gone, there was nothing to insulate him from more investigations.*

"That doesn't make any sense."

"The only answer I can give to that is that, sometimes, too much wealth and power cause people to lose their senses."

Kuuresoh shook his head. "It still doesn't make sense."

"That's the best answer I can give," said Dekkard before turning toward his desk.

Ingrella looked sideways from her desk toward Dekkard as he seated himself. "More surprises?"

"Only for those who haven't been paying attention."

A few moments after Tomas Pajiin eased in behind his desk, the lieutenant-at-arms thumped his staff.

Hasheem immediately took the lectern. "Most, if not all, of you have read the newssheets. I will not engage in speculation, but I will present those facts verified to be true that have been established as a result of ongoing investigations by the investigatory subcommittee of the Council Security Committee, by the Council Guard, and by the Justiciary Ministry." From there Hasheem gave a methodical, almost plodding, detailed account of the known facts involving the five corporacions, Capitol Services, Ulrich, Minz, and the New Meritorists.

All in all, his presentation took slightly longer than two-thirds of a bell.

After a slight pause, Hasheem went on. "There's one other announcement, of an organizational nature, that I need to make. It has become exceedingly obvious that there have been far more corporacions and even former councilors who have been implicated in connection with the New Meritorists and other felonious and treasonous activities than anyone heretofore believed. Rectifying the conditions that led to those activities will involve significant changes in both law and the oversight process employed by the Council. While this is ongoing, it is clear that, as Premier, my most important duty is to assure the successful undertaking and completion of those changes. Because of the essential and time-consuming nature of guiding those reforms, I would necessarily be neglecting my duties as chair of the Security Committee. Therefore, I am appointing as acting chair the councilor whose work as the chair of the investigatory subcommittee uncovered much of the corruption that surfaced over the past week. As acting chair, Councilor Steffan Dekkard will have the full power of the chair, subject, of course, as every chair is, to the oversight of the Premier." Hasheem paused, then declared, "The Council stands in recess until the first bell of the afternoon on Unadi." He rapped the lectern with the gavel once.

Ingrella turned and said, with an amused smile, "No surprises?"

"No surprises. It's what I've been doing for the last month, with a bit more authority, and I'll likely be doing it for months to come."

"More likely years."

Dekkard grinned. "Why not? I'm far too young for anything else." *And you're actually too young for that.* But he had Avraal . . . and Svard . . . and Ingrella, and Nincya . . . and more than a few others to help him.

73

THE IMPROBABLY QUESTIONABLE
COUNCILOR DEKKARD

Remember the questionable Councilor Steffan Delos Dekkard? How could anyone forget? The Military Institute graduate who never really served out his service obligation? The short-term former security aide who somehow manipulated members of the Gaarlak Craft Party to gain appointment to the Council, and whose principal opponent ended up mysteriously frozen to death this past winter? A councilor barely in office who bought and elegantly refurbished a house that no one on his pay could possibly afford, and in solid marks, no less?

A councilor who miraculously survived not one but two shellings of the Council, as well as the putative assassination attempt of an entire subcommittee? A subcommittee which he was appointed to chair, despite being nearly the most junior councilor on the entire Security Committee. Even more improbably, the questionable Councilor Dekkard led the investigatory subcommittee through a series of closed hearings, at the end of which a distinguished former premier was imprisoned and charged with high crimes on evidence that no one but the subcommittee and Craft political ministerial appointees have seen. And based on that withheld evidence, apparently the Navy saw fit to fire warning shells at the yacht of the presidente of Siincleer Shipbuilding, shells that in fact sank the yacht and killed the presidente and everyone else on board.

At present, Councilor Dekkard's subcommittee now has the presidente of Suvion Industries in custody facing charges of illegally shipping military explosives under false pretenses and funding the New Meritorists because minor amounts of funds were sent to a services business that few if any knew had any connections to the insurrectionists. Charges against three other corporacions have been lodged on the basis of the unseen evidence discovered, or not inconceivably fabricated, behind closed subcommittee doors.

Even more questionable is the decision of Craft Premier Fredrich Hasheem to name the questionable Councilor Dekkard as acting chairman of the powerful Security Committee. Yet few in the Council seem even aware of how much power is gathered in the hands of the most questionable councilor in the history of Guldor, or how such power in the hands of such a councilor bodes ill for continuing the proud traditions of the Imperium.

The Machtarn Tribune
29 Springfirst 1267

74

All men, all women, all children have their illusions, and those illusions both sustain and destroy them.

The counterpoint to illusion is not truth, not in the way in which truth is now and apparently always has been defined by human beings, although many would claim such. Truth is, as popularly accepted, just another form of illusion, if a well-meaning illusion, because, over time, it has been corrupted from its original meaning, which was conformity to reality. As culture and language developed, men applied the term to words, or more properly, nouns, then next to principles, and finally to beliefs. Yet none of those conform directly to reality.

Nouns are single-word terms that attempt to name or describe either something real or something unreal, but no word encompasses the completeness of whatever is being so named. Every noun is at best a name of the principal attribute of what it purports to represent.

When one applies the term "true" or "truth" to belief in a deity, how can a belief in the existence of any deity be true, or even false, when there is no demonstrable physical proof of the existence of that deity?

In the end, truth as it is, and not as so many have described it to serve their own ends, can only be the open acceptance of what is. Not what we remember, not what we hope for, not what we fear, not what we love . . . but what is. Nothing more and nothing less.

For the truths that men claim, in their vaunted principles, and in the governments that they have built based on those principles, and will build long after I am gone, are all part of the grand illusion that words can describe all of what exists.

AVERRA
The City of Truth
Johan Eschbach
377 TE